ACCLAIM FOR

COMING TO LIGHT

"These translations reveal a great and varied literature, an inheritance that white people ignored till it was almost too late. Whatever languages they spoke first, these voices speak from and of our land . . . and they can tell us things about it nobody else can."
—Ursula K. LeGuin

"An essential introduction to American Indian oral literature, with each strange, strong, and vivid contribution clarified with introductions by the translators. . . . A valuable book."
—Peter Matthiessen

"Brian Swann's book knocked me over. This is a gold and silver treasury of radiant, touchstone tales—a continent's worth—that in such ebullience one thought might have been lost. They reverberate like a sort of cross between Aesop and Homer, fabulous, haunting, funny, cryptic, and tragic."
—Edward Hoagland

"By far the best anthology on the subject ever assembled. It eclipses everything else."
—Dr. Alfonso Ortiz

VINTAGE BOOKS

A DIVISION OF RANDOM HOUSE, INC.

NEW YORK

COMING

TO

LIGHT

▲

CONTEMPORARY
TRANSLATIONS
OF THE NATIVE
LITERATURES
OF NORTH
AMERICA

▲

EDITED AND WITH AN INTRODUCTION BY
BRIAN SWANN

The Library of Congress has cataloged the Random House
edition as follows:
Coming to light: contemporary translations of the native literatures of
North America / edited and with an introduction by Brian Swann.
p. cm.
Includes bibliographical references.
ISBN 0-679-41816-4
1. Indian literature–North America–Translations into English.
2. Folk literature, Indian–North America–Translations into English.
I. Swann, Brian.
PM197.E1C66 1994 897–dc20 94-13457
Vintage ISBN: 0-679-74358-8

Manufactured in the United States of America
10 9 8 7

We have stories
as old as the great seas
breaking through the chest
flying out the mouth,
noisy tongues that once were silenced,
all the oceans we contain
coming to light.

LINDA HOGAN, "To Light"

ACKNOWLEDGMENTS

Grateful acknowledgment is made for permission to reprint from the following copyrighted works, sometimes in revised form:

Thomas Lowenstein, *The Things That Were Said of Them: Shaman Stories and Oral Histories of the Tikiġaq People,* told by Asatchaq. University of California Press, © 1992, the Regents of the University of California.

Nora Marks Dauenhauer and Richard Dauenhauer, *Haa Shuká/Our Ancestors: Tlingit Oral Narratives,* 1987, and *Haa Tuwunáagu Yís/ For Healing Our Spirit: Tlingit Oratory,* 1990, both University of Washington Press, © Sealaska Heritage Foundation.

Catharine McClellan, *The Girl Who Married the Bear: A Masterpiece of Indian Oral Tradition,* 1970, Ottawa, National Museum of Man Publications in Ethnology, © National Museum of Civilization, Canada.

Julie Cruikshank, *Life Lived Like a Story: Life Stories of Three Athapaskan Elders,* University of Nebraska Press, © 1990.

James Kari, *A Dena'ina Legacy,* 1991 © Alaska Native Language Center.

Eliza Jones, "The One Who Kicked His Grandmother's Head Along," © Yukon Koyukuk School District.

Antone Evan and Jane McGary, *Dena'ina Sukdu'a,* 1984 © Alaska Native Language Center.

Robert Brightman, *Ācaôôhkīwina and Acimōwina: Traditional Narratives of the Rock Cree Indians,* Canadian Museum of Civilization, Mercury Series, 1989 © Canadian Museum of Civilization.

Anthony Mattina, "Blue Jay," reprinted from *Parabola: The Magazine of Myth and Tradition,* vol. 2, no. 4 (Winter 1977); © Colville Federated Tribes.

Blair Rudes, *The Tuscarora Legacy of J.N.B. Hewitt: Materials for the Study of the Tuscarora Language and Culture,* Canadian Museum of Civilization, Mercury Series, 1987 © Canadian Museum of Civilization.

Larry Evers and Felipe S. Molina, *Yaqui Deer Songs/Maso Bwikam: A Native American Poetry,* 1987 © University of Arizona Press.

Acknowledgments

Barre Toelken, reprinted from *Traditional American Indian Literatures: Texts and Interpretations,* ed. Karl Kroeber, 1981 © University of Nebraska Press.

Paul Zolbrod, *Diné Bahané: The Navajo Creation Story,* 1984 © University of New Mexico Press.

William Shipley, *The Maidu Indian Myths and Stories of Hánc'ibyjim,* 1991 © Heyday Books.

CONTENTS

Contents

Contents

INTRODUCTION

▲

BRIAN SWANN

This volume presents a sampling of the magnificence and diversity of the many different Native American cultures that have existed for thousands of years and continue to exist today, despite efforts to repress, suppress, and even extirpate them. Most non–Native Americans are still ignorant of the complex achievements and amazing variety of these cultures, having been presented, for the most part, with homogenized stereotypes and misinterpretations, either ideal-istic-romantic or defective-demonic, depending on the era (often both are present at the same time). There has, however, always been some interest in things Native American, an interest at times amounting to a hunger. One of the aims of the present volume is to develop and cultivate that interest, build on it, in the hope that through their literatures, Native American cultures can be seen clearer, appreciated not only for their similarities to our own tradi-tions but for their bracing dissimilarities.

Most people are surprised to learn of the number of languages that existed when Europeans first arrived in what is now the United States and Canada—there may have been as many as five hundred. In five centuries many of these languages have disappeared. Some exist only in archival form, but against all odds others have survived, and a number still flourish, even if subject to a variety of pressures. It will come as news to many that in the United States and Canada there are still some two hundred languages being spoken, with about forty-five spoken by one thousand or more people. (In all the Americas there are still approximately six hundred Native languages spoken by about eighteen million people.)

Just as there has been what has been called a "Native American renaissance" in the arts during the last twenty or thirty years, so there has been a renaissance in the study and translation of Native languages and literatures. Fascinating work is being done by both Native and non-Native scholars and translators. From this I have selected stories, songs, oratory, and prayer that represent the cultures well and are also accessible to an audience probably unfamiliar with these cultures. I intend this book to showcase the state of contemporary Native American translation in its interpretation and presentation of these traditions. Here the reader can hear and see, as far as possible, something of the power of the original. In this volume the reader can begin to observe how translations are arrived at, how texts are put together. I have aimed at achieving a collection that not only is accurate and reliable but also reads well. It should be noted that if there is a certain lack of stylistic uniformity from contributor to contributor, this is due to the translators' particular exigencies and requirements, responses to the materials they are dealing with, and not to oversight on the part of the copy editor.

The format in which each translation is preceded by an introduction that places the work in its culture, gives it a context, explains what needs to be explained, and suggests ways to learn more is one of several features that distinguish this volume from previous anthologies. As a professor of literature, I have found it frustrating to teach Native American oral literatures because the anthologies in which the texts appear often lack sufficient background to help a reader understand them. The selections lack cultural context and are often linguistically unreliable. Disparate stories are run together and earlier versions rewritten without knowledge of the languages from which the stories had been translated. Stories are adapted or retold without the original narrator being credited, or stories are credited merely to a tribe.

The selections in this book come from all parts of North America: north, south, east, and west. Starting from Alaska, the Yukon, and the Subarctic (a convenient, not "scientific," grouping), we have stories, songs, oratory, and prayer from Yupik, Iñupiaq, Aleut, Koyukon, Dena'ina, Tagish/Tlingit, Tlingit, Dunne-za, Rock Cree, and Innu. Thence we move to the North Pacific Coast with Haida, Kwakiutl, Kathlamet Chinook, Clackamas Chinook, and Kalapuya. The Great Basin and Plateau come next with Thompson River Salish, Colville, Cayuse/Nez Perce, and Wind River Shoshone. We reach the Plains with Skiri Pawnee and Lakota. From the Eastern Woodlands we have Ojibwe, Tuscarora, Cayuga, and Passamaquoddy, while the Southwest is represented by Yaqui, Pima, Zuni, Navajo, Western Apache, Hopi, and Havasupai. The Southeast has a sole representative, Koasati. We end with California: Yana, Atsugewi, Maidu, and Karuk.

When in 1858 Jacob Hamblin and thirteen Mormon missionaries set out for the Hopi town of Oraibi in northern Arizona, they took with them a Welsh interpreter, since they believed the Hopi were descended from the twelfth-century Welsh prince Modoc.[1] Theories of the origins of Indian languages were as diverse as theories of the origins of the Indians themselves.[2]

The first serious attempt to classify North American languages was made in 1836 by Albert Gallatin, "the father of American linguistics," who believed that all the Native American language families were related. Gallatin came up with thirty-eight families, excluding California.[3] (California is a case in itself. At the time of the first European contact, it presented the greatest diversity of Native American cultures and languages in North America: some two hundred languages and dialects belonging to many different language families. To reflect this distinction, California has been given a section all to itself, concluding this volume.) For the last hundred years or so scholars have been divided on the question of just how many language families there are and on the relationship of families and languages, one to another. In 1891, John Wesley Powell classified fifty-eight families north of Mexico, but during the first half of the twentieth century the tendency was toward combining and reducing ("lumping"). Thus in 1929, Edward Sapir came up with just six families, regrouping and consolidating Powell's structures. By 1944, however, Harry Hoijer (a "splitter") returned to Powell's system and arrived at fifty-three families. Scholars are still divided between the "splitters" and the "lumpers," though from time to time someone like William Leap will make a "middle-ranged attempt" and come up with eighteen families.[4] Most controversial of all is Joseph Greenberg's return to Sapir's position that all Indian languages are connected by many threads. He has reduced all Native languages of the New World to just three: Eskimo-Eleut, Na-Dene, and Amerind.[5]

Whatever the number of languages in the United States,[6] the actual languages spoken today are under pressure. Some will die out in the near future, but a number are still in use and thriving, a tribute to the persistence of Native peoples in the face of physical and cultural genocide, past and present, official and unofficial.[7] In the name of "progress," in the nineteenth century and into the twentieth languages and cultures were ruthlessly assaulted by missionaries and missionary schools and in off-reservation manual-labor boarding schools, of which the most famous was the Carlisle Indian Industrial School, founded in 1879 by Captain Richard H. Pratt, whose motto was "Kill the Indian and save the man." Part of this process involved destroying languages. Just a decade before the founding of Carlisle, the 1868 Commission on Indian Affairs decided that the Indians' "barbarous dialect should be blotted out." One of the results of such an education was that a child returning home to a reservation could no longer communicate with his or her family, and since, as N. Scott Momaday has pointed out, the oral tradition is always but one generation away from extinction, cultural survival itself was in doubt.[8] Moreover, while some who attended these boarding schools continued to speak their own language, many refused to teach the Native language to their children, feeling they would be better off speaking only English. When from 1945 to 1961 the official government policy of Termination entailed moving people off reservations and into cities (today over 50 percent of the approximately two million Native Americans in the United States live in urban areas; there are over eighty thousand in Los Angeles alone[9]), many lost their Native language as a consequence of the need to adapt to the larger society. There are many other reasons for language decline and the dangers facing the oral tradition, not the least of which, as Vine Deloria Jr. has pointed out, is that "instead of gathering around the elders in the evening to hear stories of the tribal past, children today rent a video tape and watch 'Star Wars' or horror films."[10]

And yet despite this, and despite the continued assaults ("the new Indian wars") on Indian sovereignty, life, and culture, the battles over water and fishing rights, the mining of coal, oil, and uranium ("genocide by energy development"), and the threat of using reservations for the dumping of nuclear wastes; despite the undermining of the American Indian Religious Freedom Act (1978) by a Supreme Court decision in 1988 *(Lyng v. Northwest Indian Cemetery Protective Association)* determining that the government's management of its lands comes first, even if this means the destruction of sacred sites and lands in the name of logging or mining (or even the erection of huge telescopes in Arizona on the sacred mountain of the Apache, Dzil nchaasian, also known as Mount Graham); despite all this and more, the cultures and languages of the First Peoples persist.

The shifts in U.S. government policy—from Removal and Relocation (1828–1887) to Allotment and Assimilation (1887–1928) to Reorganization and Self-Government (1928–1945) to Termination (1945–1961) and finally to Self-Determination (from 1961 to the present, though with President Reagan "the halcyon days of self-determination ended"[11])—have finally meant some increase in local control over services.[12] Efforts in language maintenance have focused largely on the needs of children, but they could not have succeeded as well as they have without the active participation of Elders in the community. Even with budget cuts in the 1980s and 1990s and other severe financial problems, a wide variety of approaches has been developed, from the Akwesasne Freedom School's instruction in Mohawk from prekindergarten through eighth grade to the Little Wound Day School's aim to teach all students Lakota by the year 2000 (the school receives Bureau of Indian Affairs—BIA—funds but is completely controlled by a school board composed of local people). Then there is the Kickapoo Nation School in Powhattan, Kansas, dedicated to integrating traditional Indian ways with modern education, via, for example, its successful Talking Books project, which uses computer technology to teach Kickapoo to children in kindergarten and first grade. Peach Springs School in northwestern Arizona, with its bilingual curriculum, has become something of a showcase for Indian educators: Hualapai (a Yuman language) is the language of playground and computer programs. In Navajo country there are a number of schools teaching literacy in Navajo, Rock Point Community School being, perhaps, the best. (Mazii Dinełtsoi, also known as Rex Lee Jim, a Navajo poet and Princeton alumnus who publishes solely in Navajo, teaches there.) Several innovative approaches to language renewal have been instituted on the Cattaraugus Seneca Reservation near Buffalo, New York, including bilingual programs in the nearby school district and in-school instruction in Seneca from kindergarten through high school. Finally in this brief overview, teaching materials in the Flathead Salish and Kootenai languages for use in local schools are being developed at the Salish Kootenai College on the Flathead Indian Reservation in Pablo, Montana.

At the adult level there are a number of important ventures. Stanford University has offered Navajo, Cherokee, and Tlingit; the University of California, Berkeley, regularly offers Hopi and Lakota; and the University of Oklahoma has an innovative program in college-level instruction in Native American languages. The Ute Indian Tribal Audio-Visual, in Utah, has provided Ute-language instruction since 1979. Navajo is central to the curriculum at Navajo Community College in Tsaile, Arizona. Montana's Little Big Horn Community College has the only Crow Studies program in the nation, and many of the 120 courses are taught in Crow, which is the first language of 85 percent of the six thousand members of the tribe. In South Dakota, Oglala Lakota College in Pine Ridge, chartered in 1971, and Sinte Gleska University on Rosebud, also chartered in 1971, are the only four-year institutions to offer a degree in Lakota Studies, stressing the Lakota language. The aim on Rosebud is to make Lakota part of the school curriculum, all assemblies and activities, and as many public activities as possible. In Canada the En'owkin Center of Penticton, British Columbia, has stated its resolve to "restore the Okanagon language to its rightful place as the communicator of the culture, under the guidance of the Elders."

It is difficult to know exactly how many Native-language speakers there are today in North America, but Michael Krauss, Director of the Alaska Native Language Center, and Richard and Nora Dauenhauer of the Sealaska Heritage Foundation have written on the subject.[13] From them one learns that half or more of the approximately two hundred Native languages north of Mexico are "obsolescent" (Krauss says that 80 percent of them are "moribund"[14]). That is, the languages are spoken only by older people, and there are no fluent speakers under fifty. In Alaska, with twenty living Native languages, only Siberian Yupik (spoken by about 1,000 people) and Central Yupik (spoken by about 12,000 out of 18,000 people) are flourishing. Inipiaq, in Canada, Alaska, and Greenland, is spoken by about 64,000 out of 77,000 people (with about 42,000 in Greenland). About seven of the remaining seventeen Alaskan languages are spoken by some 350 people out of 1,900. Most of the speakers are over seventy years of age. Tsimshian is spoken by approximately 3,600 out of 10,000 people, while Tlingit has about 1,000 speakers, mostly over sixty years of age, out of 9,000 (95 percent of the Tlingit live in Alaska). Jane McGary informs me that "if today's trends continue, it is unlikely that any Alaskan Athabaskan languages will be spoken—except in ceremonies—by the middle of the next century." Keith Basso has made a similar point to me about an Athabaskan language of the Southwest that also hangs in the balance. Although the several dialects of Western Apache are still spoken widely and fluently—and in some communities, such as Cibecue, by almost every child—in communities such as Whiteriver and San Carlos the children speak imperfectly or not at all. If this trend continues, Basso notes, "the outlook is dire."

Despite continuing pressures for assimilation and monolingualism, including what Nora and Richard Dauenhauer term "anti–Native language sentiment" among educators, administrators, and Christian religious groups,[15] efforts have been made to revive and strengthen Native languages and cultures in Alaska. The renewal of Tlingit literature and scholarship began in the late 1960s with the Summer Institute of Linguistics, and regular workshops began in 1971. The literature gathered by Nora Dauenhauer (a native speaker of Tlingit, raised in a traditional family) and her husband, Richard, includes a series of traditional texts that resulted from taking down exactly what the elders said in a way acceptable to the oral-tradition bearers and the Tlingit community. The Dauenhauers also developed instructional materials, such as grammars and glossaries. In this way it is hoped that the language will survive at least in select cultural and ceremonial contexts.

Also in Alaska, at the University of Alaska in Fairbanks, the Alaska Native Language Center was founded in 1972 as a center for research and documentation of the state's Indian, Aleut, and Eskimo languages. ANLC publishes story collections, histories, dictionaries, and grammars for bilingual teaching as well as other classroom materials. In Whitehorse the Yukon Native Language Center does similar valuable work with the eight Native languages of the Yukon.

The strength of the Native languages in the rest of the United States and Canada varies greatly, but it is interesting to note that there are more speakers of the Na-Dene languages today than ever before. There are about two hundred thousand speakers of the Athabaskan languages, with Navajo—the only Indian language north of Mexico with more than one hundred thousand speakers—accounting for about three quarters of that number. Mikasuki in Florida, Alabama in Louisiana, Choctaw in Mississippi, and a number of languages in Arizona and New Mexico, including Jemez, Mescalero, Zuni, Hopi, and O'odham, are in pretty good shape, as are Ojibwe, Slave, Dogrib, Dakota and Lakota, and Cree in Canada—Cree is taught at Brandon University, the University of Manitoba, the University of Alberta, Saskatchewan Indian Cultural College, and other universities as well as on many reserves. Pedagogical audiotapes are available in Cree; it is estimated that there are about sixty thousand speakers.

The Sioux, one of the largest North American groups, speak

Lakota to varying degrees, even within a single community.[16] Thus, between 25 and 50 percent of the adults at the Pine Ridge Reservation in South Dakota speak Lakota, and the lowest percentage of Lakota speakers is at Pine Ridge Village (Red Cloud's community), whereas in smaller communities, such as Manderson (Black Elk's community and home to many relatives of Crazy Horse) and Kyle (the location of Little Wound Day School), as many as 70 percent of the residents speak Lakota.

In spite of determined efforts to strengthen, retain, or revive Native American languages, the problems are manifold, from pressures to give in to the dominant culture and language to the need for funding for educational programs, whether supplied by the BIA or other sources. If the language isn't a living entity, used at work, at home, at play, it will assume the difficult and ambiguous position of an object of study, retaining an aura of the most bitter kind of alienation. If it is seriously endangered, a whole range of cultural identities is rendered problematic, for as the Ojibwe writer Gerald Vizenor has noted, "The tribes were created in language." Ray A. Young Bear, the Mesquakie writer, was told by his grandfather, "These were the words you were fed to give back to the world."[17] When a language dies, its universe—a unique way of understanding, interpreting, and inventing the world—dies with it. A cultural gene pool dries up, and all of us are the weaker and the poorer for the dying of diversity.

Much of the achievement of Western culture has come down to us in written form. We can only guess at the vast amount of Native American stories, songs, and ceremonies that have been lost forever as languages have died and cultures have been destroyed since contact with the Europeans. Ishi (the only survivor of the Yahi culture of northern California and the last of his tribe, which had been wiped out by white ranchers), while presumably, as Bruno Nettl notes, "not an outstanding singer of his tribe," was yet able to sing over fifty songs (which T. T. Waterman and Alfred L. Kroeber recorded between 1911 and 1914), and he was able "to sing them, if the recordings are reliable, in an assured and self-confident manner."[18] Paintings on pottery (on Mimbres ware, for example), rock art such as that of the Chumash in California, and paintings on the walls of Horse Canyon, Barrier Canyon, and elsewhere in Utah all seem to illustrate legends and stories and suggest a rich tradition of oral literature. Much has been irrevocably lost. It is the aim of the present volume to reflect as much as possible the quality and variety of the material that has survived and continues to thrive.

When the Europeans arrived on the North American continent, they were confronted with a rich and even bewildering variety of cultures and languages. But with a few exceptions there was little interest in recording the songs, stories, or ceremonies of Native Americans for some time after first contact.

The first New World language recorded was probably Laurentian (Northern Iroquoian), when Jacques Cartier collected a word list on his first voyage to the Gulf of Saint Lawrence in 1534. The earliest grammar was in Timucuan (Northern Florida), published in 1614. Marc Lescarbot was the first to record songs. Between 1601 and 1607, he collected some Micmac songs in Acadia (Nova Scotia), writing out the words and setting down the music in the tonic system. The oldest text surviving from what is now the United States is in William Strachey's *The Historie of Travaile into Virginia Britannia,* published in 1612. Strachey discusses a vigorous literary tradition among the Powhatan Confederacy and records one of their "scornful songs." (It has always seemed a pity to me that one of the great translators of the early seventeenth century, George Sandys, Treasurer of the Virginia Company at a time of great turmoil— when Opechancanough launched his great uprising against the English—did not set his hand to translating from the native languages. He was more intent on subduing the Powhatans than learning their culture—naturally enough, given the times. He did, however, find time to write a good part of his famous translation of Ovid's *Metamorphoses.*)

In 1635, Harmen Meyndertsz van den Bogaert, author of an account of a journey from Fort Orange (in present-day Albany) to the Oneidas, recorded the words of a chief's song: "Ho schene jo ho ho schene I atsiehoene atsiehoene," after which the "savages" shouted "Netho, netho, netho."[19] In 1674, Père Marquette provided one "verse" of an Illinois Calumet Song collected on his first voyage (more words and the music were found later in a manuscript preserved by the Jesuits in Paris). But we had to wait until 1765 for the earliest translation (more version than translation) of an Indian song, when Lieutenant Henry Timberlake published his rendition of a Cherokee "war song" in heroic couplets.[20]

Despite the Romantic movement's interest in the "primitive," little else from Native American languages was translated until the early nineteenth century, perhaps because from the middle of the eighteenth century to the first quarter of the nineteenth century, the version of "savagism" (Roy Harvey Pearce's well-known term[21]) that prevailed viewed the Indians as an obstacle to "civilized" progress westward, an obstacle that the European settlers felt must vanish, one way or another. In 1819, the Moravian missionary John Heckewelder published his *Account of the History, Manners, and Customs of the Indian Nations* (which James Fenimore Cooper was to use extensively for his novels).[22] Heckewelder, as a missionary, of course had his own reasons for studying the culture of the Delaware, whom he regarded as about to pass from the world's stage "in a few years." He could not see Delaware culture in its own terms; so while, like many others of his time, he was impressed by Indian oratory, he regarded it not as the result of so much training but as a "simple and natural ability." Being "sons of nature," "they speak what their feelings dictate without art and without rule." While he collected examples of discourse and oratory, he saw the Delaware "fondness" for metaphors as something of a weakness: metaphors "are to their discourse what beads are to their persons; a gaudy but tasteless ornament" (though he did note that Shakespeare had a taste for metaphors, too). In the chapter of his book called "Dances, Songs, and Sacrifices," he describes Delaware "poetry," transcribes a war song, and appends a description of how the song is sung: "They sing it, as I give it here, in short lines and sentences, but most generally in detached parts, as time permits and as the occasion or their feelings prompt them."

THE SONG OF THE LENAPE WARRIORS GOING
AGAINST THE ENEMY
O poor me!
Whom am going out to fight the enemy,
And know not whether I shall return again,
To enjoy the embraces of my children
And my wife.
O poor creature!
Whose life is not in his own hands,
Who has no power over his body,
But tries to do his duty
For the welfare of his nation.

And so on, for sixteen more lines.[23]

Many observers believed that Indians had the "necessary qualities" to become "civilized" and that their languages, too, had possibilities for development into artistic expression, since they were composed of "the very language for poetry" (as Walter Channing phrased it in 1815). It was, said Channing in a romantic rhapsody, like nature itself, "now elevated and soaring, for his image is the eagle, and now precipitous and hoarse as the cataract whose mists he is descanting."[24] Yet interest in the "oral literature" of the "aborigines" really began with the publication of Henry Rowe Schoolcraft's work, especially his *Algic Researches* of 1839, which Longfellow drew on for *The Song of Hiawatha* (1855). Schoolcraft was the first scholar of Native American literature to collect and analyze his materials extensively, and his career inaugurates American ethnology.

His literary career began when he accepted the post of Indian agent at Sault Sainte Marie, Michigan, in 1822. A year later he married Jane Johnson, whose father was an Irish fur trader and whose mother was the daughter of the famous Ojibwe leader Wabojeeg. Schoolcraft, however, was not interested in the legends and myths he collected for their own sake. Rather, he saw them as expressions of the Indian mind, "the interior man," as he termed it in *Algic Researches,* and "the secret workings of his mind, and heart, and soul."[25] Access to the Indian soul was necessary, Schoolcraft thought, for he believed that conversion to Christianity (specifically Presbyterianism) would precede civilization, and civilization was necessary because the Indians couldn't compete, being an "idle, pastoral, unphilosophical, non-inductive race of Central Asia." The inability of a Native narrator of tales to relate "a clear, consistent chain of indisputable facts and deductions to fill up the fore ground of his history" was evidence of the noninductive Oriental mind, operating in a world populated by gods and demons.[26] It comes as no surprise to learn that by 1844 Schoolcraft was a defender of the government's policy of Indian removal. He thought of Indians as children (a common attitude of the time), and the literature he was collecting and translating with the help of his Indian family (his knowledge of Ojibwe was not extensive) he regarded as "a chapter in the history of the human heart, in the savage phasis."[27]

As William M. Clements notes in "Schoolcraft as Textmaker," Schoolcraft, in his translations, stressed the practice of leaving the stories "as nearly as possible in their original forms of thought and expression." He did alter and vary, however, weeding out what he termed "vulgarisms" and "grossness," as well as "the repetition of tedious verbal details," "redundancies" that contemporary scholars have shown to be vital to the structural integrity of oral literature (the structure Schoolcraft denied existed).[28] In fact, in common with other pre-twentieth-century collectors, such as Thomas Percy and the Brothers Grimm in Europe and Americans such as Charles Godfrey Leland,[29] he made a number of changes, including rewordings and rewritings. He also removed songs (which he regarded as brief expressions of feelings, wild rhapsodies) from their narrative matrix, "where it was necessary," and relegated them to an appendix.[30]

Between the War of 1812 and the Civil War, as a result of the rise of romanticism and the call for artistic independence via the use of specifically American subjects, the Indian became prominent in literature, but as the "safely dead Indian,"[31] in books such as *The Last of the Mohicans* (1826) and *The Song of Hiawatha* (1855), the poetic representation of a dying race, a last Noble Savage. Even though this interest did not last and by late mid-century the theme of the superiority of White "civilization" over Indian "savagery" had taken its place, the late 1890s saw the beginning of a sympathetic treatment of contemporary Indian life and an understanding of tribal cultures by Adolph Bandelier and other "anthropologically inclined writers."[32] This was also about the time that witnessed the first transcription of Native ceremonies, resulting in texts that in many cases we have come to regard as classic. Horatio Hale published *The Iroquois Book of Rites* in 1883, and Washington Matthews, a medical doctor, published *The Navajo Mountain Chant* in 1883–84, and *The Night Chant* in 1902. In addition, there is the work of Major John Wesley Powell among the Numa (1868–80), W. J. Hoffman's *The Mide'wiwin or 'Grand Medicine Society' of the Ojibwa* (1891), the work of the Mennonite missionary H. R. Voth among the Hopi, including *The Oraibi Powamu Ceremony* (1902), and James Mooney's *The Ghost Dance Religion* of 1896. Also in 1896, Frank Hamilton Cushing brought out *Outlines of Zuni Creation Myths*, to be followed in 1901 by *Zuni Folk Tales* and, in 1920, by *Zuni Breadstuff*. Frances Densmore's work spanned decades and included *Chippewa Music* (1913), *Papago Music* (1929), and *Music of the Indians of British Columbia* (1943).[33]

Much of this work appeared in scholarly journals and in the bulletins of the Bureau of American Ethnology, the American Folklore Society, and the Smithsonian Institution. Anthropology was not yet formally organized as a discipline with university curricula, and most ethnologists were on the staff of the Bureau of American Ethnology. Whatever the collector's reasons for collecting (most thought they were preserving materials that would soon be lost in the march of progress; some were intent on wiping out the culture they were recording), the collections demonstrate the complexity and beauty of the songs, stories, myths, and ceremonies.

By 1850, the idea of a superior Caucasian race had been firmly established among North Americans of European descent, based on what Reginald Horsman terms "scientific racialism."[34] By the century's end social Darwinism, or cultural evolutionism, underlay the thinking of a great many White Americans and persisted into the twentieth century. Natalie Curtis was one of the people who believed in the imminent destruction ("the night soon to come") of the "child race."[35] In 1907, in the middle of all this collecting activity, she published *The Indians' Book,* the first collection aimed at a general audience (though this claim might also be made for the more restricted *Creation Myths of Primitive America,* which Jeremiah Curtin published in 1898[36]). The Curtis book contains Indian song, myth, music. In her introduction Curtis expresses the wish that the book can be useful for Americans by providing an impetus for American art; she hoped also that it would help revive pride among the Indians themselves—this at a time when the policy of the Bureau of Indian Affairs was to destroy and suppress Indian languages and cultures. (In 1886, a federal policy forbidding the use of any Indian language had been announced. This was not reversed until 1990, with the Native American Languages Act, which acknowledged the languages to be "an integral part" of Native American cultures and identities and affirmed the right of Native Americans to encourage the use of their languages in instruction and college curricula.)

The Indians' Book attempted to place the songs and other materials in the appropriate cultural context in order to help the reader's understanding. Although she knew none of the Indian languages, Curtis consulted experts as well as the singers and storytellers themselves. She included the music to the songs, difficult to transcribe in Western terms, and made transcriptions of the songs' original languages. Her word-by-word translations at the end of the book can be read against her free translations and have proved useful for later scholars.

If Natalie Curtis was the first to collect texts and make them available to the reading public, Mary Austin was the first to popularize Indian "poetry" and the first to utilize what she regarded as its ethos and principles to suggest ways in which English-language American poetry itself could advance.[37] She was not so much interested in the translations of songs (like Curtis, she knew no Indian language) as in the absorption of the "spirit" of the original to produce new poetry, something specifically and newly "American," based on what she called "the resident genius" of the land. She wished to establish a link between "this natural product and the recent work" of the modernists, specifically the Imagists, showing that "the first free movement of poetic originality in America finds us just about where the last Medicine Man left off."[38]

This process of renewal, using Indian songs to revitalize American poetry, entailed much rewriting of collected texts by poets innocent of any Indian language. The climax was twofold: a special "aboriginal issue" of the prestigious journal *Poetry* in February 1917 and, in 1918, what Mary Austin (in her introduction to the work) termed "the first authoritative volume of aboriginal American verse": George W. Cronyn's *The Path on the Rainbow*.[39] Cronyn drew inspiration from the special issue of *Poetry,* reprinting a number of the poems as well as translations by Schoolcraft, Matthews, Brinton, Curtis, Swanton, Mooney, Boas, and others. Mary Austin supplied some of her poem versions, and Frances Densmore turned some of her own texts collected in the field into haiku or imagist poems for the "new and enlarged edition" published in 1934.[40]

But the songs in the collection, from various cultures and languages, appear in isolation as American *poems,* cut loose from context and available for assimilation, available as models for the new "American rhythm." And while this work was being done, assimilation was the official government policy. The year 1887 had seen the General Allotment Act, a massive assault on Indian land and sovereignty; and the more virulent forms of assimilationist policies came to a halt only in 1934, the year *The Path on the Rainbow* was reprinted, when the Indian Reorganization Act came into being, guided by John Collier, Franklin Roosevelt's Commissioner of Indian Affairs. Although its promise was never fully realized, the IRA was intended to promote Indian regeneration and self-government by allowing tribes to organize for their own welfare and adopt federally approved constitutions at the same time that it curtailed the power of the office of Indian Affairs.[41]

One of the problems in studying Native American literature (though it has not always been regarded as a problem) has been the creation of a critical vocabulary and a mode of presentation. At first the structural model simply used the forms of the English lyric or narrative poem for presentation, and the critical stance also relied on what lay at hand. We can see this in the first attempt at criticism, Daniel G. Brinton's "Native American Poetry" (1880), and in Nellie Barnes's more extensive *American Indian Verse* (1921).[42] Barnes worked entirely with English versions made by collectors and stated her mystical belief that "the American Indians are the poets of the cosmos." This did not prevent her, however, from denying Indians any "great" poetry, the reason being "a lack of discipline in individual life" and a poor memory: "Memory is limited even in the most exact keeper of songs and rituals." Her literary analysis is limited to a number of impressionistic and quasi technical categories, such as "spirit," "imagination," "sense of beauty," "repetition," "parallelism," "poetic diction," "onomatopoeia," and the like. Her conclusion is no surprise: Indian poetry is "imaginative, aesthetic, and emotional." It lacks, however, "intellectual quality."[43] It thus corresponds to racialist ideas about Indians themselves. (It is interesting to note that Nellie Barnes's dichotomous conclusion corresponds roughly to prevalent contemporary ideas of male and female qualities.)

If a scholar like Nellie Barnes was interested in bringing Native American literature into critical consideration and a poet like Mary Austin wanted to revitalize American poetry by means of anthropologically "interpreting the Indian," Franz Boas set out to revolutionize American anthropology and anthropological linguistics through the study of the Indian, under the banner of cultural relativity and pluralism. And time was growing shorter for saving as much as possible. As Theodora Kroeber, the wife of Boas's first student, wrote, "The time was late; the dark forces of invasion had almost done their ignorant work of annihilation. To the field then!"[44] And to the field Boas went, from his base at Columbia University, where he taught from 1896 to 1936. Boas, "founder of professional anthropology in the New World,"[45] trained many of the major figures in the discipline, from Edward Sapir, Alfred Kroeber, Ruth Benedict, and Elsie Clews Parsons to Ruth Bunzel, Clark Wissler, Robert Lowie, and Paul Radin.

From the beginning of his career, when he was an assistant curator at the American Museum of Natural History, Boas revolted against raciology and cultural evolutionism. As Ira Jacknis notes, when the museum wanted to exhibit "a series illustrating the advance of mankind from the most primitive forms to the most complex forms of life," Boas protested that "our people are not the only carriers of civilization. . . . The human mind has everywhere been creative."[46] He revolutionized museum exhibits, no longer showing items as curiosities or specimens in natural history but presenting them instead as representations of a cultural context, "the objects becoming," Michael Ames writes, "words and sentences in a three-dimensional story about a people and their lifeways."[47] Something similar might be said of the way in which Boas displayed Native American texts. The Boasian tradition was to publish, after extensive fieldwork, a grammar, a dictionary, and a collection of texts. The texts have a dual purpose: they provide data for linguistic analysis, and they serve as primary ethnological documentation. As such, translation as an art form was not uppermost in Boas's mind, nor was it so in the minds of his students. In fact, Judith Berman has suggested that the texts themselves were the end product of ethnography and their translation "a necessary evil, an aid to those without fluency" in the language (this is still the position of some linguists): "The translations were never intended to be the primary source they have become."[48] Certainly there was no explicit attention to structure, and texts were represented in plain prose, in block form, with little or no attempt to represent the verbal artistry. Dennis Tedlock has taken the Boasian tradition to task for this, although he notes that "Boas and his students were reacting against collectors and 're-tellers' who avoided direct contact with the original languages."[49]

After the 1930s there was a falling off in the collection of Native American texts, and translation made few advances until Dell Hymes and Dennis Tedlock took up where the Boasians left off. Both men are linguistically and anthropologically based, but Hymes investigates structures in *transcribed* texts, especially those of the Northwest cultures, employing rhetorical patterns that reveal themselves as repetitions or recurrent adverbial particles, to produce "measured verse." He demonstrates that texts, written in blocks of prose, tend to be organized in lines and verses by grammatical means, though he stresses that principles of structure differ from language to language and from culture to culture—a Boasian position. As Joel Sherzer has written, "Hidden within the margin-to-margin printed texts are poems, waiting to be seen for the first time."[50] Hymes also utilizes the structure of drama in the presentation of his translations, a practice derived from Melville Jacobs. Hymes's concerns are fundamentally formal. Care is taken not only in the translation and in the structure of the texts but also, as part of an "attractive, efficient and effective format,"[51] with the way sounds are reproduced visually on the page.

Tedlock breaks with the past by focusing on *voice in oral performance,* providing translations that have some of the qualities of a musical score. He works with a tape recorder, and when the time comes for transcription and translation, he utilizes typography and spacing to indicate pauses, voice quality, tempo, cadence, variations in pitch, and the like. In this way he reminds us that the literature he is working with is *oral*—spoken and enacted, not read from a page.

There has been some opposition to the approaches of Hymes and

Tedlock. Anthony Mattina, for example, has argued that both provide merely "typographical remedies" for the problems of translation or "intuited underlying structure" and that the methods are not applicable to all situations: "Not all North American Indian narrative is verse any more than all of English literature is dialogue." He argues for a variety of approaches. He himself prefers to translate into "Red English" ("roughly analogous to Black English").[52] Judging by the evidence of the present volume, however, it seems that the approaches of Hymes and Tedlock have been adopted and adapted by a good number of translators, perhaps because, as Julie Cruikshank reports, breaking lines and utilizing other "experimental" forms recapture some sense of actual performance: "Native women who know the storytellers and have read various versions of the text say that they find it easier to 'hear' the speaker's voice when reading this form."[53]

The collection of texts has been fraught with problems, many of them questions of morality of method. While Indians were being stripped of land and culture, collectors were out "in the field" doing "salvage anthropology." But for whom were they rescuing the material? Wasn't this collecting just another form of Western "possessive individualism"?[54] Wasn't it just self-enrichment in the name of "knowledge" and "science"? As James Clifford has pointed out in 1988 in *The Predicament of Culture,* collecting materials from another culture cannot be natural or innocent. All collectors and collections, he notes, embody "hierarchies of value," since "the simplest cultural accounts are intentional creations." The desire is to collect not only artifacts but the makers of those artifacts.[55]

In her essay "An Old Time Indian Attack," the Laguna Pueblo novelist Leslie Marmon Silko has remarked on "the racist assumption still abounding that the prayers, chants and stories weaseled out by the early ethnographers, which are now collected in ethnographic journals, are public property." This is an extreme statement; not all was theft.[56] Nevertheless, collectors of texts and artifacts have operated under certain assumptions, and perhaps the most prevalent is the assumption of "democratic" rights of access to any material and information. This, however, is in direct contrast to the norms of many, if not all, Native cultures. As Peter Whiteley has noted of the Hopi: communication of knowledge "is not an open free-for-all; much knowledge is privileged and valuable, and the average citizen does not have rights of access. Some forms of knowledge, especially pertaining to ritual, are highly sensitive and should not be discussed publicly."[57] Moreover, pressures brought to bear by insensitive collectors and edicts such as the Indian Religious Crimes Code, which the Department of the Interior began to enforce in 1921, driving many religions underground, have resulted in less openness than might originally have existed.

Finally, sometimes a field worker discovers that access to knowledge, once achieved, poses real perils, that "there is danger in deeper inquiry into the stories," as Barre Toelken wrote in "Life and Death in the Navajo Coyote Tales." He discovered, for example, that for the Navajo, language does not simply describe reality; it creates and controls it. And Navajo oral literature "embodies many key aspects of their worldview on reality and human health. Their concept of health is largely psychological in nature, thus any psychological intrusion can—and will—have an effect on them and on their sense of stability." Toelken's work on Coyote stories entailed asking selective and analytic questions to find out what was powerful about Coyote, dealing with parts and motifs as interesting ideas. His questions were seen as dissecting and separating rather than bringing things together. Since Navajo ritual does the latter and witches do the former, his academic-analytic questions and categories were interpreted by some Navajo as being like witchcraft behavior. This presented an ethical dilemma: "For me to actually do further work would necessitate a repudiation of Navajo beliefs and values—treasures that I feel ought to be strengthened and nurtured by folklore scholarship, not weakened, denigrated, or even given away to curious onlookers." So he decided not to go any deeper on the analytic level. Even though Toelken has modified his approach and abandoned the questions that were bothering the Navajo (no matter how fascinating they might have been for the scholarly audience), for Toelken's "fieldwork partners," the Yellowman family, there have been repercussions: deaths, injuries, accidents. Toelken is now a patient in the Blessingway—one of the approximately twenty-six rites that make up the chantway cures. It is performed for good mental and physical health, to correct disharmony. The Yellowman family considers it efficacious for him and stabilizing for them. Toelken concludes: "The enormity and complexity of the living whole have eluded the best efforts of long-range fieldwork, and that needs to be admitted and confronted. Not only were basic ideas and concepts missed and misunderstood, but the very fieldwork itself stood a strong chance of being dangerous to the informants as well as to myself and my family."[58]

Collecting and translating Native American texts are, then, replete with ironies and dilemmas. Eric Cheyfitz, claiming that translation broadly conceived was, and still is, "the central act of European colonialization and imperialism in America," argues for dialogue, not monologue, as a way of healing some of the rifts.[59] And Barre Toelken has written that fieldwork, which is "often viewed as a means of coming up with more artifacts or texts for study, needs to be reexamined as a model for human interaction. We already have plenty of 'things' to study; what we lack is a concerted effort to understand fieldwork itself as an interhuman dynamic event with its own meanings and cultural peculiarities."[60] Moreover, Native American leaders are calling for something along the same lines. Thus, Hopi Tribal Chairman Vernon Masayesva notes that "research needs to be based on the reality of our existence as we experience it" and that an "inclusive agenda" would "involve mutual study."[61]

The evidence from the present volume is that the contributors have faced up to this issue and are enacting a dialogue. Many, in correspondence, expressed dissatisfaction with the exigencies of publishing, whereby texts are presented only in translation and not along with the original language, thus reducing the value for the Native American community, which might want to use some texts as part, for instance, of a bilingual-education program or a literacy program. As Larry Evers wrote, "To erase the native language text in a trade edition sends a very negative message to those who speak and read a native American language."[62] Evers and Felipe Molina have voiced the dual aim of most, if not all, the translators in this volume: "We work for two goals: for the continuation of deer songs as a vital part of life in Yaqui communities and for their appreciation in all communities beyond. Most of the time these goals coincide."[63]

Contemporary interest in Native American cultures, boosted by the 1992 Columbus quincentenary "celebrations," has its roots in the 1960s, which saw a new ethnic awareness and the growth of civil and minority rights. This interest is both serious and trivial. Native Americans have always been seen through many and varied lenses. Euro-American perceptions have long been shaped by prejudices, desires, fears, theories—what Louise Barnett calls "the White fantasy world."[64] In a sense "Indian" and "Native American" do not exist; they were created as fictions of the Euro-American consciousness. This "fictional" process has been, and still is, insidious in that it not only affects the non-Native perception of what it means to be

"Indian," but it infiltrates part of the Native American community also.[65]

In the last quarter century or so serious interest has resulted in the growth and establishment of departments of American Indian and Native American Studies programs in colleges and universities in the United States and Native Studies programs in colleges and universities in Canada. Native American literatures are being taught at the high school and college levels and are being included in anthologies. Journals and newspapers devoted to Native Studies have been established, Native American organizations and associations have been formed, and fourteen radio stations in the United States offer Indian-language broadcasts. Important work is being carried out in film and video by such entities as the Native American Public Broadcasting Consortium and, in Canada, the Inuit Broadcasting Corporation and Northern Native Broadcasting. In 1972, growing self-confidence resulted in the establishment of the American Indian Higher Education Consortium; twenty-six colleges in the United States and Canada are members. There has also been a renaissance in all the arts, from drama and dance, poetry and fiction to film, video, and the fine arts. The new and old, "Anglo" and "Indian", are intimately linked. The novel, for instance, is often rooted in the oral tradition, as we can see in N. Scott Momaday's *House Made of Dawn,* which won the Pulitzer Prize in 1969 and ushered in the new Indian writing. Momaday draws on the living oral tradition, as well as on Washington Matthews's *The Night Chant* of 1902. Similarly, Momaday's *The Way to Rainy Mountain* (1969) draws on Kiowa storytelling and James Mooney's *Calendar History of the Kiowa* (1898). Likewise, Leslie Marmon Silko's celebrated novel *Ceremony* (1977) utilizes Franz Boas and Elsie Clews Parsons, as well as "the stories—whether they are history, whether they are fact, whether they are gossip."[66]

Unfortunately, the frivolous interest of non-Indians in matters Native American has grown at the same time, with its New Age tinsel and old stereotypes, all variations on what Robert F. Berkhofer Jr. has called the "timeless Indian."[67] The Indian as healer has given rise to wide variations on the theme of the "plastic shaman."[68] We also have new twists on the Indian as sage and environmentalist, from the well-known poster from 1972 that announces POLLUTION: IT'S A CRYING SHAME and features Iron Eyes Cody with a glycerine tear to the growing use of Chief Seattle's Speech as a primary environmental document when in fact, as Rudolf Kaiser has shown, it is largely a modern fabrication.[69] The recent burst of interest on the part of filmmakers continues to draw on such hoary stereotypes as Good versus Bad Indians and the Noble Savage versus the Demonic Savage, as in *Dances with Wolves* (1991), though there is now an attempt to use Indian actors and Native languages—witness the Lakota spoken in *Dances with Wolves* and the White Mountain Apache (a substitution for Geronimo's Chiricahua Apache) spoken in the 1994 film *Geronimo*. This is a change from the gibberish used in many old Westerns and from John Ford's substitution of Navajo for Cheyenne in *Cheyenne Autumn* (1964), though the pronunciation of Apache in *Geronimo* by non-Apache speakers leaves a great deal to be desired. Nineteenth-century eugenics is alive and well in the film *Thunderheart* (1992), where an FBI agent with one-quarter Sioux blood is visited with atavistic visions on his road to self-discovery.[70] *Blackrobe* (1991) presents a sensationalist view of Native culture and a parodic view of Native spirituality. And so it goes, from fake Indians like "Princess Pale Moon" singing the national anthem for the Washington Redskins to made-for-TV Ishis and Geronimos; from Carlos Castaneda's books to *Hanta Yo* (1979) by Ruth Beebe Hill to *The Education of Little Tree* (1976) by Forrest Carter (also known as Asa Earl Carter); from Lynn Andrews's New Age works of "self-awareness and knowledge" to the Chief Joseph Massage ("a holistic massage"), four-wheel drive Cherokees, and twin-blade Apaches—not to mention the names and mascots of sports teams, the recent forty-ounce "upstrength" malt liquor Crazy Horse ("a Product of America"), and even the annual summer "invasions" (as Carter Camp calls them) of Indian Country (the Lakota Nation seems to be a special target) by people "hungry to have an 'Indian experience.'"

All this—mostly examples of bad taste, thoughtlessness, a "need" for the "primitive,"[71] and the kind of trivialization and exploitation most people take for granted in our culture—might not be so bad if Native Americans were not "still among the most poorly housed, poorly nourished, least educated, unhealthiest and most unemployed" of any people in the United States, with the lowest life expectancy.[72] The "invasions," for example, might not be so bad if they did not adversely affect Indian life. "How," asks Carter Camp, "can Lakota children find the same respect for tribal ways our grandfathers handed down to us if hundreds of these pitiful ones are out waving pipes, pouring water, singing songs learned from cassettes and whipping a drum?"[73] It might all be easy to overlook were it not for the history of this country and the continuing ignorance of that history by many Americans, from those in positions of power, such as James Watt, Interior Secretary under Ronald Reagan, who informed a TV audience on January 19, 1983, that "If you want an example of the failures of socialism, don't go to Russia, come to America and go to the Indian reservations," and Senator Alan Simpson of Wyoming, who more recently said, "Languages of the Indian Native American people . . . have never been set down in writing. They cannot be. They have passed into history," to syndicated columnists such as Andy Rooney, "America's favorite humorist and commentator," whose racist remarks in print probably reflect the thinking of too many Americans.[74]

In 1985, Frederick E. Hoxie examined thirteen commonly used college history textbooks. He found "the persistence of inadequate and inaccurate treatment of Indians."[75] Americans know little about the Native roots of their history and are expected to know less, if we can believe E. D. Hirsch Jr., Joseph Kett, and James Trefil of *The Dictionary of Cultural Literacy,* a best-selling volume that—along with an earlier companion volume, *Cultural Literacy: What Every American Needs to Know*—created something of a stir when it entered the arena of debate over "cultural heritage" in 1988. This massive collection of "specific information that is taken for granted in our public discourse" contains very little on Native America, and even that is inadequate and misleading, which is not surprising, since the authors believe "Native Americans" (their ubiquitous term used often instead of important specific tribal identifications, as in the statement that Custer was defeated "by a large force of NATIVE AMERICANS") are long gone. Witness the entry "NATIVE AMERICANS: The inhabitants of NORTH AMERICA and SOUTH AMERICA before the arrival of white settlers from Europe." The book devotes approximately 2 pages out of 586 to these Native Americans. There is no mention of anything after about 1890.[76] (Hoxie noted the same thing in the college textbooks he examined: "The greatest gap in classroom presentation of Indian life seems to occur in the twentieth century. For the most part, Indians simply cease to exist after the Battle of Wounded Knee."[77]) If we are to believe *The Dictionary of Cultural Literacy,* Indians are mostly creatures of myth (Quetzalcoatl) or mythic popular story or history (Hiawatha, Pocahontas, Sitting Bull).

I do not wish to engage extensively here in the debate over multiculturalism and the canon. The desire to bring the texts in the present volume to a wide audience needs little justification. It can only help broaden our sense of what our real and complex cultural history really is. Native cultures, like all cultures, are valuable in and for themselves and do not need any apologia. To some, however, "other" cultures seem to represent a threat to "a common American culture," in which differences can exist so long as they are more or less assimilated. Any culture other than the one they have identified as paramount seems a challenge to their sense of order or their sense of themselves and their culture as authentically American. It was actually suggested to me by an intellectual of some note that if "minority" cultures and languages were allowed full expression (through, for example, bilingual education), the United States would end up in warring, balkanized fragments, much like Yugoslavia.

Surely in this cultural sense polyphony is to be preferred to plainsong. In place of the arrogance of Saul Bellow's statement that "when the Zulus have a Tolstoy, *we* will read him,"[78] would it not be a good idea to consider that the Zulus just might have a literature that could be worthy of our attention and that we might have something to learn, to share, something in common and something intriguingly *not* in common? Why not extend or adapt Mikhail Bakhtin's statement that "language . . . lies on the borderline between oneself and the other. The word in language is half someone else's . . . the word does not exist in a neutral or impersonal language . . . but rather exists in other people's mouths, in other peoples' contexts, serving other peoples' intentions: it is from there that one must take the word and make it one's own"?[79]

Native storytellers, orators, and singers have contributed to this collection. The great majority of the other contributors, Native and non-Native, have also worked with the indigenous languages, either in collaboration with these Native artists or via the retranslation of earlier texts. Some (for example, Catharine McClellan, Julie Cruikshank, and Anthony Mattina) have worked with multilingual people who chose to tell their stories in English.

In "Anthologies and Narrators," a 1987 critique of the Erdoes-Ortiz anthology, Dell Hymes argued that "ethnopoetics provides a foundation on which anthologies should as much as possible be based."[80] One could say that the present book is the first with a substantially "ethnopoetic" slant. And it makes certain demands on the reader. If Native American literatures are not as easily digested as some might wish, if they almost successfully resist assimilation, then that is part of the book's ethos. As William Bevis has written, "We won't get Indian culture as cheaply as we got Manhattan."[81] (The Cherokee poet and artist Jimmie Durham put it more radically and paradoxically: "I do not want to entertain you in any sense of the word. I would hate it if you all came to understand me."[82])

Initially, I thought I would have difficulty finding more than about twenty contributors to this volume. I was surprised (though I shouldn't have been) by the response. To include as much good work as possible, and to fit it all into the prescribed number of pages, I had to reduce the original page allocation for each contributor. The result might give the wrong impression that most Native American literature consists of songs and shortish stories, oratory, and prayer. The longer "epic" productions, such as the great Navajo Chantways, the Osage Wa-Xo-Be, and the Zuni Ha'lako ceremonies could not have been represented here in their totality, even if any new translations had been submitted.

An anthology omits more than it contains, but that is implicit in the word's etymology—it is only "a bunch of flowers." I was largely dependent on responses to the hundreds of letters I sent to people working in various languages and cultures and on responses to notices I placed in journals specializing in anthropology, linguistics, and Native American literatures. Much of the work that came in was from the Southwest and the North, where the Native languages and literatures are the strongest and study of them most intense. In making choices, I tried to cover as much ground as possible. But there are inevitable gaps. For instance, while I worked hard to obtain translations from Cherokee, I was not successful. And there is only one representative from the Southeast. Perhaps, given the rapid advances in this field, by the time the second, expanded edition of this volume goes to press, there will be no lack of Cherokee and southeastern material to choose from. So, while attempting to be as representative as possible, this anthology does not lay claim to comprehensiveness.

The collection has taken its inspiration not so much from previous anthologies, like Margot Astrov's *The Winged Serpent* (1946) or, more recently, John Bierhorst's *The Red Swan* (1976) and Richard Erdoes and Alfonso Ortiz's *American Indian Myths and Legends* (1984), useful as these books may be. Instead, I have followed the lead of Karl Kroeber's *Traditional Literatures of the American Indian: Texts and Interpretations* (1981)[83] and follow up my own *Smoothing the Ground* (1983), *On the Translation of Native American Literatures* (1992), and *Recovering the Word,* the latter edited by Arnold Krupat and me in 1987. These books contain many "texts and interpretations" by leading scholars of Central and South American literatures, as well as the literatures of North America. If there is a very early anthology with which I feel a certain affinity, it is Natalie Curtis's *The Indians' Book* of 1907, since it did not let the translations stand naked by themselves but attempted to provide a context, cultural and linguistic.

I would like to thank all those who have contributed to this volume: original performers, singers, storytellers, orators, and their translators. Some of these translations are reprinted (most with changes) from recent publications, but the majority were made especially for this volume. I want to thank the translators not only for their distinguished work but for responding so generously to my suggestions, queries, and requests. And I want to thank many other people, too numerous to mention, but including my dear wife, Roberta, and my friend and collaborator, Arnold Krupat; also Joseph Bruchac, William Cowan, William Fenton, Ives Goddard, Victor Golla, Frederick Hoxie, Michael Krauss, W. H. New, Joel Sherzer, and William Sturtevant. In addition, thanks to Thaddeus Gatza for help with musical transcription, to the American Indian Community House Gallery, New York City, Joanna Osburn-Bigfeather, Curator, for supplying the cover art, and to Gail Buckland for initiating this project. Finally, I am grateful to Harold Evans, President and Publisher of Random House, and LuAnn Walther, Vice President and Executive Editor of Vintage Books and Knopf/Everyman's Library, for helping Native American literatures reach a wide audience, and to Sally Arteseros for expert editorial help; also at Random House, thanks to Susan DiSesa, managing director of the Modern Library, Ian Jackman, assistant editor, Dennis Ambrose, production editor, Stephen Wolf, and Abigail Winograd.

The art used for the part title page of Alaska, Yukon, and the Subarctic is a fillet from the lower Yukon, made of sealskin and caribou skin. The art for The North Pacific Coast is a Kwakiutl Noohlmahl mask from Vancouver Island, while that for Great Basin and Plateau is a Thompson basket with a design of arrowheads. Art for The Plains is nineteenth-century Sioux. The tipi decoration shows it belonged to a member of the Black Bear subgens. The Eastern Woodlands art is a dancing garter with beaded design, part of an elaborate ceremonial costume worn by members of the Ojibwe Midé or Grand Medicine Society. Art for The Southwest and Southeast is a Laguna water jar, (Sources: Eva Wilson, *North American Indian Designs,* Dover Publications, New York, 1984; Maria Naylor, *Authentic Indian Designs: 2500 Illustrations from Reports of the Bureau of American*

Ethnology, Dover Publications, Inc., New York, 1975.) That for California is a Chumash rock painting from Cuyama. (Source: Campbell Grant, *The Rock Paintings of the Chumash,* University of California Press, 1965.) Part-title frame decorations are ancient Pueblo pottery designs.

NOTES

1. Peter M. Whiteley, *Deliberate Acts* (Tucson: University of Arizona Press), 1988, 33.

2. For a history of "the idea of the Indian," see Robert F. Berkhofer Jr., *The White Man's Indian: Images of the American Indian from Columbus to the Present* (New York: Alfred A. Knopf, 1978). The Indians' very existence was a challenge to the European world view, and Indians were regarded as Phoenician, Assyrian, Egyptian, Canaanite, Trojan, Roman, Israelite, Chinese Buddhist, Irish, Norse, Basque, and so on in order that they might be fit into this scheme. Even today their Israelite origin is part of Mormon-church doctrine, as laid out in "The Book of Alma, the Son of Alma." For more on this, see Robert Wauchope, *Lost Tribes and Sunken Continents* (Chicago: University of Chicago Press, 1963).

3. Merritt Ruhlen, *A Guide to the World's Languages* (Stanford, Calif.: Stanford University Press, 1987), 805.

4. Charles A. Ferguson and Shirley Brice Heath, eds., *Language in the USA* (Cambridge, England: Cambridge University Press, 1981), 119.

5. For this brief overview I have drawn on Harry Hoijer, ed., *Linguistic Structures of Native America,* Viking Fund Publications in Anthropology no. 6 (1944; reprint, New York: Johnson Reprint, 1946, 1963); Ruhlen, *A Guide to the World's Languages;* Lyle Campbell and Marianne Mithun, eds., *The Languages of Native America* (Austin: University of Texas Press, 1979); Joseph Howard Greenberg, *Language in the Americas* (Stanford, Calif.: Stanford University Press, 1987); and Ferguson and Heath, eds., *Language in the USA.*

6. I have concentrated here on the history and cultures of Native Americans in the United States. Clearly there are many overlaps with Canada, including policies of removal, assimilation, and suppression. But there are also differences, especially in legal and social matters. For more on Canada and the First Nations, the following books are useful: Doreen Jensen and Cheryl Brooks, *In Celebration of Our Survival: The First Nations of British Columbia* (Vancouver: University of British Columbia Press, 1991); John A. Price, *Native Studies:*

American and Canadian Indians (Toronto: McGraw-Hill, 1978); J. Anthony Long and Menno Bolt, eds., *Governments in Conflict? Provinces and Indian Nations in Conflict in Canada* (Toronto: University of Toronto Press, 1988); Bruce Alden Cox, ed., *Native Peoples, Native Lands* (Ottawa: Carleton University Press, 1988); Ian A. L. Getty and Antoine S. Lussier, eds., *As Long As the Sun Shines and Water Flows: A Reader in Canadian Native Studies* (Vancouver: University of British Columbia Press, 1983); and Penny Petrone, *Native Literature in Canada from the Oral Tradition to the Present* (Toronto: Oxford University Press, 1990).

7. For demographies see William M. Denevan, ed., *The Native Population of the Americas in 1492* (Madison: University of Wisconsin Press, 1976), and C. Matthew Snipp, *American Indians: The First of This Land* (New York: Russell Sage Foundation, 1989). Estimates of the population of North America at the time of contact vary from a low of just over one million to a high of ten million (the true number is probably somewhere in the middle). For all the Americas the population was probably about fifty-seven million. There was a massive drop in the sixteenth century, termed by Denevan "probably the greatest demographic disaster in the history of the world, and one from which the Indians never recovered" (p. 7).

8. N. Scott Momaday, *House Made of Dawn* (New York: Harper and Row, 1968), 90.

9. In 1980, the U.S. Census Bureau reported a 72-percent increase in the Indian population since 1970; an additional 38-percent increase was recorded in 1990. Clearly not only natural increase is at work here. People who never did so before are now choosing to define themselves as Indian, for a variety of reasons. (In Canada there are about half a million Native people.)

10. Vine Deloria Jr., "Commentary: Research, Redskins, and Reality," *American Indian Quarterly* 15 (Fall 1991): 460.

11. The phrase is used by Vine Deloria Jr. and Clifford M. Lytle in *American Indians, American Justice,* ed. Deloria Jr. and Lytle (Austin: University of Texas Press, 1983), 24.

12. As Stephen L. Pevar notes in *The Rights of Indians and Tribes* (Carbondale: Southern Illinois University Press, 1992), there has never been a consistent federal Indian policy. This lack has resulted in great disruption in Indian life, especially since there has been a total lack of Indian involvement and consent. Policy can change at any moment—many non-Indian groups, some well financed, want to abolish Indian and tribal rights. Pevar also observes that "no other ethnic or cultural group is so heavily regulated. Although some federal laws were intended to benefit Indians, as a whole they have placed Indians in a political and economic straitjacket" (p. 2). Virtually every aspect of Indian life is affected by the relationship to the federal government, especially to the Bureau of Indian Affairs. This means that the price of survival is dependency.

13. Michael Krauss, "Number and Viability of Native American Languages by State and Province," *SSILA Newsletter* (January 1992): 2; Richard and Nora Dauenhauer, "Native Language Survival," *Left Bank* 2 (Summer 1992): 115–22. Robert H. Robins and Eugenius M. Uhlenbeck, eds., *Endangered Lan-*

guages (Oxford, England: Berg, 1991), is a valuable source of information on the situation in the Americas. Ofelia Zepeda and Jane H. Hill's essay, "The Condition of Native American Languages in the United States," is particularly relevant for our purposes, as is M. Dale Kinkade's "The Decline of Native Languages in Canada."

14. Michael Krauss, "The World's Languages in Crisis," *Languages* 68 (March 1992): 3.

15. Dauenhauer, "Native Language Survival," 115–22.

16. Julian Rice, letter to author, 1992.

17. Gerald Vizenor, "Dead Voices," *World Literature Today* 66 (Spring 1992): 241; Ray A. Young Bear, *Black Eagle Child: The Faceprint Narratives* (Iowa City: University of Iowa Press, 1992), 67.

18. Bruno Nettl, "The Songs of Ishi: Musical Style of the Yahi Indians," *Musical Quarterly* 51 (July 1965): 460–77.

19. *Ho* is a salutation of joy or an expression of approval. *Schene I atsiehoene* is something like "It will produce peace," and *netho* is "so be it." See Charles T. Gehring and William A. Starna, trans. and eds., *A Journey into Mohawk and Oneida Country, 1634–1635: The Journal of Harmen Meyndertsz van den Bogaert* (Syracuse, N.Y.: Syracuse University Press, 1988), 44–45. Thanks to William N. Fenton for directing me to this new translation.

20. For a fuller discussion of early recording, see my introduction in Brian Swann, ed., *On the Translation of Native American Literatures* (Washington, D.C.: Smithsonian Institution Press, 1992); for an overview of the history of translation, see also Arnold Krupat's essay in the same volume, "On the Translation of Native American Song and Story: A Theorized History."

21. Roy Harvey Pearce, *Savagism and Civilization: a Study of the Indian and the American Mind* (Berkeley: University of California Press, 1967; reprint, with a foreword by Arnold Krupat, 1988).

22. John G. E. Heckewelder, *An Account of the History, Manners, and Customs of the Indian Nations* (1819; reprinted as *History, Manners, and Customs of the Indian Nations Who Once Inhabited Pennsylvania and the Neighboring States,* Philadelphia: Historical Society of Pennsylvania, 1876, and New York: Arno Press, 1971).

23. Heckewelder quotes are from the 1876 edition, xl, 113, 137, 210.

24. Quoted in William M. Clements, " 'Tokens of Literary Faculty': Native American Literature and Euroamerican Translation in the Early Nineteenth Century," in *On the Translation of Native American Literatures,* ed. Swann, 37.

25. Quoted in William M. Clements, "Schoolcraft as Textmaker," *Journal of American Folklore* 103 (1990): 181.

26. Quoted in Robert E. Bieder, *Science Encounters the Indian, 1820–1880* (Norman: University of Oklahoma Press, 1986), 175, 180.

27. Quoted in Clements, "Schoolcraft as Textmaker," 186.

28. Ibid.

29. For Leland's practices see Thomas Parkhill's " 'Of Glooscap's Birth, and of His Brother, Malsum, the Wolf': The Story of Charles Godfrey Leland's 'Purely American Creation,' " *American Indian Culture and Research Journal* 16, no. 1 (1992): 45–69.

30. Clements, "Schoolcraft as Textmaker," 186.

31. Berkhofer Jr., *The White Man's Indian*, 90.

32. Ibid., 107.

33. Horatio Hale, *The Iroquois Book of Rites* (1883; reprint, with an introduction by William N. Fenton, Toronto: University of Toronto Press, 1963); Washington Matthews, *The Navajo Mountain Chant*, in The Fifth Annual Report of the Bureau of American Ethnology for the Years 1883–84 (Washington, D.C.: Smithsonian Institution; reprinted as *The Mountain Chant: Navajo Ceremony*, 1887), and *The Night Chant: A Navajo Ceremony*, American Museum of Natural History Memoirs, Anthropology Series no. 5 (New York, 1902); John Wesley Powell, *Anthropology of the Numa: John Wesley Powell's Manuscript on the Numic Peoples of North America*, ed. Don D. Fowler and Catherine S. Fowler (1860–80; reprint, Washington, D.C.: Smithsonian Institution Press, 1971); W. J. Hoffman, *The Mide'wiwin or 'Grand Medicine Society' of the Ojibwa*, in The Seventh Annual Report of the American Bureau of Ethnology for the Years 1885–86 (Washington, D.C.: Smithsonian Institution), 145–300; Henry R. Voth, *The Oraibi Powamu Ceremony*, Field Columbian Museum Publication no. 61, Anthropological Series, vol. 3, no. 2 (Chicago, 1901); James Mooney, *The Ghost Dance Religion, and Sioux Outbreak of 1890*, pt. 2, The Fourteenth Annual Report of the Bureau of Ethnology for the Years 1892–93 (Washington, D.C.: Smithsonian Institution, 1896; reprint, Lincoln: University of Nebraska Press, 1991); Frank Hamilton Cushing, *Outlines of Zuni Creation Myths*, in The Thirteenth Annual Report of the Bureau of American Ethnology for the Years 1891–92 (Washington, D.C.: Smithsonian Institution, 1896), 321–447, *Zuni Folk Tales* (New York: Putnam, 1901), and *Zuni Breadstuff*, Museum of the American Indian, Heye Foundation, Indian Notes and Monographs no. 8 (New York, 1920); and Frances Densmore, *Chippewa Music*, Smithsonian Institution, Bureau of American Ethnology Bulletin nos. 45 and 53 (Washington, D.C., 1910–13), *Papago Music*, Smithsonian Institution, Bureau of American Ethnology Bulletin no. 90 (Washington, D.C., 1929; reprint, New York: DaCapo Press, 1972), and *Music of the Indians of British Columbia*, Smithsonian Institution, Bureau of American Ethnology, Anthropological Paper no. 27 (Washington, D.C., 1973). For a critique of Frank Hamilton Cushing, see Dennis Tedlock, "On the Translation of Style in Oral Narrative," in Tedlock, *The Spoken Word and the Work of Interpretation* (Philadelphia: University of Pennsylvania Press, 1983), 30–61.

34. Reginald Horsman, *Race and Manifest Destiny: The Origins of Racial Anglo-Saxonism* (Cambridge, Mass.: Harvard University Press, 1981), 139.

35. Natalie Curtis, *The Indians' Book: An Offering by the American Indians of Indian Lore, Musical and Narrative, to Form a Record of Songs and Legends of Their Race* (New York: Harper and Brothers, 1907; reprint of 1923 edition, New York: Dover Books, 1968), xxi, xxii.

36. Jeremiah Curtin, *Creation Myths of Primitive America, in Relation to the Religious History and Mental Development of Mankind* (Boston: Little, Brown, 1898; reprint, New York: Benjamin Blom, 1969).

37. Mary Hunter Austin, *The American Rhythm* (1923; reprint, Boston: Houghton Mifflin, 1930).

38. Austin, introduction to George W. Cronyn, ed., *The Path on the Rainbow: An Anthology of Songs and Chants from the Indians of North America* (1918; rev. ed., New York: Liveright, 1934), xxxii. Michael Castro's *Interpreting the Indian: Twentieth Century Poets and the Native American* (Albuquerque: University of New Mexico Press, 1983) traces the relationship between Native American literature and twentieth-century poets and poetics.

39. Austin, introduction to Cronyn, *The Path on the Rainbow*, xvi.

40. Here is one of Densmore's poems:

THE DEER AND THE FLOWER

**The deer
looks at a flower.**

Unfortunately, although Austin stated in her introduction that "it is the very nature of primitive verse that it should require interpretation," no notes appear in *Path*. There is no way of finding out, for example, that Densmore's little poem (and others like it that she wrote for the collection) was, in fact, a tiny extrapolation from a large ceremony: two lines (or, nontextually, one phrase) from a complex Yaqui Deer Dance that Densmore had recorded at Guadalupe, near Phoenix, in 1922 and that had appeared in her *Yuman and Yaqui Music* (Smithsonian Institution, Bureau of American Ethnology Bulletin no. 110 [Washington, D.C., 1932]).

41. For an account of American Indian history in legal and cultural terms, see Deloria Jr. and Lytle, eds., *American Indians, American Justice*, as well as Pevar, *The Rights of Indians and Tribes*. For a concise discussion of the General Allotment Act, see Wilcombe E. Washburn's *The Indian in America* (New York: Harper and Row, 1975), 238–50. Washburn points out, for example, that when the act passed in 1887, Indian land consisted of 138 million acres. By 1934, when the process of allotment ceased, about 60 percent of the land had passed out of Indian hands, had been declared surplus, and had been sold. Of the lands allotted to individual Indians to farm and held in trust by the government for twenty-five years, 27 million acres, or two thirds of the land, were lost between 1887 and 1934. For an excellent, wide-ranging account of policy, see pt. 4, "Imagery and White Policy: The Indian as Justification and Rationale," of Berkhofer's *The White Man's Indian*. For a discussion of the IRA as "another cooptation of Indians" ("Indians do not see the tribe as organized under the IRA as their own democratic, legitimate government, but as an

alien force"), see Michael G. Lacy, "The United States and the American Indian: Political Relations," in *American Indian Policy in the Twentieth Century,* ed. Vine Deloria Jr. (Norman: University of Oklahoma Press, 1992), 83–104.

42. Daniel Garrison Brinton, "Native American Poetry," in *Essays of an Americanist* (Philadelphia: David McKay Publishers, 1890), 284; Nellie Barnes, *American Indian Verse: Characteristics of Style,* University of Kansas, Bulletin of Humanistic Studies no. 4 (Lawrence, 1921), 1–63.

43. Barnes, *American Indian Verse,* 9, 21, 56.

44. Quoted by Karl Kroeber in "Reasoning Together," in *Smoothing the Ground: Essays on Native American Oral Literature,* ed. Brian Swann (Berkeley: University of California Press, 1983), 350. For more on Boas, see chap. 21, "Modernism, Irony, Anthropology: The Work of Franz Boas," in Arnold Krupat, *Ethnocriticism: Ethnography, History, Literature* (Berkeley: University of California Press, 1992). Although Boas is often praised for his linguistic accuracy, Judith Berman has demonstrated that in regard to at least one of his Kwakiutl texts, "His misinterpretations are so extreme that in the English version the story seems incoherent" ("Oolachan-Woman's Robe: Fish, Blankets, Masks, and Meaning in Boas's Kwakw'ala Texts," in *On the Translation of Native American Literatures,* ed. Swann, 125).

45. George W. Stocking, ed., *Objects and Others: Essays on Museums and Material Culture* (Madison: University of Wisconsin Press, 1985), 107.

46. Ira Jacknis, "Franz Boas and Exhibits," in *Objects and Others,* ed. Stocking, 102–110.

47. Michael Ames, *Museums, the Public, and Anthropology* (Vancouver: University of British Columbia Press, 1986), 40.

48. Berman, "Oolachan-Woman's Robe," 157.

49. Tedlock, *The Spoken Word and the Work of Interpretation,* 32.

50. Joel Sherzer in *Native American Discourse: Poetics and Rhetoric,* ed. Sherzer and Anthony C. Woodbury (Cambridge, England: Cambridge University Press, 1987), 19.

51. Dell Hymes, "Gitskux and His Older Brother," in *Smoothing the Ground,* ed. Swann, 139.

52. Anthony Mattina, "North American Indian Mythography: Editing Texts for the Printed Page," in *Recovering the Word: Essays on Native American Literature,* ed. Brian Swann and Arnold Krupat (Berkeley: University of California Press, 1987), 129, 137, 139.

53. Julie Cruikshank with Angela Sidney, Kitty Smith, and Annie Ned, *Life Lived Like a Story: Life Stories of Three Athapaskan Elders* (Lincoln: University of Nebraska Press, 1990), 18.

54. C. B. Macpherson, *The Political Theory of Possessive Individualism* (Oxford, England: Oxford University Press, 1962).

55. James Clifford, *The Predicament of Culture* (Cambridge, Mass.: Harvard University Press, 1988), 10, 218.

56. Leslie Marmon Silko, "An Old Time Indian Attack Conducted in Two Parts," *Shantih* 4 (1979): 3–5. H. David Brumble III discusses the problem of the use of Indian material and Indian "informants" in "Indian Sacred Materials: Kroeber, Kroeber, Waters, and Momaday," in *Smoothing the Ground,* ed. Swann, 283–300. Brumble engages with Karl Kroeber in debate over similar topics in the same volume ("Reasoning Together," 347–64).

57. Whiteley, *Deliberate Acts,* xv.

58. Barre Toelken, "Life and Death in the Navajo Coyote Tales," in *Recovering the Word,* ed. Swann and Krupat, 388–401.

59. Eric Cheyfitz, *The Poetics of Imperialism: Translations and Colonialization from 'The Tempest' to 'Tarzan'* (New York: Oxford University Press, 1991), 104. In this context Tejaswini Niranjana, in *Siting Translation: History, Post-Structuralism, and the Colonial Context* (Berkeley: University of California Press, 1992), has developed the idea that translation is not just "interlingual process" but "an entire problematic" that raises questions of "representation, power, and historicity" (p. 9).

60. Barre Toelken, "From Entertainment to Realization in Navajo Fieldwork," in *Fieldwork Epiphanies,* ed. Bruce Jackson and Edward Ives (Carbondale: University of Illinois Press, in press).

61. Quoted in Whiteley, "The End of Anthropology (at Hopi)?" (manuscript, 1991).

62. Lawrence J. Evers, letter to the author, 1992. It should be noted that in a number of cases (including Evers's), the reader can obtain dual-text volumes without much difficulty.

63. Lawrence J. Evers and Felipe S. Molina, *Yaqui Deer Songs/Maso Bwikam: A Native American Poetry* (Tucson: University of Arizona Press, 1987), 8.

64. Louise K. Barnett, *The Ignoble Savage: American Literary Racism 1790–1890* (Westport, Conn.: Greenwood Press, 1975), 17.

65. On this point see James A. Clifton, ed., *The Invented Indian: Cultural Fictions and Government Policies* (New Brunswick, N.J.: Transaction, 1990). For a critique of Clifton's book, see Vine Deloria Jr., "Comfortable Fictions and the Struggle for Turf," *American Indian Quarterly* 16 (Summer 1992): 397–410.

66. N. Scott Momaday, *The Way to Rainy Mountain* (Albuquerque: University of New Mexico Press, 1969); James Mooney, *Calendar History of the Kiowa,* in The Seventeenth Annual Report of the Bureau of American Ethnology for the Years 1895–96 (Washington, D.C.: Smithsonian Institution, 1898), 141–44. Leslie Marmon Silko, *Ceremony* (New York: Viking Press, 1977). The quote by Silko is from her article, "Language and Literature from a Pueblo Indian Perspective," in *English Literature: Opening Up the Canon,* ed. Leslie A. Fiedler and A. Houston Baker Jr. (Baltimore: Johns Hopkins University Press, 1981), 60.

67. Berkhofer Jr., *The White Man's Indian,* 67.

68. See, among others, Alice B. Kehoe, "Primal Gaia: Primitivists and Plastic Medicine Men," in *The Invented Indian*, ed. Clifton, 194–210. It should be noted that not all the exploiting of Native American culture is done by Whites. The late Sun Bear of the "Bear Tribe Medicine Society" comes to mind, as well as Running Water ("Mohave Spiritual Leader") and Sundance Aquero ("Métis Spiritual Guide") of the White Buffalo Robe Series and Ed McGaa, or Eagle Man, an Oglala of the "Rainbow Tribe." Hyemeyohsts Storm, a Cheyenne of *Seven Arrows* fame, probably belongs here, too. It is interesting that those who claim they wish only to share their culture with outsiders phrase their activities as a challenge to the exclusivity of "the Elders" or "traditionalists" who refuse to move with the times.

69. Rudolf Kaiser, "Chief Seattle's Speech(es): American Origins and European Reception," in *Recovering the Word*, ed. Swann and Krupat, 497–536.

70. "Blood quantum" is at the heart of the bureaucratic definition of Indian, and one-quarter blood quantum is used as the minimum requirement for entitlement. Thus, a discredited nineteenth-century belief that blood is literally the carrier of not only genetic but also cultural traits (habits of dress as much as habits of thought) is at the core of the federal definition of Indian. But the situation is even more complicated. There are at least forty federal definitions; in addition, tribal governments employ their own tribal rolls and different fractions. There is also a strong movement today toward self-definition, often linked to the issue of sovereignty. For more on this topic, see Snipp, *American Indians,* 28–35.

71. Marianne Torgovnick, in *Going Primitive: Savage Intellects, Modern Lives* (Chicago: University of Chicago Press, 1990), says this:

> A voyeuristic interest in the primitive surrounds us in what we see and hear, what we learn and read, from the cradle to the grave: it is part of the atmosphere, part of the culture we live and breathe. . . . Western desires for the primitive have not waned as primitive societies have modified or been forced to modify traditional ways of life. . . . The West seems to need the primitive as a precondition and a supplement to its sense of self: it always creates heightened versions of the primitive as nightmare or pleasant dream. The question of whether that need must or will always take fearful or exploitative forms remains pressing (p. 246).

For what Torgovnick means by *primitive* as concept, or "generalized notion," see 18–23.

72. Allogan Slagle in a review of Snipp, *American Indians,* in *American Indian Quarterly* 16 (Winter 1992): 76.

73. Carter Camp, "Sincere Doubts: 'Tourism' Diminishes Lakota Ceremonies," *Lakota Times,* August 12, 1992, A8.

74. Alan Simpson's remarks, reported by the *Lakota Times* of August 12, 1992, A2, were made on August 7, when Simpson was opposing an amendment to the 1965 Voting Rights Act to expand language assistance to Indian voters not proficient in English. Andy Rooney's remarks were reported in Nick Coleman, "CBS's Rooney Is Following in Custer's Footsteps," New York *Daily News,*

April 19, 1992 (Rooney's article appeared nationally on March 25). Rooney said that the impact of Indian cultures is slight, and Indians "hang onto remnants of their religion and superstitions that may have been useful for savages . . . but which are meaningless in 1992." They should get off the reservations, since "the time for the way the Indians lived is done." And he said much else, including that "there are no great American Indian novels, no poetry . . . no memorable music . . . no American Indian art, except for some good craft work."

75. Frederick E. Hoxie, "The Indian Versus the Textbooks: Is There a Way Out?" *Perspectives* (American Historical Association) 23 (April 1985): 18–22.

76. E. D. Hirsch Jr., Joseph Kett, and James Trefil, eds., *The Dictionary of Cultural Literacy* (Boston: Houghton Mifflin, 1988), xi, 363, 397. See also Hirsch Jr., Kett, and Trefil, eds., *Cultural Literacy: What Every American Needs to Know,* with appendix, "What Literate Americans Know" (1987); rev. and enlarged ed., New York: Vintage Books, 1988).

77. Hoxie, "The Indian Versus the Textbooks," 22.

78. Quoted in Paul Berman, *Debating P.C.* (New York: Dell, 1992).

79. Quoted in Louis Henry Gates Jr., "Editor's Introduction: Writing, 'Race' and the Difference It Makes," *Critical Inquiry* 12 (1985): 1.

80. Dell Hymes, "Anthologies and Narrators," in *Recovering the Word,* ed. Swann and Krupat, 41.

81. William Bevis, "American Indian Verse Translations," in Abraham Chapman, ed., *Literature of the American Indians: Views and Interpretations* (New York: New American Library, 1975), 308.

82. Jimmie Durham, "Those Dead Guys for a Hundred Years," in *I Tell You Now: Autobiographical Essays by Native American Writers,* ed. Brian Swann and Arnold Krupat (Lincoln: University of Nebraska Press, 1987), 163.

83. Margot Astrov, ed., *The Winged Serpent: An Anthology of American Indian Prose and Poetry* (New York: John Day, 1946); John Bierhorst, ed., *The Red Swan: Myths and Tales of the American Indians* (New York: Farrar, Straus and Giroux, 1976); Richard Erdoes and Alfonso Ortiz, eds., *American Indian Myths and Legends* (New York: Pantheon Books, 1984); Karl Kroeber, *Traditional Literatures of the American Indian: Texts and Interpretations* (Lincoln, University of Nebraska Press, 1981).

ALASKA,

YUKON,

AND THE

SUBARCTIC

TWO STORIES
FROM TIKIĠAQ

▲

TOM LOWENSTEIN
AND
TUKUMMIQ

INTRODUCTION BY TOM LOWENSTEIN

These two stories from Tikiġaq (Point Hope, Alaska) were told in the spring of 1976 by Asatchaq (1891–1980) and translated from Iñupiaq (North Alaskan Inuit) by Tukummiq, a bilingual Tikiġaq woman, and me. Tikiġaq (pronounced *tikerak*) lies on what is probably the oldest continuously inhabited site in the Americas. The village was famous in ancient Alaska, first because the Tikiġaq peninsula, jutting twenty miles into the Arctic Ocean, commanded enviably quick access to whales and seals and second because the large and powerful Tikiġaq village was an important ceremonial center.

The size of the Tikiġaq village was matched by the intensity of social, intellectual, and religious life. Crowded onto the point were more than six hundred of the thousand or more people who subsisted on the wider Tikiġaq territory. Family life was centered in semisubterranean earth-insulated iglus built of driftwood logs with entrance passages of whalebone; entry from passage to the iglu was through a circular hole *(katak)*. Tikiġaq's six ritual centers *(qalgi,* pronounced *kalgi)* were large houses built on the same principle as the iglu. Here long autumn ceremonies were organized by the community's skin boat owners *(umialiks)* and shamans *(aŋatkuq,* pronounced *angatkok)*. It was also the *umialiks* and *aŋatkuqs* who supervised the great spring whale hunt.

Whaling was vital both to Tikiġaq subsistence and to the identity of its people, their land, their rites and narratives. At the basis of this was the local origin story, which describes how Tuluŋigraq, the primal shamanistic Raven Man (his name means "something like a raven"), was created by a magical earth crone (*aana,* "grandmother"). Tuluŋigraq went on to harpoon a whalelike sea beast whose body then transformed itself into the earth of Tikiġaq Point. Before this primordial whale hunt Tuluŋigraq had tricked a female shaman (*uiluaqtaq,* "woman who won't take a husband") who lived in voluntary isolation into marrying him. The death of the whale and the creation of Tikiġaq thus flowed from the united power of the male and female shamans. The identity of the *uiluaqtaq* was also closely linked to the *aana* who created the Raven Man.

The careers of Tuluŋigraq and the *uiluaqtaq-aana* were not limited to the origin story. The primal couple also reappeared in many of Tikiġaq's legends and histories, the first story printed here being a good example.

Like most Inuit people, the Tikiġaq divided their narratives into two main classes. There were myths and legends (*unipkaaq*), and there were local histories that chronicled the lives of ancestors (*uqaluktuaq*). Both texts here are *unipkaaq,* but while each has the flavor of village social life, both reach back into the archetypes of myth time.

I recorded these stories, along with about ninety others, in Point Hope between 1973 and 1989. From 1975 to 1980, my work was mainly with Asatchaq (his Anglicized name was Jimmie Killigivuk). Asatchaq came from a strongly conservative Tikiġaq family, one with a passionate interest in the local traditions, which had started to erode after contact with Europeans in the nineteenth century. Asatchaq learned much of his repertoire when he was thirty-five, in a series of formal transmissions from his maternal uncle Samaruna. Asatchaq's mother, Niġuvana, was also a major source of lore, whereas his father, Kiḷigvak ("mastodon"), inducted him into the whale hunt. Asatchaq became an umialik in 1925, when he inherited his father's skin boat.

Among the surviving Tikiġaq storytellers, Asatchaq had the largest repertoire and perhaps the most formal style of recitation. For him the narrative process was a sacred obligation, and he refused to tell a story unless he had it perfectly in memory. Asatchaq's storytelling style was grave and unemphatic. Like his mentors and colleagues, he recited both legends and histories in a slow and rhythmic measure that was metrical only when the narrative held a song. At moments of high drama, his voice took on a crooning menace, and his gestures grew sculptural with understated violence. Even in stories of nineteenth-century contact, he was never judgmental. Asatchaq repeated each text precisely as he had learned it; the object was simply to tell things as they were and reproduce the tradition.

The first story here, that of Siġvana (pronounced *servana*), presents shamanism in the context of the domestic iglu, though with its numerous echoes of Tuluŋigraq, the tale would have had an obvious mythical resonance for its audience. But whereas the *uiluaqtaq* in the Raven Man myth is tricked with guile and magic, here the girl is simply terrorized with a display of *aŋatkuq* pyrotechnics.

As in many Tikiġaq stories, the iglu entrance passage is the locus of both vision and danger. "He was using a loon amulet [*tuullik*, 'yellow-billed loon'] to dive through the iglu ventilator," the storyteller said later. The counterpoint of the two figures shuttling toward each other through the village is conveyed with hypnotic repetition that suggests the sleep the unwilling Siġvana is due:

> *Isiqtuq* ["She enters"] . . . *Aniruq* ["He's leaving"].
> *Isiqtuq* . . . *Aniruq* . . . *Isiqtuq* . . . *Aniruq* . . .

All storied *uiluaqtaq*s are punished or raped. But the *aŋatkuq* is successful only when Siġvana has succumbed to the horror of old age and the seal's emergence. "He used a seal-fetus amulet; there's nothing stronger," said the storyteller in later conversation. The slimy nasal emphasis with which the seal is born ("*paamŋuaq* . . . *paamŋuaq* . . . ['crawling . . . crawling']") was one of the high moments of Asatchaq's often dark narrative style. Siġvana's character as quasi-mythical *uiluaqtaq* is reinforced in this episode. Just as the woman who won't marry is an aspect of the earth crone, so here Siġvana is both virgin and old woman. But smile as she does at the grisly pleasure of the seal coming through her, she is forced in the end into mundane submission.

The story of Tigguasiña (pronounced *tiggohsinya*), the subject of the second tale here, is one of many Tikiġaq narratives that outline the progress of a poor boy (*iliappaq*, "orphan") to the status of shaman. Despite Tuluŋigraq's supernatural origin, his career also has this structure; but instead of subduing a dangerous *uiluaqtaq*, Tigguasiña simply rises from destitution to a position of shamanistic power.

Despite the widespread practice of adoption, Tikiġaq society had its child outcasts, who lived rough lives, sometimes with dogs, and depended on what they could beg and scavenge. This story sketches the semidestitute life of a child shaman who made his home in one of the ceremonial houses. Tigguasiña is already an *aŋatkuq* when we meet him, and this may explain why the elders connive at his occupation of Tikiġaq's central sacred space.

The story's initial focus is Tigguasiña's lonely authenticity; its conclusion, his social and shamanistic triumph. Just as in other Tikiġaq legends and histories the spirits often chose children to revitalize a tired practice, here Tigguasiña's initiation is set in the very context of an old professional's hocus-pocus. Children in Canadian Inuit societies used to entertain their families with skits of shamans in ecstatic seizure. Gently satirical stories like this one also perhaps helped regulate the practice.

As in many stories, the whalebone entrance passage is a locus of sex or rape and shamanistic vision. Here these events converge in the image of the observing child among a mass of entrance-passage whale jaws while the wolf man has intercourse with the woman initiate. Tigguasiña is already a shaman, but his place in the sacred hierarchy of the village is secure only when he sees through what the old man's students fail to understand. The orphan's developing career, stereotyped as it is, is outlined amid a clutter of wonderfully realistic things, textures and voices, inside the *qalgi* and around the village. The conversation between Tigguasiña and his friend takes place outside, with a view through the dusk of lamp-lit domestic windows, thus providing a new visual perspective on his marginality. But the storyteller's falsetto impression of boys' voices (*"Tuuŋapiaq?* ['A *real* spirit?']"*) helps transform the dark intrigue in the entrance passage into airy, boyish chatter. The melodrama in the final *qalgi* seance is in keeping with the charade in the entrance passage. But Tigguasiña's final gesture ("Plaque is strong!" the storyteller said later) is neither boys' play nor the theater of Utkusik's (the old shaman's) order. He snatches the initiative and ruthlessly steps into Utkusik's place at the center of the *qalgi*.

Tikiġaq people frequently connected relics they picked up with the details of their oral history. Excavations in 1939–40 gave them an extensive new opportunity to do this. The jet-inlaid ivories that filled the eye sockets of a pre-Tikiġaq-culture skull found near the point in the celebrated Ipiutak excavations "came from the man with ivory eyes" whom adults used to terrify bad children. Of the present story Asatchaq commented: "Just east of the old mission house (on the north side, near Ipiutak), we dug up the bones of a dog buried in the middle of a human skeleton." According to Asatchaq's mother, this must have been Tigguasiña, "because he turned himself into a dog when people were angry with him."

I'm going to tell a story. Now, I'm going to tell a story.
There was a woman who refused to take a husband: here in
    Tikiġaq.
Now, an aŋatkuq wants her.
And this young woman has a name: Siġvana.
And she has parents.
Now an old aŋatkuq visits her parents and asks for their daughter.
The old man is an aŋatkuq.
"It's for our daughter to decide," the parents say.
"If she wants you, you can have her."
That's what they say to him.
And so the aŋatkuq comes for her one evening.
"*Naami:* No."

As soon as he comes in, Siġvana walks out of the iglu.
After she's gone out, the aŋatkuq stays inside for a while.
Then he leaves too. He goes to find her.

Well, the aŋatkuq doesn't know where Siġvana has gone.
Then he starts asking, and he finds out from the people.
And when he finds which iglu she has entered, he goes after her.
When she sees him enter, she starts leaving.
As soon as she goes out, he follows her.

Then she goes into another iglu.
But as she enters, there's the aŋatkuq in the entrance passage.
Just as she enters, there he is, approaching. He's leaving the iglu.

She'd escaped from the aŋatkuq,
but now she meets him leaving every iglu that she enters.

Every iglu that she enters, there he is already.

When she sees the aŋatkuq, she turns back and goes out again.
She turns and doesn't enter; she goes out to another iglu.

This continues.

▲

*aŋatkuq: "shaman."

Every time she goes into an iglu,
she meets the aŋatkuq coming out of it.
They meet in the entrance passage.

This young woman's getting weary of the aŋatkuq.
But now he decides he'll put a sleep on her.
And when he's made her sleep, he'll start.

Siġvana goes back to her parents' iglu.
She *still* finds the aŋatkuq in the iglu entrance passage.

Every iglu that she enters, there's the aŋatkuq.
She meets the aŋatkuq leaving every iglu that she enters.

And now the young woman is getting sleepy.
The girl who doesn't want a husband is sleepy.
Now she wants to sleep; she goes home and sleeps there.

The aŋatkuq does nothing.
The aŋatkuq doesn't even sleep with her.
He does nothing. But he will do something.

And during the night the young woman grows old.
Her hair turns gray, and her teeth fall out on her pillow.

Her parents see what's happened to her.
Their daughter Siġvana has become an old woman.
Her hair is white, and her teeth have fallen out.
She's grown old overnight.

Now she's old, the aŋatkuq still does nothing.
The man and woman stay in the iglu with their ancient daughter.
They want to see if she can stand up by herself.
The day before, she had been a young woman.

Now the father tells his wife to fetch the aŋatkuq
so he can make their daughter what she was before.
"When she knows what it's like to be old,
she will decide to take the aŋatkuq," says the father.
And he says to his daughter, "The aŋatkuq can change this.
Then he'll take you for his wife. But not as an old woman."

▲

So the mother goes out and fetches the aŋatkuq.
(Aŋatkuqs did this in the past, when a woman didn't want a
   husband.)
The aŋatkuq comes into the iglu.
And when he enters, he sees an old woman down there on the
   floor.

He sees her teeth have gone. He sees her gray hair.
And when he comes in, he sits down and does nothing.
He doesn't perform.
And as the aŋatkuq sits and does nothing,
out of the woman in her sleeping skin a seal begins to crawl.
And as the seal emerges from her, she starts smiling.
But she can do nothing.
She can't stand; she can't move. The seal crawls out.
It comes out of her and tingles,
but she can't do anything.
And once it's come out, it goes back into her.

When the aŋatkuq entered, the woman's father said to him,
"Being like this is no good for our daughter.
If she wants you for a husband, she will have you,
but she'll have to change if this is to happen.
This isn't how she wants to be. Make her normal again.
If she wants you, she will take you."
Then the aŋatkuq makes her normal, and she's old no longer.
She's back as she was.
Her hair is black, and she's a young woman.
As the aŋatkuq starts to leave the iglu, he says,
"*Qanuq?* Well? Well?" says the aŋatkuq.
She says, "I will follow."

So the aŋatkuq got a wife again without too much trouble.
And when he took her home with him,
it is said he restored her completely, creating her youth again.
This is what Siġvana, daughter of that man and woman, went
   through.

I'll tell the story of a Tikiġaq boy
who spent all his time in the qalgi.*
His home was the qalgi.
And whenever he heard there'd been a death in Tikiġaq,
he'd take a strip of baleen that was lying in the qalgi and go to the
    katak.†
And with his legs astride the katak,
he'd lower the baleen into the entrance passage.
He also worked on the baleen and sliced it into strips.
What he did was lower two strips of baleen and then raise them.
He did this when he heard there'd been a death in Tikiġaq.

Now one night he took an owl's-wing brush
and a lamp stick he had dipped in seal oil.
These are two things that spirits are scared of.
He placed these two things by the katak.
And while he sat in the qalgi, cold air started rising through the
    katak.
He kept the stick and the wing beside him. This was his habit.
And as he sat by the katak, the stick and the wing started
    bouncing;
they jumped up and down on their own, beside him at the katak.
(People used to talk a lot about spirits in those days.)
The stick and the wing chased the spirit away.
And in its flight, the spirit left some things belonging to it.
One thing a spirit sometimes leaves is its grave wrap.
The next man to enter the qalgi was heard saying,
"Some children have left a caribou skin in the passage."
This was what the spirit left: a grave wrap.
Now in the course of all this,
Tigguasiña, the boy from the qalgi,
met a boy who also played at being an aŋatkuq.
And when they met, the other boy told him,
"They're going to perform; the shamans will perform in
    Qaġmaqtuuq qalgi!"
(There were six qalgis in those days.
Today there are only two in Tikiġaq: Uŋasiksikaaq and
    Qaġmaqtuuq.)

*qalgi: "ceremonial house."
†katak: "entrance hole connecting passage and chamber."

11

And when Tigguasiña heard they were going to Qaġmaqtuuq,
he went to that qalgi; but they'd put a sled across the entrance.
They'd blocked the entrance.
But he moved the sled aside and lowered himself into the entrance
    passage.
He hid between two whalebones in the passage.
He stood between the jawbones of a whale and listened.
And he heard them starting to talk in the qalgi.
The name of the shaman was Utkusik.*
Utkusik had three people with him for instruction:
a man, a woman, and a small boy.
And while Tigguasiña stood in the passage, he heard them
    starting.
Utkusik said, "Take a light and search the passage."
He thought there might be someone hiding there.
Someone lit a stick and went to the passage. He saw nothing.
He didn't see Tigguasiña, who was hiding.
When he returned to the qalgi, he said,
"There's no one in the passage."
"*Ii*. Yes, all right," said Utkusik.
Some time later Tigguasiña noticed the sled against the entrance
    moving.
A man came down into the passage and then closed the entrance.
The man's face was invisible: he was masked in a wolf's head.
The teeth were still in it.
The man sat down in the middle of the floor with his face toward
    the katak.
Tigguasiña watched him from between the whale jaws.
Now a man's legs came down through the katak,
but the wolf man snapped at them, and the man in the katak
    retreated to the qalgi.
He said he couldn't go down to the passage.
There was a spirit down there, and he dared not approach it.
Now Utkusik told the boy to go down to the passage.
It was the boy's turn;
so he lowered his body through the katak and stopped.
The wolf jaws snapped at him, and he too retreated.
He didn't dare approach the spirit. Utkusik said,
"Whoever approaches the thing in the passage will be an aŋatkuq."
That was what the aŋatkuq told them.

*Utkusik: "bowl."

Now it was the woman's turn.

So she lowered her legs through the katak and descended.

Then the man by the katak with the wolf head took his mask off.

He beckoned the woman, and she approached him.

Tigguasiña watched from where he was hiding.

And when the woman was beside him,

the man pulled a deerskin from under his parka

and laid it on the floor of the passage.

And he told the woman to get onto the skin, and he lay down on
   her.

When they woke, the woman returned to the qalgi.

(I don't know which qalgi.)

Then they went back to their iglus. It was nighttime.

When Tigguasiña woke in the morning,

he looked for the boy who had been training to be an aŋatkuq.

When he found him, he asked,

"Did you meet a *tuunġaq** yesterday?"

"Yes," said the boy.

"A *real* tuunġaq?"

"A real one," said the boy.

Tigguasiña pointed to an iglu. Its skylight was lit.

"You see that skylight? That's where your spirit lives."

He told the boy about the man who had acted the spirit.

"The man in that iglu was your spirit."

And the boy said he'd get back from the aŋatkuq what he'd given
   for instruction.

Now he knew it wasn't a real spirit.

He said he'd get back what he'd paid the aŋatkuq.

And the Tikiġaq people were told that night to visit the qalgi.

Tigguasiña went too and sat down by the wall bench.

(Some qalgis had a narrow bench around the walls for the men to
   sit on.)

And Utkusik began his performance.

He was carrying a piece of skin and a harpoon.

Utkusik started to walk round the qalgi,

and he aimed the harpoon at everyone sitting there.

Eventually he came to Tigguasiña.

And Tigguasiña took some plaque from his teeth,

---

tuunġaq: "spirit."

and he spat it on the harpoon when the aŋatkuq pointed at him.
The harpoon point fell off.
Again and again the aŋatkuq thrust at him,
but the harpoon point kept falling.
Now that Utkusik saw he was beaten, he took aim at himself.
He harpooned his own breast. Utkusik killed himself.
He'd been shamed by Tigguasiña. The story ends here.

MARY KOKRAK: FIVE BROTHERS AND THEIR YOUNGER SISTER

▲

ANTHONY C. WOODBURY
AND
LEO MOSES

INTRODUCTION BY ANTHONY C. WOODBURY

This is a translation of a traditional Yupik Eskimo *quliraq* (myth; plural, *qulirat*) as it was performed orally in 1977 by Mary Kokrak, an elder of Chevak, Alaska. Chevak, with about five hundred people, is located a few miles from the Bering Sea, on the vast, boggy tundra between the Yukon and Kuskokwim rivers. I first visited there in 1978 to study the language, a variety of Central Alaskan Yupik unique to it and its neighbor, Hooper Bay. During that visit I was fortunate to acquire from Rosemary Kokrak Sylvester a copy of a tape recording she had made the previous year of her mother, Mary Kokrak, telling a story to several other women, probably in her tiny, one-room plywood house. Mary Kokrak, a highly respected Chevak elder, died later that year. But despite her frequent coughing and evident ill health, her voice on the tape was vivid and dramatic. Her audience sighed and laughed frequently. It was an event, a performance.

In the performance Mary Kokrak used features of her voice to highlight her story's narrative structure, to create dramatic tension, and to channel its emotional force. These techniques belong to a respected tradition of narrative performance in Yupik society. Perhaps most salient was the slow, rhythmic alternation she established between speech and silence, as in the following passage, where each line of text translates an uninterrupted stretch of speech followed, in the original Yupik, by a pause:

> There was nowhere more to look; so the remaining brothers
> quit their hopeless search. And after a while
> they no longer left their qasgiq.
> And after a while they slept all the time and no longer woke up.
> THEY HAD GIVEN UP.
> And their sister too
> *was in sorrow.*

In the first two lines this pausing scheme operates in counterpoint to syntax: the pauses after *brothers* and *after a while* occur at points of incompleteness and hence create a sense of suspense; at the same time the independent clauses ending with *look* and *search*—both marked with punctuation—are not followed by pauses, thus giving a hurried impression. But this tension-filled counterpoint does not last, for in all subsequent lines pausing and syntax come back in phase, with lines and sentences generally corresponding. One might conclude that as a literary device the counterpoint effectively captures the anxiety of the brothers' situation, whereas the resolution of the counterpoint conveys the passage from anxiety to complete despair.

TABLE OF FORMAT CONVENTIONS	
Line break	Pause (averaging slightly less than one second)
Line space	Long pause within a sentence or drop to a low pitch to mark the end of a sentence or sentence group
Large capital letter	Episode break, marked by pitch-range reset and other vocal features
SMALL CAPS	Impressionistically harsh (for example, breathy or raspy) voice quality, sometimes in an unusually low pitch register
Italics	Impressionistically mild voice quality or higher pitch register; often used by Mary Kokrak when she editorializes or utters interjections
ITALIC SMALL CAPS	Impressionistically mild voice quality, but in a lower pitch register

Other salient vocal features of this performance are voice quality and pitch: Mary Kokrak shifted vividly, from a gentle and quiet voice at one moment to a rasping bass, a high wail, or a brittle monotone at the next. In the translation different typefaces (see table) are used to give at least some idea of this (though obviously these few choices do not capture all the vocal flexibility of the original). Like pausing, these techniques construct textual meaning. In the passage quoted above, for example, the impressionistically "harsh" and "mild" voice qualities communicate subtly different attitudes toward the suffering of the brothers and the sister.

Although these features are shown in the translation, their effect is only felt when it is read aloud. To do this, the reader should take a leisurely pause after each line, suppress the tendency to pause at punctuation within any line, pronouncing commas and periods there only by slowing down or dropping pitch, and modify his or her voice quality as the typeface changes.

A final fact of this (and any) oral performance is that it unfolds in real time and is therefore accompanied by audience response, coughing, self-correction, and the like. Indeed, these occurrences are part of the performance since they can affect its course. Accordingly, they are noted in the translation (inside brackets). They should be taken not as blemishes but as reminders that the translation represents a living event.

This translation has gone through several stages. In 1978, Leo Moses and I listened to the tape over and over, he dictating each word slowly and I transcribing. At the same time, he gave detailed English glosses for each individual word and phrase, as well as a simultaneous oral translation on tape. That, along with grammatical analysis of the Yupik original, gave rise to our first translation, which appeared beside the original transcript in my 1984 work.[1] The current version is a retranslation I made in 1992, after more detailed prosodic analysis of the original and based on what I hope are improvements in my understanding of the language and its unique poetics.

Mary Kokrak's performance continues a tradition of storytelling: coastal Yupiit (plural of Yupik) of her generation describe their youth as a time when non-Natives were met only rarely, when men lived communally in the *qasgiq* ("men's house"), and when storytelling was part of both sacred ceremonies and daily life, whether among those in the *qasgiq,* among women and children in family dwellings, or within extended family groups in the various subsistence encampments that were part of the yearly cycle. Her story is a *quliraq,* one claimed to have originated with remote ancestors rather than in the experiences or imagination of some known individual. Stories of this category, recognized by nearly all Yupik and Inuit groups, are memorized precisely so that they may be transmitted faithfully through the generations. The fact that many *qulirat* are recognizable across the entire Eskimo Arctic supports this claim to antiquity. In the case of this *quliraq,* versions have been recorded several times over the last century well to the north of Chevak, in the Inupiaq-speaking region around Seward Peninsula.[2] And suggestively similar stories are recorded to the north and east in Alaska[3] and even in western Canada.[4]

Despite careful transmission, there is no strict *quliraq* canon: repertoires and stories vary, not only from region to region but also among storytellers in the same village. The two versions of "The Woman Who Returned from the Dead" in this volume present a fascinating glimpse of such variation. Likewise, very divergent versions of Mary Kokrak's *quliraq* are told in the immediate Yupik-speaking region. What vary less within the tradition, from Greenland to Siberia, are certain special functions, settings, themes, and character types: a *quliraq* often recounts the origins of the environment, living creatures, or social customs; it may be part of a ceremony; and it is likely to tell of supernatural encounters, ghosts, or contact with the underworld, of Raven and other animal characters, of their transformations into and from human shape, of oppressed orphans, killers, or young women who refuse husbands. It is these characteristics, as much as the individual stories, that constitute the inherited tradition.

Moreover, since these characteristics are expected, they inform Native understandings of *qulirat*. Granted, Mary Kokrak's oral performance has power, even outside its own cultural context, as a dramatic exploration of cruelty, violence, and the bonds of kinship, telling vividly of a hero who finds his youngest brother in the hands of a sadistic hunter and is then guided in his revenge by strange allies. As such, each reader may relate it to his or her own literary experience. To me, for instance, it strongly evokes the emotional tone of the last books of the *Odyssey* (not to mention the shared images of avenging relatives in lowly disguise, their return to a house full of revelers, and the final bloodbath inside it). But the story is more fully understood in light of the tradition and cultural context in which it arose.

Introduced with the *quliraq* formula "They lived by the bank of a river," the five brothers and their younger sister are put at the story's center (and give it its informal name—*qulirat* do not usually have set titles). They are an ideally self-sufficient family group, with the brothers hunting and the sister straining to keep up with their catch. They are likewise ideal morally, since in their ignorance of others they bear no immodest pride over their success. When their youngest is lost, they are helped by a disheveled man and his grandmother who live in the large village to which the boy has been taken. These two evoke an important family of *qulirat*, known from Alaska to Greenland, about an orphan who is abused by all in his community but an old grandparent. The orphan secretly acquires supernatural powers while carefully retaining his reserve and humility. When the moment is right, he overwhelms his former tormentors in a way that is always ironic and usually violent. He is a model of conduct, for he combines in one person patience and power, meekness and vengefulness. In this story the grandson bears all these qualities. Although not overtly abused, he is a marginal man, with poor clothes and equipment, a house on the edge of town, and a sleeping place by the drafty *qasgiq* door. His actions appear to be directed by his grandmother (just as the wicked hunter's actions seem to be directed by his old father and Uyivaangaq's by his younger sister), at least some of whose supernatural power he may have acquired: when he keeps his kayak back from shore after penetrating the siblings' curious isolation, he is acting as one who wishes to avoid the potentially dangerous consequences that actual physical contact between the real and spirit worlds might invite. Finally, of course, the grandson is effective in planning and carrying out revenge. If the grandson and grandmother do evoke the traditional orphan and grandparent, then their grievance against their village is implicit, complementing the explicit grievance of the sibling allies with whom they share many qualities.

The cruel *nukalpiaq* ("great hunter") too has a special literary and cultural context. Traditionally, a very powerful person could at times dominate a village without fear of opposition. This threat is personified in *qulirat* by a cruel and overbearing hunter, strong man, or shaman who is ultimately done in by a revenge taker. Such revenge is presented as an act of virtue and justice. In this story Uyivaangaq lectures the complicitous villagers as the wicked *nukalpiaq* shames himself by his reluctance in the face of superior strength. Next the force behind the *nukalpiaq*, the old father, is shamed when Uyivaangaq presents him with his son's body and says to him with great irony, "Look at him! You thought so highly of your son, all the time he was your son!" According to Yupik elder

Charlie Pleasant, "When they had wars, whenever enemies killed a man, to show their contempt they used to go and tell the man's father and mother that they had killed their son."[5] Finally even the massacre of the village is presented as virtue in the line "they polished off the rest of the village, the people who didn't go to the *qasgiq.*" *Polished off* translates a verb meaning "to polish, pick clean," used especially in reference to bones with meat still adhering to them. "Polishing" the bones shows respect to the game; by implication, polishing off the village is a virtue too.

One final note is in order, since Mary Kokrak assumed that her listeners were familiar with the layout of a *qasgiq.* The typical *qasgiq* in large coastal villages was a square semisubterranean structure framed with heavy driftwood logs. Above ground the four sloped sides were covered with sod and came together at the top, where there was a skylight with a removable translucent gut cover. In Kashunuk—the ancestral village of modern-day Chevakers, visited by the American ethnologist Edward Nelson in 1879—the *qasgiq* was thirty feet square, with a height of twenty feet from the floor to the skylight. In the story Uyivaangaq first sees his brother by climbing the sod sides and peering through this skylight. Inside, a *qasgiq* had sleeping benches extending along all four walls. The rear bench, where the single oil lamp stood, carried high social status; accordingly, that is where the cruel *nukalpiaq* slept. By contrast, the least desirable places were along the opposite wall, where there was a drafty entranceway used mostly in summer; it is here that the grandson had his place. This summer entranceway was not used in winter, when people went in and out through an underground passage accessed by a hatch in the middle of the floor that worked as an efficient heat trap. That is where the grandson emerges for his final revenge, it being the only unoccupied place during the *nukalpiaq*'s final spectacle.

NOTES

1. Anthony C. Woodbury, ed., *Cev'armiut Qanemciit Qulirait-llu/Eskimo Narratives and Tales from Chevak, Alaska* (Fairbanks: Alaska Native Language Center and University of Alaska Press, 1984).

2. Edward William Nelson, *The Eskimo About Bering Strait,* in The Eighteenth Annual Report of the Bureau of American Ethnology for the Years 1896–97 (Washington, D.C.: General Printing Office, 1899; reprint, Washington, D.C.: Smithsonian Institution Press, 1983), 499–505; William A. Oquilluk, *People of Kauwerak: Legends of the Northern Eskimo* (Anchorage: Alaska Methodist University, 1973), 189–94; Edwin S. Hall, *The Eskimo Storyteller: Folktales from Noatak, Alaska* (Knoxville: University of Tennessee Press, 1975), 109–114. In Nelson's version five brothers and their younger sister live with their parents at Point Rodney. The youngest brother and sister drift on a broken chunk of ice to the Siberian coast. The remaining brothers, having acquired magical powers, set off in search along the coast, where they have tense encounters at four villages along the way. At the fifth, the Siberian village of Ungasiq, the sister is said to be the wife of a powerful shaman. The oldest brother, called Ak'-chĭk-chú'-gúk, puts on shabby clothing to disguise himself as an old man while the youngest rescuer, on reconnaissance, finds the sister not in fine furs but emaciated, on the floor with her limbs, neck, and tongue bound. The next day the shaman challenges the brothers to wrestle, decapitating two of the younger ones by dashing them against a sharp-edged piece of whalebone. When Ak'-chĭk-chú'-gúk is challenged, he bursts out of his old parka, squeezes the shaman until blood gushes from his mouth, and then breaks him on the whalebone. He then restores his brothers and rescues his sister, from whom he learns that the shaman had killed their youngest brother. The villagers, glad to be rid of the shaman, treat the siblings well. But twice thereafter a host of warriors comes from elsewhere to kill the brothers. In the first battle the attackers are slaughtered. The second time, they enter the *qasgiq,* led by two old women who then kill the younger brothers by pointing at them with bones from the dead of the first battle. But the eldest restores his brothers again, crushes the old women, and uses the bones to strike dead the remaining attackers. The protagonists then return home, but failing to observe an admonition of their former hosts, they turn to stone as they come ashore at their own village.

3. Knut Bergsland, *Nunamiut unipkaaŋich/Nunamiut Stories* (Barrow, Alaska: North Slope Borough, 1987), 321–27.

4. Knud Rasmussen, *Intellectual Culture of the Copper Eskimos,* Report of the Fifth Thule Expedition (Gyldendal, Copenhagen, 1921–24, vol. 9 1932), 245–52.

5. Quoted in Edward A. Tennant and Joseph N. Bitar, eds., *Yuut Qanemciit: Yupiit Cayaraita Qanrutkumallrit/Yupik Lore: Oral Traditions of an Eskimo People* (Bethel, Alaska: Lower Kuskokwim School District, 1981), 15.

MARY KOKRAK: FIVE BROTHERS
AND THEIR YOUNGER SISTER

Well now,
this is a story
my children's father told
across there near the mountain Ingrissaareq,
when we spent the winter there;
He told it
when we lay down for bed, when the children were small.

Can'irraq told it to them when they were small.

It is said that some brothers
once lived by the bank of a river.

Their river
flowed into the ocean.
Just downstream they could see its mouth.

Aa! There weren't ANY other hunters around.
So even though each of them was a nukalpiaq,*
they had no idea just how good they were.

There were four older brothers
with a boy making a fifth;
And they had a single younger sister.

Their sister,
as best she could,
took care of their catch.

There was a lake out back for trash,
seal oil and other old stuff. *And that water didn't get ripples even
when it was windy!†*

---

*nukalpiaq: "great hunter."
†*And that water . . . windy!:* It stayed calm because so much oil floated on the
surface.

When oil went bad,
they put it in the lake, scoring the pokes*
to release and drain their contents
in the lake.

The lake was their dump
for things they no longer needed. Also,
for the oldest brother down to the youngest,

[*coughs*]

their sister made water boots for each in his turn.
No one does that for you nowadays!
These poor things.†

They probably have no one making them water boots!

For their hunting she made rainwear of seal gut and *arillut,*
which are mittens of fish skin.

All the things they needed.
While he,
the youngest brother,
served them,
as a help to his sister;
So to his brothers in their qasgiq,‡
he brought food and then took out their dishes.

Well this was how they survived;
And living this way, *they knew NO other people;*
When they hunted caribou,
they REALLY got lots.

For the oldest
of his four brothers

---

*When oil went bad . . . pokes: seal oil is stored in bags—*pokes* in local English—made from whole sealskins. *Scoring* metaphorically likens the pokes to fish, since it is the translation of a verb meaning "to cut fish fillets for drying." It also implies that they are cut on the same crosshatch pattern.

†*These poor things:* young people nowadays.

‡qasgiq: "men's house"

the youngest had a nickname.
He gave the name Uyivaangaq to him;
to the oldest of his brothers.

[*coughs*]

He called him Uyivaangaq.

One day
in summer
the youngest brother disappeared,
gone completely.

Aa! What a shame!
There was nowhere more to look, so the remaining brothers
quit their hopeless search. And after a while
they no longer left their qasgiq.

And after a while they slept all the time and no longer woke up.
THEY HAD GIVEN UP.

And their sister too
was in sorrow.
[*coughs*]

And then one day as summer was ending
and outside the cold was coming,
the cold of winter was coming,
their sister, their sister alone was up and about;
So she went out.

Upstream was a slough whose mouth they could see;
There was a slough there.

It followed the length
of the mountains beyond,
flowing in front of the mountains there.
It had mountains behind it;
the slough.

▲

She went out as usual that morning,
since her brothers
would not set out anymore.

Not long after,
there came from upstream
A SHABBY OLD KAYAK.

A kayak so shabby
that both ends pointed up;
AN UGLY LITTLE KAYAK.

And floating downstream in it,
bright and alert,
WAS AN UGLY LITTLE MAN.

[*laughter*]

With each stroke of his paddle, [*inaudible*] it yawed so badly, his
    ugly little kayak;
So shabby a kayak it was!

Well he didn't land.
He didn't land. BUT DOWN THERE A WAYS OUT,
a little ways out he went,
"Why how are you?
Are you all right?"

"Aa! See, it happens those in there,
my older brothers,
have given up;
They no longer leave their qasgiq
and no longer wake up
because our youngest brother has disappeared,
and even though they've searched, they cannot find him."

"See, your youngest brother is upriver,
my grandmother says." He was down below, not too close to shore;
floating.

▲

"*My grandmother had me come to tell you,*
  so I have come to tell you.
  See, your youngest brother is upriver.
  A nukalpiaq
  took him away
  and has tortured him there all summer.
  He shows him in the evening,
  gathering the village people in the qasgiq,
  torturing him;
  making him suffer,
  showing him as he suffers.

"*So,*
  when it's time to do something, I'll tell you,
  when I'm told to, I will come and tell you
  (and your older brothers);
  But they must get whatever weapons,
  whatever equipment they'll need!"

And then he was upriver and gone, having not even landed.

She went in the qasgiq. When she went in, she said, "How SMALL
  you are!

It happens your youngest brother
was taken away last summer
by a nukalpiaq
to his village upriver,
where he tortures him."

Oops! The grandson had told her,*
"*See it's been this way before;*
  this is not the first time he has gotten someone to torture
  from another village,
  showing him as he makes him suffer."
  That is how he does it;
  [*inaudible phrase*]

▲

* *Oops!:* This interjection indicates that the sentence belongs earlier in the story.

"So when I am told to, I will come for you."

AA! AT THAT,
WHEN SHE TOLD THEM,
LIKE A CLAP OF THUNDER
HER BROTHERS
CHANGED THE SKINS ON THEIR KAYAKS AND MADE NEW EQUIPMENT;
And as they got ready,
UYIVAANGAQ WAS RIGHT THERE.

Not long after,
it was winter—
winter was getting close;
AGAIN THAT SHABBY OLD KAYAK floated downstream.

And again only their sister was there to see it.

He came nearer this time,
saying, *"Very well now.*
Tomorrow,
early tomorrow, they must come!
Come! They must come!
I'll be here on this side, at the mouth of the slough upstream, where it
    flows out."
EVEN THOUGH THEY WEREN'T FAR AWAY, THEY HADN'T HEARD OF
    THAT VILLAGE UPSTREAM.

"Where it flows out its mouth
I'll wait for them, net fishing."

WHEN SHE WENT IN AFTER HE HAD SPOKEN,
THERE THEY WERE WAITING ANXIOUSLY.
WHEN SHE TOLD THEM,
How did they ever sleep at night?

They left their sister behind at dawn.

They departed upriver as they had been instructed,
for he had said he would wait for them beyond the slough.

▲

As they started out, led by the oldest brother,
there was the net fisher.

When they got out,
that upstream village
was there above them.
As THEY ARRIVED JUST BELOW IT,
the grandson's shabby old house was still upstream outside the vil-
    lage;
[*coughs*]
THAT HUGE VILLAGE.

Well, they did not draw anyone's attention when they arrived, since
    it was early in the morning before anyone was about.
They went into the house. When they entered,
there was an elderly matron,
a grandmother:
"So you have come?" "Yes."
"Come on!
Sit down!
But wait until it's night tonight;
Then it will be time to go ahead and see your youngest; he's over
    there in the qasgiq."

They waited anxiously for nighttime.

They passed the time.

Then finally

they got word:
"In there,
in the qasgiq, I've been keeping an eye on things,"
the grandson said.
"They're getting started there, so follow my grandmother's instruc-
    tions."

Aa! THEY TRIED TO STAND UP EVERY SO OFTEN;
BUT WITH SHARP WORDS THE GRANDMOTHER MADE THEM SIT IN SPITE
    OF THEIR EAGERNESS,
telling them, "Wait awhile."

▲

Meanwhile the grandson, without letting on, kept an eye on things.

Aa! When it finally got dark,
when it got dark, she said,
"Put on my old clothes,
  and go watch him through the skylight! The oldest, you first!"

"*Otherwise they will catch on to you;
  They will suspect you are a stranger;
  Especially those peering in because they can't get inside.*"

As they went toward the qasgiq
and approached the people,
how noisily they laughed!
And the ones peering in from above
laughed;
But Uyivaangaq climbed up anyway.

Aa! WHEN SOME OF THEM NOTICED HIM,
a nukalpiaq
disguised as a grandmother,
he was squeezed in tight:
The grandmother's worn-out parka and her old boots
were all too small for him;
And her cane,
he used her cane and her parka hood.

"POOR *thing!*
See that grandmother going to peer in!"

Wobbling, he climbed to the skylight;
When he crouched next to someone,
grabbing onto the far edge
OF THE SKYLIGHT,
they talked about him:
"GRANDMOTHER HERE HAS SUCH BIG WRISTS!

When they looked in—
Kccch! In there!
In there was this nukal——
this nukalpiaq lying down in the middle of the rear sleeping bench.
There below him

▲

was a big awful urine vessel;
It was so full
its contents were pure white.*

And next to that
was a bowhead-whale shoulder blade,
with a hole through the middle
that had sawteeth around its edge
that would make nasty little wounds.
And across
on the other side, a ways down from the people,
WAS AN OLD MAN;
sitting.

AND THE WHOLE QASGIQ WAS LIT UP!

Well then the old man spoke from across the way:

"My son!
Do not just rest there;
Let them have something to see; go on, make their evening short!"

Aa! Slowly the nukalpiaq rose in back,
and having risen, he climbed down.

There below him was something, looking scarcely human,
just covered with an ugly little blanket of worn-out caribou hide,
[*laughter*]†
where he was.

[*murmuring*]

Poor thing!

HE TORE THE BLANKET OFF
THAT ONE DOWN THERE. *KCCH!*
HE HAD NO MEAT ON HIM AT ALL; AND ON THE OUTSIDE
HE WAS COVERED WITH SORES, SCRATCHES EVERYWHERE;

**pure white:* Probably an indication that the urine had aged.
†The laughter, by one in the audience, abruptly turns to murmurs of sympathy
when the boy, rather than the shabby blanket, emerges as the dominant focus.

little wounds everywhere;
he had no meat on him;
a naked little thing.
WHAT A SHAME!
The nukalpiaq took a rag;
Wetting the boy's body with it,*
(There was the qasgiq, only its underground entrance clear of
*   people!†)*
In great pain the boy wailed,
going "Aaaaaa!"

And he put the whale thing on and off the boy, with his head
    through the hole, SO ITS EDGES WOULD CUT LITTLE WOUNDS.

When he released him,
the boy spoke out loud enough
for his brothers to understand:
"Aaaaa!
My Uyivaangaq should see me now!" *How awful!*
"My Uyivaangaq
should just see me now!"

His Uyivaangaq THIS time was able to hear him.

And then,
clenching his jaws,

HIS TORTURER WENT,
"What is it with you that when I do things to you, you blabber like
    this?"

AA REALLY!
POOR UYIVAANGAQ
DIDN'T KNOW IT,
but with a "crack!" they noticed him:
It seems he had broken in half the part he was holding on to.‡

▲

*Wetting the boy's body with it: The rag is wet because it has been soaked in the
stale urine, assumably a painful astringent.
†There was the qasgiq . . . people!: That is, the whole qasgiq, packed with people,
was watching.
‡the part he was holding on to: That is, the far edge of the skylight, which would
have been a medium-size log.

As he grew angrier,
HE STOOD UP SUDDENLY: "LET'S GO BACK TO THE GRANDMOTHER'S!"

And the people went,
"Wonder what he was doing,
pretending to be a grandmother?"
When he entered her house,
he showed no regard for the grandmother's old parka,
getting out of it from here
as if it were a coat.*

And the grandmother complained,
"AA! HE'S RUINING MY OLD PARKA! WHAT A SHAME!"
He didn't slow down for that.
"LET'S GO TO THE QASGIQ!"

Hastily they prepared, getting their clothes;
But there was the grandmother,
still lamenting her things with nobody to listen.

[*laughter*]
[*coughs*]

With nobody to listen!

[*pause of fifteen seconds, perhaps for tea*]

Heh.

They went back,
led by the grandson,
their host.

And when the grandson emerged,†

▲

*as if it were a coat: A Native parka is pulled on over the head, in contrast to a
European-style coat (*pal'tuuk,* from Russian *pal'tó,* "overcoat"), which buttons up
the front. To take off the grandmother's parka, Uyivaangaq simply rips it apart
down the front.
†And when the grandson emerged: *Emerge* implies that the grandson came in
through the underground entrance.

he went through the crowd
toward his own place above the upper entrance,
toward the sleeping bench there. Then the people inside became
    silent!

*A little more?**

[*coughs over a pause of twenty-five seconds*]

The grandson
climbed up
on one side of the bench above the upper entrance;
And Uyivaangaq, climbing right behind,
sat down beside the grandson.

Then likewise,
from the next oldest brother on down,
they followed in order.

AND ALL BECAME SILENT THEN,
AND THE NUKALPIAQ,
REMAINED SILENT;
And then he just laid himself down to rest.

The qasgiq was nicely filled with people.

Beforehand they made war clubs;
and he instructed his brothers,
telling them to CLUB *the people.*

AND THEN AT THAT MOMENT
THE NUKALPIAQ'S FATHER SPOKE FROM ACROSS THE WAY:
"My son!
You have strangers here;
Don't leave them lonely and sad!

"Give them some fun; Go on, let them have something to see."

AND HIS SON
was slow in standing up;

A little more?: Mary Kokrak is probably responding to an offer of more tea.

[*laughter*]
because of those he was seeing.

When he finally stood up
AND PULLED THE BLANKET OFF THEIR BROTHER BELOW,
Uyivaangaq jumped down:

"Such a child
will not satisfy you;
Because he is young, you won't be satisfied with him even though
  you are having some fun with him.
But if they watch the two of us,
then they will have some really good fun!
So let's get it over with, poor torturer."

AA!

WHEN HE GRABBED THE NUKALPIAQ AROUND THE MIDDLE,
HE WAS BIG, HIS HOST,* WHILE UYIVAANGAQ was smaller.

They embraced, parkas off.

Each tried to get a good hold with his arms.

As Uyivaangaq tried, trying to get a good hold,
HIS HOST WENT, "WAIT JUST A MOMENT!
Just a moment d——don't!"
But they squeezed even more.
Then,

as Uyivaangaq squeezed even more,
THE BLOOD SUDDENLY BURST OUT THE MOUTH OF HIS HOST.

UYIVAANGAQ
BROUGHT HIM OVER TO HIS FATHER:
"Look at him!
You thought so highly of your son
all the time he was your son!"

AND PLACING HIM ON TOP OF HIS FATHER,
*HE PRESSED SLOWLY DOWN, SEEMING TO FLATTEN HIM AND THE FATHER
  TOO.*

*HIS HOST: the wicked *nukalpiaq.*

Aa! THEY WERE WAILING HARD NOW.
And one of the brothers blocked the underground entrance below,
even though people wanted to leave;
He did it so they wouldn't have any weapons.

"*You ugly things here*
who have been trying to have fun!
I wonder how a child adds to it when you are trying to have fun?"
So the oldest brother was speaking to them.

Then, when Uyivaangaq swung his war club,
his blows never felled just one;
Instead, each blow sent several people down.

When they went out,
they polished off the rest of the village, the people who hadn't gone
    to the qasgiq.

Heh!

And they too went down.

The grandmother complained about her old parka;
he had gotten out of it from here;
as if it were a coat,
ripping it apart.

The brothers wanted to stay over again.

When they finally left, they said they would come back for the
    grandson and grandmother;
later when they had their boat.
They were so grateful.

They went home, and their sister and the youngest brother—*Oops!**

When they brought him, she laid the boy down,
the grandmother had them lay him down right in front of her.

▲

* *Oops!*: The storyteller indicates she has left something out. She then describes
events before the brothers' departure.

How in the world, I wonder, can someone be healed who is all cut up
and covered with scratches?

Then the grandmother,
turning to the youngest brother
of Uyivaangaq's family,
restored him to his original condition with her saliva.

She did something to him—
she treated him,
fixing him right away, healing his wounds.

Mm.
They were very grateful!

They went home the next day;
They reached their sister. *Aa! How very thankful their sister was!*

And soon after, on the next day,
they wanted to fetch the grandson and grandmother;
The brothers went off by boat the way they had come,
AND THEY BROUGHT THEM BACK;
They brought them back,
so grateful they were.

TWO TELLINGS OF THE STORY OF UTERNEQ: "THE WOMAN WHO RETURNED FROM THE DEAD"

▲

PHYLLIS MORROW
AND
ELSIE MATHER

INTRODUCTION BY PHYLLIS MORROW

Along the Bering Sea coast and the major river systems of south-western Alaska live about twenty-one thousand people who call themselves Yupik (plural, Yupiit; "real people"). Unlike their northern Alaskan, Canadian, and Greenlandic relatives (who prefer to be called Inuit), Central Alaskan Yupiit lived in densely populated winter villages, supported by rich runs of salmon, herring, and saffron cod. Before twentieth-century missionaries instituted nuclear-family households, men dwelled together in a large, semisubterranean *qasgiq* in the winter, when family groups were not dispersed in seasonal fishing, hunting, or trapping camps. In the *qasgiq* the community also held elaborate ceremonies, with masked dances and large-scale distributions of gifts, somewhat reminiscent of Northwest Coast potlatches. On dark nights in the *qasgiq,* men often told narratives, some lasting several days, to entertain each other and to instruct the youth. Women lived, and told their tales, primarily in the smaller family dwellings. In today's villages, where the Yupik language and many sociocultural traditions often remain central, individuals continue to be respected for their verbal artistry.

Yupiit group their tales into two sometimes overlapping genres: *qanemciit* (singular, *qanemciq*) include relatively recent stories of legendary people, historical events, and personal experiences, such as supernatural encounters; *qulirat* (singular, *quliraq*) are myths, and tales set in more distant times. "The Woman Who Returned from the Dead," like the preceding tale of "Five Brothers and Their Younger Sister," is a *quliraq*.

The subject of life after death is as likely to elicit the story of Uterneq (literally, "the one who returned") today as it did near the end of the nineteenth century.[1] Among other things it reminds people of the thinness of the separation between the living and the dead. In traditional Yupik narratives the earth is pictured as flat. Only four or five steps, the thickness of the earth, separate the world of the living from that of the dead. For older Yupiit that distance is a gauge of the human relationship with the spirit world. When the earth was thin, encounters with ghosts and supernatural beings were commonplace. This image and the metamorphic character of humans and animals in oral tradition may stand as metaphors for interdependence.

Through the early part of this century, maintaining close ties with the dead required elaborate care and often years of preparation. *Elriq* (literally, "throwing away") was a ceremony during which the living community provided for their dead relatives and namesakes, giving them food, water, and clothing in the afterlife. Behind *elriq* are beliefs about the dead and the afterlife that are clearly recalled, and in some cases practiced, today. The story of the woman who returned from the dead portrays the transition zone between the two worlds, describes some features of the afterlife, and offers explanations for some mortuary and postmortuary customs. It is a reminder that appropriate human actions maintain the interrelatedness of the living and the dead, and it is a caution against remaining aloof or oblivious to the needs of others. Although human disrespect in the modern era has thickened the earth, one sometimes hears that it is thinning with the revival of Native traditions and an organized move toward self-determination.

Naming is a basic means of perpetuating relationships among the living and between the living and the dead, for those who share the same name may share a spiritual essence, elements of the same identity and personality. During a naming ceremony, a pinch of food may be placed on the ground as an offering to the deceased, or it may be placed in the water or in some other beverage that the new namesake sips as the name is conferred (a custom deriving from an earlier belief that the dead were continually thirsty, like the seals, who were given fresh water when hunters brought them to land from the salt ocean). The dead person then "enters" the new namesake, who acts just like the one after whom he or she is named, causing alarm and wonder. The living namesake is called by the kin term appropriate to the deceased and is often treated as if he or she were that person. Thus a person calls a child named after his or her grandfather Grandpa. In this way naming relationships collapse generations and multiply layer kinship ties, creating a dense social network among the living and the dead. As one person explained, "You see this is the reason why we should not neglect these names while we are living. Even to this day they are with us." The essential identity of a person with his or her namesake creates linkages between the living and their ancestors. By giving gifts to the living namesakes of their deceased relatives, people maintain past kinship ties in the present. In the men's house and at the grave site, in particular, there were points of contact between worlds, through which gifts could be passed to the deceased.

Like many other Yupik concepts, ideas about the dead are nondefinitive and open-ended, consisting of multiple terms and descriptions that follow from each person's traditional knowledge and personal experience of things spiritual. The Western preoccupation with fixed nominal categories seems empirically inadequate when set against the Yupik acceptance of indeterminacy in the world. As a result, we find it both impossible and inappropriate to impose a single translation, such as "soul," on the variety of terms that refer to sensible aspects of personhood: image, breath, warmth, personality, and sound. When asked, Yupiit simply tend to confirm that a variety of terms are used by different people. In these stories those dwelling in the afterworld are called the dead, or they are designated by one of the terms for spirit(s). The dead traveled via a pathway, sometimes said to be beneath the earth "somewhere" in the Yukon-Kuskokwim Delta, the Yupik homeland. They left the other world temporarily to attend ceremonies given by the living, where they received sustenance from their kin.

The two following descriptions of a woman's return from the land of the dead are known as the origin or explanation of *elriq*. In fact, although they suggest that the woman "fixed" or "improved" certain *elriq* customs, they do not literally detail the origin of the ceremony. It is their allusive power, their evocation of a world where the dead need the living, that makes these "stories to remember by." Each narrator began to tell his or her story when Elsie Mather asked about a difficult metaphysical subject. By drawing on oral tradition in such contexts, Yupik narrators both disclaim individual authority and validate received collective knowledge as their source ("It is said . . .").

Although the two tellings are similar in style, they differ strikingly in detail and perspective. Here again Yupiit embrace contradiction without confusion. Although narrators try to remain faithful to tales as they have heard them, they say that the different tellings together constitute a collective wisdom. Storytellers often encourage listeners to add variations, ending a tale with the invitation "This is the way I heard it; perhaps others have heard it a little differently." A dynamic interplay in Yupik epistemology balances two ideas: that the world is a place of multiple possibilities and that words can actualize the events they describe. The comfortable acceptance of artistic variation reflects the former; a careful, indirect, and reserved use of speech reflects the latter. It is especially important to avoid making bad things worse by verbalizing them directly (a possibility apparent in stories where characters create or destroy by using direct phrasing). Another example of these preferences is a tendency to avoid generalized analyses of meaning and motivation. In fact, many Yupiit see the academic predilection for critical analysis as leading people from meaning toward discord and confusion. The indirect qualities of these tales should be understood in this light and not mistaken for vagueness.

In Yupik prosody there is a complex interplay among pitch and intonation contours, pausing, grammatical groupings, and affect.[2] In the following transcriptions line breaks indicate the co-occurrence of several of these features. Often these are junctures where listeners may (and Mather sometimes does) give back-channel cues, equivalent to *"mm-hmm"* or *"unh-hunh"* in English. Typically the narrator's pitch rises at the beginning of a line grouping, is maintained (perhaps with a few dramatic emphases) in the middle, and drops at the end. When narrators provide background information, their pitch contours remain relatively even, as indicated here by longer lines. A line space usually corresponds to the end of a grammatical grouping and indicates a longer pause. A large capital letter indicates a shift in setting or heightened action, as cued by changes in intonation and moments of silence. For example, Andy Kinzy, in the first telling, pauses dramatically to convey the tension of a novice shaman's cautious approach to a supernatural presence. The stories are best appreciated when read aloud, with the reminder that Yupik pauses are longer than most English speakers are used to hearing.

Details are also presented in a different order than is usual in English. The grammatical structure of a typical Yupik word is roughly the reverse of an English sentence, with suffixes indicating person, case, number, and various modifications of meaning following a stem. In the second telling, for example, Martha Mann expresses the idea "I won't come to get you" in a single word ordered as "get-won't-I-you." In translation, we reverse this Yupik syntax to conform to the English, but we have tried to preserve the organization of larger units, which are often similarly structured. By following the Yupik order, we are able to transfer the backgrounding effect to English: it builds interest and tension and contributes to the characteristically indirect quality of Yupik speech by modifying or qualifying what is to come. By following this order, we also preserve the terracing of the original, whereby the narrator layers sound, meaning, and empathy by repetition in subsequent lines. For example, the tale's themes of love, death, reciprocal relationship and being left behind echo in Uterneq's explanation that everyone, no matter how poor, should distribute gifts during *elriq:*

> when the living relative left on the earth,
> one who lost a loved one,
> did not take part,
> the dead person,
> the one for whom he had cared,
> would stay behind, feeling unloved,
> somewhere there,
> °perhaps in the place of the dead. . . .

In retaining this organization, we do intend not to make the narrative sound exotic or romantically poetic.

A bubble (°) is used to indicate a clarification or parenthetical explanation elicited in response to a question. These occasional questions have been edited out because Mather felt that for these tellings she interrupted more often than she would have if she were normally listening to a story and not also doing historical research.

Far from simply transmitting tales verbatim through the generations, each of these tradition bearers artfully elaborates the story in relation to gendered knowledge and perceptions. Less than halfway through Kinzy's account, the narrative takes a male viewpoint. Kinzy leads the listener to identify first with the young man (the budding shaman) who finds Uterneq (the woman who returned from the dead) and then with the men in the *qasgiq,* into which Uterneq is brought. Mann takes the listener into a woman's world, where a grandmother feels the pain of her granddaughter's early death and a woman's parka has a slit for nursing. Uterneq is brought not into the *qasgiq* but into the female-centered family house, and a miscarriage traps her among the living.

Elsie Mather came to talk with Andy Kinzy in the Yukon River village of St. Mary's in the spring of 1983, when Kinzy was seventy-
two years old. The two had not known each other before, but
quickly entered into a lively discussion. When Mather asked about
customs relating to death, Kinzy commented that people did a
number of different things for the dead, and then he told his story
about Uterneq.

Martha Mann, in her seventies when she told her Uterneq story in
1984, is originally from Kwigillingok. She is Elsie Mather's
mother's first cousin. Mather has known her all her life, and they sat
comfortably in Mann's small house in Kongiganak, having tea and
recording what she had to say about ceremonialism. (Kwigillingok
and Kongiganak are neighboring villages on the Bering Sea coast,
near the mouth of the Kuskokwim River.) When asked if she had
heard where people were said to go after death, Mann answered
with the second story that appears here.

Both of these stories were told to Elsie Mather in the course of
our collaborative research on Yupik ceremonialism; together Elsie
Mather and I refined the translations of these narratives and added
commentary for this collection.

NOTES

1. Edward William Nelson, *The Eskimo About Bering Strait,* in the Eighteenth
Annual Report of the Bureau of American Ethnology for the Years 1896–97
(Washington, D.C.: General Printing Office, 1899; reprint, Washington,
D.C.: Smithsonian Institution Press, 1983), 424.

2. Readers especially interested in Yupik prosody are referred to Anthony C.
Woodbury, "Rhetorical Structure in a Central Alaskan Yupik Eskimo Traditional Narrative," in *Native American Discourse: Poetics and Rhetoric,* ed. Joel
Sherzer and Anthony C. Woodbury (Cambridge, England: Cambridge University Press, 1987), 177–239.

ANDY KINZY'S TELLING

That one . . .
That one woman
who died and returned,
is said to have improved the elriq ceremony.

Upriver from here, downriver from Marshall, in the place they
    called Takcat,
lived that woman,
Uterneq.
They called the one who came back from the dead Uterneq.

They say she improved
the elriq ceremony that they used to do.

She taught the people.
They say she urged them
to make every effort to participate,
even those who had nothing to give.

For they say that during elriq,
when the living relative left on the earth,
one who lost a loved one,
did not take part,
the dead person,
the one for whom he had cared,
would stay behind, feeling unloved,
somewhere there,
°perhaps in the place of the dead,
°envying the other dead who participated.

They say that woman
was sent back by her grandmother.
They say maybe it was her grandmother who made her return.

▲

They say the grandmother was old
when she died.

So then her surviving relatives,
those who cared for her,
would clothe her
and would have her put parkas on
during elriq,

through her namesake,
her little namesake.

They say that the dead
returned to attend ceremonies
like elriq,
when those on the earth's surface,
˚the living whom they left behind,
held such ceremonies.

Well then,
on their way back from a ceremony,
the girl's grandmother cried out to her,
"Oh no! That frozen fish . . . !"
(They say that when people offer just a pinch of food,
even a very small piece,
the dead receive the whole item.)

So then
she told her dear granddaughter
to go back and get it;
she told her that she had put it
on the side of the food cache
and then forgotten it.
She had forgotten to take it.

She explained
that as she went back,
on her way,

she would come to a spruce tree
covered with sharp, ugly branches.

It would be blocking her path.

When she got to it,
she should fall on it without being afraid.

So she went on,
as her grandmother had said to do,
to get what her grandmother had forgotten, what she didn't want to
    leave behind.

She walked.
And walking along,
she came to the spruce tree,
which was just as her grandmother had said it would be.
It was terrible!
And it would be terrible to fall on it
because it had such sharp branches.

At first she paused,
but then she did as she'd been told
and fell forward
on it.

And she lost consciousness.

After a while she came to.*
She was inside
a food cache.

And she cried when she came to,

finding herself in a strange place.

▲

*she lost consciousness. . . . she came to: Consciousness/awareness (from *ella-*,
"universe," "weather," "outside," "awareness") is central to Yupik conceptions
of personhood. Becoming aware also refers to one's earliest continuous memory
and is the mark of becoming fully present in the world.

Now in that village,
among those people,
there was a young man.
They say he had begun to use a helping spirit, a *tuunraq,*
you know,
but his powers were not yet obvious.
His shaman powers were still unknown.

They say he'd begun to use a helping spirit.

In those days all of the men
slept in the qasgiq.
They used the qasgiq as their house,
and they slept there.

One time
that young man
came out of the men's house to relieve himself.

He was out there relieving himself. . . .
They say that the food cache
was not far behind him.

In those days a cache did not have closed doors,
but only wooden slats set sideways
to bar the entrance.

Standing there relieving himself,
he heard someone crying somewhere.

He listened—
the sounds seemed to be coming
from that food cache.

So, stepping sideways,*
he went toward
the cache.

▲

*stepping sideways: This indirect approach is used when encountering ghosts and
other supernatural beings.

46

When he got there,
he peeked into the cache
and saw a woman standing in there facing the wall, crying.

When he looked closely,
he recognized her as the one who had died.

He recognized her.

So then
he removed the boards
that barred the doorway.

So, when he was able to get in,
he kept his feet sideways,
and without stepping directly forward,
but moving sideways,
he went toward her.

When he got to her
and he was ready,
he gathered all his strength
and grabbed her.
But his arms came back empty.

She didn't move at all.

Then
from around him—
there are always bits of food
on the racks and floors
of food caches—
he picked up some of those scraps
and rubbed his arms with them.*

▲

and rubbed his arms with them: Anointing oneself or one's house with oily soot
or making motions of encasing oneself was a way to form a protective barrier
against the supernatural. It may also be significant that the food scraps belong to
both worlds: it was a scrap left in the cache wall that Uterneq was there to reclaim,
and offerings to the dead were customarily dropped through the cracks in the floor
of the house or *qasgiq*. Using the scraps, the young man was able to reach into her
plane without fully leaving his own. Later he could not bring her into the *qasgiq*

Then he was able to hold her.

And although she struggled,
he took her to the qasgiq.

They used to have entrances
like the opening of an animal's den.
And down there
in the floor of the qasgiq
was an opening
through which people pulled themselves up.

When he came up through that opening,
when he came up with her,
putting his hands on the floor for support,
his hands went right through the floor.

So then one of the old men
(this was when they used oil lamps)
smeared lamp oil on his hands and painted the floor with it.

Then the young man could bring her up.

And then they tried to seat her
near the back wall of the qasgiq.*

She said then
that she wanted to sit
on a deerskin that had never been used.†

So then
one of them went to fetch one.

▲

---

until the floor was smeared with lamp oil, and she refused to sit down without
another symbolic barrier, a new deerskin.
*the back wall of the qasgiq: This was a place for honored guests.
†**she wanted to sit on a deerskin:** A person who is about to be named also sits on
a skin.

And then she finally sat down.

Then they discovered
that the clothing given to her namesake,
the parkas,
were layered on her body!

At that time,
when the woman returned,
her namesake, that little one, suddenly died,
taking the young woman's place.

She took that woman's place among the dead!

They say it was that woman
who corrected the way they did the rituals of elriq.

˙She corrected
some things
that were not being done properly.
She told people what to do.

˙She talked to the people
and urged those who didn't take part,
who didn't do anything during those ceremonies,
to participate in them.

˙She said that they made their dead relatives
suffer when they didn't take part in the ceremonies.

When a person participates, even if he has nothing to share,
the dead are very happy . . .

MARTHA MANN'S TELLING

They say that young woman died.

And they say her mother's brother used to give her clothes and
food (through her namesake).

So then
when she died, she went on her way.
They say her grandmother had died before her.

I seem to recall
that the person who told this story
said that the young woman was from Qinaq.*
Kunuin's grandmother who is now dead—
it was her older sister who told this story.

So then when she died, she went on her way.

She went along a path,
coming upon various things on her way.
They used to cover the faces of the dead °with things (they used bird
   skins when they didn't have the appropriate coverings).
She came to
the places where those face coverings were.
And she put her face cover down and went on.

She came to a river
with a turbulent and confused current.
There was no way she could cross it.

On the other shore was her grandmother,
·who had died before her.

The grandmother scolded her from the other side:
"Why did you come so soon?
I'm not going to come get you!
Why did you come so early! Go back!"
She told her to go back, and here
she didn't know how to get back.

So then when she'd finished her scolding, she left.
She left the young woman behind.

After she left, the poor girl started to cry.

▲

*Qinaq: A village site near present-day Tuntutuliak, on the Kuskokwim River.

While she was crying, she heard a voice
and looked across
and saw a woman,
a younger woman doing something.
She wore a ground-squirrel parka
with an opening here for nursing a baby.

It had an opening here for nursing a baby.

She said, "Oh, you can't get across?"

And when the girl agreed,
she got two pieces of wood
for her to walk across on.

Then she went across on the wood,
and the other waited for her with outstretched arms.

When she was close enough to reach her arm, she pulled her over.

"Now go on your way."

This was her dog's. . . .
The girl had really loved her dog!

It is said that the woman was her dog's "person."*

She went on
and came to a village
where they were very rich,
with many seal guts hanging up!†

This was the place of the dogs' "people."

There were things she passed on her way.
And finally

*her dog's person: *yuit* ("their persons"; singular, *yua*) are the humanlike spirits
of animals, places, the weather, and other things. Animals might reveal their person
faces by lifting their muzzles or beaks, and humans sometimes visited or stumbled
upon the villages inhabited by a particular species' *yuit*.
†with many seal guts hanging up: The guts were cleaned, inflated, and dried for
several uses, including material for lightweight, semitransparent rain parkas.

she got to the place of the dead.
When she went into a house, there was her grandmother.

This time she did not scold her.

Well then, after some time, maybe that next year,
it was time to go back to their former village to attend a ceremony.

They used to do a ceremony with water.
They called it taking in a little water.
They feasted and gave away gifts.
Those who gave gifts to the namesakes
gave them then in the qasgiq.
And [whole containers of food]
were distributed to the people in that village
and to guests who came from other villages.

They would always identify
and explain the sources of their gifts,
the gifts that were distributed to the namesakes.

The young woman who died
was always given gifts by her mother's brother.

So they went back.
When they arrived,
her uncle gifted her as usual,
giving her clothes to put on.

They say
he gave her something in a bowl,
the kind with a wooden bottom attached to a wooden rim.
When she started to take it,
only the rim stayed in her grasp.
The bottom fell out.

So year after year
she lost her gifts like that.

They say
it happened year after year.

So then one time everyone got ready to go and attend a ceremony.
Since she and her grandmother
had a small sled,
they went to the festival with that.

They went on their way.

They got there.

When they got there, her uncle
gifted her.
He also had her put on a mink parka.

And when he gave her food,
he gave her a bowl that was constructed of a single piece,
without a separate rim.

This time she received her gift.

So then, having stayed there long enough, they returned.

But when they had gone quite far,
oh, no!
they discovered that the young woman had left her gift behind.

She told her grandmother that she had forgotten her gift,
that she was going to go back to get it since she had finally been able
    to receive the gift.

Her grandmother warned her
that she was likely to have problems and had better not go.

But since she did not want to lose that bowl, she insisted until her
    grandmother said,
"Go back then!"

And she explained that when she got near the village,
when she came to what looked like a pair of inner cones from fish
    traps,*
she should fall upon the newer ones.
So she went back.

And when she came to those,
she fell forward onto the newer ones.

She found herself getting up from a fireplace.
Long ago when a body was brought to the grave site,
they fed a fire
with wood
by the grave.
Then they took small pieces of food and placed them there.

They symbolically cooked bits of food.

She went down to the village,
and when she peeked into her family's food cache,
she saw the bowl there.
After she took it, she started to leave, but,
oh no! her pathway was nowhere to be found!

Oh no! So then,
not knowing what to do
or which way to go,
she went from the outer porch
back into the cache.

It is said that a boy
went out to relieve himself and heard her crying.
He said to her, "How . . . ?"

He rubbed his eyes.
Because he knew that she had died,

*inner cones from fish traps: Yupiit use classic cone-shaped basket traps to catch
blackfish. The fish are trapped in the inner cones. Like the spruce branches in
Kinzy's tale, these cones are sharp, and falling on one would be painful.

he thought that he was seeing a ghost.
He stopped rubbing his eyes
since she was not floating off the ground like a ghost
and asked her what was wrong.

She said that she had no way to get back,
that she had come to fetch her gift.

So then,
even though she struggled, he brought her into a house.

And then!
They took her clothes off when he brought her in,
perhaps to her parents' house.

They took her clothes off and there they were
all in layers!
The part closest to her body
had grown into her flesh.

They say that the people paid no attention to this.

And when she began to get some flesh on her body,
it came off—
the part that had begun to be absorbed into her body!

At that time they learned
one of the village women had had a miscarriage!
This had caused her to lose her path.
Her pathway was pressed shut.

The path she used before.

At that time,
when she came down to the village,
she saw those girls
playing on a lake.
One of them had on clothes just like hers.

▲

That was her namesake.

And then soon after that
they say that girl suddenly died,

that namesake.

They say that later on,
when that girl was able to,
whenever people did those rituals,
gave those gifts,
when they were going to give things to the namesakes,
when they feasted in the qasgiq—
she told them to tell about their gifts.
Even if they were gifts of food,
they should tell about the contents of the bowl.
She said that the dead ones would eat the food together.

She told the people to tell about their gifts.
They were to tell about the food they gave,
to tell about who caught the game.
They were to tell about everything,
even who fetched the water.

To tell about the fish they dried—
who caught them,
and who had stunned them as they were taken out of the net.

They were to explain all the gifts.
She said that when they didn't explain,
the dead felt uncomfortable reaching for the gifts.
They would feel shy about taking them.*

*shy: The word often translated as "shyness" or "bashfulness" actually connotes a
combination of respect, hesitance, and social deference. If one does not know the
provider of the food, one may be hesitant to accept it, out of deference to the giver.

THE BOY WHO WENT TO LIVE

WITH THE SEALS

▲

ANN FIENUP-RIORDAN
AND
MARIE MEADE

INTRODUCTION BY ANN FIENUP-RIORDAN

The Yupik Eskimos of western Alaska are one of the least known and most traditional Native American groups. They differ in both language and way of life from the whale-hunting Inupiat of northern Alaska and the relatively impoverished Canadian and Greenlandic Inuit to the east. Living along the river drainages and coast of the Bering Sea, they continue to speak the Central Yupik language, practice elaborate ceremonial exchanges, and harvest an abundance of fish and wildlife from their rich coastal environment.

Imagine a "typical" Eskimo family—peaceful hunter, wife, and child surviving on their own in an inhospitable homeland. This well-known stereotype, however, originated in the Canadian Arctic and does not apply to the Yupik Eskimos of Alaska, who are anything but typical. Far from merely surviving, they reap from their environment a wealth of resources, including seals, walrus, beluga, fish (both saltwater and freshwater), waterfowl, small mammals, moose, musk-oxen, bears, berries (from which they make the festive mixture known as *akutaq*), and greens. Although the low-lying coastal plain is treeless, every spring the rivers wash down an abundance of driftwood that the people traditionally used to build semisubterranean sod houses and elaborate ceremonial paraphernalia. Nor did families live in isolated igloos. Rather, during the winter ceremonial season people gathered in communities as large as three or four hundred. There men and boys over the age of five worked, ate, and slept together in a *qasgiq* (a communal men's house) while the women lived separately, along with their mothers, sisters, daughters, and small children, in sod dwellings. Finally, far from peaceful, these villages were plagued by violent bow-and-arrow warfare into the early nineteenth century, warfare that abated only after the arrival of Euro-Americans and the epidemic diseases that followed in their wake.

Although Yupik Eskimos remain atypical in many respects, they share an essential feature with their Iñupiaq and Inuit neighbors to the north and east. For all Inuit peoples the relationship between humans and animals is central to the construction of value. To this day they do not view animals as distinct from humans. Rather, humans and animals alike are considered both human and nonhuman "persons" possessing awareness and meriting respect. Moreover, both humans and animals distinguish themselves from one another by their acts. Boundaries between the human and animal worlds are dynamic and transitional, and passages between worlds are, for better or worse, always a potentiality.

The following *quliraq* (traditional tale) eloquently presents the Yupik view of animals and describes as well the Yupik understanding of how animals view humans. The story is well-known all along the western coast of Alaska and is told to this day. I recorded this version in 1977 while Paul John of Nelson Island told it to a group of high school students in the village of Toksook Bay. Marie Meade, a Native speaker, and I collaborated on the translation, employing a modified version of the transcription style developed by Anthony C. Woodbury.[1] Commas within sentences reflect brief pauses in Paul John's delivery, whereas longer pauses are marked by a period. Paragraph breaks mark a complete stop in speech and the beginning of a new thought.

The story describes the relationship between hunter and prey as a cycle of reciprocity in which seals—the focus of ceremonial activity for the Yupiit—visit the human world, where they are treated as guests and sent back to the sea, to return the following season. The Yupik Eskimos do not view this as a necessary response on the part of the seals but as an intentional act in which the seals willingly approach the good hunter in the ritual of the hunt. Clearing a path so that the animals may approach humans is a constant theme in Yupik moral discourse. Ideally, a young man focused all his efforts on "making their way clear" by keeping the thought of the animals foremost in his mind and physically working to clear water holes, entranceways, and windows, allowing the animals a clear view into the human world.

In the story that follows, an *angalkuq* ("shaman"; plural, *angalkut*) sends an uninitiated youth to dwell in the seals' underwater home, where the boy simultaneously views the seals as persons and is given glimpses of the human world from the seals' point of view. In the spring the boy and his mentor approach the good hunter, who—using a kayak and wearing a bentwood hunting hat—appears as a seabird, specifically, a *cigu'ur*, or Kittlitz's murrelet, in the seals' eyes. Faced with the contradiction between an ideology that emphasizes the seal as honored guest and the reality of the animal's death in the hunt, Yupik hunters were both protected and empowered by a new identity.

Another key feature of Yupik cosmology embodied in the story is the belief in the infinite, cyclical quality of both human and animal life. When the seal is "killed," it does not die; rather, its *unguva* ("life") retracts into its bladder, where it remains until it is returned to the sea the following season. During the annual Bladder Festival, Yupik hunters and their wives inflated and cared for the bladders of the seals and other animal guests. After properly hosting them, they returned them to the sea. It is at this point that the boy's journey into the seal world begins.

NOTE

1. Anthony C. Woodbury, ed., *Cev'armiut Qanemciit Qulirait-llu/Eskimo Narratives and Tales from Chevak, Alaska* (Fairbanks: Alaska Native Language Center and University of Alaska Press, 1984).

The angalkuq, observing the ways of our ancestors, compelled a young person to go with the seals out to sea.

He was a young person just like you.

He lived with the seals for a whole year. Then at the end of the winter, he finally came back.

He was a young child like you, and he was the only child of his parents.

Since he was their only child, the parents began pondering over the situation and said, "When this poor child of ours becomes an adult, he will have no one to help him, for he is alone." Then one of them asked, "I wonder how his life can be easier and less strenuous when he becomes a grown person?"

After they considered how their son's life could be easier, the father said, "Let me probe and find the most productive and powerful angalkuq so he may look into how our son can have an easier time when he becomes a hunter."

He was one of our ancestors, a person just like you and me. He decided to search for the most capable and powerful angalkuq.

It was when knives from the outside were very scarce. And since there were very few knives, everyone protected them, and they would worry about losing them. And the father of the child was well aware of how one felt about losing a knife.

As he began searching for the most powerful angalkuq, he hid his knife under the sod by the window while everyone was sleeping. He hid it in the soil where no one could see it. Since the knife was hidden under the sod, as one looked at the space where it was hidden, there was no sign of anything being there.

Now, among the many angalkut in that village, there was one who everyone thought didn't have much power. Although everyone recognized him as an angalkuq, he was considered to be the least productive. But in the view of the people, the other angalkut had all the power that it took to be an angalkuq.

The father placed his knife in this fashion, hoping that his child would become a good hunter.

In the past, when an angalkuq was asked to perform using his spirit powers, the patron would reward him in some way.

And since the father of the child was prosperous, not in the sense of material wealth but as a successful hunter, always having enough to survive on, he approached the most lauded angalkuq and said,

"Here is my reward for you. Would you administer your powers and inquire about my knife that I have been missing?"

The angalkuq began chanting, speaking in a nonsensical manner, but he did not find it.

Then he proceeded to award each angalkuq a gift, and he asked each one to look for his missing knife.

None of the angalkut he asked could reveal the knife's location.

Then finally the angalkuq who everyone thought was inferior was the only one left. The angalkut who were believed to have great powers had all been asked. He had honored each one with a gift to look for his knife, but all of them had failed to find it.

He hoped that when he found the right angalkuq his son would be helped in becoming a successful hunter.

It was during the time when people had great faith in the angalkuq and believed they could empower someone to become a great hunter.

Finally the angalkuq who, in everyone's opinion, had less power was the only one left. Since he was the only one left and had no other preference, he awarded him a small token and said, "Oh dear, I have asked all the angalkut to look for my knife, and they all have failed to find it. Oh my, whatever happened to it?"

Then he asked him, "Do you suppose you could try to find it?"

He responded and said that he could look for it.

After he had awarded bigger gifts to the angalkut who appeared to be confident, he awarded him a measly token, and he asked him to look for it.

Customarily, as the angalkuq performed, the others would attend him. They would do this when he invited his spirit to come.

As he did that and removed his gut parka (they would put on a gut parka as they did this), he disclosed the spot where his knife was hidden.

He said to the father, "Gosh, you should go get the knife that you placed up there by the window and spare yourself from losing it."

Finally there was someone who could find the hidden knife. And the angalkuq had not seen him when he hid it.

Then the father suddenly felt hopeful and thought, "I have finally found the angalkuq who will help my son become a prosperous hunter. After a long, long search one is finally found."

Then the boy's father invited the angalkuq to his house to discuss the issue privately. He wanted to be alone with his wife when he talked to the angalkuq.

Then after he escorted him into his house, he said, "Oh my!

Among all of your associates you are the only one who revealed the location of my knife. I hid it and requested the search when we decided our son needed the help of an angalkuq in becoming a good hunter. He is our only child and does not have siblings to help him. That was the reason I hid the knife."

Then that plain and simple angalkuq said to him, "Would you describe what you have in mind?"

The father answered, "Using your abilities, would you do something to him so that he may have good fortune when he is big enough to hunt?"

Then the angalkuq said, "You are now giving me permission to do this. This evening, when everyone has retired for the night, would you bring him over to the qasgiq? I will give you instructions you must follow when you bring him into the qasgiq. When you bring him into the qasgiq and come to the entrance hole and the appropriate moment comes . . ."

(The doorways of the qasgiq we saw were like this. As you entered, you would see a hole up ahead. And farther on inside there would be another depression which was the fire pit. And the surface up above was covered with flooring of split wood. Right at the end of these pieces was the hole. As you went in, you would emerge from the hole, and as you came up, you would see another hole down below the flooring.)

The angalkuq said, "When you bring him in through that entrance hole . . ."

(They used to make ropes out of sealskin which they called *taprartat*. They would allow the sealskin to dry and take the skin and cut a continuous strip around and around until they had a long cord.)

He told him that he would take a cord and tie it around his neck and pull from the doorway.

Then at the entrance hole (the boy was just a poor little one), when his neck came through the hole, the father was instructed to strike with his knife and sever his neck when he placed his neck through the hole.

This was what he had to do if he wanted his son to become a great hunter.

Then he said to him again, "Let me assure you that if you don't hit him, it is you who will destroy his chance of becoming a good hunter."

He told him that if he was too distressed and failed to strike, he would damage his opportunity to acquire the ability to hunt successfully.

So when he brought the boy over to the qasgiq, the angalkuq tied a sealskin rope around his neck and began pulling, just like I demonstrated to you.

When he positioned his neck through the hole and was given the signal to strike, the father lifted his knife.

There in front of him stood his only son.

Then, ignoring the signal of the angalkuq, he lowered his arm. He found it absolutely impossible to slash the neck of his only son.

When he lowered his arm, the angalkuq said, "I already told you that if you refused to follow my instructions, you would ruin his fate. It is over. There is nothing else I can do."

Then an immense feeling of remorse fell upon the father for refusing to sever the neck of his son. He felt tremendous regret.

When it was understood that the inquiry had ended, the father invited the angalkuq to his house again.

When he brought him into his house, he began pleading with him. He asked him if he could find another way to help his son.

Finally he said to him, "If you two can avoid mourning and grieving over him, we can let the seal bladders take him away. That's one thing I can do for him."

It was with those I mentioned earlier. I told you they would inflate all the bladders of the seals they had caught, and they would dry them and put them away. And in the winter, when a certain month arrived, just like the time we set aside to celebrate Christmas and New Year's, though they were Yupiit, they had a special month when they would do that, and they called it the time to lift the bladders. That was what they called it. I'm not certain which calendar month it was.

The angalkuq told him that he could let the bladders take him away if they agreed not to worry and agonize over the separation and to accept the fact that he would be gone the whole year.

And so the father quickly agreed, and he authorized him to do that.

Then when the time to take care of the bladders arrived, they inflated the bladders after soaking them in water and hung them up across the back of the qasgiq. Each hunter would hang all of his bladders in a bundle.

The many hunters gathered their seal bladders and hung them. Those who were successful hunters would have many, and the less fortunate ones would have fewer. This was done to return the seals they had caught to their home in the ocean.

When they caught a seal, they would save and keep its bladder, and they believed they were still alive.

Then when they went hunting, they believed that the seals they had caught the year before had come back again. They would assume the seals they caught were the same ones they had caught the year before.

According to their own perspective, they would not allow the seal to die eternally.

Their bladders would be moistened and inflated. When they prepared to send the bladders, they would chop a hole in the ice and make a pathway for them. They would chip the ice and make a hole all the way down to the bottom of the river.

After they inflated all the bladders, they would deflate them. After they let all the air out, they would let two people bring them down to the river and drop them into the hole. Then, after they sank them, they would declare that the bladders had returned to their home in the ocean through the river.

So the angalkuq said that if he enabled the child to go with the bladders, that would be his only chance to become a good hunter.

The boy's father quickly urged him to carry out the plan.

After the bladders were deflated, and when the men brought them down to the river to let them go, the angalkuq took the boy and followed them down to the hole. When the bladders had been sunk into the hole, he turned to the two men and said, "Would you two go back up? I will follow shortly."

The men went up and entered the qasgiq. Shortly after, the angalkuq came in alone. The boy who was with him was gone.

Then from that moment on, the little boy disappeared. He totally vanished from the village. . . .

So the boy stayed away all winter long.

At the time the boy came down to the hole in the river, he remembered he was suddenly captivated, and his whole being was mesmerized. Perhaps it was like a jolt.

When he woke up and was alert again, he was traveling along with other people. His traveling companions would say they were going home.

Then when they arrived, they went into the qasgiq. There was a raised platform for working and sleeping around the inside of the qasgiq just like they had back home.

There were men sitting down below on the floor. They had sores all over their bodies. They were constantly moving and scratching.

And there were other men sitting on the ground-level benches who were small with circular faces and large round eyes.

Finally there were men sitting on the elevated platform all the way around. These men were strong and full of confidence.

There was one person who had told him as they traveled that he would watch and care for him all winter. And also the angalkuq had told his parents that he had appointed a mentor for him out there. One of the men on the bench told him that he would sit next to him all winter.

All winter long those who were sitting on the floor would leave. They constantly went out. They would enter carrying fresh fish in front of their garments, and some would carry frozen fish. Then they would begin eating.

And also those little people on the ground-level bench would constantly go out from the qasgiq.

He soon discovered that the people on the floor who were covered with sores and constantly moving were spotted seals. And those small men with big eyes were hair seals. He actually saw them as human beings. And the men who sat on the elevated platform around the walls were bearded seals. They were the ones who never went out, but their companions would endlessly bring them food to eat.

So while they sat there in the qasgiq in the winter during bad weather, someone would come to the skylight in the roof of the qasgiq and clean it. And as he put his head down to look, the boy would recognize the person. It would be someone he knew from his village.

Then the person would come down lower and act as if he were sucking and drinking water. And he would stand up when he was satisfied.

The boy soon learned that during a stormy winter day one of the men back at his village had come down to the water hole and had cleared the hole to take a drink. And when he came down to drink, the men in the qasgiq would see him look down through the smoke hole. And the boy would recognize him.

His mentor would say, "You have witnessed that man up there from your home. Now when you go home and begin living on your own, you must carefully clean the water hole and drink when you are thirsty. When you do that, we will be able to see you, just like the man we saw up there."

Then another person would come and begin cleaning their window. And as the boy watched from down below, the man would clean it briefly and go away.

His mentor would say, "When you return home, you may sometimes clean the ice hole carelessly. You have just witnessed one of the people in your village who just tried cleaning the ice hole. He was very careless and left without looking down at us. His actions clearly confirmed his lack of motivation and desire in hunting."

And sometimes while he sat there, he would begin hearing chunks of snow landing on the surface of the qasgiq making a clattering sound. You know, when you toss the snow off the shovel, it makes a very distinct and noticeable sound. He would hear the chunks as they landed up above, and bits of snow would fall on the window.

His guide would say, "When you arrive at your place, you might be lazy about shoveling the doorways of others in your village when the weather is bad. Listen to someone up above, one of the men from your home who is taking care of doorways in such weather instead of lounging. And as he hurls the snow off his shovel, you can hear it land on the roof of our house. Listen to him cleaning the pathway so carefully as he clears the way he will use when he comes to catch one of us in the spring.

"The things that would block him on his journey are landing on our roof. When you clean the doorways, you might get careless at times. When people continually take care of doorways in the storm back in your village, they are only clearing the path of the animals when they come in the spring."

And sometimes the boy would hear something faintly from way in the distance. Someone was actually shoveling. And when he tossed the snow, the impact would be hardly audible.

The mentor would say, "Now observe this very carefully. You may sometimes shovel aimlessly without thinking about the path of the animal. You can hear someone shoveling up there now who is totally unaware of removing the obstacles from the path of the animal. And the snow from his shovel is landing in the path of those who will come to him."

His mentor continually counseled him.

Sometimes while he was sitting there, a bowl of akutaq would come in through the entranceway and slide in and land between the two of them.

At this time his host would say, "Your parents have provided us with food. Now let's have some akutaq." Then they would quickly devour it.

He soon understood that when the angalkuq ate the akutaq that the parents had brought to him, he had indeed shared it with them. This was done through making a food offering. When he took a bit of his own akutaq and tossed it into the air, it would come to them there in the qasgiq.

The mentor continually instructed him on how he could be a productive person when he returned and became a member of his own people.

Then soon it gradually lit up outside, and some of the many members there stopped coming back in whenever they left.

His host would say, "Since the daylight is getting longer, undoubtedly your relations back home are beginning to look down into the ocean, the place where they will demonstrate their hunting skills. When the appropriate time comes, you and I will also go see our elected host. I have returned to him year after year, for he honors my presence with great reverence and doesn't make me feel intimidated. He has been my host again and again."

Eventually, those on the floor stopped coming back inside, and only a few were left. He soon found out they had started to swim north.

When some of the young men were preparing to leave, one of the old men would say, "While you are out there on your journey, remember not to sleep too long. Please, try not to sleep very long. If you do, the hunter will capture you while you are not awake and alert."

One of the young men would say, "It is difficult to stay awake listening to the perpetual beat of the two drummers."

(You girls will not understand this.)

Down in the ocean ice when a thin layer of ice forms on the edge, it creates a murmuring sound. The jagged surface makes a ceaseless, gurgling tune.

Apparently, when seals are on an ice floe and begin hearing the sound, according to their own judgment they hear drums beating.

And while they were up and observing, and the rippling sound continued around the ice floe, they would become drowsy.

They didn't want them to be caught while they were asleep because they would get stuck as they escaped into their bladders.

They had always been advised to try to stay awake during the time hunters hunt them. And when the hunter hit him with the harpoon, he was to fly into the farthest end of the kayak with full force.

Evidently, it was his life, his soul, that would dash into his bladder. Perhaps those who were hit before running in would die forever.

Then he and his mentor began their journey when the time arrived. As they were traveling, they would sometimes see another kayak going along. The poor man's kayak would be covered with old clothes. It would be covered with old boots and tattered garments.

His mentor would ask, "Didn't you see that person who just came by?"

When he said that he did, his mentor would say, "Now remember this. When you go back to your village and acquire your own kayak, you might want to place the poles to support it too close to the houses. Some women will hang clothes anywhere outside. If you place the poles too close to the house, and women hang clothes on them, you will look like that man when you paddle out in the ocean. But when you look at yourself, you will not be covered with old clothes."

As they traveled along, they would see another kayak floating above the water. The man would be paddling while his kayak hung above the water. And the tips of his paddles would barely touch the water.

His mentor would say, "Look at that man with a kayak hanging. You can see him paddling above the water. In your lifetime you may neglect the ocean at times. The man you just saw with a kayak floating above the water was someone who never thinks about the ocean."

He was one who suddenly remembered the ocean when the other men were starting to travel out.

As they traveled along, they would see another kayak, and the man paddling inside would have a bucket over his head. He would not be able to see where he was going since the bucket covered his eyes. However, the movement of his paddle would be constant and regular.

When I was a little boy, our elders used to teach us not to stoop down and drink water from the bucket. They would tell us always to use a ladle when we drink.

Apparently, this was one of the fundamental principles from a long, long time ago.

They say those who paddled with buckets over their heads were those who drank by stooping down. They were the ones who had ignored the advice and drank without a ladle.

As they went by, the men appeared to them in that fashion.

Nevertheless, the hunter would be paddling continuously.

And when they stopped sometimes, another kayak would go by, and the man inside would have hair hanging down his mouth.

His mentor would say, "See that man? When you acquire children, you may want to bite off their louse eggs."

In those days people had many lice. And someone would bite another's hair, then squeeze out the lice, and pop them in his mouth.

He would tell him that he may want to do that when he acquired his own children.

His guide would say, "Look at that man with hair in his mouth. He is the kind who likes to bite the lice off his children's hair."

As they traveled along, they would go by a village, and his mentor would recognize the place.

They traveled toward the north.

Then one day when they were approaching a village, his mentor said, "We have reached my host's village. Let us sit here and wait for him. I know he's planning to come down early tomorrow morning."

They sat and waited. And as they waited, the boy became drowsy and began dozing off. His mentor quickly shook him and said, "My goodness, don't fall asleep now! Stay alert and watch our host. He just walked out of the qasgiq and went over to his spouse's house to get ready."

They were waiting right below the houses. And as he looked, a woman came out of a house holding a grass pack basket. She was absolutely pure, and there were rays of light radiating from the edge of her parka ruff.

The woman was busy helping her spouse as he was getting ready to leave. She was very eager to help him.

Then his mentor said, "Look at the woman up there. There are clear indications that she is not a lazy person. And the glowing shine from her confirms her cleanliness. When a woman does not sit idle and neglect what needs to be done, she will begin to appear to us in that fashion. Let's watch as her husband gets ready to come down."

They sat and watched the village from a distance, just like watching a television set.

Then her husband began pulling his kayak on a small flat sled and headed toward the ocean.

They sat on an ice floe as he came down. When he came to the water's edge, he pulled the sled from under the kayak and secured it on the back of the kayak.

Then he reached into his kayak and stood up holding a wooden bowl.

Then his mentor said, "Look at him as he gets ready to give us some of his akutaq."

And as he watched, he reached into his bowl and pulled up his hand. Then, as if he knew exactly where they were, he tossed the akutaq toward them, and the piece landed right in front of them.

Then he said, "Let's enjoy it now."

They ate the whole thing.

Back in those days, before the arrival of the Western religion, everyone who traveled down to the ocean always offered food to the animals.

They would take a little bit of all the food they had brought with them and throw it in the water. They would throw a little piece of food in the water. The food was an offering to the animal that might come to them.

Then as the hunter got into his kayak, he began paddling toward them.

Then his guide said, "Now observe his eyes as he looks toward us and see the strength in his vision. And when he looks straight at you, feel the forceful impact it creates. Examine the acuteness of his eyesight.

"Now, when you return to your village, you may want to look at women and other people straight in their faces and make them nervous. When men constantly view women right in the faces, their eyesight becomes weak.

"However, when men avoid looking at women and others straight in their faces, and they begin going out hunting, their vision is keen.

"Watch him very closely. When he glances over toward us, you will feel the force."

Then the hunter came straight toward them. And as he watched him, he suddenly felt a tremendous jolt, and his body trembled.

Then his companion said, "He has seen us. He has spotted us."

And he added, "Now when he begins to come after us, try not to fall asleep. You will experience a very strong urge to sleep. Keep alert and try not to doze off."

(The hunters used to wear tall, pointed wooden hats. I used to see some of the hats like that.)

Then the hunter slipped on his wooden hat and began coming after them. As he was approaching, he disappeared behind the ice. They waited but the hunter did not reappear.

As they waited, a little bird slowly came out, a bird that people called cigu'ur, a light-colored seabird that constantly dived in and out of the water.

(I'm sure one of you young boys will see these birds when you begin going out to the sea. They are light-colored birds and have dark spots on their wings.)

After the bird came around the bend, he started swimming toward them. After he swam for a while, he burped a little bit. When he burped, a fine haze came out of him and slowly spread toward them.

And when the pleasant little mist reached them, the boy sensed a pleasurable feeling and became very drowsy. As he was beginning to doze off and fought to stay awake, his partner gently nudged him and said, "Poor you! I thought I told you to try to stay awake."

Then he forced himself to wake up and was vigilant again.

Then the mentor said, "Now watch him. Next time he does that, the effect will be stronger, and you will become very, very sleepy. I, too, will suffer greatly when I try to stay awake. I had just become very drowsy, too, a few minutes ago.

"But if you accidently fall into sleep, as soon as you feel the impact of the force, you must dash into your bladder."

(Remember I told you that they used to save the bladders of the seals. Apparently, when that happened, they were told to run into their bladders.)

Then as the bird got closer, he burped again and let out a pleasant little mist. Then just like before, the little mist came toward them. And when it reached them, he suddenly became drowsy. He tried to stay alert but soon dozed off.

Then, just when he was falling asleep, he suddenly felt a great jolt all over his body. As soon as he felt the blow, he quickly escaped into his bladder.

The hunter caught both of them. He killed only their bodies.

And since their souls had escaped into their bladders, their immortal beings stayed there.

Then when the hunter skinned and carved him, his whole body was tingling. It was a thrilling sensation and didn't hurt at all.

After he finished cutting them up, he loaded them up and took them home.

When he arrived at the lagoon, he held his paddle aloft to indicate that he had killed a seal.

Then when he walked away, they stood there and watched him.

When the hunter got home, his wife came out putting on her belt, and she got their sled ready to fetch his catch.

When the hunter's wife arrived, the angalkuq ran into the house of the parents of the boy who had gone with the bladders, and he told them that their son had arrived.

The parents jumped up, for they thought he had arrived in human form.

Then the angalkuq said, "Oh my, don't jump up. You will not see him now. He will only appear this winter during the time they send the bladders away. You should welcome him and make some akutaq, and bring me some when you are done. He has arrived with great yearning for akutaq."

After they made akutaq they brought some over to the angalkuq in the qasgiq.

Then the parents waited all summer long, and even though they were told that their son had arrived, they began to doubt that he was there.

And when they began to be lonely, the angalkuq would storm in and say, "I have told you again and again not to be lonely. I am telling you that he's actually here now. But he will appear only when the appropriate time arrives. You must wait and be patient. You should make some akutaq and bring me some."

They would go ahead and make the akutaq and bring him some in the qasgiq.

Eventually, the time to honor the bladders arrived in the winter. They took care of their bladders and hung them. And the day came for them to send them away. They deflated them and took them down to the ice hole in the river and let them go.

But there was no sign of the boy.

Then, after the last bladders had gone, one of the women in the village went down to fetch some water.

They say when there was lots of snow in the winter, the snow would pile up high around the hole. They would make a roof on top and make a little shelter around the hole and make a doorway just like a house. They would call it *aniguyaq*. They would go inside it and fill up their buckets.

One of the women went down to the river and walked up to the aniguyaq. As she looked in, she saw a naked little boy sitting all crouched up. He was trembling and was quietly sobbing. As she looked closer, she discovered that he was the boy who had disappeared the year before, the boy who went with the bladders.

She said, "Why are you crying?"

He replied, "My companions left without me. I begged for them to take me, but they refused and left me here."

He continued to cry, saying he wished to go with them.

The woman said, "Oh my, don't cry. You should stay and come with me to your parents' house. Let's go see your own parents here."

Then she took him and ran up to his parents' house. He had just become a regular human person and had come back to his village.

When he came in, his parents were very happy and delighted and prepared new clothing for him.

After that he remained in the village and started a normal human life.

The following year they again prepared to send the bladders away. And one day when the bladders were hanging in the qasgiq, the boy removed all of his garments.

When he began removing his clothes, one of the men in the qasgiq said, "What are you going to do?"

He answered, "I'm going to go visit those people up there whom I stayed with."

He told them that he was going to visit the people he was with when he was away. Then he stood up and walked to the end of the row of bladders that were hanging. As he put his hands on the bundle at the end, he slowly vanished.

Then starting from the bundle he had touched, the bladders began quivering, and the motion moved slowly across like a wave. The bladders would tremble even though they hadn't been touched.

And as everyone closely watched, some of the bladders would shake longer than the others. And some would quiver a little bit and stop.

Then finally he came to the end. And shortly after the bladders stopped shaking, he fell out of the bladders at the end and came out exactly the way he looked [when he went in].

As he was putting on his clothes, he said, "I'm so glad I finally saw my old friends, the people I stayed with when I was away."

Year after year he would do that. Every time they were sending the bladders, he would visit them. He would enter the bladders hanging at one end and come out through the other side.

When he became a grown man, he began going out to the ocean. And he would recognize every seal he saw out there.

When he came to a seal who had not treated him well or had gotten angry with him when he was with them, he would throw his harpoon with all his might and try to hurt him.

However, when he came to those who had treated him well and those who had cared for him, he would throw his harpoon at them very gently. He would throw his harpoon and try to let the spearhead make just a little hole in the skin.

He would tell his companions in the qasgiq about all of these things.

He became an adult and never disappeared again. And he became a father.

That was usually the end of the story when people told it.

They say that the person who had stayed with the seals down in the ocean used to speak in the qasgiq. When he became an elder, he spoke to others and talked about the doorways, ice holes, and the floors of the houses. He would urge the young boys to take care of these places. He would say that when they kept these places clean, they were clearing the way between them and the animals.

This is where the story usually ends.

"THE MOON'S SISTER"

AND

"SONG OF THE ATKAN ALEUTS"

▲

KNUT BERGSLAND

INTRODUCTION

The two examples of Aleut oral art presented here in English translation relate to Aleut culture before it was dominated by the Russian
fur traders and hunters, who from 1745 on conquered the Aleutian
Islands and the mainland farther east called Alaska (a name of Aleut
origin), the land that eventually would constitute the greater Alaska
purchased from Russia by the United States in 1867. The first piece
is a cosmic myth that was told in the village of Unalaska in the winter
of 1910 by the blind Aleut storyteller Isidor Solovyov (born in 1849
at Akutan, farther east) and was written down and first translated
into Russian by the Aleut church lector Leontiy Ivanovich Sivtsov
(1872–1919) for the Russian ethnologist Waldemar Jochelson
(1855–1937). The second specimen is an Aleut song recorded in
the 1830s at Atka, to the west of Unalaska, by the Orthodox priest
Iakov Netsvetov (1804–64), whose mother was an Aleut. It was
first published, with a Russian translation, by the famous Russian
priest Ivan Veniaminov (1797–1879), who created an Aleut literary
language, consolidated the Russian Orthodox Church in Alaska,
and in 1977 was canonized as Saint Innocent, the Apostle of
Alaska.[1]

In the Eastern Aleut myth the Moon's sister is presented as living
on the upper floor of the ancient Aleut universe, digging roots in the

manner of an ordinary Aleut woman on the earth below. Digging a hole in the upper ground, she looks down and sees that there are villages on the earth below. Having spent the winter braiding a cord, she slides down it and sees two Aleut hunters in their kayaks. As they are paddling along the choppy sea, the wooden visors they wear, decorated with sea lion whiskers, look like wisps of smoke. They bring boiled salmon and water to her and have her come to their house, where she becomes the wife of both of them, as could normally have happened in the ancient Aleut world. They beget a son, who like an ordinary Aleut boy, would be educated by his maternal uncle. The mother sets out with him to visit her brother, the Moon, but it is a long walk, and she becomes too old and dies, but not before telling her son how to get up to his uncle. Ascending by a ray of sunlight, he first reaches some bowls full of blood and empties one of them, the red of dawn and dusk.

Walking on, he comes to three men looking down, called on earth the Three Stars—that is, Orion's Belt—and then to a large man looking down, the Evening Star, in Aleut usually understood as Venus but here more probably Aldebaran.[2] Passing two groups of men looking down—the Bundles-of-Codfish (the Pleiades) and the Caribou (Ursa Major)—he finally reaches the Moon's house. There, in the absence of his uncle, he finds the Sun rolled up in a grass mat, and unrolling it (against his mother's advice), he burns his face. Returning exhausted, the uncle tells him to take his place, and then he dies. The young man buries his uncle, puts on the clothes representing the phases of the Moon, and continues to live as the Moon. The Moon's task is heavy, probably the moral one of guarding taboos, and not to be made light of, for he has to pass over the filth and excrement on earth. In an earlier version of the myth, the Moon's sister may have represented the Sun, as in an Eskimo myth known from Alaska to Greenland. The story ends with a traditional formula, as if the person in the story were telling his own story.

In the Atkan song the dancing singer, with the modesty becoming to a hunter, describes how he had in vain been all alone in his kayak, chasing a sea lion, and, coming back, expresses his joy at hearing the drums calling for a dancing feast. According to Netsvetov's comments, he then stops singing, those sitting in front of him begin to beat the drums and sing, and he again dances and acts as a hunter.

NOTES

1. Both pieces appear in Aleut with a more literal English translation in Walde-mar Jochelson, *Unangam Ungiikangin Kayux Tunusangin: Unangam Unii-kangis Ama Tunuzangis/Aleut Tales and Narratives,* ed. Knut Bergsland and Moses L. Dirks (Fairbanks: Alaska Native Language Center, 1990). "The Moon's Sister" is on pp. 148–55; the Atkan song is on pp. 706–709, in an appendix that contains ancient Aleut songs and other texts originally published in the 1840s by Ivan Veniaminov, which I have re-edited here.

2. This interpretation was suggested to me by John MacDonald of the Igloolik Research Center, Northwest Territories, Canada.

The Moon's sister liked to eat lupine roots when she grew up. One time she was out digging lupine roots and pulled one out of the ground. A cold draft blew on her from the hole of the root, and when she looked down through the hole, she saw that there were villages down there. Seeing that, she filled the hole with mud, set up her digging stick as a marker, went home, sat down in her place, and without leaving it, spent the winter braiding a cord.

When spring came, she took the cord and went to the place where she had removed the lupine root and had seen that there were villages down below, and she began to dig a hole. When she thought that she had made it big enough for her body, she tied one end of her braided cord to her digging stick and, taking hold of the other end, threw herself down into the hole she had dug. But a constant strong wind blew her back up to the place she had jumped from. So, holding the edges of her skirt together, she again threw herself into the hole and began to slide down the cord. Having slid down without reaching the ground, she lengthened her cord with her braid; but still not reaching the ground, she let herself drop down, and she fainted.

Coming to her senses from the cold ground, she walked along the shore and, looking down from the top of the bank, saw two kayak men landing below her. They wore wooden visors decorated with sea lion whiskers, so they looked like wisps of smoke. She sat down there. One of the men brought up to her some boiled red salmon in a round basket made of fresh grass; the other one brought water in a wooden cup. When she had eaten the boiled red salmon from the basket and drunk the water from the cup, they told her the path for her to walk by, then left her and set out in their kayaks. When the two men were some ways from her, she went over to what seemed to be their house and went in.

When the two men returned, they entered their house and placed between them the woman they had taken as wife, and they started to eat. And she continued living like that until she had a son with her two husbands.

When her son grew and became able to talk and began to play with other boys, his mother said to him, "Whatever talk there is about the Moon you see there, don't take part in what is said about him. He is my brother and your uncle."

"But can't you take me to him?"

"He is far away up there!" she said.

She spent the night with him, but did not sleep. Next morning they set out together.

After she had walked with him for a long time, she became an old woman and her son a young man. Feeling it difficult to walk any longer, she said to her son, "The place that I am going to is not far off, but I feel the end is coming. My strength is failing, and I am no longer able to get there. When you walk on from here, you will reach the daylight coming from above. When you reach it, you will grab it and get up on it. It will try to shake you off, but don't let it drop you down and don't breathe on it. When it has taken you to the top, get off. When you walk on, you will reach some bowls containing blood. When you reach them, you will empty one of the bowls. When you empty it, there will be what here on earth is called the red of dawn and dusk. When you walk on, passing to the right side of those bowls, you will come to three men standing in a row looking down. Here on earth they are called the Three Stars. When you walk on ahead from there, you will come to a large man looking down. That's the one called here on earth the Evening Star. When you walk on, passing on his right side, you will come to a group of men looking down. Those are the ones called here on earth the Bundles-of-Codfish. When you leave those men, you will come to some men facing away from each other. Those are the ones called here on earth the Caribou. When you walk away from there for a while, you will reach the house of my brother, the Moon. That will be the end of the journey for you. You should give him my greetings. But whatever you look at inside that house, don't let your hand touch it, especially a rough grass mat that you will see rolled up in the inner part of the house. Don't let your hand touch it."

As soon as she finished saying that to her son, she died.

When his mother died, he walked on from there and after three days came to the daylight streaming from above. Having come to it, he did as he had been told, grabbing it so that he would not fall off. Having gotten up on it, trying not to breathe on it, he let it pull him up. When it had pulled him up, he got off; and when he walked away, he came to the bowls containing the blood and emptied one of them. He saw that the blood from the bowl flowed far away. Thinking that this is what is called down there on earth the glow of dawn and dusk, he walked away from it.

Seeing all those things that his mother had told him about, and passing by them, he reached the house of his mother's brother, the Moon. After he had been there for a while, all alone, he approached the grass mat that he saw rolled up in the inner part of the house and unrolled it. But when a fire appeared and flew out of it and burned his face, he quickly covered it up. He saw that that was the one called down there at daytime the Sun.

He stayed alone in the house until the daylight ended. When he saw his uncle the Moon come to him, he said, "Your sister sends you her greetings."

"Are you my nephew, then?"

"Yes."

"You have done what you ought to do. I have lost my strength, and you must take my place. It is very hard to go up from the northeast where the sun goes up and pass over the filth and excrement down there. A little way below here is a house. In that house are the clothes for the new moon, the half-moon, the waning moon, and the full moon. You will walk with all those. These clothes that you see me wearing you must wear. Now I have no more strength. I have reached my end," he said and died.

When his uncle died, he removed his uncle's clothes and put them on. He wrapped his uncle in a grass mat and buried him. Doing as he had been told, using from that house the things that the Moon is supposed to have, he walked on and continued to live as the Moon—the Moon's nephew said, so the story goes.

Sluggishly, telling no one, I went out in my kayak today.
As I was paddling along, looking around, I saw an animal, a sea
    lion surfacing joyously, and
stopping paddling in front of him, I began to think.
Thinking that, in this case, even a sluggard could succeed,
I decided I could carry it off and pulled out a spear that I kept on
    the stern of my kayak, removed the sheath, and put it in front
    of me.
Paddling toward him, I got close and speared him but not
    strongly enough for it to stick in.
In a panic, he dashed off.
I paddled after him, speared him again and again, but with no
    result except I blunted the points of my spear on him.
As I had gone out secretly so as to see nobody,
I looked around to see if there were anybody, until
I felt like crying, if I'd had someone to cry with.
After having lain still there, I started paddling again, went back,
    and when I landed,
returning to the one I love most and have as my assistant spirit,
    the drum, I kept my ears open but did not hear it.
But as I was imagining that it was still there—there you are!
Take your drums and open your mouths, now!

THE ONE WHO KICKED HIS

GRANDMOTHER'S HEAD ALONG

▲

ELIZA JONES
AND
CATHERINE ATTLA

INTRODUCTION BY ELIZA JONES

"The One Who Kicked His Grandmother's Head Along" is one of many *kk'edonts'ednee* stories told by the Koyukon Athabaskan people, and other Athabaskans. These stories are often referred to as "distant-time" stories—stories that took place before the remaking of the world as we know it today. Many Koyukon Athabaskan beliefs come from these stories. Explanations of the origin, design, and functioning of nature and proper human relations with it are found in these stories of the distant time.

The story here tells how a grandmother's spirit leads her grandson to a new life. The behavior of the grandmother, who invites a bear to come and marry her, suggests that she is probably senile. Even after the young man brings her back to life after the bear has killed her, she does not learn her lesson, saying, "Your uncle slapped me." While she may be senile, it is nonetheless the power of her spirit that directs the young man to crash the house down upon her. Then her head conveniently pops out of the caved-in house. The young man tries to dispose of his grandmother's head at each camp he comes to, by sinking it into the water hole. But none of these camps is the place for him to settle; so the head won't sink. When he finally reaches the right place, it floats downstream, leaving him on his own.

There is a great deal of power associated with skulls in these stories. In another story that Catherine Attla tells, a skull of a man's brother comes to the shore of a lake to warn him of danger, and in another story a skull saves the life of a woman and helps her avenge the death of her family members. I don't know why the young man in this story kicked his grandmother's head along. All I can say is that the characters in many of these stories do things that today are considered unacceptable. For instance, it is *hutlaanee* (pronounced hu tlAH nee; "taboo") to touch the bones of the dead. When a skull is found—which is sometimes a bad omen—it is handled carefully so as not to put the fingers through the eye sockets, and then it is reburied. Whoever finds it pleads to the spiritual power of the skull for mercy for one's family and self.

The actions of this young man do not correspond with the proper expected behavior among Koyukon people, now or in the recent past. Koyukon respect and care for their elders, loathe ruthless killing, and don't spit on one another.

It is believed the stories have spiritual power: telling a story can bring good luck to the teller. Generally stories were told in the fall. "I thought the winter had just begun, and now I've chewed off part of it" is said at the end of each story as a prayer for a short winter, because long winters bring hard times, for then game is scarce.

The *nonaałdlode* (pronounced nAW nAHł dlAW DA; the barred *l* is a voiceless *l*), or "creamed one," is also locally called "Indian ice cream." In this story it is made of whipped caribou-leg marrow, cooked, dried meat flakes, and possibly some berries.

"The One Who Kicked His Grandmother's Head Along" was originally told in Koyukon Athabaskan by Catherine Attla of Huslia, Alaska. I transcribed and translated the story, which appears in *Sitsiy Yugh Noholnik Ts'in'*.[1]

NOTE

1. Catherine Attla, *Sitsiy Yugh Noholnik Ts'in'/As My Grandfather Told It* (Fairbanks: Alaska Native Language Center, 1983). Other books by Attla include *Bakk'aatugh Ts'uhuniy/Stories We Live By* (Fairbanks: Alaska Native

Language Center, 1989) and *K'etetaalkkaanee/The One Who Paddled Among the People and Animals,* trans. Eliza Jones (Fairbanks: Alaska Native Language Center and the Yukon-Kokukuk School District, 1990), an epic-length tale of a powerful medicine person's journeys. All three books promote the Native culture of the area they serve.

THE ONE WHO KICKED HIS
GRANDMOTHER'S HEAD ALONG

In the time very long ago
a grandmother and her grandchild were living together.
It was freeze-up time again, and thin ice was beginning to run on
   the river.
They were living there.
Thin ice started to appear on the river now.
And there on the riverbank this orphan was sitting.
He was sitting there on the riverbank,
watching the thin ice running out there.
Then across on the beach a black bear was walking.
He ran back into the house to his grandmother.
He shouted, "Grandma, there's a black bear walking across
   there."
Grandmother started scurrying out the door.
She went out to the riverbank and saw it across there.
She shouted, "Husband, come across this way among the pieces
   of ice!"
He was standing by his grandmother as she said this.
He was really scared.
Now it started into the water to come across.
To his surprise, it started swimming across among the pieces of
   ice.
He ran back into the house in fear.
Grandmother came back in.
They were staying in the house.
The bear came in the door and sat down out there by the
   fireplace.
Meanwhile, he was back there really scared; he didn't know what
   to do.
It kept grimacing, as if it were going to growl.
And he asked her, "Grandma, why does it keep showing its
   teeth?"
"Oho! Your uncle is smiling at me!" she said.
There it was, baring its teeth.
When it started doing it more, he jumped up and raced out the
   door in fear.
He ran into the cache.
It is said that caches always had stakes planted all around them

so that if something started climbing up, it would fall and be
  impaled.
The stakes would pierce it in several places.
There he was, sitting in the cache.
Then, all of a sudden, he heard a lot of commotion in the house.
Now he heard it growling, and Grandmother shouted out just
  once.
Down below and over there it came back out.
It saw him on the cache, and it rushed toward him, growling as it
  came.
It was climbing up heavily from below.
He kept spearing at it from above.
Then it fell off.
All they had for a ladder was a log with notches cut into it for
  steps,
which is very difficult to balance on.
Because of that, it fell off and got impaled.
There! He killed it. Now he came back down.
Grandma—he rushed back into the house to Grandma.
There was Grandma all torn up.
He put her all back together.
He put her all back together in one place.
He covered her up with a caribou-skin blanket.
Then he stepped back and forth over her, singing a medicine
  song.
He stepped back and forth over her,
and then it looked as if the blanket was starting to move a little.
He looked under the blanket, and
there was Grandma, looking at him.
He became really happy for Grandma.
"Grandchild, oh Grandchild, your uncle slapped me,"
she said, still talking nonsense.
Now he went back out and started butchering the bear.
He cut it all up. They had acquired a lot of food now.
They also had some dried fish.
So now they had a lot of food and were living there.
A long time must have passed since then;
they had eaten up the bear meat now.
Now Grandma had brought in the last of the food.
He was starting to starve now because of Grandma,
so he didn't want Grandma around anymore.
But what could he do?

Now he went to all the house posts and chopped at them to
    weaken them.

He was fixing it now so the house would cave in.

It was this morning that his grandmother had brought in the last
    of the food.

Grandma was down in the house.

He started jumping up and down on the roof.

"Grandma brought in the last food for me this morning—

crash, crash," he shouted while jumping up and down on the
    roof.

The roof caved in. It caved in on Grandma.

Grandma's head came popping out.

Out came Grandma's head.

He got ready to leave.

He kicked her head over the bank.

Now he was going along kicking Grandma's head, kicking it
    along.

Downstream along the edge of the river, he was kicking it along.

Here and there he would spend the night, spend the night.

He came to a water hole with a well-worn path leading up the
    bank.

Then he kicked it into the water.

It floated, and he kept pushing it down into the water, but to no
    avail;

it wouldn't sink.

So now he put it at the edge of the water hole and just left it.

He started up the bank.

There was a small winter house.

It didn't look as if many people lived there.

He sneaked up to the smoke hole.

He went up to the smoke hole and there, down below, were two
    old women.

Why didn't he just leave them alone?

They had half-dried whitefish skewered on a stick up beside the
    fire.

And so here with a stick that was hooked at the end, he hooked it,
that stick of skewered fish.

He was all covered with sweat, from running along the beach,
kicking Grandma's head along.

He took the fish and rubbed his armpits with it.

Then he put it back down where it had been originally.

He put it back down there.

Because they were so old, those women didn't hear a thing.
Now one of them turned back around to face the fire.
She turned back around to the skewered whitefish.
It sort of gave off an odor, so she sniffed it.
Then she said,
"Hey! Friend, this thing smells the way we used to smell long ago
  when we were young."
I guess because they were old, they didn't have any body odor.
They were all dried up.
"Friend, let me smell it; let me smell it," she said.
They got into a really big fight over it.
They pulled each other over the fire.
Then he spit on their heads.
By doing so, they died.
Back down the bank he went.
He began kicking Grandma's head along again.
He was kicking it along and kicking it along.
Then he came to another water hole.
He kicked it into the water.
He kept pushing it down, but it kept floating back up.
So he left it there on the edge, and he went up the bank.
There was a house back there with smoke coming up from it.
While walking back, he asked,
"With whom shall I li—ve? With whom shall I li—ve?"
meaning, "With whom should I be married?"
Then from inside he heard a young girl ask,
"Hey! I wonder if the one asking that is skillful at carving the
  complicated parts of a sled?"
So, hearing this, he sneaked up to the smoke hole.
Inside he saw that it was a poor, homely young girl who had been
  speaking.
Apparently this girl had spoken like that out of ignorance.
This is the reason that people say you shouldn't speak without first
  carefully considering what you want to say, because this girl
  spoke without thinking.
She had spoken that way to a good boy who might have made a
  good living for her.
So he dropped a wad of saliva on her head.
And by doing this, he killed her.
He went back down the bank.
And he started kicking Grandma's head along again.
He was kicking it along and kicking it along.

He would spend the night here and there.
He didn't know what to do; I guess he was looking for a place
   with people,
for a home.
Now here was another water hole.
Now once again he kicked it up to it.
Now, as he usually did, he kicked it into the water.
"Koyaaluk, koyaaluk, koyaaluk,"
he could hear it saying as it floated away downriver under the ice.
He had thrown it into the water with no success before, but now
   it did,
finally, sink.
He started up the bank.
There, smoke was coming up in two places.
He looked at them.
One of the places from which smoke was rising was a small house,
and the other was a big house.
So he went into the small house from which smoke was rising.
Now he made noise in the entryway;
he came in and brushed off his feet to announce his presence.
That was their way of knocking.
He came into the house, and there a young girl was living *all* by
   herself;
so he asked her,
"Hey! What are you doing here all by yourself?"
" 'Why isn't she married?' they say to me, so I'm staying here all by
   myself
because I don't have a husband," she said.
"Oh!"
So I guess she fed him the last of her food.
"Go over to your parents and say to them,
   'Look, someone came to marry me,' to see what they'll say," he
   told her.
He told her that because he planned to marry her and to live
   there.
"When I start entering their house, Father says to me,
   'Watch it! Don't bump the dish of food into an icicle in the
   entryway.'
That's his way of harassing me for not being married.
That's his way of saying, 'Why doesn't she have a husband?' " she
   said.
"Oh!" he said.

He spent the night there.

Then early the next morning he said,

"I'm going to walk around up there in the mountains, hunting for
   caribou."

So he left.

He left and was walking around up on the mountain.

He saw caribou.

He killed a lot of caribou.

Then he broke up many leg bones, and he extracted the marrow.

He also packed up some stomach fat, all the good parts, and
   started home.

He came home now with a big pack.

They made nonaałdlode,

lots of food—she hadn't had so much good food before.

Now he said to her,

"All right, now, how about taking this over to them to see what
   they'll say?"

Filled with happiness, she started over to her parents' house with
   it.

She made noise going down into the entryway.

Then her father, who always made this remark, said,

"Watch it! Don't bump the dish of food into an icicle." She was
   coming in.

She was carrying in a dish of nonaałdlode.

They were startled.

Even her father was startled.

"My child, where did that come from?" he started asking her.

"A poor orphan, who came to me, and he went hunting up that
   way," she said.

So with great feeling he said to her, "My dear child!"

He told her,

"My child, up there, if I remember right, there are wolf-legging
   boots in the cache.

Bring them down for him.

When he goes out hunting,

he should not hang them where smoke will blow toward them,"
   he told her.

She brought down the wolf-legging boots.

She brought them into her house for him.

"Father said for you to wear these boots," she told him.

He was very happy to get them.

" 'When he's out where he spends the night here and there,

he should not hang them where smoke will blow toward them,'
he said to you," she told him.

Meanwhile, the woman was really happy because someone had
started making a living for her.

And her parents were no longer angry with her.

Now he kept going out hunting now and then.

He began spending the night out there now.

Now he wondered about his boots, "I wonder why he said that
about them?"

Then he hung them where smoke would blow toward them and
went to bed.

So, the night passed.

He woke up after the night had passed.

Then he thought, "Oho! I wonder what happened?"

He remembered his boots over there.

He looked, and they were gone.

"What happened?" he thought.

He jumped up out of bed, and he rushed over there.

It seems that right from where the boots had been hanging were
signs

that a big male wolf had walked off.

There he was; he was without boots.

The boots had turned into a wolf while he slept.

I don't know what happened to him after that.

I thought that the winter had just begun, and now I've chewed
off part of it.

"RAVEN" AND
"FOG WOMAN"

▲

ANTONE EVAN
AND
JANE MCGARY

INTRODUCTION BY JANE MCGARY

"Raven" and "Fog Woman" are traditional stories of the Inland Dena'ina, one of the Athabaskan Indian groups of Alaska; the name means simply "people." The Dena'ina, also called Tanaina, historically occupied a territory of about forty-one thousand square miles extending around most of Cook Inlet. Early and intense exploitation by Russian and American colonists led to population loss and acculturation among the Dena'ina on the western shore, around present-day Kenai and Anchorage; but on the eastern shore, between the sea and the towering peaks of the Alaska Range, the Inland people have maintained a strong, integral culture into modern times. In the communities of Nondalton, Lime Village, Pedro Bay, and Newhalen, many Dena'ina adults (but few children) still speak their ancestral language and gather for traditional ceremonies, where elders sing and tell stories like the two that follow. Especially in Lime Village, Dena'ina pursue many of their ancient subsistence practices, including the summer hunting in the mountains depicted in "Fog Woman."

Antone Evan, who told these stories, was born about 1920 at Qeghnilen ("Canyon"), a now-abandoned village on the upper Stony River. In the early 1940s the Evan family moved to Nondalton; they all were known as experts in oral tradition and survival skills. Antone lost his eyesight in his thirties as a result of snow blindness. For the remainder of his life, he dedicated himself to developing his memory, singing, and storytelling and to sharing his knowledge and craft with others. He died suddenly of a heart attack in 1983, in the village of Tyonek, where he had traveled to sing at a memorial potlatch.

The original Dena'ina tellings of these stories and many others were tape-recorded by the linguist Joan Tenenbaum between 1973 and 1976, while she was living in Nondalton and studying the language. Tenenbaum transcribed and prepared interlinear, word-for-word translations of the stories for publication.[1] In 1983, I prepared a new edition, in verse, based on oral features noted in the recordings, with parallel English translations.[2]

The format of my translations is similar to that introduced by Dennis Tedlock in his work with Zuni narrative.[3] Each line represents a "breath group," a phrase delivered by the narrator without pausing; the stanza breaks represent longer pauses. This format is not appropriate for every oral narrative, but it enhances the written record of performances by a master storyteller. By expressing the pause structure and phrase length in Antone Evan's stories, it is hoped that we can reflect some of his skills: he heightens suspense with frequent long pauses, stirs excitement with long, rapid phrases, and emphasizes topics by isolating them in a single "line." These techniques are analogous to what a good writer does with the skillful use of paragraphs, word order, and punctuation. When the recorded performance is the practiced, deliberate work of a professional narrator, representation of oral detail is more than justified.

The story "Raven" is a series of episodes drawn by the narrator from a large body of stories about the most important figure in Northern Athabaskan mythology. Raven is similar in many ways to Coyote, a character probably more familiar to readers. He is the Transformer whose deeds changed the world of myth time—when animals lived like people—to the world of historical time. Many of those deeds are achieved by deceit, for Raven is also the great Trickster, sometimes working his magic for the benefit of humans, sometimes for the benefit of no one but himself. Yet this powerful being also appears in the role of a dupe whose egotism and base desires lead to his own humiliation. It is unsurprising that irony is the major mode in the literature of a people with a god like Raven.

In this story we see most facets of Raven's nature (except lust, in which he equals Coyote). By magic he makes a canoe—in some extended versions of this episode, he invents the first canoe. When

he gets bored and lonely, he uses magic to torment and rob an innocent fisherman. In the second episode (whose serial repetition
heightens its humor, especially for children in the audience),
Raven's trickery becomes truly evil; for the Athabaskan audience,
however, the stupidity of the seal makes the story funny as well as
horrifying. Raven cannot fool all the people all the time: as usual,
when he takes on a whole village, he is discovered and humiliated by
a despised orphan. (The orphaned boy being raised by his poor old
grandmother, who doubts his abilities, is a stock figure in Athabaskan folklore.) Revived in disgusting fashion by his avian relatives,
Raven naturally denies that he was in trouble at all. His second attempt to deceive the villagers succeeds—providing a scene with a
stock Athabaskan comic character, the gullible old widow—and his
escape is followed by the usual exclamation: "That must have been
Raven!"

The reader might wonder whether Raven is in avian or human
form. Athabaskan storytellers differ in their opinion of how Raven
looked as a "person." Sometimes he must have looked quite
human; sometimes much like an actual, but very large, raven. In
some stories he is almost human, but some characteristic—often his
three-toed feet—betrays his identity. Raven's wishes have the force
of magic spells. This power is evident as he recruits the seal as both
canoeing partner and dinner and as he tricks the villagers in the last
episode.

The fisherman whom Raven tricks greets him with "I never see
any people." This formula, often used in Athabaskan stories, is a cue
that the speaker is living in isolation and is about to experience
something supernatural—and probably bad.

When Raven assures the seal that certain water holes belong to
either rich people or poor people, he reflects the Dena'ina sense of
hierarchy, similar to but not so highly developed as that of the
Northwest Coast cultures to the south. The foolish seal is certain to
consider himself a "rich man."

The story "Fog Woman" belongs to a special genre that the
Dena'ina call *dghiliq' sukdu'a* ("mountain stories"). These were
traditionally told in summer, when people migrated to the mountains to hunt game, which they preserved for the long, hard winters.
The stories were not mere entertainment. They were didactic, explaining to younger people the proper relationship of humans to
nature and the importance of valuing the survival of the group over
the desires of the individual. Other mountain stories told in Nondal-

ton may instill respect for ground squirrels or wolves; one recounts the origin of a ritual for calling for good weather. To understand "Fog Woman," one must realize how vulnerable the caribou hunters were, exposed on the chill alpine tundra in skin clothing, able to find their wide-ranging prey only by scanning from high lookout points. A period of rain and fog—not uncommon in this country— might mean death by famine for the band.

The traditional Dena'ina believed that many animals, birds, plants, and weather conditions have corresponding spirits; when humans dealt with objects in the natural world, they necessarily dealt also with the spiritual. Fog Woman is such a spirit person, an entity bound to mist and rain. She warns the young hunter that his love for her is wrong yet acquiesces to his urgings—perhaps because her watery, cloudlike nature cannot resist, or perhaps to punish his transgression. Such stories often end tragically, but this young man realizes that his family's survival is more important than his personal desire. Although grieving for the loss of his wife and child, he resumes the responsibilities of ordinary life in the end.

On another level "Fog Woman" is representative of a widespread theme in mythology, which we may term alien marriage. Stories of marriages between humans and animals or spirits are especially frequent in Northern Athabaskan and Northwest Coast traditions. They may have symbolized the experiences of women captured in war and forced into marriage among strangers; more deeply they may strike a responsive chord in anyone who senses the profundity of otherness amid intimacy. The introduction of a baby into "Fog Woman"—at odds with the apparent chronology of the story—is not only a device to heighten pathos; it is an almost constant figure in Native American alien-marriage stories.

The language used in the translation of "Fog Woman" is deliberately more literary than the colloquial language of "Raven." This choice reflects both the narrator's tone and the usual Native perception of the stories. Like most Athabaskan narrators, Antone Evan uses comical intonation and sly sarcasm in his Raven narratives. His performance of "Fog Woman," by contrast, is measured, serious, and contemplative. Note, for example, the pacing of the climactic scene, where Evan's delivery parallels the gradual progress of Fog Woman and her clouds ascending the mountainside.

NOTES

1. Joan Tenenbaum, *Dena'ina Sukdu'a: Traditional Stories of the Tanaina Athabaskans,* 4 vols. (Fairbanks: Alaska Native Language Center, 1976). The recordings and Tenenbaum's Nondalton field notes are in the archives of the Alaska Native Language Center.

2. Joan Tenenbaum, *Dena'ina Sukdu'a: Traditional Stories of the Tanaina Athabaskans,* trans. and ed. Joan M. Tenenbaum and Jane McGary (Fairbanks: Alaska Native Language Center, 1984).

3. Dennis Tedlock, *The Spoken Word and the Work of Interpretation* (Philadelphia: University of Pennsylvania Press, 1983).

RAVEN

This is a Raven story.

That Raven started walking, and he walked and walked and walked
 and
he walked, and then he got lonesome.
So then he wanted to travel by boat.
He walked out onto a sandbar.
On the sand he drew the outline of a canoe, and
he kicked it with his big toe.
A canoe lay right there in the water.
And then he paddled off.
He kept going and going and going,
and finally he came to a village.

When he came in sight of the village, there was a man standing over
 on the beach with a fish spear in his hand.
Raven paddled back out of sight.
He landed and got some birch;
he hollowed out a rotten birch log.
He got inside it.
He turned into a salmon.
He started off swimming.
In the shape of a king salmon,
he started off swimming,
and he swam along to where the man with the spear was sitting on
 the beach;
he swam by offshore from him.
The man thrust his spear at Raven.
With the man still holding on to it, Raven grabbed it and darted
 out.
He dropped the spear,
that man, and Raven darted out with it and
he swam back down the river, and where he had beached his
 canoe,
he swam ashore.
He turned back into a person,
he turned back into a person, you see.
He put the spear into his canoe, behind a rib at the bow.
He started off again.
He landed there where the man had been,
and there he was, still sitting on the beach.

▲

"I never see any people.
  Where did you come from, coming here to me?" the man said to
      him.
"Ah," Raven told him, "me, I'm just canoeing all around here,"
  he said to him.
"That spear you have there behind the rib,
  it looks a lot like my spear, the one you have behind the rib," said
      the man.
"Why, it sure does!
  That's *my* spear, but it does indeed look like your spear," said
      Raven.
And then he paddled off again.

He kept going and going, and then
he got lonesome as he was traveling.
"Who will come with me?" he said.
And then a moose appeared on the beach: it came out near him.
"Me, let me go with you," it said to him.
"You can't sit in a canoe.
  Look at yourself, how can you say that about yourself?
  If you stepped into a canoe, you'd put your hoof right through it.
  You're not the kind of creature that can sit in a canoe," Raven
      told it.
And so the moose went back into the woods,
  and Raven paddled off again.

Then once more he said, "Who will come with me?"
  And a caribou appeared on the beach; it came out near him.
"Me, let me go with you," it said to him.
"I don't think you could sit in a canoe either; look at yourself.
  You too, you'd put your hoof right through my canoe.
  You're not the kind of creature that can sit in a canoe," Raven
      told it.
He paddled off again.

He kept going and going.
"Now who will come with me?" he said.
And a porcupine appeared on the beach; it came out near him.
"Me, let me come with you," it said to him.
"How could you come with me?
  If I made you mad, you'd club me with your quills.
  I don't want you, not you either."
He paddled off again.

He kept going and going, and then:
"Now who will come with me?" he said.
  Then a beaver surfaced right beside him.
"Me, let me go with you in it," it said to him.
"As for you, if you got in my canoe,
  your tail would dry up and
  when you wanted
  to go back into the water, you'd capsize me.
  I don't want you, not you either," he told it.
He paddled off again.

He kept going and going and going,
  then once more:
"Now who will come with me?" he said.
  And then a seal surfaced right beside him.
"Me, let me come with you," the seal said to him.
"Yes! You're the one I've been asking for, friend!" Raven said to
  him.
"I've been asking for you for a long time.
  All kinds of people asked me to let them come with me, but
    you're really the one I've been asking for," he told him.
He landed and the seal got in beside him.
He paddled off with him, he paddled off and
  he talked and talked with him.
"You know, I was lonesome
  as I traveled, but you know, I'm talking now."

The sun was going down.
"Let's look for a place to camp for the night," Raven told him.
  The seal said, "All right."
He landed and
  pulled the canoe up among some willows and
  left it there.
"At this time of year, people never camp right on the beach.
  They camp way up in the woods when it's like this," Raven told
    him.
"Really?" said the seal.

And so Raven started walking inland with him.
The seal followed him with difficulty.
They walked and walked, and very far up,
  where there was no water anywhere near, he led him.
And then Raven said, "We'll camp here."

He built a brush shelter under a tree,
and he built a fire.
The sun went down.

Then the seal said to him, "Well, what are we going to eat?"
"Ah," he said to him, that Raven,
"at times like this, when we're starving, it's our feet.
We cut off one of our feet," he told him.
That Raven made two skewers.
That Raven cut off his own dried-up foot and
stuck a skewer through it and stuck the stick into the ground.
"Come on, you next, you do that with one of your feet," he told
    the seal.
"No, it'll hurt me!"
Raven made a powerful wish: "Oh, how I wish he'd cut it off, his
    own foot," he thought.
He put a knife in the other's hand.
"Lay the knife on it—it never hurts," he told him.
The seal cut into the joint, and indeed it didn't hurt.
He cut it off.
"Good, it doesn't hurt!"
"Wipe it with your spit and then your foot will grow back."
The seal did this, and it came back just as it had been before.
And then he stuck it on a stick beside the fire.

He put it on the skewer, and his foot was very oily.
The seal stuck it on the skewer beside the fire,
and the heat hit it.
Oil started dripping from it, it just flowed,
it started sizzling.
That Raven said to him,
"Friend, when we are good friends like this,
we never eat our own feet.
We eat each other's feet," he told him.
"Really?" said the seal.
Raven's own foot was hanging there on the stick, and
it curled up its toes as it singed.
When the seal looked in the other direction,
Raven took oil from the seal's foot and rubbed his own foot with
    the oil
as it hung on the stick.
Meanwhile, the seal kept looking away from him.

"Look, friend, my foot is oily too," Raven told him.
"Yes," said the seal.
So when it was done roasting,
Raven stuck his own foot in the ground by the seal,
and by himself, the seal's foot.
Well! That Raven just got sick on the oil
from that foot, and the seal tried to eat Raven's foot.
It was dried up like a hoof.

Then they went to bed.
In the middle of the night the seal said, "Friend, I'm very
    thirsty!"
"Fine, it'll be daylight soon," Raven told him.
The seal started to suffer a lot from thirst.
He can't go without water, because he is a water creature,
and he can't live without water—it's not good at all for him to be
    away from water.
"Go where there's water,
    you go get some for me," he begged Raven.
That Raven built up the fire and
he went after water.
He came to a place where there were springs, and there he dug
    three water holes.
Then, way over on the other side, he dug another water hole.
He put raven feathers all around it, that's what he did.
And then he started back to camp.
He dipped up some water.
He brought it back to him.
He came in sight of him.
"Friend, I need water bad!" the seal said to him.
"Yes, I'm bringing you water," he told him.
When he was almost back to the campfire, Raven deliberately
    stumbled and fell.
He fell down.
He spilled the water.
The seal cried, "Friend, I need water bad!"
"Well, it's dark!
    Hey, what was that, a stick I stumbled over?" he said.
"Where is the water?
    Let's go look for it.
    I'll go along with you too," said the seal.

"All right," said Raven.
They started off.

Raven led him around for a long time but
he didn't really walk too far
before he found a water hole.
The seal walked up to it, wanting to drink, when
Raven told him, *"No,* not there, that's the poor people's water
    hole.
That other one over there is no good either,
not the next one either."
The seal was really thirsty.
"Wait!" Raven told him.
"Look, here it is, the rich men's water hole!"
He found the water hole that he had circled with raven feathers.
"Go ahead, drink some water," he told him.
The seal plunged his head into the hole.
He stuck his head halfway into the water in the hole.
As he started to drink, that Raven kept walking around behind
    him and
pecking at his anus.
The seal raised his head.
"Friend, that hurts!" he told him.
That Raven said to him, "Don't you ever wipe your butt?"
The seal was just thirsty,
so he stuck his head into the water again.
Raven kept on that way until
he had pulled out the seal's guts.
He took off running with the guts,
and then the seal died.
He killed him.

There by him he sat, that Raven.
Well, the seal was really fat.
Raven ate and ate,
he kept on, and
he spent two days there living off him.
He devoured him.
He just got sick on the fat.
He went back down to the beach and walked on,
he started walking again,

and he walked and walked,
and then he came to a village.
He walked into the village and
he went into a house.

"We don't see many strangers.
Where did you come from, coming here to us?"
"Yes, well, I'm just walking around these parts, that's the way it is."
They cooked for him and
gave him food, lots of food.
"I'm not a bit hungry.
Something bad just happened to the one who was my best friend,
so nothing is good for me now."
He didn't eat.
"Just, well, I feel like crying,
but I'm holding it back," he told them.
"It's all right, now, go ahead and cry," they said to him.
That Raven just started crying.
He cried and cried, and then all of a sudden he vomited up fat.
As he kept crying, he quickly shoved dirt over it.
Then he vomited up some more fat,
and at that, the people in the house said, "He himself must be the
one who did it, he was lying!"
At that, Raven went up, *shu shu shu,* he flew up through the
smoke hole!
He landed on a big spruce tree that stood nearby.
"It was Raven who did it, he was lying!
Kill him!" they said.
They picked up bows and arrows
and shot at him.
They shot at him, but they didn't hit him.
Then this old lady's grandchild asked her, "Grandma, make a bow
and arrow for me!"
He brought her some willow,
and she made it for him, stringing it with some kind of thing.
"You? They didn't hit him, how can you say you'll hit him?" she
said to him.
He went back outside, and they were still shooting at him,
and then the boy hit him, and that Raven fell down.
When he fell down, the old lady's grandchild ran up to him and
twisted off his beak.
He ran back inside to his grandma.

"Grandma, here's Raven's beak, just the right size to wipe your
    butt with," he said to her.
"Ah, Grandchild!" she said.

That Raven lay dead there for a long time, and then
Magpie, Camp Robber, and Dipper flew to him.
They just shit all over him.
They kept doing it until Raven woke up.
"What's the matter with you guys, doing that to me?
I just laid my head down.
I was sleeping here."
"Sure, you weren't sleeping.
They killed you.
You were lying there dead.
That's why we were doing that to you," they told him.
"What bad things are you saying!
How could I die?" he said.
Magpie and the others flew away.

That Raven got up and
he went into the woods.
"Let me be a young boy, with a mustache just starting to show
    above my lip,
I wish," he said.
And that's what happened.
He turned into a nice-looking young boy
with a mustache just starting to show on his upper lip.
And then he went back to those people.
He came back to them.
He went into their house.
"Welcome!" they said to him.
"Yes,"
he said.
They cooked for him.
He kept his arm over his nose.
"Have you hurt your face?" they asked him.
"No," he said.
"When I was leaving for here, my friends tattooed a mustache
    on me,
that's why I'm like this," he said.
They served him food.
He ate, and then

he said to them, "I'll go fetch wood."
"Why, you just got here!
  Why should you go chopping wood?
  There's plenty of wood."
"Well, I just can't ever stay still, that's the way I am,
  I only like it when I keep moving."
"All right," they said.
  He went out and
  he went into the woods.
  He came out on the beach on the other side of the point.
  There was sand there.
  He drew the outline of a boat in the sand.
  He kicked it with his big toe.
  It turned into a big skin boat, lying in the water by him.
  He picked up a lot of spruce cones
  and filled it with them.
  And then: "You guys will go around this point to the village
      there.
  Just as you're coming around the point there, make a lot of noise,
  and go, *'Hwi hi hu hu!'* like that.
  Make a lot of noise when you come out around the point!"
  There weren't really any people at all in it,
  there were only spruce cones in it.
  He went back into the woods and returned to the people.
  He went back into the house.
  And then he kept going out to check, listening for them.

Once more he went out, and as he had ordered them, they were
      starting to round the point,
  and it sounded like they were yelling, and he ran back into the
      house.
"Warriors!
  Hurry, go hide somewhere in the woods!"
  Every one of those people ran outside,
  and then they heard the others yelling.
  The boat was really big.
"Go on, go somewhere, anywhere!" Raven told them.
  All the people ran away,
  they all ran in different directions.
  After they had run away, Raven ran back into the house:
      "Grandma, there are warriors!
  Let me take your needle case and things for you!" he told her.

105

That grandma threw him her sewing kit.
He ran out with it
and ripped the bag open and dug through it, but
it wasn't there:
"Your needle case!" he told her.
Next he ripped open the needle case,
and there inside it was his beak.
He slapped it back onto his face and ran outside.
"Turn back into what you were!" he said.
At that, the boat turned into sand
and sank, and then he shouted,
"I was just joking!"
Those people who were hiding all over the place said,
"*Eyi!* That must be Raven!"
That Raven took off flying.
He flew away then.

That's the way it happened, the Raven story.

FOG WOMAN

Long ago
they went up the mountain.
The parents had one son,
their boy child.
They climbed up and
built a brush shelter for hunting ground squirrels.
His mother went out after ground squirrels.
And as for him, he and his father
went hunting caribou; they were always hunting every kind of
     game.
They kept doing that constantly.

Then one day,
as he was out hunting,
he came upon a woman.
"Let me take you back with me," he said to her.
"No," she replied.
"But why not?" he said.
"By myself . . .

tomorrow, I'll return to you," he told her.
All that summer
he walked around there and
he kept returning to that woman on the mountain.
He kept doing that, constantly. . . .

Then once more he returned to her, and then,
"Please come home with me,"
he said to her.

"No, what you say to me is wrong," she told him.
"But it is all right," he said to her,
 and so she started back with him, and just then,
 it began to rain on them a little.

He came home with her.
With her, he came back to where they were staying,
and just then it began to rain on them.
It rained and rained on them,
 it never cleared up, it was always foggy, and

it rained.
They stayed there in camp, and
their food began to run out, too.
What they had hunted there that summer,
the meat and other things, was used up.

"This is the reason
    I told you it was wrong, can you see how it's raining on us now?"
It kept on that way, on and on, it kept raining on them.
It was always foggy.

"This is the way it is:
    only if I leave you will it get better," she said to him.
"As long as I stay here with you people, the weather will not be
        good for you," she told him.
"All right," he said to her.
    In the morning,
    in the morning they arose.
    They had had a baby.
    He wrapped it up for her,
    the baby,
    and tied it on her back with a blanket.

She started walking away from him.
He walked halfway up with her.
"This is far enough:
    sit down here."
The man sat down right there, and she started walking away from
        him.
    Up the hill,
    as she walked up the hill,
    the fog lifted along with her.

Upward,
    as she walked away from him,
    the rain left along with her.
He watched her, he watched her, the fog over the hill

was going with her also.
That man
    burst out weeping there.

As he watched her going upward the fog lifted along with her,
and he burst out singing:

> Upward you are
> walking; come back, uhuna*;
> you who are
> walking upward, come back!

He watched her
as she walked over the crest of the hill, out of his sight;
the fog too went over the crest of the hill.
It stopped raining and began to clear; the sun began to shine on
    them.

The man cried and cried, and then
he wiped his eyes and turned away from the mountain, and looked
    from the mountain out toward the flats.
Out on the flats were caribou: there were many caribou there.
He wiped his eyes and
he ran back down the hill and seized his bow and arrow.
Toward them,
toward them he ran.
He killed some caribou and
packed home meat.
It was good, the weather was good for them again.

That is the way it happened,
the story of Fog Woman.

uhuna: a nonsense word used in songs.

SIX SELECTIONS FROM PETER

KALIFORNSKY'S

A DENA'INA LEGACY

▲

JAMES KARI

INTRODUCTION

A Dena'ina Legacy, from which six selections have been chosen for
this volume, is a collection of 147 writings compiled over a nine-
teen-year period (1972–91) by one of the last speakers of the Kenai
dialect of the Tanaina (or, more properly, Dena'ina) Athabaskan
language of Cook Inlet, Alaska.[1] Peter Kalifornsky, who died in
1993, was a literary artist and scholar who was the great-great-
grandson of a man called in Russian Kalifornsky. Born on Columbus
Day in 1911, he was one of the last storytellers of his language and
one of the few to have written stories in that language. Although his
first two books were printed in very small runs,[2] his work attracted
attention throughout Alaska.

Peter Kalifornsky drew on unique linguistic and cultural materials. The Dena'ina language, which is spoken in four dialects in and
around the Cook Inlet Basin, is a member of the Athabaskan language family. There are today about seventy-five speakers of
Dena'ina. Cook Inlet was a prehistoric frontier on the shores of the
North Pacific. Since it was one of the main Alaskan centers of Russian occupation (from 1791 to the 1880s) and American occupation
(since the 1880s), Dena'ina has had a dramatic history of outside
contact.

The stories in *A Dena'ina Legacy* are about Dena'ina cosmology

and religious thought, animals and basic survival, and lifestyle, people, and geography; the volume includes a chronological collection
of first-person narratives, Kalifornsky's autobiography, and finally a
selection of his Dena'ina language lessons, language experiments,
and poems.

Since Peter Kalifornsky was essentially a self-taught artist and ethnographer, a discussion of his methods and approaches is of interest.
I first met him on June 2, 1972, on my first trip to Kenai, where I
went to study the Dena'ina language. During that two-week visit
my wife, Priscilla, and I became completely absorbed in the fieldwork process. In March of 1972, there had been a small potlatch in
Kenai, and around that time Peter had obtained in a dream the melody of his potlatch song[3] and had written a Dena'ina story in English.

When I returned to work in the Kenai area in 1973, Peter
watched closely as I grappled with the phonetics and orthography of
his language. In January of 1974, he began his first Dena'ina notebook. And that spring we started a small Dena'ina language class in
the evenings in Kenai. In this role as impromptu teacher, Peter
wrote a variety of lesson materials, stories, and translations.

Peter Kalifornsky wrote almost all of his material in Dena'ina. He
wrote most of the pieces spontaneously in one session and did not
revise them. Before about 1985, he usually added the English translations in a second phase. For the 1977 and 1984 books, Peter and
I often discussed the English and made minor modifications in the
translations. For most of the stories written after 1985, I made the
initial English translation, which Peter and Alan Boraas reviewed
and amplified.

From 1974 to about 1983, Peter favored handwriting his stories
and lessons in Dena'ina along with an interlinear English translation. After about 1984, Peter composed many of his stories on a
typewriter in Dena'ina alone. He strongly favored the writing process and tended to eschew the audio recording of stories.

In 1988, Peter began discussing with Alan Boraas his ideas about
a collection of his writings. On the day of the funeral of his sister
(Fedosia Sacaloff) in Kenai—March 23, 1989—Peter asked Alan
Boraas and me to team up to edit his collected writings. The book
took shape in 1990–91, with Alan and Peter meeting on a weekly
basis and coteaching a Dena'ina language class at Kenai Peninsula
College. Peter developed the story inventory of *A Dena'ina Legacy,*
although some topics were suggested to him by others (for example,
other Dena'ina speakers and his editors) in the course of discussions

about Dena'ina material. Virtually all titling of the stories, in Dena'ina and English, is by Peter.

In the late 1980s Kalifornsky developed a subgenre of writings about his own work. *A Dena'ina Legacy* includes his comments at the ends of some of the stories. Included here are his comments on "The Gambling Story," "The Lynx Story," and "The Dog Story."

The 1991 volume is circulating far and wide. It was featured on National Public Radio in January of 1992, and it won a 1992 American Book Award from the Before Columbus Foundation. The six selections chosen for this anthology are representative of Kalifornsky's work on traditional Dena'ina materials. What makes Kalifornsky a unique folk artist, however, is his breadth: his nontraditional, iconoclastic, and whimsical topics, his witty neologisms for non-Dena'ina concepts, and his linguistically based Dena'ina poems. There is, for example, an absurd hilarity to his translation of "The Pledge of Allegiance." My colleague Mike Krauss has called Peter an Athabaskan Isaac Bashevis Singer.

When reading these selections, keep in mind that they were composed in Dena'ina. Kalifornsky's program was the salvaging of the vanishing Dena'ina oral traditions and the creation of new indigenous horizons.

NOTES

1. Peter Kalifornsky, *K'tl'egh'i Sukdu/A Dena'ina Legacy: The Collected Writings of Peter Kalifornsky,* ed. James Kari and Alan Boraas (Fairbanks: Alaska Native Language Center, 1991).

2. Peter Kalifornsky, *Kahtnuht'ana Qenaga/The Kenai People's Language* (Fairbanks: Alaska Native Language Center, 1977) and *K'tl'egh'i Sukdu/The Remaining Stories* (Fairbanks: Alaska Native Language Center, 1984). For more information about Kalifornsky, see Dell Hymes, foreword to *K'tl'egh'i Sukdu/A Dena'ina Legacy,* by Kalifornsky, xvi–xx; "Ginhdi Shi Ukt'a/This Is My Life Story," in ibid., 356–61; and Alan Boraas, "Peter Kalifornsky: A Biography," in ibid., 470–81.

3. Kalifornsky, *K'tl'egh'i Sukdu/A Dena'ina Legacy,* 466.

POLLY CREEK STORY

"Polly Creek Story," written in 1974, was one of Kalifornsky's first original compositions. This story was seminal to his steady compilation of K'tl'egh'i Sukdu/The Remaining Stories. It offers a glimpse of the range of Kalifornsky's interests and his writing style.—JK

They set up a factory at Snug Harbor to can clams. Different people came to Polly Creek. Some came from Iliamna, others from Seldovia, Kodiak, Ninilchik, Tyonek, or Kenai. There were no houses there. They all pitched tents. They just stayed in them.

When the tide went out, they all went out on the flats. They gathered clams. They kept a scow anchored for them. There they bought the clams from them. They paid $1.25 for one gas box full of clams. Some people were good at clam digging. My uncle Chickalusion, with whom I stayed, was the best digger. On a good day he would gather twenty boxes.

They came back ashore when the tide came in. A boat would come to the scow and take it and leave another in its place. Then the people came back ashore. They played the stick gambling game, cards, quoits, and a game where they pushed and pulled on a pole. They played different kinds of games. And they would wrestle. Some of them would hunt in the woods for black bear, porcupine, and beaver. Some would hunt beluga or seal.

I would fire up the steambath for the old men. And they would all take a steambath. I put rocks on the fire for other people. When evening came, the old men would gather and tell stories. "Come," they said to me. And I would listen to them. Before the year 1921, I heard those songs and stories there. I don't know the names of all the people who were there because they addressed each other as they were related. When fall came, the company boat took them all back to wherever their home villages were.

THE GAMBLING STORY

In this story, the shaman's belief is in something tangible, that is something he could see. The other man's belief is "k'ech'ghelta," that is belief in something intangible which one cannot see. The story shows how one can have reversals in life because of bad luck. But the man is also a "True Believer" and that little skin represents how, through belief and proper attitude, one can rebound from adversity. In the end, it is the shaman who goes broke.—PK

The Dena'ina once used to tell stories. In this story two rich men met and said, "Let's play the gambling game." One young man was a shaman. The other fellow followed the traditional beliefs.* That shaman was winning everything from the rich man. He took all of the rich man's possessions from him. Then, all the rich man had left were his wife and children.

"What will you bet me?" the shaman said. He had his wife and children, one a small boy. He longed to keep them. The shaman had taken all of the rich man's belongings from him. He longed to keep the young boy and his wife. He bet his three girls and lost. He only had his wife and young son left.

"Bet me your wife and boy against all your things and the three girls," the shaman said. Which one did he love the most, his wife or his young son? He bet his wife and lost.

All his belongings and his daughters and his wife he bet for that boy. The shaman took the boy from him too. He had nothing. The shaman had won all that he had, even his last gun.

That young man went outside and walked a long way. When he came to a trap he had set in the foothills, a squirrel was caught in it. The squirrel was chewed up and only a small skin was lying there. He picked it up and put it into his pocket.

He walked a long way and then came to a big house. From inside someone said, "I heard you. Turn around the way the sun goes and come in."† It was big inside. A big old lady was sitting there. "My husband is away, but he'll return to us," she said. Not long after, a giant came in. "Hello. What happened to you that you come to see me?" the giant said.

The man explained what the shaman had done to him. "The shaman took from me my daughters, then my wife, and even my young boy. And somehow I came here."

*He was a *k'ech' eltanen*, a "true believer."
†the way the sun goes: clockwise.

"Good," the giant said. "Rest yourself well and I'll fix you up." The man rested well, and then that little skin he had put into his pocket started to move, and it jumped from his pocket. It became an animal again. "Yes, you have come to us with our child," the giant said. "And I had searched all over for my child that I had lost. You said the one who gambled with you is a shaman. Good. I too have powers. I'll prepare you to go back to him," the giant said.

There were animal skins piled in the house. The giant cut little pieces from all of them and put them into his gut bag. He put down feathers in with them. "You'll return with this and sprinkle these down feathers on the gut bag when no one is looking at you. It will turn back into a large supply of animal skins. You will bet with these." And he laid down three sets of gambling sticks. He wrapped these up.

"The first time you play with the shaman, sometimes he'll win from you and sometimes you'll win from him. As you continue and he thinks, 'I'll take everything from him again,' you will throw down this set of gambling sticks. They will spin the way the sun goes and you will take back all your belongings and wife and children," the giant said.

"Then you tell the shaman, 'Do to me as I did to you. I went out and went to the one they call K'eluyesh. K'eluyesh resupplied me and gave me the gambling sticks. With them I won everything back from you.' Go to K'eluyesh and tell him, 'Give me gambling sticks,' " the giant said.

The True Believer went back. This is why the True Believer won everything back from the shaman when he gambled again. When he went to K'eluyesh, K'eluyesh blocked the shaman's powers by means of the pieces he had cut from all those skins. As the shaman tried magic, as he tried to transform himself, he couldn't take the form of an animal again. He failed at magic and left, and there was not any more word of him.

The Dena'ina, they say, had some beliefs about animals. After they killed and butchered an animal in the woods while hunting or trapping, they would put the bones in one place. In the winter they would cut a hole in the ice and put the animal bones into the water. At home in the village, too, they put all the animal bones into the water, either in a lake or in the inlet, or they would burn them in the fire. They did this so the animals would be in good shape as they returned to the place where the animals are reincarnated. They say they had that kind of belief about the animals.

There was one young man. The old men would tell stories about the animals, about how to take good care of them and treat them with respect. And this man listened to the stories the old men told and said, "Look, the old men are lying."

Later that man went into the woods and built a brush camp, and he killed a caribou. He took the caribou back to his camp and butchered it and cooked it, and he started to eat. Then a mouse came out, and he clubbed it and threw it away. Then more mice came out, and he clubbed them and threw them away too. He was trying to eat, but still more mice came out, and he poured hot water on them and scalded them and threw them away, but still the mice kept coming out at him.

So he went back to the village, and he went to the chief, and he told him, "I'm in bad shape; I'm all tired out, and I'm hungry." They gave him something to eat, and then he told the chief how the mice kept coming out at him after he had killed the caribou. He said that if the men would go with him, they could bring home the caribou meat that was still good. When they arrived at the brush camp, they found the mice had not touched the caribou meat; but when the man checked his traps, he discovered the mice had chewed whatever had been caught, and he threw the meat away.

They returned to the village, and the man put his pack of caribou meat in a cache. A day or so later he went to get the meat he had brought home and discovered it was not usable because the mice had eaten on it and dirtied it with their waste. The chief told the man, "The mice are not bothering you for no reason. Maybe you treated the animals improperly."

At night when the man went to bed, the mice ran all over him. Then when he finally went to sleep, the man had a dream. He dreamed about an open country: no ridges, no mountains, no trees as far as one could see. There were all kinds of people all around. And there was a lady seated in front of him there. "I know you," she said to him. There were people there, but their faces were made differently than human faces.

The woman was beautiful. She said, "The way you are now is bad, and as a result you will have a very hard time. You have smashed the animal bones and thrown them where the people walk on them. When the animals return here, they have difficulty turning back into animals."

And she gestured, and the place turned into a different country. It was populated by horribly disfigured animals. There were people there who were tending to them. "These are my children," she said. "Look what you did to them. You scorched off their skin with hot water."

Then she said, "Now look where you came from—the sunrise side." He turned and saw that they were at a land above the human land, which was below them to the east. And all kinds of people were coming up from the lower country, and they didn't have any clothes on. When they arrived, they put on clothes, and when they did, they turned back into all kinds of animals again. The beautiful lady told the man that the animals were returning from the human people to be reincarnated. She told him, "The Campfire People have come.* The Campfire People take good care of us. They take our clothes for their use, and if the humans treat us with respect, we come here in good shape to turn into animals again. We will be in good shape if the humans put our bones into the water or burn them in the fire."

As she was talking to him, the woman was standing behind him. And when he turned to look at her, he saw a great big mouse sitting there. And the man got scared and startled, and he woke up.†

He went to the chief and said, "You told me the right thing. You said maybe I had done something wrong to the animals. I want to tell my story in front of the people." And the people of the village got together, and the man told them the story about the animals. He said, "The animals are on the west side of us, above us, and we are on the east side, below them, on the sunrise side of our country. The animals know whatever we are doing. The old men told stories about how to respect the animals, and I did not believe them. I would smash up the animal bones and throw them away. You people

---

*The animals refer to human beings as Campfire People.
†**the woke up:** that is, from his dream.

did not know it, but you were walking on the animal bones. And they (the animals) knew it too." And then he told the people about his dream.

Afterward he thought a great deal about his dream, and although he didn't exactly go crazy, he was not himself anymore.

LYNX STORY

This story describes how Lynx prefers to be hunted. It is about proper attitudes through proper behavior, and the consequences of improper behavior. It is also about forgiveness. Another part of the story is about estimating and reckoning time.—PK

Long ago, they say, the Dena'ina would tell stories. And they believed in many kinds of things, and they told stories. They told this Lynx story.

Lynx, they say, said, "When they choke me with a snare, I like that, but I don't like to get clubbed. Whoever clubs me, for seven weeks I will not look back at him,"* Lynx said.

One young man listened to the story, and he set snares. When he came back to his snare, a lynx was in it. Wondering what would happen, he clubbed it.

Later he set snares again even though Lynx had said he would not be taken for seven weeks. Seven weeks, then seven months went by. There were plenty of lynx, but he didn't catch any.

After seven years from the day when he had clubbed it, then in his snare there was a lynx.

"I have a good choke string for you," he said, and he choked it.

"Seven weeks" turned out to mean "seven years," according to the lynx, by the lynx's calendar.

*I will not look back at him: I will avoid him.

119

THE BOY AND THE KILLER WHALE

This story is of interest for its blend of the wolf, a powerful figure in Athabaskan culture, and the killer whale, which the Dena'ina encounter in Cook Inlet. —JK

A young man was going around in a skin boat, and he came into a cove somewhere. Out in the water there were killer whales. He watched them dive. And they looked like dogs that surfaced from the water. When they came near the shore, they dove down, and then humans came out of the water. They went out into the woods.

And he followed them. There was a trail there between high ridges up into the mountains. There was a village there. And he visited them, and they gave him a nice place to stay, and they fed him and clothed him. Some of them went out hunting and brought back meat. He did not know how long he stayed with them.

They were gathered together, and they said to him, "You probably are lonely for your relatives. Go on back. There is a trail you can follow. You will return there," they told him.

And he started back, and he found the trail, which came out to the ocean. When he turned to look back, the country had changed. He came down to the beach, and he came upon his skin boat, and it was rotten. He looked at himself, and his clothes were all ragged. He went back and looked at the place he had come from, but there was no trail.

Somehow he repaired his boat, and he started back home. When he got back to his village, some different people were staying there. He called out his own name, "It is me," he said. Then he called the names of the others of his village: "Where are they?" They told him, "They have been dead a long time. We are their children." He had become old.

He told them what had happened to him. And he went to sleep. And his life expired (he died).

DOG STORY

This story describes jealousy and evil-minded behavior. It is bad for one's health when conflicts occur. To resolve the accusation, one person, the chief, takes a leadership role and administers punishments and pardons according to traditional laws and customs.

To find love, the man and woman who were exiled get married. There is sickness, and they go someplace and are transformed into different people. And they have a child, and they become recognized as a different tribe. There is rebirth of the soul in another body. And there is trouble and distress. The chiefs must choose between two equally unfavorable positions. One person dreams about adopting the dog as a method of assistance. But another person asks him for a loan, and it turns out badly. And people who get lost or lose their minds hear the dog's bark. And the dog does not change; it's the same as it was. One village has problems, and because of sickness, they die out, and their language is gone. —PK

This is the story of how long ago the dog first came to the Campfire People. There was a village, they say. A man there had a wife. He went back there and saw a dog in heat. The dogs were stuck together. "Yes, if my wife has been sleeping with another man, this is what I'll do," he said. And he crossed his legs. He watched and uncrossed his legs. The dogs came unstuck. At that time that man knew that man's hearing was gone.* "In the morning I'll go hunting," he said. And when it was still dark, he got dressed and he went out.

He hid, and that wife of his went out and went into another man's house. The husband crept over and saw his wife and another man go to bed. The husband went back into his house, lay down, and crossed his legs. For three days he lay with his legs crossed. The chief came to him there and told him, "Beware! They are about to die. You ought to let them go; it's not humane to kill them. Sickness will come upon us. If you will let them go, we will drive them naked into the woods," he said.

So he let them free with no clothes, and thus the people sent the man and woman away through the village. They had become very sick. The woman took an angelica leaf and put it on as clothing. The man put on a wild celery leaf. As they walked by the door of the last house, the poor people who lived there took pity on them and gave them all their belongings, which consisted of some dog skins.

*that man knew that man's hearing was gone: He knew that his wife had been sleeping with another man and that the other man was a slow learner.

They covered themselves with those. Then they went into the woods. There they became dogs, and their babies were puppies. Men would hunt there. The dogs would bark, and they killed game for the people. The man and woman didn't realize they had turned into dogs. Then they looked at themselves and saw their skin resembled that of dogs and they had become dogs.

Then wolves came to them and killed the dog people and ate their meat. They were half-human, and for that reason they were reincarnated as people.

Two villages of people with two *qeshqa*** were reincarnated from them; they became people again. But they were stupid and dirty, and there was nothing for them to do. And the chiefs had a talk, and they married the people of the villages to one another. They gave them slaves and prepared supplies for them. "Wherever there is a place with no people, you go there," one chief told them. And they went. They didn't know where they were going.

And more news came of them. They had increased in population. All of them were unclean and didn't care about filth; that's the kind of people they were. Their name was the Half People, they used to say. Whenever they had a child, it became a puppy and it stayed in the woods.

One man in a village had a dream. "A dog will become yours, and you will take care of it well. When you feed him, put food down, and he'll eat, and he'll kill game for you. He'll learn. When he kills for you, he'll sit on whatever part of the kill he wants to eat. Butcher it well for him and feed it to him. When he kills game for you, butcher it and give the meat to the people." Thus, they say, he dreamed.

And the next morning a dog was lying in his doorway. He made a place for it and kept it well. They went hunting, and it killed for him, and he treated it just as he had dreamed.

A man from a different village came to him. "How is it with you?" he asked the dog's master. "This dog of mine here takes good care of me," the man said.

"Lend it to me," the visitor said. But the man didn't want to part with it. "We'll go out into the woods, and you watch whatever the dog does," the master said. He went to the woods with it, and the dog killed some animals for them. It sat on the part it wanted to eat. They butchered it, and the man laid down the piece of meat by the dog and said, "The rest is for us." Again the visitor asked for the dog, saying, "Lend that dog of yours to me."

* *qeshqa:* "chiefs."

"Do just as we did when we took it out," the man told the visitor. "Do not do wrong to him." And the dog killed for the visitor, and the dog went to the edge where the last animal, a good one, was and sat on it. And the man kicked the dog. "Those lousy dogs," the visitor said. He took the animal for himself and butchered the kill and slapped the dog's face with blood. And at the edge a yearling was lying, and that one he butchered for the dog. "This is what lousy dogs eat," he said.

The dog ate, and the man bundled up the one the dog had chosen for himself, but he could not get up with his heavy pack. "Help me up," he said. The dog came to him and gave him its tail. He kicked him. "You gave me your lousy tail," he told him. He tried to get up again. "Well, help me up, I tell you," he said. The dog went back to him and gave him its tail. The man took its tail and pulled himself up. The dog went away, turned its back on him, and looked back at him. Then it went back to its master.

His (the master's) door was open. The dog put his head in. His face was covered with dried blood. What could he say? The dog pulled back its face skin, and then it said, "You will swallow a dog spirit, and I'll return to my people, and they'll care for me. The man who eats the animal I chose, his offspring will have trouble on account of the way he fed me."

He pulled down his face skin again, and because it had a half person's breath, he exorcised himself. There was a big rock out on the tideflats. At low tide he disappeared into it. Then whenever it was high tide, the rock would bark. And whenever it was high tide, a puppy would bark in the woods. When people heard it and went after it, they would get disoriented. Their minds went blank. That's what happened at the village of the man who had mistreated the dog. And the people of that village became filthy. For no reason they got mad, and they fought with one another. So it happened that they wounded one another, and thus they died off.

THE GIRL WHO
MARRIED THE BEAR

▲

CATHARINE MCCLELLAN, MARIA JOHNS, AND DORA AUSTIN WEDGE

INTRODUCTION BY CATHARINE MCCLELLAN

I first heard the wonderful story of "The Girl Who Married the Bear" in 1948 when, as a graduate student in anthropology, I was doing my initial fieldwork with Tagish Indians of Carcross in southern Yukon, Canada. Maria Johns, aged and blind, volunteered the tale as a going-away present for me, telling it in Tlingit, which was the language spoken by most Tagish in the late nineteenth century. After every few sentences her daughter, Dora Austin Wedge, translated her words into excellent English. The only other person present was Dora's nine-year-old daughter, Annie, and we listened, entranced, as the tale unfolded. The narration was superb.

Maria offered the story to explain why people do not eat the meat of grizzly bears and to account for the origin of the ritual for the proper disposal of the body of a slain bear. As she described it, the ritual seemed to be part of what anthropologists identify as a circumpolar complex of bear ceremonialism, but so far it had not been reported for this part of the Subarctic. Here was something new I could add to scholarly literature. Could a novice ethnographer ask for more?

In my subsequent Yukon fieldwork I did not specifically plan to collect oral narratives, but I soon discovered that the Indians considered telling stories to be one of their most vital ways of expressing their identities and teaching their most deeply held values to their children or to an outsider like me. Despite major changes in their culture, Native narrators and their audiences still find their oral traditions relevant in the literate world. Over the years many more stories filled my notebooks, and I heard about the girl who married the bear eleven more times. Nine of the narrators volunteered it as Maria had done, five of them choosing it as their first selection; I specifically requested it only twice.

Since at first I naïvely judged the story's chief value to be that of extending the known distribution of bear ceremonialism, I paid relatively little attention to other aspects of it. Only later did I ask, Why its great popularity? Why did men and women of all ages so often choose to tell it? Actually Maria and Dora had already revealed the reason, which is simply that it is a marvelous piece of creative narrative. Indeed, because Maria was such a gifted raconteur and Dora such a fine translator, their skills had easily carried me across language differences, lifting the tale into a realm well beyond that encompassing all my earlier ideas of folklore. Even though at that time I knew little of the tale's cultural context, I could not fail to sense the tremendous psychological and sociological conflicts in the plot, and I began to glimpse the true depths of the stories I was hearing. Ultimately I came to understand that this particular story grips Yukon natives with all the power of a major literary work, evoking in them the same kind of intense responses as those experienced by Greeks hearing their great Attic dramas. That is why I called the story a masterpiece of oral tradition when I finally published it in 1970 and why I continue to think it is such. It speaks, of course, most forcibly to those most aware of its cultural context, but its messages are fundamental enough to have reached beyond the world of northern Natives, to be recontextualized in various ways by others of non-Indian heritage.

Until recently Western scholars of literature rarely have rated the stylistic qualities of oral narrative even by their own standards or paid much attention to linguistic and other criteria by which nonliterate people themselves evaluate their oral traditions. Yukon Natives do not often comment on such matters either. I believe that the gross structural arrangement of a story can remain the same in translation, but to appreciate finer stylistic points, one needs the text in the original language. Lost forever is whatever linguistic magic may have been in Maria's original telling, the subtle imagery conveyed by her choice of words, and other ineffable qualities of language. Tape recorders were not then widely available, and to have asked Maria to wait while I laboriously wrote her Tlingit phrasing would have been to destroy her gift to me. I took down only Dora's translation and added explanatory comments. She spoke slowly for my benefit, but even so I probably missed a few phrases. Nor could I catch Maria's rendition of the two songs so integral to the tale. Dora did not translate them, so I have substituted two texts from a version of the story told to me in 1951 by Tommy Peters, an Inland Tlingit of Yukon.[1]

Of course, oral societies do not value well-wrought language alone; performance also counts. Sadly lacking in my printed English version of this story are Maria's and Dora's pacing of utterances, their pauses and emphases, the changing loudness and softness of their voices, Maria's imitations of a growling bear and barking dogs. My written record of Maria's accompanying gestures as she told the story scarcely conveys the unsettling impact produced each time she passed her hand slowly across her face to indicate whether the bear appeared at that moment in his human guise or in his bear guise. Nor does it capture the effect of impending disaster Maria somehow imparted by stirring about in bed under her gopher-skin blanket and knocking on the dresser beside her at the point when the girl and her bear husband first hear her oncoming brothers and their dogs.

Yet style and performance alone do not guarantee an oral master-piece. Every great narrative must have compelling substance as well, and I believe it is the content of "The Girl Who Married the Bear" that so powerfully and consistently attracts Yukon Natives and others. I would argue too that the more that is known of a story's cultural context the greater the appreciation of the tale. Certainly as my own knowledge of Yukon Native culture has deepened, so too has my awareness of the multilayered symbolism embedded in this story. For example—though I do not develop it here—at a deep level the story may be an account of a failed shamanistic quest, illuminating just when in their life cycles females are able to absorb certain kinds of strong spiritual power. Dora's daughter, Annie, has doubtless discovered new meanings too.

The overt plot holds considerable suspense, but adult Natives all know its outcome well. The reason the story continues to grip them so forcibly, I think, lies in the dreadful choice of loyalties to others that its characters have to make and in its pervasive underscoring of the delicate and awful balance in relationships between humans and animals that Indians believe has existed since the world began. The basic concerns of everybody in the society are rendered relentlessly vivid by the tale's concentration on the actions of only a few individuals.

What of the cultural context? Southern Yukon Indians of either sex trace their consanguineous ties only through females; it is through them that one's kin group is formed. In every family also the wife and children belong to one matrilineal kin group, but the husband belongs to a different one. This is because the whole society is divided into two distinct sides, or moieties, designated as Crow or Wolf. One always belongs to the moiety of one's mother but always must marry a person of the father's moiety. Membership in one moiety also obligates one to dispose of the corpses of those in the opposite moiety, with suitable rituals.

Another crucial aspect of the social system is cross-sex sibling avoidance. After puberty, brothers and sisters should neither talk to nor look at one another directly, though in a crisis a younger brother or sister may speak circumspectly to an older sister or brother. One of Maria's most traumatic experiences occurred right after her puberty seclusion, when she had to find her older brother on his winter trapline and ask for help because the family was starving. Following the encounter, she hid and wept for several days. Yet in spite of avoidance rules, strong sibling unity lies at the heart of the society. The oldest brother looks after the welfare of his younger siblings, who ideally never question his actions, and brothers and sisters aid one another with food and clothing throughout their lives. The brother-in-law tie is equally important, for brothers-in-law link those of opposite moieties. Only the best fellowship should prevail between those who address each other as Brother-in-Law.

A Native can always find a sibling or sibling-in-law in Yukon, for anyone of one's own age within one's own moiety may be counted as a brother or sister, depending on sex, whether or not truly related by blood, and anyone of one's own age in the opposite moiety may be classed a sibling-in-law. Furthermore, the system includes animals as well as humans. I have seen a Crow man address a pack of wolves as brothers-in-law, and the term is equally appropriate for a bear.

Long ago animal people even looked like humans, until they pulled up their animal masks after Crow, the transformer, opened the box of daylight on them. Now, except in rare instances, they appear to humans only in animal guise. Yet most animals have greater spiritual power than humans, and they may use it for good or ill. A major philosophical and practical problem for humans is how to live harmoniously with animals that they continually confront and often have to kill in order to stay alive. Indians observe many rituals designed to entice the potentially beneficial powers of animals and to ensure the reincarnation of their spirits so that humans may have food. One must never say or think anything offensive about an animal or treat it or its attributes, including its excrement and its corpse, disrespectfully. An offended animal is bound to exact revenge, often drawing the culprit to its own domain and making it difficult or impossible for him or her to return permanently to the human world. Those who have come back, however, report staying in places where time is distorted, where fires are not what they seem, and where many other phenomena are illusory to humans. Sojourners in animal worlds have also learned, as does the girl in this story, how animals wish their bodies to be treated after death.

Surely the reader who knows only these few facts can now grasp the drama of "The Girl Who Married the Bear" more fully than one ignorant of its cultural context. As soon as she mocks the bear droppings, the girl is at risk. A handsome man appears, and in spite of her desire to go home, she enters a socially unarranged sexual alliance with him. Anguishing doubts and dilemmas ensue. She gradually learns that she is staying with a bear, and she betrays him by leaving signs of her presence near their den. But she also comes to love him, especially after her two children are born. Then she must decide whether to cleave to him or return to her human kin. She persuades the bear to give up his life to his brothers-in-law,[2] but the supreme irony is that in the end she herself does the unthinkable deed of killing her mother and all her brothers but the youngest. The very kinsmen who earlier have so carefully prepared her and her cub children for a brief stay in the human world and who should have continued as her protectors become her tormentors. Their irresponsible insistence that she and her children don bear hides seals the fates of them all. Every rule of sibling and affinal relationships and of human and animal relationships is violated. A young girl's careless defiance of a fundamental taboo has doomed her to join the animal world forever. How can the enormity of such events fail to shake the narrator and audience? They must realize that although he allowed himself to be killed, it was the bear-shaman husband who had the ultimate strength. So it is that grizzly bears today are held in reverence and are accorded funeral rites suitable for humans of the highest rank and power.

I believe Dora's translation of Maria's story is among the best of the Yukon versions available to English speakers today, but the existence of other versions invites comparisons. If well documented, they enable us to explore the influences that have shaped them: both the cultural context and the life circumstances of the individual narrators. For example, although this story has so far been recorded

most often in Yukon and adjacent matrilineal areas, Robert Brightman has published two versions from the Woods Cree of northern
Manitoba.[3] The Cree practice bear ceremonialism, but unlike
Yukon Indians, they reckon kinship through both the mother's and
the father's lines. Is this why some of the key interactions between
the characters in their story contrast so markedly with those in versions from matrilineal areas? The Cree say that the girl's father (not
her brothers) hunts and kills the bear husband and that she is killed
by the only brother to escape the massacre she and her sons wreak
on an entire village. If we focus on personal history as a source of
variation, we discover that more than any male narrator, Maria
stresses the items of clothing that the girl wants for herself and her
partly furred children as they prepare to reenter a world where
clothes and human odors define human identity. She also develops
themes of romantic and maternal love, both of which were significant in her own life. Men elaborate other themes—the strained relationship between the bear and his brothers-in-law, the bear's ability
to provide food for his wife, or the proper treatment of a grizzly's
corpse. Do not such variations cogently reaffirm a need to understand both content and context if we are ever to fathom the essential
components of this genuine masterpiece of oral literature?

NOTES

1. Nora Marks Dauenhauer and Richard Dauenhauer, in *Haa Shuká/Our
Ancestors: Tlingit Oral Narratives,* vol. 1 of *Classics of Tlingit Oral Literature*
(Seattle: University of Washington Press, 1987), give Tommy Peters's 1972
and 1973 version of the story in Tlingit text, with a translation by Nora Dauenhauer, discussing further his two 1951 songs that I have incorporated. They
also include a version by Frank Dick Sr. of Dry Bay, Alaska. Maria's version and
ten others, including those by Tommy Peters and Jake Jackson (see note 2),
appear in Catharine McClellan, *The Girl Who Married the Bear: A Masterpiece
of Indian Oral Tradition,* National Museum of Man Publications in Ethnology no. 2 (Ottawa: National Museums of Canada, 1970). Much of my
introduction here is condensed from that publication. Additional Yukon versions are in Catharine McClellan et al., *Part of the Land, Part of the Water: A
History of Yukon Indians* (Vancouver and Toronto: Douglas and McIntyre,
1987). In some texts, including Maria and Dora's version, I have made some
minor corrections in basic English.

2. Tommy Peters explained that only the girl's younger brother was ritually pure enough to be able to kill the bear. Maria did not say which brother did the killing, but another narrator, Jake Jackson, did. See McClellan, *The Girl Who Married the Bear*.

3. Robert Brightman, *Ācaðōhkīwina and Ācimōwina: Traditional Narratives of the Rock Cree Indians,* Canadian Ethnology Service, Mercury Series, Paper no. 113 (Ottawa: Canadian Museum of Civilization, 1989).

Once there was a little girl about as big as Annie. And she used to go pick berries in the summer. Every summer she would go with her family, and they would pick berries and dry them. When she used to go with her womenfolk on the trail, they would see bear droppings on the trail. In the old days girls had to be careful about bear droppings. They shouldn't walk over them. Men could walk over them, but young girls had to walk around them. But this girl always did jump over them and kick them. She would disobey her mother. All the time she would see them and kick them and step over them. She kept seeing them all around her. She did this from childhood.

When she was quite big, they were going camping. They were going to dry fish. They went out picking berries. She was just a young girl. She went out and was picking with her mother and aunts and sisters. She saw some bear droppings. She said all kinds of words to them and kicked and jumped over them.

When they were all coming home, they were all carrying their baskets of berries. The girl saw some nice berries and stopped to get them. The others went ahead. When she had picked the berries and was starting to get up, her berries all spilled out of her basket. She leaned down and was picking them off the ground.

Soon she saw a young man. He was very good looking. She had never seen him before. He had red paint on his face. He stopped and talked to her.

He said, "Those berries you are picking are no good. They are full of dirt. Let's go up a little ways and fill your basket up. There are some good berries growing up there. I'll walk home with you. You needn't be afraid!"*

After they had got the basket half full of berries, the man said, "There is another bunch of berries up there a little ways. We'll pick them too."

When they had picked them all, he said, "It's time to eat. You must be hungry."

He made a fire. It looked just like a fire, but it was not a real one. They cooked gopher, quite a lot of it, and they ate some.†

---

*Here Dora stopped to explain: "He was really a bear, only she didn't know it yet. This is a really old story from way back when there were only a few people. It's true." I do not think that Maria put this into her account; it would have seemed unnecessary.

†**gopher**: the local English term for the ground squirrel that grizzlies dig up in quantity in late summer.

Then the man said, "It's too late to go home now. We'll go home tomorrow. It's summer, and there's no need to fix a big camp."

So they stayed there.

When they went to bed, he said, "Don't lift your head in the morning and look at me even if you wake up before I do."

So they went to bed.

Next morning they woke up. The man said to her, "Well, we might as well go. We'll just eat that cold gopher. We needn't make a fire. Then we'll go pick some berries. Let's get a basketful."

All the time the girl kept talking about her mother and father. All the time she wanted to go home, and she kept talking about it.

He said, "Don't be afraid. I'm going home with you."

Then he slapped her right on the top of her head, and he put a circle around the girl's head the way the sun goes. He did this so she would forget. Then she forgot. She didn't talk about her home anymore.

Then they left again. He said, "You're all right. I'll go home with you."

Then after this she forgot all about going home. She just went around with him, picking berries. Every time they camped, it seemed like a month to her, but it was really only a day. They started in May. They kept traveling and going.

Finally she recognized a place. It looked like a place where she and her family used to dry meat. Then he stopped there at the timberline and slapped her. He made a circle sunwise on her head and then another on the ground where she was sitting.

He said, "Wait here. I'm going hunting gophers. We have no meat. Wait until I come back!"

Then he came back with gophers. They kept traveling. Late in the evening they made a camp and cooked.

Next morning they got up again. At last she knew. They were traveling again, and it was getting near fall. It was getting late. And she came to her senses and knew it. It was cold.

He said, "It's time to make camp. We must make a home."

He started making a home. He was digging a den. She knew he was a bear then.

He got quite a ways digging a den. Then he said, "Go get some balsam boughs and brush."

Then she went and got some. She broke branches from as high as she could. She brought the bundle.

He said, "That brush is no good! You left a mark, and people will see it and know we are here. We can't use that! We can't stay here!"

So they left. They went up to the head of a valley. She knew her brothers used to go there to hunt and eat bear. In the springtime they took the dogs there, and they hunted bears in April. They would send the dogs into the bear den long ago, and the bear would come out. That's where her brothers used to go. She knew it.

He said, "We'll make camp."

He dug a den and sent her out again. "Get some brush that is just lying on the ground—not from up high. No one will see where you get it, and it will be covered with snow."

She got it from the ground and brought it to him, but she bent the branches up high too. She let them hang down so her brothers would know. And she rubbed sand all over herself, all over her body and limbs. And then she rubbed the trees all around so the dogs would find where she had left her scent. Then she went to the den with her bundle of brush. She brought it.

Just when the man was digging, he looked like a bear. That was the *only* time. The rest of the time he seemed like a human being. The girl didn't know how else to stay alive, so she stayed with him as long as he was good to her.

"This is better," he said when she brought back the brush. Then he brushed up and fixed the place. After he fixed the den, they left.

They went hunting gophers for winter. She never saw him do it. She always sat around while he was hunting gophers. He dug them up like a grizzly bear, and he didn't want her to see it. He never showed her where he kept the gophers.

Nearly every day they hunted gophers and picked berries. It was quite late in the year. He was just like a human to her.

It was October. It was really late in the fall. He said, "Well, I guess we'll go home now. We have enough food and berries. We'll go down."

So they went home. Really they went into the den. They stayed there and slept. They woke up once a month and got up to eat. They kept doing it and going back to bed. Each month it seemed like another morning, just like another day. They never really went outside; it just seemed like it.

Soon the girl found that she was carrying a baby. She had two little babies. One was a girl and one was a boy. She had them in February in the den. That is when bears have their cubs. She had hers then.

The bear used to sing in the night. When she woke up, she would hear him:

> I dreamed about it;
> that they were going after me.

The bear became like a doctor when he started living with a woman. It just came upon him like a doctor.*

> I dreamed about it,
> that they were going after me.

He sang the song twice. She heard it the first time. The second time, the bear made a sound, *"Woof! Woof!"* And she woke up.

"You're my wife, and I am going to leave soon. It looks like your brothers are going to come up here soon, before the snow is gone. I want you to know that I am going to do something bad. I am going to fight back!"

"Don't do it!" she said. "They are my brothers! If you really love me, don't fight! You have treated me good. Why did you live with me if you are going to kill them?"

"Well, all right," he said; "I won't fight, but I want you to know what will happen!"

His canines looked like swords to her. "These are what I fight with," he said. They looked like knives to her.

She kept pleading, "Don't do anything! I'll still have my children if they kill you!"

She knew he was a bear then. She really knew.

They went to sleep. She woke again. He was singing again.

> I went through every one of those young people,
> and the last brother—I know he did the right thing.

"It's true," he said. "They are coming close. If they kill me, I want them to give you my skull—my head—and my tail. Tell them to give them to you. Wherever they kill me, build a big fire and burn my head and tail. And sing this song while the head is burning. Sing it until they are all burned up:

> I went through every one of those young people,
> and the last brother—I know he did the right thing."

So they ate and went to bed, and another month went by. They didn't sleep the whole month. They kept waking up.

"It's coming close," he said. "I can't sleep good. It's getting to

---

*doctor: an Indian doctor, or shaman; someone who can see what is going to happen and use his or her spiritual powers to prevent it.

be bare ground. Look out and see if the snow has melted in front of the den."

She looked, and there was mud and sand. She grabbed some and made it all into a ball and rubbed it all over herself. It was full of her scent. She rolled it down the hill. The dogs could smell it.

She came in and said, "There's bare ground all over in some places."

He asked her why she had made the marks: "Why? Why? Why? Why? They'll find us easy!"

After they had slept for half a month, they woke, and he was singing again.

"This is the last one," he said. "You'll not hear me again. Any time, the dogs are coming to the door. They are close. Well, I'll fight back. I'm going to do something bad!"

His wife said, "You know they are my brothers! Don't do it! Who will look after my children if you kill them? You must think of the kids. My brothers will help me. If my brothers hurt you, let them be!"

They went to bed for just a little while. "I can't sleep good, but we'll try," he said.

Next morning he said, "Well, it's close! It's close! Wake up!"

Just when they were waking up, they heard a noise. The dogs were barking. "Well," he said, "I'll leave. Where are my knives? I want them!"

He took them down. She saw him putting in his teeth. He was a big bear.

She pleaded with him: "Please don't fight! If you wanted me, why did you go this far? Just think of the kids. Don't hurt my brothers!"

When he went, he shook her hand and said, "You are not going to see me again!"

He went out and growled. He slapped something back into the den. It was a pet dog, a little bear dog,* and also a pair of gloves.

When he threw the dog in, she grabbed it and shoved it back in the brush under the nest. She put the dog there to hide it. She sat on it and kept it there so it couldn't get out. She wanted to keep it for a reason.

For a long time there was no noise. She went out of the den. She heard her brothers below. They had already killed the bear. She felt bad, and she sat down.

*bear dog: Southern Yukon Indians kept a special breed of small dogs, Tahltan dogs, to hunt bears.

She found an arrow and one side of a glove. She picked it up and all of the arrows. Finally she fitted the little dog with a string around his back. She tied the arrows and the glove into a bundle. She put them on the little dog, and he ran to his masters.

The boys were down there dressing the bear. They knew the dog. They noticed the bundle and took it off.

"It's funny," they said. "Nobody in a bear den would tie this on."

They talked about it. They decided to send the youngest brother up to the den. In those days a younger brother could talk to his sister, but an older brother couldn't.

The older brothers said to the youngest brother, "We lost our sister a year ago in May. Something could have happened. A bear might have taken her away. You are the youngest brother. Don't be afraid. There is nothing up there but her. You go and see if she is there. Find out."

He went.

She was sitting there crying. The boy came up. She was sitting and crying. She cried when she saw him.

She said, "You boys killed your brother-in-law! I went with him last May. You killed him! But tell the others to save me the skull and the tail. Leave it there for me. When you go home, tell Mother to sew a dress for me so I can go home. Sew a dress for the girl and pants and a shirt for the boy. And moccasins. And tell her to come see me."

He left and got down there and told his brothers, "This is my sister up there. She wants the head and the tail."

They did this, and they went home. They told their mother. She got busy and sewed. She had a dress and moccasins and clothes for the children.

The next day she went up there. She came to the place. They dressed the little kids. Then they went down to where the bear was killed. The boys had left a big fire. The girl burned the head and tail. Then she sang till all was ashes.

They went home, but she didn't go right home.

She said, "Get the boys to build a house. I can't come right into the main camp. It will be quite a while. The boys can build a camp right away."

She stayed there a long while. Toward fall she came and stayed with her mother all winter. The kids grew.

Next spring her brothers wanted her to act like a bear. They wanted to play with her. They had killed a female bear that had cubs, one male and one female. They wanted the sister to put on the hide and act like a bear. They fixed little arrows. They pestered her to play with them, and they wanted her two little children to play too.

She didn't want it. She told her mother, "I can't do it! Once I do it, I will turn into a bear! I'm half there already. Hair is already showing on my arms and legs. It is quite long!"

If she had stayed there with her bear husband, she would have turned into a bear. "If I put on a bear hide, I'll turn into one," she said.

They kept telling her to play. Then the boys sneaked up. They threw hides over her and the little ones.

Then she walked off on four legs, and she shook herself just like a bear. It just happened. She was a grizzly bear.

She couldn't do a thing. She had to fight the arrows. She killed them all off, even her mother. But she didn't kill her youngest brother, not him. She couldn't help it. Tears were running down her face.

Then she went on her own. She had her two little cubs with her.

That's why they claim long ago that a bear is partly human. That's why you never eat grizzly bear meat. Now people eat black bear meat, but they still don't eat grizzly meat, because grizzlies are half-human.

HOW THE WORLD BEGAN

▲

JULIE CRUIKSHANK
AND
ANGELA SIDNEY

You tell what you know.
The way I tell stories is what I know.

Angela Sidney

INTRODUCTION BY JULIE CRUIKSHANK

Angela Sidney (1902–91) always introduced her work by describing herself as a Tagish and Tlingit woman of the Deisheetaan clan. Born near the present village of Carcross in southern Yukon, she was given the Tlingit name Stoow and the Tagish name Ch'oonehte' Má. A prospector passing her parents' cabin on the night of her birth paused to warm himself at their fire and remarked that the newborn baby looked like an angel, and so she was also given the English name Angela.

Mrs. Sidney spent much of her adult life documenting the stories, the traditions, the histories of her Tagish and Tlingit ancestors. She worked with anthropologist Catharine McClellan for many years and has recorded Tagish narratives with linguist Victor Golla and Tlingit narratives with linguist Jeff Leer. It was a great privilege for me to work with her during the last twenty years of her life, when together we recorded stories, genealogies, songs, place names, and accounts of her experiences.

A volume of contemporary translations of Native American literatures raises important questions about the transformation of oral tradition into written text, particularly when the text is not recorded in an indigenous language. While Mrs. Sidney prepared booklets of place names and family names in the Tagish and Tlingit languages, she also insisted on recording her own English translations of stories. The problems involved in recording in English narratives originally told and heard in an indigenous language have long been recognized. Nevertheless, Mrs. Sidney had a clear objective in making her recordings: she wanted to produce booklets that her grandchildren would be able to read. Despite the growing enthusiasm for Native-language instruction in Yukon schools during the 1980s, all Yukon children still begin school with English as a first language. Angela Sidney firmly believed her work could provide a connection between the world of tradition and the educational system in which her grandchildren are immersed and that her own booklets should be included in the school curriculum. While elements of form and style inevitably are lost in any translation, Mrs. Sidney's English translations are lively, colorful, and highly metaphoric. As a trilingual speaker—of Tagish, Tlingit, and English—she really is her own best translator. Her translations retain her own rhythm and idiom, her own expressions, the nuances of her unique narrative performance; and they are immediately recognizable to those familiar with her storytelling style. In converting her spoken words to text, I have followed Dell Hymes, Dennis Tedlock and others,[1] breaking the lines to correspond with a pause or breath and leaving a line space to indicate a longer pause. This seems to reproduce the "sound" of Mrs. Sidney's voice more accurately than does conventional paragraphing.

In 1974, when we began working together, some of the earliest stories she chose to record for her grandchildren were those of Crow, the Trickster who plays such a prominent role in northwestern America and Northeast Asia. An ambivalent combination of good and evil, Crow is at one moment a world transformer, at another a clown, the next a selfish and petulant being. His exploits are told with considerable humor, and it is clear that Mrs. Sidney and other elderly narrators have a fondness for his roguish humanity. Punctuating accounts of his exploits with comments like "You know what that Crow is like, don't you?" she moves from one account of his adventures to another.

The generalized Trickster figure belongs to the oldest stratum of myth. He is known by many names: Wee-sa-key-jac by the Eastern Cree, Napi by the Blackfoot, Raven on the Northwest Coast, Coyote on the Plateau, Crow in the Yukon; in parts of Europe he is Reynard the Fox, in Polynesia he is known as Maui, and in Africa one of his forms is Anansi.

The Trickster is a figure of chaos, the principle of disorder. He embodies two distinct and conflicting roles: creator of the world and bringer of culture on the one hand; glutton and instigator of trouble on the other. In the Yukon, Crow creates the world, brings light and fire and fresh water. He creates human beings and teaches them the principles of culture. But he also marries Fish Mother so that he can eat without doing any work, and then he treats her with disrespect. His vanity blinds him when he mistakenly thinks he has found a beautiful Chilkat blanket. He frightens people away from their village (drowning some of them in the process) so that he can eat all the food they have stored. He adopts Deer as his brother and then kills him for his fat, shedding mock tears of sorrow at the death of his "brother." His sexual appetites are insatiable, and he even tries (unsuccessfully) to seduce his mother-in-law. Instead of becoming involved in socialized, cooperative activities, Crow wanders from place to place, a vagabond who systematically violates accepted codes of behavior. While the Trickster frequently makes people laugh—the story of his "talking eye" is a favorite with children—he is by no means a figure of light entertainment, and his appeal is based on contradictions. He remains a familiar, if shadowy, figure, representing the range of good and evil in human behavior.

Here, then, Angela Sidney tells some of Crow's many adventures.

NOTE

1. See, for example, Dell Hymes, "Anthologies and Narrators," in *Recovering the Word: Essays on Native American Literature,* ed. Brian Swann and Arnold Krupat (Berkeley: University of California Press, 1987), 41–84, and Dennis Tedlock, *The Spoken Word and the Work of Interpretation* (Philadelphia: University of Pennsylvania Press, 1983).

One time there was a girl whose daddy is a very high man.
They kept her in her bedroom all the time—
Men tried to marry her all the time, but they say, "No, she's too
    good."

Crow wanted to be born—he wants to make the world!
So he made himself into a pine needle.
A slave always brings water to that girl, and one time he gets water
    with a pine needle in it.
She turns it down—makes him get fresh water.
Again he brings it. Again a pine needle is there.
Four times he brings water, and each time it's there.
Finally she just gave up—she spit that pine needle out and drank
    the water.
But it blew into her mouth, and she swallowed it.
Soon that girl is pregnant.

Her mother and daddy are mad.
Her mother asks, "Who's that father?"

"No, I never know a man," she told her mother.

That baby starts to grow fast.
That girl's father had the sun, moon, stars, daylight hanging in his
    house.
He's the only one that has them.
The world was all dark, all the time.
The child begged for them to play with.

Finally the father gives his grandchild the sun to play with.
He rolls it around, plays with it, laughs, has lots of fun.
Then he rolls it to the door, and out it goes!
"Oh!" he cries. He just pretends.
He cries because that sun is lost.

"Give me the moon to play with."
    They say no at first—like now if a baby asks for the sun or moon
        you say,
"That's your grandfather's fire."

Finally they gave it to him.

▲

141

One by one they gave him the sun, moon, stars, daylight—
he loses them all.

"Where does she get that child from? He loses everything!"
That's what her father says.

Then Crow disappears.
He has those things with him in a box.
He walks around—comes to a river.
Lots of animals there—fox, wolf, wolverine, mink, rabbit.
Everybody's fishing. . . .
That time animals all talk like people talk now—
the world is dark.

"Give me fish," Crow says.
No one pays any attention.
"Give me fish, or I'll bring daylight!"
They laugh at him.

He's holding a box . . . starts to open it and lets one ray out.
Then they pay attention!
He opens that box a bit more—they're scared!
Finally he opens that daylight box and threw it out.
Those animals scatter!
They hide in the bush and turn into animals like now.
Then the sun, moon, stars, and daylight come out.

"Go to the skies," Crow says.
"Now no one man owns it—it will be for everybody."

He's right, what he says, that Crow.

After Crow made the world, he saw that Sea Lion owned the only
    island in the world.
The rest was water—he's the only one with land.
The whole place was ocean!
Crow rests on a piece of log—he's tired.
He sees Sea Lion with that little island just for himself.
He wants some land too, so he stole that Sea Lion's kid.

"Give me back that kid!" said Sea Lion.

▲

"Give me beach, some sand," says Crow.

So Sea Lion gave him sand.
Crow threw that sand around the world.
"Be world," he told it. And it became the world.

After that he walks around, flies around all alone.
He's tired—he's lonely—he needs people.
He took poplar-tree bark. You know how it's thick?
He carved it, and then he breathed into it.

"Live!" he said, and he made a person.
He made Crow and Wolf too.
At first they can't talk with each other—
Crow man and woman are shy with each other—look away.
Wolf is same way too.

"This is no good," he said. So he changed that.

He made Crow man sit with Wolf woman.
And he made Wolf man sit with Crow woman.
So Crow must marry Wolf, and Wolf must marry Crow.

That's how the world began.

But Crow wants to get married—he needs a wife to help him out.
One time he saw a beautiful lady sitting by the river.
She has red hair, white skin.
. . . You know how Crow is . . . ! Comes up to her sort of friendly,
   sits down . . .

"Hello," he says. "What are you doing here?"
"Just fishing," she says, kind of quiet.
They call that one Fish Mother: every time she comes to water,
   fish come to her.

Crow's thinking about this. . . . He says,
"I know what we'll do. We'll make fish rack, dry fish!
I've got no one to look after.
You've got no one to look after you.
We'll stay together! We can pick up fish from water . . . ?

▲

"No . . . ," she says. "No . . . that's all right. No, I'll just catch
   them for me."

"But I'll help you," he says. "I'll help you eat them!"

She looks at him . . . thinks about that.
He's good-looking man. . . . They cut up fish, dry them.
He stays there with her, but they sleep separate for two or three
   days.
But after he marries that woman, he does not ever see her eat!

She has a slave who brings her water.
Crow, he's always thinking about fish, but he always walks along
   beach, picking seaweed to eat.
One day Crow comes back from picking seaweed.
That slave—her slave—is sleeping across the fire, other side of the
   fire from where she sleeps.

Crow notices something funny. . . .
He sees light ashes on that slave—he wonders what this means.
Looks to him like somebody is cooking something!

Crow's smart: he starts to tickle that slave so he laughs,
and when that slave laughs, Crow sees piece of fish meat between
   his teeth!
He picks at that piece of fish with his beak.

"Where you get that fish meat from?"
Crow is greedy, and Crow is hungry!

"I went to get my boss, your wife, some water.
But *you* know that when she put her fingers in that water, fish
   come to her."

Crow thinks about that too, thinks about that.
So he did same thing. He said to her,
"My beautiful wife, let me get water for you."
When he did that, *he* got fish too.
When she sticks her fingers in water, fish come.
Crow is happy now!

Then he thinks some more. He says to her,
"Let's dry fish. Let me build a fish trap for you.

Then you put your fingers in water, and fish will come."
He wants his wife to do that every day.

So he did. He built a trap.
"Now, Wife, put your fingers in the water."

But his wife took bath there instead of just putting fingers in water,
    and he got *lots* of fish.
Fish start to come every day after that.
After those fish dry, there's not much work to do that time.

Crow's sure happy now! No more work to do!
So he starts walking again.
Every day he goes for a walk,
just walks around, like Crow.

His wife, Fish Mother, says to her slave,
"Something is going to happen.
Crow, my husband, is going to say something against me,
    something to insult me.
When he does, you go to your cache.
Make a cache in the bush for your fish.
And make long stick to protect yourself and your fish.
You are going to keep your fish, but he's going to lose all his."

One day she's hanging fish.
He's looking at her, feeling like Crow—acting kind of smart!
Under her arms he sees long red hair.

"Ha, ha, my wife, you've got red hair under your arms." He insults
    her.

She waves her arms; she's angry now!
She knew this was going to happen.
Then she goes to the beach and disappears—she turns to fog, I
    guess.
All those fish that are hanging there turn back into fish and come
    to life again.
They run back into the water!
They go away!

That slave runs back to his cache—Crow didn't know he had a
    cache.
Crow sorry now! Feels bad after that.

Shouldn't say that. . . .
He feels bad—you know how men are! Too late now!
Crow has to eat seaweed again!

After he eat all that fish, Crow goes walking along again, eats seaweed.

One time after his wife's gone, he comes on a pretty green blanket.
Looks like a Chilkat blanket, lying in the water.
So he says, "I'll take that one." He threw his old gopher blanket out in the water.
That blanket drifts out, disappears.

Then he picks up that pretty green blanket, puts it on—he's looking good now!
Little by little that blanket falls to pieces.
Pieces fall off as he walks along.
That blanket is made of seaweed! His wife did that to him—makes it look like Chilkat blanket!

"Oh, what have I done?" he sings to that gopher blanket that floated away.
"Come back from a deep place." He sings South Wind song.
    "From way out in the middle, drift back my blanket."

Pretty soon it drifted back to him.
His blanket is nice and white again.
He dries it out, starts traveling again.

"That's my wife did that to me. She didn't beat me after all."
Crow's always in trouble!

One time Crow's walking along beach. Comes to a blueberry patch.
He took his eye out and put it on a rock.

"Look for boat coming. Watch out," he tell it. He goes off to bush to eat blueberries.

That eye hollered at him. "Boat's coming. Boat is coming."
He ran out. He looked around. He sees no boat.

He picks up that eye: "Don't lie to me. That's bad luck," he told his
 eye.
He bounced that eye up and down to punish it!
He sets it back, careful, on that rock again.
"Don't lie!" he tells it.
He goes off again to pick blueberries.

Pretty soon that eye hollers again.
"Boat coming. Boat is coming now. I see boat coming. . . . Oh, oh,
 somebody picked me up!"

Crow doesn't believe him. But no more that eye hollers.
"Maybe it's true. . . ." says Crow. He investigates. He checks.
Sure enough, no eye no more!

"Too bad my eye." Where's that boat gone? He thinks. He knows.
He takes huckleberry and puts it in his eye.
He comes up to the people on that boat, where they're camping.
He comes up real sure of himself.

"*Tlagoo,* surprise. We found a talking eye on a rock," they tell him.
"Let me see it," he says, sort of polite.
They give it to him, give it to him to look at.
"Boy, you sure look like Crow's eye to me!" Bang. He sticks it in
 his eye.
He took it. He took off! Gone now!

Another time Crow is packing around jack pine wood, chopped up
 into kindling.
That's the time he saw that Whale.

"Come up close," he said. So that Whale came closer, and when
 water came up, Crow flew into that Whale.

He starts to live in that Whale's stomach—starts to eat all the fat in
 that Whale.
He makes a smudge with his kindling, makes a fire in that Whale.
That's how he cooks that fat.

Finally only the heart is left.
"What's that hanging there for?" That's the heart.

Here; he cut it off.
When the heart is gone, that Whale starts to die.

Crow says to Whale, "Land in a most capital city."
Finally it stopped in one place.

Crow said, "I wonder where there's big shot like me to cut that
    stomach open?"

Finally it took lots of people to chop that Whale open.
Took lots!
As soon as they cut that Whale open, Crow flew up and out till
    people can't see him.
He rested there. He gave them chance to make grease from that
    Whale.

He came back to people like before.
When he came to them, they said to him,
"Something strange happened! We saw an eye sitting talking on a
    rock! Then Crow took it. Now Whale comes to us. Then Crow
    flies out. Seems funny to us."

Crow says to them, "Something strange happened to me too.
I had a dream that there's a war coming.
It happened like that a long time ago too.
I dreamed like that when I was going to lose my mother and my
    father. Then war came upon them, and people all got killed.
That's why I am alone.
You people should move onto an island.

"Boats leaking," they say.

"Put fish grease on them," he told them.
So they do that. They put boats in water. They don't leak now.

"Put all kids in one boat. I'm captain," he said.

Little way out he goes and licks fat off those boats.
He eats kids' boat last.
Boats start leaking, and those kids drown. He tells them,
"Become diver—loon."

So those kids make noise like suffering, and that's why loons do
   that.
After those people drown, he eats all that whale grease.

Another time Crow walks on beach. He feeds from beach all the
   time.
"Who will go with me?" he asks the animals.
"How about me?" they all say; one by one they came out.
"No . . . no . . . no," he says to each one.

Finally Buck Deer say, "How about me?"
That Deer is sure fat!

"OK, you look fat enough. You can come with me."
They walk along upstream. Come to a canyon.

"Let's cross here," Crow say.
Crow makes a grass bridge put together of grass and horsetails.

"How do I do that?" ask Deer. "It won't hold me."

"Sure it would," say Crow. "I'll do it first."
He pretends to walk. . . . That bridge look good.
But he uses his wings.

Deer tries too.
That first step, grass and horsetails pull apart—he falls into the
   canyon. *Smash!*
Deer is fat, and that fat flies all over.
He sure makes a big splash! That's why you see white marble rock
   sometimes—that's deer fat.
Crow ate that fat.

That food lasts Crow two, three days.

Crow walks alone after that. Walks on the beach again.
"Boo hoo, I lost my brother. Who is high enough to cry with me?"
Imagine that! He just *ate* his brother!

Willow says, "Let me cry with you."
"No," Crow say. "Your paint is too pretty. It would spoil."

Poplar says, "Let me cry with you."
"No," Crow say. "Your paint is too good on your face."

Then Crow sees a tree covered with pitch—spruce tree.
"Ah, ho, ho, ho. You must have the same sadness as me!
My brother was killed. You are crying like me. You look good.
 You can cry with me."
That's why spruce tree is always covered with pitch.

Then one time Crow falls in love with his mother-in-law.
He's walking along, comes to a widow and her daughter.
He comes up, lay down, legs crossed, hand under his head,
 looking nice; he talks to them nice.
He's stuck on that girl.
She pretty soon moves over to him. Now he's got a new wife.

One year later, though, he gets stuck on his mother-in-law!
She gets sick—he wished her sick, that's why.

He said, "I'll be doctor." So he tells his wife, "I know what medicine will help your mother."
He tells his wife, "Send your mother to the bushes, to the
 meadow. Tell her to sit on the first thing she sees coming out of
 the moss."

Then he covers himself up with moss, all but his private part!
She came there. She saw it. She sat down.
Then she looked down and saw some feathers. She figured it out!
He didn't get anything from her!

She goes to her daughter. "Where's your husband?"

"He went to get water."

She tells her daughter what happened.
Funny thing, though, she got better right away.
Crow medicine, I guess that is.

That's end of Crow stories. At end he gets tired of walking around.
 So made himself into Raven.
Now he doesn't bother people anymore.

"GLACIER BAY HISTORY" TOLD BY AMY MARVIN AND "SPEECH FOR THE REMOVAL OF GRIEF" DELIVERED BY JESSIE DALTON

▲

NORA MARKS DAUENHAUER
AND
RICHARD DAUENHAUER

INTRODUCTION

The following pieces are taken from the first two books in our series *Classics of Tlingit Oral Literature*.[1] We direct readers to these volumes for the Tlingit-language texts and to their introductions and annotations for more complete information on the texts and context as well as for photographs of the regalia alluded to in the oratory.[2]

The texts function well as a pair. The story by Amy Marvin, "Glacier Bay History," explains the background for the ritual of which the speech by Jessie Dalton is the central part. Both texts are the English translations of material performed orally in Tlingit. Amy Marvin told her story in a private recording session with Nora Dauenhauer in Juneau on May 31, 1984. Jessie Dalton's speech was delivered in public, in Hoonah, Alaska, in October 1968 as part of a Tlingit ceremonial popularly called potlatch in English. Most studies of the potlatch emphasize rivalry and the economic aspects, but one of the main spiritual functions is healing through the removal of grief and the end of the mourning period following the death of a clan member. To achieve these ends, the clan that has experienced a death hosts a memorial potlatch, during which the hosts perform a ritual of lamentation, and the guests deliver to the hosts speeches for the removal of grief. Jessie Dalton was the main speaker for the guests, and her speech is recognized as an outstanding example of Tlingit oratory.

Tlingit social structure underlies all Tlingit verbal and visual art and social and ceremonial interaction. Tlingit society is organized into moieties, called Raven and Eagle. A person follows his or her mother's line and traditionally marries into the opposite moiety. Amy Marvin is of the Eagle moiety and the Chookaneidí clan; her main crests are the eagle, porpoise, and brown bear. Jessie Dalton is of the Raven moiety and the T'akdeintaan clan; her main crests are the raven and tern. In ceremonial situations the moieties interact, exchanging goods and services. In the memorial in which her speech was delivered, Jessie Dalton was a spokesperson for the Raven moiety guests, and Amy Marvin's Eagle clanspeople were the hosts. In the oratory people are often identified by kinship and clan crest; thus in the line "your father's sisters would fly out," the reference is to women of the opposite moiety who have the tern as their crest. Likewise, in the text beginning "during the warm season" and ending with "he will burrow down, with it;" (lines 160–70), the father of the hosts is equated with a frog. In all of this, the art pieces, such as the tern blanket and the frog hat, are linked with the spirits they depict as well as with the spirits of departed former stewards.

In the story by Amy Marvin, a young woman is undergoing seclusion at the onset of puberty. As the proverb says, she is "sitting for seed," because at the end of this time she will be married and will contribute to the physical survival of society. But she will also contribute to cultural survival, by learning how to act as an emotional and spiritual, as well as physical, adult. During this time of seclusion, she receives training from the female elders in how to become a contributing human being and competent member of society. Among other things she is to practice self-discipline and self-control. Bored, she calls to the glacier for companionship. She lifts the bark wall of the temporary structure and offers some dry fish, salmon that has been dried (like jerky) in a smokehouse. The story teaches us that human action can have cosmic as well as social reaction. In the end the young girl accepts responsibility for her action and stays behind, giving her life to redeem herself and her clan. Her sacrifice also establishes Glacier Bay as sacred space and the physical as well as spiritual property of her clan. The story explains the mythical relationships among the human, natural, and spiritual worlds. It explains the covenants for the kind of ritual in which Jessie Dalton delivers her speech, and it traces the migration from Glacier Bay to Hoonah, where both of the tradition bearers live.

In turn, Jessie Dalton's speech is an example of ritual, the enactment of an underlying myth. Her oratory accompanies, and takes as its main images, the ritual display of regalia depicting clan crests: carved wooden hats, dance frontlets, masks, woven Chilkat robes, and beaded button blankets. Called *at.óow* in Tlingit, these visual art forms are familiar to many from museum displays and books on Northwest Coast art, of which Aldona Jonaitis offers three excellent, recent examples.[3] But the museum displays and books are static and without sound. Readers should imagine Jessie Dalton's oratory as the sound track providing the ritual, ceremonial, social, and spiritual contexts of the great visual art of the Northwest Coast. Her speech illustrates the connection in Tlingit folk life between visual and verbal art, between the spiritual and the human, and among the clans within the social structure.

The metaphor and simile of Jessie Dalton's speech are difficult to follow and understand in their entirety, but a few words on the background and structure will help the unfamiliar reader. To perform their part in the ceremonial, the guests have put on their clan *at.óow*. One by one the orator recognizes the hats, blankets, robes, and so forth, giving the history of each piece and explaining the kinship connection of the stewards to the hosts. She identifies each piece by name, calling, for example, a hat Mountain Tribe's Dog after the image it depicts. She then makes the artwork come alive through simile and metaphor, calling to the present assembly the spirits each piece depicts, describing the spirits as removing grief in an appropriate manner and returning with the grief to the spirit world, restoring harmony to the community of the living.

In both texts the line breaks reflect pauses in oral delivery. (Wrap-around lines are simply lines that extend beyond the right margin.) The story is presented in narrative voice but with the storyteller using different voices for the narrator and each character. In contrast, the oratory is chanted in a shout, higher in pitch than the normal speaking or narrative voice. There is audience response throughout the speech, and this is indicated in italics, with the speaker's name in small capitals. The untranslated word *áawé* is something like "amen."

Guide to Pronunciation

Tlingit has about two dozen sounds not shared with English. Roman letters are modified to spell these uniquely Tlingit sounds.

Tlingit is a tone language; the acute accent indicates phonemic high tone; low tone is not marked.

Underlined letters are uvular (back-in-the-mouth) sounds and contrast with velar counterparts. *X* is like German *ich*, and *X* like German *ach*.

An apostrophe indicates a glottalized consonant.

A period in the middle of a word indicates a glottal stop.

A space between lines indicates a pause.

NOTES

1. Nora Marks Dauenhauer and Richard Dauenhauer, *Haa Shuká/Our Ancestors: Tlingit Oral Narratives* and *Haa Tuwunáagu Yís/For Healing Our Spirit: Tlingit Oratory*, vols. 1 and 2 of *Classics of Tlingit Oral Literature* (Seattle: University of Washington Press, 1987 and 1990); the latter volume received a Before Columbus Foundation American Book Award in 1991.

2. For additional cultural background, see Sergei Kan, *Symbolic Immortality: The Tlingit Potlatch of the Nineteenth Century* (Washington, D.C.: Smithsonian Institution Press, 1989), Wallace Olson, *The Tlingit: An Introduction to Their Culture and History* (Auke Bay, Alaska: Heritage Research, 1991), and George Thornton Emmons, *The Tlingit Indians*, ed. Frederica de Laguna (Seattle: University of Washington Press, 1991).

3. Aldona Jonaitis, *Art of the Northern Tlingit* (Seattle: University of Washington Press, 1986), *From the Land of the Totem Poles: The Northwest Coast Indian Art Collection at the American Museum of Natural History* (Seattle: University of Washington Press, 1988), and *Chiefly Feasts: The Enduring Kwakiutl Potlatch* (Seattle: University of Washington Press, 1991).

Now this is the way I will begin telling the story
today.
Now,
at the beginning
of how things happened to us
at Glacier Bay,
the way things happened to us there.   5
This little girl was one of us
Chookaneidí.

. . . . .

Now*
the time had come
for this young woman.
Very young
newly   60
put in confinement.
Today she would be called teenager.
This is what this young girl was.
Kaasteen.
This was when   65
they had her sit.
Not in the house.
But in an extension
of the house.
A room would be made.   70
It was like the bedrooms of today.
Someone who was in this condition would not be allowed inside
    the main house.
They would build a room for her
extending from the main house.
At the same time   75
there was a feast.
A feast was being held.
Everybody was gone;
everyone had gone to the feast.

*The preceding forty-seven lines have been omitted here.

But this young girl's mother 80
went to see her.
She gave her some sockeye strips.
"Here."
There was another little girl, a little girl maybe eight years old.
Her mother didn't want to leave her. 85
People didn't take their children out in public
in those days
because they respected one another.
This is how things were.
People didn't take children 90
even the babies.
This woman didn't want to leave her little girl.
She was weaving
a basket.
She brought her weaving out. 95
She wove.
They were all gone! It was deserted.
Then the little girl ran in by the one who had become a woman.
She sat with her.
Kaasteen 100
was eating the dry fish.
She broke them.
All of a sudden she bent down.
This is when she lifted the edge of her wall.
They say she held the dry fish out with one hand. 105
Then she bent down that way.
This is how the little girl told it to her mother.
"Hey,
glacier!
Here, here, here, here, here. 110
Hey,
glacier!
Here, here, here, here, here, here.
Hey,
glacier! 115
Here, here, here, here, here."
Then she lowered the wall.
The little girl was surprised by all this.
That was why she got up; she ran out by her mother.
"Mother! 120
Why is she saying this?

'Hey,
glacier!
Here, here, here.'
Three times she said this.   125
Mom!
Three times she said this."
"Don't say that! Go away!
You're always saying things,"
she said to her little daughter.   130
This woman was the witness.
This one who stayed home with her little daughter was the witness
about her,
about Kaasteen.
This is why   135
we tell it the same way.
We didn't just
toss this story together.
This is the way it's told.
My grandmother,   140
my mother,
my father,
were very old when they died.
This is why I don't
deviate when I tell it; I tell it exactly right.   145
At that time
the ice
didn't begin advancing from the top.
It began advancing from the bottom,
from the bottom.   150
That was why no one knew.
Not one person knew.
All of a sudden it struck
the middle of the land that people were living on.
Why was the land shaking?   155
Why was it?
People thought it was an earthquake; it didn't bother anyone.
Then another one,
then another one.
Why didn't it quit?   160
Here it was the ice crushing against itself and moving in.
That was why
they finally gathered together.

"What's happening?
  It should happen just once.   165
  Why is this?
  Oh no!
  It wasn't an earthquake, was it?
  It's becoming stronger."
The people forgot about it again.   170
Then it happened again.
Here this woman finally said,
"Oh dear! It's the one sitting in the room.
  She called it with dry fish like a dog."
Where was the glacier?   175
There wasn't a glacier to be seen.
But that was what Kaasteen gave a name to; she named it *sít'*.
What was it she named this?
There was a little piece stuck there.
That was what she gave a name to.   180
That was why the people who were wise gathered then.
"Oh!
  I guess she said a bad thing."
When a person who is ritually unclean, you see,
mistakenly does something,   185
it turns bad.
That's the reason,
that's the reason
they gathered together.
Oh, she violated a taboo, didn't she?   190
I guess she mistakenly said things about the ice.
Oh, no.
They kept gathering.
They kept gathering.
They were really troubled by the way things were turning out on
  their land; people stayed in their homes.   195
It was becoming troublesome too.
But the young girl wasn't bothered by this anymore.
Perhaps it was changing her every moment.
It was because of her;
the glacier was doing this because of her,   200
because of the way she called it over.
Here they said,
"I guess she broke a taboo, didn't she?
  Quick!

Let's get ready to get out."   205
Things weren't turning out right.
The house was already falling over on its side
from how strong the ice was getting.
[*Slap!*]
It was behaving
like it was crushing against itself;   210
[*Slap!*]
how strong the ice was.
And they knew.
It was the ice pushing the people, wasn't it?
It was pushing; it was pushing the village along.
This was when people said, "Quick! Quick! Quick! Quick!   215
Quick.
Let's move the people.
Quick!
Move the people.
It isn't right.   220
It isn't right."
This was when they said,
"Quick! Let's pack.
Her too.
It's OK to take the one who broke the taboo; it's OK.   225
Let her come aboard.
Let her come aboard."
People used to cherish one another, you see.
There was no way they could have left her there; she was a young
    woman,
a young girl.   230
Yes, like the saying, "They had her sitting for seed."
This is when this happened to her.
This was when people said,
"There's nothing wrong with her coming aboard.
Let her come aboard."   235
That was why they asked her, indirectly:
"People will be getting ready now.
Quick!
Fix your clothes.
Fix them."   240
"No!
I won't go aboard."
Oh no!

Her words spread quickly.
"She said, 'I won't go aboard,' the one who broke the taboo.   245
She said she doesn't want to go aboard."
Oh no.
Then it came to the opposite groups.
"This paternal aunt of hers should go to her,
her father's sister. Quick, quick, quick."   250
On that side of the village, people were packing; it was already like
    a whirlpool.
The village was trembling constantly,
trembling constantly; it was as if they were expecting disaster.
Perhaps it was like the storm we just had.
It was very frightening the way things were.   255
They were trying to beat it.
"Yes, because it is like this, and because it is this way, my niece,
my brother's daughter,
because things are this way, now,
let's go;   260
pack,
pack!
Pity your mother; take pity on your father."
They begged her.
"No!   265
No!
I won't go aboard.
I won't go aboard.
What I said
will stain my face forever."   270
She didn't deny it.
"What I said will stain my face
forever; this is why
I won't go aboard; it won't happen."
That was why they gave up on her.   275
That was why they said,
"Let's go!
But let's take these things
to her.
We can't just leave her this way.   280
Yes.
Let's go!"
It began to happen.
They began going to her
with things that would keep,   285

her paternal aunts,
all of them,
with all of us,
going to her
with things for her food.   290
"For Kaasteen to eat!
For Kaasteen to eat!"
In this way they brought
whatever
might keep her warm,   295
the skins
of whatever was killed and dried.
They were made into robes.
These, "For Kaasteen!"
("For Kaasteen!")   300
"For Kaasteen to eat!"
("For Kaasteen to eat!")*
"For Kaasteen!"
In this way
they turned then and left her.   305
Now,
this is the reason it became a saying;
it will be a saying forever: for whomever is mourned, people
   relinquish
the ownership of things in their memory.
Only after this do we feel stronger.   310
And "for her to eat" is also said.
Only if the food that is given is eaten with another clan
can it go to her.
This is when she will have some,
the relative who is mourned.   315
When the opposite clan takes a bite, she will also eat some.
This is the reason we call it invitation to feast.
A feast is offered
to remove our grief.
Only when we give to the opposite clan   320
whatever we offer,
only when we know it went to her, only when this is done does it
   become a balm for our spirits.
Because of her,

*In a potlatch these lines would be spoken by the audience. Here the storyteller
imitates the audience, changing her voice as she imitates the response.

Kaasteen.
And whatever we relinquish our ownership to,   325
for Kaasteen,
when we give these to the opposite clan,
only after this do our spirits become strong.
It's medicine, spiritual medicine.
Because of the things that happened to Kaasteen, this is what
    informed us.   330
When all the things were piled on her.
Yes.
Now.
They were gone.
They were all aboard the canoes.   335
That was when Shaawatséek' got angry.
Yes.
She was already old.
She was already older than me at the time.
"Isn't it a shame," she said.   340
She started going there.
Yes.
The relatives who were going to leave her were standing by
    Kaasteen
in the house they were leaving her in.
This was when Shaawatséek' pushed the door open.   345
Yes.
"Am I going to bring your next generation,
my brothers?
But take Kaasteen aboard.
Take her aboard.   350
I will take her place.
I'm expecting death
at any moment.
So I will take her place.
Yes.   355
Let her go aboard.
Let her go aboard."
This was when Kaasteen spoke, in a loud voice:
"I will not go aboard.
I said, I will not go aboard.   360
I'm staying here."
That was it.
Shaawatséek' couldn't persuade her either.

Now,
no more.   365
They gave up on her.
This was the last try
when Shaawatséek' came for her.
This was why
they left her.   370
There was enough.
It measured up.
The food
from her paternal aunts,
from her paternal uncles,   375
from her mother's people
was piled high.
They were leaving her with almost enough to fill the house.
This is when they all finally
went aboard.   380
Yes.
They didn't paddle away just then.
When they were all seated in the canoes,
they just drifted.
While they were packing, I guess, this song kept flashing on the
    mind of Kaanaxduwóos'.   385
It kept flashing on his mind.
He knew too
when they went to get her.
My!
No, she didn't want to leave the house.   390

Only when they were drifting out,
they saw.
The house was rolling over.
And it popped out of their mouths:
"It's rolling over!"   395
It fell over sideways,
and she with the house.
Yes.
That's when her mother screamed.
She screamed.   400
Kaasteen's mother screamed.
Yes.

The other women also
screamed with her.
While they couldn't believe it, it was sliding downward,   405
the house she sat in,
downward.

Their voices
could be heard from far away,
crying.   410

They had no more strength.
Today
death is not like that.
It's like something dropping.
At that time, though,   415
if anything happened to even an infant, the grief would leave us
    weak.
The way we didn't want to lose each other,
the way things were.
Yes, this was why he stood up in the canoe.
The voices were still loud.   420
They were still crying.
She was dying before their eyes
as the house slid downward.
This was when he began singing, then.

FIRST SONG

    Won't my house
    be pitiful;
    won't my house
    be pitiful
    when I leave on foot?*

    Won't my house
    be pitiful;
    won't my house
    be pitiful
    when I leave on foot?

*The vocables have been omitted from this translation.

Won't my land
be pitiful;
won't my land
be pitiful
when I leave by boat?

Won't my land
be pitiful;
won't my land
be pitiful
when I leave by boat?

Now this is what happened to them.   425
This is how they were.
Now.
This is the song from there
when they left Kaasteen.
This house became like her coffin,   430
this Chookaneidí house.
It went with her to the bottom of the sea before their eyes.
This is why the words are of the house;
when he first sang
this song: 435
"Pity my house,"
he said.
Yes.
And when they left her: "Pity my land."
Yes.   440
I guess they didn't put the comparison together
at first.
When one who was precious,
their relative,
this woman,   445
died before their eyes,
yes, no one else thought of songs.
They were just afraid.
They just trembled to go where they could be saved
because it was too much the way the land was shaking.   450
It wasn't letting up.
This was why they were afraid.
Even with all this he thought of the song.
Yes.

This is the reason it's everlasting, also for the generations coming
    after me. 455
I'm recording for them
so that they will know why this song came into being.
But no man volunteered
to stay with her.
But recently someone said that one did. 460
No!
No!
Well,
I will come to it,
the part of the story 465
why people were saying this.
After this
I guess it was
out from Pleasant Island.
When they were passing it, 470
Sdayáat,
a Chookaneidí,
also our relative,
stood up in the canoe.
Yes. 475
He also repeated:
"Stop for a moment.
Stop for a moment."

That was why they held those moving canoes motionless; yes.
"I too 480
cannot let
what I'm thinking
pass.
Please listen
to the way I feel too." 485
They began drifting; all the canoes drifted.

This is when he sang the song that flashed on his mind.

Yes.

My land,
will I ever
see it again?*

My land,
will I ever
see it again?

My house,
will I ever
see it again?

My house,
will I ever
see it again?

Now, this is Sdayáat's song.
Yes.   490
This is how the two of them composed songs
when trouble came.
Well,
they didn't just abandon her carelessly.
Now,   495
not even the T'akdeintaan
searched their minds,
or the Kaagwaantaan,
or the Wooshkeetaan.
They just left.   500
It was only these men who expressed their pain.
They didn't just leave her carelessly.
Now
only then they began leaving.
The Wooshkeetaan   505
went to the place
called Excursion Inlet today.
But the Kaagwaantaan

went to Ground Hog Bay.
I guess it's called   510

*The vocables have been omitted.

Grouse Fort.
This is where they went, the group of Kaagwaantaan.
As for us, we continued away from them.
There is
a river called Lakooxas't'aakhéen.   515
It flows there; it's still there today, where Frank Norten made his
    land,
a place like a cove.
It was there; we waded ashore.
Now
you know how tiring it is to be in a canoe.   520
It was then and there we waded ashore; this is where we prepared
    a place to live
at Spasski.
It's called Lakooxas't'aakhéen.
It was there we waded ashore.
It was like   525
after a war.
There was nothing.
This is how it was.

Does death take pity on us too,
my brothers' children,
   WILLIE MARKS: *Áawé.*
my fathers?
All my fathers,
it doesn't take pity on us either,   5
this thing that happens,
   UNIDENTIFIED: *That's how it is.*
which is why you hear their voices like this,
your fathers,
lest your tears fall without honor
   HARRY MARVIN: *Thank you.*
   WILLIE MARKS: *Thank you.*
that flowed from your faces.   10
For them,
they have all come out at this moment;
your fathers
have all come out.
   HARRY MARVIN: *Hó, hó.*
They are still present   15
is how I feel
about my grandparents.
   WILLIE MARKS: *Thank you.*
Here someone stands wearing one,
this Mountain Tribe's Dog.
It is just as if   20
it's barking for your pain is how I'm thinking about it,
   WILLIE MARKS: *Thank you.*
my fathers, my brothers' children,
my father's sisters,
yes.
Here   25
someone is standing next to it.

It's Raven-Who-Went-down-Along-the-Bull-Kelp.
Someone is standing closer, next to it.

Lyeedayéik's robe:
That is the closer one. Someone is standing next to it.   30

Yes.

 HARRY MARVIN: *Thank you.*

 EVA DAVIS: *Thank you.*

It's the Beaver Blanket
from Chilkat,
a Chilkat robe.

 UNIDENTIFIED: *Uh-uh.*

 WILLIE MARKS: *Thank you.*

Lutákl,   35
your father,
it was once his blanket,
once his Chilkat robe.

 UNIDENTIFIED: *Hó, hó.*

 HARRY MARVIN: *Thank you.*

Because of you
he came out.   40

 DAVID MCKINLEY: *Hó, hó.*

 WILLIE MARKS: *Thank you.*

Yes
at this moment
all of them seem to me as if they're revealing their faces.
Your fathers' sisters,
my mother,   45
Saayina.aat,

 UNIDENTIFIED: *That's it.*

 UNIDENTIFIED: *That's right.*

her robe,
the Tern Robe.
Yes.

 UNIDENTIFIED: *That's it.*

 WILLIE MARKS: *Thank you.*

A person who is feeling like you   50
would be brought by canoe,
yes,
to your fathers' point,
Gaanaxáa.
That is when   55
the name would be called out, it is said,
of the person who is feeling grief.
Yes.
Father! Séi Akdulxéitl'.

 DAVID MCKINLEY: *Áawé.*

Yes. 60
My grandfather's son,
Koowunagáas';
   JOE WHITE: *Áawé.*
my brother's daughter's son,
Keet Yaanaayí.
   WILLIE MARKS: *Áawé.*
Yes, 65
my father's sister's son,
Xooxkeina.át.
   PETE JOHNSON: *Áawé.*
How very much
for your grief
your fathers' sisters are revealing their faces. 70
My brother's son
   WILLIE MARKS: *Thank you.*
Kaatooshtóow,
   JOHN F. WILSON: *Áawé.*
Kaakwsak'aa,
   DAVID WILLIAMS: *Áawé.*
yes,
my brother's wife, Aan Káxshawustaan. 75
   MARY JOHNSON: *Áawé.*
Yes,
how very much it is
as if they're revealing their faces is how I'm thinking about them,
your sisters-in-law.
Yes, 80
they are revealing their faces.
The shirt that belonged to Weihá;
it was only recently
we completed
the rites for him. 85
That's the one there,

the Raven Shirt.
   WILLIE MARKS: *Thank you.*
You heard him here also,
Weihá,
this brother of mine, 90
this peacemaker of yours;
this shirt of Weihá

will remain in his hands, in his care.
> UNIDENTIFIED: *Thank you.*

Now it's as if he is coming out for you to see.
> WILLIE MARKS: *Yes.*

Yes.   95
How proud
he too used to be
wearing it,
this brother-in-law of yours.
> UNIDENTIFIED: *How very much.*

The Raven-Nest House Robe,   100
here this father's sister of yours stands wearing it.
And on the far side
is Yaakaayindul.át, your father's sister,
yes.
We had long since given up hope of their return,   105
these fathers' sisters of yours,
your fathers.
> UNIDENTIFIED: *Hó, hó.*
> UNIDENTIFIED: *Thank you.*

Yes,
Raven-Who-Went-down-Along-the-Bull-Kelp Shirt,
your father,   110
Kaadéik,
> UNIDENTIFIED: *Áawé.*

it's his shirt;
that's the one.
> UNIDENTIFIED: *Your brothers' children are listening to you.*

That's the one there; I don't feel that it burned.
Yes.   115
It's the same one in which your father's brother is standing there
   in front of you.
> WILLIE MARKS: *Thank you.*
> GEORGE DALTON: *Thank you.*

That is why,
yes,
Gusatáan,
> UNIDENTIFIED: *Áawé.*

it will be just as if I will have named all of you,   120
those who are my sisters-in-law,

yes.
Can I reach the end,
my brothers' children?
Yes.   125
Can I reach the end?
These terns I haven't completely explained,
yes,
these terns.
Your fathers' sisters would fly out over the person who is feeling
   grief.   130
    WILLIE MARKS: *Áawé*.
Then
they would let their down fall
like snow
over the person who is feeling grief.
    GEORGE DALTON: *Your brothers' children are listening to you.*
    HARRY MARVIN: *Thank you.*
That's when their down   135
isn't felt.
That's when
I feel it's as if your fathers' sisters are flying
back to their nests
with your grief.   140
    HARRY MARVIN: *Thank you indeed.*
Yes.
Here someone stands,
here,
my mother's mother's brother, his hat.
Yes.   145
To the mouth of Taku he went by boat
then for that hat,
to his grandparents,
to his grandparents.
Yes,   150
from there it's said he acquired the Frog Hat.
Along with it came
the shirt from Weihá.
    GEORGE DALTON: *That's it.*
Yes,
it also came from Taku.   155
That is why
I keep saying "thank you"

that they're standing in front of you at this moment.
    WILLIE MARKS: *Thank you*.
Yes,
during the warm season   160
this father of yours
would come out.
That's when
I feel it's as if your father's hat
has come out for your grief.   165
Yes,
    HARRY MARVIN: *Thank you indeed*.
your grandparent's hat.
With your grief
he will burrow down,
with it;   170
with your grief he will burrow down.
    GEORGE DALTON: *Your brothers' sons are listening to you*.
Not that it can heal you,
my brothers' children, my fathers,
    UNIDENTIFIED: *Thank you*.
my fathers' sisters,
my sisters-in-law.   175
And now
yes,
it is like the saying "They are only imitating them
lest they grope aimlessly,"
    GEORGE DALTON: *Thank you indeed*.
the way your grandparents said.   180
That's why
it's as if your fathers
are guiding them.
Here is one.

Here is one.   185
Here someone stands wearing one,
the hat of Yookis'kookéik,
this grandfather of mine.
    UNIDENTIFIED: *Hó, hó*.
He too has stood up
to face you.   190
Yes.
    UNIDENTIFIED: *Hó, hó*.

Your father, his hat,
Koowunagáas'.
> UNIDENTIFIED: *Thank you, indeed.*
He has stood up to face you,
> WILLIE MARKS: *Thank you.*
> UNIDENTIFIED: *Thank you.*
yes, 195
the Loon Spirit.

Yes.
And here,
yes,
is the one this brother of mine explained awhile ago: 200
how that tree rolled for a while on the waves.
Then when it drifted to shore,
the sun would put its rays on it.
Yes.
It would dry its grief 205
to the core.
At this moment this sun is coming out over you, my grandparents'
mask.
> UNIDENTIFIED: *That's it.*
> UNIDENTIFIED: *Thank you.*
> UNIDENTIFIED: *Hó, hó.*
At this moment
my hope is that your grief 210
be like it's drying to your core.
> GEORGE DALTON: *It shall be.*
> WILLIE MARKS: *Thank you; it shall be.*
Géelák'w Headdress,
yes,
your fathers' sisters
would reveal their faces from it, 215
from Géelák'w,
yes.
That's the one there now. Someone is standing there with it,
this headdress,
> UNIDENTIFIED: *Thank you indeed.*
my grandfather's headdress. 220
> WILLIE MARKS: *Thank you.*

DUNNE-ZA STORIES

▲

ROBIN RIDINGTON

INTRODUCTION

The Dunne-za, or Beaver Indians, are Athabaskan-speaking hunting people of the Peace River area of British Columbia and Alberta. Their stories, like those of many other First Nations people, circle around and touch one another in complex patterns of resonance. Before the Dunne-za came into contact with a literate tradition, they experienced the text of each story as an event, not a document. A story existed in the vibration of its voicing. It existed in the shared memory from which the storyteller called it and to which he or she gave it in return. A story's beginning or end reflected the situation of its teller and listener as well as canonical conventions of plot and character. A story took place simultaneously in the real time of its telling and in the mythical time in which it occurred. For narrator and listener beginning and end were points of knowingly woven entry and departure. They were like the entries and departures of a Dunne-za dancer when he or she moves in or out of the dreamer's dance circle.

When I first encountered the Dunne-za in the 1960s, storytelling was done very much in the way it always had been. (In the 1990s younger people have come to communicate largely in English.) Stories the Dunne-za told me reflected their understanding of me and the situation we shared. The stories were instructional: the tellers expected me to learn from what they told me. They were probably also intended to be illustrations of Dunne-za knowledge and power. Ultimately they also became archival representations of that knowledge and power. I made it clear that through the act of telling me stories that I recorded on tape, the Dunne-za were participating in the creation of written texts.

Writing down the words of a storyteller's performance calls on a variety of authorial responsibilities. The storyteller contributes through his or her performance, the translator makes decisions about the transfer of meaning from one culture to another, and the editor makes further decisions about the appearance of a text in writing. Sometimes the writer is also the translator. Less frequently he or she also takes the role of storyteller.

Frank Hamilton Cushing, for instance, wrote down Zuni stories from memory in his classic, *Zuni Fetiches*.[1] He accepted the authority of his own instruction in Zuni ways as an appropriate interpretive instrument and thus assumed the role of storyteller. Franz Boas and many of his students took the more mechanistic path of writing down stories word for word and then producing interlinear translations. The gain in accuracy of transcription, however, was sometimes submerged in a dulling loss of the story's integrity as meaningful performance. The use of portable recording equipment has made it possible to capture the moment of performance. A recording materializes an intermediate version of a story that hovers ambiguously somewhere between performance and written text. It is convenient to call this recorded version simply an audio document. Recordings are similar to photographs in that they are mechanical representations of events amenable to study in a different time frame from the one in which they were experienced as performance. It is from these documents that the translator and writer construct texts such as the ones presented in this sample from the Dunne-za archive.

The stories reproduced here are written transformations of audio documents recorded on a portable reel-to-reel Uher tape machine in the mid-1960s. They were told in response to my request for "Indian stories" that I could preserve in writing. Some stories were told in English; most of them, however, including these, were told in the Beaver language. I obtained translations through the use of a second tape recorder, into which a Dunne-za translator spoke after listening to a passage in the original document. The result was a secondary audio document, this one in the translator's own English words. I have chosen to render these tape-recorded documents as line-for-line poetics rather than right-justified prose. This should not suggest that Indians speak poetry and white people prose. It merely serves to open the text to the reader's eye and ear.

Much of the actual transformation of these texts from handwritten original transcripts is the work of Lindy-Lou Flynn. It is she who named the stories. From the hundreds of pages of "Beaver Tales" she put together while a research associate at the University of British Columbia, I have chosen three for this collection. The choice was difficult. Rather than repeating some that are already in print elsewhere, I have focused on unpublished stories that illustrate the living and changing quality of Dunne-za narrative. Two of these, "All the People in This World Come from That Brother and Sister" and "The Girl and Her Younger Brother," are in fact versions of the same story contextualized by different narrators. The third, "A Story About Heaven," gives a dreamer's perspective on Dunne-za transformations of Christianity.

In Dunne-za experience a world of myth is interior to the everyday world of sensation. "A long time ago . . . everything could talk just like people" describes a state of being that children traditionally experienced through their vision quests and adults frequently experienced in dreams. The mythical time comes to mind with each telling of a story about it. Even the events of recent history are mythologized. Aballi Field, who tells about a brother and sister who created all the people in the world, began with an account of "this new business" that "somebody just like a bishop" negotiated with the white men and their Christianity. He is referring to a dreamer known as Makenunatane, whom Dunne-za tradition credits with "dreaming ahead" to predict the coming of the white men. Aballi does not find it necessary to give more than an oblique reference to this figure, who was well known to Dunne-za listeners of his generation. He then presents episodes from familiar first-encounter stories before launching into his version of the amazing bear-husband story, which I later obtained from Antoine Hunter as well.

Antoine Hunter was a very old man when I recorded his story about the girl and her younger brother in 1968. His version is more detailed and multifaceted than Aballi Field's. He says outright what was probably an unstated understanding in the other version: the hole in the ground was a place of first-menstrual seclusion. Both stories are unusual in that a younger brother was placed there with the girl. Antoine's story briefly but powerfully runs through a cascade of shockingly powerful images. An older sister marries a grizzly bear and denies her human brothers, leading to her husband's death. Antoine's image of the dead bear husband's paws "dangling from the pack, its claws swinging as she walked along the trail," is chilling, even at a distance. This story is about families literally tearing each other apart and then coming together to make a new life. It is an intricate masterpiece, best understood when seen in relation to other information available about Dunne-za life.

The story I have placed between Aballi's and Antoine's is a dreamer's narrative by Old Man Aku. The story begins as Aku's account of a dream encounter with his father. It is about how Jesus made a new road on the right side of the trail to heaven. Is this a Dunne-za version of the Apostles' Creed or a Christian version of the shamanistic keeper of the game? In reality it is both. The bird on the pole guarding the gate to heaven is as old as shamanistic tradition itself, but the image of God dropping down messages written on paper clearly represents a Dunne-za response to the Judeo-Christian idea of script and scripture. All the new ideas blend with the old in Aku's dream, to become "the way it used to be."

These stories are tied together in more ways than I can point to here and certainly in more ways than my limited acquaintance with Dunne-za language and experience allows me to realize. The storytellers and translator, Liza Wolf, have produced evocative and beautiful texts in English. I commend them to your intelligence and imagination.

NOTE

1. Frank Hamilton Cushing, *Zuni Fetiches* (Washington, D.C.: U.S. Government Printing Office, 1883; reprint, Flagstaff, Ariz.: K. C. Publications 1966).

ALL THE PEOPLE IN THIS WORLD COME
FROM THAT BROTHER AND SISTER

A long time ago there were just Indians in this Canada.
At that time all the animals knew how to talk.
Moose, Caribou, Beaver—
everything could talk just like people.
Life was really dangerous then.
The people had a hard time.
There was a big animal—*onli nachi**—
that used to kill the people, and everyone was afraid then.
People used to fight each other then too.
That was before this new business.
Someone just like a bishop fixed everything up.
Now Indians know about God.
Somebody says the white men came across the water
in some kind of boat. I don't know myself.
First they came down the Peace River
and tried to show things to the Indians—
but they were shy.
The Indians would just look and then run away.
Finally the white men came to where some Indians were camped.
They tried to help them—
to show them all kinds of good things.
But the Indians were too suspicious.
The white men gave them a little sugar,
but at first they wouldn't try it.
They thought it would kill them,
but finally they tried a little, and it was really sweet.
Then the white men showed them all kinds of things
and helped them lots.
After that they weren't afraid anymore.

A long time ago when the animals talked
and onli nachi killed people, things were very hard,
and people were afraid all the time.
One family had a girl about thirteen and her younger brother.
The mother and father were afraid for their children,
so they made a big hole in the ground eight feet deep.

**onli nachi:* literally, "something big"; the generic name for giant animals of
mythical time.

They put the children inside the hole and covered it up.
Onli nachi had been killing people,
and they wanted to save their kids.
The big animal had already killed most of the people.
The parents put two strings down into the hole
to their children.
One string was red and the other string was black.
They told the kids—
"If you want water, pull the red string;
if you want food, pull the black string."
The children lived down in the hole for some time.
When they got hungry, they would pull the black string,
and their mother would send them down food.
When they got thirsty, they would pull the red string,
and their mother would send them down water.
One day they pulled the string, and no one came.
"What's the matter?" said the girl.
"Why does nobody come when I pull the string?"
Her brother told her to pull the other string—
but nobody came.
"What's the matter?" said the girl again.
"Maybe you should go and see."
The boy went out of the hole and looked around.
There was nothing there—no people—nothing.
Onli nachi had killed all the people.
The brother and sister had a hard time after that.
There was no one to feed them.
They had to learn to make fire themselves
and set snares—but they managed to stay alive.
They lived like that for some time.
Finally when they were out hunting, they came to a big hill.
They went around different sides of the hill
until they came to a big tree standing up by itself.
They met at that place.
It was there that they decided to marry
and make more people.
From that they started all the people up again.
When they had kids, they put them together to make more kids.
All the people in this world
come from that brother and sister.

My father was talking from a beautiful place.
He said, "Son—it's very hard to get to heaven.
Even if you're around people swearing, stealing,
doing things like that—don't be like that.
When somebody carries stories around—
lots of people kill each other for that.
That kind of person carrying stories around—
he makes good people turn to bad—
steal, lie, pack stories around—
he makes really good people turn to bad.
That kind of person can't get to heaven.
The man that made us, His son, Jesus,
knew if that road to heaven was straight up
it would be too hard to get to heaven.
But when they killed Jesus, He made the road good.
He made it shorter; He made that road easier
for good people to pass to heaven.
He made that new road with lots of turns.
That's how the new road Jesus made looks.
When Jesus went to heaven after they killed Him,
He thought it would be really hard if the road was straight.
On the new road, on the right-hand side there is a house.
When we get to that house—
from there you can see a beautiful place.
The one who keeps the gate to heaven,
the keeper of the game,
watches over the animals too—
moose, caribou, everything that lives on earth.

From the house Jesus watches the world.
He sees everything people do.
Nothing is hidden from Him—
like if somebody does something, you know it.
When there is fresh meat, if a woman eat that,*
that's no good; the moose don't like that.
The moose know. Whenever women do that,
His people have poor moose with no fat
and are really hard to find—even if there is lots.

*if a woman eat that: that is, if a menstruating woman eats it.

Jesus looks down and sees,
and He give the people a hard time for doing that.
God made Jesus look after this world.
That's why Jesus do that.
On this world Jesus looks after the people—
Like the little people who live in caves
in the mountains.
That's the same kind of person as Jesus,
Who lives on the right side of the road to heaven.
Moose are just like that too.
They know what people are doing to their meat.

The people who look after their meat really good—
they don't have hard time.
When women who aren't supposed to eat fresh meat
stay away from the fresh meat and eat drymeat,
that kind of people who look after meat like that,
when they kill moose, it's fat and good to eat.
That's a gift from Jesus for keeping the meat good.
Inside the house on the right side of the road to heaven,
Jesus divide up something really beautiful.
And beside there, there is a pole
with a bird sitting on top of it—
and when a good person die on this world,
he sees the person go through the gate.
He starts to sing to welcome him,
and he's really happy.
He welcomes them really beautifully.
As soon as the bird starts that,
everyone up above in heaven hears it.
They say,
"Somebody is coming; somebody is coming, that bird says,"
they say.
That's what *chie* said*
when he tells us a story about heaven.
My father said that. My father said that.

God first made the world.
He is so beautiful and powerful that nobody sees Him.
There are houses just like a town,

* *chie:* "my father."

and it's so beautiful
that even people are sometimes shy to step on it.
God made that for good people.
Still God doesn't stay there.
He has a special place for only Himself,
still on top of heaven.
He is so beautiful for Himself that nobody sees Him.
He's above the people who go to heaven.
When He sees something not going right,
He writes a paper and drops it down—
and they pick it up, and Jesus tells the people what to do.
That's how the Father talks to the Son,
when He wants something his way
(He couldn't come in person because He's so beautiful).
That's what chie used to say.
And when a person appear in heaven,
that person is made into a new person.
That's what Jesus does to a good person.
Jesus came to a beautiful lake.
He is just like his Father,
and He wash that person in the lake
with His beautiful hands.
He washes them in the lake,
and that person turns out just like white man.
On this world Indians look poor.
You know how Indians look.
But in heaven we are the most beautiful people—
just like those white women in the books.
Just like those white women in the books.
Jesus shows you
lots of different pictures of people's faces.
You choose the one you want to look like,
and hair too.
In heaven everyone doesn't have the same color hair.
What kind of hair you choose, what kind of face you choose—
you'll look exactly like that.
After you choose your face and hair,
He takes you to another room, and you choose your dress—
the most beautiful dress you've ever seen.
After you put on that dress,
you are no longer the poor-looking Indian of this world.
After that, when you're all ready—

He lets you go to your relatives.
You will never have a hard time or be sorry.
You will always be happy.
That's why we tell you to be good.
The young people think you die forever,
but it's not that way.
Some bad people die, and they can't see the road to heaven.
When a good person dies, his soul just goes to heaven—
from earth to heaven through the part between.
When you get to heaven,
that's when you leave the world for good.
The minute a good person dies, his soul goes out,
and he just can't wait.
He sees the road to heaven for his own goodness.
He goes to the beautiful country up there.
That's why we tell you young people to pray and to be good.
For you bad people it's going to be hard.
That's what chie used to say.
That's the way it used to be.

One time there was a young girl
who started her period first time.
They put her in a sideways hole in the ground,
"her house over there."
Great big, so she could sew and things.
They put her younger brother in the hole too,
so he would be a good hunter and get all kinds of game.
He would always have good luck.
The animals would never run away from him.
That boy would grow up to be a famous hunter.
He would be a good hunter and get all kinds of game.

They put two strings out of the hole.
When they wanted meat, they pulled one string,
and they drew in meat for the boy and drymeat for the girl.
When they wanted water, they pulled the other string,
and they got water.
They were going to stay in there ten days.

That girl had a sister who was married to a grizzly bear.
She had gone off in the bush with her grizzly bear husband
a long time ago.
That girl also had some brothers,
and they went out in the bush to hunt.
Those two brothers came across a grizzly bear's hole.
Then they went and cut green sticks and peeled off the bark.
With those white sticks they started poking in the hole.
The grizzly told his wife—
"Tell my *klase* you are in there."*
But she wouldn't.
So the grizzly ran out to kill the brothers.
Before he could strike at them, they shot him and killed him.
They killed their grizzly brother-in-law.
They made a mistake.
They didn't mean to do that,
but their sister didn't speak, so they didn't know.

After the grizzly was dead,
the brothers told their sister to come out.

*****klase:** "brother-in-law."

But she wouldn't.
They told her all kinds of things,
but she wouldn't come out.
Finally they told her
she was going to pack her husband's head and hide and backbone.
Then she came out, and she was really happy.
They made a pack for her
with the hide and backbone and head,
and they started off.

The two brothers walked in front,
and their sister followed a little ways behind.
Every time she was behind a little hill—
every time there was a little hill
between her and her brothers,
the dogs would start to bark.
"Why are the dogs barking like that?"
her brothers asked.
"They are afraid of your brother-in-law," she said.
One of his paws was dangling from the pack,
its claws swinging as she walked along the trail.

Finally they got back home.
The grizzly man's wife didn't come back close.
She made her camp a little ways from her brothers' camp.
All night long the dogs barked at her camp,
but the brothers didn't bother to see what was the matter.

The next morning
the girl in the hole and her brother
pulled the string for water.
But nobody came to them.
They called and called,
but nobody came.
The older sister said to her brother—
"I'm going to lift up the tarp on top of us,
and you look out and see if you can see anybody."

The boy crawled out of the hole and looked around.
He didn't see anybody.
He went to his mother's camp.
His mother was sleeping there with her neck chewed off.
His brothers too.

Their necks were chewed from their bodies,
and they were lying where they were sleeping.
The little boy went to his oldest sister's camp—
the one who was married to the grizzly bear.
She was sitting there by a big, big fire
with her legs spread apart.
Her younger brother remembered her.

He went back to his sister in the hole.
He told her everything that had happened.
He was worried about how they were going to live after that.
He was afraid they would starve.

His older sister said—
"I'll make you a bow and arrows.
You see if you can get something."
"All right," the boy said.
"You go and see if you can kill our older sister," she said.
  So she made him a bow and arrows,
  and she came out of the hole too.
  They went to their older sister's camp.
  They talked to her.
"Why did you kill our mother and our brothers?
"What did you do that for?" they said.

"I'm a grizzly bear now. I'm not their sister.
  Those aren't any relations of mine.
  Besides—they killed my husband."
"Where's your heart?" they asked—
  and their sister opened her hand,
  and there was her heart pulsating away.

The boy shot through her other hand.
She fell on the fire,
and they put more wood on her
to make sure she wouldn't come alive again.
The woman and her brother ran outside.
They were worried about how they were going to live.
"We're the only people alive in this world,"
she told her brother.
"We may as well get married and have some children."

But her younger brother didn't want to—
it was his own sister.

He cried and cried.
So his sister said—
"I know! You run around the hill on this side,
and I'll run around the hill on the other side,
and if we meet in the middle, we'll get married."
So the younger brother ran around one side,
and his older sister ran around the hill on the other side,
and they met halfway around on the other side.

The woman put her arms around the boy.
"All right, we're going to get married.
You be my husband," she said.
But the boy still didn't want it.
He cried and cried.
"I have an idea," the woman thought.
"I'll paint around your eyes."
She got something, and she painted circles around his eyes.
That was for hunting.

That boy was too young to kill animals with a bow and arrow.
He didn't know how to make the arrowheads.
But every time he looked at an animal—
moose, bear, caribou, chicken—
it just dropped dead.

That woman must have been a medicine woman.
She must have known something about eyes.

And that boy didn't even touch that girl,
and she had a baby every year.
Every year till they had a big bunch of kids.
Then the brothers married the sisters,
and their children married each other,
and so on.

And that's how all the people in this world were made.
That's the end.

MISTACAYAWĀSIS,

BIG BELLY CHILD

▲

ROBERT BRIGHTMAN,
ANGELIQUE LINKLATER,
AND HENRY LINKLATER

INTRODUCTION BY ROBERT BRIGHTMAN

The narrative translated here was recorded at Brochet, the northern-most Cree community in Manitoba and one of several communities in northern Manitoba and Saskatchewan whose members identify themselves as Asinīskāwiðiniwak, "people of the country of abundant rock." Nomadic hunter gatherers, the Rock Cree entered the European fur trade as middlemen and trappers in the late seventeenth century, exchanging furs and meat for European goods. Throughout this period they lived in groups of two to five families, moving frequently to exploit different regions and resources. With the inception of dog traction and intensified food storage in the late 1800s, groups occupied small log-cabin settlements, the men making extended round trips into the bush to hunt and trap. A number of factors converged around 1950 to produce microurban reservation towns with band administration offices, schools, churches, stores, and nursing stations; most but not all Cree families have long since become permanent residents of such communities.

Television, comic books, and other media today coexist with the indigenous oral literature, the latter comprising a theoretically infinite number of narratives. At least in the communities with which I am familiar, children continue to learn Cree as their first language, and the prospects for the perpetuation of the indigenous language and literature appear favorable.[1] The unmarked term for story is *ācimōwin*, which refers inclusively to any variety of cohesive narrative. The noun *ācaðōhkīwin* refers more narrowly to a story exhibiting characteristics we call mythological, one situated in an earlier condition of the world and having as characters either anthropomorphic animals or other humanoid beings distinct in kind from modern humans. These narratives include stories about the trickster character Wīsahkīcāh and also, as in the example here, sagas in which heroic characters overcome formidable adversaries and perils. Stories of the *ācaðōhkīwin* class are understood, at least by many individuals, as representations of events that actually occurred: they are not fictions.

"Mistacayawāsis: 'big belly child' " was one of five stories I recorded as they were told by Mrs. Angelique Linklater during the winter of 1979. Retired at the time, Henry and Angelique Linklater occupied a log cabin several miles to the north of Brochet village. Mrs. Linklater, monolingual in Cree, was an accomplished storyteller, and her husband, multilingual in Cree, English, and French, was a patient and careful translator. I began by taping Mrs. Linklater's oral narrative. Each taping was followed, at the narrator's request, by a replay, during which we listened to the narrative. I then undertook a transcription of the Cree text, assisted by Mr. Linklater, who took control of the tape recorder and painstakingly redictated the passages that exceeded my command of Cree vocabulary. The transcription then provided the basis for a literal interlinear translation from Cree to English, again in collaboration with Mr. Linklater. A sample of this translation, with grammatical labeling, appears below.

The graphic representation of the Mistacayawāsis narrative that appears in this volume draws somewhat eclectically on certain conventions introduced and developed by Dell Hymes,[2] primarily in relation to Chinookan materials. Each line represents either a sentence of the text or a clause that introduces a new grammatical agent or subject. The dialogue of each character is set off on indented lines. Spaces between sequences of lines represent the narrative transitions signaled by Mrs. Linklater's use of the discourse particle *īkwāni*. I have elsewhere glossed *īkwāni* as "so" or "so then" but have left it untranslated here. *Īkwāni* occurs typically, although not exclusively, in the initial position of a sentence and, as the translation makes clear, indicates narrative transitions of diverse kinds, including changes of scene, action, characters, and focus from one interacting character to another. In addition, I have introduced line spaces to indicate those many transitions in the text that are seemingly comparable to those marked by the particle but from which it is absent. A more detailed analysis would indicate whether transitions with and without the particle exhibit systematic differences. The most inclusive units into which I have divided the text are based on transitions in narrative content. They are usually marked by *īkwāni* and involve a major shift in scene and the introduction of new characters or the reappearance of existing ones. I have given each of the ten sections titles drawn from the relevant span of the text. Further subcategorization is, of course, possible. The first three segments, for example, form a unit by virtue of the presence of the *witiko* ("cannibal") woman as the antagonist.

There has been, as yet, relatively little examination of the narrative and poetic functions of the grammatical categories (such as tense, mode, aspect, and case marking) specific to particular American Indian languages. In oral performances of myths and folktales, the narrator's choices from among "different ways of saying the same thing" directly influence how the audience interprets and appreciates the story. In the translation of "Big Belly Child," I have signaled how Angelique Linklater used one such strategy to indicate which character is in focus. In Cree and other Algonquian languages there is a grammatical contrast between the third-person referent upon whom the narrative is at that time most clearly focused (the proximate) and the other third-person referent or referents (the obviative[s]). The proximate third person can be characterized, in general terms, as being in the narrative foreground, the character whose perspective the narrator is adopting, whose actions he or she wishes to emphasize, or with whom he or she has maximal empathy. As the story unfolds, the focus shifts, of course, as different characters move in and out of the foreground. The translations signal these shifts by introducing spaces where the focus shifts and by highlighting with larger type the nouns and pronouns that refer to the proximate character. The following sentence demonstrates the latter form of signal:

1. Īkwāni   īkwa ōkō   iðiniwak kapīsiwinihk anima īkota ī-kostācik
   So then, then those people   in the camp, that   there, they fear him,

Mistahōōōwatimwa   anihi.
Great Howling Dog,   that one.

The obviative character is grammatically marked by the suffix *-a*. In sentence 1, *people* is proximate and *Great Howling Dog* is obviative, as indicated by the suffix *-a* (in boldface) that is attached to his name. Additionally, verbs are conjugated in such a way as to indicate the proximate or obviative status of their subjects and objects. The suffix *-ācik* (in boldface) on the verb for *fear* tells us that it is the people who fear Great Howling Dog and not the reverse.

2. Ispi pī-takosiniki māna ī-nipahāt mīna kā-mōwāt kahkiðaw
   When he comes, always he kills them, and he eats them, all

iðiniwa kapīsiwinihk īkwa awa Mistahōðōwatim.
people in a camp then, this Great Howling Dog.

In sentence 2, the proximate and obviative are reversed. Great Howling Dog is proximate, and *people* is now obviative, taking the suffix *-a*. The suffix *-āt* on the verbs for *kill* and *eat* indicates that Great Howling Dog is doing the killing and eating. Mrs. Linklater could have kept *the people* as proximate in sentence 2, but one can conjecture that the spectacular behaviors she here ascribes to Great Howling Dog prompted her to shift him into focus as the proximate character.

The social and natural landscape in which the narrative is positioned is one of transiently occupied winter camps, extended family networks, frequent hunting expeditions, and occasional encounters with hunger. Elements in the narrative that will strike the non-Cree reader as "mythological"—cannibal monsters, magical impregnation, caribou transformations, and the like—do not differ qualitatively from events and experiences that some Cree recall from the recent past or recognize as persisting into the present. The *witiko,* or cannibal monster, for example, into which the oldest sister transforms, is an entity that has figured in the personal experience of persons still living. Crees say that *witikos* were originally human beings, transformed into their monstrous condition by spirit possession, dream predetermination, or famine cannibalism. Like the oldest sister in the narrative, *witikos* acquire spiritual and physical strength that allows them to overcome their victims. Also like this character, some *witikos* are said to undergo lucid periods during which they lament their crimes and request execution.[3] Big Belly Child's magical impregnation of his future wife and the theme of the paternity test occur in other narrative contexts, contexts not limited exclusively to the mythological age.

Such spectacular events as the hero's use of a magically expanding knife, his autometamorphosis into a tall and handsome man (with Euro-Canadian phenotypes), and his transformation into a caribou do not exceed the capacities attributed to exceptionally powerful medicine men alive in the recent past. The use of the sweat lodge and the drum to secure magical objectives likewise figures in the contemporary practice of some individuals. From the perspective of the Cree, the narrative is an *ācaδδhkīwin*, a "myth," not because it includes such motifs but because it is temporally situated in a remote past, prior to the occupancy of the earth by modern humans. Certain events occurring during this epoch produced changes that thereafter became perpetual, persisting into the contemporary period of "modern" humans. Thus, when Big Belly Child, temporarily in the form of a caribou, survives an arrow wound, Mrs. Linklater has his wife assert formulaically that "in the future, when many people dwell here on the earth, they will often shoot the caribou just there, below the ribs" and that "they will never succeed in killing them when they strike them there."

To my knowledge no other versions of this narrative have been recorded from Cree or other sources, although three of its constituent episodes—the impregnation, the paternity test, and the hero's self-transformation—occur in an Ontario Ojibwa narrative in which they are ascribed to a dwarf character found in a tree.[4] Mis-ta-ta-o-wa-ses, the hero of a Plains Cree myth, is closely cognate in name, but the stories about him show no resemblance.[5] More than other stories I have heard from Crees, "Mistacayawāsis" exhibits simultaneously elements of tragedy, horror, adventure, comedy, and the miraculous, all within a morality play celebrating the successes of an (at first) unlikely hero and juxtaposing improper and correct conduct: murder and atonement, abandonment and rescue, the refusal and offer of food.

It is worth noting a dimension of meaning that Mr. Linklater reflectively ascribed to the story. He stated that the narrative contains three major disasters: the appearance of the murderous *witiko* woman, the appearance of the anthropophagous Great Howling Dog, and the hero's abandonment by his relatives. He speculated that these three calamities referred to and prophesied what he identified as the three primary health disorders to which the Cree people have been subject: the *witiko* disorder, widely believed to be the only disease prior to contact with whites; tuberculosis, which devastated many northern communities in the late nineteenth and early twentieth centuries; and cancer, whose occurrence many Crees today believe is increasing among them. Mr. Linklater's remarks exemplify the continually emergent relevance of the "old stories," their capacity to take on reference to new circumstances and historical experiences.

Pronunciation

ð is the *th* sound in *this*.

Vowels have the following approximate English equivalencies:

ō is the *oa* of *boat* or the *oo* of *boot*

o is the *u* in *put*

ā is the *o* in *pot* or the *a* in *pat*

a is the *u* in *but*

ī is the *ea* of *beat* or the *ai* of *bait*

i is the *i* in *bit*.

NOTES

1. Robert Brightman, *Ācaðōhkīwina and Ācimōwina: Traditional Narratives of the Rock Cree Indians,* Canadian Ethnology Service, Mercury Series Paper no. 113 (Ottawa: Canadian Museum of Civilization, 1989).

2. Dell Hymes, *"In Vain I Tried to Tell You": Essays in Native American Ethnopoetics* (Philadelphia: University of Pennsylvania Press, 1981) and "Use All There Is to Use" in *On the Translation of Native American Literatures,* ed. Brian Swann (Washington, D.C.: Smithsonian Institution Press, 1992).

3. See Robert Brightman, *Grateful Prey: Cree Human-Animal Relationships* (Berkeley: University of California Press, 1993).

4. James Stevens, *Sacred Legends of the Sandy Lake Cree* (Toronto: McClelland and Stewart, 1971), 64–65.

5. Verne Dusenberry, *The Montana Cree: A Study in Religious Persistence* (Uppsala, Sweden: Almqvist and Wiksells Boktryckeri, 1963), 260–66.

"That's Not the Meat I'm Hungry For"

Once then and long ago two brothers were married to two sisters.
They lived together there in a camp in the bush.
Really, those people loved one another.
The youngest sister had two young sons.

Ikwani,
it happens, while those two men were away hunting,
that eldest woman turned witiko.
   "I'm hungry," she said.
   "We have plenty of meat for you to cook if you're hungry."
   "No. That's not the meat I'm hungry for."

Ikwani,
she seized those two young boys, the children of her younger
   sister, and she murdered them.
Halfway she roasted them in the fire, and then, really, she ate
   them.
Their mother, that youngest sister, could do nothing.

Ikwani,
that young man (younger brother) returned to camp.
Really that witiko woman was immensely strong.
She threw him to the floor and murdered him and half-roasted
   him in the fire, and then, really, she ate him.
Only her younger sister that woman did not wish to kill because,
   perhaps, she yet loved her.

Ikwani,
in late evening that man (older brother), the husband of that
   witiko woman, returned to the camp.
He was able to divine before he came to a place what had
   happened there.
He came into the lodge.
   "I know everything that you have done here," he told her.
She tried to wrestle him down, but three times he threw her to
   the ground.

He was stronger than that witiko woman.
That witiko woman begged her younger sister, she whose
  children she had eaten, for help.
Her sister did not help her.

That man told her then,
  "I could kill you now, but you've already killed all those I love
    in this world, my brother and my nephews.
  Because of this, I'll let you overpower and kill me."

Ikwani,
she murdered him and only half-roasted him in the fire and ate
  him.

"We'll Go to Visit Our Parents and Brothers"

Close by, in the bush, the parents of the two sisters were camped
    with other people, and with them were their three young
    sons, the younger siblings of those two sisters.
That witiko woman could command her sister to do anything,
    and she could in no way resist.
  "We'll go," said that woman, "to visit our parents and
    brothers."

Ikwani,
they came there to that camp.
That old lady asked that witiko woman,
  "Where are your husband and your brother-in-law and your
    two nephews?"
  "They went off hunting," she answered, "and for two nights
    they will be camping away."
And really that youngest sister could say nothing.

Ikwani,
the following day, that witiko woman asked the oldest of her
  three young brothers to accompany her into the bush to hunt
  ptarmigan.
Really, that little boy was excited and happy to be doing that.
He carried with him a small bow and small arrows that the old
  man, his father, had made for him.

When she saw a ptarmigan, that witiko woman helped him aim his
  bow at it.
Really, that little boy was very excited about shooting the
  ptarmigan.

Ikwani,
she grabbed him around the neck, strangling him.
She murdered him and built a fire and half-roasted him and ate
  him.
And once again her younger sister could do nothing.

Ikwani,
they came back, in evening, to the camp.
  "Where is your younger brother?" those people asked them.
  "Lost far in the bush," said that witiko woman.
  "All day and into the evening, we sought him out."
Those people believed what she told them, and they mourned
    for the little boy.

Ikwani,
but one man among them thought to himself,
  "I wonder if this that she says is true?"

Ikwani,
the next day that witiko woman asked the next youngest to come
  out into the bush with her and hunt ptarmigan.
And all happened as before.
When that boy aimed at a ptarmigan,
that woman strangled him and half-roasted him and ate him.

That one man, he who doubted her story, thought that she
    might be doing something evil.
He followed them unobserved into the bush and watched
    everything that she did.
He ran back ahead of them to the camp and told the people,
  "She is witiko."

Ikwani,
the people took spears and bows and arrows and went through
  the bush to find that witiko woman.

Ikwani,
they shot their arrows and threw their spears at those two sisters.

▲

Ikwani,
they killed that younger sister, she who always stayed with that
    witiko woman, for they thought this of her:
  "She, too, is witiko."

But that witiko woman, really, the arrows and spears broke upon
    her body.
Really, all of her body was frozen into ice.
She had no fear at all of the spears and arrows.
  "I'll overcome all of you. I'll kill and eat all of you," she told
    them,
  "but not before I've finished eating my younger brother."

Ikwani,
she finished her eating and fought all of those people—perhaps
    twelve people—and killed them all.

And This Way He Killed That Witiko Woman

Ikwani,
before the fight the old lady concealed her youngest son in the
    spruce-bough flooring of their lodge.
And this was he who was named Mistacayawāsis, "Big Belly
    Child."
But his first name was Mahkicās, "Large of Girth."

That witiko woman knew exactly the number of those in that
    camp, and when she counted the dead, she said,
  "One is missing!"

Ikwani,
now she recovered her reasoning.
Once again, really, she became a human being.
She looked on what she had done.
That woman lamented for what she had done.
She went to the camp and found Big Belly Child under the spruce
    boughs in the lodge.
  "Really, I grieve for all I have done," she said to him.
  "There is only one way that I can be killed, and so I will tell
    you how you are to succeed in it.
  Take this small ax, and sever my little finger."
In her sickness her heart had grown small and come to lodge in
    her little finger.

"Don't be frightened," she told him, "if you strike the blow
and I scream because the ax does not immediately sever
my finger but only glances off it."

Ikwani,
Big Belly Child struck at her finger with the ax.
And it happened as she had said.
The ax glanced off her finger; that finger that was frozen into ice.
That woman screamed.
He was frightened.
He jumped back, dropping the ax.
  "You must strike one more time," she told him.
He struck again, and this time he severed the finger containing
  her heart.
And this way he killed that witiko woman, she who was his eldest
  sister.

Those People at That Camp Feared Great Howling Dog

Ikwani,
Big Belly Child left that place and traveled through the bush to
  another camp.
That old man, his mother's father, was living there, and also his
  grandmother on the other side was living there.

He spoke proudly when he strode into the camp and told those
  people that he had killed a witiko.
But none of those people believed him; all of them laughed at
  him.
All but his grandmother, who was kind to him.
And so he lived there with his grandmother.

Ikwani,
those people there in that camp feared Mistahōōōwatimwa,
  "Great Howling Dog."
When he came, this Great Howling Dog would kill and eat all
  the people in a camp.
The old man divined that Great Howling Dog was running
  toward them on its great dog trail leading across the frozen lake
  to the camp.

Along this great dog trail, where it traversed the lake, the people
   chopped out three holes and covered them with snow.
They hoped in this way to drown Great Howling Dog.

Ikwani,
Great Howling Dog came running toward them across the lake.
He fell through the ice into the first hole.

Ikwani,
he crawled out from the water and dried himself, rolling over and
   over in the snow.
The same at the second hole and at the third:
Great Howling Dog fell through the ice but crawled out and
   dried himself.

Ikwani,
he looked across the lake to the camp and, howling, came running
   forward.

Ikwani,
Big Belly Child said to them,
   "I myself will go out on the ice and kill it."
The people laughed and said,
   "He will be eaten in one bite."
Big Belly Child took a small knife from his sack.
   "I will kill it with this," he said.
They laughed at him.

Ikwani,
he went out on the lake, face-to-face with Great Howling Dog,
   who bounded forward.
He took out the little knife, and it grew forth and became three
   feet long.
He struck Great Howling Dog only lightly on the rib, and, truly,
   he killed him.

Now all the people in that camp were happy to see that Great
   Howling Dog was dead.

"Perhaps He Is the Father"

At a nearby camp a beautiful young woman was living.
Presently Big Belly Child loved her, wanted her for his wife.

▲

Ikwani,
he watched to see where she urinated and then urinated himself
   just at the same place.
Whenever she went into the bush, he followed and urinated in the
   same place.

Ikwani,
from this that young woman became pregnant and conceived.

All the men from those camps met together to divine who was the
   father.
In that time they determined the father by handing the baby
   around the circle.
The baby itself would urinate on the one who was its father.
One man there, *Macikaðawis,* "Good for Nothing," hated
   Big Belly Child.
Good for Nothing had already one wife, but he desired that
   young woman as his second wife.

Ikwani,
when they handed the baby around, he dribbled saliva on himself
   so as to be named the father.
Those men saw him do it and said,
   "Good for Nothing is not the father."
Big Belly Child stood watching outside the lodge door.
That old man, his grandfather, said disparagingly,
   "Give the baby to him. Perhaps he is the father."
Big Belly Child sat down in that circle of men.
They handed the baby over to him.
And, really, that baby began urinating before he had a good hold
   of it.
Truly, that baby wet all over his chest.

Ikwani,
they all knew that he was the father.

"What Does a Handsome Man Look Like?"

But, nevertheless, that young woman did not want Big Belly Child
   for her husband because, at that time, he was short and fat.
Always his grandmother would ask that young woman to come
   to their camp.

Always she refused, saying,
  "Big Belly Child is ugly."

Ikwani,
Big Belly Child built a sweat lodge.
He took a big drum into the lodge and built a fire.
He heated rocks and sweated himself and drummed.
He called out to his grandmother,
  "What does a handsome man look like?"
  "Kind of stout, with blue eyes and brown hair," she told him.

Ikwani,
really, he made a new appearance for himself in that sweat lodge.
Really he transformed himself into a handsome young man.
He came out, and his grandmother was astonished at his
  appearance.

Right away she went to the camp where that young woman was
    staying.
  "You should see the stranger who is staying at my camp," she
    said to her.

That young woman became curious.
Without being seen, she went there and observed Big Belly Child.
Really, she liked the way he looked, and she lived there with him
  as his wife.

"Leave Us Twelve Beaver Tongues"

Ikwani,
the food at those camps began to run short.
That old man, Big Belly Child's grandfather, hated him, and
    Good for Nothing also hated him.
  "He will not be capable of hunting," they said about him.

Ikwani,
when they were all but out of food, they moved to a lake far
  away, abandoning Big Belly Child and his grandmother and his
  wife.
They took with them all the food.

▲

"Leave us twelve beaver tongues," said Big Belly Child.
"He doesn't ask for much," said the old man.
"What can he do with beaver tongues?
Give him the tongues, if he wants them."

Ikwani,
they moved away.

Big Belly Child took those tongues into the lodge.
Right there he dug a hole in the snow beneath the pine boughs.
He put the twelve beaver tongues into the hole right there.
For a long time he waited there, drumming.

Ikwani,
water appeared at the bottom of the hole.
Up and down the water slopped in the hole just like the water in a
    beaver runway when beavers are swimming.
The old lady was almost crying because they had fasted for so
    long.
Then from the hole Big Belly Child extracted beavers.
Twelve beavers in all he pulled out from the hole.
    "Good," he said, "we will be able to feed ourselves now."

"Come Back to My Camp, and I Will Hunt for You"

Ikwani,
many days passed.
Big Belly Child knew that those people, those who had
    abandoned them, were starving.

Ikwani,
he told his grandmother to pack dry beaver meat in skin bags.

Ikwani,
he carried that dry meat through the bush to where the others
    were living at another lake.
Just outside their camp he hung the bag in a tree.
The first lodge he found belonged to Good for Nothing.

Good for Nothing looked pitiful from starvation.
He gazed on his genitals.
    "I wonder if I could eat them in order to live?" was what he

thought.
He didn't recognize Big Belly Child and wondered who he was.

Ikwani,
Big Belly Child went to the lodge of his wife's parents.
They didn't recognize him at first,
but then that old woman said,
    "It's our son-in-law."
He told them that all was well at his camp, that food was
        plentiful.
He told them about the dry meat he had brought.
He instructed them to send someone to retrieve it.

They sent Good for Nothing, but he was so weak he could hardly
    walk.
He wasn't able to lift the bag down and had to push it off the
    branch.
He reached down to the ground to pick it up but was so weak he
    fell over.
Finally he struggled to his feet and dragged the bag back to camp.

All those people, those who had been starving, ate that dry meat.

Ikwani,
Big Belly Child said,
    "Now I will go back to my camp.
    Eat the dry meat until you become strong.
    Then come back to my camp, and I will hunt for you."

"That Lead Caribou . . . Will Be Me, Myself"

Gradually, those people recovered their strength by eating the dry
    meat.
Finally they were strong enough to travel.
They moved to where Big Belly Child was living with his wife and
    grandmother.
They had many platforms filled with beaver meat there.

Ikwani,
those people had eaten most of the meat.
When the food was nearly gone, Big Belly Child told them he
    would go drive barren-ground caribou.

"Build a long brush caribou fence," he told them, "and group
   yourselves at the end of the fence with your spears and
   arrows.
Many caribou will pass through the fence.
The first caribou will be a large male leading all the others.
Don't shoot that lead caribou because it will be me, myself."

All the people listened and agreed,
except Good for Nothing was thinking this about him:
   "I intend to kill him."

The people did what he told them and built a long brush fence on
   the lake and waited at the end with their arrows and spears.
Truly, just as they were told, many caribou came down between
   the fences with a large male in the lead.
None of them fired on that lead caribou
except Good for Nothing, who fired an arrow and struck the
   caribou just below the ribs.
The arrow passed through the body, the point protruding from
   the other side.
That caribou fell to the ground.

Big Belly's wife was standing at the fence with their baby in a
   cradleboard.
She ran to where the caribou lay and, kneeling beside it, pulled
   the arrow from the body.
She held the arrow up in front of the people.
   "In the future, when many people dwell here on the earth, they
   will often shoot the caribou just there, below the ribs," she
   told them.
   "They will never succeed in killing them when they strike them
   there," she told them.

Then that caribou transformed into Big Belly Child, who stood up
   alive and unharmed.

"It Is Time for Me to Overcome Him"

The people killed many caribou, and for a long time there was meat
   in the camp.
At length they had eaten nearly all of it.

▲

Good for Nothing was always jealous of Big Belly Child.
He told the people,
  "I will drive the caribou just as Big Belly Child did."

Big Belly Child thought this of him:
  "He will always try to harm me.
  It is time for me to overcome him."

And, really, Good for Nothing did as the other had done.
He gave the people the same instructions and himself became a
    caribou and led other caribou through the fence.

Ikwani,
when that lead caribou passed by, Big Belly Child shot it with an
    arrow in the ribs.

Good for Nothing's wife stood there at the fence, carrying her
    child in a cradleboard.
That woman ran to where the caribou had fallen and kneeled and
    extracted the arrow from the ribs.
But when she pulled the arrow out, that caribou became a whisky
    jack—only a whisky jack, which flew immediately away.

Anima tīskwa. "That's finished."

WOLVERINE:

AN INNU TRICKSTER

▲

LAWRENCE MILLMAN

INTRODUCTION

The landscape of the Labrador Peninsula is made up of dense forests, no-man-fathomed barrens, Canadian Shield granites, and the labyrinthine trails of caribou. It is not a hospitable landscape, yet it is the home of a band of Native Americans, variously known as Naskapi, Montagnais, and Naskapi-Montagnais. Nowadays these people prefer to be called Innu, a word that simply means "The People" and is not to be confused with Inuit, which also means "The People." The Innu have had contact with the white world since the arrival of the Jesuits in the seventeenth century. Even so, they remain the least assimilated Native group in eastern North America.

I first scraped the surface of the Innu world in 1986, when I visited the ramshackle little village of Davis Inlet, Labrador. There I met a man named Uinipapeu Rich, a local jack-of-all-trades who was then serving as a paralegal. Seated in his small office in the jerry-built Innu Association Building, with a single, outdated law tome on his desk, Uinipapeu began telling me a story in English about the Innu culture hero–trickster Wolverine, "Why Certain Creatures Live in Rotten Tree Stumps." It took him a while to finish this story, not because he couldn't remember it, but because he kept breaking into uproarious laughter.

To understand Wolverine (or, as the Innu call him, Kwakwadjec), it is a good idea to know a little about the wolverine itself, the canniest, most indomitable member of the mustelid family. Wolverines are born survivors. They have no difficulty whatsoever managing the rigors of the Subarctic. Indeed, they're the only northern mammal whose fur actually turns darker, rather than lighter, in the winter. A wolverine will stand up to a bear ten times, no, twenty times its own weight. It is one of the few mammals capable of shading its eyes with its paws in order to see better. Wolverines are loners, self-sufficient, relentlessly nomadic—much like the Innu of thirty and forty or more years ago.

The mythological Wolverine has similar powers of survival. He created our present world to keep himself from drowning. Yet there is a flip side to his adaptability. It's the same flip side you find in other infinitely adaptable creatures whom the Native imagination has turned into trickster figures. Like the Haida Raven, the Oglala Iktoni, or the ubiquitous Coyote, Wolverine tends to make a mess of things. Either he's getting stuck inside a bear's skull, being duped by a woman, or mistaking his ass for caribou jerky. This aspect of Wolverine's behavior is at least as significant as his other attributes for the Innu. For it allows them to shrug off their own shortcomings by implying that it's not so bad, after all, to get stuck inside a bear's skull.

Wolverine stories are usually told in bunches, as if they formed a cycle. But they don't form a cycle like, for instance, the Wasah-ketchuk cycle of the Cree or the Nanabozho cycle of the Ojibwa. I daresay they're much closer to dirty jokes, which are often told in bunches too. Indeed, one storyteller, Apinam Ashini from Shesha-shui, would grace the stories he told me with scatological frills and furbelows of his own invention. In rendering Apinam's stories ("Wolverine Creates the World," "How Rocks Were Born," "Wolverine Eats His Own Ass," and "How Wolverine Tried to Destroy the World"), I had to determine what was genuine scatology, as it were, and what was more or less gratuitous.

This wasn't the only decision I made in composing English texts for Innu *atnukan* ("stories"). Sometimes I would hear a version of a story that was livelier, albeit less obviously traditional, than another version. Sometimes a Davis Inlet version would be slightly different from a Sheshashui version. Rather than print every version I heard, I tried to come up with a sort of protoversion, one that would get at the heart of a story even if it obliged me to use my own words. "How Wolverine Got Stuck in a Bear's Skull," for example, was synthesized from versions told by John Poker, Tshinish Pasteen, and Thomas Pastitshi, all from Davis Inlet.

As befits an endlessly creative character like Wolverine, I tried to be flexible in my renderings. One story, "How Wolverine Tried to Destroy the World," I heard in English and set to paper almost exactly as I heard it. Others, like "The Giant Skunk," I translated freely from Inueimun, the dialect of Eastern Cree spoken by the Innu (the Innu and the Cree, however, find each other's languages almost unintelligible). Occasionally I would use a Sony tape recorder to take down a story; more often I'd rely on note-taking or my own ability to recall a story's salient features at the expense of mnemonic devices or localisms, for tape recorders espouse a literal-mindedness alien to the spirit of Native American storytelling.

Like other languages in the macro-Algonquian linguistic phylum, Inueimun leans heavily on verbs and verb constructions. Whereas an English speaker might say, "It's lousy weather," a speaker of Inueimun will say, "It lousy weathers." That sort of tortured syntax is fine in the original, where it isn't tortured at all, but not much fun to encounter in English. It has the additional drawback of making one's Native informants sound a little demented. Thus, I have chosen a fairly standard vernacular for my renderings. Likewise, I've tried to convey an oral style in a readable written format—if a story falls easily on the ears, it should also be easy to read—without descending into the self-conscious simplicity of all too many folkloristic renderings.

Most Innu storytelling happens away from the settlements, usually around a winter campfire in the bush. Before a story can be told, the teller has to make sure there aren't any evil spirits lurking nearby, or else his story will attract them in much the same way the scent of blood attracts a predator. Wolverine stories, on the other hand, are told anywhere and at any time, since they tend to be anecdotal rather than ritualized. Also, they invite the one response that makes life in an unhappy, government-sanctioned community livable: laughter.

Long, long ago was a time of great floods. Almost the whole world lay underwater. Wolverine was able to keep dry only by leaping from stone to stone. He said to himself, "If these floods get any worse, even my stepping-stones will be submerged, and that'll put an end to my wandering, perhaps my life, too."

So he called a meeting of all the water animals. He asked each to help him save the world from drowning.

First he talked to Otter. "Dive down, Otter," Wolverine said, "and bring me some ground."

Otter dived down, but he came up without any ground. He said he couldn't see anything down there except weeds and a few fish.

Next he talked to Beaver. He said, "If you bring up some ground, I will find a pretty little wife for you."

Beaver also went down, but he didn't bring back any ground either. "I can't swim deep enough to reach the bottom," he gasped, "and as for a wife, I'd rather live without one than drown."

So Wolverine asked Muskrat to bring him some ground. "I'll try," Muskrat said, "but only if you tie a thong to my leg."

The thong was tied, and Muskrat jumped into the water. He was down there for quite a while. "I hope he didn't drown," Wolverine thought. He pulled up the rope, and when he did, up came the thong . . . without Muskrat.

Too bad, thought Wolverine. That means only water, water, and more water from now on.

But just when he had given up, Muskrat surfaced. His mouth was so full of ground that he couldn't talk. Nor could he breathe. Wolverine put his lips to Muskrat's ass and blew as hard as he could. Out came the ground from Muskrat's mouth, more and more ground, heaps and heaps of it, seemingly without end.

This ground is the very earth we walk on today.

Once upon a time there weren't any rocks in the world, only one very large boulder. Wolverine went over to this boulder and said, "I bet I can outrun you, friend."

To which the boulder replied, "That's probably true, for I can't run at all. In fact, I've been sitting in this same place for as long as I can remember."

"*Can't run?* But even Lemming can run. Even Ant can do it. You must be the lowest of the low, friend."

And with that Wolverine gave the boulder a strong kick. The boulder did not like this kick, or Wolverine's insults, so it began rolling toward him.

"Well, at least you can *move,*" Wolverine laughed, and he took off down a hill with the boulder rolling after him.

"Are you pleased now?" the boulder said.

"I am, but I wish you'd slow down. You're hurting my heels."

"I thought you wanted to see me run. . . ."

Suddenly Wolverine fell down, and the boulder rolled right on top of him. "Get off! You're breaking my body!" he yelled. But the boulder just sat there and went on breaking his body.

Now Wolverine called on his brothers to help him.

"Wolf, get rid of this damn boulder!"

"Fox, get rid of this damn boulder!"

Neither Wolf nor Fox would help him. They said it was only fair, since he'd insulted the boulder, that he be stuck under it.

"Frog, come here and help me get rid of this boulder!"

Frog tried to lift the boulder, but his hands were so slippery that he couldn't move it at all.

"Mouse, can you help me?"

"Sorry, brother," said Mouse, "but I'm too small."

At last Wolverine called on his brother Thunderstorm. Thunderstorm took one look at him and roared with laughter. "What are you doing under that boulder, brother?"

"Being silly again," sighed Wolverine. "Now will you please help me get up?"

Thunderstorm called on Lightning, who zigzagged down from the sky and struck the boulder *bamm!* It broke into many, many little pieces.

That's how rocks were born.

From then on Wolverine said only kind things to these rocks.

For he did not want his body broken again.

Wolverine was searching around for a hunting partner. He came to a place where two women, a mother and her daughter, had put up their camp. The daughter said she would hunt with him.

"But you're a woman."

"Not really. It's just that someone has been conjuring with me, and now I look like this."

"If you're a man," Wolverine said, "let's see you piss."

She squatted down.

"Just as I thought," Wolverine said. And he wandered on. But wherever he wandered, he couldn't seem to find a man who would hunt with him. Indeed, he couldn't find a man—any kind of man—in all the world. He thought to himself, "Maybe men haven't been made yet. That's something for me to do one of these days."

But he still needed a hunting partner. So he went back to the women's camp. "Pack up your things," he told the women, "and come with me."

The first night, Wolverine offered the women caribou heads for supper. The daughter took her head and tried to pull apart the jaws. She kept pulling and pulling until she pulled so hard that she fell over on her back.

"*Ehe!*" Wolverine exclaimed. "I can see you're not a man." And he leaped right on top of her.

"Don't let him do that," said the mother to her daughter. "You'll have a baby, and then you won't be able to hunt at all."

But the girl had already stuck Wolverine's penis between her legs. The old woman grabbed the penis from her. "I'm your mother," she said, sticking it between her own legs, "so I'm supposed to go first." When she'd finished, the daughter took it and stuck it back between her legs. And when she'd finished, the old woman grabbed it again.

Next morning Wolverine got up early to go hunting. As the two women were still asleep, he decided to hunt by himself. But he was so tired from the night before that he only got as far as a little clearing near his tent. Then he lay down on the moss and fell asleep.

Along came a spider, a caterpillar, and an ant. They saw Wolverine's penis sticking up in the air. The spider took a whiff of it and said, "There's a woman around here somewhere."

"A woman! A woman!" shouted the others.

And off they all went to find her.

A while later Wolverine woke up. What's my blanket doing in the sky? he said to himself. Then he realized his penis was holding it up there. "Little brother," he said to the penis, "it seems as if you would like some more work . . . even after last night." So he returned to the two women in the tent.

The women were stretched out asleep, as before. Wolverine started to wake them, but then he noticed the spider, the caterpillar, and the ant crawling in and out of their vaginas. And as they crawled, they sang: "What a sweet taste! How lovely! We can't get enough of it!"

Wolverine reached down and seized all three of them.

"Hey! Why did you do that, short legs?" they cried.

"Because creatures like you aren't allowed in women's vaginas, that's why," Wolverine said, adding, "You want a place to crawl? Well, I'll give you a place to crawl."

Whereupon he flung them into the stump of a rotten tree.

"That's where you'll be living from now on, friends," he said.

And in rotten tree stumps all three of them have lived to this very day.

One winter Wolverine was wandering through slush. Everywhere he went, he'd sink up to his thighs in this slush. He couldn't cross rivers because there was never enough ice on them. Nor could he cross lakes because there was always too much water on the ice. At last he said, "What's wrong with Tciwetinowinu? If he really wants to prove himself a man, he ought to send a real winter."

A while later Wolverine came upon an enormous man dressed entirely in white. The man said, "I'm Tciwetinowinu. I hear you're not satisfied with the weather."

Wolverine repeated what he'd said about the winter not being cold enough.

Tciwetinowinu smiled. "I'll see what I can do," he said.

Next summer it was very warm. Fall was also warm. Winter started out as if it was going to be warm too.

"Tciwetinowinu is a woman," thought Wolverine.

Then snow started coming down in thick clumps, and Wolverine's camp was buried. Also, it grew very cold.

One day Tciwetinowinu dropped by for a visit. Wolverine's teeth were rattling, his feet were nearly frozen, but he would not let on that he was cold.

"How do you like this weather, friend?" Tciwetinowinu asked.

"It's all right," Wolverine said, "but I was hoping for something a little colder."

Next day the snow came down in even thicker clumps. Then the snow stopped, and it grew so cold that branches were snapping off trees. Wolverine sat in front of his fire, pouring grease on it. Tciwetinowinu dropped by for another visit.

"How do you like the weather now?"

As before Wolverine would not give in. Instead he began to tell his guest all the gossip he'd heard that year—who'd stolen the most wives and that sort of thing. And as he talked, he kept pouring grease on the fire.

Tciwetinowinu was beginning to melt. On and on Wolverine gossiped, even as his guest was melting away.

At last Tciwetinowinu said, "You're stronger than I am, friend. You have beaten me at my own tricks. There's nothing for me to do now but say good-bye."

He walked out of Wolverine's tent, and the very moment he left, the cold became less severe.

And so it is that ever since that time, winters have been winters, neither too cold nor too hot, just right.

One day a giant skunk came to a camp and sprayed two old women. One of the women said to the other, "That's a mighty powerful fart you've got there, sister."

"I haven't farted, sister. But your fart is a killer. . . ."

And soon both women were dead from the smell.

Now the skunk moved on to where a man was frying bear fat to make oil. The man said to himself, This fat smells real bad. *Kue!* I seem to smell bad myself. . . .

Before long he was dead too.

Through the camp went the skunk, spraying women and children, babies and old people, even dogs. Whoever got sprayed fell dead in his tracks. At last only the headman and his two sons were left alive. The headman said, "We must get our brother Wolverine to help us. Otherwise we'll die too."

So they visited Wolverine in his den. "I've killed wolves, bears, even human beings themselves," said Wolverine, "so I can easily get rid of a mere skunk."

But when Wolverine saw all those dead bodies, he changed his mind. Too late! The giant skunk was already advancing toward him. Suddenly it turned around and aimed its ass in his face. Wolverine clamped down his jaws directly on the skunk's ass and kept them clamped, knowing that if he let go, the skunk would release its fumes, and he'd die.

Now the headman and his sons came out from their hiding place. "Good job, Wolverine, old friend!" they said. Then they began hitting the skunk's head with their clubs. They hit its head again and again until it collapsed on the ground. Wolverine eased his jaws. And just before the skunk died, it sprayed him in the face.

"It got me! It got me!" Wolverine cried.

He ran right down to the sea and jumped in. There he washed himself until he'd managed to wash off all the smell . . . into the sea.

And ever since Wolverine washed there, seawater has smelled bad, tasted bad, and been of no use whatsoever to anyone.

One day Wolverine saw a flock of geese flying across the sky. "If geese can fly," he told himself, "I ought to be able to fly too." He flapped his front paws, but nothing seemed to happen. He flapped them again, but again nothing happened. So he visited some geese and asked them to teach him how to fly.

The geese dressed him in feathers and gave him a pair of wings no one was using, and soon he was flying just like a goose.

"You must beware of human beings, brother," the geese told him, "for they will kill you if they see you."

Said Wolverine, "I haven't been afraid of human beings before, and I won't start being afraid of them now."

So he flew as he pleased until he flew over a camp. Down in this camp he saw an old woman. "Ah," he said, "it's one of those stupid human beings." And he shouted, *"Stupid human being! Stupid human being!"*

The old woman took up her bow and shot an arrow, which went right through one of Wolverine's wings. While he was trying to shake loose this arrow, she shot an arrow into his other wing. He plummeted down to where the old woman was standing. She dropped her leggings and squatted over him, saying:

"I've always wanted to shit on a wolverine."

Wolverine said to her, "Don't shit on me, grandmother! I'll find you a partridge for supper, a hare, anything, only don't shit on me!"

The old woman shat all over him.

That's when Wolverine decided to give up flying.

So it was told long ago.

For a long time Wolverine had eaten only lemmings and shrews. He craved fat, real fat, with lots of grease. So when he noticed a big she-bear prowling around, he formed a plan to get her into his stewpot.

"How are you doing, sister?" he said.

"Why are you calling me 'sister'?" the bear replied. "I'm a bear, and you're a wolverine, two entirely different creatures."

"A wolverine? Your eyesight seems to be failing you, sister. I'm a bear just like you. Indeed, I'm your brother."

"Your legs are too short for you to be a bear."

"Admit it, sister. You're losing your eyesight. Why, I bet you can't even see that patch of ripe berries over there."

He pointed to a barren hillside.

"I see only moss and rock. . . ."

Now Wolverine conjured berries all over the hillside. The two of them went over there. The bear exclaimed, "How did your eyes get to be so good?"

Said Wolverine, "Our father used to squeeze berry juice into my eyes. And as everyone knows, berry juice improves the eyesight."

"Think you could squeeze some into my eyes?"

"I'll be glad to, sister. But first you must lie down."

The bear did as she was told.

"Next you must remember this: your eyes will get worse before they get any better."

"I'll remember, brother."

And so Wolverine began squeezing berries into the bear's eyes. The juice blinded her.

"You're doing fine, just fine, sister," he said. He grabbed his lance and pierced her heart with it.

"That was almost too easy," he said to himself.

After Wolverine had dressed the bear's carcass, he got an urge to eat the brains. Usually he left brains for dessert, but now all he wanted to do was crack the skull and eat them. However, the skull would not crack. Even when he threw it against a rock, it wouldn't crack.

"Well," he thought, "I'll just have to conjure myself into a maggot."

That's exactly what he did. Then he crawled right in through an eye socket and began sucking on the brains. He sucked . . . and sucked . . . and sucked. And he grew bigger . . . and bigger . . . and bigger.

At last Wolverine was such a big maggot that he couldn't crawl out of the eye socket.

"Help!" he cried. "I'm trapped inside a bear's skull!"

But no help came. For who would ever want to help a maggot?

"I suppose I'll starve to death now," Wolverine thought.

But he didn't starve to death. Instead he got thinner and thinner until he was thin enough to crawl out the eye socket. Once he was out of the socket, he got back his old shape again. And not having eaten since he ate the last of the brains, he was now very hungry.

"It's a good thing I have all that bear meat," Wolverine told himself.

But where was this bear meat? He couldn't seem to find it anywhere. He even peered under rocks to see if he'd cached it, but it was nowhere to be seen. That's because a wolf had found the meat and dragged it off while Wolverine was stuck inside the skull.

So now Wolverine went back to eating lemmings and shrews.

And he never conjured himself into a maggot again.

Once it happened that Wolverine couldn't stop farting. And these farts were scaring away all the game. "Shut up!" he told his ass.

"You shut up," the ass replied, "or else stop eating so much moss. That's why you're farting all the time."

"No, *you're* why I'm farting all the time, friend, and I'm going to punish you for it."

So he heated a large stone and sat down on it until he'd burned his ass to a reddish crisp.

"You're killing me!" cried the ass.

"Maybe that'll teach you not to fart when I'm trying to hunt," Wolverine said.

Over the next few days his ass began to heal, and one of the scabs fell off. Ah, thought Wolverine, a piece of dried meat. Just my luck that someone dropped it. He picked up the scab and ate it, saying, "*Um-m-m,* not bad at all . . ." Later another scab fell off, and he ate that one too. And then another. And another.

So it was that Wolverine lived all winter by eating his own ass.

And so Wolverine made the world. But once he tried to get rid of it. I'll tell you about that.

It was winter and very cold. Wolverine didn't have any wood, so he was burning bones for their fat. Then he ran out of bones too. "Well," he said, "maybe I can find some sort of female who'll keep me warm." A while later a pretty young girl showed up at his camp. Wolverine said to himself, "I'll get under her dress tonight." He invited her to share some caribou hearts with him.

"Only if you cook them," she said.

"I don't have any wood," he replied, "no bones either."

"Well," she told him, "if you won't cook them, I'm not going to eat them." And off she went on her snowshoes.

Now Wolverine was so angry that he started tearing up the earth, grabbing it and throwing pieces into the sky. Most of these pieces just came back down again . . . they're the mountains. But some stayed up there . . . never came down . . . stayed up there forever. That's the Milky Way.

Isn't it wonderful how things came about?

THE
NORTH
PACIFIC
COAST

JOHN SKY'S

"ONE THEY GAVE AWAY"

▲

ROBERT BRINGHURST

INTRODUCTION

A hundred miles off the northern coast of British Columbia lies a forested archipelago less than two hundred miles long, though its shoreline extends for something closer to four thousand miles. Maps and gazetteers persist in labeling these islands the Queen Charlottes, after the wife of George III of Great Britain. Most residents (and the local tribal government) now call them Haida Gwaii, "the Islands of the People." Older speakers of the Haida language call them by an older Haida name, Xhaaidlagha Gwaayaai, "the Islands at the Boundary of the World."

People who depend on hunting and foraging are almost always mobile, while gardeners and farmers stay put and build towns. In Haida Gwaii, as elsewhere on the Northwest Coast of North America after the last glaciation, this rule ceased to hold. Shellfish are there for the taking twice each day, when the tide recedes, and salmon, halibut, cod, herring, eulachon, sea lion, seal, and other species pass like an edible calendar through the maze of inshore waters. The Haida of precolonial times planted no crops, and yet they lived, like wealthy farmers, in substantial towns. The rich tradition of Haida visual art and oral literature is simultaneously rooted in the powerful social forces of the village and in the hunter's acutely personal relations with the wild. It is also rooted in the constant presence of the sea. Manna does not descend from heaven; it emerges from the waves. And the primary realm of the gods, in Haida cosmology, is not celestial; it is submarine.

The Haida divide both the gods and themselves into two sides, or moieties, known by their primary emblems: Raven and Eagle. The laws of marriage and inheritance, the means of commemorating the dead, and other essentials of the social order are framed on this basis. The result is a complex web of reciprocal relations between the two sides. Each side is divided in turn into a number of matrilineal families, or clans. Rank within the family is hereditary, and family ownership of fishing grounds and other resources is recognized. Status nevertheless depends in the long term on the character, skill, and luck of individual hunters and traders. The superstructure is very nearly feudal, but the base is not. As in any hunting culture, the system rests not on control of the land as such but on control of the human demands that are placed on it.

Europeans intruded on this world at the end of the eighteenth century, first as fur traders, then as direct exploiters, taking the whale oil, timber, gold, and fish. After a hundred years of European contact, the indigenous economy and culture were in ruins. Island sea otter and caribou had been hunted to extinction; whales were badly overhunted, salmon and cod were overfished, old-growth forest was disappearing rapidly, and disease—chiefly smallpox—had killed about 90 percent of the human population. Of the fifty or sixty major villages, four—two in Haida Gwaii and two newer settlements in Alaska—were still inhabited. One was the site of a cannery; the other three were the sites of Christian missions. Fewer than a thousand Haida survived, and many of those had scattered to the mainland, seeking wages. Under these conditions a young and gifted anthropologist, John Reed Swanton, arrived to spend a year taking dictation.

Classical Haida literature consists of the roughly 250 narratives and songs Swanton recorded, in two distinct dialects of Haida, during the winter of 1900–1901. Swanton prepared all his Haida texts for publication, and a large number were published as planned.[1] Many others were issued only in English translation,[2] while the originals languished in manuscript. The most important unpublished collection is held by the American Philosophical Society Library, in Philadelphia,[3] and it includes the Haida text translated here.

No other extensive recording of Haida oral literature was undertaken until the 1970s. Some of the songs and stories Swanton heard in 1900 are still in circulation, and new ones are still made, but a century of churchgoing, Bible study, and English-language schooling, abetted in recent years by television and films, has also left its mark on the narrative tradition.[4]

One of the finest Haida poets Swanton met was an old man known to his friends as Skaai (this is the Haida name for the small mollusk known in English as a periwinkle). Skaai belonged to a family called the Qquuna Qiighawaai ("descended from [the village of] Qquuna") of the Eagle moiety. For most of Skaai's life, the head of this family lived in the village of Ttanuu, just south of Qquuna, in southeastern Haida Gwaii. Skaai was a member of his household.

Names are an important form of wealth among the Haida, and Christian baptism had its attraction, even for nonbelievers. In January 1894, Skaai too allowed himself to be baptized by a visiting Methodist missionary. He must have been in his sixties then and was probably recognized as the best surviving male myth teller from the southern part of the islands. Knowingly or otherwise, the visiting preacher christened him John. By this means Skaai acquired the name of another fisherman turned symbolist poet and myth teller, and one whose totem matched his own. Saint John's evangelical emblem, the eagle, is also Skaai's primary family crest. By the late 1890s, when he moved with the other survivors from Ttanuu into the mission village of Skidegate, Skaai was known to both whites and the younger Haidas as John Sky.

"One They Gave Away" is one of thirteen narrative poems, or stories, dictated by old John Sky to young John Swanton. To the best of my knowledge, no other versions of this story have been recorded in any language or at any time; yet the story does not exist in isolation. Its central characters are known throughout the Northwest Coast; it is part of the large and living body of Haida mythology; and in John Sky's mind it was only a third of an evening's work. Skaai liked to tell stories in sets, or suites, the way many solo musicians like to play, and he told this story as the opening movement in a suite of three. The two stories he joined to it are set in Tsimshian country, and both are well-known in Tsimshian versions. Swanton, in fact, protested that these tales had nothing to do with one another, but Skaai insisted the link was real.

Swanton was looking for continuity of character or setting, which is scant. But structural and thematic echoes abound. A close analysis of the relations among the three stories would fill many pages, but the rudimentary outlines are as follows:

· In the present story the daughter of a chief who lives in the islands comes of age and is ready to marry. When all suitors are refused, the son of a chief who lives on the floor of the sea abducts her. A servant locates her lying mindlessly in a cave in the other world. This exploratory voyage or dream, which occupies much of the story, involves the death and resurrection of the girl's mother. The girl's two brothers (one of whom is very young) then take superhuman wives. One marries Mouse Woman; the other marries a powerful shaman who is unnamed. These women take charge of the expedition to reclaim the girl. Back at home the girl bears a child who is her father-in-law—her abductor's father—reincarnate. In accordance with his instructions, she returns this child to the sea, midway between the islands and the mainland.

· In the second movement of the suite, the wife of a chief who lives on the mainland refuses food. A creature from the forest kills her, enters her skin, and returns in her stead to the village, eating like a fiend. The woman's two sons (one of whom is very young) then marry superhuman wives (Mouse Woman and another, unnamed, who is a powerful shaman's daughter). These women take charge of a voyage to find and revive the boys' mother and to kill the impostor.

· In the third movement the shaman's daughter from the second story has borne her husband seven boys and a girl. The boys are married; the girl is not; and the children have settled, with their mother, on a coastal island just across a narrow strait from a larger town. When the eldest brother dies in an accident, the cause is divined as his wife's infidelity. This suspicion is confirmed, and the youngest brother kills the adulterer, whose father is the chief of the opposite town. This murder is discovered, war ensues, and the six remaining brothers are killed. Their mother and sister escape alone into the trees. There the mother offers her daughter in marriage. Animal suitors emerge from the forest and are rejected one by one. The son of a chief who lives in the sky then presents himself, is accepted, and marries the girl. In the world above the clouds, she bears eight sons and two daughters. (The numbers five and ten, like the number two, are of special importance in Haida mythology.) These children return to earth, resettling their deceased uncles' town. War breaks out again with the town across the channel. The eight brothers are fine warriors, and both sisters have miraculous powers as healers; even so, they are beaten back. The youngest brother seeks their celestial grandfather's aid, and the grandfather drops a deadly cloud on his grandchildren's opponents. Here the story ends.

Human beings, in Haida, are called *xhaaidla xhaaidaghaai,* "surface people," or, in the language of the poets, *xhaaidla xitiit ghidaai,* "ordinary surface birds." This idea is widespread in Native American philosophy. The corresponding Navajo term, for example, is *nihokáá dine'é,* "earth-surface people." But the Haida term evokes in particular the surface of the sea. The story of "One They Gave Away" is a map locating the world of surface people in relation to the world beneath the waves, which is of special concern to the Haida. The full narrative suite, or triptych, extends that map to include the forest and the sky. We can pass from one world to another, according to these stories, by paddling a canoe across the horizon or by making a moral choice.

This is the first story Skaai chose to tell John Swanton and only the third Haida text Swanton transcribed; not surprisingly there are glitches in the transcription. But I think Skaai chose this story for a reason. Skaai himself was multilingual, fluent in Haida and Tsimshian at least. He knew that riding a story across the boundary of translation can be nearly as informative as crossing under the sky's rim—and that it can even pose similar risks.

Skaai had spent his lifetime watching a long and, in more than one sense, inhuman cultural war. The old matrilineal order was centered on reciprocal relations between Raven people and Eagle people and between human beings and the sea. Skaai had seen this system crushed under the force of insatiable greed and then displaced by a new order, patrilineal and fixated on the powers of a father in the sky. Even the pun that the new language makes of Skaai's name records this transition. The war he had witnessed was a catastrophe on a scale the older myth tellers, who taught him his art, had never known. Yet I think they had left him a means with which to address it.

Skaai was an oral poet in a mesolithic culture. He spoke his stories in a supple, stylized language, but the style is of an oral, not a literary, kind. I call these stories poetry because they are dense, crisp, and full of lucid images whose power is not confined by cultural fences—and because they are richly patterned. But the patterns are syntactic and thematic more than rhythmic or phonemic. For all the acoustic beauty of these poems, that is not where their obvious formal order resides. They are distinguished by a thinkable *prosody of meaning* more than by an audible prosody of sound. The language is not verse (in the familiar Indo-European sense) any more than it is prose, and it has no established typographic form because it has not yet been absorbed, like the language of Greek and Hebrew oral poets, into a literate tradition.

We know that Skaai was an animated performer, because Swanton wrote down some of his cries, chuckles, hoots, stretched syllables, and other vocal gestures; and we know it from his handling of dialogue. He uses forms like "he said" and "she said" very rarely, much less often than do most other Haida myth tellers. Clearly he dramatized dialogue more than he narrated it. But there is a phrase that appears more frequently in Skaai's work than anywhere else in the Haida canon: *wansuuga,* "they say," or "it is said." He uses it shrewdly, to distinguish between his own fallibility and the durable truth of the myth and to emphasize certain passages by slowing the pace of events. He also uses it—the twinkle in his eye is clearly audible—to dance back and forth across the boundary between the credible and the outlandish. Speech itself is neither verse nor prose, and myth itself is neither fact nor fiction. Myth is a species of truth that precedes that distinction. But even in Skaai's world it must wear the appearance of one or the other, and Skaai can skip at will between them. I have therefore made it a point, in my translation, not to downplay, omit, or relocate these marks of oral style.

But how should one read a poem that was never meant to be written—a story carved in the air like spoken music, a voice in the dark that could only be stored as a light in the mind? The answer is clear. This oral voice, masquerading as written text, should be respected for what it is, and that means reading the text aloud.

Skaai's language is simple and direct, but there are several basic terms that have substantially different meanings in his world than they are likely to have for his readers. I have listed a few of them here.

Cape, blanket, or *robe.* Four or five different types of garments are mentioned in the story, and three are of special importance. (1) The cedar-bark cape *(qqaaix)* has remarkable powers in this narrative, but it was an everyday garment in precolonial times. Woven red-cedar bark is breathable, waterproof, comfortable, and warm. (2) The figured blanket *(naaxiin)* is what is now commonly known as a Chilkat blanket: an ornate, fringed cape bearing a stylized portrayal of an animal, woven of mountain goat wool and yellowcedar bark.[5] (3) The sky blanket, or cloud blanket *(qwiighaalgyaat),* is a cape of white mountain goat wool, plainwoven or with stylized rain clouds added in black. Sky blankets are more widely known now as Raven's-tail blankets, a translation of their Tlingit name.[6]

In real life capes or robes of all the kinds discussed are normally worn one at a time. In this story, where the number two is of great importance (just as it is in the Haida social order), blankets are worn in pairs. I can think of no other Haida narrative in which this happens—but I am intrigued to know that one of the few surviving *qwiighaalgyaat* (the Swift robe, now in the Peabody Museum of Archaeology and Ethnography, Harvard University) is woven in such a way that, when worn, it appears to be two blankets in one.[7]

Canoe. A Haida canoe *(tluu)* is an oceangoing redcedar dugout, typically thirty to sixty feet long and four to eight feet in the beam. The crew and passengers might number anywhere from five to thirty. Smaller dugouts were used for solo travel. Some Haida had surely seen the skin boats of the Eyak, Aleuts, and Yupiit, but the self-propelled harbor-seal canoe *(xhuut tluu)* mentioned in the story has no obvious counterpart in real life.

Grease. *Tau* is edible grease or thick oil, usually from eulachon. It is eaten like mayonnaise on dried berries or fish. Here it appears only in the metaphor *gudaagha tau la gutga'istlghaayang,* "he thought grease into [her] mind." This is of course to say he transformed her mind into an opaque and turgid mass, like congealed fish oil.

House. In Skaai's experience a proper house *(na)* was a solid, square structure with a gable roof sloping gently to the central smoke hole. The frame was made of enormous redcedar posts and beams, and the walls were of redcedar planks, vertically set. Light and air could leak through the chinks, but there were no windows, and there was only one door. The house of Skaai's family head at Ttanuu, for example, was forty-eight feet square and about twenty feet high at the central beam. An area about thirty feet square—the entire center of the house—was excavated to a depth of several feet, with the walls descending in one or two tiers. At the center of this sunken gallery was the fire. Before the smallpox epidemics the typical population of such a house would have been twenty to thirty people. The head of the house had his private quarters at the rear, often separated from the rest by a painted wooden screen. But the submarine house in this story, in which the floor descends in *ten* tiers to the fire and a fleet of canoes can pass through the smoke hole, is bigger than any house Skaai or his friends could have seen outside their dreams.

Guide to Pronunciation

Doubled vowels are lengthened, and doubled consonants are glottalized. The *x* is a velar fricative, like *ch* in the German name Fichte. *Gh, q,* and *xh* are uvular *g, k,* and *x;* in other words, they are like *g, k,* and *x* pronounced farther back toward the throat. *Xh,* therefore, is like the *ch* in Bach.[8]

NOTES

1. John Reed Swanton, *Haida Texts: Masset Dialect,* Publications of the Jesup North Pacific Expedition, vol. 10:2 (Leiden, Holland: E. J. Brill, 1908) and *Haida Songs,* published with *Tsimshian Texts: New Series* by Franz Boas in Publications of the American Ethnological Society no. 3 (Leiden, Holland: E. J. Brill, 1912).

2. John Reed Swanton, *Haida Texts and Myths: Skidegate Dialect,* Smithsonian Institution, Bureau of American Ethnology Bulletin no. 29 (Washington, D.C., 1905), and *Contributions to the Ethnology of the Haida,* Publications of the Jesup North Pacific Expedition, vol. 5:1 (Leiden, Holland: E. J. Brill, 1905).

3. Franz Boas Collection of Manuscripts, N1:5 (Freeman no. 1543), American Philosophical Society Library, Philadelphia.

4. For examples of recent Haida narrative, see Carol Eastman and Elizabeth Edwards, *Gyaehlingaay: Traditions, Tales and Images of the Kaigani Haida* (Seattle: Burke Museum, 1991).

5. For photographs and further information see Cheryl Samuel, *The Chilkat Dancing Blanket* (Seattle: Pacific Search Press, 1982), and Robert Bringhurst and Ulli Steltzer, *The Black Canoe: Bill Reid and the Spirit of Haida Gwaii,* 2d ed. (Vancouver and Toronto: Douglas and McIntyre, 1992).

6. See Cheryl Samuel, *The Raven's Tail* (Vancouver: University of British Columbia Press, 1987).

7. See Ibid., 94–103.

8. For more details see Bringhurst and Steltzer, *The Black Canoe,* 163.

There was a favored child, they say.
She was a girl, they say.
They wove the down of peregrine falcons into her dancing
    blanket, they say.
Her father loved her, they say.
She had two brothers:
one who was older and another still quite young.

And then they came to dance at her father's town, they say,
in ten canoes.
And then they danced, they say.
And then they waited, they say.
And someone—one of her father's servants, they say—questioned
    them,
"Why are these canoes here?"

"These canoes are here for the favored child."

Then, they say, someone said, "The woman refuses."

They went away weeping, they say.

And again on the following day in ten canoes they came to dance,
    they say.
And again they were questioned, they say.
"Why are these canoes here?"

"These canoes are here for the favored child."

And then they refused them again.
And they went away weeping.

Now, on the following day someone was there,
in a harbor-seal canoe, in a broad hat, at early morning, they say.
Surfbirds lived in his hat, they say.
After they had looked at him in his harbor-seal canoe,
they asked him, they say,
"Why is this canoe here?"

He said nothing, they say.
They refused him.

They said to him, so they say,
"The woman refuses."

Something encircled his hat.
It was white, they say.
It was breaking like surf, they say.
It was foaming and churning, they say.
And when they refused him, the earth became different, they say.
Seawater surged over the ground.
When they found themselves half underwater, the villagers feared
    that they might have to give him the woman.
And she had ten servants, they say.
And they dressed one to resemble her, they say.
And they painted her also, they say.
They painted red cirrus clouds on her face, they say,
and gave her two sky blankets to wear and sent her out to their
    visitor.
He turned her down, they say.
He wanted only the favored child, they say.

And again and again they painted one, they say.
They painted one with seaward dark clouds
and gave her two marten-skin capes to wear and sent her out, they
    say.
He refused her too, they say.
He refused all ten the same way.
Then the villagers took their children into her father's house, they
    say.
And they wept,
and they let her go down without painting her, they say.
And her ten servants went with her, they say.
When she stood by the sea, the canoe came of itself, they say.
And the visitor placed his hat on the shore as a gift for her father,
    they say.*
She and her ten servants boarded, they say.
No one could see what moved the canoe.
When the favored child had boarded, they saw the canoe standing
    offshore again.

▲

*And the visitor . . . they say: Swanton's interpolation, evidently in consultation
with Skaai.

Then they poked holes in the housefront, they say.
Through these they watched the canoe departing, they say.
After watching awhile, they saw nothing in any direction, they say.
They did not see that it had gone back down.
And then they did not know which way the favored child had
    been taken.

Day after day her father turned to the wall, and he cried and cried
    and cried.
And her mother turned to the wall and cried and cried and cried.
Her father's head servant stood with them day after day.
Her father, still weeping, said to him,
"Find where my child was taken."

"Cousin,* I will be absent for a while.
I will find where your child was taken."

Later, one day at first light, he stirred up the fire and bathed, they
    say,
while those in the house were still sleeping.
The day began well for him,
so he took care that no one should see him.
Now, as his skin dried, he turned to the wall,
and he spread out his fishing tackle, they say.
He opened a bundle and took out a cornlily stalk†
and set it afire.
When it had burned for a while, he extinguished it,
smearing the ash on a flat stone.
He marked himself with it.

Now he set out, they say.
He went after the favored child, they say.
And the favored child's mother was with him, they say.

From then on he moved like a hunter.
He had a sea-otter spear, they say.

*Cousin: The form of address here, *kkwaai,* suggests close and respectful relations.
It could even be rendered as "elder brother." This is the first of many signs that this
is no ordinary servant.
†cornlily stalk: in Haida, *gwaikkya.* The cornlily is *Veratrum viride,* a highly toxic
plant widely used by shamans of the Northwest Coast.

He pushed off, and he threw the sea-otter spear,
and it wiggled its tail and made ripples.
It towed them, they say.

In time the canoe ceased moving, they say.
So, they say, did the sea-otter spear.
And then, they say, he beached the canoe.
The lady stepped out of the boat, and he turned it keel-upward.
Green seaweed grew from the hull.
This is what slowed the canoe.
They had traveled for one year, they say.
And he took off his redcedar cape,
and he rubbed the canoe with it.
He rubbed the lady as well,
and he rubbed his own body
until he was clean.
Again he launched the canoe,
and again he threw the sea-otter spear,
and again it swam forward.
Again the sea otter towed him along.
He went on and on and on and on,
and then, once again, the canoe ceased moving, they say.
He beached the canoe again,
and he turned it keel-upward.
Green seaweed had covered it,
and seaweed had covered the lady.
It covered him also.
And again he took off his cape.
And he rubbed the canoe and the lady.
He rubbed himself also.
When he was clean, he launched the canoe.
And again he threw the sea-otter spear,
and it towed him along.

Farther on he encountered floating charcoal, they say.
The canoe made no headway, they say.
He brought out his tackle box and looked in.
He had old scraps from repairing his halibut hooks.*
When he threw these ahead, a passage opened,

*old scraps . . . halibut hooks: Halibut hooks were of wood (usually alder) with
a bone or metal barb, the parts fastened together with spruce-root twine. The
scraps, then, might be spruce root, metal or bone.

and then he passed through it, they say.
Not far away the channel closed over.
Again when he put what he had in the water,
the passage was opened, they say.
Then he went through it, they say.

And he came to the edge of the sky.
When it had opened and shut four times, he thrust in his spear,
    propping it open.
In that way he went under, they say.
Then he pulled out the spear.
From then on he kept it inside the canoe.
At that time he took out his paddle and used it, they say.

Now, they say, he could see the smoke from a large town.
He beached the canoe to one side of the village, they say.
He turned it keel-upward and seated the lady beneath it, they say.
Then he walked to the village, they say.
It was low tide when he came to the edge of the village.
There at one end of the beach he sat down.*

A woman with a child on her back had come down on the foreshore.
She carried a basket and digging stick, probing for something.
As she placed something into her basket, she looked at him sitting
    there.
She returned to her work; then she looked up again.
She was prying up stones and gathering sea slugs† into her basket.
Wealth Woman it was.

The next time she looked at him sitting there,
she spoke to him, they say.
She said, "I know you."
Then he stood up, they say.
Then he went down on the beach and stood near her.
And she said to him, they say,
"You are here in search of the favored child."

▲

*There . . . he sat down:** my interpolation.
†**sea slugs:** holothurians, especially the yellow and white *Eupentacta quin-
quesemita* and the red or yellow *Parastichopus californicus.* These are the food of
the poor. Wealth Woman is commonly met collecting them.

"Yes" was his answer.

"You see here a town.
  The one who took the favored child gave away his father's hat.
  Therefore, his father thought grease into his son's wife's mind.
  In this condition she lies in that cave.
  In the headman's house go around to the right, and walk back of
    the screen.
  There you will hear what people are saying."

Then he set out, leaving Wealth Woman there,
and he entered the cave of the favored child.
She lay still, but her eyelids were fluttering.
He took off his redcedar cape and used it to rub her,
trying to rouse her.
Nothing.
He tried once again and failed again and grew angry.
Then, having failed, he went on his way.

He dressed in two figured blankets and wandered among them.
They did not see him.
Then he went into the headman's house, they say,
going round to the right.
They say that the floor descended in ten tiers to the fire.
On the upper tier, on one side, a figured blanket hung on the
    weaver's frame,
and a voice came from the blanket:
"Tomorrow one of my faces will still be unfinished, unfinished."

Then, they say, he went back of the screen,
and there, they say, something surprised him.
A large bay lay there, with sandspits and beaches, and cranberries
    ripening on the outcrops.
Women sang songs there.
Near the stream flowing into the bay a fire was built for heating
    salt water,* they say.
Women emerged from the berry patch then and walked past him.
The last one was sniffing, they say.

▲

*heating salt water: Warm salt water is drunk as a purgative before important
undertakings.

"I smell a human being."

"Hello," he said. "Are you speaking of me?"

"My dancing blanket came from one of the favored child's ten
    servants,
  the ones who were eaten," she said.
"It is me that I smell."

Mink Woman, that was.

Now he went to the fire they had made for salt water.
When he came near, one of those who were sitting there said,
"What will he do when they come here to look for the favored
    child?"

"What are you saying?
  The favored child's family must return his father's hat.
  When it is returned, he will make her sit up."

After hearing what was said, he turned around.
Thinking of the lady, he ran back to the canoe
and lifted the hull, finding only her bones.
Then he took off his redcedar cape and moved it across her.
She stirred and sat up.
She was sweating.

He righted the canoe and pulled it to the water.
When the lady had boarded, he paddled in front of the town.
There, they say, he roped her to her seat.
He roped himself to his seat as well.
Wealth Woman had told him to tie himself down—and also the
    lady.
Roped to their seats, they floated offshore from the headman's
    house.
Someone came out of the house, saying,
"Cousins, they ask the lady to wait where she is
  while they make preparations."

When they had floated there awhile, lightning struck the house,
    they say.
After that the point of a feather rose from the smoke hole.

It came up; then it broke off.
It veered toward them, striking the two of them, knocking them
   cold.

Now he awoke on the upper tier of the house floor.
There he untied himself, they say.
There he untied the lady as well.
When he could walk, he came to her aid.
Her son-in-law sat toward the rear,
and they say that they spread out a mat for her, lower down.
Then she came forward
and sat in the center of one of the tiers.
Food was brought in a basket, they say,*
and they offered it to the lady.
They offered her food.
When this had been eaten, another basket was brought to the
   hearth.
Fresh water was poured into the basket.
Stones were put into the fire.
When the stones had been roasted, they lifted them into the
   basket with tongs.

Now it was boiling.
Her host spoke to a youngster who stood near the basket.
The boy went into a storeroom in the corner.
He returned with humpback whale on the end of a stick.
This he put into the basket.

Soon he tested it with the stick.
When it was soft, he lifted the whale flesh onto a tray like a red
   chiton†
and set it in front of the lady.

Her host spoke again,
and the boy brought her the rotten shell of a horse clam

---

*Here I have deleted one sentence because it conflicts with later developments in
the story. The sentence says, "There were horse clams and butter clams and two
mussels also, they say." I think this is a formulaic sentence, appropriate to many
other meals in the storyteller's repertoire, but not to this one.
†**red chiton:** in Haida, *sghiidaa*, a large, leathery mollusk, *Cryptochiton stelleri*, that
is common in Haida waters. When Skaii says the tray is like a chiton, I think he
means that it is carved with the stylized representation of a chiton, not that it
literally resembles one.

to spoon up the soup.
She was unwilling to eat in this way.
Reaching into her purse,
she took out two horse-clam shells and two mussel shells.
Silence fell in the house.
Even her host looked at nothing except the shells.
She paused when she noticed his eyes fastened upon them.

Then she handed the shells to the servant,
who passed them in turn to her son-in-law.
He cradled them in his cape.
When he had admired them for a while, he spoke again,
and they put them away behind the screen.

Then it was evening.
The house went to sleep.
The servant slept also, they say.

At daybreak a seal pup cried in the corner, they say.
And as day broke, the servant prepared for departure, they say.
The canoe sat on the upper tier of the house floor.
There he tied the lady to her seat.
He tied himself to his seat as well.
Behind the screens set end to end in the rear of the house,
    lightning struck, they say,
and the point of a feather came forward and struck them, they say,
knocking them cold.

They awoke floating on open water, they say.
And the servant untied himself and went to the lady.
He untied her as well.
They had left in midsummer, they say,
when the seal pups cry.*
Now he took up his paddle and used it, they say.
After taking two strokes, they say, he arrived at his master's town.

The lady entered the house and sat down.
They say she revealed to her husband what she had learned of her
    child's position.
Then the head servant went to his master.

*They had left . . . when the seal pups cry: The implication is that a year has
passed, and it is midsummer again.

He revealed what he had heard from those near the fire for
   heating salt water.
He spoke precisely as they had spoken.

His master spoke to the fire keepers, they say.
Two of them went through the village calling, they say,
and the people came.
The house overflowed with them, they say.
Then he brought food from the storeroom, they say.
He fed them and fed them.
When they had eaten, they say,
he told the people his thinking.
He told the villagers he was going to take back his daughter.
He proposed that the headmen travel in ten canoes.
They agreed to do it, they say.
Then on the following day his elder son had vanished, they say.
And the day after that, when they started their work,
the younger also had vanished, they say.

For the father and mother, cumulus clouds were painted on ten sets
   of clamshells, they say.
Ten mussel shells were within them.
For the elder son ten were painted.
Ten were painted for the younger son as well.
Each of the villagers who was preparing to go gathered ten, and
   the women five.
And when they had gathered them, they sat waiting.
The two who were missing had gone to get married, they say.
The others were ready to search for their sister
and tired of waiting, they say.
The villagers were fully prepared
and were waiting.

The elder returned at midday
with cedar twigs tied in his hair.
"Mother, I bring you my wife,
who is standing outside.
Will you welcome her?"
So he spoke to his mother, they say.

"*Aiii!* My child has come!"

She went out.
A woman with whiskers and round eyes was standing there.
It was Mouse Woman, they say.

The younger was gone somewhat longer.
He too, they say, returned at midday.
He entered with fern fronds tied in his hair.
Haiiii, hai hai hai haiiii!
"Mother, I bring you my wife,
    who is standing outside.
Will you welcome her?"

Something astonishing stood there, they say.
One could not look at her.
Something with short hair, wearing armor.*

"Lady, come in."

She declined to come in.

"She declines to come in.
    She refuses.
My child, your wife refuses."

"She is given to doing things backwards."

He got up and went out to his wife and escorted her in.

On the following day they set off at first light.
The villagers launched their canoes and went seaward.
The elder son's wife sat on a thwart toward the bow,
and the younger son's wife concealed herself in the crowd.
The one sat up high to see well, they say.
A small purse was with her wherever she was.
When they went seaward, she opened it.
Reaching inside, she brought out her sewing needle, they say.

*wearing armor: Haida armor was generally made of wooden slats and hide, but
Swanton understood this armor to be made of copper. It has thus become customary to identify the younger son's wife as Xaalajaat, "Copper Woman." If that is who
she is, this is her only appearance in extant Haida literature. But copper, *xaal,* is not
mentioned in the text.

She tossed it into the sea, they say,
and it sliced through the water, they say.
They lined up behind it, they say,
and the needle towed them, they say.

When it had towed them awhile, they say,
they saw the smoke of a town drifting seaward.
Some distance away, the elder son's wife told them to land.
She gave them directions.
They say she had married the elder son so she could advise them
Mouse Woman had.

Going ashore, they cut long poles, they say.
They cut them in pairs.
The younger son's wife concealed herself,
while the elder son's wife gave them directions.

The ten canoes stood offshore.
At the bow and amidships they linked them with poles.
They lashed the poles to the thwarts.
They were able to do it, they say.
Then they paddled in front of the town.

They took the most favored position, they say,
and someone came out of the headman's house, they say.
"Cousins, they ask you to wait where you are
while they make preparations."

After waiting awhile, they lost track of themselves, they say.
They awoke in the house, they say,
on the uppermost tier of the floor.
There they unfastened the lashings.
There they untied the poles that linked the canoes.

Mats were spread on the upper tiers,
and on either side of the house pit, the people assembled.
The favored child was not to be seen—
the one they had come to reclaim.
Only her husband was seated there.
They spread out two mats directly in front of him,
and he continued to sit there, they say.
The voyagers piled their clamshells in front of him.

They heaped them up as high as the house.
Ho ho ho hoooo! Up to the top!
And they placed the hat at the top of the pile.

"Call in my father.
Ask him not to delay."

A youngster set off on the run, they say.

"Is he not here?"

"He is close by."

Hwuuuuuuuuuu!
The house quivered, they say,
and the earth shook.
Together they all shied away.
No one looked upward.
But the youngest son's wife raised her head as they cowered, they
    say.
She looked to the rear of the house, and she looked to the door.

"Raise yourselves up!
Have you no power?"
She spoke in this way.

The house quivered again,
and the earth shook.
Hwuuuuuuuuu!
And again those in the house lowered their heads.
"Raise yourselves up!
Have you no power?"

At that moment he entered, they say.
And what entered amazed them, they say.
His eyes bulged so that no one could look at him.
When he planted his foot, they say, he stood there awhile.
He took one more step, and the earth and the house shuddered,
    they say.
And he took one more step, and the house and the earth
    quivered,
and all together they cowered.

▲

She said once again,
"Raise yourselves up!"

As she lifted her face, something powerful came to her,
and their heads rose like the tide.

"A powerful woman you are."

After that he sat down,
and the tremors subsided.
He sat near his son.
But he laid his hand on his hat before he sat down.

With his father's staff, the son divided the shells.
He took fewer for himself.
He gave more to his father.

"Have you not yet sent for your wife, my son?"

"No. I have waited for you."

"My spokesman, my son, send someone now for your wife."

A youngster went to call her then, they say.

"Is she not here?"

"Yes. She is close by."

Soon the one they were looking for entered, they say.
She came from the cave where she had been lying.
She went at once to her mother, they say.
She did not go down to sit next to her husband.

And his father began to summon his power, they say.
He began to dance.
After a time he fell over, they say,
breaking in two.
Feathers came out of his body and out of his neck.
One of the servants emerged from his body.
Another came out of his neck.
And another came from his body, and one from his neck.

He restored the ten that he had eaten.
He danced for that reason, they say.
Because of the hat, he had eaten the ten servants, they say.
He had also thought grease, they say, into the favored child's
  mind.
Because of the hat, they say, they had put her into the cave.

After a time his body grew whole.
He ended his dance.
He sat down.

They built up the fire then, calling them forward.
They started to offer them food, they say.
They continued till midnight.
And then it was finished; then it was finished.
They gathered the dishes, they say.

At daybreak a seal pup cried from the corner, they say,
just as before,
and then they prepared for departure, they say.
The canoes were still there, on the highest tier of the house floor.

Her father-in-law summoned her then, they say.
"Lady, come here. I have something to tell you."

He took her aside, they say,
and she sat down beside him.
Then, they say, he advised her.

"Lady, you will give birth to me from your body.
Do not be afraid of me."

He gave her a skull made of copper, they say.
Something stuck out from it at each side.
Its name, they say, is Between-the-Neck-and-the-Body.

"Let Master Carver make my cradle, lady.*
Let cumulus clouds be placed on the top of it, lady,

*Master Carver: *Watghadagang,* the nonhuman embodiment of artistic skill in
painting and woodworking. Master Carver lives in the forest, not in the sea. The
literal meaning of his Haida name is "Maker of Flat Surfaces."

and also below.
Let the clouds be flat on the bottom.
When the sky is like this, even human beings may come to me to
  feed.
When they see me like this,
common surface birds may come to me to feed."

Her family was waiting on the upper tier, they say,
while her father-in-law was advising her below,
and she was listening, they say.
When he ended his speech, she went up to her father.
They had already lashed the canoes together
and already roped themselves into their seats.
When the favored child boarded, they say,
they lost track of themselves.
They woke on the open water, they say.

At once they set off.
And at once they came to the village, they say.

Time passed, and the favored child was also with child, they say.
When she started her labor,
they built her a separate shelter, they say.
They drove in a stake,* placed her hands upon it, and left her,
  they say.

Now he emerged,
and when she saw him, she was astonished by him, they say.
Something stuck out of his eyes.
She raised herself up and drew back from him, frightened, they
  say.

"Awaaayaaaaa!"
Her cry shook the houses, they say.

Then she turned back to him, they say, picking him up.
"Aiii! I am here, Grandfather."

This is the term by which she addressed him, they say,
and the town was like something lifted and dropped.

▲

*a stake: The birthing stake—a handhold for a woman in labor—was widely used
on the Northwest Coast.

She brought him into the house, they say,
and her father brought out his own urinal for him.*
In that they bathed him, they say.
Now Master Carver was sent for.†
They summoned him, and he came directly, they say.
He had started his work in the forest
and brought it half finished, they say.
The moment he entered, they say, he made the design
as the favored child described it.
He drew cumulus clouds together in pairs.
He drilled holes for the laces to straighten his legs.

Then they placed him in it, they say.
Two sky blankets were brought,
and they wrapped them around him
and laced him into the cradle.

Then, they say, they launched the canoe.
Five of them, and the favored child as well, went aboard with her
    child,
and they started seaward, they say.
They traveled and traveled and traveled.

To the landward towns and the seaward towns it was equally far;
    they could see that it was,
when they put him over the side, they say.
When they put him over the side, he turned round and round and
    round and round to the right four times
and lay quiet, they say,
like something lifted and dropped.
And they left him
and went to the place they had come from, they say.‡

---

*her father brought out . . . for him: The urine of healthy humans is a sterile
fluid, chiefly water, ammonia, and carbonic acid. It makes an excellent biological
cleansing agent, useful in treating insect bites and wounds as well as baptizing the
newborn. A bath in a grandparent's urine—so long as the donor is free of disease—
is not just a ritual honor for the child but a perfectly defensible obstetric procedure.
†Now Master Carver was sent for: my interpolation.
‡As a postscript to the story, Swanton recorded the following comment, perhaps
from his Haida tutor Henry Moody: "He was one who resides in mid ocean, they
say. Sometimes when sickness was coming they saw him, they say. He was a reef,
they say—the One They Gave Away was."

NIGHT HUNTER

AND DAY HUNTER

▲

JUDITH BERMAN

INTRODUCTION

"Night Hunter and Day Hunter" is a story from the North Pacific Coast, from a native group that is often called the Kwakiutl, but is more correctly known as the Kwakwaka'wakw. Like their neighbors, the Kwakwaka'wakw traditionally lived on the shores of the many islands and inlets of the region and subsisted largely on the resources of the sea. They placed a strong emphasis on rank and inherited social position.

The Kwakwaka'wakw story translated here was written down in 1921 in the Kwak'wala language by a man named George Hunt. Although Hunt was the son of a Tlingit Indian noblewoman and a Hudson's Bay Company employee, he lived his whole life among the Kwakwaka'wakw, and he came to be considered a cultural expert by many of the Kwakwaka'wakw of his time. Hunt is an important figure in the history of anthropology and folklore because of his forty-five-year collaboration with Franz Boas, during which Hunt wrote down thousands of pages of Kwakwaka'wakw myths, folklore, family histories, dreams, and much more. Unfortunately, although Boas was a pioneering linguist and acquired a thorough knowledge of the Kwak'wala language, his translations of Hunt's materials are stilted and awkward and sometimes contain errors and unexplained omissions.[1]

Hunt learned the story of "Night Hunter and Day Hunter" from a man named T'labid, a member of one of the Kwagulh (Fort Rupert) divisions of the Kwakwa̱ka'wakw whose mother came from another division called the A̱'wa'itla̱la, the "Inside People." The story concerns the ancestors of the hereditary chiefs of one of the three kin groups of the Inside People. It belongs to a category of Kwakwa̱ka'wakw myth that tells how the ancestors of the hereditary chiefs, through encounters with the spirit world, established institutions and acquired names and prerogatives that were passed down to their latter-day descendants.

One Kwakwa̱ka'wakw institution whose origins lie in myth was the seal feast. In the nineteenth and early twentieth centuries a feast of harbor seals *(Phoca vitulina)* was one of the most prestigious events a chief could host, and precise etiquette governed the inviting, serving and eating. "Night Hunter and Day Hunter" presents the Inside People's version of the origin of the seal feast.

Another important myth-derived institution was the T'sit'se̱ka, a name difficult to translate but that I have rendered as "the Masking." This wintertime ritual complex, connected to world renewal, included a number of dramatic masked dances performed by initiated members of the Kwakwa̱ka'wakw elite. In "Night Hunter and Day Hunter," though this is not explicit, the ancestor-hero acquires the prerogative of initiation for his descendants through his own initiation by spirits. As is typical in many ancestor-initiation stories, the hero disappears into the spirit realm, is healed and resurrected by spirits, and later returns home too full of spirit power to be comfortably accommodated in the human realm. He performs dangerous and bizarre feats but is ultimately tamed and returned to a more or less fully human state—though he will retain some spirit power.

The geography in the story is, with the exception of the hero's trip to Charcoal-at-the-River-Mouth, quite real. The Inside People were so-called because they dwelt "inside" Knight Inlet, a twisting, narrow fjord that cuts over fifty miles into the rugged coastal mountains of the British Columbia mainland. The fjord, rarely more than two miles across, reaches depths of over 250 fathoms and is walled in by mountains that rise steeply to heights of over a mile above sea level. Night Hunter's village, an historical Inside People village site, is located partway into Knight Inlet, near the mouth of the Anhuati River (the "Having Humpback Salmon" of the story). In the Kwak'wala of the original text, the mountain Feet-on-Water, where the eldest hunts for seals, lies "downriver" from the village, that is, oceanward. The head of Knight Inlet, Having Oolachan, where the

younger brother hunts, is upriver. In nineteenth-century Kwak'wala,
the terms *upriver* and *downriver* apply to the entire world, rivers and
ocean together constituting a kind of World River; at the extreme
upriver pole are the interior mountains; at the extreme downriver
pole is the far side of the ocean, the River Mouth, where the sea
monster lives. We infer that at the River Mouth the World River
flows out into some vast cosmic ocean, but such an ocean is never
described in any Kwakwaka'wakw myth.

A few words should be said about the form of the story as it is
given here. As Dell Hymes[2] and others have shown, the stories from
oral traditions frequently have internal "rhetorical" structures of
lines and groups of lines that are marked by particles and built out of
patterns of narrative action. These patterns are nearly always influenced by the pattern number or numbers of the culture from
which the story comes—the number of ritual efficacy, of completion. In European-derived traditions the most common pattern
number is three. A fairytale's hero is the third of three sons or
daughters; there are three magical objects or three magical helpers;
the third repetition of an action is the successful one. In Kwakwaka'-
wakw oral literature, as in many other Native American traditions,
the basic pattern number is four, though two is also important.

The basic rhetorical unit of Kwakwaka'wakw oral literature is a
unit I refer to as a stich. In George Hunt's narrations each stich
begins with the particle *we*. I have not translated this essentially untranslatable particle, but in the English below, stichs begin at the
left-hand margin. Most stichs are made of a single sentence. The
English sentences correspond exactly to those of the Kwak'wala
original.

In the story, groups of stichs form larger rhetorical units that are
demarcated by shifts in setting, character, and focus and by the pat-
terning of action. "Night Hunter and Day Hunter" is divided into
two nearly equal parts by the shift of setting to the interior of the
seals' cave. Each part is divided into four rhetorical scenes, which in
the translation are marked by time headings (for example, "Day
1"). All scenes are divided into four stanzas, except for the very first
scene, which has two stanzas in the original text and one here, as will
be explained below. Stanzas are marked in the translation by asterisks. Stanzas are in turn divided into verses, distinguished by line
spacing; most stanzas have four verses. Verses are often subdivided
into two or four smaller units, but to simplify the presentation, these
are not marked in the translation. The very complex rhetorical form
of "Night Hunter and Day Hunter," along with many other details
of interpretation, is discussed elsewhere.[3]

The translation remains quite close to the original text, with one important exception. The original contains a stanza-long digression regarding nineteenth-century political events that begins during the first stich. Because of space limitations, the digressive stanza has been removed, and the very first stich and the first stich following the digression have been compressed into one. The original text of "Night Hunter and Day Hunter" can be found in Boas.[4]

Although Kwakwaka'wakw oral tradition has diminished in vitality, it has not disappeared altogether. Most Kwakwaka'wakw communities have instituted Kwak'wala-language curricula in their grade schools in an attempt to reverse the trend toward language loss. The effectiveness of these curricula has varied. At Alert Bay, the largest Kwakwaka'wakw community, a Kwak'wala immersion program is currently in the planning stages, with the goals of producing a new generation of fluent speakers and perpetuating the rich tradition that depends on the language.

NOTES

1. See Judith Berman, "Oolachan-Woman's Robe: Fish, Blankets, Masks, and Meaning in Boas's Kwakw'ala Texts," in *On the Translation of Native American Literatures,* ed. Brian Swann (Washington, D.C.: Smithsonian Institution Press, 1992), 125–67.

2. Dell Hymes, *"In Vain I Tried to Tell You": Essays in Native American Ethnopoetics* (Philadelphia: University of Pennsylvania Press, 1981).

3. Judith Berman, *The Seals' Sleeping Cave: The Interpretation of Boas' Kwakw'ala Texts* (Ann Arbor, Mich.: University Microfilms International, 1991).

4. Franz Boas, *Kwakiutl Tales, New Series,* Columbia University Contributions to Anthropology, vol. 26, pt. 1, "Texts," and pt. 2, "Translation" (New York: Columbia University Press, 1935 and 1943).

DAY 1

Head Copper Maker was dwelling with his clan, the Ancient Ones,
   in a village at Beach-Behind-the-Points.
Head Copper Maker had four sons.

Head Copper Maker and his four children were relaxing on their
       seaside platform when the eldest began to speak.
He said,
   "What work could I do for my father?
   I will work as a seal hunter for him,
      so he can always be giving seal feasts for the people of our vil-
         lage,"
      so he said.

Then the next eldest also began to speak.
He said,
   "I too will work as a seal hunter,
      and I will have our youngest brother as my steersman."
   "You will have my younger brother as your steersman.
   You will hunt at night,"
      so he said to the eldest of the brothers.
   "I will hunt in the day,
      so our father can always be giving seal feasts for the people of
         our village,"
      so he said.

From that point on the eldest brother had the name Night Hunter.
The younger brother had the name Day Hunter after that.
Their words made Head Copper Maker happy because he had
   wanted his children to work as hunters of seals.

DAY 1, NIGHT 1, DAY 2

Night Hunter and his steersman, the third brother, began their
   preparations.
Night Hunter singed clean the bottom of his hunting canoe.
As soon as he had finished, he went inland with his steersman and
   dug hellebore roots.

When he had four hellebore roots, he broke off tips of hemlock branches that had spirit power in them.

They went to the headwaters of the stream at Beach-Behind-the-Points.
He took two of the hellebore roots and gave them to his steersman.
Two of the hellebore roots were rubbed on his own body.
His younger brother, his steersman, just copied his eldest brother.

When they had finished with the hellebore, they took the hemlock twigs and rubbed them on their bodies at the same time.
When they had both finished, they sat down on the stream bank.

They waited for evening before leaving the woods to go seal hunting.
As soon as it began to grow dark, the two of them went out of the woods to their hunting canoe.

*

They carried the canoe down to the water and climbed aboard.
They headed toward Hanging Skulls Rock, down the inlet from Beach-Behind-the-Points.
Then they steered for Hollow Point.
At Hollow Point they heard a seal barking above them, atop the great mountain named Feet-on-Water that is not far from Hollow Point.

Night Hunter paddled and stopped the canoe near the foot of Feet-on-Water.
They kept motionless as they drifted there, waiting for the seal to bark again.
Soon the seal began to bark again, high above them.
At once Night Hunter paddled to the foot of Feet-on-Water because the seal was barking on a high ledge Night Hunter had seen before.

He stepped out of his traveling canoe and climbed up from the water toward the ledge on the mountainside.
He took his cedar-withe rope—the long anchor line of his canoe—and his seal club.
Night Hunter had reached another ledge, halfway to the ledge on the mountainside, when he saw a ball of fire.

He approached it. But what did he see? A great seal lay on the
ground with a quartz crystal in the back of its head.
The fire he had seen was the crystal glowing in the great seal's nape.

When the great seal saw Night Hunter, it jumped down into the
mouth of the seals' sleeping cave.
There was the noise of many seals growling at one another inside a
hole in the rock face, which was, he was amazed to see, a door
leading downward, the breathing hole of the seals' sleeping cave.
Night Hunter walked over and looked down into it.
A strong wind blew on his face from the inside of the seals' sleeping
cave.

*

Night Hunter put his cedar-withe rope on the rock.
He carried his club with him as he went down to the water, calling
his younger brother, his steersman, whose name was They-
Purify-for-Him.
He reached the place where his canoe lay. He said to his younger
brother,
"I have found a treasure, the seals' sleeping cave.
You will not talk about this to our brother Day Hunter.
If you talk about this to anyone, even our father,
I will kill you with this club,"
so he said, threatening his younger brother with his club.
The younger brother begged for mercy from the eldest, saying that
he would tell no one about the treasure of the seals' sleeping
cave.

When he had finished promising this, Night Hunter told his
younger brother that they would both go up the mountain
that night.
They both went up.
Night Hunter still carried his club.
They reached the hole in the rock face, the mouth of the seals' sleep-
ing cave.
Night Hunter took the cedar-withe rope and tied the end to a tree
that stood at the side of the hole in the rock face, the mouth
of the seals' sleeping cave.
He told his younger brother that when he felt a tug on the rope,
"You will haul it up,"

so Night Hunter said as he took hold of the rope and went down.

It was not long before he tugged on the rope.
They-Purify-for-Him hauled up the rope, which was very heavy with a large seal.
He untied the rope from the seal.
Again They-Purify-for-Him let down the end of the rope.
Again Night Hunter tugged on the rope.
They-Purify-for-Him hauled it up.
Four large seals were pulled up by They-Purify-for-Him.
Then he pulled up Night Hunter.

They both rolled down the four seals.
Night Hunter told They-Purify-for-Him to wash off the seals' bodies and the insides of their mouths and eyes until all the soil and hemlock needles came off.
When he had finished washing off the soil and hemlock needles, they loaded them into the work canoe.
When all four large seals were on board the work canoe, they headed home.

*

They reached Having Humpback Salmon as day came.
They reached the beach at their house at Beach-Behind-the-Points.
They saw Day Hunter as he was paddling out. He was heading toward Having Oolachan.

They-Purify-for-Him unloaded the four seals because Night Hunter had already gone up the beach into the house.
At once Head Copper Maker made a fire on the beach and singed the hair off the four seals.

When he had finished, he cut the seals into pieces.
He boiled them with hot stones.

When the seals were cooked, he invited his village.
Then Head Copper Maker gave the very first seal feast, with the seals his child Night Hunter had caught—the first seals ever to have been caught.

It was evening when Day Hunter returned to the beach, having taken only one yearling seal.

He was terribly ashamed when he learned that his eldest brother had brought in four large seals.

It was evening when Night Hunter set off seal hunting with his younger brother They-Purify-for-Him.

They just went along to Feet-on-Water.

They reached the foot of the seals' sleeping cave.

They both stepped out of their work canoe.

Night Hunter took his club.

They reached the seals' sleeping cave.

He took hold of his cedar-withe rope.

He went down.

It was not long before he tugged on the rope.

They-Purify-for-Him hauled it up.

He untied the rope from a large seal.

Eight large seals were hauled up by They-Purify-for-Him.

Then he hauled up Night Hunter.

Today the place where the seals were piled up is called Heap-of-Seals.

*

They rolled down the eight seals.

They-Purify-for-Him washed off the soil and hemlock needles from the round bodies of the seals and from the insides of their mouths and from their eyes.

When he had finished, Night Hunter took his harpoon and speared the sides of the seals to make it appear they had been killed that way.

When he finished, they loaded the seals into the work canoe.

They came home.

As soon as they reached Having Humpback Salmon, daylight came.

They reached their house at Beach-Behind-the-Points.

Night Hunter saw his younger brother Day Hunter as he was setting out on his seal hunt.

▲

Day Hunter saw that the work canoe of his eldest brother, Night
  Hunter, was very low in the water.
He turned back up the beach and went into his house.
He was ashamed that his eldest brother had taken so many seals.

Night Hunter stepped out of his work canoe, went into his house,
  and fell asleep.
His father, Head Copper Maker, went down the beach to the water
  and unloaded the eight seals from his child's work canoe.

*

Now Day Hunter whispered to his younger brother, named They-
  Wish-for-Him, to go secretly to look in the mouths of the seals
  and in their eyes for any needles or soil that might be sticking
  inside the mouths or on the skin or in the eyes of the seals, because Day Hunter and his whole village guessed that Night
  Hunter had won the treasure of the seals' sleeping cave.
That was why Day Hunter sent his steersman, They-Wish-for-Him,
  to look at the seals.

They-Wish-for-Him pretended to help his father, Head Copper
  Maker, unload the seals from the canoe.
Right away They-Wish-for-Him saw soil in the eye of a seal.
He saw hemlock needles on the skin of a seal.
They-Wish-for-Him took the hemlock needles and secretly gave
  them to his elder brother Day Hunter.

Day Hunter said,
  "Do not tell anyone I have learned that Night Hunter won the
     treasure of the seals' sleeping cave,"
    so he said to his younger brother.
Day Hunter was happy because he had found it out.

Head Copper Maker singed all eight seals.
When he was done, he cut them into pieces.
When he finished this, he invited the people of his village.
As soon as they were all in his house,
Head Copper Maker set raw seal before his guests.
When he finished, all the feasters went out.

*

Night Hunter and his steersman, They-Purify-for-Him, went out
  to sit on the platform on the ocean side of their house.

They had not been there long when Day Hunter and his steersman,
    They-Wish-for-Him, also came out of the house to sit on the plat-
    form.
Now Day Hunter and his eldest brother, Night Hunter, were sitting
    next to each other.

Night Hunter began to speak to his younger brother Day Hunter.
He said to him,
    "Why didn't you paddle out today, Day Hunter?"
        so he said to him.

Day Hunter answered.
Day Hunter said,
    "Oh, you before whom I am a dog, this is why I did not paddle:
        I openly say I am ashamed that you get so many seals.
    I got only a single yearling seal.
    I beg you, let our names go to each other;
        let me be the one named Night Hunter.
    You will be the one named Day Hunter,"
        so he said to his eldest brother.

The eldest one laughed.
He said,
    "All right, *Night Hunter,* since you say that's your name!
        Go out tonight.
    You will still go where you always go.
    I will be named Day Hunter.
    I will go out in my canoe in the morning
        to go day hunting where I always go with this little boy,"
        so he said.

NIGHT 3, DAY 4, NIGHT 4

When it got dark that evening, the new Night Hunter, the
    younger brother, started by canoe.
He headed for Having Oolachan.
As daylight came, he returned home.
He had taken two seals.

Then the eldest, now named Day Hunter, set off seal hunting.
He headed toward Hanging Skulls Rock.
As soon as he was hidden beyond the point of Beach-Behind-the-

Points, the new Night Hunter boarded his canoe with his steersman, They-Wish-for-Him.
They started paddling, heading toward Hanging Skulls Rock.

As soon as they came around the point, they saw their eldest brother heading for Hollow Point.
When their eldest brother was hidden beyond Hollow Point, the new Night Hunter started paddling.
He reached Hollow Point. He paddled along, staying close to the rocks.
There was nothing of them to be seen.

He neared Feet-on-Water. Then he saw the work canoe of his eldest brother tied up at each end at the foot of Feet-on-Water.
Before he reached it, he stepped out of his canoe, taking his club of crab apple wood.

*

He went up from the water.
He had not gone very high when he came upon an animal trail.
He followed the trail, which led straight above where their canoe lay on the water.

It had not taken him far before he saw someone hard at work, hauling a rope out of a hole in the rock.
That one was They-Purify-for-Him, Day Hunter's steersman.

While the boy was hauling, the new Night Hunter came straight up and stood behind him.
A large seal came up tied in the middle with the rope.
They-Purify-for-Him put the seal on the pile.
They-Purify-for-Him did not see Night Hunter standing behind him.

Night Hunter struck him with his club.
They-Purify-for-Him was dead.

*

The new Night Hunter took hold of the rope and let it run down into the breathing hole of the seals' sleeping cave.
Soon the new Day Hunter tugged on the rope.
The new Night Hunter pulled up the rope.

He saw that he was hauling up his eldest brother, the new Day
    Hunter.
Night Hunter saw him. At once he stopped hauling him.

The new Night Hunter spoke first.
He said to his eldest brother, the new Day Hunter,
    "Oh, you who have erred, would it have been wrong for you to
        tell me, your younger brother, to come help you with your
        great treasure, the seals' sleeping cave, that is not often won
        by a man?
    Now you will become a seal,"
        so said the new Night Hunter to his eldest brother, Day
        Hunter.

Night Hunter was already cutting the rope when Day Hunter
    spoke.
He said to him,
    "Don't be so hasty, brother;
        it would be good if you could look ahead and see that only we
        together possess this treasure, the seals' sleeping cave,"
    so he said.

In spite of his words, the new Night Hunter cut through the rope.
His eldest brother dropped into the hole.
He was dead.

*

Night Hunter did not take any of the seals lying around because he
    did not want anyone to guess that he had murdered his eldest
    brother.
That was why he filled his canoe with firewood.

He returned home.
He was questioned by his father, Head Copper Maker, about why
    he had paddled out.
Night Hunter said that he had been fetching firewood, because he
    knew that the first of the clan Ancient Ones of the Inside People
    was wondering if he had murdered his eldest brother.

It was evening.
The time for Day Hunter to come home passed by.
He did not come home the next day.

▲

None of the men guessed that he had been murdered by his younger
brother.
This made Night Hunter very happy.

* *

Now I will stop talking about Night Hunter.
Now I will talk about his eldest brother, Day Hunter, who I said was
dead inside the seals' sleeping cave.

*

DAY 4 THROUGH NIGHT 8

This is what happened when Night Hunter cut the rope that Day
Hunter was holding.
Day Hunter fell on the rocks of the beach inside the seals' sleeping
cave.
Day Hunter knew that his belly had split open, because his intestines
were scattered over the rocks.
But his mind remained steady.

He lay as if dead where he had fallen.
He heard many men speaking to each other, talking about how he
had dropped down.
All the men were glad that someone they called Keeps Us Sleepless
had died from a fall,
so said the voices he heard.
Many men gathered around him.

Day Hunter heard someone shouting loud, saying,
"What are you crowding around over there?"
so said the distant voice.
One of the men standing alongside the motionless Day Hunter
replied.
He said,
"Keeps Us Sleepless fell down into our house.
Now he is dead over here,"
so he said.
The one who had questioned the crowd said,
"It serves him right that he is dead,"
so he said.

That is why the heart of Day Hunter became strong, so that he

stood up quickly on the rocks.
Some of the seals had no time to dress in their sealskins.
Many of them had time to dress.
Day Hunter just stood there waiting for the men to speak to him or
kill him.

*

The chief, named Seal Face, began to speak. He was the largest of
all the seals, the one on whose nape was the round quartz crystal.
He said,
"Oh, people of my village, we have been profaned by our friend
Keeps Us Sleepless, because now he has seen that we are people
like him.
Go on, ask him! Does he not want us to set him right?"

There was a man among those standing around Day Hunter.
This man began to speak.
He said,
"It is his desire that you do so, chief,"
so said one who had wonderfully good hearing, as he stood in
the crowd around Day Hunter.

There was a man in the corner by the great carved house posts.
He brought what looked like a feast dish that was full of water-of-
life.

The man sprinkled it over Day Hunter's body.
Day Hunter was put right.
His wounds healed up.

*

The chief began to speak again.
He said,
"What does our friend want for his spirit treasure?
Will he not take the property grower?"
so he said.
Day Hunter thought that he did not want it.
At once the man with wonderful hearing said that he would not
take it.

The chief began to speak again.
He said,

264

"Will he not take the carved house posts and that pool of water-
    of-life in the corner?"
    so he said.
Day Hunter thought, "What is the use of it?"
At once the man with wonderful hearing said,
    "What is the use of it?"
    so he said.

The chief became annoyed.
He said,
    "Does our friend want the death-bringing wand?"
    so he said.
Day Hunter thought, "That is what I want, a death bringer."
At once the man with wonderful hearing said,
    "That is what our friend chooses, the death-bringing wand, so he
        can take revenge on his younger brother,"
    so he said.

Day Hunter won the spirit treasure of the fire-making death-bring-
    ing wand—that was the full name of the death-bringer.

*

The chief said,
    "I will engage someone to take our friend home after he has been
        four days in my house, people of my village,"
    so he said.

Day Hunter stayed with the seals, and they were all people when
    they came home to their houses inside the seals' sleeping cave.
The Seal People called their village Wealth Ground, and every night
    the Seal tribe began the Masking.

The ceremonies were the Sea Grizzly and the Grizzly and the
    Attack and the Laughing-Goose Dancer;
there was the Killer Whale Dancer;
    there was the Greedy One of the Seal People, and they were truly
        afraid when it was aroused.
These initiates were seen by Day Hunter.

Day Hunter did not know that, amazingly, it was winter at night;
    that was why the Seal People held the Masking every night.
That is why there are few seals abroad in winter.

To them the summer is daytime.

Day Hunter was always called Keeps Us Sleepless during the time he
   stayed with the Seal People.

DAY 9

In the morning the chief called the people of his village to an assembly.

Day Hunter was told to sit among the guests.

He was told to go to the place of honor at the rear of the house.

As soon as he sat down, the chief arose.

He began to speak.

He said,
   "It is I who called you, people of my village, on account of our
      friend Keeps Us Sleepless, so he can go home to the place he
      came from.

   I now engage someone to bear him home.

   I engage our friend Crossing-the-World-in-a-Single-Day, be-
      cause his dive is long, and the entrance to our houses is far
      away.

   I know that our friend Keeps Us Sleepless is anxious to return, for
      he has been four days in my house.

   Come, friend Crossing-the-World-in-a-Single-Day, bear our
      friend home,"
      so he said.

A man in very fancy clothes stood up.

He said,
   "Come, friend Keeps Us Sleepless, so I can measure the length of
      your breath,"
      so he said.

At once Day Hunter stood up and went to him.

That was when the death bringer was given him by the chief.

*

Crossing-the-World-in-a-Single-Day told him to lie down on his
   back,

and also to pinch his side when he came to the end of his breath,
   so said Crossing-the-World.

As soon as the man was ready to dive, he became a Loon.
He dived.
He had not been long underwater when Day Hunter pinched him.
At once he came up to the surface.

He dived again.
This time he stayed a little longer under the water before Day
  Hunter pinched him.
He came up.
Now he went deep underwater.

Crossing-the-World began to speak.
He said,
  "I am happy that your breath is long.
  Go on, try to hold your breath as long as you possibly can,"
    so he said.
He dived again.
Day Hunter did not pinch Crossing-the-World, and the Loon came
        up where he had been coming up, by the beach of the Seal
        People's village inside the seals' sleeping cave.
Day Hunter's breath proved longer than the breath of Crossing-
        the-World.

*

Crossing-the-World began to speak.
He said,
  "My breath has been defeated by your breath.
  Now I feel satisfied that we will reach the mouth of this place.
  Get ready, because now we will go all the way out,"
    so he said, and he dived.
Day Hunter knew when they emerged from the mouth of the seals'
        sleeping cave, because the light under the water changed,
        because it was always dark in the daytime in the seals'
        sleeping cave.
They came up seaward from Egg Island, on the open ocean.

Crossing-the-World-in-a-Single-Day, the Loon, began to speak.
  "Here now, friend Keeps Us Sleepless, I know that your younger
        brother Night Hunter hurt you.
  I want you to take revenge.

We shall go to Sea Monster Forehead at his village at Charcoal-at-
the-River-Mouth and engage him to return with us,"
so he said.

He told Day Hunter, the so-called Keeps Us Sleepless, to draw in
all the breath he could, for they were going a very long way,
so he said.
He dived.
He went out across the open ocean.
He came up at Charcoal-at-the-River-Mouth.
Day Hunter saw much charcoal floating there.

Crossing-the-World began to speak.
He said,
"Be careful, friend, when we go to the house of Sea Monster
Forehead beneath the sea, because it is in a different world,"
so he said.
He dived straight down.
Soon they passed all the way through the salt water.
They arrived at a sandy beach.
There stood Sea Monster Forehead's house.

*

Crossing-the-World became a man when they entered the house.
A big, fat man was sitting inside.
As soon as Sea Monster Forehead saw Crossing-the-World, he
greeted him in a friendly way.
At once Crossing-the-World began to speak to him.
He said,
"We come to engage you, friend, to help us take vengeance on
the younger brother of Keeps Us Sleepless,"
so he said.

This speech made Sea Monster Forehead very happy.
At once he got ready.
He called what he referred to as his dogs, the many seals staying in
his house.
The seals came to him.
He took hold of a small seal, the one he called Dirty.
He took the sealskin from him.
"I will take your sealskin along in case I want it, little Dirty,"
so he said.

At once they got ready.
They left his house.
They both came up to our world.
Crossing-the-World again became a Loon.
Sea Monster Forehead became a large Halibut.
Day Hunter lay on the back of Crossing-the-World.

They went together as they dived.
They depended on the equality of their spirit power; that is why they
    traveled together as they came landward from Charcoal-at-the-
    River-Mouth, which is not far from where the walls of the upper
    world rest upon the lower world.
They came up near Day Hunter's village, at the place called Water-
    fall.

DAY 9 CONTINUED

Sea Monster Forehead took the seal mask of Dirty and dressed
    Keeps Us Sleepless, Day Hunter, in it.
Sea Monster Forehead said to Keeps Us Sleepless,
    "Go on, friend, stretch your head above water in front of your
        father's house.
    As soon as the people of your village see you, they will send your
        younger brother Night Hunter to spear you.
    When he comes near you, you will dive and head seaward to
        where I will be.
    As soon as he goes onto my flat side, I will pull him into the water.
    When the tide starts to run out, you will go aboard his work
        canoe.
    You will stand up in the canoe and aim your fire-bringing spirit
        treasure here and there,"
        so he said.

*

Day Hunter dived.
He went across and emerged in front of his house.
Right away the men sitting outside saw the seal.
Night Hunter was told to go spear it.

He went out to it at once in his canoe.
As he came near the seal, he picked up his harpoon.
He was getting ready to spear the seal when it dived.

It was not long underwater; then it emerged seaward from where
   Night Hunter's canoe was floating.

He began paddling and tried again, in vain, to spear the seal.
Again the seal dived.
Again it did not go far before it came up.
Again Night Hunter paddled and went to it.

Again he was about to spear the seal when it dived.
It only went a little farther seaward, and then it turned back and
   came up behind the canoe.

*

Night Hunter was trying in vain to follow when the tide began to
   run.
Night Hunter saw that the water was shallow where his canoe was
   floating.
He poled with his harpoon on the flat side of the monster Sea Monster Forehead. He couldn't move against the currents pulling him
   seaward.
His harpoon stuck to Sea Monster Forehead.
His hands also stuck to his harpoon.

Night Hunter was standing helpless in his canoe.
Then Day Hunter pulled off the sealskin of Dirty and boarded
          Night Hunter's canoe.
Day Hunter began to speak.
He said,
   "You are Night Hunter, my brother.
   You will go where you wanted me to go,"
      so he said.

Night Hunter had no time to speak because his harpoon pulled him
   into the water.
He was dead after that; when he stepped onto the sandbar running
   across in shallow water between Beach-Behind-the-Points and
   Waterfall, the water was just knee-deep.
But the current was powerful.
It was the back of Sea Monster Forehead, the surface of the bar of
   sandy gravel.

▲

Sea Monster Forehead always showed himself like this to the old-time Indians; therefore the old-time Indian hunters used to say that they had seen Sea Monster Forehead as they returned home.

The hunters would be asked,
  "Have you any news?"
    so they would be asked by the people of their village.
They would often say, "I was met by the shallow water of Sea Monster Forehead."

*

The sea was smooth as Night Hunter sank.
The Loon, Crossing-the-World-in-a-Single-Day, just sat on the water not far from Night Hunter's canoe, where Day Hunter now stood.

All the old-time Inside People came rushing out of their houses, astonished at what had happened to Night Hunter.
The one standing in his canoe was a different man, one whom they did not recognize because the old-time Inside People no longer thought about Day Hunter's disappearance.

DAY 9 CONCLUSION

The Loon cried as if he were awakening Day Hunter.
Day Hunter sang this sacred song:

> I was set right by spirit power,
> for I was made to come back to life by spirit power.
> *Hai hai hai hai.*

> I was made powerful by spirit power,
> by the excellent High-Tide Being, the spirit power.
> *Hai hai hai hai.*

> The fire maker was given into my hand
> by him, the excellent spirit power.
> *Hai hai hai hai.*

> Therefore I will burn all with my fire bringer;
> I will burn you, most worthless commoners.
> *Hai hai hai hai.*

When he came to the end of his sacred song, he stretched out his right hand, holding the death-bringing wand, pointing toward Grooves-in-Stone Mountain.

At once that mountain burst into flames.

He pointed toward Waterfall. Again that mountain burst into flames.

He pointed toward Magetani.

Again that mountain burst into flames.

He pointed at the lands upriver from Beach-Behind-the-Points.

Again they at once burst into flames.

He stopped after this.

He did this so his father would know that he was still alive, that he was the one who had obtained the spirit treasure, the death-bringing wand.

*

Crossing-the-World-in-a-Single-Day, the Loon, cried, for he was still sitting there on the water.

He dived.

He went under the canoe in which Day Hunter was standing and pressed his back against the canoe bottom, carrying him to the beach in front of his father's house.

As soon as he arrived on the beach, Head Copper Maker went to meet his son Day Hunter.

He called him out of his canoe, and they went into his house.

*

The old-time Inside People were very much afraid of Day Hunter, for all of them had seen flames ignite when he stretched out his hand. Therefore, the people of his village gave all their property to him, so he could give potlatches.

He was truly treated as a chief.

That is the end.

THE SUN'S MYTH

▲

DELL HYMES

INTRODUCTION

Charles Cultee told "The Sun's Myth" to Franz Boas in 1891.[1]
Cultee, indeed, is the source of all the texts we have from the two
Chinookan languages that at the beginning of the century dominated the lower Columbia River. One of these, Shoalwater, was the
variety spoken around the mouth of the river on the Washington
side by the Chinook proper. Shoalwater and the somewhat distinct
Clatsop, spoken on the Oregon side of the river, are known collec-
tively as Lower Chinook. The language of "The Sun's Myth," Kathlamet, was spoken on both sides of the river from a little east of
Astoria for some distance inland. Kathlamet and the more easterly
Clackamas and Wasco-Wishram have usually been considered a single language, known as Upper Chinook. Nonetheless, Kathlamet
differs enough to count as a separate, third language.[2]

"The Sun's Myth" is remarkable for its theme of human hubris
and for its transformation of a framework widely known in western
North America. A favorite Kwakiutl myth is an analogue of the
Greek Phaëthon story. The trickster Mink is born to a woman who
has been impregnated miraculously by the sun. Teased by other
children for having no father, he goes to seek him, is welcomed, and
is allowed to take the sun's light about the world. He goes too low,
causing fires, and the light has to be taken back. In the Southwest

273

the Navajo and other groups have a story in which twins are born to a woman in a similar fashion, seek their father, are tested by him (at risk of death), show themselves to be true sons, and take back to earth the powers of lightning with which to destroy dangerous beings. Such testing occurs in many myths in which a man seeks to destroy his prospective or actual son-in-law. In all these instances the story is set before the present people have come, and the world they will inhabit still is being formed.

Cultee's narrative tells not of the establishment of that world but of its end. The one who comes to the sun is a prosperous chief (he has five towns of relatives); he is not tested but accepted as a son-in-law; he is given gifts willingly and unendingly. I believe the story is a reflection of sudden destruction by disease. The wish for power beyond that proper to the people may reflect the desire to obtain and monopolize the control of goods brought by whites to the mouth of the river. The stem for "myth, nature, character" was applied to whites, presumably because of the natives' amazement at their ways and possessions. The experience of sudden destruction went as far back as the later eighteenth century, when some villages were depopulated by smallpox; it became general in the epidemics of the early 1830s and 1840s, when almost all the Indian people west of the Cascades died. Whether Cultee created this myth or absorbed it from another, it almost certainly arose in response to that recent history. Notice that the explanation is in terms of the Indian world itself. Destruction comes because the terms of a providential relationship with the greater powers of the world are violated.

I first encountered "The Sun's Myth" as a graduate student in Los Angeles, turning the pages of Boas's *Kathlamet Texts* one by one at night to copy out the words and enter them into a file (so as to prepare a grammar and dictionary). The myth has been with me ever since. A retranslation and an analysis of the story were part of my presidential address to the American Folklore Society, given, fortuitously, in Portland in 1974,[3] a few miles from where I was born and not many more from the Trojan Nuclear Plant, at the edge of what was once Kathlamet territory.

This translation was prepared in the summer of 1979 in the Mount Hood National Forest. A copy has been made available to a descendant of Cultee's people, but it has not been published. The relations among lines and verses have been reconsidered, as have the words. For example, "that which he held" is now more literally—and more effectively, I think—"that which he had taken"; "in vain" *(kinwa)* is now at the beginning of sentences in English, as it is in Kathlamet; "give up" is now "abandon hope" (drawing on the use of *taminua* in Wasco as "forever"); in the catalogs of what is on the walls, "goods" and "things" have become "property," and "head ornaments" has been replaced by the term in current use in Indian country, "regalia"; "wrench" has become the more accurate "shaken"; and so on. The changes began in a further effort to be exact. They require adjustment of English expectations, but the effort is worthwhile, I hope, for the sake of the effectiveness of the original.

Boas published the myth as a series of sentences grouped in paragraphs. We know now that narratives in Kathlamet, and other languages, are told as a series of lines. Intonation contours and other features of the voice signal the lines. Although we have only a written record, the patterns of the original still can be approximated. A verbal phrase is usually a line, and the larger organization of the narrative consists of relations among lines. These relations can be inferred. They are marked by parallelism and repetition, by indications of change of time, place, actor, or incident, and by patterned relations.

Each culture favors one or more numbers (pattern numbers). Among the Kathlamet and many others in the region (including the Kalapuya and the Clackamas), the principal pattern number is five. In a ritual or a narrative, a series of actions will be five (or its correlate, three) in number. A dialogue will consist of three or five exchanges. (Sometimes a set of three consists of three pairs). These sequences are not mechanically counted out. They express a rhetorical logic, an arousal and satisfying of expectation. There is an onset, a continuation, an outcome. Often a five-part sequence will consist in effect of two series of three. The third element will be the outcome of one series of three and at the same time serve as the onset of another.

Narratives such as "The Sun's Myth" display a consistent architecture. They are made of lines that constitute verses, sets of verses that make up stanzas, stanzas that go together in scenes, scenes that go together in acts. In a long myth such as this, there may be more than one part, or set of acts. Here there are two such parts, one for the journey to the Sun, one for the return. Each has three acts. Each part reaches a time of stable quiet in its third act.

A narrator such as Cultee, then, coordinates two sequences, one of incident, one of form. He or she may skillfully adapt each to the other in a variety of ways, sometimes amplifying and pressing the limits of the frame, sometimes contracting, while maintaining the coherence of the whole. With patience, we can learn to recognize that shaping skill.

NOTES

1. Franz Boas, *Kathlamet Texts,* Smithsonian Institution, Bureau of American Ethnology Bulletin no. 26 (Washington, D.C., 1901).

2. Of the three languages, Shoalwater and Clatsop may continue to be called Lower Chinook, or Chinook proper; Kathlamet may continue to be called Kathlamet; and Clackamas and Wasco-Wishram may be called by their own name for their language, Kiksht.

3. Dell Hymes, "Folklore's Nature and the Sun's Myth," *Journal of American Folklore* 88 (1975): 35–69.

<table>
<tr><td></td><td>One</td></tr>
</table>

They live there, those people of a town.   Preface
Five the towns of his relatives, that chief.

In the early light,   I(A)
 now he used to go out,
  and outside,   5
  now he used to stay;
   now he used to see that sun:
   she would nearly come out, that sun.
Now he told his wife,
 "What would you think,   10
  if I went to look for that sun?"
She told him, his wife,
 "You think it is near?
  And you will wish to go to that sun?"

Another day,   (B)15
 again in the early light,
  he went out;
   now again he saw that sun:
   she did nearly come out there, that sun.
He told his wife,   20
 "You shall make ten pairs of moccasins,
 you shall make me leggings,
  leggings for ten people."
Now she made them for him, his wife,
 moccasins for ten people,   25
  the leggings of as many.

Again it became dawn,   (C)
 now he went,
  far he went.
He used up his moccasins;   30
 he used up his leggings;
  he put on others of his moccasins and leggings.
Five months he went;
 five of his moccasins he used up;
  five of his leggings he used up.   35
Ten months he went—

now she would rise nearby, that sun—
    he used up his moccasins.
Now he reached a house,
    a large house;   40
he opened the door,
    now some young girl is there;
he entered the house,
    he stayed.

Now he saw there on the side of that house: II[i](A)45
    arrows are hanging on it,
    quivers full of arrows are hanging on it,
    armors of elk skin are hanging on it,
    armors of wood are hanging on it,
    shields are hanging on it,   50
    axes are hanging on it,
    war clubs are hanging on it,
    feathered regalia are hanging on it—
        all men's property there on the side of that house.
There on the other side of that house: (B)55
    mountain goat blankets are hanging on it,
    painted elk-skin blankets are hanging on it,
    buffalo skins are hanging on it,
    dressed buckskins are hanging on it,
    long dentalia are hanging on it,   60
    shell beads are hanging on it,
    short dentalia are hanging on it—
Now, near the door, some large thing hangs over there;   (C)
    he did not recognize it.

Then he asked the young girl,   [ii](A)65
"Whose property are those quivers?"
    "Her property, my father's mother,
        she saves them for my maturity."
"Whose property are those elk-skin armors?"
    "Our property, my father's mother [and I],   70
        she saves them for my maturity."
"Whose property are those arrows?"
    "Our property, my father's mother [and I],
        she saves them for my maturity."

"Whose property are those wooden armors?"   (B)75
    "Our property, my father's mother [and I],

she saves them for my maturity."
"Whose property are those shields,
    and those bone war clubs?"
    "Our property, my father's mother [and I]."   80
"Whose property are those stone axes?"
    "Our property, my father's mother [and I]."

Then again on the other side of that house: (C)
"Whose property are those buffalo skins?"
    "Our buffalo skins, my father's mother [and I],   85
        she saves them for my maturity."
"Whose property are those mountain goat blankets?"
    "Our property, my father's mother [and I],
        she saves them for my maturity."
"Whose property are those dressed buckskins?"   90
    "Our property, my father's mother [and I],
        she saves them for my maturity."

"Whose property are those deerskin blankets?"   (D)
    "Our property, my father's mother [and I],
        she saves them for my maturity."   95
"Whose property are those shell beads?"
    "Our property, my father's mother [and I],
        she saves them for my maturity."
"Whose property are those long dentalia?
Whose property are those short dentalia?"   100
    "Her property, my father's mother,
        she saves them for my maturity."

He asked her about all those things.   (E)
He thought,
    "I will take her."   105

At dark,
    now that old woman came home.   [iii]
Now again she hung up one [thing],
    that which he wanted,
        that thing shining all over.   110
He stayed there.

A long time he stayed there;   III
    now he took that young girl.
They stayed there.

In the early light,   115
  already that old woman was gone.
In the evening,
    she would come home;
  she would bring things,
    she would bring arrows;   120
 sometimes mountain goat blankets she would bring,
    sometimes elk-skin armors she would bring.
Every day like this.

                                       Two
A long time he stayed.   IV[i](A)
Now he felt homesick.   125
Twice he slept,
  he did not get up.
That old woman said to her grandchild,
  "Did you scold him,
    and he is angry?"   130
[—]* "No, I did not scold him,
  he feels homesick."

Now she told her son-in-law,   (B)
  "What will you carry when you go home?
  Will you carry those buffalo skins?"   135
He told her,
  "No."
"Will you carry those mountain goat blankets?"
He told her,
  "No."   140
"Will you carry all those elk-skin armors?"
He told her,
  "No."

She tried in vain to show him all that on one side of the house. (C)
  Next all those [other] things.   145
    She tried in vain to show him all, *every*thing.
He wants only that,
  that thing that is large,
    that [thing] put up away.
When it would sway,   150

*A dash in brackets indicates a change in speaker.

that thing put up away,
  it would become turned around,
  at once his eyes would be extinguished;
    that thing [is] shining all over,
    now he wants only that thing there.   155

He told his wife,   [ii]
  "She shall give me one [thing],
    that blanket of hers, that old woman."
His wife told him,
  "She will never give it to you.   160
  In vain people continue to try to trade it from her;
  she will never do it."
Now again he became angry.

Several times he slept.   [iii](A)
  Now again she would ask him,   165
  "Will you carry that?"
    she would tell him.
She would try in vain to show him all those things of hers;
  she would try in vain to show him those men's things;
    she would try in vain to show him all.   170
She would reach that [thing] put up away,   (B)
  now she would become silent.
When she would reach that [thing] put away,
  now her heart became tired.
Now she told him: 175
  "You must carry it then!
  Take care! if you carry it.
  It is you who choose.
  I try to love you,
  indeed I do love you."   180

She hung it on him,   (C)
  she hung it all on him.
Now she gave him a stone ax.
She told him:
  "Go home now!"   185

He went out,   V[i](A)
  now he went,
    he went home;

he did not see a land;
    he arrived near his father's brother's town.   190
Now that which he had taken throbbed,
    now that which he had taken said,
      "We two shall strike your town,
      we two shall strike your town,"
        said that which he had taken.   }*   195
His reason became nothing,   (B)
    he did it to his father's brother's town,
      he crushed, crushed, crushed it,
        he killed all the people.
He recovered—   200
    all those houses are crushed,
      his hands are full of blood.   }
He thought,   (C)
    "O I am a fool!
    See, that is what it is like, this thing!   205
    Why was I made to love this?"
In vain he tried to begin shaking it off,
    and his flesh would be pulled.   }

Now again he went,   [ii](A)
    and he went a little while—   210
Now again his reason became nothing—
    he arrived near another father's brother's town.
Now again it said,
    "We two shall strike your town,
    we two shall strike your town."   215
In vain he would try to still it,
    it was never still.
In vain he would try to throw it away,
    always those fingers of his would cramp.

Now again his reason became nothing,   (B)220
    now again he did it to his father's brother's town,
      he crushed it all.
He recovered:
    his father's brother's town [is] nothing,
      the people all are dead.   225
Now he cried.

▲

*A closed brace indicates the end point of a pair of units. There are three pairs of stanzas in this scene.

In vain he tried in the fork of a tree,   (C)
   there in vain he would try squeezing through it;
in vain he would try to shake it off,
   it would not come off,   230
     and his flesh would be pulled;
in vain he would keep beating what he had taken on rocks,
   it would never be crushed.

Again he would go,   [iii](A)
   he would arrive near another father's brother's town.   235

Now again that which he had taken would shake:
   "We two shall strike your town,
   we two shall strike your town."
His reason would become nothing,   (B)
   he would do it to his father's brother's town,   240
     crush, crush, crush, crush;
   all his father's brother's town he would destroy,
    and he would destroy the people.
He would recover;
   he would cry out;   245
    he would grieve for his relatives.

In vain he would try diving into water;   (C)
   in vain he would try to shake it off,
    and his flesh would be pulled.
In vain he would try rolling in a thicket;   250
   in vain he would keep beating what he had taken on rocks;
    he would abandon hope.
Now he would cry out.

Again he would go.   [iv](A)
Now again he would arrive at another town,   255
   a father's brother's town.
Now again what he had taken would shake:
   "We two shall strike your town,
   we two shall strike your town."

His reason would become nothing,   (B)260
   he would do it to the town,
    crush, crush, crush, crush,
     and the people.
He would recover:

all the people and the town [are] no more;   265
    his hands and arms [are] only blood.
He would become
  "Qa! qa! qa! qa!"
    he would cry out.

In vain he would try to beat it on the rocks,   (C)270
    what he had taken would not be crushed.
In vain he would try to throw away what he had taken,
    always his fingers stick to it.

Again he would go.   [v](A)
Now his too, his town,   275
    he would be near his town.
In vain he would try to stand, that one;
    see, something would pull his feet.

His reason would become nothing,   (B)
    he would do it to his town,   280
    crush, crush, crush, crush;
    all his town he would destroy,
      and he would destroy his relatives.
He would recover:
    his town is nothing;   285
    the dead fill the ground.
He would become
  "Qa! qa! qa! qa!"
    he would cry out.

In vain he would try to bathe;   (C)290
    in vain he would try to shake off what he wears,
      and his flesh would be pulled.
Sometimes he would roll about on rocks;
    he would think,
      "Perhaps it will break apart";   295
        he would abandon hope.
Now again he would cry out,
    and he wept.

He looked back.   VI(A)
Now she is standing near him, that old woman.   300
"You,"

she told him,
  "You.
In vain I try to love you,
  in vain I try to love your relatives.   305
Why do you weep?
  It is you who choose;
    now you carried that blanket of mine."
Now she took it,   (B)
  she lifted off what he had taken;   310
now she left him,
  she went home.
He stayed there;   (C)
  he went a little distance;
there he built a house,   315
  a small house.

COYOTE, MASTER OF DEATH, TRUE TO LIFE

▲

DELL HYMES

INTRODUCTION

This myth, told by William Hartless in Mary's River Kalapuya, begins with death and ends with life. It shows Coyote as the shape-changing chameleon familiar from many stories, but after showing foresight, devotion to a child, and mastery of the land of the dead. To experience tricks and transformations as a sequel to that makes them appear not the foibles of a scamp but a lesson learned, a way to say, as if Coyote might quote T. S. Eliot's "The Love Song of J. Alfred Prufrock" and add a line:

> "I am Lazarus, come from the dead,
>   Come back to tell you all, I shall tell you all,—
>   Live exuberantly."

The first act, the origin of permanent death, is a well-known frame.[1] When a friend's child dies, his partner ordains that the dead should not come back; when his own child dies, he wants to change the rule and cannot. But what follows is not an Orpheus myth, as in some nearby traditions (Wasco-Wishram, Nez Perce).[2] There two partners set out to bring back their dead and would succeed but that Coyote is unable to control his curiosity, looks before they are all the way back, and so the dead are gone forever. He may try to go a second time but cannot find the way.

286

Here, however, Coyote goes without a partner, not to bring his child back but to be with her. When he returns, it is after having mastered the other world. He stumbles as he goes, and makes mistakes when first there, but learns the ways of hunting and is praised. There follow contests, an allusion to myths in which a party travels to another land, perhaps under the ocean, and engages in contests in which life is at stake. The protagonists need advice and trickery to win. Here Coyote has the help of those he is among in gambling (they sing his gambling song with him), then in other contests simply wins.

In the land of the dead, this Coyote does well what a man should want to do well, almost as if he were a chiefly character, like Eagle or Salmon. But the desire that has led him to follow his daughter becomes a reason to leave. He cannot be with her enough. The dead are active at night, not during the day. She agrees it is right for him to return. He goes back from a world of darkness to a world of summer (though it will be a year before he says so).

And what is he now? A prankster, leading frog women who have importuned him for salmon to open a pack of hornets. Autocoprophagous, eating his feces as if they were camas. Scaring off the woodpecker that could help him escape confinement in a tree, unable to resist attempting to copulate with her. Self-dismantler, taking his body apart, piece by piece, throwing it out, putting it together again. One eyed, without an anus, forgetting the latter until a wind blowing into him reminds him to go back to get it. As for his eye, stolen by Blue Jay, he steals it back, and that is the rest of the story. He makes himself appear wealthy, then a headman, then an old woman, each time fooling the people he needs to fool. Again and again he makes others think something, mostly himself, what it is not.

This quicksilver Coyote, protean, polymorphous, a carnival of identities, is that, I think, because of his having come from the dead. In each land, that of the dead and that of the living, he first pays a price for what he tries to do and then succeeds. Foreseeing that the interests of the world require death to be forever, he loses his own child. Following her, he stumbles. Taking a part in the hunting of the people in the land of the dead, he fails. But these three failures are followed by success. He learns the way of hunting, and wins at gambling, at the games of women's shinny and men's shinny, at wrestling—five successes. In the land of the living, he pays the price for tricking the Frog women: he must enclose himself in a tree to escape the weather they bring. He fails when he seeks help from the birds. And he loses his eye when he attempts to throw himself out piece by piece. But these three failures are followed by success. He gets the information he needs from one old woman and then from another; he goes unrecognized among the people as he gambles (despite the warning from another coyote), outruns those who pursue him (including his initial partner, Panther, who is the one who almost catches him), and goes unrecognized by those who catch up with him (despite some who doubt he is really a blind old woman)— five successes. Within the architecture of scenes and acts, then, is a doubling that invites reflection.

Mastery in the land of the dead is learning practices that are the opposite of what one has known. Mastery in the land of the living also may involve the opposite of what is expected. The land of the dead has ways that stay the same. The land of the living can be play, a stage for improvisation with whatever is at hand—hornets, an ash tree, rose hips; it can be a stage for the invention of an identity—rich man, headman, blind old woman. Or so the sequence of these adventures seems to say.

There is a direction within the doubling. Coyote begins as a partner and a father. He leaves his partner to follow his daughter to the land of the dead. He leaves his daughter to return: two social ties, then one, then none. The last words are his, "You beat me indeed," translated as "You never can beat me!" That finally is his nature, it would seem, to be beyond social ties and against them, to be forever the possibility of what is not.

This myth ends with Coyote sarcastically exultant and alone. It is as if the narrative had created an icon. Its doubling and its zest invite a thought of *post hoc propter hoc* and the reflection that coyote's exultation is earned. In each half of the myth, he pays a price before he succeeds. This is true both when he seeks the good of others and when he seeks only to satisfy himself. He earns, then, success in the land of the dead and earns, one can think, success in the land of the living. This doubling points to an implicit constant.

The first success consists of adaptation, the second of deception, but in one respect both are alike. If deception is a counterpoint to the living, so is adaptation in the land of the dead. For the ways to which Coyote adapts are opposite those of the living. Day is night, and so forth. Perhaps that is why Coyote succeeds there at what others do. Perhaps he ultimately is a principle of inversion, a form of what Kenneth Burke might call the negative, somehow kin to the helpful Satan of Burke's great essay, "Prologue in Heaven."[3]

In stories Coyote can be an object lesson, doing what should not be done, being fooled or scorned in consequence, or teaching others not to be fooled. He can also be a source of fun. In this myth, as shaped by William Hartless or those from whom he learned it, I sense a reflection on Coyote's nature that can be linked with something Burke describes. There is a feeling of transcendence, of reaching out to a farther shore.[4] The beginning bespeaks recognition that a human condition should remain fixed, and a choice is made that it be so (death is to be permanent). The middle involves discovery that a condition that is fixed for others can be mastered by someone unlike them. The last part exhibits a lesson learned, the exploration of being something other for its own sake, as if self-mastery is self-transformation, making oneself a pure principle of transformation among others who (so far as the story tells us) are always what they are.

The genre of the story, myth, implies a further step. In the myth, whether adapting or deceiving, Coyote is unlike others: alive among the dead, ever changing among the living. But these are the living of the world of myth people. They will not, after all, stay what they are. They themselves will be transformed when the myth period ends, and the Indian people, who tell these stories, come. The entire genre and its world is based on inversion, on consideration of the counterfactual. The people of the myths, and Coyote, become again what they were when the stories are told. But Coyote, at least in this myth, becomes almost a pure example of the principle of myth itself. He becomes almost inversion itself, imaginative experiment with experience, play with appearance, transformation and transcendence of identity—and he does so, I conjecture, because the mind of William Hartless, thinking and telling these events and details in this sequence in these proportions with these details, was party to the kinds of exploration of verbal resource, of logical and temporal order, of carrying through and perfecting of motive that Kenneth Burke has done so much to show is inherent in the human use of language.

The integration of the full myth may not have been the accomplishment of Mr. Hartless alone, but what is known suggests as much. The incidents and sequence of the second part (the Frog sisters, the hollow tree, the loss and recovery of the eye) are shared Kalapuya tradition. John B. Hudson told a fine version of the myth in Santiam Kalapuya,[5] but he told the story of the origin of death separately and without a role for a daughter.[6] Mr. Hudson's sequence differs in details. It has Coyote hungry but not lecherous—the birds he calls to help him are "brothers," and what he wants from the last bird are feathers for regalia. It has no sudden rush of sexuality. It lacks the steps by which Coyote builds up his impersonation and participation in the gambling. Rather, Coyote simply comes, uses his power to keep the people from noticing him, grabs the eye, and runs off. It elaborates the pursuit with three deceptions; only the last is as another person (the first are as a digging stick and a hole in the ground).

Eustace Howard (the husband of Victoria Howard, who tells the myth of "Seal and Her Younger Brother Lived There") dictated to Jacobs a somewhat different version of the full myth. It does not begin with a decision as to the permanence of death. The focus is on the daughter and a series of suitors, and she dies as a result of her encounters with them. Coyote then follows her to the land of the dead and returns. Mr. Howard's narrative may have some of the implications of the telling by Mr. Hartless, but it is expressed in a more leisurely manner. Permanent death comes about after the return from the land of the dead, somewhat in the Orpheus manner found in the Wasco-Wishram and Nez Perce traditions. Coyote valiantly attempts to carry the souls of the dead the full way but cannot. The effect of this placement is quite different from that in Mr. Hartless's narrative, where permanent death occurs at first.

Mr. Hartless stands out in his expression of character and human nature through narrative, though he is not unique in this. The genre itself serves that purpose, analyzing motive or character through consequences exhibited in a story. Charles Cultee in "The Sun's Myth" and Victoria Howard in "Seal and Her Younger Brother Lived There" and others (for example, Mrs. Howard again in "Gitskux and His Older Brother Lived There") also used the genre profoundly.[7] No doubt there were many who did, pondering the stories they had heard and finding further meaning in them. In Charles Cultee's and Victoria Howard's narratives are instances remarkable for the transformation in point of view. Mr. Hartless stands out for the depth he gives to familiar incidents through extended sequencing and organization.

The form of the story can be sketched as follows. There are twelve scenes in three acts. Each act can be summarized in terms of what it is about and what Coyote does at the end of it. The acts are about, successively, the origin of permanent death, the ways of the dead, and the ways of the living, as disclosed by a Coyote who has returned from the land of the dead. The acts end with Coyote going to the land of the dead, returning from the land of the dead, and going on alone.

Kalapuya tradition makes use of three kinds of relations among elements, a sequence of three, a sequence of five, and a sequence of three or five pairs. These relations obtain first of all among verses. Verses themselves are frequently marked by an initial *lau'mde* ("now then") or *wi·naswi·* ("sure enough"). A major time reference, such as "five days" or "five times" or "a whole year," may mark a verse. A turn at talk is always a verse.

There are exceptions, however. At a few points in this narrative, there are simply pairs. The narrative begins with two verses that introduce Panther and Coyote and the fact of each having a daughter. It ends with two verses in which Coyote and then the narrator say, in effect, "that's all." Perhaps the two pairs are a sort of envelope to the narrative proper, and their pairing is felt appropriate to the role.

Again, the second and third contests in the land of the dead, women's and men's shinny, each are pairs of verses. Here pairing does not seem to have a formal significance. It may be just an expeditious way to get from gambling to the wrestling with which the scene culminates.

At the end of the second act, there is a scene whose first stanza consists of three verses in a familiar pattern: Coyote stayed there, he got lonesome, he said such and such. There follow two exchanges between Coyote and his daughter and a verse of departure, five verses in all. If they make up a stanza, the scene has only two. The text is presented this way, although there is no apparent reason for the lack of a third stanza. It remains possible that Coyote's three announcements ("I'll go back," "Now I'll leave you," "Well now I go back") show the scene to have three stanzas. They would have three, two, and three verses, respectively, with no apparent reason for just two in the second.

This myth was dictated by William Hartless to Leo J. Frachtenberg in 1914. In 1936, it was checked by Melville Jacobs with the help of John B. Hudson, a speaker of the mutually intelligible Santiam dialect, who had known Mr. Hartless well. The edited text was published in *Kalapuya Texts*.[8] I have checked the published text against a photocopy of Frachtenberg's manuscript and have followed the Jacobs-Hudson text, which differs in orthography, word and syllable divisions, and sometimes morphemes from that transcribed by Frachtenberg. I have reconsidered the translation of each sentence. The present translation is more literal, in that it retains patterns of repetition and structural cues more consistently. Sometimes it is more colloquial. Jacobs published the myth with a title that enumerates its actions. The title given here attempts to state its theme.

NOTES

1. Stith Thompson, *Tales of the North American Indians* (1929; reprint, Bloomington: Indiana University Press, 1966), 285*n*.

2. Jarold Ramsey, *Reading the Fire: Essays in the Traditional Indian Literature of the Far West* (Lincoln: University of Nebraska Press, 1983), ch. 3.

3. Kenneth Burke, "Epilogue: Prologue in Heaven," in *The Rhetoric of Religion: Studies in Logology* (Boston: Beacon Press, 1961; reprint, Berkeley and Los Angeles: University of California Press, 1970).

4. Kenneth Burke, *Language as Symbolic Action: Essays on Life, Literature, and Method* (Berkeley and Los Angeles: University of California Press, 1966); cf. Angus Fletcher, "Volume and Body in Burke's Criticism, or Stalled in the Right Place," in *Representing Kenneth Burke,* ed. Hayden White and Margaret Brose, Selected Papers from the English Institute, new series vol. 6 (Baltimore: Johns Hopkins University Press), 150–71.

5. Melville Jacobs, *Kalapuya Texts,* University of Washington Publications in Anthropology no. 11 (Seattle: University of Washington Press, 1945), 96–103.

6. Ibid., 137–38; cf. note 16 in that volume.

7. See Dell Hymes, "Victoria Howard's 'Gitskux and His Older Brother': A Clackamas Chinook Myth," in *Smoothing the Ground: Essays on Native American Oral Literature,* ed. Brian Swann (Berkeley: University of California Press, 1983), 129–70.

8. Jacobs, *Kalapuya Texts,* 226–36.

Panther and his brother lived there,   I[i](A)
  he together with Coyote.
Coyote had a daughter,
  Panther indeed also had a daughter.

Now then Panther's daughter fell ill,   (B)5
  she died.
Now then Panther said,
  "I will go see my brother."   }*
Now then he said to his brother, Coyote,
  "How is your heart about it?   10
  When a person dies,
  The fifth day he will come back?"
Coyote said nothing.   }
Again indeed he said to his brother,
  "How is the thing I told you?"   15
Coyote said,
  "No. It must not be that way.
  If it were to be that way where people live,
    the number of people would be endless.
  Better that a person die for all time.   20
  For all time he will be gone."   }
Panther said,
  "Ohh no! Brother!
  Better really that they come back."
Coyote said,   25
  "Not now!
  Everything that is,
    the black water bugs themselves would say,
      'Where are we to stay?'"   }
Coyote said,   30
  "Let it be that way when a person dies.
  That way he will indeed die for all time."
Panther said,
  "Your own heart."   }

---

*A closed brace indicates the end of a pair that counts as a unit. In this scene there are five such pairs of verses.

Now then Panther went back.   (C)35
  He wept.
    He buried his daughter.

Now then one year later Coyote's daughter fell ill,   [ii](A)
  she died.
Now then Coyote said,   40
  "Well now brother!
  Let it be the very way you told me."
Panther said,
  "It cannot be that way now."
Coyote said,   45
  "Ohh it would be better that people come back,
  on the fifth day they awaken."
Panther said,
  "Not now!
  You already said,   50
    'When a person dies,
    he is to be dead indeed for all time.'
  You spoke that way,"
    Panther said.

Now then Coyote went back,   (B)55
  he wept and wept,
    he got back home,
      he said,
        "I will go myself."
He said to his daughter,   60
  "I will go myself.
  We will go together."
His daughter said,
  "You can't follow me now.
  It is another kind of country where I am going."   65
Coyote said,
  "It's no matter that I go myself."
Now then he made a rope.

Five days he made a rope.   (C)
  "All right then, let's go!"   }   70
Sure enough Coyote tied it to himself.
Now then the girl went up [in the air].   }
Now then she told him,

"When you get tired,
    don't actually call out.   75
I won't hear.
When you call out,
    just say 'hahh.'
Now then I will come down,
    I will wait for you."   80
"Ohh," Coyote said,
    "I will certainly know that."   }

Now then they went along.   [iii](A)
    Coyote ran along on the ground,
        the dead one went along up above [in the air].   85
Coyote was running along.
Now then he got tired.
Now then he called out,
    "Ohhhh I am getting *tired!*
    Ohhhh I am getting *tired!*"   90
The dead one never heard him.

At last Coyote got tired,   (B)
    he nearly fell down,
        his heart nearly gave out [in faint].
He just opened his mouth [a gasp].   95
Now then the dead one heard,
    she arrived below,
        she scolded her father.

Five times they went on that way;   (C)
    they arrived.   100
Well now they arrived at the ocean.   }
The dead one called out.
Sure enough, a canoe came.   }
Now then the dead one told her father,
    "It won't come close.   105
        Jump.
        We will both jump.
        And when we are across,
        we will jump that very same way again.
    Now then I will go to a house,   110
        you yourself will also go to a house.
        You must stay there five days.

You will not see me.
  For five days and for five nights,
    and then you will see me.   115
  I will be standing at my dance that long a time,
    and then I will be right again."
Sure enough, Coyote stayed all alone.   }

Now then his daughter got there.   II[i](A)
Now then she said,   120
  "Who is this old man?
  He is raw.*
  Let us go hunting."   }
Sure enough, the raw one was taken along.
And now the raw one was put along the deer's trail.   }   125
Now then some of the people encircled the mountain,
  they were driving [deer].
Now then they were crying out.†   }
Sure enough the people came closer.
Coyote noticed nothing,   130
  he saw only snails.
  He could see no deer,
    he saw only that.   }
Now then the people arrived.
"Ah dear! The old man spoiled the deer!"‡   }   135

Sure enough they fed him only bones,   (B)
  they were heaped in a pile.
    The meat they threw away.
And now they went back.   }
He went along there to the rear,   140
  he threw away those bones he had been given,
  he picked up the meat thrown away,
    that is what he took along,
    he got back to the house.
Now then the bones he had brought turned into meat.   }   145
Now then his daughter scolded him,

*He is raw: Or, "he is green"; that is, he is not in the right bodily condition to be there.
†they were crying out: They were crying, "Hí hí hí," as in guardian spirit songs and sweathouse songs.
‡spoiled the deer: let it escape.

she told him,
   "What you call a snail,
      that is our deer.
   Those here call it deer."   150
Now then Coyote said,
   "Now I know."   }

Sure enough, again indeed he was told,   (C)
   "Let's go hunt."
Now then indeed they went away again.   155
Again he was placed on the deer's trail.
Now then the people encircled the mountain,
   they drove.
Sure enough, now then they drove it.

In a little while, sure enough, a snail went by.   (D)160
Now then he poked it with a stick,
   he threw it aside.   }
In a little while again a snail again indeed went by,
   again indeed he poked it with a stick,
      he threw it out of the way.   165
Now then a number of snails went by,
   he killed them all.   }
Now then the people arrived,
   they said,
      "Ohh the old raw one is fine!"   170
Now then Coyote looked to the rear,
   he noticed great numbers piled up,
      great numbers of deer and elk.
      Ohh he felt glad at heart.   }

Now then they skinned and butchered.   (E)175
Now then they piled them up.
   They threw away all the meat,
      only the bones were taken along.   }
Coyote also actually packed bones.
He reached the house,   180
   now then those bones turned into meat.   }
Now then it was said,
   "The old man is fine now!"
They liked the old man now.   }

▲

Now then some of the people said,   [ii](A)185
  "Let's gamble."
Now then Coyote said,
  "Not here!"
Now then some of their dead ones said,
  "We will help you [sing your gambling songs]."   190
[—]*"Ohh that's fine."
Sure enough now then they gambled.
  Some of the dead helped him,
    Coyote won.

Now then again Coyote was actually told,   (B)195
  "Let's play woman's shinny."
Sure enough Coyote actually played woman's shinny,
  indeed he also won.

Now then again he was actually told,   (C)
  "Let's play men's shinny now."   200
Sure enough, they played men's shinny;
  indeed Coyote also won.

Now then Coyote was told,   (D)
  "Tomorrow we will wrestle."
Now then Coyote wrestled;   205
  he was pretty nearly thrown.
Now then he threw him.

Five times he wrestled.   (E)
Now then on the fifth time *again* he was actually nearly thrown,
  again Coyote actually threw him.   210
Now they quit their gambling.

Now then Coyote remained there.   [iii](A)
Now then he got lonesome.
Now then he said,
  "I'll go back.   215
  I'm lonesome.
  There's no one here to talk with.
    In daylight I don't see anyone,
      only in the dark do people then go about.

*A dash in brackets indicates a change in speaker.

I don't like it like that,   220
  and so I say,
    'I'll go back.' "

Now then he told his daughter,   (B)
  "Now I'm going to leave you.
  I'm lonesome.   225
  Even you I do not see in the day."
His daughter said,
  "That I cannot help.
  That is our way."
  In the dark we get up,   230
    we go about,
      in the day we sleep.
  That is how we do."

He said to his daughter,   (C)
  "Well now I go back."   235
"Ohh it's quite all right you go back,"
  his daughter said.
Sure enough Coyote was taken across.
Now then he came back,   III[i](A)
  he was halfway [to his] place,   240
    he saw five girls digging camas.
He said,
  "They'll come over to meet me.
  —Ohh I'll go back,
  I'll fetch what I saw."   }   245
Sure enough he went to get those hornets.
Now then he put it [the nest] in his sack.   }
He went on again.
  He got to where the five girls were digging camas.
Sure enough the girls said,   250
  "Ohhhh Coyote!
  Give us food!
  Aren't you carrying along a little dried salmon?" }
Coyote kept going,
  rather as if he really didn't hear them.   255
Again the girls halloed in the very same way:
  "Uhhh Coyote!
  Give us food!
  Aren't you carrying something along?

Give us a little food!"   } 260
Now then Coyote said,
    "Hu! What is it?"
[—]"Ohh give us food!"   }

[—]"What shall I give you?   (B)
    I'm not carrying anything.   265
    I am carrying a little.
    Well, come over here!"
Sure enough those girls came.
[—] "Sit down here!
    Look at it carefully!   270
    Sit close!
    All of you smell it
    And then unpack it."
Sure enough they unpacked it.
Now then out came hornets.   275
    They stung all those girls,
        they all fell there [unconscious].

Now then Coyote snorted [a forced laugh especially his own]. (C)
Now then Coyote went on.
Now then Coyote said,   280
    "You can indeed make fun of me."

After a long time one of the Frogs woke up.   [ii](A)
Now then she dragged her sisters to one side.   }
Now then they all got up.
Now then they said,   285
    "Let's go after Coyote."   }
Now then the youngest said,
    "What do you know [of spirit power]?"
Now then the oldest said,
    "I know nothing.   290
    I know a little smoke fog."   }
Now then she said to another also,
    "What do *you* know?"
[—] "I know nothing.
    A little of the sky [up above] pours down [that is, rain]. } 295
Now then she spoke the same way to another also.
Now then the fifth time she herself said,
    "I will cause snow and a north wind."   }

▲

Sure enough, the youngest said [that].   **(B)**
Now then snow came down.   **300**
Now then a north wind blew.

Now then Coyote hurried along.   **(C)**
At last snow got to his knees.   }
Now then he kept going along.
Now then it got to his upper thigh.   }   **305**
Now then Coyote said,
  "Now they've gotten me.
  Maybe they won't have gotten me.
  Open up!
  Tree!"   **310**
To be sure, an ash tree opened up.   }
Now then Coyote went inside there.
  "Shut!
  Tree!"
Sure enough the tree shut.   }   **315**
    Coyote remained inside the tree.
Now then the Frogs were going after Coyote.
  They got there,
    they lost his trail.
Now then those Frogs went back.   }}*   **320**

One whole year Coyote remained inside.   **[iii](A)**
He woke up:
  "It's really as if I hear birds singing."
Now then Coyote said,
  "Ohh it must really be summertime now!"   **325**
Now then he felt around,
  he found "cooked camas"
    —he called it "cooked camas,"
      what he called "cooked camas" were his feces.
Now then he ate really his feces.   **330**

Now then he halloed,   **(B)**
  "Open it for me!"
Sure enough, the Sapsucker came.
[—] "Not you!"

---

*The double brace indicates that this is the end of the second of a pair of scenes.
The third act consists of three pairs of scenes, having to do with the Frogs [i, ii],
confinement in the tree and escape [iii, iv], and recovery of his eye [v, vi].

Now then the Yellow Hammer came.   335
Now then he said,
  "Not you!"

Now he began halloing indeed again.   (C)
Now then the Mountain Woodpecker came.
Now then that one pecked.   340

Sure enough he could see a little.   (D)
Now then he could see somewhat farther.
Now Coyote said in his heart,
  "I'll catch her as she pecks close here.
  I'll fuck her—   345
  It's a woman."

Sure enough, he leaped on her,   (E)
  he missed.
Now then the Woodpecker went back to the mountains,
  she said,   350
    "Gagagagagagag."
Now then Coyote said,
  "Come back!
  I was only joking with you."

Now then Coyote was left there.   [iv](A) 355
Now then he told his anus,
  "Could you take care of yourself right away?"   }
Sure enough he pulled off his leg,
  he pulled off his other leg also.
Now then he pulled off his anus,   360
  he threw it outside.   }
Now then he pulled off one of his arms,
now then he pulled off his head,
  he threw it outside.   }

Now then the Blue Jay went by on the run   (B) 365
  he stole Coyote's eye.
The Blue Jay said,
  "Qwácha qwácha qwácha,
  Coyote's anus broke wind!"
Coyote got angry.   370
Now then he threw everything,

he threw his body.
Now then he put himself together.
  One of his eyes was missing,
    Blue Jay had stolen it. 375

Now then he left his anus there. (C)
  He felt cold,
    wind was coming in.
Now then he went back,
  he went to get his anus. 380
Now then he went along.
  He made his eye from a rose hip. }}*

Now then he went along again, [v](A)
  he got to where one house was standing,
  one old woman stayed there; 385
    he went into it:
      "Where are all the people?"
[—] "Ohh they went away to the hand-game gambling,
  All the people went away to the hand-game gambling."
Coyote said, 390
  "Ohh! In what direction?"
Now then the woman said,
  "This direction!"
    She named the place.
Coyote said, 395
  "Ohh good indeed."

Now then Coyote went along. (B)
Now then he made money [dentalia] from stalks of camas sprouts,
  that was what he made into money.
Now then he made beads of several kinds from rose hips, 400
  that was what he made into beads.

Now then he went along, (C)
  he got to still another place,
    one house had smoke coming out.
Now then he went in there, 405
  an old woman is staying there. }

*Again the double brace indicates that this is the end of the second of a pair of scenes.

[—] "Who are you," said the old woman.
[—] "Ohh just me.
  Where have they gone to?"   }
[—] "They went to the hand-game gambling."   410
[—] "In what direction?"
She named the place.
[—] "Ohh," Coyote said.
  "What is going on?"
[—] "Coyote's eye is being rolled."   415
  "Ohh," said Coyote.   }

Now then he went along,   [vi](A)
  he got to this place.
Sure enough he had already fixed himself up,
  he had made himself a headman.   420
Sure enough.

It was said,   (B)
  "Let's gamble."
Now then another coyote said,
  "Be careful!   425
  That's a coyote there!"   }
Now then they wanted to whip him.
Now then Coyote sat [remained sitting].   }
Now then they said,
  "Let's gamble!"   430
Still he sat.   }}*

After a long time he said,   (C)
  "Ohh all right then, really!"†
Sure enough, he poured out his bet [money dentalia].
Now then Coyote's eye was rolled,   435
  Coyote missed it,
    he was beaten.

Again indeed he bet.   (D)
Again he [another player] rolled it,

*In this scene the double brace indicates the end of the second of a pair of stanzas. There are five pairs of stanzas in the scene.
†"Ohh . . . really!": Of course the reluctance is feigned. He has come just for that purpose.

he missed indeed again,   440
    Coyote was beaten.
At the fifth time Coyote said,
    "Now I'll get it."   }}

That other coyote on the opposite side kept saying,   (E)
    "That's a coyote there."   445
Now then he was scolded by them.   }
Now then they rolled it,
    the people forgot their hearts [grew careless a moment],
        they rolled the eye again.
Now then he got it,   450
    he jumped up,
        he ran,
            he was chased,
                he left them behind.   }
That other coyote was told,   455
    "Run!
    You are fast!"
He said,
    "You won't catch him now.
    I did tell you."   }   460

Now then all the kinds of people ran,   (F)
    Panther also indeed,
        he pretty nearly overtook him.
He twisted around to the other side of a hill,
    he set up a house,   465
        he went into it.
He made himself an old woman;
    she had no eyes,
        she was washing.   }}

Now then the people arrived there,   (G)470
    they entered,
        they said,
            "No one has gotten here?"
The old woman said,
    "No one has gotten here."   475
[—] "Search around for him!"
Sure enough they searched around for him,
    everywhere close and outside;

they did not find him.
Now then they said,   480
  "Ohh let's go back.
  We can't find him."

Some of them said,   (H)
  "It must be he himself!" [the old woman]
Some others said,   485
  "No!
  That's not really him!"
Now then they went back,
  they gave it up indeed.   }}

Now then Coyote said,   (I)490
  "You indeed [can never] beat me!"

That's all of that now.   }}   (J)

SEAL AND HER YOUNGER
BROTHER LIVED THERE

▲

DELL HYMES

INTRODUCTION

Victoria Howard dictated "Seal and Her Younger Brother Lived There" to Melville Jacobs in 1930, shortly before her death.[1] It is recorded in the last notebook (number 17) of their collaboration along with a number of other texts considered incomplete. Incomplete, in one sense, it is. In origin it is a scene of suspense from a story of revenge. A man has killed his wife; her brother disguises himself as her to gain access to the house and take revenge. (In other forms of the theme, two men recapture the older man's wife, or two sons recover and restore their father). The avenger survives a series of near detections. Finally, going up to bed at night, a knife (or a penis) is seen beneath his clothes by a small child (as in the Coos versions). The child calls out but is shushed by an older person. The revenge succeeds.

Mrs. Howard heard the story from her mother-in-law. In it (and in what Ida White and George Forman, Wasco speakers of the Yakima Reservation in Washington, once recalled to Michael Silverstein and me), the event is seen from the standpoint of women of the family revenged upon. It is one of several myths Mrs. Howard told in which male adventure is transformed into female experience.

The title is her own. It calls attention to the mother as the one whose conduct determines the outcome of the story (death and separation). But there runs through the story a second consequence, that of the daughter's emergence into maturity and of her independence.

I have discussed this story several times over some twenty years and each time have found something more.[2] It has been reprinted in the *Longman Anthology of World Literature by Women* and in a Japanese translation.[3] The present form supplants that of earlier articles,[4] recognizing that in the second scene the mother's second *"shush"* must, like that in the first scene, be heard as a close; change of location initiates the third scene as well as the first and second.

NOTES

1. Melville Jacobs, *Clackamas Chinook Texts*, Research Center in Anthropology, Folklore, and Linguistics Publication no. 11, International Journal of American Linguistics, vol. 25, pt. 2 (Bloomington, Ind., 1959) and *The People Are Coming: Analyses of Clackamas Chinook Myths and Tales* (Seattle: University of Washington Press, 1960).

2. Dell Hymes, "The 'Wife' Who 'Goes Out' Like a Man: Reinterpretation of a Clackamas Chinook Myth," *Social Science Information, Studies in Semiotics* 7 (1968): 173–99, and "Discovering Oral Performance and Measured Verse in American Indian Narrative," *New Literary History* 8 (1977): 431–57, which also appears in Hymes, *"In Vain I Tried to Tell You": Essays in Native American Ethnopoetics* (Philadelphia: University of Pennsylvania Press, 1981) as chs. 8 and 9; see also Hymes, "Notes Toward (an Understanding of) Supreme Fictions," in *Studies in Historical Change*, ed. Ralph Cohen (Charlottesville: University of Virginia Press, 1992).

3. Victoria Howard, "Seal and Her Younger Brother Lived There," trans. Hymes, in *Longman Anthology of World Literature by Women, 1875–1975*, ed. Marian Arkin and Barbara Shollar (White Plains, N.Y.: Longman, 1989), 106–9, and Hymes, trans., "Seal and Her Younger Brother Lived There," *Hermes* (Tokyo; July 1991): 132–33.

4. Hymes, "The 'Wife' Who 'Goes Out' Like a Man" and "Discovering Oral Performance and Measured Verse in American Indian Narrative."

They lived there, Seal, her daughter, her younger brother.   [i](A)
After some time now a woman got to Seal's younger brother.

They lived there. (B)
  They would "go out" outside in the evening.
The girl would say, 5
  she would tell her mother,
    "Mother! Something is different about my uncle's wife.
    It sounds just like a man when she 'goes out.'"
[—]* "Shush! Your uncle's wife!"

A long long time they lived there like that. (C)10
    In the evening they would each "go out."
Now she would tell her,
    "Mother! Something is different about my uncle's wife.
    When she goes out, it sounds just like a man."
[—] "Shush!" 15

Her uncle, his wife, would lie down up above on the bed.   [ii](A)
Pretty soon the other two would lie down close to the fire,
  they would lie down beside each other.

Some time during the night, something comes onto her face. (B)
She shook her mother, 20
  she told her,
    "Mother! Something comes onto my face."
[—] "Mmmmm. Shush. Your uncle, they are 'going.'"

Pretty soon now again she heard something escaping. (C)
She told her, 25
    "Mother! Something is going *t'uq t'uq*.
    I hear something!"
[—] "Shush. Your uncle, they are 'going.'"

The girl got up, [iii](A)
  she fixed the fire, 30
    she lit pitch,
      she looked where the two were:

*A dash in brackets indicates a change in speaker.

Ah! Ah! Blood!
She raised her light to it, thus: (B)
  her uncle is on his bed, 35
    his neck cut,
      he is dead.
        She screamed.
She told her mother, (C)
  "I told you, 40
    'Something is dripping.'
  You told me,
    'Shush, they are "going." '
  I had told you,
    'Something is different about my uncle's wife. 45
    She would "go out,"
      with a sound just like a man she would urinate.'
  You would tell me,
    'Shush!' "
She wept. 50

Seal said, (D)
  "Younger brother! My younger brother!
  They are valuable standing there.
  My younger brother!"
She kept saying that. 55

As for that girl, she wept. (E)
She said,
  "In vain I tried to tell you,
    'Not like a woman,
    With a sound just like a man she would urinate, my uncle's
      wife.' 60
  You told me,
    'Shush!'
  Oh oh my uncle!
  Oh my uncle!"
She wept, that girl. 65

Now I remember only that far.

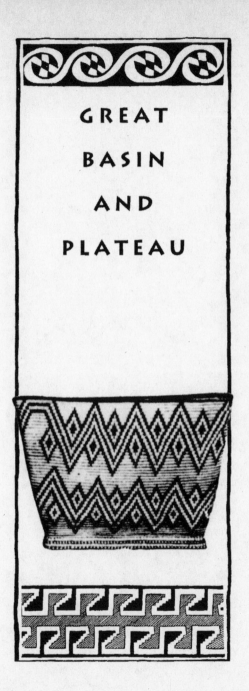

GREAT

BASIN

AND

PLATEAU

HILDA AUSTIN'S TELLING OF "Qʷíqʷλ'qʷəλ'T: A TRADITIONAL NłEʔKÉPMX LEGEND"

STEVEN M. EGESDAL
AND
M. TERRY THOMPSON

INTRODUCTION

In the pantheon of the legendary beings of the *Nłeʔképmx* (a Salishan people, described more fully below), one rises above the rest: Qʷíqʷλ'qʷəλ't, literally, "the smiling one." More affectionately, he is Smiley, as the Nłeʔképmx have carried his name into the reader's tongue. Smiley outdoes even his closest transformer peers, Coyote (Snk'y'ép) and Son of Carrot Root (Q'ʷəq'ʷilehíhiʔt), who otherwise could lay claim to being *the* culture heroes of the Nłeʔképmx. Qʷíqʷλ'qʷəλ't tames monsters, ogres, and cannibals. In this legend Smiley vanquishes Grizzly Woman (Səxʷsuxʷínek)—a monster easily on a par with Clytemnestra—with the aid of his grandfather Sqʷnéyqʷeʔ, himself revered as a grandfather of the real Nłeʔképmx.[1] Smiley stands alone as culture hero of the Nłeʔképmx. His exploits are written in tomes on the tongues of the Nłeʔképmx elders, of which the translation below is a chapter.

The translation that follows invites the reader to enter the world of Nłeʔképmx legend, *sptékʷł*, "when animals talked and walked as men." *Sptékʷł* perhaps is not so much a time or place as a dimension, another reality, in which elements of the landscape—fauna, flora, and even natural phenomena, such as thunder and ice—are anthropomorphized. As "real people" of the *sptékʷł* stage, legendary dramatis personae act out the quintessence of their personalities, wearing different skins on transformed shapes. Coyote always was Coyote; he just looks more doglike in the here and now. Importantly, the teller avoids the word *myth* in the reader's tongue, she explains, because "*myth* means it is not true." The events occurring in the *sptékʷ*ł world, she emphasizes, "are true."

The legend begins with Grizzly Woman slaying Smiley's mother and father, who are her co-wife and husband, respectively. She cuts off his penis and her breasts and cooks them for her dinner. She then instructs her four cubs to murder Smiley and his three elder brothers, who are her stepchildren and their stepbrothers. Her plan also calls for the murdered Smiley to be roasted and set on a stake for her next meal. Her plan backfires completely. Smiley and his brothers kill Grizzly Woman's cubs. Her youngest cub is roasted and set on the stake instead. Grizzly Woman devours her cub, thinking him to be Smiley. Meadowlark sings out that ghastly truth just as Grizzly Woman places the last little paw in her mouth. Horror seizes Grizzly Woman, then rage. Berserk, she races after Smiley. Smiley uses his wiles to elude Grizzly Woman during the entertaining chase that ensues. Finally, when Smiley can run no more, he enlists the help of his grandfather Sqʷnéyqʷeʔ. The legend closes with Sqʷnéyqʷeʔ leading Grizzly Woman into a painful death trap.

The *Iliad* is not so much a story about Troy as it is a story about Achilles. Similarly, this chapter of the Smiley epic is perhaps not so much about Smiley's victory as it is about Grizzly Woman's defeat. The legend begins with Grizzly Woman's actions, grows with her reactions, and ends with her death. She is the developed character. She expresses jealousy, horror, rage, and pain; Smiley shows little emotion. Likewise, Achilles is a killing machine, almost two-dimensional; Hector has texture and depth. Grizzly Woman has jagged edges where Smiley has clean lines.

As Achilles needs Hector, Smiley needs foils like Grizzly Woman to establish his prowess. Grizzly Woman, in fact, is the perfect foil for Smiley, almost his diametric opposite. She is evil, irrational, treacherous, and fierce. He is good, calculating, elusive, and cunning. Oddly enough, these two opposites never engage in head-to-head combat (as Smiley does with Son of Carrot Root or the ogre He Eats Men). Grizzly Woman attempts to have her children murder Smiley; Smiley needs his grandfather's trickery to kill Grizzly Woman. Both respect the other's powers; they joust but never duel.

The legend's content raises questions about which one can only speculate. Why is Grizzly Woman so vicious? What motivates her to murder her husband and co-wife, ingest his penis and her breasts, and then plot to kill her stepchildren? The noted anthropologist and Amerindianist Melville Jacobs advanced the notion that Native American oral literature acted as a "psychological safety valve" to release social pressure in a highly structured culture. In the safe domain or other reality of the performance, motifs would have had a cathartic effect on the members of an audience, allowing them to release negative, pent-up emotion.[2]

Implicit in the legend is Grizzly Woman's status as a remarried widow. Grizzly Man is dead, perhaps even having been killed by Grizzly Woman. According to Nłe?képmx custom her expected replacement husband is her deceased husband's brother, here Bear Man (taxonomically a natural association). Perhaps Grizzly Woman embodies the anger and jealousy of the new wife and the fear and insecurity of the old wife, where they both have to share a husband and a household. Teit's version of this same legend explains, "He paid most attention to the Black Bear wife; so the other [Grizzly wife] became jealous, and made up her mind to get rid of her rival."[3] Such emotions would have to have been suppressed, except on the *sptékʷł* stage, where myth was allowed to be truer than truth.

A less abstract explanation also exists. Linguistic and archaeological evidence indicates that the Nłe?képmx migrated from the Northwest Coast to the Interior Plateau. Yet through trade and marriage they maintained considerable contact with tribes on the Northwest Coast, such as the Halkomelem. Franz Boas traced the Smiley legend to transformer myths of the Northwest Coast,[4] which provenance is suggested elsewhere.[5] With that context, one might look to Northwest Coast oral literatures as a spawning ground for the Grizzly Woman motifs. Certainly the trickster-dupe Coyote and Lynx of the Interior Plateau share parallels with Mink and Raven of the Northwest Coast. Grizzly Woman similarly has a likely analogue in the Northwest Coast's Basket Ogress. Basket Ogress (Slápu?) is an evil, witchlike being who carries on her back a large basket filled with snakes, crabs, or other such biting, creepy-crawly creatures and into which she places children she has stolen. Reshaping Basket Ogress into Grizzly Woman (or repackaging motifs from Basket Ogress legends in those with Grizzly Woman) would have been a natural process. In this legend, for instance, Grizzly Woman scratches the stripes into Chipmunk's back (the Bear cubs had enlisted Chipmunk's aid in delaying Grizzly Woman). The same motif to explain the origin of Chipmunk's stripes occurs in a Coast Salish Clallam legend about Chipmunk and Basket Ogress, thus suggesting a parallel between Grizzly Woman and Basket Ogress.

▲

To appreciate the structure of the translation below, one must understand one salient aspect of Nłeʔképmx oral literature. Melville Jacobs observed that a special contrast exists between characters' spoken lines and lines of narration concerning their relative importance in developing and advancing the narrative.[6] He described Northwest Native American oral literature as "terse, staccato, or rapidly moving" and not overly embellished with narrative description. In what he termed "tersely delineated narrative," lines of narration compress expressions of content and are limited to a succinct description of setting, movement in time or space, and characters. Any important feeling or idea of the dramatis personae is conveyed through the mouths of the actors themselves.[7] He wrote, "A recitalist never once verbalized a motivation, feeling, or mood of the actors of a myth or tale . . . the succinct recitation of actors' deeds [narration lines] and discourse [characters' lines] alone revealed sentiments meant to be elicited."[8]

That characters' lines would carry the performative load of a narrative stands to reason. Native American oral literature is drama. It follows that characters' lines have much greater performative value than "stage direction"—narration lines. To highlight that important difference typographically, the characters' lines are indented and italicized in the translation that follows.

The translation into the reader's tongue is as literal as it needs to be in order to remain faithful to the Nłeʔképmx and prevent images of the reader's tongue from interfering with those of Nłeʔképmx. The translation likewise is as free as it needs to be to reveal the legend's artistry, wit, and elegance and to convey presupposed cultural information needed to appreciate the legend fully. For instance, the legend begins with the formulaic opening line *"Húmeɬ,xʷuyʔ ptékʷ ɬetimn,"* which literally means, "All right, I will tell you a legend." But such a simple, literal translation ignores important cultural knowledge shared by the teller and the audience. The first line really tells the audience this:

> All right, I will take you to the world of legend.
> You know that time, that place well,
> where animals talked and walked as men,
> untamed, unchanged, real people still.

The freer translation conveys what the first line should invoke in the eye of the reader—what the original invokes in the ear of the Nłeʔképmx audience. It also captures beliefs the teller offered concerning the *sptékʷł* outside of its performance. The engrafting of that editorial commentary helps to frame the legend for the non-Native reader.

The original legend repeats material, often inverting slightly the order of words in adjacent lines. Such repetition is a common rhetorical device in Nłeʔképmx narrative (and, more broadly, in Salish languages) to show emphasis. In the reader's tongue, however, literal translation of that repetition often appears wooden or superfluous. The translation of such repetition is therefore handled more freely, by using synonyms of the repeated words, to add a similar but more natural emphasis in the Euro-American narrative.

Several final points require brief discussion. First, in the legend the Bear cubs and the Grizzly cubs have a pudding-making contest. The term *pudding* refers to a favorite Nłeʔképmx food, *nkéxʷ*, which contains saskatoons (serviceberries), bitterroot, flour, butter, cream, sugar, and sometimes tiger lily bulbs, avalanche-lily corms, deer fat, black tree lichen, and salmon eggs, all boiled together until thick. Second, Qʷíqʷλ'qʷəλ't refers to the youngest of four Bear-cub brothers introduced below. The teller refers to Qʷíqʷλ'qʷəλ't as the youngest Bear cub throughout the legend, calling him Qʷíqʷλ'qʷəλ't only much later, and then somewhat parenthetically. This legend was well-known to the audience, whose presupposed knowledge likely accounts for the teller's not identifying the character earlier and more significantly. Third, Qʷíqʷλ'qʷəλ't and Grizzly Woman's youngest cub were near twins in appearance. Grizzly Woman had tattooed her child's fingernails to distinguish him from the youngest Bear cub. The significance of these facts will be evident below.

The legend's teller was Hilda Austin, an Nłeʔképmx elder. (The Nłeʔképmx are a Salishan people of southern British Columbia; they are called Thompson in English, after the Thompson River Gorge, the lower part of which is central to their territory.) Ms. Austin was born around the turn of the century, one of the last Nłeʔképmx women raised in the traditional manner. She was reared by her maternal grandmother, who forbade her to attend the "white man's school." Ms. Austin therefore never learned to read or write, which may help to explain her phenomenal memory. She learned many Nłeʔképmx legends as a girl, of which her favorite was the one translated below. She has performed it on a number of occasions, winning awards at Elder's Day contests. It is perhaps her signature legend. At her daughter's request she performed the version below in July 1981, which Steven Egesdal recorded. Egesdal then transcribed, analyzed, and translated the legend with Ms. Austin's help. Egesdal and M. Terry Thompson later refined the translation for this publication. It has never been published before, although James Teit and Charles Hill-Tout provide similar versions in English.[9] The authors are preparing a collection of Nłe?képmx traditional legends for publication that will include this legend.

Pronunciation

The text contains several unfamiliar Nłe?képmx letters:

ł is like the English *l* but very breathy. One should whisper *please*, holding the *l*. As the air is released, the sound should then approximate ł.

? is similar to the catch in *uh-uh* (meaning "no").

kʷ is like the *qu* in *quick*.

qʷ is like *kʷ* except one makes the sound by touching the back of the tongue farther back in the mouth.

q'ʷ is like *qʷ* but with a sharp popping sound. One makes the popping sound by preparing to make a *?*, holding it, and then saying *qʷ* simultaneously.

xʷ is like the *wh* in *wheat*.

The sound of the vowel ə varies, depending on the consonants surrounding it. In Qʷíqʷƛ'qʷək't the ə sounds like the *u* in *cut;* in Səxʷsuxʷínek the ə sounds like the *oo* in *cool.*

k' is like *k* but has the same popping sound described for *q'ʷ*.

ƛ' is similar to the English *tl*, with the same popping sound. One should place the tongue to say *tl*, keeping it closed against the roof of the mouth. The air should then be released quickly, with a pop.

NOTES

1. James A. Teit, Farrand Livingston, Marian Gould, and Herbert Spinden, in *Folktales of Salishan and Sahaptin Tribes,* ed. Franz Boas, Memoirs of the American Folklore Society, vol. 11 (Boston: Houghton Mifflin, 1917).

2. Melville Jacobs, *The Content and Style of an Oral Literature: Clackamas Chinook Myths and Tales* (Chicago: University of Chicago Press, 1959).

3. James A. Teit, *Mythology of the Thompson River Indians,* Publications of the Jesup North Pacific Expedition, vol. 8:2 (Leiden, Holland: E. J. Brill, 1912).

4. In James A. Teit, *Traditions of the Thompson River Indians,* Memoirs of the American Folklore Society, vol. 6 (Boston: Houghton Mifflin, 1898), 11.

5. Ibid., 42, 217.

6. Jacobs, *The Content and Style of an Oral Literature* and *The People Are Coming Soon: Analyses of Clackamas Chinook Myths and Tales* (Seattle: University of Washington Press, 1960).

7. Jacobs, *The Content and Style of an Oral Literature,* 266.

8. Jacobs, *The People Are Coming Soon,* x.

9. Teit, *Traditions of the Thompson River Indians,* 69–72, and *Mythology of the Thompson River Indians,* 218–20; Charles Hill-Tout, *The Thompson and Okanagan,* vol. 1 of *The Salish People: The Local Contribution of Charles Hill-Tout,* ed. Ralph Maud (1899; reprint, Vancouver: Talonbooks, 1978), 1:21–28.

Qʷíqʷⱡ̓qʷəⱡ̓'t:
A TRADITIONAL NⱢEʔKÉPMX LEGEND

All right, I will take you to the world of legend.
You know that time, that place well,
where animals talked and walked as men,
untamed, unchanged, real people still.

This legend is called Qʷíqʷⱡ̓'qʷəⱡ̓'t. Qʷíqʷⱡ̓'qʷəⱡ̓'t is its name.

Bear Man and Bear Woman lived there with their four children, the
    Bear cubs.
Grizzly Woman also lived there. She too had four children, the
    Grizzly cubs.
Grizzly Woman was married to Bear Man.

They were living together there.
One morning they went climbing to forage for food,
to dig roots, gather chokecherries, and pick saskatoons.
They set out at daybreak.

Grizzly Woman was rummaging around, looking for something.
She was searching for her husband and co-wife.
They were there on the mountain, gathering food.
Grizzly Woman finally came upon her co-wife and said,
    Let's sit down right here. We need to talk.
They sat down, and Grizzly Woman told her co-wife,
    I'll delouse you. I'll delouse you.
Bear Woman replied,
    Fine. Delouse me. Delouse me.
As Grizzly Woman deloused her friend, she told her,
    Oh, your husband loves you so much.
    And you're just covered with nits and lice!
    They're all over you.
Grizzly Woman went on,
    I'll chew them for you. I'll chew them for you.
Bear Woman consented:
    Fine. Chew them for me. Chew them for me.
Grizzly Woman chewed them, her friend's nits and lice. She was
    chewing,
    crack crack crack crack,
feigning the sound of crackling nits and lice.

She kept up the pretense, setting herself just so;
then quickly she bit down on Bear Woman's neck,
sinking her teeth into her co-wife's jugular.
Instantly Bear Woman died, Grizzly Woman's co-wife.

Grizzly Woman left her, looking for their husband. She searched
    for Bear Man.
She combed the area until she found him. She told him
    affectionately,
    Let's have a little sit here. We need to talk over a few things.
Her husband sat down, and she scooted right next to him.
She told her husband,
    How about I delouse you?
Bear Man replied,
    Fine, delouse me.
She deloused her husband. As she did so, she remarked to her
    husband,
    Your wife loves you, passionately.
    And you're just covered with nits and lice.
    I'll chew them for you.
Bear Man agreed:
    Fine. Chew them for me.
She chewed them for him:
    crack crack crack crack,
it crackled as she chewed the pretend nits and lice.
She was smacking like that when she fixed a sudden death bite to
    his neck.
He fell dead.

She killed her co-wife, then her husband.
She snipped off Bear Man's penis, then headed back for Bear
    Woman.
Grizzly Woman sliced off her co-wife's breasts, both of them.
She sliced them off and headed home, holding the breasts and
    penis.

She arrived at their house.
The children were waiting, the Bear cubs and Grizzly cubs.
It was not even dusk, but she sent them to bed:
    Time to sleep. Off to bed.
She herded them to their beds.
The children lay down to sleep, the Bear cubs and Grizzly cubs.

Soon they fell fast asleep.
She fried the breasts of her co-wife next to her husband's penis.
They sizzled. The youngest Bear cub shrieked,
  My mommy's titties! My mommy's titties!
That's what the youngest Bear cub said.
Grizzly Woman cut him off crossly:
  Go to sleep up there! Shut your mouth! Sleep!
  It's just venison I'm frying.
The baby Bear cub pulled the covers over his head.
They sizzled. The baby Bear cub cried out,
  My papa's pee-pee! My papa's pee-pee!
She scolded him:
  Go to sleep! It's bedtime!
  It's just venison I'm frying.
He pulled the covers back over his head.
Grizzly Woman kept on frying there her co-wife's breasts and
    husband's penis.
Then she ate them. Gobbled them up. When she finished, she
    went to bed.

Early the next morning Grizzly Woman woke up.
She woke up her children, the Grizzly cubs, and instructed them:
  When the Bear cubs wake up, tell them this:
  "We're going to make pudding for one another.
  You'll make pudding, and we'll make pudding."
  Then you're going to eat the pudding, slurping it up.
  Afterward you'll tell the Bear cubs,
  "All right, we're going to bathe."

Grizzly Woman instructed her children further:
  When you're in the water, bathing, grab the Bear cubs and dunk
  them.
  Hold them under until they're dead.
  Then roast that youngest Bear cub.
  Skewer him through the ass, and barbecue him.
  Roast him, and then impale him on a post,
  pointing in the direction I'll be coming from.
The Grizzly cubs told her,
  All right.
She left her children.

The Bear cubs woke up. The Grizzly cubs told their friends,
  All right. We're all going to make pudding.

You're going to make pudding,
and we're going to make pudding.
We're going to slurp pudding.
The Bear cubs agreed:
All right. All right. We'll make pudding.
The Bear cubs made some pudding, and the Grizzly cubs made
    some pudding.

The youngest Bear cub said to his older brothers,
Make your pudding thick! Make it thick!
He told his brothers that, and they agreed:
All right.
They made the pudding thick.
The Bear cubs' pudding was thick. But the Grizzly cubs' pudding
    was runny.
The Bear Cubs said,
All right, we're going to swap our puddings.
You eat our pudding, and give us your pudding to eat.
The Grizzly cubs said,
All right.
They exchanged puddings.
The Grizzly cubs ate the Bear cubs' pudding.
The Bear cubs ate the Grizzly cubs' pudding.
The Grizzly cubs ate and ate the Bear cubs' pudding,
but they couldn't finish it. They were completely full.
The Bear cubs started to eat the Grizzly cubs' pudding. Right
    away it was all gone.
But the Grizzly cubs could not finish their pudding. They were
    too full.
The Grizzly cubs remarked,
We didn't even finish their pudding, and yet we are full.
The youngest Bear cub said,
All right. Hand me my pot of leftover pudding then.
I'm going to lick it.
They handed over his pot to him. The little Bear cub licked his
    pot.
He just licked it, and the leftover pudding was gone.
Right away the Grizzly cubs said,
All right, we're going to take a bath.
We're all going into the water.
The Bear cubs replied,
Fine. Let's go! We'll take a bath together.

▲

They all were strung out in a line facing the water.
There was water nearby.
They stood in a column, wading in one by one. They started to
  bathe.
The youngest Grizzly cub and the youngest Bear cub paired off,
one dunking the other.
The youngest Grizzly cub got held under the water.
It wasn't too long, and he ran out of air.
The others dragged him to shore and laid him down.

The youngest Bear cub gave a signal:
  All right.
The others put the youngest Grizzly cub before him.
The youngest Bear cub started to jump over him. He came alive,
  opening his eyes.
The youngest Bear cub told them,
  We're all going to jump over one another like that after a good
  dunking.
  Then we'll feel better.
The Grizzly cubs agreed:
  Sure.

The Bear cubs dunked the Grizzly cubs.
They did that just a little, and one Grizzly cub was dead. He was
  dragged from the water.
They dunked the next Grizzly cub. He died quickly too.
They pulled him from the water, and they turned to the next
  Grizzly cub.
The eldest Grizzly cub said,
  You jump over my little brothers for me now,
  so they get better.
The youngest Bear cub told him,
  Here's how I'm going to do it: I'll jump over all of you at once.
  After you've all been dunked. Then you'll be better.
But the eldest one was afraid.
The Bear cubs held him under the water until he drowned.
He was dead. All of them died.
All four of the Grizzly cubs died.

The youngest Bear cub instructed his brothers,
  Roast Grizzly Woman's youngest child. She had told her children,
  "You roast that youngest Bear cub for me.

He's going to be my meal.
Stick him up in the direction I'll be coming from."
So we'll just roast her own child for her. And stick him up for her.
They roasted the youngest Grizzly cub. They whittled a stick.
They shoved it through his anus and propped him next to the fire.
They kept turning him on the stick until he was roasted.
Once he was roasted, they stuck him up in the direction of his
    mother's approach.

The youngest Bear cub said,
    Let's go. We've got to get out of here, or we're dead.
    Our parents already have died. Grizzly Woman killed them.
    Next it's us she'll kill.
His elder brothers agreed:
    All right.

They gathered some rotten logs. Then they piled them up where
    they usually slept.
They piled the rotten wood up there.
Qʷíqʷƛ'qʷəƛ't, that youngest Bear cub, said,
    All right, let's go now. We've got to run away.
The children took off, running.

They ran for some time. The youngest Bear cub said,
    She's coming after us.
Grizzly was coming along, approaching where that meal was stuck
    up for her.
She came upon it, running. She said,
    Hmm, now where is it? Aren't I the lucky one!
She ran to it. She grabbed what was stuck up there.
She ate it, gobbled it up. There was nothing left except little
    tattooed claws—
her own child's. She held on to it.
At that moment Meadowlark sang out,
    She's eating her child's little tattooed claws.
    She's eating her child's little tattooed claws.
Grizzly Woman shot back,
    Whatever are you saying?
Meadowlark repeated its song:
    She's eating her child's little tattooed claws.
    She's eating her child's little tattooed claws.
Then she looked at it, what she held in her hand.

Grizzly looked at his little paws, his fingers.
It was her child's fingernail tattoos.
She stuck her finger down her throat until she retched.
There she was vomiting, but she already had finished off her child.
She heaved her guts out.

She ran to where the children slept, where those piles of rotten
    wood were.
She mauled them, clamping down with her teeth.
She thought those piles were the Bear cubs asleep.
She attacked one, biting into it. It was just dusty, rotten wood.
She attacked another one. Just another bite of rotten wood.

She stood there. Then she rushed to where her own children used to
    be.
They were all dead. She ran around in a frenzied rage. She
    screamed.

She looked for those children's footprints.
She searched for their tracks. She spotted their tracks,
signs showing where those children were running.
She followed them. She chased after the Bear cubs.

The Bear cubs kept on running. The youngest Bear cub said,
    She's after us. She's almost upon us.
    Grizzly Woman's almost caught up with us.

There was an ant's nest there, ants and a huge ant's nest.
The youngest Bear cub gave instructions:
    Here we go. Take the ant children, and tie them in a bundle.
They had something to bundle them in. They dug up the ant
    children.
Then they poured them in there and tied it at the top.
They climbed a tree. They climbed up.
The eldest was first, followed by the second,
then the younger one, and the youngest was last.
The one next to the youngest was the one who carried him on his
    back.

Immediately Grizzly came along.
Grizzly could not climb. She went to the bottom of the tree.
She called to those children,

Come here! Come here! Your parents are about to kill me!
They've lost you. I'm looking for you.

The youngest told the eldest something. The eldest one told her,
Oh, all right. Lie down at the bottom of the tree! Lie down!
We're going to throw our youngest brother to you, so he won't get
hurt.

Grizzly said,
All right.

Grizzly lay down. She lay on her back.
They told her,
Open your eyes! Open your mouth! Spread your legs!

She said,
All right.

Grizzly Woman lay there.
She opened her eyes. She opened her mouth.
She spread her legs. She extended her arms and legs.
They said,
All right. We're going to throw him to you.

They threw it down to her. The bundle of ant children.
They threw it. Immediately Grizzly was filled with ant children.
Her mouth was filled up. Her eyes were filled up. She couldn't see
a thing.
Those children climbed down. Away they ran.
Grizzly writhed on the ground with her eyes, mouth, and vagina
full of ants.

Those children scurried off. They escaped. They ran until they were
far, far away.
Grizzly stayed there a long time, cleaning out the ants.
Then she resumed her chase.

Those children were going along, and the youngest Bear cub said,
She's about caught up to us from there.

Chipmunk was there. They talked with Chipmunk.
There was a rock there, where Chipmunk lived.
He was perched up there. They said to Chipmunk,
When Grizzly Woman comes by here, you're going to call her
names.
You're going to slow her down. She's after us. She's going to kill us.

Chipmunk said,
All right.

Those children ran away from there.

It wasn't very long, and Grizzly came running.
Grizzly said,
   Did you see those children come by here?
Chipmunk said,
   Yes. Just now they came through. Already they passed by.
Grizzly was about to leave when Chipmunk spoke up.
He called Grizzly names. Chipmunk came out, and he called her
   names.
Grizzly turned back to grab him, but Chipmunk went inside a
   crevice in the rock.
Grizzly turned to leave, but Chipmunk came out and called out
   again, berating Grizzly.
Grizzly got angry and went back to catch Chipmunk.
She was about to grab him, but he slipped inside the crevice in the
   rock.
He kept doing that, name-calling and then hiding,
until the time she almost caught him.
He came out and called her names.
She went after him and got a hold of him.
That is why Chipmunk has a striped back today. Grizzly clawed
   him in the back.
Then Chipmunk didn't come out again.
Grizzly ran off from there, chasing them.

Those children kept on running. The youngest said,
   She's about to close in on us.
But they had reached the river's edge.
Their grandfather Sqʷnéyqʷeʔ was on the other side.
They called to him,
   Take us across, Sqʷnéyqʷeʔ?! We're about to die.
   Grizzly is after us, Grizzly Woman.
   She's going to kill us. She's killed our parents already.
Sqʷnéyqʷeʔ said,
   All right, I'll take you across.
Sqʷnéyqʷeʔ crossed over in his canoe. He landed there.
He boarded those children and took them across.
He took them ashore. He told those children,
   Go to your grandmother. Your grandmother will feed you.
   I'll fix Grizzly myself.
Those children said,
   All right.
They went away from the water. Those children went to where

she lived.
Sqʷnéyqʷeʔ's wife was there.

Sqʷnéyqʷeʔ stayed there. He was making a hole in the bottom of
   his canoe.
He made a hole in the bottom of it, pounding:
  bang bang bang bang.
He was hammering on his canoe.
Along came Grizzly Woman on the other side of the river.
She called out,
  Where are you, Sqʷnéyqʷeʔ? Did those children come by here
  already?
Sqʷnéyqʷeʔ said,
  Yes. Those children already passed by here.
Grizzly said,
  Take me across! Take me across!
  I'm following those children. I'm following them.
  Their parents are going to kill me. They'll kill me.
  I'm following them. They must have run off. I'm following them.
Sqʷnéyqʷeʔ said,
  All right. I'm fixing my canoe. I'll take you across. Just wait.
Grizzly said,
  Work fast! Hurry up!
Sqʷnéyqʷeʔ said,
  All right, I'll take you across.
Sqʷnéyqʷeʔ was over there, still pounding:
  bang bang bang bang.
He was making that hole in his canoe.
He finished making that hole in his canoe.
He went across. Sqʷnéyqʷeʔ crossed over the river.
He got to Grizzly. He told Grizzly,
  Listen, I've got a hole in the bottom of my canoe—a hole.
  When I take your friend across, she sits on that hole.
  You're going to sit on that hole, so we won't die.

But Sqʷnéyqʷeʔ already had made a plan with Sturgeon. He had
   told Sturgeon,
  You're going to eat out Grizzly's insides.
  She's going to kill those children.
Sturgeon said,
  All right, we'll do that.

Grizzly sat there. Sqʷnéyqʷeʔ got aboard and pushed off in his
  canoe.
He told her,
  Sit there! Squat on that hole! We won't die then.
  Your friend does that when we cross the river.
  She sits right like that, so we don't die.
Sqʷnéyqʷeʔ pushed off in his canoe. Grizzly squatted on the hole.
He told her,
  Squat! Squat! If you don't squat there, the canoe will take on
  water.
  And we'll die.
Grizzly said,
  All right.
She squatted on the hole. They didn't get very far, and Grizzly
  screamed,
  Ouch!
Grizzly said that.
Sturgeon was biting her bottom. She popped up.
Water gushed in from the hole in the canoe. Sqʷnéyqʷeʔ told her,
  Stop that! Sit! Sit! We'll die. Sit on that hole!
  Look, the canoe is taking on water. We'll die. We'll drown.
Grizzly sat down. They continued on.
Right away she screamed,
  Ouch, ouch, ouch, ouch.
Sturgeon and all kinds of fish were biting at Grizzly Woman's
  anus.
They didn't get very far, and Grizzly's intestines were gone.
  Disappeared.
Sturgeon and all kinds of fish ate her insides out.
All kinds of fish, even the frogs, were biting her.
They didn't get very far, and Grizzly Woman was dead.
  Disemboweled.
Sqʷnéyqʷeʔ threw her overboard. Grizzly Woman was dead.

Sqʷnéyqʷeʔ crossed over there. He got to those children. They
  asked him,
  Where is she now? Where is she?
Sqʷnéyqʷeʔ said,
  I threw her overboard as I came across.
  I threw Grizzly Woman away. Don't be afraid anymore.
Those children said,
  Oh, it's good you threw her away. We won't be afraid.

Sqʷnéyqʷeʔ said,
> *Yes. It's good I killed Grizzly Woman on my way over.*
> *Don't be afraid.*

They said,
> *Oh.*

They told their grandfather their story, all that Grizzly Woman
    had done to them.
They said,
> *She'd already killed our mother. She'd already killed our father.*
> *Then her children were going to kill us. She told her children,*
> *"You're going to make pudding. You'll dunk one another in the*
> *water.*
> *You'll hold the Bear cubs under water, so they die.*
> *I've already killed their parents.*
> *When you've killed the Bear cubs, roast the youngest one for me."*

The Bear cubs said,
> *We killed Grizzly's children. We killed the Grizzly cubs.*
> *We roasted her child for her. We put him on a spit for her,*
> *in the direction of her approach. Then we ran away.*

Their grandfather said,
> *Oh, you're safe. You won't die. I killed her. I killed Grizzly—*
> *Grizzly Woman. Don't be afraid.*

Those children said,
> *Oh, that's good.*

Those children went way from there.
That's as far as I know. They did a lot of things after that.
Those children went on from there. Qʷíqʷƛ'qʷəƛ't. But I forget.
That's as far as I know. Yes. That's it. The end.
The legend is finished.

BLUE JAY AND HIS
BROTHER-IN-LAW WOLF

▲

ANTHONY MATTINA

INTRODUCTION

"Blue Jay and His Brother-in-Law Wolf," a Colville narrative by
Peter J. Seymour, was tape-recorded on August 9, 1968, at Seymour's Hall Creek residence near Inchelium, Washington, a small
town located at the eastern edge of the Colville Reservation, on the
western shore of the Columbia River (or the Franklin D. Roosevelt
Lake, as this dammed section of the river is known), about one hundred miles northwest of Spokane. I had begun studying the Okano-
gon-Colville language continuum earlier that summer, using
practices that included the collection of texts. My knowledge of the
language was still barely above zero.

Seymour and I had agreed on what to do, and when I prompted
him with "the story of Blue Jay," he clarified: "Blue Jay and his
brother-in-law the Wolf. That's the way I heard it; that's how they
. . . started the story." Then after another pause (of about fifteen
seconds) he said, *"Way' axà? qʷ Sásqi? na?ɬ nkʷ əlmúts, nc'ícən, ixì?
ikscaptíkʷləm* [Well, this here Blue Jay and his brother-in-law Wolf,
that's what I'm going to tell]." The tape then ran to its end, sixteen
minutes and five seconds. The narrative interrupted, we started a
new tape. Seymour summarized the story up to the interruption and
continued for another twenty-six and a half minutes.

Three years later, in July and August of 1971, I transcribed the story with Madeline DeSautel, my long-time Colville collaborator, an excellent speaker of the language and my best teacher. We dedicated four sessions to the task, Madeline translating as we went along. At the time, I recorded three of Madeline's comments in the margins of my notebooks. Two are about the character of the older sister: "She's kind of jealous, ain't it?" and "She must be hell of a sister, ain't it?" A third concerns the people as they question Blue Jay about the meaning of the ears; commented Madeline, "That's what they should have done [ask Blue Jay] a long time ago."

Of all the other Okanogon narratives I have heard or read in any dialect or in English translation, I know of none that matches the richness of any of Peter J. Seymour's stories. If I extended this statement to include all the Interior Salish languages—Lillooet, Thompson, Shuswap, Columbia, Kalispel, and Coeur d'Alene—I would not be overstating my belief. In fact, I do see the extant narrative collection of the Okanogon (and that of the other Salish tribes of the Interior Plateau) as a corpus of works that sets its own standard of literariness. In other words, these narratives are average Okanogon Salish works, whereas Seymour's texts are the richest in Okanogon literature—and some of his texts are works of art.

While all narrations probably fall somewhere on a continuum between mime and prose reading, good prose doesn't need any theatrical accoutrements; and once a story is written down, it is written prose—prose that can be read aloud but nevertheless is written. I do not buy any of the claims that an Indian story shines in its splendor once it is versified, and I reject the implication that all Indian stories are verse. A story is good if its words are good and put together well. Techniques that lead to the discovery of linguistic patterns have not given me anything that I can use to enjoy a story more. Nor can they be used as devices to detect a good story.

The content of the story that follows is a more interesting topic, and an open-ended one. Although the story provides a glimpse of Colville life, many readers will want to learn more. An appreciation, for example, of such questions as jealousy or rivalry between sisters that relied on some intuited notions of (presumably universal) primal emotions would not be as satisfying as one that took into account questions of Colville social organization and practices. Similarly, the character of Blue Jay, who is better understood when seen in the context of other Interior Salish stories. For texts that elucidate these and other subjects, see the Suggested Reading at the back of this volume.

Pronunciation

Colville has more consonants than English and fewer vowels. The intended
significance of the more unfamiliar symbols in the material that appears
in Colville is as follows:

ʷ   following a consonant marks the lip rounding that accompanies that
consonant.

ˀ   following a stop (for example, *t'*, *c'*, *k'*, or *q'*) marks an ejective stop—
the stop is immediately followed by a popping sound made by the
forceful expulsion of air at the point of closure. Following a resonant
(for example, *y'*), this symbol signals that the resonant is immediately
followed by a glottalic constriction and release.

ˊ   (*á, í, ú*) marks the most prominent syllable of a phrase.

ˋ   (*à, ì*) marks the second most prominent syllable of a phrase.

Unmarked syllables are the least prominent.

ʕ   represents a pharyngeal resonant, similar to the fricative 'ayn of Semitic
languages.

ʔ   represents a glottal stop, the catch between the vowels of such utterances as *oh oh*.

ə   represents a central vowel sound like that of the last vowel (the *u*) in
halibut.

ƛ   represents a *tl*-like sound.

q   represents a *k*-like consonant produced with the back of the tongue
against the uvular region.

ł   represents a sound sometimes referred to as a wet or slurpy *l*. It is like
the English *l* but without any vibrations of the vocal folds.

x   stands for a sound similar to that of the *ch* in the German *ach*.

c   stands for a sound intermediate between those of the *tch* in *batch* and
the *ts* in *bats*.

Well, this here Blue Jay and his brother-in-law Wolf, that's what I'm going to talk about. Wolf was married with the oldest one. And he was their leader. There were also others, the chief's children, the chief's law relations. And long ago what comes first for the people is their riches. Those who are good providers of fish or of deer, since at that time they didn't know what money was—they put them above all others. Yes, those providers, they put these above all else. They are the highest. And this being so, that's when Wolf proposed to the chief for his daughter, and he consented because Wolf is smart at getting food, deer. He was told, "All right." And so they got married, he and his daughter. And when they go hunting, they put Wolf at the head—because at that time the people didn't stay alone but in a group. They stick together in winter; they winter *sənʔístktn'*, "a wintering place," they call it. They don't have buckskin tipis. They use all kinds of things to cover their houses, maybe these tules; they use tree bark as cover or anything—boughs, cedar boughs; those which sprout from the limbs, they call these *qʷilcən*, "palm boughs." They grow from cedar trees. Like, look at fir trees; they call these *kcq'əɬpíkst*, "fir boughs"; that's how it grows. And those that grow on the cedar . . . Well, no, I can't remember its name, the cedar when it has boughs. That's how they cover their houses. And they don't get wet, and it's warm. And these board houses, it's bark that they board up, and they board them on top. And they call them boarded houses.

Well, Blue Jay got to them. Well, he proposed to the chief. The youngest one also had grown up. In Indian one would say *t'ak' əmxwílx*, "she had become a young maiden." She had grown up. Yes, she wants a man. Well, he began to flirt. Blue Jay likes his daughter, the chief's daughter. He got stuck on her, and she said to her father, "Well, you had better consent." To no avail her father said to her, "But we don't know him. We don't know in what things he is smart, in getting things to eat; maybe you'll suffer from it. If it turns out that he's good for nothing, it might not be long, and you'll throw him away. The one who will do us good, take him for your husband." But no, his daughter: "He's going to be *my* husband, not your husband; even if I get hard up, it is I who would be hard up." He told her, "Well, if that's how you feel." That was that, and Blue Jay got his answer. So he got married. Blue Jay honeymooned. They were together, Wolf and his wife and Blue Jay with his wife and his law relations, the couple of the chief. And there they are all together, in one house; I don't know in how many tipis put together, maybe four, maybe three, since there are three couples. Well, all Blue Jay does is play with his wife. He sleeps until noon, then he wakes, and he and his wife get up, because they are honeymooning. By that time they are gone.

They hunt, they go get things to eat, and Wolf is their leader because he sure is smart in getting things to eat. He knows where the wintering places of the deer are, and he's smart with snowshoes. When they make a drive for the deer, Wolf chases them. The deer don't go far, and he catches up with them, and then he slaughters them. Then he overtakes his law relations, the other people. And then he gives them the deer. And then they drag the meat home; they don't even have to shoot, and they get meat. That's when Wolf gives it to them to eat. Because he's great, smart at hunting. That's why he's their leader.

Well, the oldest daughter, this here Wolf's wife, she started eating her feelings. She's always watching her brother-in-law. She hates her brother-in-law. She even said to her younger sister, "What's the matter with you? It's been many days, and you're still honeymooning. You should be getting tired of one another already. And your husband should be getting things to eat. That's all you do is play. You know, your brother-in-law, I guess he sure gets tired that all you do is play; he doesn't try to get anything to eat. He should be going, even if he doesn't kill, just so he goes along. And his brother-in-law would feel good. I guess he has all kinds of different thoughts." She kept a-nagging at her sister. Then she believed her.

At first she tried to take up for her husband; finally she believed, she understood. "That's true; my older sister is telling the truth." The parents never say anything. They tried to stop their oldest daughter when she hates her brother-in-law; she backbites him. Well, she told her Blue Jay, "Listen here. It's been too many days, and we're still honeymooning. Listen, think about getting something to eat. We have sponged too much. Maybe they are getting tired of us. Just look at your sister-in-law. They hate us very much. And they are your law relations. They tried to take up for you. They tried to stop their daughter, the oldest one. They said to her, 'Listen, leave your brother-in-law alone.' "

He said to his wife, "Give me a piece of skin since you complain with me. I haven't any snowshoes or bow and arrow. I'm going to prepare myself." Well, Blue Jay got a bow. Well, the bow he made wasn't even that; it was awful. It wasn't any good. And the arrows he got are just the same. And even when he put the feathers on the arrows, he just sticks them on. And his arrows are not good enough. His things are bad; the snowshoes no, they're bad; they aren't much, they are new shoots he made the frame with. Well, it's not fit. She asked her mother for some lacing skin. She asked her, "And what is it for?" She said, "Your son-in-law, the one I'm married to, he's going with the hunters, and he doesn't have snowshoes, and now he's made frames, but he doesn't have anything to lace them in. That's why he told me, and I interpret him to you; maybe you have some hide." She said to her, "Yes, I keep some in stock. I'll give you some." She started cutting it.

Blue Jay started stringing the shoes. It took him one day to fix his bow and arrow and his snowshoes. And those who are used to it, takes them several days to finish shoe work or arrow work. But in one day he already had finished his arrows and his snowshoes. They can't be good enough. Those who know how to fix them take pains. The sticks for the arrows have to be dry, and then they straighten them. Then they fix the feathers on, they fix the arrows, and the bow the same way. They dry the sticks dry, they whittle them, and they dry them. They make it shine in the center of the bow, and then they wrap it with sinew, and they glue it with pitch, and it doesn't come loose, and it's solid; the bow is good and strong, but because Blue Jay maybe has weak arms, what he made is no good.

The next day it was still dark when Wolf started hollering, "Daylight will overtake us, we will be late, we are going far, get up." Goodness, the people got up, the young people. They ate, they drank, they were all ready. Wolf was hollering, proclaiming, "All right. We are going." The young folks started coming out. Blue Jay came out too. Blue Jay coaxed his wife to put on him his snowshoes from inside because he doesn't even know how to tie his shoes, the loops around the ankles—that's what we call it. Well, it was his woman who put on him his snowshoes; right from inside she put his snowshoes on him. These young folks that are used to it. . . . They go far, like where there is no road, and then they put their snowshoes on. Goodness, they made fun of him. The people laughed at him because he put his snowshoes on from inside; Blue Jay takes just one step, and he hooks on something, and he has to protect himself with his hand. It must have been from the snow, and his hands got cold because I don't suppose he has gloves. He started sucking his fingers because they are cold. The young ones said, "Well, no, maybe he'll get out of sight, and then he'll come back, because Blue Jay is way behind; he will give up there, he'll come back. He's making us lose time." They walked away, and this Wolf is way ahead, fixes the trail for his friends. Then they find tracks, then they scatter. Wolf'll point to where to go; this Wolf is the leader, the smartest of all; he goes where the deer go—because he's smart and strong. And he can go fast.

They were going. Then they see the tracks—lots of deer where they are feeding. They scattered. There were many deer. He stopped. There's a hollow place, it's a big place. The deer must be there: "We didn't scare them. Here are their tracks; they might still be eating." It was broad daylight. They stopped, and he asked them, "Are you all gathered here?" They said, "Yes, we are all here. Just your brother-in-law Blue Jay hasn't yet come in sight. Just as we left, he was falling around, because he doesn't know anything about snowshoes; he might have turned back. Let's not wait for him. We are wasting time."

Wolf said, "Well, that's right; we saw tracks of deer, fresh tracks. I don't think they went anywhere far. Maybe they're in that hollow, in those slate rocks. We are going to scatter. There on the top there's a hollow. That's where we will get back together. If they've gone over, then we'll think more how they might scatter." They agreed: "Yes." He pointed for them where to drive the deer: "And those on the outside, half of them will go where they'll be watching to walk under.* There will be two groups; as for me, I'll be from this half; I will be on the outside, I am going to walk under." Only the smart ones can be on the outside because they're doing their best to get to where the deer go; that's where they always go; it's a low place where the deer go, and these who drive the deer take their time; when they see tracks, they follow them. They drive them. The deer tracks go straight to the low pass, and those who went to watch, these kill them. When he who drives the deer accidentally catches a glimpse of it, he shoots it; or when they come down and turn around, they see the ones who are watching, and they come down on their same tracks; they run across the others, then they kill them; that's when the ones that are driving kill their own deer. And that's what's called in the language *iʔ sɔck'awsk'ɬcahmíx*, "the ones that go and set watch"—the smart ones, those who watch. They said, "Maybe when Blue Jay comes out of sight, he gets tired, his hands'll get cold, he might turn back. He doesn't know anything about snowshoes. We'll waste too much time if we wait for him." They scattered. He told them, "You know the place where I told you to go; there will gather."† They scattered.

---

*they'll be watching to walk under: They'll be watching for deer to walk under.
†". . . there will gather": There we will gather.

Blue Jay's been watching for them. He saw his friends scatter. He must have good hearing; he heard every word of it. His brother-in-law is the one who's going to watch. Blue Jay was just putting on, and that's why he fell deep in the snow; he didn't know snowshoeing. Blue Jay just rised up, kicked the trees. The wind started blowing. The snow on the trees came down to the ground. The snow was floating around the land. He ran up the hill. The land was like that, and the deer did their best to get to where they could get shelter, to a place for shelter, where the air is still, where the snow doesn't reach, where the wind is still.

Blue Jay went up the hill. He went, he got there to the top where that low place is. The deer had already gone over. His partner, his brother-in-law, has already gone over. He started following, he run right in his brother-in-law's tracks. Wolf hadn't gone very far. He heard something, he got the chills. He looked behind him; well, he was being overtaken by his brother-in-law Blue Jay. Then he runs, he's doing his best. He thought, "Ah. And we thought he couldn't make it. And I am the best in hunting, and then he overtakes me. It won't be far he will give out." Not until he overtakes the deer, that's when Wolf'll turn back. Well, Wolf ran down the hill. *Dust, dust, dust,* go his snowshoes; and with the corner of his eye, he saw his brother-in-law. *Dust, dust, dust,* go his snowshoes. He had got used to his snowshoes. He didn't get to the bottom, and he got give-out, because it isn't for nothing that he's Blue Jay.* Wolf used to not get tired. He just overtakes the deer, he slaughters them. He doesn't get tired, then he gets back; I suppose Blue Jay changed him around, that's why he's tired; he's just tired. Wolf turned around. He was too tired. He told his brother-in-law, "Go ahead, maybe you are a little better off. I am plum to the end with tiredness. You are stronger," he said. Wolf gave him the way. Blue Jay jumped. Like Wolf didn't move. He started to go. Just like that Blue Jay was out of sight; he tried his best. Finally Wolf got to the bottom, because he always tracks the deer; his tracks, Blue Jay's, are right along. It got dark, it was dusk when he got to the bottom. There are deer laying all over. Well, he was busy doing something. That was the last. Blue Jay got done taking the guts out. That's when he overtook him. He has the deer all killed.

Wolf thought, "From the time I was born, from the time I got my senses, not anybody could step in front of me. Now this brother-in-law of mine steps in front of me. I'm not going to believe it. Maybe I am just dreaming." Blue Jay told him, "Hurry, let's turn back. We

---

*Blue Jay has done something to weaken Wolf.

might be too late. Our women are far away, our camp." Wolf told him, and he figured it's all uphill to the top, then it's downhill to their houses; he said, "No. I fear it. I have no more breath from fatigue. It's true that I could barely catch up with you. I can't make it up the hill. I am going to camp here." "Ah." He said, "OK," and Blue Jay had already figured out what to do. The biggest, the leader of the deer that he had killed. There was very much fat in the inside of it, he thought. He lay the deer gift down. They dug until the deer came in sight. He broke up the stitches on the deer because he had stitched up the deer. He told his brother-in-law, "Here, you go into this deer." He told him, "And then you will live. Look how clear it is, it's very cold. You will freeze. What can you do to make fire, what can you do to get wood? There's snow on trees, lots of snow. What can you do to get fir boughs in the dark? And you are tired besides. That's the only way you can save your life. Don't refuse. If you refuse, you will die. Don't you get stingy of your wife? You want to stay alive." He coaxed his brother-in-law. He believed him. He thought, "Well, I am too tired. I can't even try to get fire; and if even I make fire, I still have to get wood. No. It's still early in the night. And I have got to have something under me. And I am done in from being tired. What he said to me is true." He said, "I'll take your advice." He told him, "Get in." He went into the deer because it's big. He stitched the deer back, and he put snow back on it. After he got snow on top, Wolf got warmed up. Because he still wasn't too cold, he was warm; he hadn't gotten cold. He really liked how he was getting warm. It was very warm. But he's very hungry. He felt something, fat. He cut some off. And then he ate. That was delicious. He cleaned off the inside of his deer gift. Since it's fresh meat, in a little while he got diarrhea. He couldn't do anything to get out, because he's sewn up in there. Then Wolf did something pitiful, Wolf that used to be boss. Blue Jay ran up the hill. He *raaaan,* got to the top, he ran down the hill.

Now I am going to splice my fairy tale. The Blue Jay group with Wolf, they are brothers-in-law. They were hunting when Wolf got tired. And Blue Jay was newly wed. And he wasn't tired, and he was lonesome. He didn't like to camp by his brother-in-law. So he picked out the biggest, fattest deer. That's where he put his brother-in-law. And he said, "You might freeze, and you are tired; what can you do to make fire or to get wood or to get the boughs? It's too cold. You will freeze. This place is nice and comfortable."* Wolf

---

*This place: that is, inside the deer.

thought, "Yes, he's telling the truth." He said, "OK." He put him in the biggest deer. He sewed him up there with a twisted twig, then he covered it with snow. In a little while Wolf felt warm, I guess from his breath—from where else could the air come?—the deer in his insides, and besides he had snow on it. Blue Jay ran up the hill, got to the top; he ran down the hill. He got halfway, closer to home. He hollered repeatedly because they don't go to sleep when they have relatives. They always wait up for them. They sit around. If nobody shows up, then the next daylight they go looking for them. Something could have happened to them; they're either hurt or give out.

They heard. He was hollering. They answered him. They thought, "That's Wolf." Wolf's wife pushed her. She pushed her younger sister. She said, "Fix the fire. That might be your husband that is hollering. Put the coffeepot on the fire. He must be awful hungry." Now she's making fun of her younger sister—because Blue Jay put his snowshoes on from inside. He didn't know his snowshoes. He was falling around and then he got out of sight. Because the oldest one is sure that the smartest one is her husband— that's why she is making fun of her younger sister. The younger sister jumped up, stood up. She fixed the fire. And she started sup-per. She warmed up some leftovers, some soup, whatever was cooked for them. She warmed it over. The hollering continued. They answered it. Then she rushed her younger sister. She said, "Fix that fire, that's your man." Their parents tried to stop her because they knew for sure that she's making fun of her younger sister when she says, "That's your husband." Because it never came close to their minds. They thought, "The one who gave up is Blue Jay, be-cause he's new at hunting, since he got married." Well. They heard him because the snowshoes are loud, because it's frozen. *Dust, dust, dust, dust.* That's snowshoes. It's a good sound, clear snowshoes. He came in. He raised the curtain. He came in. He still had snowshoes on. And he sat down. His wife rushed to him, she rushed to him and kissed him on the face. She said to him, "I bet you are tired." He said, "Yes, yes, I am tired. I have traveled far. I was done in when I got back. Take off my snowshoes." She took off his snowshoes, and then he said, "Also my moccasins, because my feet are wet." Because he had moccasins on. "I covered the deer with snow."

Well, she took his moccasins off. She started drying them. She gave him his bedroom slippers. The white people call them house slippers. She set the dishes down—they don't have a table; she set dishes for him, just spread something down for him and then put dishes on that, a whole pot for his food. Blue Jay was just about to eat, and he pulled something from his chest. And he threw it at his father-in-law. He said, "Take it. Look at this. Then you'll know what it is, whatever it is." His father-in-law took it. He started to unwrap it. What is it, deer? He lay it down. He did like that, shook it, and put it down. He can't figure out what it is. It doesn't come out right.

Blue Jay started to eat. He ate and got done eating. My, his sister-in-law had a frown on her face, the one who made fun of him, his sister-in-law. And sure enough it was he who came in, and she was making fun of her younger sister—and said, "Your husband is coming. Fix that fire." And sure enough, Blue Jay came in. His sister-in-law was disappointed. She got ashamed, felt cheap when she made fun of her brother-in-law. Blue Jay got done eating.

The old man went out, and because he's chief, he yelled. All the people are listening. It was all of them, and they said, "Ah, the chief is talking. It's important." He said to them, "I'm calling all of you. My son-in-law Blue Jay came back. And he gave me this tied-up bundle. And I can't get them to match, I can't get it right. I want you to figure it out for me, that's why I am calling you." My, the people ran over there, because that's surprising news. They all came in, at the chief's. It was a full house with young folks. The old man gave it to them. They figured it out. Rather, no, they couldn't figure out the ears. They knew it's deer's ears, but they wouldn't match. They even laid them out. It doesn't fit to one half one with the other. Well, no, it doesn't match. Then they asked Blue Jay. They said, "We are puzzled. What is wrong with this ear that it doesn't match?" Blue Jay laughed at them, and he said to them, "You got no sense. You know that it won't match. Each deer has one ear. I marked all of them on one side. And if it comes out right, it will show. And it will be easy to count." That's when they all agreed. They understood, and they knew the ears. They counted them. There were lots of deer if there are so many ears.

Her brother-in-law told her, because maybe the oldest one got over her shame, his sister-in-law asked him, she said, "And what became of your brother-in-law? Didn't you see him?" And he said, "Yes, we scared the deer, and then I did my best to where they're going, to a low place where it joins the little mounds; that's where the deer went. And he went to the outside of those who drive. I got there. The deer are gone. Went over the mountain, I was too late. He was also behind, I guess he didn't even get a shot at it, and then he started chasing the deer, many of them. And also I started chasing. I followed the tracks. They hadn't got to the bottom yet on the other side of the mountain. From there to the other side, and there was a bigger valley; they hadn't yet got to the bottom. They were gone halfway when I overtook my brother-in-law. He didn't go far, and he made room, he told me, 'I am getting tired. I will never get near them. You go ahead,' he said, and I went ahead of him. I left him. The deer just got to the bottom and I overtook them. I killed them, finished them all. And all had ears. And I just had got done gutting them, I was going to bury them, when my brother-in-law overtook me. He's played out with fatigue, he's just walking. Then he told me, 'You cleaned them deer all out.' I said, 'Yes.' And he said to me, 'Well. With me, I got tired. I got give-out. And I am discouraged to go. And I'll camp here with these deer.' And I told him, 'No.' He told me, 'I am too tired.' And I said, 'No. You will freeze to death. It's late and dark. Gee, the stars are bright.' I said to him, 'You just said you are tired, tired. And what can you do to make fire? And if even you did make fire, what can you do to get wood in this dark night? And also things to put under you?' I said, 'You will freeze to death. You want to camp, and I will put you away here, in the biggest of the deer, because they are all open. I will put you here, and you won't freeze to death. The deer is quite warm, still warm. And then I'll bury you, and you won't freeze to death.' I put him there, and I sewed him up. I twisted a stick. I sewed up the deer. I tromped the snow, and it made a hole there. There I stuck him, and I buried him with snow. And then I stepped away."

He told the chief. He told his father-in-law. Blue Jay told them, "All of you that are related will get up early, the women folks too; we are going to get the dead deer. Because it's far." They said, "OK." The folks never even went to sleep. The morning came, and they woke up and started hollering. They got up, got busy, and got done eating. Then the chief went out. "Now we will walk." They said, "We are all ready." It got broad daylight. "You women folks go with your husbands." Because the women are smart with snowshoes. That's the only way they can travel anyway, because they don't have horses; who does in wintertime? That's all they travel in, on snowshoes. Especially the North Halfs. They went, and Blue Jay led them. Gee, Blue Jay is smart on snowshoes. He didn't know how, and they made fun of him.

Blue Jay's wife had gone along too, and his sister-in-law was right behind him too, also his mother-in-law and father-in-law, they're behind, and then the rest of the folks string along. They went.

There's a big valley at the end of a little mountain. That's where the low place is. They went climbed that hill. Then they went down the hill. They went, got to the bottom. He told them, "Here." There are snow mounds all over where the deer are buried. He told his father-in-law, "You are the boss, my father-in-law. You distribute the meat. That's the whole catch." The father-in-law said, "No, even if I am the chief. It's you that killed them; you're the one that worked hard. You pass it around. And here I was only sitting around, I lay on my back, I pull my whiskers with tweezers, and for me to take the lead to pass it around . . . You do it." He said, "OK," and he passed it around. He knew where he put him in the deer. He told his sister-in-law, "That's what I'm going to give you, this is your lump. You dig that out, do what you please, drag it home, or skin it, pack it back, do what you want. Whatever you think." My, his sister-in-law was glad; I suppose his sister-in-law kissed Blue Jay, she was so tickled. His sister-in-law used to hate him because he was good for nothing. She started digging the deer. She took off the snow, she got to the deer. It was sewed up twisted with the sprig. She undid the stitches; she did like that, she opened it where it was cut open and sewed up. She opened it. All of a sudden out came her husband. He's nothing but shit.

Goodness, the stench hit the woman's nose. Her husband really stunk. She tried. She's going to try to skin it. She couldn't stand it. The deer is nothing but shit. And her husband got tired, because people get hungry when they get tired. He got warmed up there when he got rested, and then he thought of being hungry. He felt around, he felt the fat. He cut off from there, and he ate it. It bulged here and there, it's fresh meat. In a while after he was done eating, he started to ache with diarrhea. He tried to get out. He couldn't. It's sewn from the outside, and there isn't anything to do to get out. He came to the end. He crapped right in there, in the deer. Until daylight he crapped in the deer. That's why the deer is nothing but shit. Goodness. The woman just frowned. She got after her husband. She said, "You have done something awful. Why, that's our eats, and you messed it up." He told his wife, "You talk pitifully. I didn't do it on purpose. I got give-out; I was tired. If I hadn't slept inside the deer . . . my brother-in-law did my thinking, I would have frozen to death. He left me. In a while I got rested, that's when I felt hungry. And I ate the fat. That's what did me bad, and then I got diarrhea. There isn't any way for me to get out. That's when I did that pitiful thing inside there, I didn't do it on purpose."

They started packing the deer. He became boss Blue Jay. They got the meat home. They started drying meat, the menfolks roasting it—and the women cutting it open; they started drying it over the fire. Lots of deer, each one gets a whole deer. And Wolf's woman, she will not throw it away, whatever she did with it, maybe she washed the deer. She aired it out, and when it had no more smell, then she roasted it.

And because it's fairy tales I tell them, "The sun is coming high on me," *Way' kən xixaʔyápəlqs;* I am going to end, as they say in the Moses language, with us we say, *Nc'ayxʷápəlqs,* "it's the end of the story."

FISH HAWK'S RAID

AGAINST THE SIOUX

▲

JAROLD RAMSEY

INTRODUCTION

The rousing story of "Fish Hawk's Raid Against the Sioux" was told in Nez Perce–Sahaptin by Gilbert Minthorne to Morris Swadesh on September 20, 1930, in Pendleton, Oregon. Swadesh was just twenty-one, a recent graduate of the University of Chicago (where he had studied with Edward Sapir), and he was probably undertaking in Pendleton the first linguistic fieldwork of his illustrious career. Perhaps that is why—despite Gilbert Minthorne's evident satisfaction in getting the story written down ("now there, we have made it, / and it will always be the same story")—Swadesh never prepared his transcriptions of this and other Sahaptin narratives for publication, eventually filing them instead in the form of two notebooks labeled "Cayuse Interlinear Texts" in the Franz Boas Collection of the American Philosophical Society Library—where, following up on a hunch, I found them in 1971.[1]

Fish Hawk and his heroic companions were in fact historical figures in the Nez Perce community of Oregon and Idaho (Fish Hawk himself lived into the 1920s and is the subject of a famous photograph by Colonel Lee Morehouse). They were renowned as the Us-ka-ma-tone (*atsqa'ma'to*), the "Brothers," whose feats of derring-do in buffalo country (apparently in the 1870s) became a widespread part of postcontact Nez Perce oral tradition—Minthorne told Swadesh that he had heard the story of the raid "from several people, including Fish Hawk himself and Alex Hayes."[2] I have discussed what is known of the Us-ka-ma-tone cycle of adventures in *Reading the Fire*[3]; what is important to notice here, however, is that of the three versions of Fish Hawk's raid in print, two present themselves as Nez Perce hero stories, and only the version given here is explicitly, emphatically Cayuse, although given in the Nez Perce language.

Notorious in Northwest history because of the Whitman Massacre (1847), the Cayuse were already extensively affiliated with their Nez Perce neighbors by the time of the Massacre; and within a few decades after that calamity, they had ceased to be a tribal entity, losing their distinctive non-Sahaptin language completely. Yet in Gilbert Minthorne's 1930 telling, Fish Hawk stands forth as a self-consciously Cayuse hero, and the Us-ka-ma-tone's heroic qualities of reckless courage, hardihood, and solidarity are presented as Cayuse virtues, in which the two unnamed Nez Perce men presumably share. Thus, old allegiances and identifications can endure drastic social and cultural change, even the loss of a people's linguistic identity.

When I first read through Swadesh's very literal interlinear translation of Minthorne's story, I was immediately struck by its performative qualities. Beyond most Native texts from the Northwest, this one seemed to be coming, however obscured by transcription and translation, from a storyteller who was consciously, artfully exploiting the narrative situation and the language itself to make the most of his hero. The insistent repeating and paralleling of verbs, accentuating the onrushing action ("and he came up to them, / one Sioux, a tough man, dog disguised; / he came up singing"); the use of heroic epithets to glorify Fish Hawk ("pipe leader," "thinker in travels," "chief in war") and his mates ("tough ones," "little brothers"); the strategic appearance of interjections like *ki·ye,* having the force of "lo!" or "behold!" and emphasizing the visualization of the action—all such features surely suggest the stylistic formality of verse, specifically (in Anglo terms) that of epic poetry.

Not knowing Nez Perce/Sahaptin, at first I was content to rework Swadesh's literal translation into readable prose—so that

> they discovered them and they yelled Sioux and he told them brothers good think go slow lo they are going to take us and now horses they swept along Sioux and they took not far

became

> Then the Sioux discovered them and yelled in Sioux! Fish Hawk said, "Brothers, think good, and take it easy—they are going to try and take us." And now they swept them along a little ways. . . .

But further consideration of the story as story, including the experience of reading it aloud to a variety of audiences, convinced me that reducing Fish Hawk's geste to neat blocks of prose was a reduction indeed; a verse measure was called for. But if not Homeric hexameters or Byronic anapests, what?

The scheme arrived at here experimentally owes something to the ethnopoetic procedures of Dell Hymes and Dennis Tedlock,[4] although it is not based on the kind of linguistic rigor that informs their work. Unable to find in Swadesh's Nez Perce transcription any evidence of a system of line measure, based on either pauses (as in Tedlock) or grammatical or syntactic markers (as in Hymes), I resolved to devise a system of lineation that would, unlike prose, highlight the verb-intensive, incremental, paratactic narrative progression of the original. It seemed clear from the start (as it is in the work of Hymes and Tedlock) that incorporation of white space ("typographical silence") would be crucial to the enterprise.

What emerged was a simple stanza form made up of indented lines: each stanza generally including one complete sentence in the original; a new line, progressively indented, for each additional verb phrase, until the sentence is completed. Lines of speech are divided on the same basis but are not progressively indented, so that they stand out as speech. Stanzas are separated by line spacing, and what turned out to be the ten main narrative segments of the story are indicated by numerals. (That fives and tens are sacred numbers in Nez Perce culture may be coincidental, but it is a pleasing coincidence.)

I can't claim that the following reworking of Gilbert Minthorne's narrative is founded on new linguistic evidence of poetic measure in Nez Perce–Cayuse oral tradition—and I certainly don't want to claim that my experimental scheme for recasting Fish Hawk's exploits in lines necessarily breaks new ground for the translation of other Native American oral material. But the scheme—simple and arbitrary though it may be—does seem to me to bring into play far more of the wonderful zest and narrative acumen I sensed in Gilbert Minthorne's telling than my original prose adaptation of Swadesh's wording did. To that extent, at least, I'm satisfied. But of course what Fish Hawk and Minthorne and the Cayuse heritage really deserve is a full-scale translation by someone fluent in Nez Perce–Sahaptin, according to ethnopoetic principles. Then surely this little masterpiece of narrative art will fully arrive in its improbable outward course from the notebooks of Morris Swadesh's apprenticeship to full literary recognition alongside others of its heroic kind, like Lord Byron's "Destruction of Sennacherib" and the battle episodes of *The Song of Roland*.

NOTES

1. Morris Swadesh, "Cayuse Interlinear Texts," Franz Boas Collection of Manuscripts, 12:1 (Freeman no. 567) American Philosophical Society Library, Philadelphia.

2. Jarold Ramsey, " 'Fish-Hawk' and Other Heroes," in *Reading the Fire: Essays in the Traditional Indian Literature of the Far West* (Lincoln: University of Nebraska Press, 1983), 141.

3. Ibid., 133–51.

4. See, for example, Dell Hymes, *"In Vain I Tried to Tell You": Essays in Native American Ethnopoetics* (Philadelphia: University of Pennsylvania Press, 1981) and his "Anthologies and Narrators" in *Recovering the Word: Essays on Native American Literature,* ed. Brian Swann and Arnold Krupat (Berkeley: University of California Press, 1987): 41–84, and Dennis Tedlock, *The Spoken Word and the Work of Interpretation* (Philadelphia: University of Pennsylvania Press, 1983).

1

A long time ago,
  when many Nez Perce and Cayuse lived to the east,
    they used to go buffalo hunting.

Once a man dreamed of the Sioux;
  he saw them in his sleep,
    and he told the young men,
      "Now I am going on the warpath day after tomorrow,
      and I shall travel to the Sioux."

He was a tough man;
  many times he had fought and come out all right.
    His name was Fish Hawk.

Four Cayuse men and two Nez Perce men were going,
  the one named Fish Hawk
    and one named Come-with-the-Dawn
      and one named All-Alighted-on-the-Ground
        and one named Charging Coyote
          and two Nez Perce men.

Fish Hawk took the lead;
  he held the pipe;
    he was the thinker in travels.

2

They all had red jackets;
  they were on the warpath, all six of them.

They traveled, and it snowed;
  it snowed like winter on the prairie.

They traveled on horseback,
  and they came upon the prairie
    and went down into a canyon.

Many Sioux lived close by there.
Fish Hawk stopped, and he turned around toward his friends.

"We've come right into camp;
see, here are the tents,
and they don't know we're here."

Tents were all around,
maybe two hundred or more;
they saw the tents.

Then the Sioux discovered them
and yelled in Sioux!

Fish Hawk said,
"Brothers, think good, and take it easy—
look! they are going to try and take us."

And now they swept the Sioux horses along with them;
they drove them along a little way,
and then they all turned.

"Look! they are catching up with us,"
he told the others,
the pipe leader told them.

"Younger brothers, move on from here;
don't shoot yet;
from now on they will try and take us.
Look, there is brushy ground ahead;
there will we dismount,
and soon they will try and get us.
We shall not desert each other;
look to your guns—"
and the Sioux chased them along.

And the people's chief in battle turned his horse,
and he waved at the Sioux;
he told them,
"I am Cayuse, we all are!
We are only six,
and you are three hundred or more!
Come on! You are only Sioux,
and you are just like old women;
you will never kill us, for we are Cayuse!"

3

So they yelled at the Sioux during the chase,
   and shot at them;
      they killed them as they went.

He told his brothers, the pipe leader,
   "Now turn your horses loose,"
     and they got off,
       and they took off the bridles
        and took off their jackets
         and left it all behind
          and took only the guns and bullets into the brush
          among the cottonwoods.

He told them, the pipe leader,
   he told them,
     "Younger brothers, look:
     we can dig trenches
     and fight well from there."

They dug out the ground
   and crossed cottonwoods over the trenches
     and got under it all.

They yelled at the Sioux;
   the Sioux yelled back at them and hurled insults,
     they yelled back again.
They were killing Sioux.

4

Now then one of the Sioux used up his bullets,
   and he came up to them,
     one Sioux, a tough man, dog disguised;
      he came up singing.

Fish Hawk said, their chief,
   "Little brothers, now he comes;
   take good aim!"
     and they hit him close by the trench.

He came on
   and now he shot at Fish Hawk with a bow and arrows.

Fish Hawk cried,
   "Little brothers, he shot me!"

He got mad, the one the people call Fish Hawk.
He told them,
   "Look, friends, watch your leader, now!
   He shot one of us;
   now know me;
   now I am going after him,
   and I am going to drag him right into the trench!"

And he stood up suddenly
   and threw himself out of the trench,
     and they yelled, the Sioux;
      they shot at him,
       and he hopped;
        he grabbed the Sioux warrior by the legs
         and dragged him along;
          he threw him into the trench,
          and he hit him.

They took his bullets and gun
   and scalped him.

5

Fish Hawk told them,
   "Little brothers, maybe I am dying;
   now pull out the arrow—"
     and they pulled it out,
      and the pipe leader, chief in war, breathed good again,
       but he was bleeding and getting weak,
        and they tied up the wound.

He started shooting again;
   he told them,
     "Little brothers, think carefully;
     look, they are many,

and they are trying to get us.
Try to shoot straighter—"
    and they yelled.

6

He saw now that there was fire all around them,
    below and up above,
        and he told them,
            "Now, look, it's burning;
            they are trying to kill us by burning.
            Dig deeper now;
            we are going to be burned.
            See! they're scared and that is why
            they are trying to burn us to death.
            But we will never die of fire;
            we are younger brothers, tough ones with guns;
            they can't get us killed,
            and they will never kill us with fire."

So he told them,
    and when night came,
        he gathered them in the mouth of the thicket;
        he told them,
            "We killed many Sioux;
            now we're going;
            we're going out.
            We're in the midst of them,
            but with my knowledge soon we will get through
                anyway."

And he told them,
    "A little wind will come up presently;
    now get ready, little brothers;
    let's travel!"

And it came, the whirlwind,
    and they got out of the trench.

When the fire flared up, they went down;
    they passed the Sioux all huddled up in a ditch;
        they passed by unseen;
            they traveled on.

7

Dawn came.
The Sioux said,
   "Now, look, they're all burned up—"
      and they went up to the trench.

When they got there, they found nobody.
The Sioux were surprised.
   "Where are they?
   How could they live?
   On which side of us did they pass?"

They were greatly surprised;
   and as they went home, they cried on their way;
      they took many bodies home.

8

The Cayuse got out from the trench all right,
   and from there they traveled without pants,
      shirtless,
         pantsless,
            shoeless—
All they had were guns,
   and he told them, their chief, the pipe leader, he told them,
      "Younger brothers, now we have traveled far,
      and one of us is getting cold
      and can travel no farther."

It was Charging Coyote;
   he told them,
      "Friends, now leave me;
      I will be too much bother;
      I'll stay, I'll stay right here.
      My forefathers died too;
      I'll just rest my body."

Then the others told him,
   "No, friend, it's the same with all of us:
   without shoes,
   without pants,
   without shirts,
   somehow we will all get back.

This is what we went looking for,
and now we are coming back together."

9

Then they came upon a buffalo bull,
   and Fish Hawk told them,
     "We have traveled far without eating;
     now kill it."

And they killed two buffalo;
   from them they made shoes and pants and shirts,
     and they ate buffalo meat,
      and they went on traveling.

But they had no tents;
   they got black from freezing
     and were awful to look at;
      thus they came back to the tents of their own people.

10

This is all of the story about the raid on the Sioux:
   now they told it at the big war dance at celebration time,
     how this man,
      Fish Hawk, the pipe leader,
       went on the warpath;
        he was the man!

"Only six of us, and you couldn't get us killed,
only six, and maybe you were three hundred and maybe more!"

Thus they told the story,
   and now all the people know it.

This is a true story;
   now there, we have made it,
     and it will always be the same story.

POETRY SONGS OF THE
SHOSHONE GHOST DANCE

▲

JUDITH VANDER

INTRODUCTION

The poems presented here are religious song texts that the Wind
River Shoshone of Wyoming sang during Ghost Dance performances of the past. They are part of the Ghost Dance repertoire of
147 songs that I recorded in the late 1970s as they were performed
by two Shoshone elders, Emily Hill and Dorothy Tappay.[1] The
women learned these songs at Ghost Dance performances of their
youth, beginning around 1921 and continuing on until the religion's demise, in the late 1930s. Emily and Dorothy, however,
maintained belief in the religion until their deaths, in the 1980s.
They disapproved of the English name, as it bears no relation to the
Shoshone name for the religion, Naraya, literally, the side-shuffling
step of the dance. For this reason, I shall use Naraya when referring
specifically to the Wind River Shoshone Ghost Dance.

The Ghost Dance religion began in 1889 and spread rapidly to
many tribes. It was received in a dream by Wovoka, a Northern
Paiute prophet from Nevada. In his dream he also received songs
that were to accompany the dance of his revealed religion, which
prophesied the end of the present world, the return of the dead, and
a new world of aboriginal abundance free from disease and death
itself. While calling for peaceful relations with non-Indians in the
present world, Wovoka did not mention non-Indians in his proph-

ecy, and many inferred from this that they were not to be included in
the world to come. The date for fulfillment of the prophecy changed
several times, after each successive date came and went uneventfully.
The 1890 massacre, by troops of the U.S. Army, of Sioux who had
gathered at Wounded Knee, South Dakota, for a Ghost Dance performance, delivered a powerful message to other adherents of the
religion. In the end Wovoka called for the abandonment of Ghost
Dance performances.

Emily Hill and Dorothy Tappay disclaimed any connection between Wovoka's Ghost Dance religion and the Naraya. They maintained its pure Shoshone identity and lineage and never talked of
Ghost Dance prophecies for the return of the dead and a new world
to come. Nonetheless, a few Naraya songs they sang do mention
these themes, and the two women translated these texts and talked
of these beliefs in connection with those songs. There is also documentation for Shoshones going to Nevada to learn firsthand about
the Ghost Dance and of Wovoka's visit to the Wind River Reservation in 1910. I believe, therefore, that Ghost Dance belief and doctrine did, in fact, have some impact on the Naraya during the late
nineteenth century.

From studying all of Emily and Dorothy's Naraya repertoire,
however, it is clear that the subject matter of the Naraya is, with few
exceptions, very different from usual Ghost Dance texts. A detailed
poetic vision of the natural world, this world, is the great subject of
Naraya songs—miniature ecological scenes, compressed and complete. Emily explained the meaning of the Naraya to me in this way:

> "They say when you sing those songs it makes berries grow and make
> grass grow, make water run. Plenty of berries for in the fall, fish,
> everything. Sing for them, our elk and deer and all them. That's what
> it's for. . . . Well, some men, they dream that something's going to be
> wrong or some kind of sickness or some kind of storm. They know it.
> Well, we going to dance. It ain't going to happen when we dance. Flu
> or measles or scarlet fever or a sickness that's some kind of hard
> cough—one person knows when he's asleep, he knows it's coming.
> . . . We better be dancing, sending it back, sending it back. We just
> make it go back. That's the way they dance it. It isn't just a dance.
> . . . Well, it's a song for health. . . . When you don't feel good, when
> you feel sick or something, you dance with them. You feel good then.
> That's what it's for. It ain't just songs."[2]

Thus, the purpose of the Naraya was to protect adherents' health
and ensure the abundance of water, plants, and animals. Men and

women held hands in a circle, step-sliding clockwise. Male song leaders started off the song, and then those dancers who wished to sing joined in. There was no instrumental accompaniment to the dance, which was performed on four consecutive nights and concluded after a fifth daytime performance. The dreams of recognized Naraya leaders determined when a Naraya dance series should be held. A dream was the time and place in which to receive sacred knowledge and power. In a dream the Naraya leader saw the dangerous approach of flu or measles. Sacred songs, songs that have power, were also received in a dream. The receiver did not compose the song and its text but heard them and learned them immediately.

The Wind River Shoshone have two distinctly different cultural heritages—that of the Plains and that of the Great Basin. If you visit them today in Wyoming, there is much evidence of their history from the eighteenth and nineteenth centuries. At that time they traveled widely on the Plains as hunters of the bison and warriors competing for hunting grounds. But that phase of their cultural history does not appear in Naraya songs. In order to understand the Naraya, one must dig down into Wind River Shoshone history prior to 1500, when they still lived in their ancestral homeland, the Great Basin. This region lies in Nevada, Utah, and western Colorado and in parts of Oregon, Idaho, and Wyoming. Bounded on the west by the Sierra Nevada and on the east by the Rocky Mountains, it is a dry environment with scarce food resources. Prior to their movement out onto the Plains, the Wind River Shoshone were one of many Shoshone groups in the Great Basin. They gathered a great variety of plant foods, supplementing it when they could by hunting. Sufficient water for plants and people was ever a prime concern.

Because food was scarce, there were relatively few occasions for large gatherings. When they did occur—for example, at the time of the pine nut harvest—an event called the Round Dance was performed. The likenesses between the Round Dance and the Naraya are striking: a Round Dance performance lasted five nights, men and women sang and danced in a circle, and a dance leader offered prayers for health, an abundance of wild foods, and rain. As in the Naraya, song and dance were central to the occasion and its religious functions.

I believe that in its form and content the Naraya is basically a Wind River Shoshone religion that is rooted in ancient religious practices of the Great Basin Round Dance. At a certain point the Ghost Dance doctrine influenced the Naraya, but the Ghost Dance movement came and went, and the Naraya endured. Traces of

Ghost Dance doctrine and images remained in Naraya songs but were absent from Emily and Dorothy's religious beliefs.

In short, Naraya songs have two aspects, and in this they occupy a special place within published Native American song texts. They contain Ghost Dance references and allusions, and in one sense they are the largest collection since James Mooney's *Ghost Dance Religion* of 1896.[3] In another, larger sense they are a twentieth-century connection to the ancient religious Round Dance traditions of the Great Basin, for which there are very few published examples at all.

Naraya songs and their poetic texts occupy a unique place in Shoshone music. They are the only genre with full Shoshone texts. Sun Dance songs, War Dance songs, Round Dance songs, Hand-Game songs, and Peyote songs of the Native American Church may include bits and pieces of Shoshone, but they have primarily vocable texts; that is, their texts consist of nonlexical syllables, for example, *we ya ha he yo*. Consonants and vowels are combined according to certain conventions. Each song has its own set pattern, a kind of abstract poetry that singers learn in conjunction with the pitch and rhythm of the melody.

Beyond their historic and religious significance, Naraya songs deserve attention for their high poetic achievement. On the surface they are simple forms. Each song has two or three lines of text, and each line has three or four words. With very few exceptions, every line is repeated: *aa, bb,* and so on. I will, however, point out some of the multitudinous complexities and subtleties that complement these seemingly simple structures.

The term *poetry song* was coined by Beverly Crum, a linguist and native Shoshone speaker from Nevada. She wrote, "Poetry songs are composed in an elevated and figurative form of language. They are often detailed descriptions of what authors observed in their environment, with several levels of meanings."[4] I am happy to extend the use of this term to Naraya song texts, which I believe share these qualities and relate to the Round Dance traditions of the Western Shoshone and other Great Basin peoples.

Because form is such an essential part of poetry, I have included a literal translation, in small type, for every text. (Songs 10 and 11 are exceptions: they are essentially literal translations, the only changes being the addition of punctuation.) I also provide commentary by Emily and—in one case—Dorothy.[5] My English translation is guided by the letter and spirit of the foregoing discussions.

In the original, six of these poems have no rhyme, five rhyme, and four have the same final word. In general, I have tried to be faithful to the original, although in Poetry Songs 3, 10, and 12, I found no appropriate rhyme in English to match that of the Shoshone. Finally, unlike haiku, limericks, Shakespearean sonnets, and other literary genres, Naraya songs and their texts have no one rule dictating their rhythm and meter.

The translation from Shoshone to English is only one aspect of a more radical transformation—from something heard to something seen. As these texts come from an oral-aural, not a visual, tradition, I strongly encourage readers to read the translations out loud, to match the oral aspect of Emily and Dorothy's performance. Recite each text several times. These songs were never sung through just once. In their performance for me, Emily and Dorothy sang each song four or five times. When recording by and for themselves, they repeated a song many more times than that. In actual Naraya performances a song was sung as many times as was necessary for the circle of dancers to complete at least one revolution.

I gratefully acknowledge that this work was made possible through the support of a research grant and fellowship from the National Endowment for the Humanities.

NOTES

1. Judith Vander, *Ghost Dance Songs and Religion of a Wind River Shoshone Woman,* Monograph Series in Ethnomusicology no. 4 (Los Angeles: University of California, 1986). Beyond the transcription of music and texts, the focus of this study is the musical and textual analysis of seventeen Naraya songs. It includes historical background of the Naraya and compares it with other Wind River Shoshone ceremonies. Poetry Songs 1, 3, 4, 5, 6, 7, 8, 10, 11, 12, and 14 appear, respectively, on pages 38, 43–44, 42, 39–40, 45, 45–46, 48, 49, 52, 53, and 54–55, under different numbers.

2. Quoted in Judith Vander, *Songprints: The Musical Experience of Five Shoshone Women* (Urbana: University of Illinois Press, 1988), 11–12. In this volume and on the accompanying audiocassette, Naraya songs and other song genres are placed within the context of five singers' lives, including that of Emily Hill. The book records the women's discussion of the songs they sing

and their meaning. Poetry Songs 1, 4, 5, 10, 11, 13, and 14 appear, respectively, on pages 17–18, 19–20, 19, 24, 25, 14, and 26, under different numbers. Emily and Dorothy's performance of Poetry Songs 1, 4, 11, and 14 are recorded on the audiotape, again under different numbers (2, 5, 10, and 11, respectively).

3. James Mooney, *The Ghost Dance Religion, and Sioux Outbreak of 1890,* pt. 2, The Fourteenth Annual Report of the Bureau of Ethnology for the Years 1892–93 (Washington, D.C.: Smithsonian Institution, 1896; reprint, Lincoln: University of Nebraska Press, 1991).

4. Beverly Crum, "Newe Hupia—Shoshoni Poetry Songs," *Journal of California and Great Basin Anthropology Papers in Linguistics 2* (1980): 5. This publication presents music and detailed linguistic analyses of four Shoshone poetry songs and provides as well descriptions of their rich cultural context.

5. The commentary following Poetry Songs 3, 6, 7, 8, 12, and 14 is from Vander, *Ghost Dance Songs and Religion of a Wind River Shoshone Woman,* 38, 45, 46, 48, 53, and 55, respectively. That following Poetry Song 5 is from previously unpublished quotes that are very similar to those published in the same publication, 40. The commentary following Poetry Songs 1, 4, 10, 11, and 13 is from Vander, *Songprints,* 18, 20, 24, 25, and 15, respectively. Both the text and commentary for Poetry Song 2 are from Vander, "Nature in Numic Myth and the Shoshone Ghost Dance," a paper presented at the 1990 Great Basin Anthropological Conference. The text and commentary for Poetry Song 9 have no prior source, published or unpublished.

POETRY SONG 1

Fog over our mountains—lying, moving.
Fog over our mountains—lying, moving.
Fog, fog, fog—lying, moving.
Fog, fog, fog—lying, moving.

> Our mountain above fog lying while moving.
> Our mountain above fog lying while moving.
> Fog fog fog lying while moving.
> Fog fog fog lying while moving.

EMILY: *It's a fog over the mountains.*
DOROTHY: *It's fog on the mountains, a long ways.*
EMILY: *Fog, you see it on the side of the mountains. . . . You see it moving towards this way or that way. It just keeps saying that fog, fog.*

Water in all its many forms, including fog, is one of the most frequent images in Naraya songs. This is not surprising, as abundant water, itself a goal of Naraya performance, is essential for two of its other concerns: plant life and animal life. Fog on the mountains waters the environment for all life. But hovering over this text is a second possible meaning of its key image. Fog is also the Shoshone concept for the soul when it leaves the body at death. Fog over the mountains might also refer to a crowd of souls returning to life according to Ghost Dance prophecy. Poetic construction of the second pair of lines focuses on fog by reiterating it three times; the lengthening of the text through time serves as a metaphor for the lengthening of the fog through space.

POETRY SONG 2

Sunlit showers on the mountains, sunlit showers on the mountains
ena.*
Sunlit showers on the mountains, sunlit showers on the mountains
ena.
Pine needles in pools of mountainside gullies after sunlit showers
on the mountains *ena.*

---

* *Ena* is a vocable used by the Wind River Shoshone exclusively in Naraya songs as a cadence marker.

Sun rain mountains sun rain mountains *ena*.
Sun rain mountains sun rain mountains *ena*.
Pine leaves or needles pools side low place sun rain mountains *ena*.

EMILY: *Our mountains, you know, it kind of sprinkles up the mountains like, towards the light. That's afternoon showers. It's raining [but] not too much. And there's on the mountains, there's them water pools. Just like lakes, but only smaller. You know how it is, puddles under them mountains. It's kind of, you know, in a low place. And those pine tree leaves all over on the water. Pine needles in the water. That's what it means. Clouds go over, clouds behind that—shadow, shadow on them puddle things. It gives that shade where the water puddles are.*

With exquisite poetic economy this text collects in its reflected image mountains, trees, greenery, sky-rain-water—the natural world of the Naraya. Emily and Dorothy did not repeat the second line of text in this song, contrary to this strong stylistic norm in Naraya and Ghost Dance songs.

POETRY SONG 3

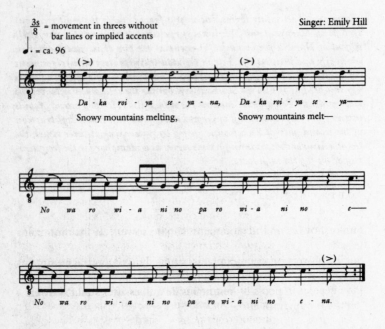

$\frac{3s}{8}$ = movement in threes without bar lines or implied accents

♩. = ca. 96

Singer: Emily Hill

Da - ka roi - ya se - ya - na, Da - ka roi - ya se - ya—
Snowy mountains melting, Snowy mountains melt—

No wa ro wi - a ni no pa ro wi - a ni no e—

No wa ro wi - a ni no pa ro wi - a ni no e - na.

Snowy mountains melting.
Snowy mountains melt——
No wa ro wia ni no pa ro wia ni no e——
No wa ro wia ni no pa ro wia ni no ena.

Snow mountain melting,
Snow mountain melt——
No wa ro mountain pass *ni no* water *ro* mountain pass *ni no e*——
No wa ro mountain pass *ni no* water *ro* mountain pass *ni no ena.*

EMILY: *Snowy mountains, melting. You know, when the sun's on the mountains, you see that snow shining . . . when it's kind of going to melt. . . . The mountains go like this,* wiaph, *like this—sloped down like this and some melting.** *

The power of the song, its performance, its images of melting snow and water on the saddle of the mountains—all were to help bring into being that which is envisioned. Song, text, and dance influenced the natural world. Concern for water and the speedy return of spring, symbolized by melting snow, took other forms in Shoshone culture. Myths characteristically end with references to melting snow, and the proper telling of a myth was to help bring about this natural phenomenon.

One source of the complexity in Naraya song texts comes from the transformation of words in everyday language into Naraya song language. For example, wia, *Shoshone for "mountain pass," is abbreviated from* wiaph. *Vocables, used as prefixes or suffixes and even inserted into the middle of a word, are another source of endless variation. All the italicized words in the literal translation of Poetry Song 3 are vocables, which are used to an exceptional extent in this song text. To read them, the reader need know only that the Shoshone vowel sounds correspond approximately to the English vowel sounds* a *as in* father; e *as in* pay; i *as in* elite; o *as in* no. *Because I have left in Shoshone the two words that are tucked into this vocable line (*wia *for "mountain pass" and* pa *for "water," given in the literal translation), the second pair of repeated lines needs no translation.*

The line in which the vocables appear has a strong lilting quality enhanced by the melody and three-beat patterns of its musical setting. To help the reader appreciate this, I have indicated when to hold a vowel sound through a second rhythmic beat of the song. For example, the o *in* no^o *is twice as long as the* o *in* no. *A dot* (·) *indicates a silent "beat." Finally, the vertical lines above the vocables indicate individual beats in the rhythm.*

---

*sloped down like this: like the saddle of a mountain; that is, a mountain pass.

| | | | | || | | || | || | | || | || | | | |||| |
No͡ o wa ro͡ o wia͡ a ni no · pa ro͡ o wia͡ a ni no · · e͡ e͡ e——
No͡ o wa ro͡ o wia͡ a ni no · pa ro͡ o wia͡ a ni no · · e͡ e͡ ena.

POETRY SONG 4

Wild ducklings, wild ducklings so small,
Wild ducklings, wild ducklings so small.
In good water swimming,
In good water swimming.

Wild ducklings, wild ducklings so small,
Wild ducklings, wild ducklings so small.
In good water swimming,
In good water swim.

Duck's ducklings duck's ducklings very small.
Duck's ducklings duck's ducklings very small.
Good water swimming.
Good water swimmi——

EMILY: *They're wild ducks, little baby ducks, going along following each other. They're swimming in the good water.*

Poetry Song 4 is one of many texts that places animals in a pristine setting and mentions a burgeoning new generation. Good in Shoshone has many more uses than in English. In this context, it means "clean," "clear," "fresh," "sparkling," and probably more.

Repetition is an important part of Naraya songs, but it is often inexact. Tiny variants in melody and rhythm give the songs the texture of a hand-woven fabric and affect the text. One such effect is the omission of a final vowel sound at the end of a line, especially in the last repetition of the song. Swim—the last word in the last line—is only a roughly translated equivalent of this.

POETRY SONG 5

Eagle's wing is skying.
Eagle's wing is skying.
Grass and shining water lying . . . flowing . . .
Grass and shining water lying . . . flowing . . .

Eagle's wing is skying.
Eagle's wing is skying.
Green or grass water shiny under lying while moving.
Green or grass water shiny under lying while moving.

EMILY: *You've [been] flying on an airplane? You see it from way up there—water, rivers, and grass on the ground. That's the way that eagle's looking down from the sky way up there. For the water's shining. Shining where the ground is green.*

The eagle is the sacred bird of the Wind River Shoshone and many other Native American tribes. Eagle-feather fans play an important role in religious ceremony and in the healing of the sick. This complete scene from the natural world includes, in addition to the eagle, two of the most important Naraya images, water and greenery.

POETRY SONG 6

Pine-tree butterflies, pine-tree butterflies.
Pine-tree butterflies, pine-tree butterflies.
Through gaps in pine-shade darkness—flickering.
Through gaps in pine-shade darkness—flickering.

Pine tree butterfly pine tree butterfly.
Pine tree butterfly pine tree butterfly.
Dark pine tree holes underneath dark flickering or fluttering.
Dark pine tree holes underneath dark flickering or fluttering.

EMILY: *You see the mountains where the pine trees are dark. It's kind of shady-like. That's where those butterflies fly.*
Emily *"held up one hand, motionless, with fingers spread apart and moved her other hand behind it. This was her demonstration of how one saw the butterflies (moving hand) flying under or through the shady pine boughs (motionless hand)."*

POETRY SONG 7

Our Father's mountain lion walks down the mountainside roaring,
  *wainda.**
Our Father's mountain lion walks down the mountainside roaring,
  wainda.
Our beloved Father's dear game animals with their young, so
  small, on the mountainside sit, *wainda.*

* *Wainda* is a vocable.

Our beloved Father's dear game animals with their young, so
small, on the mountainside sit, *wainda*.

Our Father's mountain lion.
Mountain side below walking down yowling *wainda*.
Our Father's mountain lion.
Mountain side below walking down yowling *wainda*.
Our Father's* game animals* offspring* sitting *wainda*.
Our Father's* game animals* offspring* sitting *wainda*.

EMILY: *Our Father's, our Creator's mountain lion walking around on the
sides of the mountains. All the animals, different kinds of animals that belong
to Him—deer, elk, moose, mountain sheep, and antelope—little ones with the
older ones—sitting down on the side of the mountain.*

*"Our Father," or God, does not appear frequently in Naraya songs. On
one occasion Emily suggested this relationship: "It's [Naraya song] a religious song that you sing to God." Game animals and, especially, their
offspring, on the other hand, are important and frequent Naraya personae. This brings us back to another statement by Emily regarding the
purpose of the Naraya and its songs: "Sing for them, our elk and deer and
all them. That's what it's for."*

*My translation of the second pair of lines neglects the form of the origi-
nal: it omits the special rhymed endings that give affectionate and/or diminutive meaning to the words they tag. All of them are set to the same
little musical motif, which brings out the rhyme and itself sets up a rollick-
ing repeated pattern. Although somewhat awkward, the following translation is a closer equivalent to the form of the original:*

Our Father's (dear He), game animals (dear they), their young (so
sweet), on the mountainside sit, *wainda*.

Read this as an alternative to the second pair of lines.

POETRY SONG 8

Our sun's face, radiant white, is setting.
Our sun's face, radiant white, is setting.
Our sun's going . . . sun is setting.
Our sun's going . . . sun is setting.

*To each of these words is added a diminutive, affectionate suffix.

> Our sun's face white set while moving.
> Our sun's face white set while moving.
> Our sun's going or moving sun set while moving.
> Our sun's going or moving sun set while moving.

EMILY: *It's a prayer song to sun. It's about the sun; the sun's face is white. You can't see it. . . . You can't look at the sun, it's too strong. . . . The sun's face is white, warming up the world. It's a-going—sundown. . . . When it's going down it cuts the light. Light shining like a can is shining.*

POETRY SONG 9

> On new earth all the birds singing together at the same time.
> On new earth all the birds singing together at the same time.
> Yellow-edged rim.
> Yellow-edged rim.

New earth on different kinds all birds sounding all together at the same time.
New earth on different kinds all birds sounding all together at the same time.
Yel[low] edging or rim.
Yel[low] edging or rim.

EMILY: *Next morning, daybreak and all the different kind of birds singing. You know the light early in the morning, you see that light just coming up, that yellow along there. That's the time those birds all wake up and sing, different kind of birds. That's what it means."*

As in English, Shoshone has a word for sunrise, the topic of Poetry Song 9. Without using the word itself, the text defines sunrise by what one hears (birds) and sees (sunlight just barely outlining the horizon).
  Is the "new earth" a compressed poetic statement, shorthand for the sunrise that heralds the new day and its new earth? Or is it literally the new earth, the new world of Ghost Dance prophecy? Or both? Naraya songs are rich in ambiguities. Only the person who received the song knows definitively. As to its form, note the unequal length of the two pairs of lines. This is typical of Naraya songs and their texts, one of many asymmetrical characteristics.

POETRY SONG 10

> Our Morning Star coming up.
> Our Morning Star coming up.
> Clear sun rays streaming out.
> Clear sun rays streaming out.

Star sitting lightly.
Star sitting lightly.

EMILY: *Morning Star, song about Morning Star. When you see the daylight coming up, when it's coming up, the Morning Star coming up with that light. It's sitting up there just before daybreak.*

Like Poetry Song 9, this song may be a connection between the Naraya and Ghost Dance doctrine and practice. The Morning Star adorned Ghost Dance clothing, and many tribes concluded their all-night Ghost Dance performance with a song to that star. Emily recalls dancing only until midnight; it may be, however, that Poetry Song 10 is a relic from an earlier time, when Naraya performance adhered to this Ghost Dance custom.

The ten song texts presented thus far represent the majority of Naraya songs in that they evoke images of the natural world. A few songs, including Poetry Songs 11 and 12, sing of the soul after death—this, too, is embodied in images from the natural world.

POETRY SONG 11

Soul-fog, soul-fog.
Soul-fog, soul-fog.
Soul flying up, soul flying up.
Soul flying up, soul flying up.

EMILY: *The soul is like a fog when it gets out of the body. Well, when a person dies, the soul goes out of the body and flies in the air. It flies away from you. Then they go to God's home when the body's already in the ground.*

Water, in every conceivable form and state, appears throughout Naraya songs. The soul, the essence of life itself, assumes the form of water as an amorphous airy fog. In the original Shoshone, Poetry Song 11 is exceptional in that the number of beats in all four lines—and therefore the length of the lines—is identical. The English translation does not match this rhythmic regularity.

POETRY SONG 12

Whirlwind-shrouded soul, whirlwind flying up.
Whirlwind-shrouded soul, whirlwind flying up
mountain road through green pass—lying while moving,
mountain road through green pass—lying while moving.

Small dust small flying up.
Small dust small flying up
road mountain's green lying while moving,
road mountain's green lying while moving.

EMILY: *When a person dies they go in a dust whirlwind. They go up in the mountains. There's a road for that, there's a green pass through there, where they go. . . . There's a road up the mountains where the whirlwind blows where the person when he dies he [his soul] goes, in the middle of the whirlwind.*

There is a sequence of possible translations of the first line, beginning with the literal: "Small dust small flying up." In all subsequent translations I have felt it necessary to bring soul from the implicit to the explicit: "Small dust-soul, small, flying up," or "Small dust-shrouded soul, small, flying up." The latter translation is inspired by the image of the soul wrapped in the swirl of dust. Finally, I take Emily's translation for small dust, which in this text is a sung poetic reference to whirlwind, and arrive at "Whirlwind-shrouded soul, whirlwind flying up."

The last choice, which I used in the song, attempts to retain some formal aspects of the literal translation. The repetition of small *in the first line of the literal translation is an abbreviated reference to "small dust," which begins the line. For this reason I repeat* whirlwind *in my translation, a shortened version of "whirlwind-shrouded soul." I invite the reader to experiment and read the translation using the alternative first lines given in the previous paragraph. Is it the road that lies on the mountain and moves through the pass, or is it the soul that lies in the whirlwind as it climbs the road? This is another ambiguity of the literal that remains in translation.*

POETRY SONG 13

White-Clay Man, White-Clay Man.
White-Clay Man, White-Clay Man
with Wood-Stick Man, flying on,
with Wood-Stick Man, flying on.

White clay man, white clay man.
White clay man, white clay man.
Wood or stick man keep flying on.
Wood or stick man keep flying on.

EMILY: *It's mud, the dough [white clay], they take it. They bring it out to dry. That's for dressing, putting on your buckskin. It's something like chalk. It's for the Sun Dance—white, smells good. . . . That man's made of that kind, and man made of wood. . . . Get up, up, flying on.*

371

White-Clay Man and Wood-Stick Man are personifications that capture the essence of the religious focus of the Naraya and the ancient Round Dance of its roots. White clay is used in the Sun Dance religion for purification. Shamans used it to dry out disease. So important was the use of clay that it was a standard part of the shaman's paraphernalia. White-Clay Man epitomizes concern for health. Wood-Stick Man was addressed in prayer at Round Dance performances of the Northern Shoshone as the Maker of Green Things. Health and vegetation were foci of the Great Basin Round Dance, and they carried over to the Wind River Shoshone Naraya.

Where are White-Clay Man and Wood-Stick Man going? Flight in Naraya songs is either to the land of the dead or to the new world of Ghost Dance prophecy. White-Clay Man and Wood-Stick Man are flying to this new world, bringing to it ancient Great Basin and Wind River Shoshone concerns and responses to them—the Round Dance and Naraya.

POETRY SONG 14

Our dead mothers stir as resurrection day is dawning.
Our dead mothers stir as resurrection day is dawning.
From above, looking down for us children—they will keep
 coming, keep coming.
From above, looking down for us children—they will keep
 coming, keep coming.

Our mothers day or sun come out* lying while moving.
Our mothers day or sun come out* lying while moving.
Looking down to or for us above will keep coming, will keep coming.
Looking down to or for us above will keep coming, will keep coming.

EMILY: *When our mother comes, when the end of the world—coming, looking for her children. Coming down see, she's above us and looking down and looking for her children. The day, the day, the Judgment Day comes. It's that time. The mothers come, looking down, coming, coming, looking for her children.... Everybody's coming back. End of the dead, people that dead coming alive, you know.*

Poetry Song 14 is one of the few Naraya texts that I believe clearly expresses the earlier Shoshone belief in the Ghost Dance prophecy for the return of the dead. Emily denied any connection between the Naraya and the Ghost Dance and any belief in the return of the dead. Her explanation of Poetry Song 14 draws on Christian terminology and context for an event in the far future. It was the one and only mention of Judgment Day by Emily to

---

*A diminutive, affectionate suffix is added.

me and was perhaps an attempt to provide a context that I could under-stand.

    Unique to this song is a second possible translation, one that removes the dissonance of promised resurrection. It hinges on the Shoshone word for "day," which is the same as the word for "sun," and on the interpretation of "mother" as Mother Nature.

EMILY: *When the sun comes up Mother Nature, our Mother comes looking.*

POETRY SONG 14: VARIANT

Our Mother Nature stirs as the sun is just rising.
Our Mother Nature stirs as the sun is just rising.
Looking down toward us from above, she keeps coming, coming.
Looking down toward us from above, she keeps coming, coming.

This is the sole appearance of Mother Nature in Emily and Dorothy's Na-raya repertoire. Mother Earth, on the other hand, appears in a few Na-raya songs. Like White-Clay Man and Wood-Stick Man, personification of the earth and elements of the natural world is part of the religious ori-entation of Great Basin cultures. In this way people speak and communi-cate with a landscape made of human kin and kind.

THE
PLAINS

THREE SKIRI PAWNEE STORIES

▲

DOUGLAS PARKS

INTRODUCTION

For most of the nineteenth century, the Pawnee Indians lived along major tributaries of the Missouri River in central Nebraska and northern Kansas. The rhythm of their life was characterized by an annual round that began in the spring, when they resided in permanent villages of dome-shaped earth lodges. During this season their activities centered on horticulture—women prepared and planted gardens of corn, squash, and beans, and older men engaged in associated rituals. In June, once the crops were growing, the members of each village traveled west onto the high plains; there they lived in tipis and hunted buffalo. By late August the people returned to their earth-lodge villages, where they harvested the mature crops and again took up various ritual activities. In November, with the onset of winter, they traveled back onto the western plains for their winter buffalo hunt, which lasted until February, when they returned home once again.

In the eighteenth century, when first encountered by Europeans, the Pawnee were organized in independent bands, some of which comprised more than one village. The most numerous of these groups were the Skiris, who lived in as many as thirteen villages centered primarily on the Loup River and actually formed a separate tribe. South of them were three other independent bands, often called the South Band Pawnee, who lived in one village each: the Chawi, or Grand; the Kitkahahki, or Republican; and the Pitahawirata, or Tappage. Members of these three bands spoke a single dialect of the Pawnee language that was different from Skiri, but the two dialects were mutually intelligible, and were in turn related to the speech of the Arikara, a composite of bands living to the north along the Missouri River in South Dakota and, later, in North Dakota. By the late nineteenth century the speech of the Pawnee and the Arikara had already become mutually unintelligible. More distantly related linguistically to the Pawnee were the Wichita, of northern Texas and Oklahoma, and the Kitsais, of eastern Texas. Even more remotely related to them were the Caddos, of eastern Texas and western Louisiana. Together their languages constituted the Caddoan linguistic family.

In 1825, by treaty with the U.S. government, the four Pawnee bands were treated as a single tribal entity, and in 1857, again by treaty, they were confined to a reservation in central Nebraska. In 1874–76, they were removed to a reservation in the north-central part of Indian Territory. The relocation there transformed their lives dramatically, for traditional culture—especially subsistence, religion, and doctoring—gave way to the acculturative pressures of Anglo-American society. In Indian Territory their population also continued a dramatic decrease, from at least 10,000 people in the late eighteenth century to a mere 633 individuals in 1910.

The Pawnee Reservation in Indian Territory was broken up during the early twentieth century, and land was allotted to individual families. Today the Pawnee continue to live in the area of their old reservation, in what is now Pawnee County, Oklahoma. Although their population has increased during the twentieth century, their former oral tradition has ceased as the number of people speaking the Pawnee language has dwindled to a mere handful of elders.

The earliest collection of Pawnee narratives was compiled and published in English translation by the naturalist George Bird Grinnell in his book *Pawnee Hero Stories and Folk-Tales.*[1] Subsequently, the most extensive collections of Pawnee oral traditions were compiled during the first decade of the twentieth century through the collaborative efforts of James R. Murie, a mixed-blood Skiri born in 1862 and educated at Hampton Institute in Hampton, Virginia, and George A. Dorsey, curator of North American ethnology at the Field Columbian Museum (now Field Museum of Natural History) in Chicago. Murie recorded and translated the stories, which appeared in two publications under the authorship of Dorsey: *Traditions of the Skidi Pawnee,* and *The Pawnee: Mythology.*[2] During this same period Murie and Dorsey also recorded on wax cylinders a large collection of narratives—personal reminiscences, religious traditions, and ethnographic descriptions—from a monolingual Skiri priest named Roaming Scout. The latter, however, were not published.[3] Nearly three decades later the anthropologist Gene Weltfish recorded another collection of narratives, which in contrast to the previous ones were published in Pawnee together with English translations.[4]

I recorded the three stories presented here in Pawnee in 1965. The narrator is Harry Mad Bear (1894–1972), one of the last generation of Pawnee storytellers and an exemplary raconteur. A Skiri, he was the grandson of Mad Bear, a prominent late-nineteenth-century doctor.[5] While a student Harry contracted trachoma and became blind. When I met him, he was living alone, not far from the old Pawnee Agency, the Bureau of Indian Affairs administrative headquarters. He was one of a small number of men who were able to relate a large repertoire of stories in the traditional style. Mad Bear's narrative style and vocabulary, in fact, do not differ significantly from those of narrators who lived early in the century.

The first story presented here, "Speaks-in-Riddles and Wise Spirit," was recorded in a shorter version by Murie.[6] Mad Bear's rendition, recorded a half century later, is a longer, stylistically natural one. Its theme, a riddle, is unusual among Plains tribes—indeed, among tribes throughout North America—and is in type unique in the Pawnee oral tradition.[7] The story tells of two men, one who speaks in riddles and one who is noted for his ability to understand everything and respond quickly to what is said to him. When the two men finally meet each other, Speaks-in-Riddles tells the other, Wise Spirit, about the various things he saw on his journey to Wise Spirit's village and then asks the latter to interpret what each object or activity he saw really was. He stumps Wise Spirit, who becomes sick from his inability to interpret the riddle. At the end Speaks-in-Riddles returns to Wise Spirit's lodge and explains the actual identity of what he had seen.

The second narrative, "The Story of Comanche Chief," falls into the genre of historical stories that typically tell of war exploits. This one explains the source of a man's name, Comanche Chief, and illustrates how men obtained personal names through acts of bravery or some other deed, most often accomplished on a war expedition. The event recorded here took place in the mid-nineteenth century when a large Pawnee war party set out in two or more groups to go south, apparently to capture horses. Another, longer version of this story was recorded by Grinnell almost a century earlier.[8]

The third story, that of Eagle Chief and his beautiful young wife, Plum Bush Woman, represents the fable, another major genre in the Pawnee oral tradition. Pawnees called fables Coyote stories, after the trickster Coyote, even though the genre included many other story types. One such category comprises stories of Witch Woman (Ctu'u'), a character known for being sexually loose and possessing supernatural powers. In this story Witch Woman, here called Old Woman Rat, removes the spirit from Plum Bush Woman's body and replaces it with her own in order to obtain Eagle Chief as her husband. In contrast to the explicit sexuality of many stories about Witch Woman, in this telling there are only implicit references to her sexual proclivities: she is said to approach other men at dances and to keep Eagle Chief up all night. Moreover, as is typical of fables, the story portrays various species of animals as doctors, who try to cure Plum Bush Woman after Old Woman Rat has entered her body. These animals are organized in groups like their Skiri counterparts, and they reflect the Pawnee concept that the healing powers of their doctors were given to them by the animals on this earth.

The English translations of these stories were made in collaboration with Mrs. Nora Pratt, an elderly Skiri who is an unusually fluent speaker of her language. They follow closely the original Pawnee, modifying it only as necessary to create an idiomatic, comprehensible version for the English reader, yet retaining, insofar as possible, most of the stylistic features of the Pawnee oral tradition. Hence such frequently occurring particles as the sentence introductory *ráwa* ("now," "well") and the emotive *aáka* ("oh my," "why," "well"), which expresses mild surprise, are retained despite their seeming overuse to an English ear. Preserved in these translations, too, is the frequently used introductory statement "This is what he did" followed by a statement of the character's action. Similarly, expressions that indicate a narrator's inability to be specific—to tell, for example, how many men were in a war party, where a party camped, how many days elapsed—are retained in close translation, rendered as, for example, "however many went," "however many days elapsed," "wherever they camped." These expressive features, although sometimes giving the English version a somewhat stilted countenance, nevertheless convey integral features of Pawnee oral style.[9]

Finally, two formulaic statements that indicate the end of a narrative are illustrated here. One, which translates literally as "Now the gut extends," has no meaning today other than to indicate that the narrator has finished his story. The other statement, "Now you are the winner," not only closes the narrative but also conveys the narrator's opinion that the listener has heard the story for the first time.

NOTES

1. George Bird Grinnell, *Pawnee Hero Stories and Folk-Tales* (New York: Field and Stream, 1889).

2. George A. Dorsey, *Traditions of the Skidi Pawnee,* Memoirs of the American Folklore Society, vol. 8 (Boston: Houghton Mifflin, 1904) and *The Pawnee: Mythology,* pt. 1, Carnegie Institution of Washington Publication no. 59 (Washington, D.C., 1906).

3. See Douglas R. Parks and Raymond J. DeMallie, "Plains Indian Native Literatures," *boundary 2* 19 (1992): 105–47.

4. Gene Weltfish, *Caddoan Texts: Pawnee, South Band Dialect,* Publications of the American Ethnological Society no. 17 (New York: G. E. Stechert, 1937).

5. James R. Murie, *Ceremonies of the Pawnee,* Smithsonian Contributions to Anthropology no. 27, ed. Douglas R. Parks (Washington, D.C.: Smithsonian Institution; reprint, Lincoln: University of Nebraska Press, 1981), 2:228, 274, 322.

6. Dorsey, *Traditions of the Skidi Pawnee,* 300–301.

7. For a survey of riddles among American Indians, see John Bierhorst, ed., *Lightning Inside You and Other Native American Riddles* (New York: William Morrow, 1992).

8. Grinnell, *Pawnee Hero Stories and Folk-Tales,* 25–44.

9. For a description of Arikara oral style, which is nearly identical to Pawnee style, see Douglas R. Parks, *Traditional Narratives of the Arikara Indians,* 4 vols. (Lincoln: University of Nebraska Press), 1991.

There were two bands of Indians, and in one of the two there was a person who was very wise. They called him Wise Spirit. And living in the other band was another person, named Speaks-in-Riddles. And each of them wanted to see the other one, but the day had not yet come for them to meet.

And then eventually Wise Spirit thought, "Oh, I wish I could meet Speaks-in-Riddles."

Then Speaks-in-Riddles thought, "I wish I could meet Wise Spirit."

Now this is what Speaks-in-Riddles did: he went to see Wise Spirit. That band where he lived was camped not far away. And he arrived there.

Then he said, "I guess you have heard that I've come. I am Speaks-in-Riddles. I hear that you're named Wise Spirit. I've come looking for you. Now I want to say what I want to say. It won't take long, and then I'll go."

Then Wise Spirit said, "Now sit down there, and say what it is that you want to say!"

Now Speaks-in-Riddles sat down. "Now I'm going to tell you about things I saw on my way here. My, while I was coming along the bank of that rapidly flowing river, it seemed as if there were someone with me. And now after I crossed the river and looked back, there appeared to be dead red birds lying there on the ground.

"Well, after I came up the hill, I also saw these things. And again this is what I did: while I was watching things as I looked off into the wide valley, why, off in the distance in the wide valley, there appeared to be lines of black rope.* Why, there appeared to be lines of black rope. Well, now, I looked around at the valley with many streams of water extending through it—with those streams spreading out in different directions—and there appeared to be tree roots sticking up out of the water in those streams that were spread out in different directions. And now there seemed to be roots sticking up out of the water.

"And in the distance I saw people walking around throughout the valley. Why, in the distance, in that wide valley, those people were standing all around by the water—they were standing there by the

*lines of black rope: The Pawnee braided black ropes from buffalo hair. One of their many uses was as a tie around the waist of a man to hold his buffalo robe in place.

water. And this is what they were doing: it looked as though they were crying and wiping their tears—as if they were crying while they were returning to their village in the wide valley—wiping the water off themselves the way one does when perspiring, when a person breaks out all over in perspiration.

"And when the people were coming into their village from different directions, into that large village," he said, "why, what I saw was a truly unbelievable number of people! It seemed, as they say—it seemed as if they were bending over and whistling.

"Then this is what an old woman did—in front of those lodges, why, this is what a grandmother was doing: she was rocking back and forth—all the while sitting by the fire, rocking back and forth."

And he said, "And this is what I did when I got into the village. And this is what I did when I went into that lodge: I pushed the door open and went inside. And I looked all around. Why, there appeared to be human skulls scattered all around along the wall of the lodge. Now I saw the same thing throughout the rest of the village. I saw the same thing throughout that village. Well, then I came out.

"Now I kept walking until I arrived here where you're living. Now I'm going to go back to my village. In the meantime let's see if you can interpret a little of what I've said—of what I've told you."

Well, then this is what this person Wise Spirit did: he said, "Repeat what you said!"

Speaks-in-Riddles said, "No, I have already told you once."

"Just tell me again what you told me before! Just tell me again what you told me before." He repeated, "Just tell it. Say it again! Say it again!"

Now this is what Speaks-in-Riddles said. Then he said, "Now I'm leaving. I'll come back sometime." That is what he said.

Then he got up. Then he went off.

Now after he left, this man Wise Spirit pondered what he had said. Wise Spirit pondered it for days. Now he would not eat, and he would not even drink. My, all he would do was ponder it! Why, they say that he was the wisest person in this village—in this entire village. There was no one else like him here, and it was said that if someone did not know something, this Wise Spirit would know. That one knew everything.

"Now I certainly don't know the answer to this riddle! Now see if you can bring him back to me!"

Now they went to get Speaks-in-Riddles, and after a number of days he came.

And Wise Spirit said, "Well, now sit down! Why, I'm lying here truly at the end of my wits! My mind is totally exhausted. Why, what they say is true! You are rightfully named Speaks-in-Riddles. You are rightfully named that. Now interpret for me the meaning of what you said you saw!"

"First it seemed as if someone were with me while I was coming— while I was coming down through the valley along the bank of the river. Now I meant that it seemed as though there were someone with me as I came down through the valley while the sun was setting. Now my own shadow appeared in that rapidly flowing river, and it made it seem as though there were someone traveling along with me.

"Thereupon I crossed the stream, and on the other side, why, what appeared to be red birds were really ripe plums that must have fallen off the trees. They appeared to be red birds whose feathers had been plucked and were lying there spread out over the ground. The plums were *so* red!

"Well, then this is what I did: I came up the hill. After I came up it—when I was coming up to this village of yours—why, I looked back while I was coming along, and there in the distance in the wide valley through which I had come, there appeared to be lines of black rope on the ground. They were buffalo that looked like lines of black rope. And people were driving the buffalo into that stream, where they killed them. And a buffalo would fall in the water, and it would be lying on its back—and it would be lying on its back in the water with its hooves upright. And those buffalo lying in the water looked like tree stumps sticking up. Well, then people were picking them up. Then this is what they did: they came on foot, and then they apparently started butchering them. Then they packed them on their backs. Thereupon they carried them through the valley. While they were carrying them on their backs, they got hot and broke out in perspiration and were wiping the perspiration off while they were going into the village.

"And meanwhile the women were preparing everything by spreading the buffalo hides out and staking them." They say the women used to scrape the buffalo hair off them. They would also take all the flesh off. They would dry the hides to make them into robes after they were nice and dry.*

---

*And meanwhile the women . . . after they were nice and dry: What the narrator leaves unsaid is that the people whom Speaks-in-Riddles earlier saw bending over and whistling represented these women bending over the hides and scraping them.

"Why, now there was grandmother, rocking back and forth all the while. And by grandmother rocking back and forth, I mean first she made a hole in the ground and then took kettles of boiling bones off the fire. Then she poured the broth from a kettle into the hole and blew on it. And in that way it became marrow grease, or tallow, after it hardened. Now this is what people were doing: they would shape the marrow grease into balls and then take them into their lodges. And when they put those balls of tallow along the wall of the lodge, they would look like human skulls lying there.

"Well, now after I saw these things, I knew these people had plenty," he said, "and then I came here. I came to see you, Wise Spirit. Now I have told you about everything I saw while I was coming here. And these things are what I meant by the riddle."

And now Wise Spirit sat up, after he had made himself sick from worrying about its meaning. "Well, now, old woman, at least give him some coffee to drink! Well, at least bring some food! Now he and I will eat!

"Now sit down! We're going to eat. You have outdone me."

Now the gut extends. I have finished the story.

In another version of this story, the whistling sound is said to represent the women sharpening their knives (Dorsey, *Traditions of the Skidi Pawnee*, 301).

They used to tell about a war party that set out from where the Pawnee tribe used to live—about a group that left ahead of the others. And among the group was a certain Pawnee who left ahead of the others, however many people were in it, and they were going along there. They were going along there. It was a long time later—however many days later it was—and they were going along, and then they reached a certain place.

And one man who was talking to a companion said, "I want to tell you something: I'm going to stop here, and in the meantime the rest of the party can go on to wherever they want to go. But I'm going to go this other way. I'm looking for something special that I want to find."

Now this other man said, "No. You can't go alone. I'm going to go with you." Then he started off with him.

The first man said, "No. You go on with the party, to where they're going."

But the other said, "No. I'm going to go with you. I'm going to go wherever you go."

And so they went on for however many days it was, and they got close to the place. Well, in due course of time, they reached the place, wherever it was.

When they reached it, wherever it was, the man knew the place. "Now it's right here where the ones I wanted to find are living. I wanted to see if I could find the place. This is where they live—they are called the Comanche tribe."

Now this is what the man said: "Eh, you stand right here! I'll go up this hill and look around."

"No. Why, we'll both go!"

"Now you must keep watch."

Then they went up the hill. There was a range of hills, and they went up one.

"Now you must keep a close watch."

Well, after a while he said, "Now, ha! Look at that village way off over there." He said, "That's the village there, the one whose layout I know."

This was the way they used to organize a village when they made one: standing out in front—it was not far out in front—way over there on the west side of that large village was the lodge of the man who was the Comanche head chief, and he lived there with his wife and children—his daughters—and whatever warrior assistants he had and the old man who was his crier.*

Now right at that moment the man said, "I'm going to go over there, and you stay here. You should wait for me for one, two, three, four days. If I don't return, don't be concerned. You should get up and go back home. You should conclude, 'They must have captured him. They must have killed him.'

"Now I want you to do what I have said so that you can go back and reach our village, and you can tell them, 'I know where the village is—where he went. The people in it undoubtedly captured him. They killed him. I waited four days for him, and he didn't return.' "

Now this is what the man told him, and then he started out for the village. The sun had already set. The sun had already set when they went to look around. The sun had already set, and it was now just about night, and then that Pawnee man—the Look Like Wolves man—set out.†

Then he went to that village. And the people there were doing whatever they usually did.‡ Then everything became quiet. Finally the sounds of activity subsided. And their horses were standing all around. They must have brought their best horses into the village to be close to their lodges. The most valued horses—the best horses— would be tied close by, in front of their lodges.

Now that Pawnee man went right up to a certain lodge. He went slowly. The blaze of the fire that had been burning inside was slowly dying down.

Now the time must have been drawing near. When the time was drawing near—when the time was drawing near, just before dawn, this is what he did: after he opened the door of that tipi, he went inside. He knew the arrangement of the lodge, however it was arranged. He had been there before and had seen it. So when he went there this time, he went resolutely. As we say, he did not hesitate at all. Then he just went over to the west side.

---

*This was the way . . . crier: The organization of the village and chief's lodge imputed to the Comanches is, in fact, that of the Skiris.

†Look Like Wolves man: One of the names by which the Pawnee referred to themselves was Look Like Wolves, which was their designation in the Plains sign language. They also called themselves ourselves or our people and Pawnee (*Paari*). The latter designation was borrowed into the Pawnee language from one of the Siouan tribes living east of them.

‡And the people . . . did: a reference to their dances and games that were under way.

He knew where the chief's bed was and where his daughter's bed was.* And she was lying there on it. And he sat down. He took off the things he had on. Then in front of the bed he laid down all of the things he was wearing: his bow and knife, leggings and moccasins. He was sitting on the kind of bed that Indians used to make when they made beds. That girl was asleep. Then this is what the man did: he quietly raised the covers and got under them.

The girl must have woke up. Slowly she reached her hand out to his face. She touched the man's face. With her hand she felt all over his face. She stroked his head—and she stroked him there on top of his head. And, why, he had an Osage roach!† They say it was an Osage roach—an Osage roach—when she felt his head. And she knew right away that he was a Pawnee. Those Pawnee men never hesitated to do anything.

Then she just spoke softly. She said, "Father, are you awake? A person has come to my bed."

And he said, "Why, I'm awake, daughter."

Then her father got up. Then he called to his errand man by the doorway. He said, "Build up the fire!"

He answered, "It's ready!" He threw dry grass and wood chips into the fireplace. The flames just came up slowly.

And he said, "Build the fire up! I want a really big fire so it'll be light in here!" And he said, "Now, you people inside here, get up! Just get up slowly! Don't anyone do it—don't do anything rash!‡ Let's find out who this person who came into our lodge is."

He said, "Crier, go outside. Announce this—say, 'You people in this village, the chief wants you to come right away and be ready! But don't anyone do anything rash. And the ones who get there first should go inside. Then everything will be in order after you have gone inside. And after as many as possible are inside the lodge, you others should station yourselves all around outside. You should sit or stand around so far apart in case there are others with this stranger.

" 'And be ready for anything! A person has come into our lodge. Now the stranger was lying with the chief's child, his daughter. His hair is cut; it is an Osage cut. His hair is cut.' "

---

*where his daughter's bed was: The daughter's bed is next to that of her parents.
†Osage roach: A hair style favored by many Pawnee men was the roach, a ridge of hair running down the middle of the head from front to back, with the hair on either side shaved off. Although characteristically Pawnee, the hair style was literally termed an Osage cut by the Pawnee themselves.
‡Don't . . . do anything rash: He is instructing them not to take up their weapons.

It was not long before the people gathered and came inside the lodge. It was not long before the interior was full.

The chief said, "Now let me ask, what do any of you people in this lodge think? What do you people think now that you have seen this stranger who has entered our lodge?" The Comanche chief was asking that. He was the head chief of that village. He said, "Well?"

One group said, "Let the people there on the south side of the lodge say what they think!"

And they said, "Let that man sitting over there say what should happen! Now let it be this way: let the girl's uncle speak! You who are closely related to her should say how you feel!"

Her uncle said, "Ah, the chief has told you people that *you* should decide."

Now an old man sat there. And now this old man was the father of the Comanche chief. Then the old man said, "You people have just been sitting here speechless for a long time. So now I'm going to say what I have to say, since there is something I have always wanted to do. I am old now. I have lived for a long time, and there is something I have always wanted to do. I would like to go to visit the tribe of this person."

Then he made signs. "What tribe are you?"

Then the man answered, "I'm a Look Like Wolves."

"Now that is what we thought you were. Oh, they always say the Look Like Wolves are brave people. No one else would do what you have done here."

Now this old man said, "There is something I have always wanted to do. I would like to go visit these people while I'm still alive. And I want whatever this child of mine, my son who is now chief, wants done—that we should do what he decides. But this is what I want to say: I like this young man, this Look Like Wolves. *Ooh,* this one is brave! This one is brave! He didn't reach for any of his weapons—his bow or his knife. It seems that he doesn't know fear. And look at this woman my grandchild, this girl of mine. Why, she wants him. I don't have anything against it. Now he is taking her from me. Now she is his. He can marry her if she wants to. That is why he came here. And now I am giving her to him.

"But it won't be long before it's spring, and it won't be long before everything ripens and food is plentiful. And I want to go—to go there—where this man's tribe is. Then I'll finally be able to eat everything they eat. They say that of all the tribes of Indians living here on earth, the Heavens blessed that tribe with planting seeds for food. They have every kind. And this is what I want to do: I'll finally be able to eat those different kinds of food! They have every kind there where they live. I wish I could eat them. There is the kind they call squash. The vines of that plant just climb on their earth lodges. The vines climb on them. *Ooh,* those squashes grow on top of them!"

He said, "Uh, since they taste good, why, I want to eat some of them while I'm still alive. Now in due course of time, we'll come back here. Now I wanted to say this. You people weren't going to say anything. Now I have given her to that man."

The head chief said, "That's good, my father. Now you people have heard him."

The warriors said, "Now there's no longer any need for us to stay here." And they went out.

"No one should stay around! Go on! Go home. Would any one of you do what he has done? Uh, this Look Like Wolves is brave. He has taken our young Comanche woman."

Now the man was married to this girl. It isn't known how many children she later bore for him.

When spring came, they started out. The young couple took the old man and his wife with them to where our people were living on Beaver Creek. And they arrived there.

That man was Knife Chief. And, uh, he said, "Now they named me Comanche. Comanche Chief is what they decided to name me. Comanche Chief." Now they named the man Comanche Chief. And that one was still a young man. Now that man was named Comanche Chief.

They brought the old man with them here. Now he arrived.

Meanwhile there was the other young man who had been left there on the hill, the one who had been told, "You should stay here and keep watch for four days." After he saw nothing happening and his companion did not appear, he thought, "They have undoubtedly killed him. I'm not going to go home alone." And this man who had been his companion apparently killed himself. But the other members of the war party returned to the village.

Meanwhile, the first man had found what he went after. Now it happened that way, according to what the old people said, and that man, Comanche Chief, looked after the old man, the Comanche girl's grandfather.

But later on, while he was still living, this Comanche Chief mar-

ried All-the-Chiefs Woman.* They say today that that old man Comanche Chief was later called Knife Chief, the name that the family
carries today.† Good Chief was the son of that man.‡

I wonder what the stories of these different names are? When the
older people told stories, they told me this one when they would
talk about that old man Comanche Chief.

Then later on the couple arrived back among our people, and
Comanche Woman—that young woman—*ooh,* she was a beautiful
young woman! Now this Comanche Woman was a pretty girl, when
our people used to live there in Nebraska.

It wasn't long ago when I was telling this story in Osage country
that I met a Comanche. He was at a peyote meeting with Good
Chief, when he was still alive.§ And this Comanche said, "I'm a
relative of that man. This old man is a relative of his, too." He was a
relative of that old man. He was related to that old man Comanche
Chief, the one who took the girl from their tribe. Now when he
became an in-law to Comanche Chief's family, they say that that
Comanche was named whatever his name was. Now among the
ones who were his offspring, there was one who was named White
Wolf. The name refers to a wolf that is white in color: White Wolf.

Now this story I am telling is true. It is not a Coyote story, and I
did not just make it up, and it is not a dream story; but it is a story
about the people who used to live.

They used to tell young men, "Now you have grown up. Now
you must live your own life. You must make your own way and find
your own good fortune."

Now today you are learning the story behind the name of that
Pawnee man, the one whose descendant is named John Knjfe Chief.
I am saying his name in English so that if he wants any of his son's
children to be named Comanche Chief, he'll know they have the
right to that name. That's what I want to say.

---

*This Comanche Chief married All-the-Chiefs Woman:** Comanche Chief's Co-
manche wife died before he did, and Comanche Chief then married this Pawnee
woman.
†Knife Chief:** When Comanche Chief received an English name, presumably at
the time of enrollment, he was given the surname Knife Chief.
‡Good Chief was the son of that man:** Good Chief was the last of three different
Pawnee names of Charley Knife Chief, who was the son of Comanche Chief.
§Good Chief:** apparently Charley Knife Chief.

There was a village, a large village. This was how Indians used to live: we lived together in villages after we were put here on earth. We did not just wander around, but this tribe occupied a number of villages.

Well, a man lived here once. His name was Eagle Chief. And this Eagle Chief had a wife. He must have just recently married the young girl—she was still a young girl. *Ooh,* she was beautiful! Everyone in this village looked to this girl, the wife of the chief, for leadership. And when this woman would say how she wanted something to be, all the women would gather, and they would agree to whatever she said, such as "We are going to do this"—the things they used to do when they planted gardens and when they went to get wood and when they went to gather fruit growing on trees and bushes, like plums and grapes.

Now this Eagle Chief loved his wife. Oh, she was *so* beautiful!

And from time to time, his wife would say, "We're going to go get some wood over there."

When the women used to go gather wood, they would go into the woods on foot. They would make bundles of it that were as large as a person could carry on her back.

Now when they went into the woods, this woman would say, "Don't be long. And after you've gone into the woods, if someone calls to us, that means that everyone should come—that we should gather together and we should start out all together for our village over there."

Now they would go into the woods, and the woman would say, "Now you should be alert like I said."

Well, that young girl, Eagle Chief's wife, would have someone to help her. She would not have to work but would only watch the other women while they were going around in the woods. They would fix up a bundle for her. It would be a small one. Then she would say, "Someone should call out to the women to gather together." And they would all come out of the woods. Then all of them would do it. She would see that they were all there—that everyone was there. Then they would start back to the village.

Now in this story that I am telling—the women went off to get wood not just once but several times on this one day. The chief, who had a crier, wanted the crier to make an announcement, and he told him, "You must make an announcement; you must say, 'From now on the girl who is my wife will be known as Plum Bush Woman.' " Plum Bush Woman was her name from then on. Ah, she was a beautiful girl!

They went to get wood several times that day.

Now in this village, well, she would say, "We're going to go to the gardens. Now we're going to work there, planting our gardens."

Now they would take whatever they had—it used to be hoes, the kind that Indians would make from the shoulder blade of a buffalo when they made a hoe. A woman would use it to till the ground. She would not plant several acres, as they now say, but just enough for a garden. And they would plant the seeds that they had in this village.

There were men who kept guard over everything. And whenever some women went to their gardens, those braves whom the chief used to have would go onto the ridge and watch over everything. For these people were not living alone here, but different tribes of people used to come together, and the different ones used to fight each other. All of them used to be on guard against the others.

Now that was how things would be there during the year.

And once in a while the chief would say to his crier, "You must make an announcement for Plum Bush Woman: 'Now you should get ready to go swimming.' "

Then as the season progressed, they would pick grapes when they ripened and would bring them home after they had gone swimming. There used to be sandbars along the creeks, and they would play in the water by them, and, oh, it was so nice!

Now these grapes and plums that grew abundantly on bushes were not the only things that the women would pick, but there were other fruits, what we call these things that taste good, like cherries.

Now in addition to that, there were other things that they would go to look for. They would dig Indian turnips and wild potatoes. Now when the season for collecting them came each year, this woman who was the leader in that band would do it. Why, everyone esteemed her!

And, moreover, some woman would come into her lodge. "I've come here to visit you. I've brought these things for you—moccasins, a deerskin dress, and leggings," decorated with everything that these people used to put on them: elk teeth and everything—pendants, cowrie shells—everything that they used to wear and decorate with designs. They would outfit that chief's wife in everything they used to make.

Well, that Eagle Chief, the head chief, certainly liked what they did for her. This man loved his wife. Everyone would look after her and bring her food. Sometimes someone would make mush, and other times someone would make pemmican, or someone would bring dried meat, or sometimes someone would go hunting for game, and he would kill one of the animals they used to eat—deer or elk—or one of the animals they used to trap. Or sometimes when a man went fishing, he would bring fish or else he would bring beavers—all of the things they used to eat.

Now these were the things this tribe of Indians used to eat, for there were no white men around at that time but only these Indians and those other tribes or bands.

Now when the season arrived, this would take place. That woman would say, "It's time now for us to go gather wood." If the weather should change suddenly, they would already have wood stacked beside their lodges.

Well, then the crier would announce, "Plum Bush Woman says this: 'Today is the day for all of you to get wood. Hurry! Get yourselves ready!' "

Then after he had finished, after walking through the village crying out, he would come back into the lodge.

Now it would not be long before each woman arrived with ropes; they took ropes for tying their bundles of wood. After they gathered the wood, they would tie it up into a bundle and put it on their backs and then return to the village. Then they would do it again: they would go back into the woods. Why, that was sure a good way to gather wood. And they would hurry, going to get wood every day. They would go to get it.

Also when they went to the place where they got wood, they would pick everything growing there, gathering everything that was food.

Then it was the end of the work season, and it was time for the dances we used to have.

Some woman would say, "Plum Bush Woman, we're going to put on a dance for you, and we'll all dance."

And they would all cook different foods after harvesting the crops they had planted, when they had bountiful crops. And, why, they would all dance in a lively manner in that village!

And then one day Plum Bush Woman said, "We're going to go get them. I think we'll go get poles. The weather is changing—it's getting cloudy."

And the chief would say, "Now the crier will announce what I say again: 'Plum Bush Woman wants to go get poles. The weather is changing. It looks like it's going to rain. It looks like it's going to turn cold. The next season is arriving. Hurry! You all must come!' "

Then they went. It was not very long before they all gathered together. Then they went into the woods. Those guards were watching over everything. Well, there was a stand of trees there where they went when they went into the woods. A little way beyond that stand the woods were thicker. Well, that is where Plum Bush Woman led them.

Now Plum Bush Woman said, "This is where we'll stop. Now you must go off into the woods there. Don't be long."

Now Plum Bush Woman would take one of the rawhide ropes they used to have and would rope a limb. Why, before long she had a pile of nice pieces of wood! The women tied them into a bundle just large enough so that she would not tire from its being too heavy. Some of these other women would also carry wood for her.

Now after they were all standing there with their wood, Plum Bush Woman said, "Now we'll go back."

And now some were coming out of the woods, but there were still others who were not coming. And one of them, whoever it was, said, "There is a woman here. And she says, 'I want to meet Plum Bush Woman. Hey, I want to tell only her herself what I want to say. It wouldn't be good if the rest of you were to hear it. But, yes, I'll tell her alone. All of you go around to the other side of that tree!' "

And now Plum Bush Woman went over to her. "Let's see what she wants!"

And the woman came up to her and said, *"Ooh,* Plum Bush Woman, you are a beautiful girl! Now it's no wonder that Eagle Chief has you for his wife and is always consumed with thoughts of you. Why, it seems that you two don't have any problems, and that's really good. Now let's see! It seems that your load of wood is heavy."

"Why, no."

"Lie down on your back! And I'll tie this rawhide rope securely here. Ah, then I'll take hold of your hands to help you up."

Oh my, the woman did that after Plum Bush Woman lay down. Oh my, whatever happened, that woman was one of those people they call a witch. She was one of those witches.

Then that witch said, "Take a good look at me! Why, you sure are pretty! I would like to kiss you even though I am a woman. Why, I really want to do that!"

Why, as soon as the witch stooped over to do it, to kiss her, she blew on her! And, whatever happened, well, that is what she intended to do! Now the witch went into Plum Bush Woman's body and threw out Plum Bush Woman's spirit. Her body was only a bag. Then she threw Plum Bush Woman's spirit somewhere, wherever it was. Apparently she threw it into the creek there. Now the witch entered the bag that was Plum Bush Woman's body.

Oh, and then the women came back. "Oh, what happened?"

"Oh, this bundle is heavy!"

Then they took some of the wood from her bundle. Then they lifted her up.

"Now hurry! We'll go back."

Then they were returning. Now everyone who returned had seen it. Now everyone was going back to the village.

And Plum Bush Woman went to her lodge. "Well, I now have a pile of wood! Oh, Eagle Chief, are you inside? Come out! Why, you should help me!"

Then Eagle Chief thought, "I wonder if that's Plum Bush Woman. I wonder if it's my wife, Plum Bush Woman. Why, this is *her* lodge!"

He said, "Well, I wonder why you're doing that." Then he went to her the way he always did when he would take her and hold her in his arms. Then they went inside the lodge where they lived.

"Oh, Eagle Chief, that's good. They gathered the wood in a short time. That's why we returned so quickly."

Now meanwhile the other women went to their lodges. And afterward that old witch woman wondered what they were going to do.

Then Eagle Chief asked, "Plum Bush Woman, what has happened to you? You're different. I wonder what you have done?"

"You shouldn't make me out to be that way. No. I *am* Plum Bush Woman. Now that's all I can say."

And this is what she did: she asked, "I wonder what is the best thing for us to do?" as she tried to think what she should do to get the others there to work. She asked the women who lived in the lodge, the ones who would assist her, "Oh, daughter, what do you think we should do now?"

Well, then they said, "She must have decided to have a dance."

And now they used to have different dances. And so they went there. Thereupon Eagle Chief said to the crier, "You must announce, 'Hurry! You all must come. Plum Bush Woman wants you women to dance for a while.' "

Now it happened that way. Then while Plum Bush Woman and Eagle Chief were there, Plum Bush Woman would go up to different men. Why, Plum Bush Woman had never done that before! And then when the dance was over, they went home.

Then Eagle Chief asked her, "Why, what has happened to you?"

"*Nothing* has happened to me."

Well, after it became night, the witch would lie in bed with Eagle Chief and keep him awake. And, why, he would not fall asleep until morning.

Now Eagle Chief said, "You there, crier, make an announcement. Go through the village, and tell them that today Eagle Chief wants them to see Plum Bush Woman, his wife. Whatever it is, there's something wrong." He was summoning the doctors.

Then the crier summoned them. And so they came inside.

"Hurry! You must come right on inside!" He wanted the turtles to examine her to see what the problem was.

They came inside.

And Old Woman Rat* was sitting there. "Well, now, look who's coming in! Just who do they think they are, these who are planning to doctor me! They aren't going to find anything wrong."

Now they did what Eagle Chief had asked. Eagle Chief was suspicious when he had asked them to come. And so the turtles gathered around her. Then they examined her, and one of them said, "Eagle Chief, you had better call another group! We can't determine what's wrong. All of us have examined her."

Now the next day the same thing happened. Eagle Chief wanted a different group to come inside and examine her carefully, to look her over carefully, too, to see if they could do it—to see if they could take out of her whatever was wrong with her and take it away. Eagle Chief would say, "When I look at her, it really is Plum Bush Woman that I see—her eyes and her face. Yet when she talks, she doesn't sound right, and the way she acts isn't normal."

They were sitting there. Here they were listening.

Then later, when the women went to get wood, they would hear a faint sound in the distance: a woman was saying something. A woman was crying there in the woods. The sounds were coming from that creek over yonder.

And this old witch woman was just nervously eyeing everything while these doctors were telling Eagle Chief, "Let the animals that live in the woods come to see if they can do something!"

The crows were chosen—these crows that fly around. "They'll come."

And the crows arrived. The old witch woman just looked at them.

*Old Woman Rat: the witch.

This old woman was named Old Woman Rat, this woman who was inside Plum Bush Woman's skin. And when she saw the crows, she said, "These who are coming—my, why are they coming? Well, I doubt that they'll find out who I really am. But now let them examine me, if that's what they want to do."

"Now, Eagle Chief, let some other group come in!"

Well, then the crows started to leave. There was nothing wrong with the way Plum Bush Woman was, they said. She was no different from the way she used to be.

The women inside the lodge would say, "Oh, let's go outside awhile!" Then the women would go outside and then come back inside. And when they were outside, they would listen, and they would talk about it. "There in that creek she is singing, and you, Eagle Chief, are the one who is being named. She is singing in the stream." While they were listening she was singing:

> Eagle Chief, you are embracing Old Woman Rat,
>   oh, Old Woman Rat.
> Plum Bush Woman's voice is floating down the stream,
>   oh, Plum Bush Woman.

> Eagle Chief, you are embracing Old Woman Rat,
>   oh, Old Woman Rat.
> Plum Bush Woman's voice is floating down the stream,
>   oh, Plum Bush Woman.

> Eagle Chief, you are embracing Old Woman Rat,
>   oh, Old Woman Rat.
> Plum Bush Woman's voice is floating down the stream,
>   oh, Plum Bush Woman.

> Eagle Chief, you are embracing Old Woman Rat,
>   oh, Old Woman Rat.
> Plum Bush Woman's voice is floating down the stream,
>   oh, Plum Bush Woman.

And Eagle Chief said, "That's why I'm suspicious. Let's ask another group of doctors to come examine her."

A man said, "You in this group taking care of the chief, what does your group suggest?"

He said, "We say, 'Let these birds called buzzards come!' "

Wherever these birds see a dead animal lying somewhere that

seems to be starting to spoil, they soar overhead crying. There might be a single one flying over the carcass, or there might be several of these buzzards. We call them buzzards.

Now they were coming. "Now here they come. Now, oh my, hurry!"

And they came inside. That Old Woman Rat said, "Uh, it's a different group. And now what does *this* group think it's going to do?"

They examined her all over. And these buzzards said, "Why, now this problem is too difficult for us."

Then these terrapins that go around arrived. They lived there in the tall grass and weeds in the valley. There in the grass is where these terrapins crawled around.

Now those others who had come, the crows, were flying around there. Early in the morning all of the crows were flying around watching things. When it gets dark, they are the first ones to go into the woods—the woods that cover this land. That is where they go.

"Now when we were coming, we didn't notice anything at all there while we were flying around. Now we didn't notice anyone coming over there by the creek."

And thereupon this is what they did: they left. One of them said, "We can't do anything."

Then Eagle Chief said, "It's good that you tried anyway."*

As soon as the sun had set, a person would go close to the place where the voice came from:

> Eagle Chief, you are embracing Old Woman Rat,
> oh, Old Woman Rat.
> Plum Bush Woman's voice is floating down the stream,
> oh, Plum Bush Woman.
>
> Eagle Chief, you are embracing Old Woman Rat,
> oh, Old Woman Rat.
> Plum Bush Woman's voice is floating down the stream,
> oh, Plum Bush Woman.
>
> Eagle Chief, you are embracing Old Woman Rat,
> oh, Old Woman Rat.
> Plum Bush Woman's voice is floating down the stream,
> oh, Plum Bush Woman.

*Then Eagle Chief said, ". . . anyway": He is thanking them for their efforts.

Eagle Chief, you are embracing Old Woman Rat,
oh, Old Woman Rat.
Plum Bush Woman's voice is floating down the stream,
oh, Plum Bush Woman.

The chief's assistants were coming back. Then they were going around watching things. "The skunks live there in the ground. See if they will come! They must be around here in the woods."

Over there the skunks were going into the woods. And there among all those trees in the woods is where the skunks live. Now they came too.

As soon as they came inside, the old woman saw them. "Oh, indeed, here they come! All of those skunks have really nice stripes. It seems that skunks have pretty stripes like that—that their hair looks as if it were colorfully painted all over. Oh, they are unusual!"

"Now you should do whatever you intend to do."

And meanwhile, why, that Eagle Chief was exhausted. And during the day women would gather in groups after they came out of the woods. That is what they would do. They would go with that old woman who was Plum Bush Woman. And the women would say, "She really *is* different, and yet it really is her."

And before they could finish what she wanted them to do, she would change her mind and have them do something else. "And then she just says odd things to us. Her behavior isn't what it should be." That is what happened.

Now when they would dance over there after the sun had set, after it had become dark, this is what the person singing over yonder in that stream would do: she would cry, and she would sing these songs. And it was Plum Bush Woman singing, the real Plum Bush Woman.

About that time they summoned the beavers. And so the beavers were the ones who came.

Well, now the old woman said, "Oh my, here they come! Oh, he has a flat tail!" They are the ones who swim in the water. "Why, now you can do whatever you think you're going to do."

Then those who had come examined her. Those beavers are the ones who eat all kinds of roots—all the different kinds. Before they came, they had put herbs into their mouths, the herbs that smell nice, so that, well, they could spray the old woman with medicine!

Oh, the old woman liked it! "Why, these animals are powerful! Eagle Chief, why, now I smell nice!"

They said, "Well, now, Eagle Chief, don't be concerned about it, but there isn't anything we can do. Let someone else try!" Now they also left.

The old woman said, "Now there they go. They couldn't do anything."

Now the people were doing what they always did as the season passed when it was becoming winter. Then when the water in that creek started getting colder, the woman began to sing louder. When the winds were blowing, when the winds were ice-cold, the voice of that woman—of Plum Bush Woman—was getting louder when she sang:

> Eagle Chief, you are embracing Old Woman Rat,
> oh, Old Woman Rat.
> Plum Bush Woman's voice is floating down the stream,
> oh, Plum Bush Woman.

> Eagle Chief, you are embracing Old Woman Rat,
> oh, Old Woman Rat.
> Plum Bush Woman's voice is floating down the stream,
> oh, Plum Bush Woman.

> Eagle Chief, you are embracing Old Woman Rat,
> oh, Old Woman Rat.
> Plum Bush Woman's voice is floating down the stream,
> oh, Plum Bush Woman.

> Eagle Chief, you are embracing Old Woman Rat,
> oh, Old Woman Rat.
> Plum Bush Woman's voice is floating down the stream,
> oh, Plum Bush Woman.

When they heard her, she was really singing, telling Eagle Chief that it was Old Woman Rat he was embracing.

Now it was time for them to summon one of the kinds of animals that live along the creeks. And so they called the water dogs.* This is what water dogs liked to do: they could be quite some distance

*water dogs: Contemporary Pawnee speakers are unable to identify this animal. Perhaps it is a brown mink *(Mustela vison)* or a fisher *(Martes pennanti).*

away from a person and just take his intestines out.* Someone said, "Why, that is what they can do." Those animals, the water dogs, were powerful.

They were summoned, and they agreed to come. "All right, we'll go. But you must tell Eagle Chief, 'It's about time that you called us, Eagle Chief. It won't take us long.' "

Well, they pushed the door open. There lay the old woman. When she looked up, it appeared that her eyeballs were rolling in fear. Then this is what she just did: she was gagging as if she had to vomit.

Well, it was about that time when they came inside. "Now where is she?"

"She's lying over here."

"Now it won't take us long. Let's do it quickly, . . ."—whatever plan they had for examining the woman. "Why, it won't take us long."

Then they were looking that woman over. They jerked her up. They set her upright even though no one was seen pulling her up. Suddenly they caused her to have cramps all over. Now whatever those water dogs did, they say—now whatever happened, one water dog did it, however he did it.

Meanwhile Eagle Chief saw his wife. "I have just arrived." His wife was now herself again. Oh, he was *so* thankful!

"Now, Eagle Chief, don't think anything of it! There isn't anything that you can do for us. But you are the leader of this village of yours. It was good that you thought to invite us. Now here is your wife."

And the water dogs went out. They had eaten the stomach out of Plum Bush Woman's skin, and the spirit of Plum Bush Woman had returned to it.

Now this story that I've told is a Coyote story. This is one kind that we used to tell when we lived in our old villages. "I think I'll tell a good story, a good story about Witch Woman," as we used to call them when they would tell one, when they would do that.

Now you are the winner.

---

*they could . . . just take his intestines out: These animals were said to possess mystical power that enabled them to remove a person's intestines from a distance.

TWO ROADS TO LEADERSHIP:

GRANDMOTHER'S BOY AND

LAST-BORN BROTHER

▲

JULIAN RICE

INTRODUCTION

The first priority of Lakota culture has always been the preservation of its spiritual identity in the physical world. The culture hero in the oral narratives grows into a keeper of tradition, and he never leads the people to a better place than the circle of day-to-day social existence. As an individual, however, the hero's experience may include periodic infusions of mysteriously sacred thoughts and deeds. In the following stories supernatural guides assist two young men in offering food, social order, confidence, and joy to everyone in their camp circle. In each young man spiritual receptiveness combines with skill in war, hunting, and social supervision, incarnating the male virtues of a whole adult generation in one person.

The culture hero often begins as an outsider. In the first story the boy who lives with his grandmother has the identity of many protagonists before they earn a name and enter adult reality. A grandmother's boy is understood to be an orphan, and he and his grandmother live just outside the camp circle, because they do not directly contribute to its collective life.[1] Such a boy presumably has an unpromising future as far as learning the arts of war, hunting, and vision questing from attentive male relatives. But he may also represent the general anxieties of adolescence, even for boys with many human guides and protectors. All Lakota boys are outsiders until they earn their place among the people by demonstrating courage and generosity.

In the stories as in life, a young man rarely marries simply because he has fallen in love or decided to settle down. Marriage is a rite of passage to adulthood and a social validation of manhood. In the most well-known instance of Lakota wife winning, "High Horse's Courting" in John G. Neihardt's *Black Elk Speaks,* the young man learns the hard way that a wife cannot be "stolen." Nothing worth having can be had easily, and everything worth having is earned by contribution, not just to one's immediate relatives but to the tribe. When High Horse finally buys his wife by stealing enemy horses instead of trying to steal her, his father-in-law comments, "It was not the horses that he wanted. What he wanted was a son who was a real man and good for something."[2]

In a hunting society everything depends on what the hunters bring home. Lakota boys were raised to anticipate hardship and un-certainty in their lifelong occupation of killing animals for food, shelter, clothing, and tools. Returning hunters also brought home confidence in the people's ability to live on and live well. The inter-tribal horse stealing that all Plains tribes approved and valued for the qualities it evoked in their young men was also a form of hunting; and as it involved greater risk, it infused greater energy and confidence. Expeditions to rescue captives were still more dangerous and inspiring, and they too derived technique and direction from the hunt.

Even spiritual seekers traced a hunter's circle. Vision questing required fasting from one to four days outside the camp, thereby incurring potential danger from both human enemies and spirits. If the seeker offended the Thunder Beings, he would be struck by lightning. Other spirits might require dangerous or self-destructive deeds if the seeker was insincere, unworthy, or careless in his prayers. But if the vision quester was as disciplined in his ritual preparations as a hunter tempering arrows, he would find the spirits compassionate and generous.[3] When an individual received powers from several spirits, implementing them might require teamwork, both human and supernatural. Rushing homeward with the Thunders in hot pursuit, the young man in the first story calls serially on each of his powers to release new bursts of energy. In the same way returning warriors or horse-takers alternately took the lead or assumed positions of defense. This is a common motif, and in some stories the guardian animals take these actions to keep distance between the oncoming enemy and their relatives.[4]

The principle of spiritual specialization for battle finds a parallel in the allocation of social responsibilities. In addition to the two to four highest chiefs chosen by consensus, the council selected four men to see to matters of war and police duty, and four other men to oversee domestic matters, including the settlement of disputes, the arrangement of ceremonies, and the regulation of the hunt.[5] The young man in the first story is probably one of the four war chiefs, or "shirt wearers," since he has acquired the lightning power to defend the people and free them from fear. The young man in the second story probably becomes a *wakiconze* (magistrate) entrusted to feed the people and free them from want.

Leaders and other responsible adults sustained social confidence by guarding physical objects that had manifested spiritual presence in the past. The sinew, the feathers, the animal hairs, and finally the buffalo-horn club acquired by the young man in the first story correspond to the *wotawe* (individual war medicines) used by all warriors. Before going to battle, Crazy Horse chewed and rubbed a mixture of dried eagle heart and wildflowers on his body. He would also rub dirt from a mole tunnel into his hair and onto his horse. One medicine imparted the obvious virtues of the eagle, whereas the other made him hard to see.[6] A similar reliance on animal hairs and feathers makes it possible for the grandmother's boy to move into an uncertain future with tangible proofs of protection. The sinew, however, becomes a defining symbol, teaching the necessity of ritual inspiration for spiritual travel.

The second story shifts emphasis in presenting the male ideal. The hero begins by killing an enemy, but he proceeds to bolster domestic stability, harmonious social relations, and an uninterrupted supply of food. His war powers are less prominent than those of the grandmother's boy. As a last-born brother, another culture-hero convention, he looks to a future that is almost as unpromising as that of an orphan. But both boys have strong motives to be brave. The first wishes to marry and assume responsibility for people he does not yet know. The second recovers and preserves people he has already come to love in childhood. As a last born he is likely to have lived in the shadow of his older brothers' achievements, but according to the convention and its lesson, he feels no jealousy. Instead, he mourns their loss and implicitly fears that he and his mother will be helpless without them. In his initial need for empowerment, a last-born brother, like a grandmother's boy, represents the struggle of each new generation to assume independent strength.

The oral narratives often base a boy's strength on the respectful

love he feels for women. By gaining motivation and discipline from
an adopted older sister, the second story's young man enacts a variation of Lakota culture's idealized brother-sister relationship, which
exemplified harmony throughout the circle. Young warriors often
conceived of their bravest deeds as honoring sisters rather than wives
or mothers.[7] The sister in this story also represents a supreme spiritual relationship by evoking the White Buffalo Calf Woman, bringer
of the sacred pipe. In a version of her story given by Lone Man to
Frances Densmore in 1915, the woman explains the pipe's use in
terms of her kinship role: "By this pipe the tribe shall live. It is your
duty to see that this pipe is respected and reverenced. I am proud to
be called a sister. May Wakan Tanka look down on us and take pity
on us and provide us with what we need."[8]

The two stories that follow are part of Father Eugene Buechel's
Lakota language collection, *Lakota Tales and Texts,* edited by Father Paul Manhart.[9] Translated here for the first time, with Father
Manhart's permission, they were originally told by anonymous
Oglala Lakota narrators to another Oglala, Ivan Stars, on the Pine
Ridge Reservation in approximately 1915. Like the other stories in
the collection, transcribed between 1904 and 1923, Stars wrote
them down syllable by syllable and then returned them to Buechel,
who rewrote them into the words, sentences, and paragraphs of
standard prose. *Lakota Tales and Texts* includes trickster tales; culture-hero myths; monster and ghost stories; legends of the origin
and practice of major ceremonies and healing rites; accounts of war
parties, scouting, hunting, food preparation, and weapon making;
descriptions of courting and child rearing; testimonies to the war
deeds and oratory of Red Cloud, Spotted Tail, Crazy Horse, and
Sitting Bull.

In "One Who Lives with His Grandmother" and "A White Buffalo Woman Helps a Last-Born Brother," the oral technique of
exact repetition reflects the hunter's virtue of persistence. Repetition is especially pronounced in the ordeal of outward-bound journeys, where the outcome is unknown, but in a different tone and
rhythm it often accompanies a homeward rush with enemies in hot
pursuit. I have highlighted the repetition by converting Buechel's
prose into poetic lines. I have also maintained the Lakota style of
direct quotation that Buechel preserved. When a narrator has one of
his characters speak, he first names the character and then orally
changes to that character's voice without preceding the quote with
"he said." Instead, "he said" immediately follows the quote:

"And—'Younger brother, you will not travel alone. From the start this will guard you,' she said." When quotations recur in an extended exchange, they suggest that a young man grows by learning to hear, heed, and help those he calls *mitakuye oyas'in* ("all my relatives").

NOTES

1. See Ella C. Deloria, *Dakota Texts,* Publications of the American Ethnological Society no. 14 (New York: G. E. Stechert, 1932; reprint, New York: AMS Press, 1974), 112*n*.

2. John G. Neihardt, *Black Elk Speaks: Being the Life Story of a Holy Man of the Oglala Sioux* (New York: William Morrow, 1932; reprint, Lincoln: University of Nebraska Press, 1979), 76.

3. See Nicholas Black Elk, *The Sacred Pipe,* ed. Joseph Epes Brown (New York: Penguin, 1971), 44–57.

4. See Deloria, *Dakota Texts,* 82–86, and Nicholas Black Elk, *The Sixth Grandfather,* ed. Raymond J. DeMallie (Lincoln: University of Nebraska Press, 1984), 408–9; for illustrations of this strategy in actual battles, see Helen Blish, *A Pictographic History of the Oglala Sioux* (Lincoln: University of Nebraska Press, 1967), 314–400.

5. See Royal B. Hassrick, *The Sioux: Life and Customs of a Warrior Society* (Norman: University of Oklahoma Press, 1964), 26–28, and James R. Walker, *Lakota Society,* ed. Raymond J. DeMallie (Lincoln: University of Nebraska Press, 1982), 29, 30, 38–39.

6. See Edward and Mabell Kadlecek, *To Kill an Eagle: Indian Views on the Last Days of Crazy Horse* (Boulder, Colo.: Johnson Books, 1981), 89.

7. See Hassrick, *The Sioux,* 109, and Black Elk, *The Sixth Grandfather,* 341.

8. Frances Densmore, *Teton Sioux Music* (1918; reprint, New York: Da Capo, 1972), 66.

9. Eugene Buechel, S.J., *Lakota Tales and Texts,* ed. Paul Manhart, S.J. (Pine Ridge, S.D.: Red Cloud Lakota Language and Cultural Center, 1978).

ONE WHO LIVES WITH HIS GRANDMOTHER
BRINGS HOME A BUFFALO-HORN CLUB

A Lakota band was encamped.
A woman lived in the center,
and she had a message proclaimed:
"Young men of this band!
If you bring home the buffalo-horn club,
this woman will take you for her husband."
Then the young men went out as if for war,
but though they traveled far, they did not bring it back.

And then suddenly a young man who lived with his grandmother
    said,
"Grandmother, make me moccasins.
I will seek the thing that woman wants."
And his grandmother—"No, Grandson, the bravest young men
    could not bring it back.
And even if you brought it, she would not marry you," she said.
Still—"Grandmother, make them for me," he said.
So she made them.

Then one day he set out.
Exactly where he was heading was not clear,
but he was going west.
He traveled far and became very tired;
so he headed over to rest beside a river.
And when he arrived, he saw a buffalo bull lying there;
so he charged and killed it.
After taking a piece of the neck muscle and the meat,
he lay down to rest and fell asleep.

And he dreamed.
And on each of several high mountains, he saw something
    standing at the summit.
Then he woke up.
For some reason his eye was drawn to the sinew from the buffalo
    neck muscle.
He also noticed that the high blue mountains were very far away.
He did not want to exhaust himself ascending them;
so he stopped on a ridge and felt impelled to try something.
First he made a fire and sat down next to it.

Then he passed the whole length of a strand of sinew through the
 fire
until one end curled up.
Next he dropped the middle part in the fire,
and finally both ends drew up.
Suddenly, amazingly, he was standing next to one of those
 mountains.
He started right out to climb with a feeling of elation.

From this mountain he traveled far.
Once again he stopped before a high blue mountain;
so he performed that same ritual
and again set out to climb.
On top of that second mountain sat an old man painted red;
so he went over to him.
And—"Grandson," he said, "you are having a hard time
 searching for the buffalo-horn club.
Although my power by itself cannot achieve this,
I will give you my power," he said.
Then—"Look at me," he said.
So the young man looked.
And the grandfather made an animal sound
until somehow a buffalo appeared.
"*Ho,* in this body I live," he said.
And he gave him some buffalo hair and—
"With this, Grandson, go to where your next grandfather sits
and say, 'Grandfather, Grandfather told me to come,' " he said.

Once again he traveled far
until he came to the next mountain;
so he went over to it.
A very large tipi stood there,
and from it someone quickly emerged;
so he went over to him.
And—"Grandfather, Grandfather told me to come; so I have
 come," the young man said.
And—"Good!" the grandfather said.
And—"Sadly, Grandson, you are having a hard time searching for
 the buffalo-horn club,
but you have come this far; so you will bring it home," he said.
And—"My power by itself cannot achieve this, but I will give you
 my power," he said.
Then he gave him one hair and—"Look at me," he said.

So the young man looked,
and the old man sprang up into a tree and came back down.
He had become a red squirrel—
"You may use this to live, Grandson,
  but when you come to the mountain where your next grandfather
    sits,
  say, 'Grandfather told me to come,' " he said.

So he set out from there.
Eventually he arrived at the foot of the next mountain.
He could no longer proceed by ordinary walking;
so again he took up the sinew and performed the ritual.
When the sinew drew up,
  he set out to climb and moved on.
Suddenly something flashed like lightning;
so he approached it.
There sat a man painted black.
Like the last grandfather, he made a quick movement;
so the young man—"Grandfather, Grandfather told me to come,"
    he said.
And—"Good!" the grandfather said.
"Sadly, Grandson," he said, "you are having a hard time searching
    for the buffalo-horn club,
  but you have come this far; so you will bring it home," he said.
And—"Although my power by itself cannot achieve this,
  I will give you my power," he said.
And he gave him one hair, and—"Look!" he said.
So the young man looked,
  and a swallow was flying away.
Then, in the manner of the other guides, he spoke like this:
"*Ho*, from here go to where your next grandfather sits
  and say, 'Grandfather told me to come; so I have come,' " he said.

Armed with this additional protection, he set out.
After a long journey he came to the next mountain.
Something indistinct stood there;
so he went over to it.
There sat another man painted black,
and—"Grandfather, Grandfather told me to come; so I have
    come," he said.
And—"Good!" the grandfather said.
So the young man now felt free to come to his side.

And—"Grandson, you are searching for the buffalo-horn club.
Soon you will come to it,
but you will have a hard time," he said.
And—"Although my power by itself cannot achieve this,
I will give you my power," he said.
First he pulled an eagle plume from his hair and gave it to the
    young man.
Then he took it back.
And—"Use it like this," he said;
he let the plume float on the wind
until it rose high into the air:
"*Ho,* Grandson, whenever it looks like you are going to die, do
    this," he said.
Now your last two grandfathers await you;
so look to them, and go ahead from here.

When he came to the top of the next mountain,
there sat an old woman;
so he went to her.
And—"Grandmother, I have traveled far," he said.
And—"Grandson, you are searching for the buffalo-horn club,
but you are having a hard time.
Grandson, I will give you a sprig of cedar.
When it seems that your pursuers will surely overtake you,
then you will burn it."
So she broke off a piece and gave it to him.

With this added power he set out.
Another mountain came into view; so again he went there.
And a man painted blue, a great blue heron, was sitting there.
And the heron spoke like this:
"Grandson, you are searching for the buffalo-horn club,
but you are having a very hard time.
To help you bring it home sooner,
I will give you my power," he said.
He drew out one of his feathers and gave it to him.

From there, with greater power, he set out.
And another man painted blue sat there;
so he went over to him.
And—"Grandfather, Grandfather told me to come; so I have
    come," he said.

And—"Good!" he said,
and—"Grandson, from here on you will live.
Though the buffalo-horn club is hard to gain,
you will survive. But keep your wits about you.
After you capture it, you must fly straight for home," he said.
"For four days and nights do not sleep.
Be sure to follow your grandfathers' directions exactly.
Ho! Do it like this," he said, and he made a repeated cry.
Taking the form of a great hawk, he swiftly flew away and circled
    back;
then he gave the young man a war club.
And—"With this you can kill anything," he said,
and—"No pursuer will be able to kill you," he said.
"Now go on your way," he said.

A tall mountain stood on the opposite shore of a great lake.
It was due west.
And so with the eagle plume he had received,
he flew high above the water for two days.
Next he drew upon the heron's power
until, on the morning of the fourth day,
another blue mountain came into view.
He went straight toward it.
When he came near, he changed himself into a swallow
and flew across the remaining water to the shore.
There, under a giant tree, he sat down.

A camp was nearby,
and from it came a sound like buzzing.
A barking dog ran up to him,
and a woman came toward the tree from the same direction.
So he used the great hawk's club to silence the dog.
Then he used the squirrel's power to blend into a fallen log.
As she came closer, he could see that she carried something.
Whenever she came to a tree, she took up the object and struck
    the trunk.
Each tree splintered from a single stroke.

Soon the woman, who had extremely long hair, came near the
    "log."
Just as she was about to shatter the giant tree where he had rested,
she saw the dead dog.

Without the slightest pause she started running back toward her
    camp.
But the young man became a buffalo and charged and threw her
    up onto his horns.
Then he caught her and tossed her up a second time,
and when she fell on the ground, he turned back into a man.
Again he charged and seized her:
first he tore off the buffalo horn tied to her wrist;
then he took a second club she carried;
last he pulled out some of her hair.
Then, taking up the hawk club,
he was ready to depart for home.

It wasn't long before the Thunderbirds were chasing him.
When they were dangerously close, he took up the swallow's
    feather and swiftly lengthened his lead.
The feather of the blue heron brought him across the lake;
next the eagle feather sped him to the place of the great hawk—
"Grandfather, take this club back," he said.
A heavy thunder and hail storm began to close on him,
but he burned the cedar, and the storm let up.
So he went straight ahead to the old woman and gave back the
    cedar.
He continued on his way, returning gifts to the eagle, the buffalo,
    and his other helpers.

Now, having only his own legs, he walked on until he was ex-
    hausted.
Then he remembered the buffalo sinew.
He took it out and burned it
until it drew up on both ends.
Confidently he set out for the summit of the next mountain
and continued traveling home.
After he had rested at the top of the very first mountain he had
    climbed,
he decided to try the buffalo-horn club.
He drew it out next to a great pine tree and shattered it.
Then he packed it up with the second captured club.
His people had moved their camp to the foot of another high
    mountain;
so he rested at its summit before entering the circle.

Once more he tested the buffalo-horn club on an even larger tree.
This one also shattered.

He descended at dusk and entered the camp at night.
After searching in the dark, he found his grandmother's tipi.
Just outside she had hung out a sacred root used to bring travelers
    home safely.
He went inside and—"Grandmother, I am back," he said.
The little grandmother was very happy, and she gave him food.
When he had eaten it all, she asked,
"Grandson, this morning the woman who lives in the center had it
    announced that when someone brings home the buffalo-horn
    club,
    a set of strong tipi poles should be made.
So, with this in mind, I went ahead and made them.
"Grandson, did you bring it?" she said.
And—"Grandmother, I brought it," he said.
Then the grandmother trilled the screech owl cry.

They had a joyful morning together.
In the afternoon the young man who lived with his grandmother
    summoned a camp crier,
and—"People, gather some wood, and come over here," he said.
The crier walked all around the camp circle, repeating the
    announcement:
"Hereby the boy who lives with his grandmother has earned a
    name—
Thunder Shoots they will call him," he said.
The crier completed the circle.

The people gathered quickly.
And the boy who lived with his grandmother came to the center.
He carried the buffalo-horn club, and he said,
"*Ho,* it was said that the woman who lives in the center would
    marry the one who brought home the buffalo-horn club.
So I left to search.
As you have heard, I brought it back, and now that I am home,
you will see it," he said.
And he turned toward a tree and drew out the buffalo-horn club.
When he struck, the tree exploded as if shot by lightning.

▲

"*Ho,* why are the people gathered?" the woman from the center
   asked.
She sent messengers, and after their return—
"Go to the man who has brought it
   and bring him to my tipi," she said.
They took her blanket and put it over the one who lived with his
   grandmother.
Then they brought him to the woman in the center's home.
And the woman—"The buffalo-horn club could only be taken
   with much suffering," she said.
"I called for this sacrifice so that the people would not fear the
   Thunder," she said.
"And now I will have a husband," she said.

From then on the young man who lived with his grandmother was
   not as he was.
He lived in a large tipi as a chief,
   and the people followed him.
He had many robes and horses,
   and the people honored him with the name the crier had
   proclaimed—
Thunder Shoots they called him.
Of course, they also made much of the little grandmother.

After doing many things for the people,
   one day he invited them to assemble.
When they had gathered, he said,
"I am going to perform a ceremony.
On my hunt for the buffalo-horn club,
I learned something that the people do not know.
And now you will see it," he said.
He took out a strand of sinew,
   and when he laid it in the fire,
   the ends drew up.
Then he led the people to the nearby mountain,
   where they quickly climbed so high
   that their former campsite disappeared from view.
Since then travelers always carry sinew.

The people revered and heeded this man.
To this day they travel as he taught.

A WHITE BUFFALO WOMAN HELPS
A LAST-BORN BROTHER

A Lakota band was encamped,
and four young men lived there as brothers.
One day the people sent out hunters,
but they did not return.
So they sent out more hunters,
and they found nothing,
neither the lost ones nor sufficient food.
Then the oldest of the four brothers set out to hunt,
and he did not return.
Then the second oldest brother set out,
and he did not return.
Then the third brother went looking,
and he did not return.

And so the last-born brother wandered about, crying.
Suddenly a young woman came to him and spoke like this:
"Why are you crying," she said.
So—"Older Sister, I have three older brothers, but they are all
    lost,
And only I am left to search.
That is why I am crying.
I live with my mother, and there are few men left in the camp,"
    he said.
"Many of them went out hunting and were lost,
and that is why my older brothers went to look for them,
    But they did not return," he said.

And the young woman responded,
"Younger Brother, I have come to live with you and Mother and to
    restore my older brothers.
But you must do as I tell you," she said.
Immediately he returned to the camp and entered his tipi.
His older brothers' arrows hung untouched along the wall.
He told his mother about the woman: "Mother, you are going to
    have a daughter and I an older sister," he said.
At night he lay awake,
and the woman came and stood nearby;
then she came to the entrance.

The mother came out,
and—"Daughter, come in," she said.
And she embraced the woman and brought her inside.

First thing in the morning the young woman spoke to the boy:
"Younger Brother, cut four arrows.
  Then paint one red," she said,
"and paint one blue," she said,
"and paint one brown," she said,
"and paint one black," she said.
  Then she gave him a medicine and spoke again:
"Four days from now you will come to where the Double-Face
    Monster lives,
  the one who has eaten up all the men from your camp.
  Go into the wind as you approach,
  and when you are close, blow some of the medicine on yourself.
  Then go straight up to him.
  He will be taking his afternoon nap when you arrive.
  Rub some medicine on an arrow, and drive it into his head," she
    said.
"And when he is dead, rip open his stomach," she said,
"and draw out your older brothers.
  They are still alive in there, and soon you will see them," she said;
"and tell them, 'Now we have an older sister,' " she said.
  And—"Younger Brother, go into the sweat lodge, and then I will
    dry you off,
  and you will live," she said.
  And so he purified himself.
  Then his older sister came and dried him with sage and blew some
    medicine on him.
  When she was finished, she tied the medicine to his scalp lock,
  and—"Younger Brother, you will not travel alone.
  From the start this will guard you," she said.
"Now that I have placed it here, it will never leave you," she said.

He set out and traveled all day
and slept at night on top of a hill.
In the middle of the night,
someone pulled his topknot,
and—"Wake up," it said.
He looked, but there was no one there;
so again he lay down.

Then, just before dawn,
again someone pulled his topknot,
and—"Now it is dawn; wake up," it said.
From then on he knew it was the medicine fastened in his hair.

He arose and traveled
until it was night.
Again he lay down on top of a hill.
The medicine woke him in the middle of the night,
and again at dawn it woke him.
So he arose and traveled
until it was night.
As before he lay down on top of a hill.
Again the medicine woke him in the middle of the night,
and again at dawn it woke him.
So he arose and traveled.
The next evening he slept on top of a hill.
When the medicine woke him,
he arose and traveled.

At twilight he came to a very big mountain.
He went to the top to rest,
and in the middle of the night, the medicine woke him.
Later, at dawn, it spoke like this:
"The one you are seeking is at the bottom of a snowcapped
    mountain.
Lay a sharpened stick next to you while you sleep,
and when I wake you on this hill, then go," it said.

So he arose and traveled
until he came to that high, snowcapped mountain.
As he sat down to gather his strength, he heard a sound like
    buzzing,
and he could see something like a white hill standing next to a
    stream;
it was the Double-Face's giant stomach,
and from inside it came the buzzing sound.
The young man became sleepy, but something roused him.
And—"Go now, he is sleeping . . . hurry," it said.
He jumped up and ran over to Double-Face.
There lay that hill-like stomach,
and the force of its breathing was so strong

that it staggered Last Born, and he started to run away.
But the medicine in his scalp lock—"Your power!" it said.
Immediately Last Born turned around, took up the medicine,
    chewed it, and rubbed some on an arrow.
Next he blew some on the sleeping Double-Face,
and he drove the arrow right into the middle of the huge
    forehead.
The monster instantly sat up, but the young man sent another
    arrow into his forehead.
Four times he shot him before he died.

Now he took a knife and cut open the stomach.
From inside a group of people began to come forth.
There were very many of them, and some were so deep inside that
    it was hard to draw them out.
His older brothers were among the last to emerge.
And saying, "Older Brothers, I came to find you," he embraced
    each one
and led the whole party homeward.

At the end of the second day, they rested beside a stream.
Here the medicine spoke to Last Born:
"In the morning you must provide for the others.
    Many buffalo are near this stream.
    Use your power, and go to them.
    As soon as your companions can no longer see you,
    choose four arrows, blow the medicine on them, and kill the
        buffalo."
The next morning he led the group to the top of a ridge.
"Wait for me here. I will bring you something," he said.
    He went straight to the buffalo.
    First he blew the medicine on his arrows and on his body.
    Then he went up close and killed one.
    And again he killed one.
    And again he killed one.
    And again he killed one.
    He killed four, and the rest fled.
    Then he wiped himself down with sage,
and he waved a blanket to signal the others.

They came straight over, and because they were starving,
they wolfed the meat down raw until they were full.

Then they roasted the rest and ate all of that.
Altogether they consumed four buffalo before they resumed their
  journey.
They traveled and rested,
and at dawn they traveled again
until finally they neared their camp.
Many women who had thought they were widows ran to greet
  them,
and the reunited couples embraced.
That same older sister, who lived with her mother, also came
  forward,
and she hugged her brothers,
and her mother hugged her sons.

That is how Last Born found his relatives and returned them to their
  home.

After a time he told the people he would bring them something.
Soon a large herd of buffalo approached, and he led the people
  out to hunt.
He told them this: "Do not draw blood from the buffaloes'
  heads," he said.
And they hunted and took home meat, hides, bone,
  sinew—everything they needed.
They had four hunts and lived in abundance.

Now the people gathered and decided to give Last Born a wife.
They summoned all the eligible young women,
and after questioning them, they selected one.
So now that young man became a husband.
His older sister was very happy with her sister-in-law,
and they lived happily together.

Then the people moved their camp.
First they set up their tipis near a wide stream.
From there they moved again and camped.
Here the people assembled and unanimously decided that the
  young man should become their chief.
And so he led them, and the band lived well.
One year later an infant son was born,
and the young man gave his son a name:
Sacred Cloud, he called him.

▲

One day his older sister unexpectedly said,
"Mother, Older Brothers, Younger Brother, and Sister-in-Law,
  I love all of you,
  but today I am traveling to my home, and I will not return for one
    year," she said.
"Mother, now I will go," she said.
  She stood up and went over to a hill, where she lay down.
  Then she arose and turned to go,
  and there, where she was standing,
  suddenly there was nothing at all.

So the young man watched over his people,
  and then about one year later he had a dream.
  He saw his older sister returning from the north with many
    horses.
  Then he saw her stop to rest,
  and from there she continued on into the camp.
  He woke up and told them, "Mother, Older Sister is on her way
    and will soon arrive," he said.
"Afterward she will explain her journey," he said.

Soon she approached.
  It was his sister, but she was nervous and seemed to fear the
    people.
  The young man and his little son went straight out to greet her.
  As soon as they met, he chewed some of his medicine and blew it
    on her.
  And right away she cried and kissed her nephew.
  Now, recovered from her fear, she entered the circle and
    embraced her mother and her older brothers.
  So they were full of joy and lived happily together.

After a long time the woman had another message:
"Younger Brother, Elder Brothers, Mother,
  before Younger Brother led you, the people were starving,
  and that was why I came," she said.
"From now on whenever this tribe tells me they are in need,
  then their power to grow will be renewed," she said.
"And the people will rejoice, multiply, and never live in fear," she
    said.
"Tomorrow there will be a hunt, and then three more hunts,
  and so you will have all you need," she said.
  The crier repeated the message, as criers do, by circling the camp,

and the people were very happy.
In the morning she led the whole camp to the hunting grounds,
where they hunted and prospered.
From then on the people were able to hunt without her
and to bring in deer, buffalo, and every other kind of game.

One day in midmorning, shortly after that hunt, the older sister fell
   asleep.
Her breathing was loud and hoarse,
and she lay with her legs under her like a buffalo cow.
At first the people thought she was sick and were alarmed.
But then, because she slept in broad daylight, breathing like a
   buffalo,
they knew she was a white buffalo woman.
When she woke up and came outside,
everyone was very happy.

And she said this: "Mother, Younger Brother, Older Brothers,
soon I must return to my home; this will be our last night
   together," she said.
"All the people must watch me depart," she said.
The next morning the people were called together for the
   leave-taking.
When they were assembled, the young woman spoke:
"Mother, Younger Brother, Older Brothers, Sister-in-Law, and my
   little nephew—come over here," she said.
So they came up, and she embraced them and cried.
Then she stopped crying and started toward a nearby hill.
At its top she lay down and rolled over,
and in full view of the people,
a white buffalo arose and galloped toward the next hill.
There she ran a zigzag line
until she disappeared for good down the other side.

The people dispersed sadly to mourn.
By this means they assuaged their grief.
Next, after the mourning had sufficed,
they honored their chief and also his wife and son.
Ever since then last-born sons have been wise and brave.

WILDERNESS MENTORS

▲

ELAINE A. JAHNER

INTRODUCTION

Throughout the world foundational myths and epics commemorate relationships between humans and wolves. We can look at the Lakota creation story of a wolf leading the people from a lower world to this one, or we can turn to Virgil's *Aeneid*, with its tender evocation of the she wolf mothering the founders of Rome, or we can read the Old Norse *Poetic Edda*, which announces that wolves will participate in the final undoing of our world. In these and countless other texts we find that the wolf, with its notable intelligence and social nature, has had an eminent place in imagined mediations between the world of the wilderness and that of human society, to which he refuses to accede even while seeming to gaze upon it from a fascinated distance.

Literary references to interactions between wolves and humans lead us culture by culture through a history of compacts between society and nature. Of course, the image of the wolf evokes fears just as it registers awareness of how animal intelligence can support human activities; and one feature of the Lakota stories presented here is that the affect bound up in stories about the wolf includes both hope and fear, with no simple separation of these emotions. Since society's mythically negotiated compacts with nature precede and support any institutionalized ecological politics, the wolf retains its role as a compelling imaginative mediator now that we are re-thinking balances of power in our entire ecosystem. Nowhere is this mediation more richly realized in narrative traditions than among the Lakota of the North American Great Plains. Lakota beliefs recognize the wolf's fiercely protective stance toward family; but beyond that, they link the wolf with a quality of seeing, a discerning vigilance and foresight that only the wolf teaches.

One nineteenth-century text comments on qualities that marked the wolf as a being deserving of attentive consideration. This text links a quality of guarded and dissembling watchfulness with the frequently narrated story of the woman among the wolves:

> The man who dreamed of the wolf was not very much on guard, but would haughtily close his eyes, it is said; yet the man was very much on guard. Long ago a woman lived with wolves, it is said. Then the wolves took great pity on her. The wolves went scattering away and when it was evening, they came home to the woman with meat, it is said. Therefore they believe the wolf to be *wakan* ["mysterious"]. Well, so it is. Even now they consider the wolf *wakan*.[1]

Keeping in mind that the critic too comes under the kind of scrutiny that the Lakota associate with the gaze of the wolf, I want to preface my presentation of two brief Lakota tales about encounters with wolves by stating my recognition that the stories achieve their full, complex richness only within Lakota culture. Nevertheless, they can function interculturally as a narrative analysis that acknowledges interspecies dependence, and they can do so without sentimentalizing the images that allow us to represent that dependence.

The story about a woman rescued by wolves is part of a living tradition throughout the Great Plains. In her book *Dakota Texts*, Ella Deloria published a remarkably detailed version of it.[2] At the conclusion of that tale, the woman who has spent time with the wolves is gifted with prophetic powers. The previously unpublished version of that story that I am presenting here is shorter than the one Deloria published; but it is a rich evocation of the emotions that sustain the narrative today.

As is the case with all stories that live on in tradition, the circumstances that prompt a particular telling are as much a part of the story's significance as the details of its plot. One day a friend rode with me from her home on Standing Rock Sioux Reservation to a nearby city. She was worried about what she had to do in the city, and as we drove along, she became more and more anxious. The words of the story began in the rhythm of worry and slowly took on the energy of confidence. I was only incidentally the audience for that narration; she was really telling the story to herself, reminding herself that some risks just have to be taken. Against this background her story takes on all the calming assurance of necessity. As we drove, she told the story in English. Later she recorded it for me in Sioux. My translation retains the rhythms and idioms of her original English narration. Her version of the story is less about exceptional perceptive powers than it is about how routine tasks anchor us in the ordinary when the strange threatens to overwhelm us. Her heroine does not acquire prophetic abilities, but she is notable and memorable for what she can accomplish as a consequence of her practical foresight; and this puts her in direct contrast to the hero of the second incident published here. The man among the wolves turns out to be remarkably deficient in practical foresight. Rather than peaceful coexistence with wilderness beings, he experiences sheer terror. Finally, though, wolves lead him back home too.

In the first story the heroine learns what the wolves have to teach, but she never allows herself to take her mentors and protectors for granted. Their difference imposes a respectful awareness of unbridgeable difference, and the way in which the story includes details that show how such difference is respected and honored deserves its comment. These details are important clues to the way in which the wolf functions as mediator and protector. He guides, but he is definitely not a companion. When the wolves lead the woman back to her own people, the narrator notes, "They didn't walk close to her. They walked quite far away." The story seems to include motifs that resist sentimentality toward the wolves and leaves them established in their proper place in the culture's network of relationships among all living beings.

Although the story of the woman among the wolves is the most commonly narrated example of human-wolf interactions, there are also tales about encounters that men have with these wilderness mentors. The second brief text presented here is an example found among George Bushotter's unpublished manuscripts. It was first translated by Ella Deloria,[3] and I have retranslated it. There is a compelling eeriness evoked in this tale, which begins by evoking the lulled atmosphere that presages any good mystery story. A man is enjoying a calm, pleasant walk and forgets about the dangers of his situation. He relaxes, simply giving in to the moment, and he fails to envision his goals. In this story the verb *envision* takes on an increasingly literal meaning. The link between seeing and receiving structures the tale. But this is no tale of idyllic wish fulfillment; it touches on terror, with the wolf finally leading the man to the other side of his projected fears.

A thunderstorm overtakes our hero. To his great relief he notices a shelter, and he announces his presence to those within. Something—the tale does not tell us what—triggers an awareness of danger, and he decides to get away as fast as possible. It is the right reaction because that shelter is the home of ghosts, who pursue him, one on each side, whispering unintelligible sounds. The man thinks that seeing his otherworldly companions might help dissipate his terror, but he can discern nothing, or at least nothing of them. Then his imprecisely formulated wish for company is granted. But because his foresight is vague, he conjures up what he most wants to escape: he sees a woman whose weeping echoes his own terror, and he decides that he can, at least, have companionship in his fear.

Then comes the element that gives the turn to the screw. The woman announces that since he has wished for company, she will run with him. He notices that she has no feet, and thus he realizes that his wish for company has called yet another ghost to his side. Next there is a psychological twist that makes this tale unique: the ghost woman forbids him to fear her. If he cannot overcome his fear, she will disappear, but she will refuse to go away. He must not fall back into the depersonalized anxiety he experienced with the first two spirits. As soon as he confronts this necessity to gaze at his own worst fears and to control his terror lest the situation get worse and worse, he can start to think clearly about what might happen to him. But when his thoughts do get precise and he envisages the real danger of his situation, the ghost woman goes away. Or at least we assume that she does, because the text implies her genuine absence and not just her invisibility. At this point in the story, the wolf comes to lead the man back to human community.

What is the connection between the ghost woman and the wolf? That question gets to the essential mystery of the tale. Does the tale suggest that the wolf requires those whom he protects to look straight at fears before he can rescue them? Or is it a story about a need to visualize clearly what one wants?

At this point issues of translation come to the fore. What Deloria initially translated as "aimlessly" involves an unusual stylistic construction in Bushotter's text that brings in a word that seems to take on strong visual force in many tales about wolves. That word is *taišni* (*i* indicates a nasal sound; *š* is *sh*). At its most literal level it means "invisible." Yet of the three times it is used in the Bushotter text, it can be translated only once as "invisible": the ghost woman's legs are literally invisible. The two usages that are most pivotal to the story's meaning refer to the man's intentions regarding his journey. We know from the beginning that he has not clearly visualized his goals in traveling because his travel itself is *taiśni*. What Deloria translated as "aimlessly" I have retranslated as "not very clear about his goals" in order to bring in some of the connotations surrounding *taiśni* that imply the necessity of foresight. Examining the word in the context of other stories told around the turn of the century, we can note that it was used to indicate not just invisibility but an inability or refusal to see the essential nature of something. And that inability could lead to dangerous misjudgments about how to treat something or someone. Seeing clearly is a form of precautionary discipline.

As Bushotter's text implies, *taiśni* can also imply failure to foresee with enough precision what one seeks or wants. We might say that Bushotter's text suggests that what you fail to see can be what you get, even if that seeing—or lack of it—is just prevision. And if you see or foresee clearly enough, the wolf will help.

NOTES

1. James R. Walker, *Lakota Belief and Ritual,* ed. Raymond J. DeMallie and Elaine A. Jahner (Lincoln and London: University of Nebraska Press, 1980), 160.

2. Ella C. Deloria, *Dakota Texts,* Publications of the American Ethnological Society no. 14 (New York: G. E. Stechert, 1932; reprint, New York: AMS Press, 1974).

3. George Bushotter, "Lakota Texts," trans. Ella Deloria, manuscript 4800, National Anthropological Archives of the Museum of Natural History, Smithsonian Institution, Washington, D.C. Bushotter was a Dakota Sioux who was educated at Hampton Institute in Virginia and who transcribed a series of oral literary texts that remain unpublished. In 1894, James Owen Dorsey published *A Study of Siouan Cults,* in The Eleventh Annual Report of the Bureau of American Ethnology for the Years 1889–90 (Washington, D.C.: Smithsonian Institution, 1894), 351–544. Much of Dorsey's information comes from the Bushotter manuscripts.

I remember a story about a woman that this man married. He had two wives, and one got jealous; so the other sneaked away one night. She traveled all day, all night, and the next morning she lay down in a hole. She was hiding from enemies. So she slept during the day and walked at night.

When she woke up, she started walking again.

She walked all night.

She didn't know which direction she was going in or anything.

When daybreak came again, she found a wooded place. She sat down there to look for a place to hide again, and just then a wolf came by, and just like a human he said, "Say, woman, you stay here with me. I'll take care of you and your brothers and grandfathers; they'll take care of you too." (He meant the other wolves.) "So the enemies won't come to find you."

He said that, and she stayed there. Of course she had been carrying some lunch, but she had eaten all that.

He said, "What are you crying for?"

"I'm hungry," she said.

So he said, "I'll call my brothers, and they'll bring you food." The wolves came, and they brought a fawn. They had killed that. And she had carried some kind of knife; so she cut the meat up and sliced it thin. There was a great rock there, and she put the meat over that rock to dry.

Again, she wanted to cook; so she asked for a fire.

"Well," the wolf said, "your grandfathers will make a fire for you." And that night a storm came with lightning that struck fire to the wood, and she went over there, and she fried her dried meat. That's what she was eating. She had a little stick, and she dug wild turnips, and she braided them and hung them to dry; and when they were dry, she had them to eat too.

One night she was crying: she was so lonesome and wanted to go back to her relatives. And so the wolf said, "Tomorrow, well, I'll call your grandfathers, and they'll take you back to where your relatives are."

And here he hollered again, and the wolves came, and he said, "They're ready to take you." So she got up, but they didn't walk close to her. They walked quite far away.

They were just leading her; so she went on walking, walking.

Every once in a while she got tired and took a rest. She carried some water; so she took some of that. She kept on going and going.

They all came to a big hill, and they sat down.

She just sat there, in a hidden spot, and then she saw a large camp far off. They both began to walk again. She had to walk slowly, she was so tired. They got to the big camp, and she was a little scared, but she just kept on going slowly.

And here the wolves gave her a little push. There was a tipi and she came right up to it, and she recognized the voices of her mother and her aunts. They were in there talking. She just crawled to the door, and she called her mother: "Mama, it's me."

So her mother and her aunt and her father came out of the tipi and looked.

"My daughter," her mother called out. Everyone came to see what had happened. The next morning the people put up a tipi in the center of the village, and they did a dance. And they looked at her, and they ate. They were just overjoyed because they had thought she was dead, and here she was alive.

So now a man was traveling away from camp all by himself. He was just going along, not thinking very clearly about where he was going. Then he thought to himself, "I have come this far; so I might as well just keep on going."

He went along, sometimes singing a little to keep up his courage.

Night came. So did storm clouds, and the thunder roared, and the rain poured, and he thought, "I better find myself shelter for the night."

And now he walked along the edge of a wooded place, cautiously stopping now and then because it was so very dark, and then he saw a fire in the distance; so he thought, "I'll just go on over there."

Listening, listening, he walked carefully. And then he stopped. There was a shelter shaped like a sweat lodge. Two men sat on either side of the fire.

Soon one of them said, "Friend, someone has come, and he is standing outside. Let's invite him in."

When he heard that, the man fled. Now he knew those two men were really ghosts. They caught up with him and ran, one on either side of him, but when he tried to see them, he couldn't see a thing. He knew they were there because they kept whispering something in his ear that he couldn't quite catch.

He decided the best thing to do was to pay no attention to what he was hearing and to run as fast as possible to the hill. Now as he was running along the clay crest of the hill, he heard a woman cry out, and he thought, "Well, at least she and I can travel together. We'll both enjoy the company."

Instantly someone caught up with him and said, "OK, since you want us to travel together, here I am."

That scared him even more. As soon as he saw her, he knew she was a ghost too. Then the ghost woman said, "Don't be afraid of me. If you are, you'll never see me again; but I'll still be here."

And so the two went along together without speaking. When daylight came, he saw that the ghost woman's legs were invisible. She just floated along effortlessly.

Suddenly he thought, "What if she should choke me!"

Then immediately the woman vanished, as if she were just a breeze of wind.

For a while he went on alone.

Soon after that a wolf came up to him and said, "Where are you going?" When he replied that he had no clear goal, the wolf said, "In that case follow me, and I will lead you to a camp."

So he went along, following the wolf, who ran off well ahead of him. Finally the man caught up with the wolf, who was sitting atop a hill, howling.

And there, beyond the hill, the man saw a village on the plain.

The wolf said to him, "Here is where you should live. These people will feel kindness toward you."

The man went into the village, and the people received him. They treated him well.

From that point on he realized the goodness of wolves. Whenever he killed game, he gave some to the wolves.

WAKINYAN AND
WAKINYAN WICAKTEPI

▲

CALVIN W. FAST WOLF

INTRODUCTION

The text presented here is a free translation of the first two of thirteen narratives in "The George Sword Ledger Book": "Wakinyan" and "Wakinyan Wicaktepi" ("Thunder" and "Those Killed by Thunder"), which can be found in the James R. Walker Collection of the Library of the Colorado Historical Society.[1] The greatest part of the material that George Sword and others provided James R. Walker with was subsequently typewritten, lending itself more easily to translation by non-Lakota speakers. "The George Sword Ledger Book," however, remained handwritten, thereby raising problems with understanding both Sword's calligraphy and the subtler nuances of meaning in his narratives.

Sword wrote in syllables, and the reconstruction of his narratives into discrete word units presented a somewhat difficult task. It is only in the past several years that I, a native speaker and writer fully versed in the old Lakota, have put the material into typescript. No other free translation of "The Ledger Book" narratives has been done to date, with the exception of Sword's account of the Sun Dance.[2] In 1928, Ella Cara Deloria was asked by Franz Boas of Columbia University to undertake a free translation of that narrative. Deloria was a native speaker of Lakota, and her translation is impeccable. It was published in the *Journal of American Folklore*.[3]

I have chosen these particular narratives as they deal with the Heyoka and the Thunder Beings. The Heyoka were those who dreamed of thunder; their role in Lakota society has been a matter of great interest to, and speculation by, ethnographers. Often referred to in ethnographies as contraries or clowns because of their need to do everything in a backward fashion and because of their clowning actions, they had a definitive role in Lakota society. The Heyoka were the sacred scoffers who, because they were not bound by societal constraints, could freely critique established custom. They were feared because of their power, which could incorporate the positive and the negative aspects of the sacred. Doing everything in an antinatural manner, they freely violated cultural taboos.

The Heyoka had the power to deflect the destructive thunder and lightning storms that so often struck the Plains. By the same token, however, they could refuse to deflect them. They were healers who could also reverse healing. In their powers were incorporated the dark and the light sides of the Ultimate Mystery (Taku Wakan).

The Heyoka also played a valuable role in the day-to-day life of the camp circle. By their clownish actions they would amuse the people; at the same time they could draw attention to deviancy by burlesquing actions and deeds not acceptable to the society. In this role they were social critics. By making people laugh, their antics provided a necessary release from the Lakota code of conformity to social customs, which the Heyoka were free to ridicule. Creating amusement in times of stress, they also were capable of acting out an admonition when the society felt too complacent; they would point out the potential danger by burlesquing the possible consequences of ignoring a potentially hazardous situation.

Other accounts of Heyoka ceremonies have been recorded, most notably in John G. Neihardt's book *Black Elk Speaks*,[4] where Nicholas Black Elk recounts his own acting out of the Heyoka ceremony as dictated to him by his vision. Sword's account is unique, however, in that over and above explaining the relationship between the Thunder Beings and the Heyoka, he provides us with a detailed account of the initiation into the Heyoka Society of a man who had dreamed of thunder.

Because these two narratives of Sword's overlap, being somewhat repetitive and disjointed, I have merged the two narratives while remaining faithful to Sword's text. For purposes of clarity, I have occasionally added footnotes to clarify those Lakota nuances of meaning that do not translate literally into English.

George Sword's life (1846–1910) spanned the era when the Lakota lived freely and openly on the Plains and extended into that of a rapidly changing society enforced by the establishment of the present-day reservations. Sword, who taught himself to write in Lakota, acted as an informant to Dr. James R. Walker, the agency physician at Pine Ridge (1896–1914). James Riley Walker had become intrigued by Lakota myth, ritual, and social custom. Encouraged by Clark Wissler, curator of the American Museum of Natural History in New York, he increased his efforts to secure ethnographic material for the museum. From Sword and others he obtained a large quantity of material dealing with myth, ceremony, and belief. To this collection Walker would put his own sometimes problematic interpretation and structure.

Why Sword entered into this collaboration is speculative. Had his relationship with Walker been of great significance to him, it is reasonable to assume he would have mentioned it in his autobiography,[5] as that autobiography covered the years 1844 to 1909, a time when Walker was at Pine Ridge. He does mention the military men with whom he had contact: Generals George Crook and Philip H. Sheridan, both noted military leaders, not unlike Sword himself. Although he lauds himself in the autobiography for "having tried to help my people," he makes no mention of having passed on to this white physician a legacy of myth, custom, and belief. The preservation of this material for future generations of Lakota would certainly qualify as being of great help to his people, but it is not mentioned by him.

There is little doubt that Sword learned to accommodate himself to two worlds. An *akicita* ("soldier"), he was selected as a Shirt Wearer at a young age for his outstanding characteristics of leadership in battle as well as for his conduct in the day-to-day life of the camp circle. By 1876, however, his autobiography indicates that he had become friends with the white man. This was the same year in which General George Custer's Seventh Cavalry was wiped out at the Battle of Little Bighorn. Obviously Sword had made a choice, opting for cooperation with the white man, rationalizing this by stating that he was trying in vain to prevent an inevitable confrontation between the Lakota and the trespassers on their lands.

By 1880 Sword had become captain of Indian Police during Valentine McGillycuddy's tenure as superintendent of the Pine Ridge Agency (1879–86). By the early 1890s he had become a judge of the U.S. Indian Court.

Early photographs of Sword as captain of Indian Police at Pine

Ridge show him with his hair cut short in the approved white military fashion, but by the time of his death, he had grown his hair long, and he mentions this with great pride when he describes himself in his autobiography.

George Sword was truly an enigmatic man.

NOTES

1. "The George Sword Ledger Book," document FF 184, James R. Walker Collection, no. 653, Library of the Colorado Historical Society, Denver, Colo.

2. "The George Sword Ledger Book," narrative 9.

3. George Sword, "The Sun Dance of the Oglala Sioux," trans. Ella Cara Deloria, *Journal of American Folklore* 42 (October-December 1929): 354–413.

4. John G. Neihardt, *Black Elk Speaks: Being the Life Story of a Holy Man of the Oglala Sioux* (New York: William Morrow, 1932).

5. "The George Sword Ledger Book," narrative 5.

It is said that the Thunder Beings live to the west because that is where they come from. They are considered to be the warriors of the Ultimate Mystery. They have their home in the Great Mountains to the west. Whoever ignores their commands is killed by them.

The Thunder Beings, it is said, live in the manner of ordinary people. Moreover, they travel all over the world, nurturing it, causing the rain to fall as they travel about. They make it possible for the earth to grow many beautiful and wonderful things, and by doing this, they help the animals and man to flourish abundantly. Where the earth is blighted, they come and cleanse it with rain, driving out everything that was causing the blight.

There are sky, earth, and water beings that the Thunder Beings esteem the most. Of all the four-leggeds of the earth, this is the horse, although all other four-leggeds are significant to them also. Of the winged ones of the sky, these are the gulls, nighthawks, horned larks, forked-tail swallows, and all other swallows. Of the water beings the most esteemed are the frogs and the lizards. Whenever the lightning is very heavy, it is said that frogs and lizards come down to the earth with the rain.

Although there are many reasons for things, including animals, to be struck by lightning, it is said that when a person dreams of the Thunder Beings and makes a commitment to perform a certain ceremony, failure to fulfill the obligation will result in his death by lightning. Whatever is struck by the Thunder Beings is called killed by lightning.

It is said that someone who had been killed by the Thunder Being warriors was struck on top of the head. The one struck by lightning had the hair on the top of his head twisted and ruffled into a ball. It therefore became the custom for the Heyoka* to twist the hair on top of their heads into a knot.

It is said that if someone does not do as instructed by the Thunder Beings in his dream or vision, the lightning will do it for him. It will travel down his body and curl his limbs, marking them in the way that he should have painted himself; therefore it was customary for ones who dreamed of thunder to paint their bodies and limbs in that fashion.

When a person who had been killed by lightning was put up on a

*the Heyoka: those who dreamed of the Thunder Beings.

scaffold for burial, it was said that the lightning surrounded the burial scaffold and constantly struck that spot.

The person struck by lightning was taken back to the dwelling of the Thunder Beings and lived there with them. When the Thunder Beings come from the west, such a one comes with them and is permitted to hurl the lightning bolts and to kill, so they say.* The one killed by lightning was told by the Thunder Beings, "You will go quietly and softly to where your people are.† You will feel compassion for them. Their beliefs they hold to be the correct ones, but the wisdom that each learned man holds to be true is not so," they said, "and you will reveal the truth to all of them."

The other Heyoka honor and pray to such a one for their wants and needs, it is said.

A man who had dreamed of thunder told of his dream. "I dreamed that I had gone to the land of the Thunder Beings. A horned lark came for me from the west, and so I left like a lightning bolt. When I regained consciousness, I was in the great village of the Thunder Beings. I saw them as ordinary men who had painted their torsos whitish gray. Their limbs were painted red in zigzag stripes that were about a hand width wide.

"They said to me, 'As a boy, as a man, and as an old one,‡ always be acutely aware that the rituals you now see are those that you will take back and reveal to your people.' "

One Heyoka,§ because he was impatient to perform the Heyoka ritual of pulling out of the boiling kettle, appealed to the man who had made the journey to the land of the Thunder Beings. He told him, "I dreamed a vision. From that time forward whenever the Thunder Beings come, I hear the shouts of warriors." To this the one who had visited the Thunder Beings replied, "They are telling you to pull out of the kettle in the Heyoka manner. Now you can show the people how to do this ritual in the proper fashion." The Heyoka was now ready to perform the ritual.

A small tipi made up of old, smoky discarded tipi hides was erected in the middle of the camp circle by a group of Heyoka who had already revealed their dream of the Thunder Beings. They did not use as many poles as for an average-size tipi, and they also set up two poles for the smoke flaps.

---

*to kill: that is, to kill those who did not fulfill their obligations.
†quietly and softly: in dreams.
‡As a boy . . . as an old one: at every age.
§One Heyoka: one who had dreamed of the Thunder Beings.

They then invited all the other members of the Heyoka Society who had already performed their ritual to come forth. The group of Heyoka chose one of their number. The new Heyoka who was to perform his ritual for the first time was touched by this chosen one who became aware of the new Heyoka's nascent power.

This chosen Heyoka, as he painted the new one, talked of how he would be painted. He also told him that he was to ride a multicolored horse. Then all the other Heyoka joined in the painting. His torso was painted a whitish gray; his limbs were painted a reddish color with red zigzag lines like those of lightning bolts. His hair was pulled forward, twisted, and tied so that it would hang down over his forehead. A Psoralea plant was tied to this forward-hanging topknot.*

The other Heyoka now dressed themselves. They made leggings of the old discarded tipi hides and cut ragged holes in them. These they wore as leggings. Out of the same hides they made shirts, in which they also made holes, and they wore these. They used the pericardium of the buffalo as a head covering, which covered the face as well. They cut a hole on the top of this head covering, and from this dangled a single braid. Taking two pieces of the old discarded tipi hide, they fashioned two earrings about the size of the palm of a man's hand. These they attached to their ears. From the back of their heads hung a row of crow-wing feathers attached to a strip of rawhide and beaded at the base. A hastily put together bow, shield, and two or three arrows constituted the remainder of the costumes. These bows and arrows were not really functional, as they were made quickly and carelessly.

Now the Heyoka who was about to fulfill his obligation was, as I said, arrayed in this fashion. He was painted grayish white and was mounted on a multicolored horse, holding spear in his hand. He sang a Heyoka song, of which these are the words:

A circular cloud is coming this way.
A circular cloud is coming this way.
I put myself on a sacred path by offering sacred vows for myself.

A circular cloud is coming this way.
I put myself on a sacred path by offering sacred vows for myself.

He then pierced a buffalo tongue with his spear and pulled it out of the boiling kettle.

*Psoralea plant: *Ticanica hu,* a prairie plant similar to the wild turnip.

All the Heyoka then moved closer to the kettle and pulled out pieces of buffalo tongue with their bare hands. They then dispersed among the crowd, bringing pieces of tongue to wherever middle-aged and older men were sitting, offering the pieces to them. The men replied, *"Haye,"* and partook of the food offering.* Everyone paid homage to the Heyoka leader and the new Heyoka.

The Heyoka then performed many droll and comical actions, as was their nature, much to the amusement of the crowd. The new Heyoka had fulfilled his obligation to the Thunder Beings, and the people were very happy for him.

One day, it is said, another man dressed himself in a Heyoka costume and went around the camp circle doing Heyoka tricks.† His hair hung loosely, and on a solitary topknot on his head he attached a row of crow-wing feathers. He painted his torso red, and on his limbs he painted zigzag vermilion stripes to represent the Thunder Beings. On his hands and feet he drew forked designs. He wore his buffalo robe with the hair on the outside and tied in front at the throat.‡ He carried an imitation bow and some crooked arrows along with a red painted drum. This was the song he sang as he pounded on his drum:

> The profound power of the sun is making my heart beat.
> The profound power of the sun is making my heart beat.

He turned his body from side to side as he danced around the camp circle, looking left and right. At intervals he would blow on an eagle-wing-bone flute. He did not do the Heyoka ritual of drawing from the kettle, as he was still afraid of the Thunder Beings.§ This time, however, he did ritually draw from the kettle. He did this again a second time and then a third time. From that time on he was no longer afraid of the Thunder Beings and considered himself to be fully a Heyoka.

The Heyoka were called the non–big brothers.||

*Haye: a male (oral) exclamation (point) used to denote approval.
†another man: another man who had dreamed of thunder.
‡with the hair on the outside: contrary to the usual way.
§as he was still afraid of the Thunder Beings: that is, because he had not yet performed the Heyoka ritual.
||non–big brothers: *ciyeku šni*. As the members of the Heyoka Society could evoke both the light and the dark sides of the Ultimate Mystery (Taku Wakan), they were not viewed as role models by the younger males in the camp circle. Members of the warrior societies, however, were the big brothers *(ciyekupi)* of those young men

The Heyoka spoke backward. They formed their own Heyoka Society and would select a day to have a feast. Then they would sing their Heyoka songs and do their rituals and ceremonies for the people. They would circle the camp, doing their dance, singing their songs, and beating on a drum as they sang. They did not dance in the usual way but playacted by jumping up and down as they danced.

----

who showed promise as warriors. Noted warriors would take an interest in promising youngsters, who would follow them around, learning the skills of warfare from them. In much the same way youngsters who showed a likelihood of becoming healers would follow around the holy men of the camp.

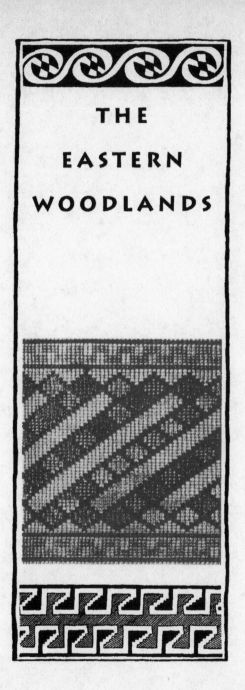

THE
EASTERN
WOODLANDS

NANABUSH STORIES
FROM THE OJIBWE

▲

RIDIE WILSON GHEZZI

INTRODUCTION

The power and beauty of Native American literature lie in the stories' dual roles as conveyors of tradition and vehicles for individual artistry. Represented here are three examples from the Nanabush (or Nanabozho) cycle of stories in the Ojibwe narrative tradition. The name of this cycle comes from the central trickster figure of the Ojibwe Indians, the stories' main character. The Ojibwe are an Algonquian-language-speaking Native group extending throughout southern and western Ontario and into northern Minnesota, Wisconsin, and Michigan. Traditionally a hunting and gathering society, the Ojibwe have continued to thrive, making up sixteen bands in the United States and sixty-seven in Canada.

The narratives presented here were collected in northern Minnesota by William Jones between 1903 and 1905. Jones, a member of the Fox tribe, had been a graduate student of Franz Boas's and was trained in the Boas tradition of Native American text collection, which demanded a working knowledge of the Native language and accuracy in transcription. These stories were included in a two-volume collection comprising not only the narratives in translation but a transcription of each story in the original Ojibwe as well,[1] another one of Boas's prerequisites. The Nanabush stories presented here were collected from two of Jones's primary storytellers.

Waasagunackank, or He-That-Leaves-the-Imprint-of-His-Foot-Shining-in-the-Snow, is the narrator of two of the three stories here. He was living at Pelican Lake, near the Bois Fort Reservation in Minnesota, when he worked with Jones, although he had grown up north of the reservation, near Rainy River and Lake of the Woods. The first story was narrated by his nephew Midaasuganj, or Ten Claw, who was living at Bois Fort as well.

As with any traditional oral literature, Ojibwe narratives were important for the transmission and reinforcement of a traditional worldview. In the Ojibwe tradition of verbal art, two basic categories are recognized. The first generally connotes "news or tidings," anecdotes and stories referring to the events in the lives of human beings. These stories range from everyday occurrences through more exceptional experiences to those verging on the legendary.

The second category of narratives involves the myths of the Ojibwe, sacred stories about the *manitok* (powerful other-than-human beings), and about deceased humans. These narratives were more traditional and formalized than the others. Their narration was restricted to the winter, when the Ojibwe were in their smaller family units, hunting for food. The Ojibwe told their traditions in the winter, they explained, so that the underwater *manitok* who hibernated then would not hear them.

The bulk of this latter category of stories told of the trials and tribulations of Nanabush. Of this material half of it describes him as a culture hero, the other half in his role as trickster, a role represented by a variety of characters throughout world literature. As hero he created the present world, in which we live. The Ojibwe creation myth presents major actions of Nanabush from his birth through his creation of the present world following a flood.

Nanabush is a complex and critical aspect of Ojibwe oral tradition, central to the tribe's worldview. The relationship between the Ojibwe and Nanabush was one of intimate identification: his mythical actions confirmed the Ojibwe as hunters. "He secured the right and ability of humans to hunt; he instituted vital cultural elements; he created the present world and formed Ojibwe identity. Without Nanabozho the Ojibwes in their own estimation would not exist."[2] As a culture hero Nanabush created the present world and all its orderly patterns. He interceded between humans and *manitok;* he served as an ideal; he invented important aspects of material culture, taught subsistence skills, and discovered wild rice; he told humans how to use medicines from wild plants to protect themselves.

As trickster Nanabush was a fool, a witch, a manipulator of his relatives, and an example of behavior to avoid. His behavior broke the rules of Ojibwe society at every turn, providing a negative form of education for all ages. His actions served as a reminder of appropriate behavior and of the consequences of disobedience. Stories from the creation myths and other Nanabush stories could be strung together endlessly, one after another in long or short series of adventures and exploits for the education and entertainment of all who listened. One Ojibwe attested to the large number of narratives: "I have known some Indians who would commence to narrate legends and stories in the month of October and not end until quite late in the spring, sometimes not until quite late in the month of May, and on every evening of this long term tell a new story."[3] Ron Evans, a Chippewa-Cree from North Saskatchewan, compared this procession of trickster tales to a piece of beadwork: one could create a different picture depending on how one strung the beads together.[4] So it is with these Nanabush stories: the way they are joined together depends on the artistry and the intentions of the narrator.

The Nanabush stories were much more than entertainment; they were the major means of keeping the tribe alive. Their messages provided the major source of educational and moral teachings for the members of each band of Ojibwe and for the tribe as a whole. Ron Evans also quoted a saying from his tribe that is equally relevant to the Nanabush tales of the Ojibwe oral tradition: "By going backwards, we move forwards."[5] Each time the stories were told, one's place in the world was held up for reexamination and reaffirmation.

The three Nanabush adventures represented here fall easily into this tradition. All of them contain examples of Nanabush at his best and at his worst, more often the latter. Consistently, Nanabush disobeys rules and makes a fool of himself. Yet within these stories the consequences of disobedience are educational: when a new vegetable and its effects are discovered, for example, the audience receives a natural science lesson and is entertained by Nanabush's predicaments and by his creative means of dealing with them.

Native American literature, while once oral, is usually presented on the page in prose form. There is, however, strong evidence from within the narratives themselves that a consistent prose rendering of these stories conceals important internal patterns and rhythms that would have been fundamental to their oral performance. Although William Jones transcribed these three narratives in paragraph form, the rearrangement of the prose form into lines and groups of lines initiates the recognition of patterns in the text, presenting natural relationships between form and content. In addition to presenting these texts in line rather than prose form, I have retranslated Jones's Ojibwe transcriptions into modern English so that they read more clearly and more consistently.

In "Nanabush Is Given Power by the Skunk but Wastes It," narrated by Midaasuganj, the narrative centers on Nanabush, who receives power from Big Skunk only to abuse the power and lose it. Finally Big Skunk takes pity on Nanabush once again and restores his power, saving him and his wife from certain starvation. As with all Nanabush stories, the first line of the narrative connects this story to the previous Nanabush story and, at the same time, starts Nanabush on his next adventure. The didactic nature of the story is clearly evident as Nanabush foolishly disobeys the manitou's instructions for survival. The lesson to be learned in this particular narrative is one of profound significance in the context of a traditional hunting and gathering culture. The procurement of food, especially in the harsh winter months, required that one follow specific instructions and be respectful of and responsible toward both the natural environment and the supernatural helpers from whom one drew power. The Nanabush stories and the antics they portrayed provided important lessons on the consequences of disregarding prescribed patterns of behavior and, subsequently, suggested the rewards to be gained through responsible action.

The two subsequent texts, narrated by Waasagunackank, represent even more sides to the complicated image of Nanabush. Whereas "Nanabush Eats the Artichokes" is highly entertaining, due to Nanabush's misunderstanding of the nature of the noise following close behind him, and would be even more hilarious if performed orally, it also plays the typical role of the creation myth as Nanabush discovers and then names a particular item. In this case the item in question is an artichoke. It is difficult to tell from either the translation or the narrative in the original Ojibwe whether the narrator was referring to an actual artichoke or to some form of raw vegetable in general.

It is certainly possible for the Ojibwe to have known about artichokes. The regular artichoke, native to Italy, would have been introduced by the French long before this narrative was collected. The Ojibwe word translated as "artichoke" here is referred to in other sources as a descriptor meaning "raw." In his collection of Menomini texts, Leonard Bloomfield includes a similar story that refers to "the sweet root."[6] This question opens a small window into the difficulties of working with texts that were translated much earlier. Whatever vegetable was originally intended here, it is clear that the story refers to a vegetable that, when eaten, produces a great deal of flatulence!

"Nanabush and the Caribou" also provides the listener (or the reader, in this case) with an educational message imbedded in one more entertaining adventure involving the trickster. As Nanabush is going along, he sees a caribou in a field and plots a way to kill it. Calling the caribou over, he acts out a story of some people he had seen shooting arrows, subsequently tricking and killing the animal. After debating how to cut up his kill and then foolishly giving away the location of the meat to a group of wolves, Nanabush is left with only the caribou's brains to eat. Turning himself into a snake so as to be able to reach the brains, something—as usual—goes wrong, and he becomes a human once more, now with the caribou head stuck over his own.

Unable to see, Nanabush proceeds to find his way to the lake by identifying five types of trees. Through his knowledge of these trees, this identification also tells him his location, where he is in relation to the lake. In a traditional setting this type of information within a narrative might have provided an important natural science lesson for a Woodlands people depending on survival in the bush. As literature it provides a lovely image of the different trees as Nanabush comes closer to the edge of the lake. The story finishes in a typically humorous fashion as Nanabush fools the people who think they have found a caribou to hunt.

These Nanabush stories offer a glimpse into the complicated but beautiful world of Ojibwe literature. As with all literature that was originally oral, part of the success of the story was in its telling. Yet, as is evident here, the beauty of the narratives is such that they are clearly able to stand on their own.

NOTES

1. William Jones, *Ojibwa Texts,* Publications of the American Ethnological Society no. 7, ed. Truman Michelson (New York: G. E. Stechert, 1917), pts. 1 and 2.

2. Christopher Vecsey, *Traditional Ojibwa Religion and Its Historical Changes* (Philadelphia: American Philosophical Society, 1983), 78.

3. George Copway, in ibid., 84.

4. Ron Evans, interview with the author, 1980.

5. Ibid.

6. Leonard Bloomfield, *Menomini Texts,* Publications of the American Ethnological Society no. 12 (New York: G. E. Stechert, 1928), 215–17.

NANABUSH IS GIVEN POWER BY THE SKUNK
BUT WASTES IT

Now again he was off traveling on foot.
Now presently he came out upon the ice of a lake;
  he saw a balsam standing.
And then he thought;
  "Some people, no doubt, are living there,"
    he thought.

On his way he continued.
Now truly he saw a hole from which they drew water;*
  they had made the hole with the anal gut of a moose.
The sac was really large.
He really wanted it.
He laid his hands upon it.

He heard the voice of someone speaking to him:
  "Hey, Nanabush! Leave that alone.
  You will make us need another!"
    he was told.
Then he truly left it alone.
  "Come here,"
    he was told.
Then he truly went up from the lake.

Now he was given food;
  then he ate.
It was Nanabush's intention to save some of the food.
  "Then eat all that I have set before you,"
    he was told.
Then truly he ate all of it.

He saw that the one who was speaking to him was really big.
  "Nanabush, it really seems as if you were hungry."

  "No,"
    he said to him.

▲

*he saw a hole: that is, in the ice.

"No, Nanabush, but you are really hungry. I know that you are
hungry. I am speaking this way to you so that I may bestow a
blessing upon you,"
    he was told.

"Yes, my younger brother, I really am hungry,"
    he said to him.
"Well now then I will teach you what you are to do,"
    he was told.
He was given a small flute.
    "Then this is what you shall use,"
    he was told.
    "Then when you go back home,
      your old woman will make a long lodge;
        let it be a long one.
And then after she has finished it,
    I wish to give this to you,
      so that with it you may kill them that come into your
        lodge.
Then as I instruct you, that is what you'll do,"
    he was told.
It was the Big Skunk that was addressing him.
    "I will give you the means to use twice what you are to use to
      kill them,"
    he was told.
    "Now go down upon your hands and knees,"
    Nanabush was told.
Then truly now he got down on his hands and knees.
Now from the other direction faced the rear,*
    who farted into [Nanabush].

Then that was what he had done to him.
And this he was told:
    "Please be careful, Nanabush,"
    he was told.
    "You will do your children harm,"
    he was told.

    "Now this is exactly what you will do when you reach home.
    You will blow a tune upon this flute of yours,
    and then some moose will come into that long lodge of yours.

▲

---

*the rear: the rear of the skunk.

And after many have entered, this they will do:
they will walk around inside of your long lodge.

Then the leader will come outside;
then you will fart so that you make it go into your lodge.

And then all that are within will die.
Then you will have some food to eat.

Again after you have eaten them up,
again you will blow upon your flute for them.
Then you will live through the winter;
not again will you be hungry.
Then that is all I have to teach you,"
    he was told.

Now Nanabush started on his way.
    He was truly very proud.
Now presently while walking along,
    he truly saw a large tree.
    "Wonder if my younger brother is telling me the truth,"
      he thought.
    "Hey, I'm going to fart at it,"
      thought Nanabush.
Then truly he farted at the big tree;
    then he wrecked it completely.
    "Why, my younger brother *is* telling me the truth!"
      he thought.

Then now presently while walking along another time,
    again he saw a large rock over beyond the hill.
    "Hey, I wonder if he really told me the truth,"
      he thought.
    "Hey, once more I'll make a test on that great rock,"
      he thought.
Then truly now again he farted at it.
    He looked, and there was nothing left of the big rock.

Well he who had taken pity upon him heard the sound of
      [Nanabush] doing this.
    "How stupid of Nanabush to bring disaster upon his children
    by not paying attention."

▲

Well Nanabush rose to his feet.
  Well he went to where the big rock had been.
Only after persistent search could he find where here and there lay
      shattered pieces of rock.
  "Then it was a fact that my younger brother told me the
     truth,"
    thought Nanabush.

On his return home
  "Old woman, I have been blessed,"
    he said to his old woman.
Now then he said to her,
  "Tomorrow let's build a long lodge!"
    he said to his wife.
Then truly now they built the long lodge.
Now he and the old woman had finished it.
  "Sit down!"
    he said to his old woman.
Then truly now they were seated.

Now he blew a tune upon his flute.
  Now truly did he see some moose running toward the place.
  "I suspect that no doubt you have been disobedient again,"
    his wife told him.
Then truly the moose came into the lodge.
  Now out started the one that was in the lead.
Now [Nanabush] tried to fart;
  then he was unable to fart.

Truly had he angered the woman.
  "Truly you never pay attention to whatever is told you by
    anyone!"
    his old woman told him.
Well all he could do was open and close his anus.
  Then he was unable to fart.
And then he angered his wife;
  truly had he angered her.
Well out went all the moose that had entered.
  And then he had angered his wife.

And then now all the moose were on their way out.
  The old woman then struck the last one coming out.
She broke the leg of the young moose.

"What a simpleton he is!
Wonder if he could have been told what to do?"

"Yes truly! Wasn't I given [the means of] twice killing all the
    game filling up the place?"
Then the poor things had little to eat.
And then she had turned the little anal gut of the moose inside
    out.
And then she laid it across the place where they drew water.

He knew that they were very much in want of food,
    he who vainly had taken pity upon [Nanabush].
    "Therefore I will go where he is"
    was the thought Nanabush received from him.
And then truly now off started the Big Skunk.
Then now in a while he came to where they were.
    "What, Nanabush, has happened to you?"
        he said to him.
Then the little anal gut of the moose was lying across the place at
        the lake where they drew water, the watering place.
    "How foolish of Nanabush to have done so!"
        he laughed at him.
Well then now this was what Nanabush was told:
    "What has happened to you, Nanabush?"
        [the Skunk] said to him.

    "My little brother, at the time when I left you,
        when I had come about halfway,
        I farted at a great tree and at a great rock.
        Then that was what I did, and I feel painfully sorry for it."

Then he was told:
    "Well again I will take pity upon you,"
        he was told.
    "Then I came here because I want to bless you."
Now again [Nanabush] was farted into by the other.
    "Now don't do it again!"
Well again he was given what he should use twice.
    Then he went on his way back home.

And then his wife prevented him from farting.
    Then it was true.
Now truly again he played a tune upon the flute.

Then now again he saw the moose coming;
    truly now they were entering the long lodge.
Now they were coming out;
    he farted at the one in the lead.
Then he had killed it.
    Now they looked;
        the place where they lived was completely filled with all the
        moose they had killed.

Well the poor creatures had all the food they wanted to eat.
Now he was told by his wife:
    "Please be careful lest you starve the children by wasting what
        you have left."
Well then they got along comfortably on the moose they had
        prepared for use.
    "It is quite likely that we will now go through the winter,"
        he said to his wife.

    "It is quite likely,"
        he was told.
    "Truly we have been greatly blessed,"
        said the woman to her husband.

Then that is as much as I know.

And then he went slowly along upon his way.
Now presently he saw some creatures.
  "What are you called?"
    he said to them.
  "Wonder if you may be eaten."

  "Yes,"
    they said to him.

And then he was told,
  "Yes, we really are eaten."

  "Well, what is your effect after a lot of you is eaten?"

  "We have no effect.
  Then we make one farty in the stomach."
And then he ate them.
  Well, he was told they were good to eat.
Eventually he ate his fill and left them.
  "You really have a pleasing taste,"
    he said to them.

And then he kept straight along upon his way.
Now presently while traveling along,
  suddenly at the rear,
  "PO!"
    came a sound.
He started running.
  "Who made that noise?"
    he thought.

He was getting far on the run.
Again he was traveling along.
  "PO!"
    was the sound something made.
He whirled around.
  "Who made that noise?"
    he thought.

Again he was traveling along.
  Suddenly he farted.

He started running.
  "Well, I will leave the one making that noise behind,"
    he thought.

Just as he was about to slow up,
  suddenly again,
  "PO!"
    came a sound.
Then he became afraid.
  "Well, I will look for the one making that sound,"
    he thought.

He lay in wait for it beside the path.
Then he went back a little ways.

And then he watched for it beside the path.
Suddenly again he heard some creature at his back.
  Then quickly came the sound:
  "PO!"
He leaped to his feet.
  "Holy smoke! Wonder what's following me.
  Must be a great manitou!"
    he thought.

He started running at top speed.
While he was running,
  suddenly again,
  "PO!"
He landed a great distance off.
He whirled around.
Well he did not see the one that he tried in vain to hit.
Suddenly again there at his back he heard something.
  "PO!"

  "Holy smoke!"
    he thought.

He started running.
Then there where he started running,
  "PO!"

▲

"Holy smoke!"
   he thought.

He started running really fast.
He ran a short way. He ran fast.
Then quickly toward him the same sound.
   "PO!"
At last at every step he took,
   "PO!"
      "PO!"
         "PO!"
            "PO!"
               "PO!"

"Then it is just what my little brothers told me
      when I saw the artichokes:
      'We make people farty in the stomach,'
         I was told.
   Hey, I am farting!
   Then that is what the people,
      my uncles,
         shall say to the end of the world."

While he was traveling along,
suddenly again,
   "PO!"
"Hey, I am farting!"

Well then he continued steadily on his way.
Now presently he was walking along;
   he came to a wide field of high grass.
He looked toward the other end of the meadow;
   a big bull caribou came walking out upon the stretch of grass.
He really wanted to get him.
   "Wonder how I can get hold of him?"

Nanabush was seen;
   "Surely he will have something to say to me,"
      thought the caribou.
   "I think I will draw him on."
The caribou started running off.

Now truly the voice of Nanabush was heard saying to him,
   "Hey, my little brother, I wish I knew why you acted like that
      whenever I see you. Wait! I want to tell you something. A
      really great time is going on over there,"
   he said to him.
   "Hey, come on over here. You have no reason to be afraid of
      me!"

And then truly [the caribou] went to where [Nanabush] was.
   "Ah, but there truly was a great time going on yesterday; they
   were killing one another. They were killing one another for no
   reason. They were shooting each other with arrows!"

Well, when he was telling this story, he was stringing his bow.
   "This was the very way they did it at the time."
He kept aiming there at the caribou's side.
   "This was just the way they did it,"
      he said to the caribou.
He shot him in the side.

   "Darn that Nanabush! Truly that was the very thing I thought he
   would do!"

Well then after he had killed [the caribou],
   he set to work stripping and cutting him up.

The caribou was incredibly fat;
  he went and hung up his fat.
He boiled all of it.
After he finished cooking it,
  he laid the meat out upon a sheet of birch bark.

And then this is what he said when he came to where the meat lay:
  "Wonder what part of the body I should take?"
    he said.
  "I think that I will take what I want to eat from the head.
      Perhaps that would not be proper and I would be laughed
      at by my relatives,"
    he thought.
  "I would be laughed at by my relatives."

  "Wonder if I should eat him from the back?
  No, perhaps I would be laughed at.
    'Maybe he shoved the big bull caribou forward while he ate
      him,'
    would be said of me by my relatives."

  "Wonder if it would be good for me to eat him from the side?"
    he thought.
  "No, indeed, maybe I would be laughed at.
    'He tried to push a great bull caribou sideways when he ate
      him,'
    would be said of me by my relatives."

While engaged in this talk,
  he laid the grease around the foot of the tree.
And then he heard the creaking of trees rubbing.
  "Truly someone is looking for me.
  Perhaps someone else wants to eat."
After slicing off a piece from the fatty part,
  he climbed up the tree.

And then he went and placed the fat.
  He put the fat in where [the tree] was creaking.
A great gust of wind came up;
  he was caught fast by the creaking tree.

Ah, then there he hung!
  For a long while after, he was hanging.

Now presently while looking toward the other end of the meadow,
  some wolves were running toward him!
And then he addressed them:
  "Don't you come this way!"

"Nanabush has no doubt slain something.
  Come on, let's run over there!"
It seemed as if they tried to race.
  They came running up to his place.
They saw his caribou.
  Right away they grabbed it from each other.

Ah, there was nothing for him to do,
  the caribou was entirely gone.
He addressed the wolves:
  "My little brothers!
Don't you come look around this tree."

"Come on, he's probably laid something out!"

And then truly they grabbed the grease from one another.
Now they were about to race away when—
  "Don't look in the sky, my little brothers!"
Well the wolves looked up:
  nothing but fat hanging there.

Well the wolves grabbed that away from one another.
After they had eaten it up,
  away they went racing.
He was let loose from the grip.
  It was over.
He was set free by the creaking tree;
  he climbed down.

Then he went in vain to see what he had left.
  Well there remained only the head.
Well he tried in vain to gnaw upon what he had left of the head.
  Well only the brain was left.
Well he had no way to get at it.

"Then I will take the form of a little snake,"
    he thought.

And then truly that was the form that he took,
    on account of the brain there.
While busy with the brain, he became a human being.
    Then he started off.
And then there were some horns.
    Ah, well what was he to do!

He bumped against a tree.
    "What sort of tree are you, my little brother?"

"Ah, I always stand deep in the forest."

"Oh, my little brother, you must be a tamarack."

"Yes,"
    he was told.

Again he bumped against a tree.
    "What kind of tree are you, my little brother?"

"I always stand on the mountain."

"Oh, you must be pine."

Again he bumped against a tree.
    "What kind of tree are you?"

"I always stand somewhere in sight of a lake."

"My little brother, you must be a birch."

Well he continued going along.
Again he bumped against a tree.
    "What kind of tree are you, little brother?"

"I always stand somewhere near a lake, a short way back in the
    forest."

"Oh, my little brother, you must be a poplar."

"Yes."

Again he continued going along.
Again he bumped against a tree.
　"What kind of tree are you, my little brother?"

"I always stand by the bank of a lake."

"Oh, my little brother, you must be a cedar."

"Yes,"
　he was told.

Well, he continued going along.
When he took another step,
　he walked into the water.
Well he waded out into the water;
　he began swimming.
He swam around.

Now presently he heard someone.

　"*Eeee,* there's a caribou swimming along!"
　　they said.
Well,
　"Ah, go after it!"
Well then they truly started after it.
Well he swam with all of his strength.

The sound of their voices grew nearer.
　"He is landing ahead of us!"
　　This is what they said.
He came to where he could touch bottom.
　He was soon there where he could touch bottom.
Well so it was a slippery bank where he ran out of the water.
　While running along, he slipped and fell upon a rock.

He burst open his head;
　the people looked.
Nanabush went running from there;

"Truly it was a caribou swimming along!
Truly it was a caribou swimming along!"
    said Nanabush, falling headlong, laughing.
He never stopped on his way to look back at them.
    He continued straight on his way.

TWO TUSCARORA LEGENDS

▴

BLAIR A. RUDES

INTRODUCTION

When first encountered by English explorers in the seventeenth century, the Tuscarora occupied most of the territory between the fall line and the Piedmont region of what is now the state of North Carolina. Following their defeat in a series of wars with the European colonists in the early eighteenth century, the majority of the Tuscarora moved northward. They finally settled in New York State and southern Ontario and were adopted by the League of the Iroquois, joining the original five nations (the Cayuga, Mohawk, Oneida, Onondaga, and Seneca). The adoption of the Tuscarora by the League was facilitated by their having much in common with the other five nations, including a cognate language, a kinship system based on matrilineal descent, and many of the same traditions and beliefs, as expressed in their legends.

With the rapid decline in the number of speakers of the Tuscarora language in this century, much of their oral tradition has been lost. Fortunately a sizable number of Tuscarora legends were written down at the turn of the century by the ethnographer and linguist J.N.B. Hewitt, himself a Tuscarora.[1] Recently the original Tuscarora versions of these legends, together with preliminary translations, were published by the Canadian Museum of Civilization.[2] Two of the stories that follow are taken from that work, with the permission of the museum, and are presented here in new translations.

The structure of Iroquoian legends—that is, the way in which major events are presented—is different from that with which most readers are familiar. The stories seem to begin abruptly, to change topics without warning, and to lack definitive conclusions. These features result from the style traditionally employed in oral presentation, as well as from the manner in which the legends were written down.

Seventeenth-century missionaries who visited the Huron, a related Iroquoian nation, noted that detailed knowledge of myths and traditions was the domain of certain male elders. During winter nights in the longhouse and at feasts, these men were called on to recite their stories; narrations of the longer legends could last several days.[3] This tradition continues to this day among the followers of the Longhouse religion, who gather once each year or so for three or more days to listen to a recitation of the credo of their religion, the Good Message, or Code of Handsome Lake.

Speakers organize the major events of Iroquoian legends into units comprising several sentences. Each unit describes a single episode, or set of closely related events, and begins with a series of adverbs that describe the time and place of the event (for example, *long ago, at that time, in the dense forest*). During a presentation the listener is alerted to the beginning and end of a unit by changes in both the speaker's intonation and the rhythm of his speech.[4] These individual episode-units connect only loosely to those that precede or follow. This organization of the narrative into semi-independent units, as well as the fact that the associated changes in intonation and rhythm cannot be adequately represented in the written version, is largely responsible for the feeling of abruptness in the transition from one paragraph to the next.

The traditional manner of relating legends had largely died out among the Tuscarora by the late nineteenth century, when Hewitt did his research. As a result, he did not record the legends under natural conditions. Rather, he elicited them out of context, writing them down by hand. Occasionally he misheard and mistranscribed a word or phrase and asked the speaker to repeat what had been said. Because of the lack of audience participation, as well as the interruptions to correct mishearings, the speakers' presentations were strained and the stories abridged. Thus, the written versions of many longer legends are incomplete.

Tuscarora legends were intended both to entertain and to pass on cultural beliefs and values from one generation of Tuscarora to the next, and they were frequently repeated. Therefore, most of the audience at any given recitation already knew many of the characters, concepts, and activities of the story, and the presenter could omit "unnecessary" details. This circumstance creates problems for the non-Tuscarora reader. Although it is impossible to explain here all of the foreknowledge a Tuscarora audience brings to the telling of these tales, a few pieces of information may prove helpful.

Both of the stories that follow involve characters whose roots go back to the *Iroquoian Cosmology,* the legend of creation.[5] It begins at a time when the universe was divided into two parts—one of light, called Skyland, where the forebears of humans dwelt, and one of darkness, which comprised the primordial sea. The story covers a complex series of events that result in a great chief's casting his wife out of Skyland. She falls toward the sea and is caught on the back of a giant turtle, which in turn becomes the earth.

In most versions of the legend, the woman is pregnant at the time she falls. After landing on the back of the turtle, she gives birth to twin sons (or, in other versions, to a girl who grows up and gives birth to twin sons) called by the Tuscarora Good Mind and Bad Mind.[6] Good Mind creates the sun, the moon, and the stars, the rivers and streams, the useful plants and animals of the earth, and humans. Bad Mind, in turn, trying to copy his brother's acts of creation, forms high mountains, steep cliffs, waterfalls, snakes, and other beings harmful to mankind. Bad Mind then forms two images of humans out of clay but errs while giving them life, and they become giants.

The acts of Bad Mind and the trouble his creations cause greatly disturb Good Mind, and eventually the two fight for control of the earth. After a long battle Good Mind drives Bad Mind and his evil creations to the bottom of the primordial sea, where Bad Mind rules. Ever since, whenever Good Mind is inattentive, Bad Mind and his creations visit the earth to cause trouble. Both the Giant Snake of the first story and the Stone Giants of the second are creations of Bad Mind.

It has been suggested that the dualism of good and evil, such as that found in the Iroquoian cosmology in the aspects of Good Mind and Bad Mind, is alien to Native American belief systems and that where it is found today, it results from the influence of Western civilization in general and the biblical story of Cain and Abel in particular.[7] However, when the Iroquoian cosmology was first described in 1623–24 by the Récollet missionary to the Huron,

Gabriel Sagard-Théodat, the twins representing good and evil (called Iouskeha, "the Good One," and Tawiscaron, "Flint," by the Huron) were a feature of the legend.[8] Although it is impossible to know the extent to which this missionary's own Christianity colored his description of the legend, it appears that Sagard-Théodat and his fellow Récollets had only marginal success in bringing Christianity to the Huron during their short stays and that it was not until later visits by Jesuit missionaries that the effects of Christianity and other aspects of Western civilization were strongly felt by this nation. Thus, the evidence suggests that the dualism is old and predates the introduction of Christianity.

A Tuscarora listening to these stories would also share the knowledge of *útkę?* (pronounced *oo-tgin*[*t*]). *Útkę?* is the Tuscarora word for a force or power that runs through everything created by Good Mind and Bad Mind. In great amounts it endows the possessor with supernatural characteristics or abilities, which may be either good or evil. For example, creatures such as the Great Snake and the Stone Giant possess malevolent *útkę?*, whereas the hunting charm in the story of the Stone Giant (the finger) exhibits beneficent *útkę?*.

The use of medicines in Tuscarora culture is also linked to the concept of *útkę?*. For example, in the story of the Stone Giant, two powerful medicines associated with *útkę?* are used: rose willow and the bark of the basswood tree. Rose willow *(Salix purpurea)* is a powerful purgative. Traditionally, small pieces of the bark or wood were pounded until they released a liquid. This liquid, when drunk, caused diarrhea, sweating, and vomiting and, it was believed, purged any evil *útkę?* from the body. The bark of the basswood tree *(Tilia americana)*, on the other hand, was used as a philter, a means of attracting a mate. Women would rub their genitalia with the bark in order to attract a man with whom they wanted to have sex.

The first of the two stories presented here will be familiar to many who have taken the boat ride under Niagara Falls. It is a Tuscarora version of the legend of the Maid of the Mist. The legend is shared by all the nations of the League of the Iroquois, and though it is a Seneca version that one hears when visiting Niagara Falls, a Mohawk version was recently transformed into a ballet at the Arts in Education Institute of Western New York.[9]

In the Mohawk and Seneca versions the legend begins with the kidnapping of an Iroquois maiden by a giant serpent. The Thunders fight with the serpent for the maiden's freedom and slay the monster with lightning bolts. As the dying serpent writhes, he creates the great gorge through which the Niagara River flows. The serpent's body finally comes to rest across the river and forms the brink of the falls. The Tuscarora version picks up the story at a later point.

The second story presented here is one of many legends told by the Iroquois, as well as by some of their neighbors, such as the Shawnee, about a race of giants that plagued mankind in prehistoric times. Although the Tuscarora consider these giants to be malicious cannibals, they also see them as rather lumbering, dim-witted, and easily fooled. The tricks that humans often play on the Stone Giants to thwart their actions add humor to the legends about this race.

NOTES

1. J.N.B. Hewitt, "The Sun Myth and the Tree of Language of the Iroquois," *American Anthropologist* 5 (old series; 1892): 61–62; *Iroquoian Cosmology,* pt. 1, The Twenty-first Annual Report of the Bureau of American Ethnology (Washington, D.C.: U.S. Government Printing Office, 1903); and *Iroquoian Cosmology,* pt. 2, The Forty-third Annual Report of the Bureau of American Ethnology (Washington, D.C.: U.S. Government Printing Office, 1928).

2. Blair A. Rudes and Dorothy Crouse, *The Tuscarora Legacy of J.N.B. Hewitt: Materials for the Study of the Tuscarora Language and Culture,* Canadian Ethnology Service, Mercury Series Paper no. 108 (Ottawa: Canadian Museum of Civilization, 1987).

3. Bruce Graham Trigger, *The Huron: Farmers of the North* (New York: Holt, Rinehart and Winston, 1969).

4. Wallace L. Chafe, *Differences Between Colloquial and Ritual Seneca, or How Oral Literature Is Literary,* in Reports from the Survey of California and Other Indian Languages, vol. 1, ed. Alice Schlichter, Wallace L. Chafe, and Leanne Hinton (Berkeley: University of California Department of Linguistics, 1981).

5. Hewitt, *Iroquoian Cosmology,* pt. 1 and 2.

6. Rudes and Crouse, *The Tuscarora Legacy of J.N.B. Hewitt.*

7. See, for example, the comments regarding Mesoamerican belief systems in Dennis Tedlock, *The Spoken Word and the Work of Interpretation* (Philadelphia: University of Pennsylvania Press, 1983).

8. Elisabeth Tooker, *An Ethnography of Huron Indians, 1615–1649* (Syracuse, N.Y.: Syracuse University Press, 1991).

9. Allan Jamieson and Jolene Rickard, "Maid of the Mist," *Turtle Quarterly* (Spring-Summer 1992): 41–46.

In a large village lived a young girl with her elderly mother. The girl was deathly ill, and because of this none of the eligible males in the village had taken her as his wife. For a long time these two lived thus together.

One day the old woman said to her daughter, "I'm going to another village to visit and will be gone for some time. I want you to fasten the door shut tight. Don't let anyone in until I get back." "OK," said the young girl, and the mother left on her trip.

Later, when everyone in the village was asleep, someone came to the door and knocked to get in. The young girl was woken by the noise and called out, "What do you want?" The intruder replied, "I want you to open the door for me. I have been thinking of you." He sounded so sincere and gentle that she ignored her mother's orders and opened the door for him. The girl was surprised to see how handsome he was. Never had she seen anyone so good-looking, or so well behaved.

The man was unattached and asked her to marry him. She consented, and the two of them then slept together. While they lay together, she noticed that he wore a necklace of silver-white clamshells that increased in size, from small ones in the front to larger ones where the necklace reached his shoulders.

When the man woke up, he told her that he would be returning home. He then removed one of the larger clamshells from his shoulder and gave it to her, saying, "Remember me by this." Realizing he was leaving her, the young girl asked, "Will you be coming back?" He answered, "No." When he saw how this upset her, however, he said, "Someday I will come back to visit you." But he said this only so she would not forget him.

The next morning her mother returned. When she entered the house, she became suspicious and asked her daughter, "Who was here?" The girl answered truthfully, "It was a young man, and he was more handsome than any man I have ever seen." The girl went and got the clamshell, which she had wrapped and put away. She and her mother examined it thoroughly and were startled to find that it was not made of silver but was instead a body scale, like that of a snake or fish, and was about as big around as the areola of one's nipple. The old woman wept for her daughter and said, "Because of your illness, you were deceived. It was not a man you married but a giant snake."

The young girl continued to live with her mother while her stomach grew bigger; each day she slept more and more. When she had become very large, all she would do was lie in the sun and sleep. One day her mother came upon the girl sleeping in a hollow log and saw a mass of little snakes appear next to her. However, as soon as the snakes saw the old woman, they ran back into the body of the young girl. The mother tried for a long time to catch another glimpse of the snakes and was finally rewarded by seeing the little *útkę?* beings again. The old woman then told her daughter about the hundreds of snakes living in her stomach. This news greatly upset the young girl, and she fled to escape her mother's words. She ran to a nearby river that possessed a great waterfall, threw herself over the edge where the current was swiftest, and was carried over the falls.

As her body crashed down, the Thunders reached out and caught her and halted her fall. There were four Thunders, three young males and the fourth a much older man, who made their home behind the waterfall. They took the young girl into their dwelling, and the old man started administering to her a medicine that caused the great slithering mass of snakes to come out of her. The elder Thunder explained to the girl, "These snakes are our food." The Thunders proceeded to boil the snakes and ate up every last one of them. They continued to give the girl the medicine until she was fully recovered.

She had been with the Thunders for about a year when she met another man with whom she slept. This man was also a Thunder, and before long she was again pregnant. The elder Thunder then told the Thunder who was responsible, "You must return the girl to her mother so she can take care of her during her pregnancy." And the younger Thunder took her home. He told her that he must return to the other Thunders and would never see her again. He also explained to her that when the baby was born, it would be a boy and that the boy would want to crawl all over the place. But, he warned her, "You must not let him play with other children because if he ever gets mad, he will make lightning. Also, when the boy grows older, the Thunders will call to him, and when this happens, you must keep him indoors with the doors securely fastened shut."

The time came when the boy wanted to go outside and make friends with other children. But his mother kept him in the house even though he cried and cried because he wanted to go outside so much.

One day after the boy had grown into a young man, the mother left the house and forgot to secure the door behind her. The boy, seeing his opportunity, quickly ran out of the house. From out of the sky he heard the Thunders speak to him, and he went to them. As he journeyed toward them, the Thunders continued to speak.

Long before the white man arrived, Indians shared the land with another race, the man-eating Stone Giants. One of the frequently told stories about these times concerns a man and his wife who had gone hunting, taking with them their infant, which the mother carried in a cradleboard on her back.

They had journeyed for about three nights when they arrived at the hunting lodge that the husband had built deep in the forest. Every day the husband would go out to kill some game. On one such day the wife thought to herself, "I should do some wash," and so she went to a nearby river. To free herself to work, she leaned the cradleboard holding her child up against a tree. The woman did her work quickly and was soon finished. As she turned to head back to the lodge, she saw that a Stone Giant had picked up the cradleboard and was staring intently at her child. The woman had but one thought: "I must get my child back." As she headed to where the Stone Giant was standing, an idea came to her. She approached the Stone Giant and greeted him, saying, "Hello, Father."

The Stone Giant replied, "Whatever happened to you, my child?" She replied, "One day when we had gone for a walk together, you stopped to relieve yourself by a hollow log, and I hung back to play. When you finished, you continued on your walk until you were out of my sight, and we were separated." This confused the giant. The woman added, "And that's your grandchild you've got there." This made the Stone Giant very happy, and he said, "It is good that we have found one another again, Daughter. We should all be together—you, me, and my grandchild—don't you think? However, since I see that your husband is not here now, I will leave and return tomorrow, for I want us to meet one another." Then the Stone Giant left.

When the woman's husband returned, she told him about the Stone Giant and what had happened. The man said, "We've got to run away from here right now." "No," she said, "we can't do that. In three days' time the Stone Giant will come back, and I have to make up another lie to tell him so that then we can escape." This convinced the husband to stay. However, the next day, when the husband heard branches breaking in the nearby woods, he almost abandoned camp. When she saw that her husband remained, the woman showed him how the Stone Giant would greet him by clasping his arms in an embrace and saying, "Hello, my son-in-law."

And so the Stone Giant embraced the hunter. The Stone Giant

was so tall that the man was lifted off the ground. Then the Stone Giant told the man, "This woman is my daughter, and we have promised that we will all live together. But we will have to build an addition on your lodge, for it's too small for me." Then the Stone Giant snapped off a huge pole from a tree and said, "I will bring back trees this size." The Stone Giant proceeded to bring back enormous trees, which he stacked, and used to build an addition to the lodge. He was so strong that these huge trees were like mere branches to him. When they had finished enlarging the lodge, the Stone Giant took a great tree and split it, using the two halves to fashion a bed for himself.

Then the Stone Giant said to the man, "I will give you one of my living fingers for hunting. To use it, hold it up on your hand and ask it to locate for you the place where the greatest number of whatever kind of game you want can be found. The finger will immediately obey your wish and point to the spot."

A short time later the man went out hunting. Everything went as the Stone Giant had promised, and soon he had killed more than enough deer. This was because the finger was able to stop animals in their tracks just as they thought to themselves, "I can escape this hunter," and bring them together in one spot. Only then did the hunter stand up and shoot. The quantity of game he killed was more than the hunter could handle, so the Stone Giant carried the bodies back to the lodge. There he piled all the carcasses crisscrossed on top of one another. The hunter skinned them and gave the Stone Giant some of the meat to eat. Though of great size, the Stone Giant limited what he ate to the same amount as the humans.

Thus they all lived together until one day the Stone Giant said, "Today at noon my spouse will arrive. You two must help me, or else she will kill us." The Stone Giant explained to them what they should do. He told the husband to make a wad of basswood bark about the size of a human leg. "When she arrives, I will fight her and throw her to the ground. Then you must hit her as hard as you can in the crotch with the wad of basswood bark."

At noon they all heard a great snapping of branches in the forest, and the Stone Giant said to the humans, "You two stand aside and watch while I fight my wife." When Stone Giant's wife arrived in the camp, she said to her husband, "My, but you look well fed. I, however, am starved. I guess I'll eat this human you've made friends with." "Leave her alone!" said the Stone Giant; "she's my daughter." The two Stone Giants then began to fight. They butted their heads against each other's in what was a very close contest, for the two were of nearly the same strength. Each time the Stone Giant succeeded in throwing his wife to the ground, the hunter would strike her in the crotch with the wad of basswood bark. And each time she was struck, the female Stone Giant would get back up and continue the fight. Finally the medicine of the basswood bark took effect, and the stone outer layer of the female Stone Giant split in two. Pieces of the coat fell from her body, and she became violently sick and died. The living finger that the Stone Giant had given the hunter had attached itself to the female Stone Giant's crotch. Most of her stone covering remained attached to her, the portions covering the arm and leg remaining unbroken. Around her neck, however, the covering was greatly splintered, and her head could be neither raised nor turned. Only the body below the neck could be moved.

Stone Giants normally ate only raw meat. However, this Stone Giant knew that if he and his daughter were going to live together, he would have to learn human ways. Therefore, he said to his daughter, "I must eat the same cooked food as you." So she made them a meal, cooking the food in a large kettle so there would be enough for the Stone Giant. When the food was ready, she dished out a huge plate for the Stone Giant as well as some for herself and her husband. No sooner had the Stone Giant emptied his plate than he threw up everything he had eaten and said, "I just can't get used to this stuff." The husband asked him, "Would it help if I give you something that will make you vomit again?" and the Stone Giant said, "Yes." So the man prepared a medicine by breaking off pieces of a medicine stick made of rose willow. He mashed up the pieces and made a vile, greenish, scummy liquid. This he gave to the Stone Giant to drink. After the Stone Giant had drunk about half of the medicine, he grew pale and nauseous and vomited once more. Mixed in with his vomit were all kinds of bugs and crawling things, for the medicine had knocked the evil out of him. Again he drank of the potion and vomited up more of the vile matter. Finally the Stone Giant stopped vomiting and was rid of the evil that had possessed him. Then the outer layer of stone that covered his great body began to loosen and crumble into sand, and he was left naked.

The man went to his aid and made clothes for him to wear. First he took a bear hide and split it in two. He wrapped half of the hide around the giant and tied it over his chest. Then he made leggings and moccasins for him, as well as a coat from the other half of the hide. He also made him a fearsome hat from the finer fur of the bear. Out of the remaining bearskin he made rawhide strips that were many arm spans in length.

Then the man and the Stone Giant went out hunting together and used the finger to help them. Each day they would kill about six or seven animals, which the Stone Giant tied together with the raw-hide strips and dragged back to their hunting lodge. There the hunter skinned the deer and made a huge pile of the carcasses. Much of what they killed they ate then and there. What they didn't eat, along with the skins, they dried for later use. They tied the meat like strings of beads or wampum and set it out to dry in batches of three or fewer. The man then made braids of the dried animals' hides, intertwining over a hundred of the skins for each braid. When this was done, they left their hunting camp and returned home, the Stone Giant carrying the fruits of the hunt fastened to his back. On their way back the Stone Giant said to the man, "We must stay together, for your wife is my daughter." (The Stone Giant really wanted this and was now able to eat cooked food because of the medicine he had taken.) However, the Stone Giant added, "I do not want to live in the village. We must build our home outside of it so that no one will notice me."

So a ways from the village, near the forest, they built their home. The villagers considered them to be witches and would come out to visit them to learn their ways. The husband and wife would dance for the visitors and play ballgames for them to watch. All this time the Stone Giant remained out of sight and, thus, was not credited with the witchcraft. The people of the village, however, knew of his presence and none of the women there would get married, for each desired to have the Stone Giant for herself.

THE IROQUOIAN
THANKSGIVING ADDRESS

▲

MICHAEL K. FOSTER

INTRODUCTION

Whenever Longhouse Iroquois meet as a group, whether it be to conduct a ceremony or take up some purely secular business, one of the men present rises to deliver a speech, which in Cayuga, one of the Northern Iroquoian languages, is called Kanǫ'hǫnyǫhk (ganō'hōnyŏʰk). Grammatically the word is an imperative that translates as "Let it be used for greeting and thanking!" It contains a verb root, -nǫhǫnyǫ-, whose meaning is broader than that of the English "to greet" or "to thank" and in fact embraces both senses. The unity of the acts of greeting and thanking in the Northern Iroquoian languages can be seen in the overlapping elements of the everyday vocative forms nya·wę' skę'·nǫ? (nyaawæ̃' sgæ̃æ̃'nō?), "hello," and nya·węh, "thank you." In the Iroquois view the coming together of a group of people in a cooperative enterprise is sufficient reason to share in mutual rejoicing. It may also be noted that in general the Iroquois make a good deal more of event openings than of event closings.[1]

The Kanǫ'hǫnyǫhk is not a memorized speech of set length. For small secular gatherings short versions lasting only a few minutes are usually given. At the beginning of ceremonies in the longhouse, however, versions of thirty or forty minutes are common. Yet Longhouse Iroquois consider all these versions to be equivalent, because the ground covered in long and brief versions is fundamentally the same, although the points may be treated schematically or developed at considerable length. Moreover, the language of the speeches is drawn from a stock of familiar, tirelessly repeated formulas, such as "He who in the sky dwells" (a reference to the Creator) and "The people who remain on the earth" (a reference to the assembled group). The flexibility of the oral composition process comes from the ways in which the formulas are combined to produce a familiar arrangement of ideas.[2]

The speaker begins by mentioning the people who have "brought their minds together as one" on the particular occasion: they are expected to exchange greetings before taking up any other business. To conclude this first part of the speech, he utters an expression built, as the name of the speech is, on the verb root *-nǫhǫnyǫ-*, which best translates as "We now greet one another." Next the speaker mentions the earth and the things contained in it that have been provided by the Creator for the people's benefit. At the end of this section, he again utters an expression based on the verb root *-nǫhǫnyǫ-*, best translated here as "We now give thanks for it [the earth]." Following a prescribed pattern, he then "carries his words upward" to mention certain spirit forces in the sky: the Thunderers, the Sun, the Moon, the Stars, and the Wind. For each of these, he again utters the group's collective thanksgiving, but now directly addressed to the spirit force in question. Next he takes up more ethereal forces, the Four Beings and Handsome Lake, explained at greater length below, coming finally to the Creator himself, who is said to live on the "other side of the sky."

In shorter versions the spirit forces on the earth—bodies of water, medicinal plants, "hanging fruit," trees, animals, birds, and the Three Sisters (corn, beans, and squash)—are covered in a single section of the speech; in longer versions each of these is accorded a separate section. The spirit forces in the sky are treated in separate sections in all but the briefest versions of the speech, where some grouping may occur. The same structure that underlies the Kanǫ'hǫnyǫhk underlies several other Longhouse speech events with varying purposes and delivered in different spoken styles.[3]

The text presented in the translation below is of medium length (twenty-two minutes). It could be given at the beginning of a Longhouse ceremony but would more likely be the kind of version given at a secular gathering. It groups all the items on earth into one large section but has separate sections for the Thunderers, the Sun, the Moon, and the Stars. It combines the Four Beings and Handsome

Lake in one section and has a separate section for the Creator. Sections are marked by the opening formula "And now we shall speak about another thing" and the closing formula "And so our minds shall be." Following the utterance of the closing formula, the men present signify their affirmation of the speaker's message with the term *yę·h* (y ǽǽh). If the speech is given in the longhouse, the men in the moiety opposite that of the speaker utter this term.

The speaking styles for the Kanǫ'hǫnyǫhk and the speech events related to it have been defined for Seneca and Cayuga versions.[4] Among other things, the lines, which are set in paragraph form and numbered, have a distinct intonational contour for each type. These lines are units of discourse that may or may not coincide with grammatically complete sentences in Cayuga. They may translate into English as parts of sentences, whole sentences, or groups of sentences.

The original recording on which the translation is based was made in 1970 at the Six Nations Reserve in southern Ontario, named for remnants of the Five Nations Iroquois (Mohawk, Oneida, Onondaga, Cayuga, and Seneca) plus some adopted Tuscaroras who chose to migrate to western New York State and southern Ontario late in the eighteenth century. About one quarter of the fifteen thousand residents of the reserve follow the traditional, or Longhouse, way today; the remaining population is divided among various Christian sects. The principal languages of the Longhouse community are Cayuga and Onondaga. Mohawk is spoken in the longhouse on occasion, although on this reserve it is associated more with the Christian community. Oneida and Seneca, which are spoken on other reserves, are seldom heard at Six Nations, and Tuscarora is moribund there.

The speaker who supplied the present Cayuga version of the Thanksgiving Address was Howard Sky (1900–1971), or Cloudy-on-Both-Sides, a member of the Wolf clan and head "faithkeeper" (longhouse official) of the Wolf moiety at the Onondaga Longhouse, one of four longhouses located on the reserve.[5] A Cayuga by birth, Mr. Sky also knew Onondaga and some Seneca. He is best remembered as a "prompter," a man who did not speak often for his moiety in the longhouse but who served as a master of ceremonies. Such men usually sit behind the front bench in the longhouse, where the speakers sit, and can often be seen whispering instructions to the more active members during ceremonies. The present version was not recorded during an actual ceremony, as the use of recording or photographic devices in the longhouse is prohibited. Rather, it was recorded in a motel room in Brantford, Ontario, a town near the reserve. I believe that this recording "out of context" in no way affected the substance or quality of the performance; Mr. Sky would have given the same speech in the longhouse had he been asked to do so. I initially transcribed and translated the speech with the help of Mr. Sky himself, and was later helped by my long-time linguistic collaborator Alta Doxtador in further refining it.

Certain points within the text require comment. In line 7, the Iroquois Confederacy is denoted by a sequence of two circumlocutions that translate as "They who are in the relationship of elder to younger brothers" and "They who are in the relationship of fathers to sons." The first term refers to the members of the tribal moieties that sit on "opposite sides of the fire" in the Confederacy council, the Three Brothers (the Mohawk, Onondaga, and Seneca) on one side and the Four Brothers (the Oneida and Cayuga along with assorted adopted nations) on the other. The second term refers to the council as a whole.[6] The two terms often occur in sequence. The Onondaga, who play a mediating role in Confederacy council proceedings, are referred to ceremonially by the circumlocution the Name Bearers.

Lines 14–16 refer to the Maple Festival, one of the calendrical ceremonies that is scheduled in the spring, when the sap begins to flow. Lines 17–20 allude to the Strawberry Festival, another calendrical ceremony, and to the fact that at the time of the festival two hundred years ago, the Seneca prophet Handsome Lake began to have his visions of a renewed social order. The Four Sacred Rites mentioned in line 26 are the Drum Dance, the Great Feather Dance, the Men's Personal Chants, and the Bowl (or Peach Stone) Game; these are the main events at the Green Corn Ceremony, held at the height of the growing season, in August or September, as well as at the Midwinter Festival, held in January.[7] The latter event is alluded to in line 33.

The Thunderers are anthropomorphic beings who are responsible not only for replenishing natural bodies of ʻwater but for keeping certain vaguely defined but very powerful monsters underground. Unlike the Thunderbird of the Plains and the Northwest Coast, the Iroquois Thunderers do not have the specific form of a bird, but their role in controlling creatures of the underworld links them to a mythological theme of wide distribution in North America and beyond.

With regard to the duties of the stars mentioned in the section on "The Stars," some speakers explicitly acknowledge that people today have lost the knowledge of star lore the Iroquois are reputed to have once had.[8]

The Four Beings referred to in line 72 are the most powerful of the Creator's special "helpers": they act as intercessors between human beings and the Creator. The Seneca prophet Handsome Lake, also mentioned in this section, lived through the Revolutionary period and into the nineteenth century.[9] Over a number of years, his visions were codified into a set of moral precepts known as the Good Message, which guide the Longhouse Iroquois in their behavior today and have been handed down as oral tradition through a succession of specially qualified "preachers."[10] The Good Message is still preached in the fall at many of the Iroquois longhouses in Canada and the United States.

The epilogue is marked by a change of voice, to a more conversational style. Speakers usually offer a ritual apology for any errors of omission or commission at this point and invite others present to make corrections. Mr. Sky simply says, "It fell to me to make the speech you have been listening to." In fact, speakers have variable reputations within the community for eloquence and rate their own and others' abilities quite frankly in private.[11] The ability to speak effectively in the longhouse is regarded as a special gift from the Creator.

Pronunciation Guide

Cayuga words are written first in a standard phonemic form as used by linguists. To the right, in parentheses, the first occurrence of each word has been retranscribed phonetically as a guide to pronunciation.

a is pronounced like the *a* in *father*.

õ is pronounced like the *on* in the French *bon*, "good."

æ is pronounced like the *en* in the French *bien*, "well."

ʰ indicates weak aspiration.

ʔ is the glottal stop. It is a significant sound in Cayuga, but not in English, although it can be heard as a substitution for the *tt* in the Cockney pronunciation of *bottle*.

ʹ marks word stress, which occurs on the vowel to the left.

A doubled vowel indicates vowel length.

NOTES

1. Michael K. Foster, "Iroquois Interaction in Historical Perspective," in *Native North American Interaction Patterns,* ed. Regna Darnell and Michael K. Foster, Canadian Ethnology Service, Mercury Series Paper no. 112 (Ottawa: Canadian Museum of Civilization, 1988), 22 ff.

2. Michael K. Foster, *From the Earth to Beyond the Sky: An Ethnographic Approach to Four Longhouse Iroquois Speech Events,* Ethnology Division, Mercury Series Paper no. 20 (Ottawa: National Museum of Man, 1974).

3. For transcribed and translated original-language versions of the Kanǫhǫnyǫhk and some of the speech genres related to it, see Wallace L. Chafe, *Seneca Thanksgiving Rituals,* Smithsonian Institution, Bureau of American Ethnology Bulletin no. 183 (Washington, D.C., 1961) and Foster, *From the Earth to Beyond the Sky* and "The Cayuga Kanō'hōnyōk (Thanksgiving Address)," in *Northern Iroquoian Texts,* ed. Marianne Mithun and Hanni Woodbury, International Journal of American Linguistics, Native American Texts Series, Monograph no. 4 (Chicago: University of Chicago Press, 1980), 9–25. In *From the Earth to Beyond the Sky,* I relate these genres to the context of Longhouse ceremonialism generally.

4. The Seneca styles have been defined by Chafe in *Seneca Thanksgiving Rituals,* 146–48; the Cayuga versions by Foster in *From the Earth to Beyond the Sky,* 188–99.

5. William N. Fenton, "Howard Sky, 1900–1971: Cayuga Faith-Keeper, Gentleman, and Interpreter of Iroquois Culture," *American Anthropologist* 74 (1972): 758–62, and Michael K. Foster, "The Obsequies for Howard Sky, or Cloudy-on-Both-Sides," *American Anthropologist* 74 (1972): 762–63.

6. See Hanni Woodbury et al., *Concerning the League: the Iroquois League Tradition as Dictated in Onondaga by John Arthur Gibson,* Algonquian and Iroquoian Linguistics Memoir no. 9 (Winnipeg: University of Manitoba, 1992), xvi–xvii.

7. See Annemarie Anrod Shimony, *Conservatism Among the Iroquois at the Six Nations Reserve,* Yale University Publications in Anthropology, vol. 65 (New Haven, Conn.: Yale University Press, 1961), 140–91. Reprinted with a new introduction: Syracuse University Press, 1994.

8. William N. Fenton, "This Island, the World on the Turtle's Back," *Journal of American Folklore* 75 (1962): 288.

9. See Anthony F. C. Wallace, *The Death and Rebirth of the Seneca* (New York: Knopf, 1970).

10. See Arthur C. Parker, *The Code of Handsome Lake, the Seneca Prophet,* New York State Museum Bulletin no. 163 (Albany, N.Y., 1913).

11. Foster, *From the Earth to Beyond the Sky,* 30–34.

KANQ'HQNYQHK

PROLOGUE: THE PEOPLE

[1] And now today, on this our day,

[2] We see the light of another dawn spreading over the earth.

[3] He who in the sky dwells gave us this kind of light to make us happy.

[4] Now we have entered the council house. He decided, "This is where the people will gather, those who follow my way."

[5] The first thing we always do when we come together is to greet one another.

[6] Today a number of people have arrived at the place our forefathers established long ago.

[7] It is the place where the tribes comprising the Iroquois Confederacy still meet, and where the Onondaga meet separately.

[8] So let us now join our minds together as one and greet one another in the prescribed way. And so our minds shall be.

RESPONSE: *Yę·h*

THE EARTH

[9] And now we shall speak about another thing: the place from which our voices go forth.

[10] First we mention the earth, the island he created for the Indians.

[11] He decided, "People will live in different settlements here and there from one generation to the next."

[12] He provided everything that is on the earth, the one we call our Mother.

[13] For he planted all the things that grow here. When it turns warm again and the planted things begin to grow, the people who remain on the earth are contented in their minds.

[14] The first thing we see every year is the sap flowing from a certain tree. We call it the maple, and it is the leading tree in the forest.

[15] He decided, "People will come together and give thanks when they see the sap flowing, the people who still remain."

[16] And it has come to pass. At the prescribed time we did come together and thanked him, he who in the sky dwells, our Creator.

[17] And now another thing. He decided, "There will be berries hanging close to the earth. It starts with the strawberry." The

time of the strawberry is important, because that is when our Creator decided to send his word back to the people remaining on the earth.

[18] At that time long ago our Creator's word, the word we still understand, alighted on the earth.

[19] It is guiding us today, and it will continue to do so all our days. For our Creator's word still comes to us from the time it first alighted, the time when the strawberries were beginning to ripen.

[20] Indeed we saw them again at the prescribed time this year, and this brought us together in a gathering to rejoice and to thank our Creator for what he did so many years ago.

[21] And now another thing he left with us. He decided that people should have food.

[22] "They will make it their business, those who remain on the earth, to plant crops. And at a certain time it will happen:

[23] "They will place the seeds underground." That is what he gave the people for food, he who in the sky dwells.

[24] These are the life-giving plants: corn, beans, and squash—native squash. He gave us these plants for food. He decided, "These will strengthen the breath of those who remain on the earth.

[25] "They will bring contentment to the people." And he also decided that when the people see the food crops again, they should come together and give thanks to him who in the sky dwells. They should address the Creator with the Four Sacred Rites, which he provided expressly for this purpose, he who in the sky dwells. "They will do this when they see the food crops growing again."

[26] And indeed it took place. At the prescribed time we came together and thanked him, he who in the sky dwells. It was the gathering he had expressly provided for this purpose: it consists of the Four Sacred Rites, which he brought to us from his world. And it continues even to today. So let us again bring our minds together as one and express our gratitude.

[27] He also provided medicinal plants. He decided, "Whenever the need arises and people are sick, medicines can be used to help them prolong their days."

[28] And indeed they are still growing. When the wind turns warm, we always see them. It is all coming to pass as he planned it, he who in the sky dwells.

[29] Also among the things he created are creeks, rivers, and springs and the various larger bodies of water here and there,

some of them very large. He decided, "These will bring strength to the earth and contentment to the people who remain on the earth."

[30] And this also he decided, "There will be fish moving about in the water, and people will subsist on them and obtain their happiness from them. Their breath will be strengthened by them." And it is still going on.

[31] He also created many kinds of wild animals, and he determined that they would benefit the people remaining on the earth.

[32] Among the animals is the deer, which is the leader of the wild animals.

[33] He decided, "Venison will be used to flavor the soup the people make when the Four Sacred Rites are celebrated. It will make the soup taste good. So the warriors should go out and bring a deer down for this purpose."

[34] We still see the wild animals from time to time approaching our settlements as they roam about.

[35] Different wild animals keep returning, and the breath of the people is strengthened by them.

[36] All of these things are contained by the earth, our Mother, as we call her, that which supports our feet.

[37] And now, for the many things that she holds, let us join our minds together as one and give thanks for the earth, our Mother, as we call her, that which supports our feet. And so our minds shall be.

RESPONSE: *Yę·h*

THE THUNDERERS

[38] And now we shall speak about another thing: the time when he completed the island for the people born here.

[39] When he made the island for the people to dwell on, he created such a vast area that he thought the people might need some helpers.

[40] The first ones he appointed were those that come from the west, our Grandfathers, as we call them.

[41] They are the Thunderers, and we call them our Grandfathers.

[42] He gave them the power to carry water around with them. They have a responsibility to replenish the springs, the creeks, the rivers, and the larger bodies of water, the lakes.

[43] They supply all of the fresh water, our Grandfathers who come from the west.

[44] And this we also understand: when he made the island for us, there were certain creatures roaming about that he did not create, and he saw that they could bring harm to the people born on the earth.

[45] And this too became a responsibility of our Grandfathers, who come from the west. Our Creator forced the creatures underground and appointed the Thunderers to keep them there so that they would never emerge again to threaten the people who remain on the earth.

[46] And up to the present time they are still carrying out the duties he assigned them, he who in the sky dwells.

[47] Truly, they are carrying out all their duties, and they too bring us happiness. So let us join our minds together as one and thank the ones we call our Grandfathers, those who come from the west. And so our minds shall be.

RESPONSE: *Yę·h*

THE SUN

[48] And now we shall speak about another thing.

[49] He decided, "Light will shine over the creation at certain times as the people remaining on the earth move about. People will do what they have to do for their well-being during these times." A great deal depends on the light, and so he appointed him, the Sun, our Elder Brother, as we call him.

[50] He gave him the power to provide light and to warm the circulating winds so that all the planted things would thrive and benefit the people remaining on the earth.

[51] And up to the present time we have been obtaining our happiness from there. It is all coming to pass as it was planned for our Elder Brother, the Sun.

[52] So let those of us who have gathered join our minds together as one and thank him in the prescribed way, the Sun who gives us light. And so our minds shall be.

RESPONSE: *Yę·h*

THE MOON

[53] And now we shall speak about another thing he made, he who in the sky dwells.

[54] He decided, "At a certain time darkness will descend upon the earth.

[55] "And at this time the people remaining on the earth will rest.

[56] "They will be refreshed at daybreak, when they will again travel about over the creation." So diligently he set about it: he appointed the Moon, our Grandmother, as we call her.

[57] He gave her certain responsibilities to last as long as the earth lasts:

[58] She regulates the times our children are born.

[59] And he also decided, "The Moon will have phases, and people will tell time by her, the people remaining on the earth."

[60] We are still obtaining happiness from her, those of us who have gathered here today. So let it be our thought that we now join our minds together as one in the prescribed manner and thank the Moon, our Grandmother. And so our minds shall be.

RESPONSE: *Yę·h*

THE STARS

[61] And now we shall speak about another thing.

[62] When darkness descends on the earth, there are stars arrayed against the sky.

[63] And we continue to see them. The way we understand it—the way we were told—they are there to assist the people who remain on the earth.

[64] Long ago people understood what the duties of the stars were.

[65] For he had assigned certain duties to them, the stars arrayed against the sky, the ones we call our Grandfathers.

[66] We still owe our happiness to them. So let it be our thought that we now thank them in the prescribed way, the stars arrayed against the sky. And so our minds shall be.

RESPONSE: *Yę·h*

THE FOUR BEINGS AND HANDSOME LAKE

[67] And now we shall speak about another thing.

[68] As we understand it, the Sun is on this side of the sky,

[69] And on the other side there is another world where he exists, he who in the sky dwells, our Creator.

[70] After he had completed the earth, he kept close watch over the activities of the people left on the earth.

[71] He listened intently to what was on the people's minds, those who remained on the earth.

[72] And this is what he did: he appointed the Four Beings to protect us.

[73] That is where Our Protectors come from, the world of our Creator.

[74] Every day and every night they look after our welfare.

[75] They have the power to keep us from going astray in our thoughts and in our deliberations.

[76] Up to the present time what we have been receiving from him makes us happy. Now in days gone by he had another matter to consider, he who in the sky dwells.

[77] He thought, "I will send my word down for the people to hear, the people who remain on the earth."

[78] He thought about what he would do. He appointed a certain man to work with the Four Beings, Our Protectors. That is how he determined it, he who in the sky dwells, our Creator.

[79] So he appointed Handsome Lake and decided on a mission for him.

[80] And in those days Handsome Lake fulfilled his mission.

[81] Now every year when the strawberries begin to ripen, we come together to celebrate the time when our Creator's word alighted on the earth.

[82] Again this year at berry time the people gathered to express their gratitude that the way to the sky world is always open to them—for no one is excluded. There is a place for all of us, when we have used up the days allotted to us.

[83] It is from Handsome Lake that we have learned our Creator's plan.

[84] So now we group them together, the Four Beings and Handsome Lake, and we join our minds as one and thank them in the prescribed way. And so our minds shall be.

RESPONSE: Υ̧ǫ·h

THE CREATOR

[85] And now we shall speak about another thing:

[86] The person of our Creator.

[87] He decided, "Beyond the sky lies another world, a world of everlasting life, and this is where people go when they have used up the days allotted to them on the earth."

[88] And this we understand: whoever follows the way of our Creator will remain in happiness in that world forever.

[89] Every day and every night we are receiving his concern and his love.

[90] He shows us the way to our happiness. We shall not want for

anything. Up to the present time all our happiness comes from him, from our Creator himself.

[91] And this is why the people have gathered here today. So let us now join our minds together as one and thank our Creator in the prescribed way. And so our minds shall be.

RESPONSE: *Y̨ę·h*

EPILOGUE

[92] Up to now we have spoken as with one voice.

[93] We have touched on what he gave us to keep our minds clear, and we have thanked him. This is where we have ended up. And so our minds shall be.

[94] There are people present with duties to perform for the one who in the sky dwells. These are the faithkeepers, who will attend to the ceremonies that caused us to come together today. It fell to me to make the speech you have been listening to. And that is it.

TALES OF THE
DELAWARE TRICKSTER

▲

JOHN BIERHORST

INTRODUCTION

The Delaware, or Lenape, who once inhabited what are now the New York and Philadelphia metropolitan areas, have been regarded by anthropologists and historians as a "classic" North American people. This is an indirect way of saying that the Delaware participated in wars of the colonial period and that Euro-American historical records are filled with Delaware references. But it also alludes to the "classic" ethnographies prepared by the eighteenth-century Moravian missionaries David Zeisberger and John Heckewelder and to the Delaware notices published by no less a scholar than Thomas Jefferson.[1]

In more recent years and continuing into the present, knowledge of Delaware religion, language, material culture, and archaeology has been deepened by the studies of M. R. Harrington, Frank G. Speck, Ives Goddard, Bruce Pearson, Herbert Kraft, and other investigators.[2]

Delaware oral literature, however, has remained a neglected topic. Harrington repeatedly promised a work to be entitled *Lenape Folklore* or *Lenape Mythology*, but it never materialized. Writing nearly fifty years ago in the *Journal of American Folklore*, the distinguished Americanist William N. Fenton could comment that Delaware folklore, rather the apparent lack of it, "presents an enigma."[3]

In a book-length study of 1978, *The Delawares: A Critical Bibliography*, C. A. Weslager found no need to treat oral literature and even failed to list two relevant titles: Richard C. Adams's *Legends of the Delaware Indians and Picture Writing* and Carl F. Voegelin's "Delaware Texts."[4] The omissions are forgivable since *Legends*, written in Victorian English, contains some dubious material, and Voegelin's "Texts," though glossed, are not Englished in the full sense of the term.

My own desire to know Delaware folk literature comes, simply enough, from living in Ulster County, New York, which is within the territory once held by the Lenape, or Delaware. I wanted to know what stories had been told—or might have been told—here.

The search has yielded a surprising 220 texts (far more than had been expected), many of which are just now being published.[5] Though uneven in quality, these are sufficient to give a rounded view of Delaware narrative art and to make possibile a meaningful anthology. A glimpse of the material can be offered at this writing, as well as a small sampling of the texts themselves.

Of the 220 stories, 34 are from the northern Lenape, or Munsee, now located in Ontario. The remainder are from the southern group, which may be designated Unami, now in Oklahoma. Prominent in the older sources are fragments of a creation epic, in which the earth is formed on the back of a turtle and life begins with a woman who falls from the sky. In addition, the repertoire includes hero tales, star myths, animal stories, charter myths for the Delaware ceremonies, and a well-developed trickster cycle.

Among Delaware specialties are tales that may be generically titled "Snow Boy," "The Water Monster and the Sun," "Why the Turtle Phratry Is Best," "Bear Pet," "Thunder's Helper," and "The Man Who Visited the Thunders." "Snow Boy"—for example—tells of a strange child who bites other children's fingers, turning them black and stiff as if frozen. When a little older, he departs on a stream, magically causing ice floes to cohere. After instructing the people to leave him an annual offering of corn, he promises to return each winter to show hunters the route of wounded game on his "body the snow."

A number of Delaware narrative types, however, are by no means unique. They are shared by neighboring or not-too-distant tribes, showing that Delaware folklore can be securely placed within the Northeast tradition. Tribes that share four or more Delaware types (with the number of shared types in parentheses) are Cherokee (4), Menomini (4), Ojibwa (5), Onondaga (8), Seneca (15), Shawnee (8), and Wyandot (6). "Earth Diver" (in which animals take turns diving for mud to create the earth), "Mudjikwis" (which tells of a band of brothers seeking a bride), "The Origin of the Pleiades" (about a group of star children), and "The Woman Who Fell from the Sky" are among the more familiar stories. Less familiar, yet widespread, are "Bear Boy" (in which a human boy is adopted by a bear), "The Fortunate Hunter" (a good-for-nothing bags game by accident), and "The Serpent's Bride" (a young woman's bridegroom becomes a monster).

On close examination the tales reveal a lively storytelling tradition marked by conscious craft and touches of humor. Opening formulas include such phrases as "Many snows ago" or "Long ago when the Lenape people lived in the east" or even so subtle an expression as "My story camps." In the latter case the narrator is drawing upon a far-flung Algonquian idea that the story itself is a person accustomed to walking over the earth; the story cannot be heard until it stops and makes camp. The closing formula, if there is one, may be no more than a simple "This is my story, an ancient one." Or, more dramatically, the teller may pick up a stick and snap it across his knee, saying, "I break it off."

Stories for the most part must be told only in winter. But the late Nora Thompson Dean of Dewey, Oklahoma, used to say that you could tell them in summer if you warded off the worms and insects (that otherwise might crawl all over you) by announcing, "I'm sitting on twelve skunk skins."[6]

Over the years the Delaware story repertoire has changed, perhaps considerably. A number of stories do not make their appearance in the record until the middle of the twentieth century, whereas others, told formerly, seem to have disappeared. After 1900, the creation epic drops out almost entirely (allowing for an occasional fragment), possibly because many Delaware had become churchgoing Christians.

An interesting exception to the rule of change is the Delaware trickster cycle, which tells of a misfit hero who, in the words of one twentieth-century narrator, "worked miracles" despite his shortcomings.[7] Known as Wehixamukes (approximately way-he-cha-MOO-case, with the *ch* as in German *ach*), this popular character has been called Jack, Crazy Jack, or simply "the strong man" by English-speaking Delawares. In its modern form the cycle is probably related, though indistinctly and only in part, to the Aarne-Thompson folktale types 1692 ("The Stupid Thief") and 1693 ("The Literal Fool"); such stories, in European tradition, have also been called "Jack the Numskull" and "Jack the Trickster."[8]

The earliest clear reference—which is early indeed, considering the scant attention paid to folklore in pre-1900 accounts—appears in a manuscript of 1823–24 by the ethnographer Charles Christopher Trowbridge, who mentions the "long story" about a "great" man named Weekharmookhaas.[9] Notices prior to Trowbridge are less convincing. Arguably the earliest reference of all is in Peter Lindeström's journal of 1654–56 from New Sweden, his *Geographia Americae,* in which he describes a legendary hero, born of a virgin, who after performing "many miracles," disappeared from the earth, promising to return.[10]

The modern Wehixamukes, likewise, promises to return; and although the details of his birth are not given by latter-day narrators, it is said that a virginal young woman will be his mother when he is reborn in the future.

Folkloristically, Wehixamukes is related to the proverbial man who misunderstands, the eccentric who misapplies ambiguous instructions and bungles every time—known from Cayuga, Onondaga, Seneca, and Wyandot lore.[11] In Wyandot stories he is also said to be magically powerful. But only in Delaware tradition does he rise to the status of a folk hero.

Of the thirteen stories presented below, all but the second are published here for the first time.[12] The second, "He Puts His Nose to the Ground," is adapted from Voegelin's "Delaware Texts."[13] Minor alterations, mostly in punctuation and paragraphing, have been made in these occasionally rough manuscript materials. It should be emphasized that the translations obtained by Harrington and Truman Michelson are by the storytellers themselves, who have re-created the texts in English.[14]

A few odd expressions that might have been reworded have been left in their original form. Thus the verb *duck,* meaning "dunk," in the sixth story ("He Dips the Turkey in Grease") and the Delaware interjection *flu,* meaning "shucks," in the second story ("He Puts His Nose to the Ground").

Finally, it may be mentioned that the memory of Wehixamukes has persisted into the 1990s, at a time when the Delaware language, now fragile, continues to be used by only a few older speakers. Among the most eminent is Lucy Blalock of Quapaw, Oklahoma, who today gives classes in spoken Delaware for the benefit of a younger generation. In a recent communication, James Rementer, secretary of the Delaware Culture Preservation Committee, tells me of a conversation he has had with Lucy Blalock on the subject of storytelling. According to Blalock, the stories that must be recited only in winter are the fictitious stories, or folktales. Wehixamukes stories present a different case. Since Wehixamukes is said to have actually existed and may yet return, tales about him can be told at any time of the year, summer or winter.[15]

Grateful acknowledgment is made to Bruce Pearson, James Rementer, the American Philosophical Society, the National Museum of the American Indian, and the Smithsonian Institution for permission to publish texts from their collections.

NOTES

1. David Zeisberger, "History of the Northern American Indians," ed. Archer B. Hulbert and William N. Schwarze, *Ohio State Archaeological and Historical Quarterly* 19 (1910): 1–189; John G. E. Heckewelder, *An Account of the History, Manners, and Customs of the Indian Nations* (1819, reprinted as *History, Manners, and Customs of the Indian Nations Who Once Inhabited Pennsylvania and the Neighboring States,* Philadelphia: Historical Society of Pennsylvania, 1876, and New York: Arno Press, 1971); Thomas Jefferson, *Notes on the State of Virginia* (Chapel Hill: University of North Carolina Press, 1955), 43, 205.

2. M. R. Harrington, *Religion and Ceremonies of the Lenape* (New York: Museum of the American Indian, 1921); Frank G. Speck, *A Study of the Delaware Indian Big House Ceremony* (Harrisburg: Pennsylvania Historical Commission, 1931); Frank G. Speck and Jesse Moses, *The Celestial Bear Comes Down to Earth* (Reading, Pa.: Reading Public Museum and Art Gallery, 1945); Ives Goddard, *Delaware Verbal Morphology* (New York: Garland, 1979), and "Delaware," in *Handbook of North American Indians,* ed. William C. Sturtevant (Washington, D.C.: Smithsonian Institution, 1978), 15:213–39; Bruce Pearson, *A Grammar of Delaware* (Dewey, Okla.: Touching Leaves Indian Crafts, 1988); Herbert C. Kraft, *The Lenape: Archaeology, History, and Ethnography* (Newark: New Jersey Historical Society, 1986).

3. William N. Fenton, "Iroquois Indian Folklore," *Journal of American Folklore* 60 (1947): 395.

4. C. A. Weslager, *The Delawares: A Critical Bibliography* (Bloomington: Indiana University Press, 1978); Richard C. Adams, *Legends of the Delaware Indians and Picture Writing* (Washington, D.C.: 1905); Carl F. Voegelin, ed., "Delaware Texts," by Willy Longbone, *International Journal of American Linguistics* 11 (1945): 105–19.

5. John Bierhorst, *Mythology of the Lenape: Guide and Texts* (Tucson, Az., University of Arizona Press, 1995).

6. Nora Thompson Dean, "Stories in Lenape and English," interview by Nicholas Shoumatoff, November 17, 1977; cassette tape; call no. 52a, catalog no. 2DE-18 and/or 2DE-21, Delaware Resource Center, Trailside Museum, Cross River, N.Y.

7. Voegelin, ed., "Delaware Texts," 111.

8. Antti Aarne and Stith Thompson, *The Types of the Folktale*, 2d ed. (Helsinki: Suomalainen Tiedeakatemia, 1973); Stith Thompson, *European Tales Among American Indians* (Colorado Springs: Colorado College, 1919), 416–26.

9. Charles Christopher Trowbridge, manuscript transcribed in C. A. Weslager, *The Delaware Indians: A History* (New Brunswick, N.J.: Rutgers University Press, 1972), 476.

10. Peter Lindeström, *Geographia Americae with an Account of the Delaware Indians Based on Surveys and Notes Made in 1654–1656,* tr. Amandus Johnson (Philadelphia: Swedish Colonial Society, 1925), 208.

11. Bierhorst, *Mythology of the Lenape*.

12. "He Baby-Sits," trans. from Munsee by Josiah Montour and Frank G. Speck, is from Josiah Montour, Texts, 1931, ms. 1173, American Philosophical Society Library, Philadelphia; "He Goes Hunting Again" and "He Sinks into the Earth: Variant," trans. from Unami by Nora Thompson Dean and Bruce Pearson, are from Nora Thompson Dean, "Wehixamukes Story As Told to Bruce Pearson: English and Delaware Text," with Delaware respelled by James A. Rementer, ca. 1970 (floppy disk; James A. Rementer, Dewey, Okla.); "He Finds a Bear Hole," "He Drives Out the Bear," and "He Dips the Turkey in Grease" are Unami stories told anonymously in English, from M. R. Harrington, Papers, ca. 1907–ca. 1910, box OC-163, folder 9, National Museum of the American Indian, New York; "He Oversleeps," "He Alerts the Enemy," "He Defeats the Enemy Single-Handedly," "He Hunts Everything Alive," "He Lives Alone," and "He Sinks into the Earth" are Unami stories told anonymously in English, from Truman Michelson, Ethnological and Linguistic Field Notes from the Munsee in Kansas and the Delaware in Oklahoma, 1912, ms. 2776, folder 9, National Anthropological Archives, Smithsonian Institution, Washington, D.C.

13. Unami text with English glosses by Voegelin and Willie Longbone, in Voegelin, ed., "Delaware Texts," 111–12.

14. See note 12.

15. James A. Rementer, letter dated March 15, 1991. Letters on Delaware Folklore and Other Delaware Topics, 1990–93, with an index compiled by John Bierhorst, American Philosophical Society Library, Philadelphia.

My story camps, called by name Jack.

Jack nursed the baby when all had gone away. While nursing, he had been told, he must drive away the flies.

Well, this Jack got angry at the flies and said, "Just wait a little and I'll kill you." He went and got an ax.

When he came back, the flies were flying on the child's face. He raised the ax, and as hard as he could he hit the flies on the little child's face—he killed the child.

Then Jack was scared. "Now what shall I do?" he thought to himself. "Here's what I'll do, I'll kill the goose and wear its feathers. I'll just be sitting when they all come back."

This Jack had killed the child, this Jack was scared. Then he went and sat where the goose had been sitting on eggs.

The woman's little boy and all the other people said, "Where could this Jack be?" They found him under the house where the goose should have been. Crawling toward him they saw him, this Jack. He was sitting there.

He made a loud noise like a goose sitting on eggs. Just like a goose: *sssss,* it sounded. And there were Jack's buttocks sticking out of the feathers. *Ihi!*

Jack was a small person, though yet a man.

HE PUTS HIS NOSE TO THE GROUND

He set off with the hunters. When they'd gone a little distance, the headman said, "Over there! You people go that way, over to that brush." And the ones that were to go had to flush out the bears.

Then the headman said, "You people here, put your noses to the ground!" He said to Crazy Jack, "Here, you! Put your nose to the ground."

"All right. I can do it," he said.

Now the ones that had gone to the brush scared the bears from the other side.

Immediately Crazy Jack dug a hole in the ground, putting his nose into it as far as he could. When the others came around, look at this! somebody's buttocks sticking out.

The headman asked him, "Did you see any bears?"

"No."

He still had his nose in the hole.

"That's not what I told you to do," said the headman.

"Flu!" he said. "You should have told me what you really meant."

HE GOES HUNTING AGAIN

Here again is a Wehixamukes story.

A long time ago the Delawares lived in the east in the faraway land of Pennsylvania. There must have been many of them at that time, and there must have been many different tribes as well.

A person had to be always on the alert, and it must have been difficult for a person to live. People had to look for food, because there were no stores the way there are now in our lifetime.

The people used animals, they lived from them. A person had to hunt all the time to kill deer, and to fish, and to kill the fur-bearing animals. They used those fur-bearing animals when they made clothing, when they made bags to store grease, and when they made moccasins and other things.

The Delaware men camped at many different places, at big rivers, and in big forests where they all went hunting when they wanted to find food.

One time when these Delaware men went hunting, Wehixamukes went along with them.

HE FINDS A BEAR HOLE

And they went on that evening and camped and the headman said, "We'll stay here all day tomorrow and try to kill a bear to eat, for we are getting hungry."

And next morning the headman said, "Now we will go out and try to kill a bear. And if anybody finds a hollow tree, hallo or whoop, and we can get together, and sure there will be a bear in it."

And they started out next morning. And when they got a little ways, somebody whooped, and they went over and saw this strong man standing beside a big stem of grass, and he was looking at a hole in the grass, and they told him that's not what they mean.

"We mean a big tree."

The strong man said, "Why didn't you tell me before?"

And they started on a little farther and they heard someone whoop again, and when they got there they found a big tree.

And the headman said, "Now who can climb up there and drive the bear out?"

The strong man said, "I can."

And he climbed into the hole and drove the bear out. And the bear was killed.

HE DIPS THE TURKEY IN GREASE

And they went back to camp. And that day there was one man that had a bucket, and he fried some grease and took bark from an elm tree and made another bucket. And whenever he would get lots of grease in the bucket that he already had, he would pour it into the bark bucket.

And that evening the headman said, "Tomorrow we will hunt turkey, for it would be good to duck it in the grease."

And the strong man said, "All right."

And next morning they started out to hunt for turkey. And the strong man had not been gone very far until he caught a turkey alive and he took it to camp, and he was there alone, and he went to ducking the turkey in the grease until the turkey was nearly dead.

And when one of the hunters came back, he saw the strong man running around one side of the bucket and the other, catching the turkey and ducking it in the grease.

And when the hunter came close, the strong man said, "Will you duck this turkey awhile in the grease? I'm getting tired."

And the hunter said, "That's not what they mean. They mean kill the turkey and cook it. And when it's done, eat it. And dip the cooked pieces in the grease—and eat it."

And the strong man said, "Why didn't you all tell me before? I would have had that turkey cooked."

Wehixamukes when he was grown was very ornery. He was dirty, lay down anywhere, and had no get-up to him.

A bunch of Delawares went out looking for enemies, so he wanted to go along. They hardly liked to take him, as they didn't think he amounted to anything, didn't care to be bothered with him.

They took him along.

And where they camped, he slept so long the next morning they just left him there. So when he woke up, his men had all left him.

So he caught up with the gang of men where they were camped. When he got there, he just lay down by the fire and went to sleep.

Next morning they woke up, ate their breakfast. And they left him, then again just let him sleep. They said, "Just let him stay there."

He knew all about it beforehand and was well satisfied.

So then he caught up with them again—he got up early.

HE ALERTS THE ENEMY

Then they went on, and they struck a big prairie country.

While going along, they ran into a big body of men that it was impossible for them to whip. So the headman said, "We'll now have to hide in the high grass so they'll pass us and we can go on."

So Wehixamukes, this is how he acted: squatted down as much as he could, and every now and then he would stick his head out.

"Look out, the people will see you," he was told.

So he couldn't stand it when the enemy passed him a bit. He jumped up and beat his breast, crying out, "Here we are, we're a big body of men."

NARRATOR ASIDE: There were only thirty or forty in the bunch and four or five thousand enemies.

HE DEFEATS THE ENEMY SINGLE-HANDEDLY

So after he did that, the others with him jumped up and told him he'd have to throw down all the enemy, since he had got them started.

So then he said, "All right" and threw his blanket away.

NARRATOR ASIDE: He *understood* them to say "Grab them and throw them down but don't kill them."

So he grabbed one and then another and laid them down.

So the headman told him, "That isn't what I told you to do. I told you to kill all of them because they're going to kill all of us."

And Wehixamukes said, "Why in the world didn't you say so in the first place?"

And he grabbed his little ax and went right after them, till he killed every one of them with his ax but one.

So the one he left was told by him, "Come here! Well, I'm going to cut your ears off." He took his knife and cut the man's ears off, just left little pieces hanging there, cut his nose off too and told him, "The rules are among men you don't want to look good, you want to look mean. That's why I cut your ears and nose off."

Then he said, "Stick out your hands." He did so. Wehixamukes split his fingers far up.

"Look here, did you ever notice men have long fingers? You didn't look like a man. Your fingers were too short. That's why I split them."

So he told him to go back to his people and he would wait for them to come too.

HE HUNTS EVERYTHING ALIVE

Some said, "We'll go on a hunt and kill everything alive that we see, and we'll take it home with us." So Wehixamukes said, "All right."

While he was hunting, he saw one of his companions ahead. He thought, "Well, he's alive, I believe I'll get him."

So he killed him. He cut holes in his legs so he could carry him on his back.

When he went on farther, he saw another one of his companions. So he did the same to him, strung him up, went on home looking for anything that was alive.

When he got home, he threw the two men down in front of the people. "Well, this is all I could find alive."

NARRATOR ASIDE: The instructions were to kill anything alive.

So the headman said, "Now the thing's happened just as I told you he'd do. So now he's played this trick on us, he's killed two men. I always told you that you should explain everything fully to him so he would understand it right."

So the chiefs notified their bands that they had discovered he had such power he could do anything.

The chiefs told the bands hereafter to be very particular in talking to him, that when they tell him anything, they must explain it fully and kindly so he would understand it right.

At that time Wehixamukes became a very powerful man. So he kind of left the tribe and went a ways off, built him a bark house for himself.

One day a bunch of men came and surrounded him. They told him, "We've got you, we've got you now."

So he said, "Yes, you've got me. Come in." He rolled the flap. They all came in.

Pallets were spread down around the fire at the center of the house. "Well, sit down, men. I'll cook dinner before we go."

So he went to work and started dinner, put some big kettles on the fire, put lots of venison in them and water, so as to make plenty of soup.

So when he got the cooking done, there was lots of boiling soup, so he asked the men, "Where's your *ila?*"

NARRATOR ASIDE: That's a war leader.

They thought he was going to feed him first, so they pointed him out to him.

So he grabbed one kettle full of soup and threw the boiling soup right square on the ila's face.

So he had a big wooden spoon in his hand, so he dipped it in the kettle and commenced to hurl the hot soup on the others. So they all started to run out of the house when he did that, so he kept on throwing hot soup on them, and they ran out of the house as fast as they could.

After they were all out, he grabbed his little ax and he whooped at them, and they could run no farther. They fell on the ground.

So he killed them all with his ax. Except one. He cut his ears off, split his fingers—split his hands—and cut off his nose and told him to go back and tell the people, and to come back again with some people with him. "I'm going to live here all the time."

He had a sister-in-law living. She went off to the creek and started to chop down a tree.

At the time it was ready to fall, Wehixamukes walked up just where it was going to fall, and this woman saw him just as he got even with the tree. She said, "Wehixamukes, you are so powerful and can do anything, let's see you catch this tree as it falls."

He said, "Oh yes, I can catch it," and he threw his hands up.

So she chopped the tree and it fell right on him.

He held the tree up, but he sank into the earth clear up to his knees—but kept the tree from the ground.

He kept on sinking till he sank into the ground till he sank to his neck, so the last word he told his sister-in-law was "So! I guess I'll have to leave you all. I'll be back when the big general war on this earth comes off."

He said that whenever a girl had a baby with the little finger cut off at the joint, that boy would be him, and there would be a general war.

When he finished talking, he sank into the ground.

But he was still alive.

It was as if someone were going someplace.

HE SINKS INTO THE EARTH: VARIANT

One of the men told him, "It is true. You are possessed of great powers, and you are strong."

Wehixamukes answered him saying, "Yes, my friend. Since long ago I have known that I am strong and possess powers because the manitou gave me their own strength and power. And now I must tell you that I feel that soon my life will come to an end, but I will come again when these white people will treat you badly, and you will all know me because when I am born, a finger will be off on one of my hands, and my mother will be a young woman who is a virgin."

Those men were all very surprised when Wehixamukes said that, because they all knew that since long ago he had acted and talked silly. Then they all went home together.

When they arrived where they lived, they began to cook: deer meat and corn mush and deer tongue, because Wehixamukes liked to eat deer tongue. Those men must have wanted to treat him well because they were still surprised at the way Wehixamukes had talked.

Then when they finished eating, they went to sleep. The next morning they all left again. They went to cut wood and trees.

Then when one man was cutting down a tree, the tree fell and mashed Wehixamukes, and at that place he disappeared into the ground.

Wehixamukes just disappeared under the ground. The men hurried; they wanted to dig him up. But they couldn't do anything. It was too late now.

Then the men left and went home. And when they got to where they lived, no one said anything, and no one could eat. They just stuffed their pipes and smoked. They were all in a sad state of mind. The men now missed Wehixamukes.

But there was nothing they could do. It was too late.

That is all I can say of what was told to me by my late mother. For a long time I have heard our old people say, "We will wait for Wehixamukes."

THE INDIAN DEVIL,

MISCHIEF-MAKER

▲

DAVID A. FRANCIS
AND
ROBERT M. LEAVITT

INTRODUCTION BY ROBERT M. LEAVITT

The tale of "The Indian Devil" Laks (pronounced LAHKS) is an eclectic concatenation of themes, protagonists, events, and lessons found throughout Passamaquoddy oral tradition. It reflects Passamaquoddy values and understanding of human relationships, which the Native language expresses in distinctive ways.

The Honorable Lewis Mitchell—or Oluwisu, as he was known in his Native community of Pleasant Point, near Eastport, Maine—was born in 1847. Self-taught and unusually well educated for his time, he served as the tribe's (nonvoting) representative to the Maine State Legislature, where in 1887 he delivered an eloquent and impassioned speech in support of Native land and subsistence rights. David A. Francis, a Passamaquoddy elder and teacher, remembers Mitchell from his childhood and Mitchell's reputation as a scholar, a man who devoured everything in print that came his way. Mitchell also had a broad knowledge of the oral tradition of his people, from contemporary songs and poetry to ancient myths and legends. Many of these he transcribed on his own, later sharing them with John Dyneley Prince, who eventually published the version of "The Indian Devil" offered here. The present translation is based on the Passamaquoddy edition published by Prince in *Passamaquoddy*

Texts.[1] This collection was in turn based on Mitchell's earlier texts, dating to at least the 1880s. Prince and Mitchell's Passamaquoddy version had the title "W'skidcinwi Wahant Malikapiu" (in modern orthography and pronunciation, "Skicinuwi Wahant Malika-piyiw").

Passamaquoddy is an Algonquian language spoken in eastern Maine at Pleasant Point, near Eastport, and Indian Township (Peter Dana Point), near Princeton. Along the St. John River in New Brunswick and northern Maine, this same language is called Mali-seet. Today there are few speakers younger than thirty. The languages closest to Passamaquoddy-Maliseet are Micmac to the east (still a first language for many children) and Penobscot-Abnaki to the west (now with very few speakers). The oral traditions of these groups have much in common, in particular the cycle of stories about Glooscap, the culture hero, and a number of separate stories about persons Glooscap encounters.

Several versions of the tale of "The Indian Devil" were published in Mitchell's time, all quite similar in content, and he may have seen one or more of them, although this is not certain. Nor is the date of his first writing down the tale. The Micmac version published by Silas T. Rand in 1894 was told by Susan Christmas in 1870.[2] Charles G. Leland, in whose *Algonquin Legends of New England* the tale also appears, identifies "The Merry Tales of Lox, the Mischief Maker" as both Micmac and Passamaquoddy. He records the Passamaquoddy version as having been given to him by Tomah Josephs, the governor at Peter Dana Point, whereas "so much of it as is Micmac was told to Mr. Rand by a highly intelligent Indian, named Benjamin Brooks, who was certain that the story was of great antiquity."[3] Mitchell himself used Micmac names for some of the protagonists, a feature also of some of his other Passamaquoddy texts.

In any case the story—at least in part—is not unique to Passamaquoddy or Micmac tradition. The star wives in particular are well-known from across the continent, from the Arctic and British Columbia to the Great Lakes and the East Coast.[4] The accounts differ somewhat in details and focus, but the essential ingredients are there—the women choose stars for husbands, escape from star land through a hole in the sky, become stranded in a tall tree, and offer themselves to passing men in order to be rescued. The rolling Rock appears in a Flathead tale from Montana, pursuing Coyote and his companions.[5] And readers will no doubt recall countless other escapes over water facilitated by a cooperative ferryman, who, like Heron in this tale, then stymies the pursuer.

Leland's version, though distorted by its flowery language and the author's penchant for interpreting the oral tradition in European terms, does offer the reader a number of interesting annotations. When the star wives become stranded in the hemlock, Leland tells us that "a want of patience or of dignity, and restlessness, are more scorned by every Indian than any other fault. This is not the only story in which people are . . . punished for being unable to bide their time." There is a "joke" embedded in the tale in that "the animals who pass by the tree each mate at the season of the year when they declare that they were married." The wolverine is a likely candidate for "Indian Devil" because "his ferocity is equal to his craftiness," and the hair string "occurs very often in Indian legends, generally as gifted with magic." Interestingly Leland says that in Tomah Josephs's Passamaquoddy version, when Laks is dismembered, it is ants who reassemble him; yet he also notes that "the dead body of a sorcerer must lie until addressed by some human being. Then it revives."[6]

Mitchell's Passamaquoddy text, as published by Prince, contains a number of Anglicisms, and its many abrupt narrative shifts are uncharacteristic of traditional oral storytelling, which is remarkable for the purity and grace of its language. These qualities the present translators have attempted to restore, first in the Passamaquoddy and then in the English. Although Mitchell's own efforts to write Passamaquoddy in a "literary" style doubtless contributed to the awkwardness of his work, much of this may also be traced to Prince, the collector and translator of the tales. In his introduction to the *Passamaquoddy Texts,* Prince explains that the manuscripts "came into my possession some years ago, but were all destroyed by fire in 1911, since which time Mr. Mitchell industriously reproduced them at my request from memory."[7] It is more than likely that Mitchell also relied on prompts or notes from Prince as he retranscribed the tales.

Nevertheless, because the story comes to us from a native speaker, a sense of the Passamaquoddy worldview and personal and social values comes through. The language reflects a Passamaquoddy understanding of the relationships among the protagonists and between them and the natural world. We find that the people in traditional tales communicate with the elements and features of the natural world as directly as they do with the other human and animal dramatis personae.

The protagonists appear in pairs who exemplify contrasting behavior: clever Marten and plodding Moose give way to the unsavory

Laks and his adjutant brother. Caught in their schemes are two sisters, first appearing as underwater women, later as star wives, the elder more temperate than the younger. All of these encounter other personages—a pair of stars, two Mohawk boys, various monsters—who aid or thwart them according to their just deserts.

The natural world makes its presence felt in the form of explicit and implicit persons. There is Rock, who kills Laks twice and eventually takes revenge not only on him but on all humankind. The star husbands have faces and personalities that match their astrophysical attributes. Small birds flock to the women's aid, bringing them "thorns, briers, burs, bees of all kinds"—and sharp flints: vengeful Rock in a different guise. Another bird, Grandfather Heron, helps the women escape. Even bone, in the form of Laks's disembodied spine, has power and is able to reassemble the other, scattered pieces of its body.

In the Passamaquoddy language *rock* and *bone* (even bone as a body part) are grammatically inanimate. Yet Rock the avenger takes on animateness and personhood when he challenges Laks with his power; and when Laks's spine speaks out directly, grammatical animateness again establishes its power. The first time Laks is smashed, on inanimate earth, we hear his spine only from the point of view of the younger brother—*Metiyewestuwik* (meh-dee-eh-WEST-oo-weeg), literally, "It is heard speaking"—and even though it is said to speak, it remains inanimate. But the next time, when Laks is crushed by animate Rock, it is an animate Bone who replies to the word of power, shouting, "My hip, come here! My legs, come here!" Such events and the language in which they are couched remind listeners of the truly personal connections between human beings and the other beings who inhabit the universe.

One further example of what the language of the tale reveals is the verb root *-hponol-*, "to fight against by spiritual power," which appears in the Passamaquoddy text four times. Marten's grandmother is "caught out" and shamed by Moose when she conceals the meat she has cooked; the underwater women "play" innocent "tricks on" one another as they frolic in the water; Laks is alert for ways in which the Mohawk boys might "get the better of" him by force; and later he is "challenged" by Rock, who turns his own dust into stinging flies. These confrontations reflect diverse uses of power rather than a diversity of types of power. Spiritual power is in itself neither beneficial nor harmful; instead, one must look at how a person uses the power.

It may seem to the reader of "The Indian Devil" that Laks and his brother and their counterparts, Marten and Moose, are inadequately punished for the suffering they cause. This apparent failure to exact "just retribution" reflects the purpose of many tales, which is to teach moderation rather than condemn evil or extol virtue. In the Passamaquoddy worldview, neither absolute evil nor saintly virtue is possible in human nature; rather, persons seek to maintain an appropriate balance between their own needs and those of the society in which they live, a balance between using knowledge and power for their own benefit and using them for the good of all. Thus, in this story Moose *may* not—and in fact *cannot*—keep secret the bear meat he has brought home, nor may he try to arrogate Marten's extraordinary powers in order to get himself a wife.

In another tale written down by Mitchell, Laks kills the children of two fishers *(Martes pennanti)* and tricks a group of nursing mothers into drowning their babies. His punishment? At the end of the tale, he eats (by choice!) too many rose hips; these give him hemorrhoids, and in an effort to relieve the itching, he scrapes his hind end bare. Listeners will understand that the fishers trusted a selfish stranger and that the nursing mothers wanted to have their children grow up without doing the work of raising them. Such tales provide cautionary examples to those who would act in self-interest or do anything in excess. "The Indian Devil, Mischief-Maker" is no exception. With both humor and cruelty, passion and detachment, it helps us keep our lives in balance.

A Note on Pronunciation

The five vowel sounds of Passamaquoddy are *a* (as in *father*), *e* (as in *bed*), *i* (as in *ski*), *o* (as in *apron;* represented by an apostrophe in the phonetic renderings below), and *u* (as in *sue*); the combination *eh* sounds like the vowel in *tack*. Vowel blends are *iw* (as in English *few*) and *ew* (short *e* followed by lip rounding, a sound not found in English). Thus, the Passamaquoddy title of the story is "Skicinuwi Wahant Malikapiyiw" (ski-JEE-noo-wee wah-HAHNT mah-LEE-gah-bee-yeew). Protagonists are Apistanewc (ah-bee-stah-NEHWCH, "marten"), Tiyam (DEE-yahm, "moose"), Cipehlahq (JEE-ba-lahkʷ, a monster), Laks (LAHKS, perhaps "wolverine"), Kasq (GAHSKʷ, "great blue heron"), and Kollu (G'L-loo, a spirit person). Apistanewc and Tiyam are actually Micmac words. Motewolon (m'-DEH-w'-l'n, "person with extraordinary spiritual powers") does not have a convenient English translation free of stereotypes; wikuwam (WEE-goo-ahm) is the source of *wigwam*—the familiar English word for a house made of birch bark fastened over a frame of poles.

NOTES

1. John Dyneley Prince, *Passamaquoddy Texts,* Publications of the American Ethnological Society no. 10 (New York: G. E. Stechert, 1921).

2. "The Badger and the Star-Wives," Micmac version of the tale of "The Indian Devil," told by Susan Christmas, in *Legends of the Micmacs* by Silas T. Rand (1894; reprint, New York and London: Johnson Reprint, 1971), 306–20.

3. Charles G. Leland, *The Algonquin Legends of New England* (London: Sampson Low, Marston, Searle and Rivington, 1884), 145, 166.

4. See, for example, Tristram P. Coffin, *Indian Tales of North America: An Anthology for the Adult Reader* (Philadelphia: American Folklore Society, 1961); Richard Erdoes and Alfonso Ortiz, eds., *American Indian Myths and Legends* (New York: Pantheon, 1984); and Stith Thompson, "The Star Husband Tale," in *The Study of Folklore,* ed. Alan Dundes (Englewood Cliffs, N.J.: Prentice Hall, 1965).

5. See, for example, Coffin, *Indian Tales of North America.*

6. Leland, *The Algonquin Legends of New England,* 147, 148, 149, 150, 155, 158.

7. Prince, *Passamaquoddy Texts,* 2–3.

A great many years ago, according to the old tradition, behind an island, along the shore of a little stream, dwelled Apistanewc and Tiyam—"Marten" and "Moose." They lived in separate wiku-wams, and their grandmother was the one who looked after them. That clever Tiyam is a hunter, but Apistanewc is a lazybones—so that even when the two of them do plant corn, they depend on the sun to smile upon it. And wherever anyone is storing preserved meat, that's where Apistanewc hangs around.

It happens one day that Tiyam kills a bear. He drags the whole thing home in a single toboggan-load. He doesn't worry himself about feeding those who don't feed him and certainly not ingrates. He says to himself—and indeed, he says it to his grandmother—"Apistanewc won't be seeing this or smelling it; he won't even touch his tongue to it. Nobody tell him what good luck we've had."

"Oh yes," the old woman answers. "My son, I take your meaning quite clearly. Our cooking pot is broken. I'll get his pot for us to cook in; then I'll wash it and wipe it dry so it will be impossible to tell anything has been stewed in it. And then I'll return it."

So she does, but that lazybones Apistanewc senses a feast like an animal on the prowl. He knows from the smallest sign that a big load of meat has been brought in, and whoever borrows a cooking pot will be boiling food.

Always the motewolon, just by stepping into his friend's house, just peeking in the door, Apistanewc sees the bear meat piled up. Here comes Tiyam's grandmother bringing back his pot. As soon as she enters the wikuwam, the smell of nicely stewed bear meat wells up from it, and when she looks inside, it is full of meat, all perfectly cooked. Apistanewc thanks her politely. Caught at her trick, she is embarrassed and runs from the wikuwam, her feet leaving her behind. In the morning, however, the two friends go walking together in the woods; all is well.

Then something happens to Apistanewc that might happen to any-one else. One day he walks all the way to a remote and lonely lake in the mountains. He steps along quietly as a cat. Behind a rock, where the grapes hang thickly, he hears girls laughing and splashing them-selves, refreshing themselves in the lake. These are the underwater women, who hide from earth dwellers. Apistanewc notices their clothes piled up on the shore of the lake and tries to catch sight of a girl who is pretty. Then, just like a marten, he sneaks across without being seen, until he can grab their clothes with his hand—because he has unusual talents. Those underwater beings—when a man takes their clothes, they fall under his control. Apistanewc knows how "little people" behave and other spirits: their extraordinary powers lie in their clothes.

Apistanewc manages to grab them; he runs this way and that along the shore. He hollers. When the underwater women hear him, they get angry; they chase after this thief who has stolen their clothing. The first to catch up with him is the one he was admiring, and when she gets close, he gives her just a little tap on the head. (This is how the Indians used to get motewolons under control long ago.) And then right away—sooner!—they are husband and wife. The underwater woman is surprised at how suddenly she got married. She faints dead away. He takes her off quietly. As for the others, Apistanewc gives them back their clothes.

Now Tiyam is a good man and well behaved. When he sees that Apistanewc is married and he hears how it happened, he says to himself, "That's all right; it's not difficult; it's as if I were already wed." He goes to the little lake in the mountains, off among the rocks, where the grapes grow. He too sees the virgins leaping about, splashing one another, playing tricks on one another like crazy fish in the water—he must have been very excited; without even looking at them, he snatches the clothes of those poor underwater women and runs off.

The one he thinks is prettiest catches up with him first. Then he thinks about how he can get his wish. He grabs hold of an enormous stick and hits her on her little head. But by accident the poor thing is killed—that's why Tiyam isn't married.

Meanwhile, Apistanewc's wife wants to go back; she wants to see her people. Apistanewc suggests that he fetch one of her sisters so he can marry her too. And so he goes off to where he'd gone before, to the mountains, among the rocks, by the little lake where the grapes are hanging. And once again he captures an underwater woman. He goes off with her, and they marry.

Now Tiyam doesn't like that. He says to Apistanewc, "Wouldn't you give me the second one—or the first one—to marry?" Apistanewc doesn't approve of the idea at all. Tiyam begs and begs him, but Apistanewc still refuses. But Tiyam just has to have one of them or Apistanewc will have to go get one for him. Apistanewc answers that Tiyam may start paddling to hell if he likes, and Tiyam gets so angry that he picks up a big stick and chases Apistanewc. Then they go after each other.

Apistanewc answers him gently. He makes white flint arrowheads. He shoots them straight at Tiyam's scalp—that's how they began to fight with each other day after day. Every night they made arrowheads and dreadful weapons; in the mornings they shot them at each other.

The underwater wives aren't used to that kind of fighting. So they look for a way to remove themselves. One morning Apistanewc and Tiyam are really going to kill each other. The two Apistanewc women run so far away that at sunset they hear the voice of Cipehlahq, the spirit person, whose cry originates in the remotest places. The moon rises and moves higher; the place looks so lonely. Apistanewc's wives lie down near some oaks, where there is an opening in the woods, and they remain there for some time, watching the stars and waiting—as children might do.

One of them says to the other, "If these stars were to become men, which one would you take for a husband? I would take the little red twinkling one."

"The only one I'd marry would be the shining yellow one, because I like a big star."

They are just joking, those two, but in the morning when they wake up, they find themselves married again—as it is ordinarily done, simply with a word.

The one who wanted the fierce shining one, when she opens her eyes—there is her husband, a handsome man. He says to her, "Quiet, you will ruin my war paint."

The other one, who said, "I like the shining little red one," when she wakes up and begins to move, she hears someone speak: "Quiet, you will knock over my eye medicine." It's that little shining star, that one she wanted—a very feeble-looking little old man; he has tiny eyes, and they wobble shiftily—yes, the ones they wanted were the ones who came to them.

But yellow or red, young or old, within a few days the two women are weary of being in star land—where they have been taken—and they want very much to go back to earth. This is how it comes about:

They are more and more impatient to go back. One day the star husbands aren't around. They hunt all day, and they have told their wives, "Do you see that big flat rock over there? Don't ever lift it up." Until now they have obeyed. Today, however, as soon as the star husbands walk away, the younger one dashes over to the rock and opens it up. She is eager to see the hole underneath. But when she has lifted it, a surprising sight confronts her—the cloud cover stretches out below, and beyond it the earth they came from. She can even see where they used to live when they were young: the lake, the woods, and the streams. When the older one looks too, their hearts almost break with longing.

Those stars are evil-minded men, as one might think of them. They see with their motewolon powers that their wives have looked down through the hole; they know it when the women deny it. But they give them the pleasure of going back to earth. They say to them, "We will sleep together tonight, and when you wake up, don't be in too much of a hurry to open your eyes. Don't uncover your faces until you hear the chickadee's song; even then do not get up, but lie still until you hear the red squirrel. Again, even then do not uncover your faces until you hear the chipmunk singing. Only then may you leave your beds and look all around."

The younger one has so many things to think of! Each time Chickadee calls, she jumps up. When this happens, the older one tries to stop her: "Wait, my sister, until we hear Chipmunk." And she manages to lie still until Red Squirrel begins his chatter and his morning rounds. She can't wait any longer. That's when she jumps up—and the older woman too. And of course they do find themselves on earth, but they have landed on top of a tall, big-branched hemlock and become caught. They can't get down without help.

It so happens, however, that with each song the birds sing, and the squirrels, they bump down a little closer to the earth. They keep getting nearer and nearer as long as the sun shines. But they do not get far enough. And so they are stranded for the night.

Those star wives make a nest of lichen for themselves in the hemlock. While they are sitting there, it goes along toward dawn. Men of different clans pass by them; to each one they call out tearfully, "Help us!" And of all the forest animals and the men who walk through the clearing, who should show up first but Tiyam—first!

"Oh, our older brother, release us! Get us down!" He stares up at them intently: "I already got married last fall." Then he goes off.

Another one showed up, they say, a nasty bear. They even offered themselves to him in order to get his help, if only they could be lowered gently from their nest. The bear just growled, "I got married last spring. One wife, that's enough for any man." Then he went away.

And then who should show up but Apistanewc, the very one they left behind! Joyfully they shout to him. They beg him to take them home. But he lies to them, as if they were strangers. He replies, "I too got married, the spring before last." And he goes off as well, leaving the underwater women all alone.

Last of all Laks shows up, the one they call the Indian Devil. He's gentler than any other kind of animal in the woods and crueler than all of them put together. When they ask for his help, he thinks about how he can torment them and be kind to them. But the ones he is dealing with are no less clever than he, and they have had many different experiences—because they left the earth, went to the heavens, changed husbands. These underwater women are really catching on.

The older woman thinks Laks can be talked into doing just what she wants him to. Quickly she unties her hair string and wraps it around a twig, knotting and tangling it so that it will be a long time before he can undo it. By now Laks has gotten the other sister down to the ground, as he was persuaded to. Then he goes to get the older one, and he helps her down too. She thanks him, but she asks him one more favor—to climb up into the branches where she left her hair string. She warns him, "Don't you dare snap it in two or damage it in any way. Just untie it carefully, one knot at a time."

While Laks is busy, the underwater women make something novel, a well-furnished house unlike anything ever seen before. These underwater women are close friends of the birds. They all flock together. "Go get thorns, briers, burs, bees of all kinds. Bring them to the wikuwam"—the one they have made for Laks—"all kinds of bees, ants, and other winged stinging insects." And they stick sharp flints into the floor. For the groom's bed they spread out bees; his chair is an anthill.

It takes Laks all day to undo the hair string. By the time he climbs down, it has gotten dark, and when he sees the wikuwam, he is happy: "Oh, but I will rest well." As he goes in, he bumps his head against the briers and impales his nose. He cuts his feet on the flints. It hurts! He yelps and yelps. He hears someone talking: it's the younger underwater woman. He sobs and moans. She says, "Go to my sister, over this way." He heads in that direction and, poor thing, steps right on the anthill. That's worse than the briers. Someone else's voice speaks; he hears a laughing call: "Go to my sister; she is younger than I am." Then suddenly he is groping in the dark, and he steps on the beehive. That's even more painful. Now he realizes he's being mocked, and he gets angry. Laks can behave very violently—and he will. No man or animal has ever been as furious.

▲

He follows the trail of the underwater women as they flee in the night, beating a path through terrible thickets. Just before dawn the women come down to a wide river. They cannot cross it. On the opposite bank stands Kasq, the tall, long-legged heron—ferryman Kasq, who always wants people to speak nicely to him and tell him how wonderful he is. It makes him proud of his beautiful figure. The girls sing to him, "Beautiful-necked heron! Beautiful-necked Kasq!" He likes the sound of that very much, that foremost ferryman. They tell him, "Grandfather, hurry!" Oh yes, he's ready right away. He stretches out his long bill across the river so that the girls can climb across. And once ashore, they immediately set out on foot again, into the bushes.

As soon as they are out of sight and the heron is standing in place again, Laks comes down to the bank. He tells the heron, "Take me across too."

"I'll take you across only if you think I am handsome. I am so good-looking. Aren't these legs of mine beautifully straight?"

"Yes," Laks answers him, "and beautiful in color."

The color makes Uncle Kasq proud. "And aren't my feathers smooth and well groomed?"

"Yes, well groomed and smooth; it's too bad how muddy and filthy they are."

And: "Isn't my neck so straight, straight just like this?"

Laks grabs a crooked stick and sings to him, "Crooked-necked heron! Crooked-legged heron! Kasq has crooked legs, Kasq has a crooked neck! And Kasq's neck is dirty—you'd better hurry, grandfather!"

Kasq says nothing at all, but he takes Laks onto his bill. When his passenger has climbed halfway across, where the water is deepest and most dangerous, the heron shakes himself; he tips his bill. All of a sudden Laks is spinning around like a little wood chip in the strong current. He keeps flailing for a while as he is swept downstream, but then he bangs his head on the rocks and strikes shore where the ground is soft. The impact kills him—Laks at that time was a great motewolon, but his strength would sometimes leave him.

It turns out that after several days two boys find Laks lying on the rocks, where he died in the bright sunshine. Those boys are Mohawks. Laks is all maggots crawling out of his mouth.

But when they touch him, he comes back to life. They stand him up, one on either side—like the proud and fierce warrior that he is. However, just as soon as he is alive again, he looks for ways they could attack him. Their bows are well made; he gets them and breaks them. Then he makes the sound of children playing far off, at a point of land. He tells the boys, "Run there, go join in all the different games." So they wander away—he made such a convincing noise! It sounded farther and farther off, but it was just the sound of the river flowing.

As they walk away, he does not go with them. Farther along they go out of sight. Laks knows that these boys are young *kollus*.* When he sees how much meat they have in their house, he wants to be related to them. Laks can live in many different ways: he knows how almost everyone behaves.

So he puts on kollu behavior. He sees a child, and he begins to sing a kollu song: "Sealskin suspenders, shoulder strings." A woman says to him, "You can't fool me," and that makes Laks angry.

He grabs an ax and kills her with a blow. He sees water boiling in a pot nearby; so he cuts off her head and puts it in. He hides her body. That's how wicked hearted he likes to be. It makes him very happy.

After a while the boys come back, and they miss their dear mother. When they look in the cooking pot, they find her head— they know very well who did that. Bravely they take off after Laks. They are unarmed; so they do not make a mark on him; they just take his gloves. They are bringing these back when their uncle Crow arrives. He joins the chase too, but all he can do is knock Laks's hat off. Laks isn't ashamed to go bareheaded. He tells the uncle, "Thank you! My head has been sweating for a long time." He shouts at him, *"My head was getting hotter and hotter!"*

Another one of the uncle's relatives comes along, an eagle. He too joins the chase. He manages to pull off Laks's coat; but Laks still says thank you: "If only my younger brother were here; he would carry my coat for me. Thanks!" he replies.

Now Kollu himself comes—assuredly the most fearsome of all living creatures. He catches right up with Laks, grabs hold of him, and carries him off in his talons, way up high, right to the top of the clouds. There he lets go of him. Laks is all day traveling, falling back down through the clouds, from sunrise until sunset. That's when he crashes onto the earth. But before being let drop, still high up in the heavens, he sings mockingly about what he sees, in these words: "Our country seems lost—heigh-ho, heigh-ho! Our country looks blue!"

* *kollus*: huge birds with evil ways.

While he is falling, this mocking, bold Laks, all the time he pretends to fly, flapping his arms up and down like wings. He makes a sound with his mouth as if he were imitating broad-winged Kollu. Just before he hits, he calls faintly, like a motewolon: "Don't let my back hit on anything!" Then he is completely smashed; his blood splashes everywhere, and his brain is scattered in all directions. But his spine is intact—and that's where his life is.

After a few days his younger brother comes along. "What happened here?"

He hears Laks's spine talking: "My hip, come here!"—and his leg suddenly appears. Again he hears it speak: "My arm, come here!" Every last joint gets up.

There he is, still the brave and mocking Laks himself, still the Indian Devil. "I haven't died yet," he says—nothing can kill him; he's hard to get rid of.

Then the two brothers start walking. Eventually they arrive at the top of a high mountain. There they position a great round boulder, and they say to it, "Well now, let's have a race." They pry it up with a big pole, and it begins to roll downhill, faster and faster, until it crashes to a stop at the bottom. But they run right along with it, always teasing it, begging it to race them.

They don't have long to wait for it at the bottom. They are sitting there cooking when they hear something coming—a noise as if something were rushing through the bushes. But it's that huge boulder! It must have gotten angry and sulked for a little while. Suddenly Rock comes through the brush, crushing the strong trees, rolling like thunder, cutting down trees like grass, roaring along as if the path were already there, passing over the thicker bushes like a rock in motewolon flight. The younger brother darts aside like a snake, but the older Indian has just uttered his motewolon's words: "My spine remains nice and whole as always." And the big rock keeps rolling on through the air until the sound of its thundering fades away on the wind.

Then the younger brother says to Spine, "Why are you lying there?"

When it hears the word of power, Bone shouts, "My body, come here! My hip, come here! My legs, come here!" and everything is jointed just as before—until what was broken is fixed, and he who died lives again. He says, as if he were just waking up, "What did I do?"

His younger brother tells him all about it. Then he is very angry.

When Laks is upset, it isn't just a little bit. He says in his wrath, "Shall I, the Indian Devil, be killed by a bird and by rocks and not defend myself?"

They walk into the woods and start tracking the rock through the thick brush and into the trees. As soon as they come upon it, they build a fire all around it. They pound it with boulders until they have beaten it into grains of sand, until it is dust—this is how Laks repays! This is how he defends himself!

But something strange happens: Rock, who challenges them with *his* power, turns the dust into blackflies, midges, and other vicious creatures who infuriate men and animals—thus, Rock's hatred shall last until the end of time.

When they have finished raging against the rock, when they see the flies, these two take off through the brush until they come to a little village, a village of good people. They know very well how the men behave there. Laks decides upon something to do to make mischief with them—of all living creatures none gets so much enjoyment as he from making fun of people. The more he does it, the happier he is—now an idea comes into his head.

He turns himself into a beautiful girl. The people are pleased with him. Soon the oldest sons are coming to call; they welcome such a beautiful virgin. The son of the village chief wants her right away. He doesn't bother himself long in catching her, nor does he hide himself. Suddenly there is a great wonder in the village: the young chief's wife is about to be a mother!

The time comes. Laks tells his husband that it is the custom among his people to be alone when a child is born. When the hour arrives, the people hear a baby crying inside the wikuwam. The women who are waiting there run in, but they are met by the mother, who is just coming out and gives them the child, all wrapped up. They take it to the young chief. He is quite surprised when he opens the outer wrapping—there is another layer, tied securely—then another—and yet another, stitched tight. When he opens this one, way down inside he finds two dried-up moose fetuses.

The young chief is so furious that he dashes their brains out in the fire. Then he grabs his ax and goes to kill his wife. But Laks is now a man again. It occurs to him that he does not want anyone bothering him; so together with his brother he flees into the woods. They hurry away down to the river.

Laks thinks it would be better if he could escape his pursuers for good. He and his brother make a fir-and-earth dam. The water barely trickles through downstream. Then he hides in a cave under the earthwork, where he imitates the sound of flowing water. No one else knows where he is. Laks has caught *himself*. The water collects upstream until it forms a lake. Then the dam bursts; the water mows him down and drowns him. No one mourns.

And thus Laks comes to an end—no more is told about him. But whether he is finished or not no one knows for sure. Maybe he'll be found alive again. There are many good stories, all of which confirm that Laks will never die.

The telling ends.

THE
SOUTHWEST
AND
SOUTHEAST

RUNNING THE DEER

▲

LARRY EVERS
AND
FELIPE S. MOLINA

INTRODUCTION

Yaqui Indian people call themselves Yoemem, "the People." Their aboriginal homeland is just south of Guaymas, along the Rio Yaqui in southern Sonora, Mexico. About thirty thousand Yaquis continue to live there, on a rich alluvial plain where the Sonoran Desert meets the sea. During the late nineteenth and early twentieth centuries Mexican attempts to exterminate the Yaquis and appropriate their lands resulted in intense warfare and a Yaqui diaspora. During this time many Yaquis fled north across the border to the United States and established villages. Some seven thousand continue to live in southern Arizona today. As Edward H. Spicer put it, the Yoemem continue in the United States and in Mexico at the end of the twentieth century as "one of the enduring peoples of the world."[1] Perhaps the most visible sign of their endurance as a people is the deer dance, a ritual that celebrates a cycle of life, death, and spiritual continuance.

The Yoemem know the deer dancer as *saila maso*, "little brother deer." When their little brother deer comes to dance for them, he has a voice. The voice speaks to all through the songs to which the deer dancer moves. The deer songs are the voice of *saila maso*. "All that he should talk about, that is what we sing," one deer singer told us. "He does not talk, but he talks in an enchanted way."

Deer songs are a traditional kind of Yaqui song usually sung by three men to accompany the performance of the deer dance. Yaquis regard deer songs as the most ancient of their verbal art forms. Highly conventionalized in their structure, their diction, their themes, and their mode of performance, deer songs describe a double world, both "here" and "over there," a world in which all the actions of the deer dancer have a parallel in that mythical, primeval place called by the Yaquis *sea ania*, "flower world." The flower world is associated with such other spiritual places as the *yo ania*, "enchanted world," and the *huya ania*, "wilderness world," and is home to both *saila maso* and Yevuku Yoleme, the prototypical deer hunter. Deer songs describe equivalencies between these two real parts of the Yaqui universe. They are verbal equations, developed richly with phonological, syntactic, and rhetorical parallelisms and repetitions. The songs link the dusty world of the dance with the ethereal flower world, a world seen with one unseen, a world that is very much here with one that is always over there. *Sewam*, "flowers," are a key part of this equation. *Flower* in this sense is anything from the flower world that is good and beautiful. Anything that is informed, influenced, or touched by the *sea ania*, the "flower world," may be termed "flower." The *rama* (from Spanish *ramada*), the location of the deer dance, is constructed of mesquite, cane, cottonwood, and other plants from the Sonoran Desert and suggests an opening in a desert thicket. The *rama* is said to become the flower world during the ceremony.

Usually the deer dance is performed during a *pahko*, a ceremonial occasion when Yaquis gather to perform religious rituals and celebrate. Ritual clowns, called *pahkolam* ("old men of the *pahko*"), serve as hosts and speech makers at these events. They also perform their own dances alongside the deer dancer but to different musicians. On certain occasions—for example, the first anniversary of the death of a loved one—special forms of the *pahko* are held. At such times the deer dancer and the *pahkolam* enact extended dramatic performances, burlesques. Yaquis call these *yeuwame*, "games." They are accompanied by whole sets of deer songs.

The translations that follow form the song set of one of these games, called *maso nehhawa*, "running the deer." The song words describe the drama of a deer hunt, using the point of view of both the hunters and the hunted. The deer dancer, *saila maso*, is the hunted. The four ritual clowns, the *pahkolam*, take on the role of Yevuku Yoleme, the "hunter person." One is called father, two are sons, and the fourth plays the part of their dog. Armed with little wooden bows and corncob-tipped arrows, the clowns jabber and bungle their way through a hunt for the deer in a series of slapstick episodes. All while this extended burlesque unfolds, the deer singers, according to Don Jesus Yoilo'i, "just sit and sing for the deer." Their words take the audience beyond the burlesque, beyond the earthly death the *saila maso* experiences, to describe how he "becomes flower" and is received back into the sentient wilderness world from which he was taken. We relate this combination of the farcical and the serious to other dramatic traditions of Native America, most especially those of the Hopi, the Yaquis' Uto-Aztecan relatives, who create a similar combination each time they bring their clowns and *katsinam* (transcendent beings who are embodied by masked dancers) into the same place. When the Yaqui *pahkolam* clown their exuberant slapsticks, they open the audience to laughter and remove any hint of sentimentality from the words of the deer singers. In this way the absurd burlesques of the clowns provide a context in which the words of deer songs can achieve an emotional intensity that is rare in any poetic tradition.

Don Jesus Yoilo'i (1904–82) was a very accomplished deer singer who lived in Potam, Sonora. As a teenager he fought to protect his homeland from colonists and was wounded. The songs that follow he sang for us in May of 1981 at Yoem Pueblo, a Yaqui community near Tucson, Arizona. Don Jesus's use of the first person singular pronoun *ne* in his songs is an important aspect of his style. It is most prominent in the *tonua,* the concluding stanza, which in almost all of Don Jesus's songs we recorded, began *"ayaman ne." Iyiminsu* and *ayamansu* are two locatives that many other singers use in the same position. All three words mean "over there." When we asked Don Jesus about his use of *ayaman ne,* he told us that it was used in the running-the-deer songs and that he used it in other songs because he liked it. Other singers use the form, but none in our experience uses it quite so pervasively. Don Jesus's use of *ne* at the beginning of his concluding stanzas provides a constant personal presence in his songs. We wonder whether he felt a special affinity near the end of his own life with the "I" of the deer he perpetuated. By the time we thought to ask that question, he was gone. In any case what Don Jesus accomplishes through the use of this I is not the celebration of his individual ego but rather an identification with an I that has endured as long as any other in Yaqui culture. He accomplishes what Kenneth Burke calls a rhetoric of identification: "Only those voices from without are effective which can speak in a language of the voice within."[2]

Repetition is an important part of the songs. Our translations present the words as Don Jesus sang them, with all repetitions represented. Following each of our translations are comments that Don Jesus made as we played the songs back for him. For transcriptions of these songs in the Yaqui language, as well as more extensive discussion of them, see *Yaqui Deer Songs/Maso Bwikam: A Native American Poetry*.[3]

NOTES

1. Edward H. Spicer, *The Yaquis: A Cultural History* (Tucson: University of Arizona Press, 1980).

2. Kenneth Burke, *A Rhetoric of Motives* (Berkeley: University of California Press, 1969), 39.

3. Larry Evers and Felipe S. Molina, *Yaqui Deer Songs/Maso Bwikam: A Native American Poetry* (Tucson: University of Arizona Press, 1987). For a visual presentation, see Evers and Molina, *Seyewailo: The Flower World* (New York: Norman Ross Publishing), videotape, 50 min.

1

First you just look;
   later you will find, find.
First you just look;
   later you will find, find.

First you just look;
   later you will find, find.
First you just look;
   later you will find, find.

Over there, I, in an opening
   in the flower-covered grove,
     I went out;
       then you will find, find.
First you just look;
   later you will find, find.

"First just take a look for him," it says. "When he goes out in an opening of the grove, then you will find him," it says. "First you just look, while later you will find him," the deer hunters, the pahkolam, they are the ones who are speaking in it.

Then, then the pahkolam will go out. Somewhere in the wilderness they will look for the tracks. Yes, in the wilderness. Well, not really in the wilderness, but just around there in front of the rama, they will walk, walk. Later they will really look for him out there. But like that they look, and like that they will come back inside the rama again. Like that the song goes.

2

Here, we, where the mescal agave
   like mescal agave stands,
     together we will meet.
Here, we, where the mescal agave
   like mescal agave stands,
     together we will meet.

Here, we, where the mescal agave
   like mescal agave stands,
     together we will meet.

Here, we, where the mescal agave
   like mescal agave stands,
      together we will meet.

And you are an enchanted, enchanted black vulture.
And you are an enchanted, enchanted turkey vulture.
Here, we, where the white wood stands,
   together we meet;
      together we will talk about this animal.
Here, we, where the mescal agave
   like mescal agave stands,
      together we will not meet.

The black vulture and the turkey vulture will meet where the white wood is standing. "When we meet, we will talk about the animal," it says. They will talk together, the turkey vulture and the black vulture, about the deer. The black vulture wants to say that. The deer will dance with that. The turkey vulture and the black vulture want to talk together themselves where there is white wood standing.

They come out here when they see something lying dead, like cows or horses. They live somewhere here on top of us. They live on top of us. They want to come down here to eat. That turkey vulture, that black vulture. The song says that.

The black vulture and the turkey vulture want to hunt, want to eat there. That's why they say this. Over there they say they will meet where the white wood is standing. Maybe it is a dead tree. Sitting together there, the sun hits them, warms them. They will talk about the animal, where they are going to overpower him. So these are the ones who are going to eat him. They are sitting somewhere out there.

3

Around there
   look for tracks;
      go get him for me.
Around there
   look for tracks;
      go get him for me.

Around there
   look for tracks;
      go get him for me.
Around there

   look for tracks;
      go get him for me.

Around there
   look for tracks;
      go get him for me.
Around there
   look for tracks;
      go get him for me.

Over there, I, in an opening
   in the flower-covered grove,
      I go out; then
         you will get him for me.
Around there
   look for tracks;
      go get him for me.

"Around there look for tracks. After a while we will get him," it says. "To-ward the flower opening, when he goes out there, we will get him," the pah-kolam say that. Then when he has gone out, they will get him. He will run out with this song, run out.

The deer will stand at the patio cross there. And these who wait for him will sit here. All four of them will sit behind some brush. When they are out there, the deer singers will start this song. When the song is starting, the deer will run toward them in the brush. They will fall backward and knock one another down. They will tell one another not to make noise. The pahkolam will joke around.

Then during the concluding stanzas the deer will push aside the one sitting there and run out. Then that pahkola will fall over backward. When he shoots, when he shoots, he will shoot upward, up into the air, and he will throw his bow.

Then the pahkolam who are the sons, they will say, "As an elder why did you do that, Father, Papa?" They will start spanking him. They will spank their father!

"Where is my wiko'i, 'bow'?"

"He is at Vicam Switch."*

"There at Potam is another."

In that way the pahkolam will joke among themselves. But then one will say, "No, not the men named Wiko'i but the wooden bow." Then they will look for it.

*He: Wiko'i is a family name as well as the word for "bow." Thus, there is a play on words here.

"Here it lies, the one that belongs to you."

That is after the deer has already run out of the rama. There at the patio cross, the pahkolam will make a round looking for him. The dog will already be there with them. The dog will look for tracks. After he finds them, the dog will bark loudly.

"The dog found it over there," they will say. And again the dog will chase the deer out. The dog will take off after him. The song goes like that.

4

Toward a place where
   I could not find safety, I went.
Toward a place where
   I could not find safety, I went.
Toward a place where
   I could not find safety, I went.

Toward a place where
   I could not find safety, I went.
Toward a place where
   I could not find safety, I went.
Toward a place where
   I could not find safety, I went.

Over there, I, in an opening
   in the flower-covered grove, I am
      here where these enchanted
         bow people are walking about.
Toward a place where
   I could not find safety, I went.
Toward a place where
   I could not find safety, I went.

Like that the deer ran out, went out in the world, saw the grove and went out. "Nowhere could I find safety," it says. "Well, here where the bow people are, toward them I went," it says.

Well, he isn't sure of himself. That is why he went toward where they were. "Toward a place where there is no safety, I went," it says, toward the wilderness grove and the wilderness world. The deer talks about that. The deer himself says that. He ran out to the wilderness world. The song says that.

5

Although unseen in the wilderness,
   I am just running.
My antler crown with these three branches
   is showing, moving.

Although unseen in the wilderness,
   I am just running.
My antler crown with these three branches
   is showing, moving.

Although unseen in the wilderness,
   I am just running.
My antler crown with these three branches
   is showing, moving.

Although unseen in the wilderness,
   I am just running.
My antler crown with these three branches
   is showing, moving.

Over there, I, in the center
   of the flower-covered grove,
     I am walking.
My antler crown with these three branches
   is showing, moving.

The deer is hiding, running. In a desert like this, he is running out. But his antlers are seen moving. That is what tells on him. That is why it says this. "Although unseen in the wilderness, I am just running," it says. "But my antlers are out. They are seen moving," it says. The deer himself says that. He has big antlers. The song goes like that.

6

Flower-covered grove, as I am walking to you,
   I am talking to you, flower-covered grove.

Flower-covered grove, as I am walking to you,
   I am talking to you, flower-covered grove.

Flower-covered grove, as I am walking to you,
   I am talking to you, flower-covered grove.

▲

Flower-covered grove, as I am walking to you,
  I am talking to you, flower-covered grove.

Over there, I, in an opening
  in the flower-covered grove,
    as I am walking,
      these enchanted bow people,
        behind me I see.
These I see,
  I am talking to you, flower-covered grove.

*The deer will be running during this song. As he is running, he is talking to
the wilderness world. As he is going, he is talking to the wilderness world.
"Flower-covered grove," it says. "As I am walking to you, I am talking to
you," it says.*

  *He wants someone to talk for him. He wants the wilderness world to talk for
him. How will it talk for him? The song, the song just says that. The poor thing
wants someone to talk for him. Not wanting to die, the deer himself says that
in the song. The song goes like that.*

7

You who are each other's brothers
  are shouting well, beautifully together,
shouting well, beautifully together,
  shouting beautifully together.

You who are each other's brothers
  are shouting well, beautifully together,
shouting well, beautifully together,
  shouting beautifully together.

You who are each other's brothers
  are shouting well, beautifully together,
shouting well, beautifully together,
  shouting beautifully together.

Over there, I, in the center
  of the flower-covered opening,
    we are running.
Just I, in flower fawn's
  flower dust,
    we are running,

shouting well, beautifully together,
　　shouting beautifully together.

The deer hunters, the pahkolam.
　　Well, this song is the four pahkolam chasing the deer, running, shouting,
chasing the deer. It is like when the children chase and shout at something.
They are running that way.
　　"Running there in an opening in the grove," it says. "Running in flower
person's, flower fawn's dust," it says. "Shouting well, beautifully together," it
says. "You who are each other's brothers," it says. The four pahkolam, the
"deer hunters," pahkolam. The song says that.

8

Where is the shouting?
　　Outside in the opening is the shouting.
Where is the shouting?
　　Outside in the opening is the shouting.

Where is the shouting?
　　Outside in the opening is the shouting.
Where is the shouting?
　　Outside in the opening is the shouting.

Where is the shouting?
　　Outside in the opening is the shouting.
Where is the shouting?
　　Outside in the opening is the shouting.

Where is the shouting?
　　Outside in the opening is the shouting.
Where is the shouting?
　　Outside in the opening is the shouting.

Over there, I, in the opening
　　in the flower-covered grove,
　　　　in the flower fawn's flower dust,
　　　　　　we are running.
Where is the shouting?
　　Outside in the opening is the shouting.
Where is the shouting?
　　Outside in the opening is the shouting.

The pahkolam will be running and shouting after the deer. "Where is the shouting?" it says. "Well, outside in the opening is the shouting," it says. The pahkolam are running after the deer while we are inside singing. "Over there in an opening in the grove, in flower fawn's flower dust, they are running," it says. "The shouting is outside in an opening," it says. The song says only that.

9

Not wanting to die,
   dodging through the wilderness.
Not wanting to die,
   dodging through the wilderness.

Not wanting to die,
   dodging through the wilderness.
Not wanting to die,
   dodging through the wilderness.

Not wanting to die,
   dodging through the wilderness.
Not wanting to die,
   dodging through the wilderness.

Not wanting to die,
   dodging through the wilderness.
Not wanting to die,
   dodging through the wilderness.

Not wanting to die,
   dodging through the wilderness.
Not wanting to die,
   dodging through the wilderness.

Over there, I, alongside
   the flower-covered grove,
     as I am walking,
      each enchanted thicket,
       dodging, moving.
Not wanting to die,
   dodging through the wilderness.

Toward the wilderness he is walking. The deer himself, to save himself there, he wants to enter the wilderness. "I want to enter the wilderness," it says. "Not wanting to die, I want to enter the wilderness," the deer himself says that. The deer himself, while he is walking, he is saying that in that way.

10

Exhausted from running, you are walking;
   exhausted from running, you are moving;
      exhausted from running, you are walking.

Exhausted from running, you are walking;
   exhausted from running, you are moving;
      exhausted from running, you are walking.

Exhausted from running, you are walking;
   exhausted from running, you are moving;
      exhausted from running, you are walking.

Exhausted from running, you are walking;
   exhausted from running, you are moving;
      exhausted from running, you are walking.

Over there, I, in an opening
   in the flower-covered grove,
     as I am walking,
  alongside
    the flower-covered grove,
      as I am walking,
with my head hanging down
   toward the ground,
     as I am walking,
with foam
   around my mouth,
     as I am walking;
exhausted from running, you are walking;
   exhausted from running, you are moving.

"Exhausted from running, you are walking," it says. "Exhausted from running, you are walking," it says. Tired, walking, moving, there at the edge of the grove, the deer is walking. With his head hanging down to the ground, with foam around the mouth, he is walking. Tired, walking, the deer himself says that in that way.

11

Never again I,
  will I on this world,
    I, around will I be walking.
Just I, never again I,
  will I on this world,
    I, around will I be walking.

Just I, never again I,
  will I on this world,
    I, around will I be walking.
Just I, never again I,
  will I on this world,
    I, around will I be walking.

Over there, I,
  in an opening in the flower-covered grove,
    as I am walking.
Just I, Yevuku Yoleme's bow
  overpowered me in an enchanted way.
Yevuku Yoleme's bamboo arrow
  overpowered me in an enchanted way.
Never again I,
  will I on this world,
    I, around will I be walking.

*This is where he falls. "Never again I, will I here, around will I be walking,"
it says. The deer himself is going to be killed, going to die. "Yevuku Yoleme's
wooden bow," it says. It means with a wooden bow I am overpowered in an
enchanted way. "With Yevuku Yoleme's cane arrow I am overpowered in an
enchanted way. Never again I, will I on this world, I, around will I be walking," it says.*

    *The deer himself says that like that. He talks like that. As he is going to die,
while dying as he is going to die, he says that like that. Just as all will say yes
while being taken somewhere to a war, they will be walking there to die. As if
to say "Never again are we going to walk about on this earth." Like that this
deer speaks in the song. "Never again I, will I on this earth, I, around will I
be walking." The deer says that like that. He is talking about himself.*

12

What happened to me that my hands
   are over my antler crown?
What happened to me that my hands
   are over my antler crown?

What happened to me that my hands
   are over my antler crown?
What happened to me that my hands
   are over my antler crown?

What happened to me that my hands
   are over my antler crown?
What happened to me that my hands
   are over my antler crown?

Over there, I, in an opening
   in the flower-covered grove,
      as I am walking.
Just I, flower person's wooden bow
   has taken me.
Flower person's flower-cane arrow
   has overpowered me in an enchanted way.
What happened to me that my hands
   are over my antler crown?

The deer, the deer, he is saying this as he is being carried. The hunters killed him, the pahkolam, the ones who are the hunter persons.

I also kill deer. I always place the hands on the top of the antlers when I carry one after killing it. The song says that: "What happened to me that my hands are over my antler crown?" Well, it is because his hands are placed there by the hunters, and he is being carried. He himself is saying that in that way and singing about himself.

He is killed, killed by a wooden bow.

13

Killed and taken, killed and taken,
   there in the wilderness,
      I am killed and taken.

Killed and taken, killed and taken,
  there in the wilderness,
    I am killed and taken.

Killed and taken, killed and taken,
  there in the wilderness,
    I am killed and taken.

Over there, I, in the center
  of the flower-covered wilderness.
Just I, Yevuku Yoleme overpowered
  me in an enchanted way.
Enchanted Yevuku Yolemem overpowered
  me in an enchanted way.
Killed and taken,
  there in the wilderness,
    I am killed and taken.

Here he will enter the rama again; he will be carried into the rama. Here he is talking about himself. "I am killed and taken. There in the wilderness, I am killed," it says. "The enchanted hunter people have gotten me," it says. He is talking about himself. "Dead, I am being taken," it says.

14

On branches you lay
  flower-covered person's flower body.
On branches you lay
  flower-covered person's flower body.

On branches you lay
  flower-covered person's flower body.
On branches you lay
  flower-covered person's flower body.

On branches you lay
  flower-covered person's flower body.
On branches you lay
  flower-covered person's flower body.

Over there, I, in Yevuku Yoleme's
  flower-covered, enchanted, enchanted flower patio,

gather each plant
   from the enchanted wilderness world.
On them you lay
  flower-covered person's flower body.

Here the singers are saying that to him. "On branches you lay flower-covered person's flower body," it says. "In Yevuku Yoleme's flower patio gather each plant from the wilderness world, and lay him on them," it says. Lay the deer on them.

Any plant can be used. At the pahko there is always cottonwood. On the rama there will be some cottonwood stuck there and out in the roadway. That can be used to place on him, on the deer.

This is where he will be butchered, where the pahkolam will butcher him. Once he is placed there on the branches, he will be covered with an old sack or blanket. I will say this song when they lay him on the branches. But then the tampaleo, *the "flute player," will sing differently; he will start to play a different one. While he is being placed on the branches, the tampaleo will start playing the spotted-fly song. The deer singers do not have the spotted-fly song, only the tampaleo. Then the pahkolam will play with that song, they will play with it. They will play round the deer; then they will pretend to defecate on him, on the dead deer. They will walk around him and pretend to defecate on him. Then they will say, "Let's butcher him right away." So they butcher him.*

15

Put a flower on me
  from flower-covered person's flower body.
Put a flower on me
  from flower-covered person's flower body.

Oh, put a flower on me
  from flower-covered person's flower body.
Put a flower on me
  from flower-covered person's flower body.

Oh, put a flower on me
  from flower-covered person's flower body.
Put a flower on me
  from flower-covered person's flower body.

Over there, I,
  in the flower-covered flower opening,
    as I am standing,

covered with dust,
   as I am standing,
covered with mist,
   as I am standing,
put a flower on me
   from flower-covered person's flower body.

Well, you see it is windy now, a dusty wind, a dusty wind. Tolosailo *is when it is dusty and not too clear. That is the way it is also somewhere in Yevuku Yoleme's flower patio out there.*

   That tree, like those standing over there in the patio, yes, well, that tree is talking to him. This is what the tree is saying. In the patio a tree will be standing. When the deer is laid there on the branches, the tree will ask for the tail, for the deer's tail. All the deer hunters cut off the tail and hang it on the tree. That is what the tree is asking for. The tree is asking for the tail. "Put a flower on me from flower-covered person's flower body," it says. The tree is saying that to the hunters, to the pahkolam. *It wants to tell the deer hunters to hang the tail on it. The tree will stand with the flower. The tree that is standing in the patio is the one that wants it as a flower, the deer's tail.*

16

My enchanted flower body,
   fire, above the fire,
      side by side is hung.
My enchanted flower body,
   fire, above the fire,
      side by side is hung.

My enchanted flower body,
   fire, above the fire,
      side by side is hung.
My enchanted flower body,
   fire, above the fire,
      side by side is hung.

My enchanted flower body,
   fire, above the fire,
      side by side is hung.
My enchanted flower body,
   fire, above the fire,
      side by side is hung.

Over there, I, in Yevuku Yoleme's
  flower-covered flower patio,
    here I am scattered;
      I become enchanted;
    here I am scattered;
      I become flower.
My enchanted flower body,
  fire, above the fire,
    side by side is hung.

*The meat, as it is being roasted in that way, it speaks. There it will be skewered.
"My enchanted flower body above the fire side by side is hung, skewered," it
says. "Yevuku Yoleme's flower patio," it says. "Here I am scattered and
become flower," it says. The deer's spirit stays in the wilderness. The deer says
that about himself. He sings like that.*

17

My enchanted flower body is glistening,
  sitting out there.
My enchanted flower body is glistening,
  sitting out there.

My enchanted flower body is glistening,
  sitting out there.
My enchanted flower body is glistening,
  sitting out there.

Over there, I, in Yevuku Yoleme's
  flower-covered flower patio,
    I am just glistening,
      sitting out there;
    here I am scattered;
      I become enchanted.
My enchanted flower body is glistening,
  sitting out there.

Guts, deer guts, it is the guts the song talks about here.

18

But one stick,
  not good and beautiful,

is standing.
But one stick,
   not good and beautiful,
      is standing.

But one stick,
   not good and beautiful,
      is standing.
But one stick,
   not good and beautiful,
      is standing.

But one stick,
   not good and beautiful,
      is standing.
But one stick,
   not good and beautiful,
      is standing.

Over there, I, in the center
   of the flower-covered wilderness,
      there in the wilderness,
         one, good and beautiful, is standing.
But one stick,
   not good and beautiful,
      is standing.

*With this song it is finished. The pahkolam, they themselves, will cut one an-
other down. The one who is made into a post will be cut and will fall there. He
will fall down, lie down backward, and straighten out. Forcefully he will
point his head toward the post in the rama. Then, after pointing his head in a
certain way, they will get an old sack or a blanket. They will wet it in some
water and cover him up. In that way they tan the deer hide.*

*After that is done they will be out there hitting the Yaquis in the audience
with it, saying that they are still tanning it. That will be the last; nothing else
will there be in the game. There it is ended. The run lasts to that point.*

PIMA ORIOLE

SONGS

▲

DONALD BAHR
AND
VINCENT JOSEPH

INTRODUCTION BY DONALD BAHR

In northern Mexico and a great part of the western United States, including the Great Basin, southern California, and Arizona, there was a Native singing tradition that the musicologist George Herzog called the "dreamt mythic song series."[1] Now there is relatively little left of it, but as these Pima Oriole songs will show, the tradition can still surprise and reward us. In fact, the main theme in these songs is precisely a combination of pleasure and anguish over finding songs, as if the tradition were pleading for itself through this one Oriole singer.

The Pima live in southern Arizona immediately south and southeast of Phoenix. Songs belonging to the same tradition have recently been published by Larry Evers and Felipe Molina—from the Yaqui of Arizona and Sonora; by A. M. Halpern—from the Yuma of the Arizona-California border; by Judith Vander—from the Wind River Shoshone of west-central Wyoming; and by me—from the Pima and the adjacent Papago, or Tohono O'odham.[2] I cannot discuss the knowledge of the full extent and varieties of the tradition, but I refer the reader to Herzog's original paper, to remarks by Alfred Kroeber, and to my own writings.[3] And I now venture that the present set of forty-seven songs is the fullest, most carefully constructed, and poetically richest "dreamt mythic song series" to be published to date.

The singer of this material was Vincent Joseph, a Pima who, I regret to say, died in 1987. According to tradition, the actual author of the songs was an oriole whom some Pima or Papago met in a dream. Joseph and I encountered the songs in the early 1980s through the Pima singer Blaine Pablo. During about ten visits at that time, Vincent Joseph, Joseph Giff, also a Pima, and I, a White, asked Pablo to sing ever more Oriole songs. Though Joseph and Giff were singers, they didn't know this type of song. I taped the sung portions of the sessions and gave copies of most of the tapes to them. Because he apparently didn't learn the songs from the sessions whose tapes I inadvertently failed to give him, I'm sure the tapes he did receive aided Joseph's learning of the songs. Altogether, Pablo sang sixty-eight Oriole songs. Of the forty-seven songs presented here, forty-five were on the tapes in Joseph's possession. He added two songs on his own.

Pablo and Giff died around 1983. I believe that more people than Pablo knew Oriole songs in the early 1980s, and I know that Emmett White, a Pima, learned them from Vincent Joseph. White sings them today, perhaps with additions from other singers or his own dreams.

Perhaps because of his character (but also perhaps because his health was better than Pablo's), Joseph was determined to put the Oriole songs in a fixed order and keep them constantly ready for use. Thus, three times when I dropped in on him unannounced, he sang essentially the same set through perfectly, in very nearly the same order. Moreover, and rare among singers in my experience, he was able to say what each song said, literally and fully, in ordinary language, immediately before singing each one. (Song language is a step removed from ordinary language.[4]) His ordinary language, or "prose," statements are given along with the song texts below.

A chatterbox in ordinary life, Joseph did not use his gift of talk to weave a narrative from the songs. As will be seen, the first twenty-two songs constitute a kind of travelogue tour of Pima-Papago country (thereafter the songs become topical), but Joseph did not say who made the tour or why. His comments on these and all the songs are limited to the songs' texts. (I have translated his comments as if the traveler were a male oriole.) Connections between texts are rarely discussed. I'm sure this was not an oversight on his part. It was his, and is his people's, custom to let song series suggest stories but to avoid speculating or telling about events that would link one song to another. Each song is a short word-pictorial story; the sets are elaborate, exquisite montages or collages.

Joseph apparently wanted to find a place in his repertoire for each Oriole song on the tapes (plus the two he added); so I cannot say he was selective in the songs he included. Nor did he revise any texts; like all participants in the regional tradition, he did not consciously create or change texts but, on the contrary, took pains to reproduce them exactly as he heard them. Thus, his one outlet for creation was in sequencing the songs—in other words, in executing the montage.

It should be noted that Joseph had excellent materials to work with. There is not a bad or humdrum song in the lot, and more to the point, the full set is quite varied. Most but not all of them contain an "I" (a first person singular pronoun), which is a hallmark of Pima-Papago song and seems to set the songs of these people apart from those of other traditions of dream-song singing. And relative to other Pima-Papago sets, this one, whose original "I" was presumably an oriole, includes a wide variety of experiences, ranging from the pure observation of nature to encounters with ancient and recent characters (borrowings, one may say, from prose narratives) to episodes of shamanistic power getting. Joseph needed to make these short sketches resonate sequentially.

The key to what he did, I believe, lies in the placement of songs 2 and 31. (The numbering follows Joseph's sequence; another singer could order them differently.) Pablo once sang the two contiguously, and this pairing undoubtedly impressed Joseph. Song 31 answers song 2 in a way that establishes the set as a plea or defense of dreamed-song singing; and song 2 is itself an unusual turn on the normal way to commence a Pima-Papago song set.

Let us consider the unusualness of song 2. By convention, nearly every Pima-Papago song set begins with references to the commencement of singing and the sunset. The idea is that the actual singing should start at sunset and last until dawn. Regardless of what happens to internal time references, the opening and closing songs should adhere to that rule. Song 1 adheres in a normal manner, being about the onset of singing, but song 2 fulfills the sunset requirement unusually. It is really about the creation of the sun and refers to the sunset only in a perfunctory but happy last line: the new sun sets in the west; the diurnal course is established. Also unusual is that the sun is not mentioned again until song 31. Most Pima song sets begin with a long sequence of four, eight, or twelve songs on the sunset.

Now we may consider the originality of song 31, which is about the sun's death, not about its setting. This death harks back to the unusual dwelling on creation in song 2: what was originated can also end. But it is not metaphysics that makes the song remarkable: it is the implication for singing. When the sun dies, the song says, all the birds but one terminate their singing; the exception is the mockingbird, who is understood by the Pima-Papago (as well as ornithologists) to imitate the calls of other birds. The Pima-Papago conclude that mockingbirds do not give fresh information on themselves or the universe but merely regurgitate, or "parrot," what they have heard. Accordingly, song 31 describes a dismal scene: the end of the sun entails the end of fresh bird calls.

One more step takes us to the plea for singing. Oriole songs are a variety of bird songs, and Pima-Papago singing is replete with sets dreamed from birds: the oriole, blackbird, woodpecker, hummingbird, and buzzard, as well as the bat and butterfly (conceived as birds—"flying things") and more. So far as I know, there are no mockingbird songs, because they are considered unoriginal birds. Of course, one could make the same case about human song dreamers—they are like mockingbirds because they too only repeat the songs that other more original spirits give them. I believe this is exactly the point. The lone mockingbird singing at the end of song 31 is like a human singer who can no longer dream, or at least can no longer dream songs—analogous to a washed-up poet in our society. I never asked Joseph whether he had dreamed songs, but I suspect he could and would have if he thought people had a real use for them. I am not sure what he thought about this last, but his strategic placing of song 31 implies an intelligent doubt.

To complete the survey: the bulk of the songs between 2 and 31 are in effect an oriole's tour of Pima-Papago land, apparently, thanks to song 2, a tour made in daylight. Geographically the tour begins a few miles from Pablo's home and goes to the eastern edge of the universe (song 3), then south into Papago country (songs 5 and 6), back to Pablo's neighborhood (songs 7–11), then north (songs 12–16), and finally west, ending at the Gulf of California (songs 17–22). Songs 23–30 are dedicated to the various bird species mentioned above; then comes the key song 31. Soon after (song 33) is a conventional song about the sunset, such as one might find at the start of other sets. Then follows a series on medicine men (songs 34–39) and whores (songs 40–44), and finally are three songs on the end of a night of singing. These last make further comments on the fragility of song.

It is not possible to discuss all the songs here, but I will comment briefly on the series on medicine men and whores. These seem to be the favored male and female human character types in all bird-song sets. Such sets have been used in "social dancing," in which men and women clasp hands to dance in a circling line in celebration of harvests, war victories, girls' reaching puberty, and in this century, American national holidays. Thus, although it is rare and welcome to find the character of the medicine man, or shaman, paired with a nonshamanistic alter in a tribal literature, this particular pairing owes much to the social-dancing context and must be seen in exactly that light. As I read it, the set says that both medicine men and whores seek songs. The seeker is away from home, alone in nature, in the first case (songs 4, 7, 12, 13, 14, 15, 16, and 26) and away from home adulterously, in society, at dances, in the second (songs 40, 42, and 43). The first search enables the second, and it is not clear whether the second motivates the first. Thus says this social-dancing poetry.

The translation of Joseph's prose given below is literal in that it follows his word order rather closely and preserves his ambiguity and terseness.[5] Joseph spoke quite grammatical, "good" Pima, but I have bent English grammatical and stylistic norms, generally to avoid saying any more than he did. The same is true of the song translations. I have not tried, or have tried rather little, to make the translations into beautiful English poems. Word order was changed some, in deference to English, but the content of each line is limited to the content of that line in the original. In general, I find the Pima poems understated on the surface and boiling underneath. The translations imperfectly reflect this.

I thank Adelaide Bahr, John Bierhorst, Arnold Krupat, Brian Swann, and Emmett White for discussing these translations with me.

NOTES

1. George Herzog, "Musical Styles in North America," in *Proceedings of the Twenty-third International Congress of Americanists* (New York, 1928), 455–56.

2. Larry Evers and Felipe Molina, *Yaqui Deer Songs/Maso Bwikam: A Native American Poetry* (Tucson: University of Arizona Press, 1987); A. M. Halpern

(credited to W. Wilson), "Excerpts from the Lightning Song," in *Spirit Mountain: An Anthology of Yuman Song and Story,* ed. L. Hinton and L. Watahomigie (Tucson: Sun Tracks and University of Arizona Press, 1984); Judith Vander, *Ghost Dance Songs and Religion of a Wind River Shoshone Woman,* Monograph Series in Ethnomusicology no. 4 (Los Angeles: University of California, 1986); and Donald Bahr, "A Format and Method for Translating Songs," *Journal of American Folklore* 96 (1983): 170–82, and "Pima Heaven Song," in *Recovering the Word: Essays on Native American Literature,* ed. Brian Swann and Arnold Krupat (Berkeley: University of California Press, 1987).

3. Herzog, "Musical Styles in North America"; Alfred L. Kroeber, *Handbook of the Indians of California,* Smithsonian Institution, Bureau of American Ethnology Bulletin no. 78 (Washington, D.C., 1925; reprint, New York: Dover, 1976), 754–90; and Bahr, "A Format and Method for Translating Songs" and "Pima Heaven Song."

4. For a discussion of this, see Bahr, "A Format and Method for Translating Songs."

5. Pima-language transcripts of Vincent Joseph's prose and song performance, as well as an audiotape of the performance, are available (Donald Bahr, Arizona State University, Tempe, Ariz.).

1

"Here I sit, here feather-down topknot sticks to me.* It waves nicely with my song." Thus says this, which is the first [song] and says,

I'm seated,
crowded by people,
crowded by feather-down topknots,
wavering with songs.

2

Look, and this tells when the sun will rise where it is called—uh—Casa Grande Ruins.† Here the sun was newly made: "Sun is newly made. Away in front of the east, toss it, and it rises. Here above us it goes, and away westward it sets," so says this song. It says,

Make a new sun.
Toss it east.
It will climb,
will light the ground,
will pass over me,
will sink in the west.

---

*feather-down topknot: Orioles, the source of these songs, do not have topknots. The reference is to people—social dancers—who crowd around as a singer sits down for a night of singing. People's fancy ceremonial feathers, little used by the Pima, are called by the same word that is used for topknots: *siwoda*, or *siwdag*.

†Casa Grande Ruins: Joseph said this name in English. The ruins are a national monument about twenty miles from where Pablo lived, just outside the eastern boundary of the Pima reservation. The Pima name for the place is Siwan Wa'aki, "Rainmaker Rain House." Joseph thought that the sun making occurred there. Song 3 names a different rain house, called Shining Rain House, which is considered to stand at the eastern edge of the earth, far from Rainmaker Rain House, which is "central." Songs 7 and 8 refer explicitly to Rainmaker Rain House. For the last hundred years the Pima have debated whether they are the descendants or the exterminators of the ancient people who built Rainmaker Rain House. They call the people the Huhugkam, "Finished Ones," but those who champion descent do not consider that the name implies extermination. The archaeologists' term Hohokam refers to the same people and was borrowed from the Pima.

3

Look, and that which stands there is the Shining Rain House.* "In front of the east, the Shining Rain House stands. Who sings there? Inside a song is locked. I unlock it and see"; so this one sounds.

Who sings?
Away where the East Shining Rain House stands,
inside, various kinds of song
are locked.
I then unlock them and
then see.

4

Then is the one that says, "Where will you take me? Away far is the Witch's Making Place. Upon it bring me. On the Witch's Bed the land sparkles."†

Where are you taking me?
Where are you taking me—
bringing me to the Witch's Making Place?
On the Witch's Bed earth sparkles.

5

Then [the Oriole traveler arrives] there, where Santa Rosa is,‡ where there is the Children's Burial, as we call it.

Children's Burial,
Children's Burial
I come upon,

***there:** far in the east.
†**Witch's making place . . . Witch's bed:** Witch, Ho'ok, is an important character in Pima-Papago mythology, a female feebleminded monster who grew claws as a child and ate children as an adult. See F. Russell, *The Pima Indians,* The Twenty-sixth Annual Report of the Bureau of American Ethnology (Washington, D.C.: U.S. Government Printing Office, 1908; reprint, Tucson: University of Arizona Press, 1974), 221–24, for the story. Her birthplace is generally considered to be Rainmaker's Rain House. Her bed is on the Pima reservation and is pictured in Russell, 255.
‡**Santa Rosa:** A village eighty miles south-southwest of Pablo's village. There is a shrine there for children who according to legend were sacrificed by the Hohokam to stop a flood. See D. Saxton and O. Saxton, *Legends and Lore of the Papago and Pima Indians* (Tucson: University of Arizona Press, 1973), 243–61, 281–304, for the story.

where ocotillo flowers enclose me:*
such I come upon.

6

*Then the Red Rock, as it is called, which is Red Rock Hill.† "There behind it
I circle. There behind it burned bows crumbling lie, and I see it. Then my
heart hurts."*

Red Rock Hill,
Red Rock Hill
I circle behind,
where burned bows lie crumbling.
While I watch, my heart hurts.

7

*Look, then he [the traveler] comes to Rainmaker Rain House where two
[songs] stand. It [the first song] says, "Rainmaker Rain House stands. Inside
[I] enter. Inside rainmaker drink lies, and I drink it and get drunk. Much
talk," it says.*

Rainmaker Rain House stands.
Rainmaker Rain House stands,
and I enter.
Inside rainmaker drink lies,
and I drink it and, drunk,
many will sing.

8

*There is also this about Rainmaker Rain House. "Rainmaker Rain House,
where Bitter Wind jumps out.‡ There back and forth it staggers and, like a*

*Children's Burial . . . ocotillo flowers enclose me: The ocotillo is a cactus that
grows long, straight, green sticks from a central point in the ground. The Children's Burial is fenced with these sticks, which are ceremonially renewed every two
or four years. The shrine sticks are stripped of their green skin; so they cannot take
root and flower as this song implies. Unstripped ocotillo sticks, used as fences, do
take root and flower in season.
†Red Rock . . . Red Rock Hill: Joseph said this place name first in English, then
in Pima. A small group of Papago was killed by Apaches there in the nineteenth
century. Their bows, burned by the Apaches and left undisturbed by the Pima-
Papago, were visited by the Oriole.
‡Bitter Wind: A wind, or wind person, referred to in myth, especially in Frances*

rainbow, curves across. There on top of Feeler [Mountain] it stops," sounds
this song.*

Rainmaker Rain House
from which Bitter Wind jumps out,
back and forth staggering
rainbowlike across staggering,
then stops at Feeler Mountain.

9

*Look, from here he reaches Black Water, where he says, "Women spring out
from Black Water.† And they run to us; all crowned with cattail leaves they
come running. Green dragonflies sit on them," sounds this Black Water
[song].*

Black Water lies,
from which women jump out,
run up to us,
all crowned with cattail leaves,
clung with green dragonflies.

10

*Look, and then behind the [Gila] River is White Pinched [Mountain].
"From inside a shining wind jumps,"‡ as it says. Another mountain also
stands. "On top it [the wind] stops," this song says. It is called Grey Hill. Over
that way [from Joseph's house] it stands.*

White Pinched,
White Pinched,
from which a shining rainbow comes out and, spinning,
stops atop Grey Hill.

11

*So he says and then reaches what is Zigzag Connected [Mountain]. "Zigzag
Mountains so connected. On top he rests. There alongside a black cloud zig-
zags. He likes it and watches"; thus this sounds.*

Densmore, *Papago Music*, Smithsonian Institution, Bureau of American Ethnology
Bulletin no. 90 (Washington, D.C.: 1929; reprint, New York: Da Capo Press,
1972), 35–55, and especially 36–39. Densmore misheard "bitter" as "beater."
*Feeler Mountain: Newman Peak, east of Eloy, Arizona.
†Black Water: a village on the Gila River Reservation, named for a nearby pond.
‡shining wind: He misspoke. He should have said "shining rainbow."

Zigzag Connected,
on top I pause.
There beside me
a black cloud floating zigzagged,
pleasant for watching.

12

*Then [he comes] this way, to what is called Red Split [Mountain], where "in-
side a song sounds." He circles behind but can't enter because, they say, it's a
devil's house. "Yet what can I do to enter? In there are many songs to learn,"
it sounds.*

Red Split,
Red Split.
Inside songs sound
and do me ill.
I circle behind.
Oh, what can I do?
Now enter;
then know many songs.

13

*Then in this direction stands, where stands the Long Grey [Mountain]. It
says, "Long Grey below sings. Companion [Coyote] runs toward it and has a
reed flute. He runs and runs, then dances toward me, then hoots and tells
songs with me," thus sounds our companion.*

Long Grey beneath sings.
Companion runs near,
then runs up,
then dances to me,
then hoots
and tells songs with me.

14

Then afterward he reaches Bent, Remainder Bent [Mountain]. He says,
"[from] inside a shining wind comes out." It's an oriole bird that takes him
there. "No one sings; no one knows," sounds this Bent song.*

*Remainder Bent Mountain: This large mountain by Apache Junction, Arizona,
is called Superstition Mountain in English. It is said that there are petrified people
on top of it—the "remainders." See Russell, *The Pima Indians,* 211–12, for the
story.

Bent Remainder,
Bent Remainder,
from which a shining rainbow comes out.
Oriole bird leads me there,
and I enter.
No one sings;
no one knows.

15

Then is another on this Bent. "Inside a song sounds loudly. He heard and hurried there. It seems to be Rock People; it is they who loudly sing." People once turned to rock there. They speak and are Rock People.

Bent Remainder,
Bent Remainder,
where songs excitedly sound,
I hear it and run to sing;
must be Rock People
who sound there excitedly singing.

16

Look, and then away beyond Camel-Back [Mountain] stands what is called Iron Mountain. "Not invitingly it sounds"; it makes frightening sounds. "Wind runs there, and there is hooting inside." There really is an Iron Mountain. I have gone there, gone and crossed the [Verde] River, and reached Iron Mountain.

Iron Mountain,
Iron Mountain,
uninviting sounds.
Wind runs there,
then stands,
then hoots.

17

Look, and then next he arrives where a mountain stands, where an Apache spoke. He was named Thin Leg. "Pitifully slumping, they did it to me, and [I] slump pitifully.* [My] feather is already wet," sounds this Thin Leg song, and it says,

*named Thin Leg. . . . "They did it to me": Thin Leg was a nineteenth-century Apache raider with a shriveled leg (he rode a mule or a horse). He was captured by Pimas near the mountain Ajik, near the present-day village of Goodyear. Joseph is referring to the taunts of his captors who are about to kill him.

Many people gather off
while my head slumps.
This, my feather tip,
is already dying.

18

Thus said Thin Leg. Then he [the traveler] lands at Greasy [Mountain],*
where he says that I'itoi came out from below.† "Below Greasy, I'itoi comes
out. He poses on a peak. Like the morning star he seems, and [his] flames
shine."‡ Thus says this I'itoi song.

Below Greasy little I'itoi comes out,
then poses at the peak
like the morning star,
distant flame lighting.

19

Look, and then he crosses the [Gila] River again. At Broad [Mountain] he
arrives, and two [songs] stand there. He says, "Broad [Mountain] stands. In
front drizzle stretches. I go in front of that; my wings are already wet."

Broad stands
with drizzle passing in front.
And in front I go,
my wings already wet.

20

Then one more [song] sounds, which is also [about] Broad. "Broad Mountain
stands," it says; "inside it speaks very windily. And I circle behind it and peep
in and hear that it sounds rainy inside," he also says.

Broad Mountain,
Broad Mountain,
inside speaks windily.

*Greasy Mountain: South Mountain, Pima name for the southern boundary of
Phoenix.
†I'itoi: a man-god, the central character of Pima-Papago mythology. He was
killed, went to the underworld, and reemerged.
‡flames: The word for "flames" is the same as the word that was used for "topknot," or "head feathers," in song 1—*siwoda*. Thus, these flames could be interpreted as feathers—or a hat full of feathers could be interpreted as a hat full of
flames.

From behind
I slowly peep in and listen.
Broad Mountain,
inside speaks rainily.

21

Look, and then there, down that way [is] the Hot Water [Spring]. *"Hot Water distantly, noisily lies. I arrive above it and look, and above are various-colored dragonflies. Above it they hover—hovering lies," he says.*

Hot Water far and noisily lies.
I arrive above and watch.
Above, many colors of dragonflies hover;
a hovering lies.

22

Look, and next I end the line where the oceanfront is,† which is called Spongy Water, where "above it many times [I] come. Behind it people's running path shows,"‡ sounds this one.

Spongy Water lies,
And I above often come.
There around it
people's running path appears.

23

Look, this [song string] we lined up. From here are those that you call birds [songs]. He says, "What kind of bird goes low?" And he says, "It must be a pelican bird that goes low. Everywhere the land is foggy." Fog exists there.

What bird goes low?
What bird goes low?
Must be a pelican going low,
earth fogged.

---

*down that way: sixty miles northwest of Joseph's house.
†I end the line: that is, the series of travel songs.
‡people's running path: The Pima-Papago went on pilgrimages to the ocean to get salt.

24

Look, and this one I will tell with them [the bird songs], about a bird flying. It sounds as if a mother bird's children flew away somewhere, as birds will do. Eventually they grow large and fly off.

Oh! Oh! my children, where did you fly?
Oh, oh, my children, where did you fly?
So I just cry and wander below,
oh, oh, my children,
each day filled with following you.

25

Of course it's true that it [the last song] is also a God song,* but it belongs with the birds, since it says, as I have spoken, "Oh, oh, my children, where did you fly?" for birds grow large and fly. . . . This [next] is surely an Oriole song, it is

Oh, oh, my children, what can I do and go with you—

Now, how does it sound?†

Oh! Oh! my children, my children,
what can I do to go high with you
now that my wings are shredded?
My poor children,
what can I do to go high with you?

26

This [last song] is an Oriole song because it means and says, "My poor children, what can I do to go high with you? My wing is shredded." . . . Yes, then [comes] the bird singing place. This one sounds, "Bird singing place lies," since birds sing there. "And I go to it. Here beside me a song stretches" like a rope. Look, "Beside me a song stretches, and I grasp its middle, then coil it, then grab it up, then go," heh, heh, heh, heh.‡

Bird singing place lies,
and I go on top.

*it is also a God song: I had commented that I knew this as a God song, not as an Oriole song. It was absent from Pablo's Oriole songs that I had taped in Joseph's company. Apparently Joseph had learned it elsewhere and decided to treat it as an Oriole song.
†how does it sound? He had made a false start.
‡heh . . . heh: This song has tricky words, hence the chuckling.

Here beside me songs form a line.
Oh, how I like it,
grasp its middle,
coil it, grab it, and go.

27

Here is the next, that tells of darkness, of flying at night. "Night-flying birds, and they go. During the night, topknots burn."* They shine toward them.†

Night fliers,
night-flying birds
going away,
topknots burning in blackness.

28

Look, this now is an oriole bird [song], since it says, "Oriole bird takes me to the sky. There brings me to Down-Nested Medicine Man.‡ His soft down shakes, encloses my body, and lowers me home," as this song says.

Yellow oriole, take me to the sky,
where is Down-Nested Medicine Man;
take me.
Soft down shakes,
encloses my body, and lowers me home.

29

He [the Oriole traveler] further says that something is a wren, a bird. "Grey wren, cholla flower makes into wine and [then] runs up to me." He says "runs up," but he means "summons." "And I drink with him and get drunk. I don't know [myself], slantingly running," heh, heh, heh, heh.

Grey wren
makes cholla wine and comes to me.

***topknots:** This is the same word, *siwoda*, that was discussed in relation to songs 1 and 18. It can also be translated as "flames."
†**toward them:** toward the Oriole traveler and his companion.
‡**Down-Nested Medicine Man:** that is, Down-Feather-Nested Medicine Man, a god who lives in the sky in a feather-down nest. At the time of an ancient flood, he is said to have suggested that various birds save themselves by making nests from their own down. The birds did so, the nests floated, and the birds were saved (Russell, *The Pima Indians*, 211).

I drink with him and, drunk,
alas for my knowing,
slantingly run.

30

*Look, this is another [about the flood], when it happened that we were [an-
ciently] drowned. The land everywhere bubbled water—flooded, that
means—when the water came out.* "Then they [the birds] forgot their flapping. Pitifully they huddled in a bunch." Having gathered, they couldn't fly.*

It will drown us;
earth everywhere floods.
Just then all the birds forget their flapping;
they feel pitiful, bunched and clinging.

31

*Look, and then this one says the sun died. The other [the last song] said it
flooded them. At that time the birds didn't know their flapping, how to fly.
Look, and this one then says that the sun died. "Sun dies, sun dies. Just then
every kind of bird dropped its cooing," it says. Then it says, "The lying land
nowhere echoes." Quiet is the land everywhere.† "Just the mockingbird pitifully speaks, but it just talks to itself," as it [the song] also sounds.*

Sun dies,
sun dies.
Earth everywhere dark.
Just then every bird stops cooing.
Earth doesn't echo.
A mockingbird speaks pitifully,
alone distantly talks.

32

*Look, and then he reaches this one. Above [songs 28, 30], our drowning was
told and that the sun also died [song 31]. Now here I say that it [the sun]
burned us. He says just, "Alas, we burn. From every mountaintop steam
comes out. It will burn us, and I already knew it," says this oriole.*

***The land everywhere . . . flooded:** This flood was not from rain, as in the
Sumerian and Judeo-Christian traditions, but from an abandoned baby's salty tears
(Russell, *The Pima Indians,* 209–13).
†**Quiet:** Here Joseph used the English word.

Oh! Oh! It will burn us;
oh, oh, it will burn us.
All mountaintops steam.
Oh, oh, it will burn us,
as I had thought.

33

Look, then he says, "Sun now sets. Darkness comes and covers me"—it's still darker—"and then I sit down and rasp my scraper."* He means, "I do it, rasp and sit," thus to tell you an Oriole song.

Sun now sets.
Darkness comes,
here covering me
as I sit down,
rasping my scraper,
Oriole songs to tell.

34

Look, and next he reaches the medicine men. This says, "A medicine man's stick he four times cuts"—cuts apart, to make a scraper. "Using that, one tells nice-sounding Oriole songs," as sounds this song.

Medicine man stick
cut in four
to make scrapers,
to make singing sound nice.

35

Look, and this is also a medicine man,† that "Earth bumps and comes out,"‡ molds it, one might also say. "Much cloud comes out with him. He stands it [the cloud] and breaks it into bits and throws them." And of course he did it, now there are clouds above us.

Earth Medicine Man,
Earth, he bumps and comes out.

*scraper: a musical instrument that is used to accompany singing.
†this is also a medicine man: This song is about the second most important character of Pima-Papago mythology, Earth Medicine Man, or Earth Doctor. He created the universe, including clouds and people, and so was the first god. But he was rivaled and replaced by I'itoi. See Russell, *The Pima Indians*, 206–14.
‡Earth bumps: Earth Medicine Man bumps with his head.

Much cloud comes with him.
Off he stands it,
breaks it in short pieces,
and throws them over all the earth.

36

Look, this [song] is also Earth Medicine Man. It surely says, "Earth Medicine Man has his own rock and makes stars. He tosses them in front of the sky. They cover the sky and shine," and that is what this says.

Earth Medicine Man
has his own rock and makes stars.
Here above me he tosses them.
They fill the sky,
great sparkling.

37

Now I've reached this one, and I'll tell it: "Ill it does to me. And I sink, here at the world beneath us I stay. Oh, oh, ill it does to me."* This means that he was killed, he was buried, he remained there, and he said this:

Oh, oh, you really do me ill.
Oh, oh, you really do me ill;
so I sink.
Below us is land,
where I'll stay.
Oh, oh, you did me ill.

38

Look, and next is this, which is "Silver lightning, there in a cloud met and killed me. I was four days dead; then I remembered again.† Now you can call me Silver-Lightning Meeting Man," thus sounds this Lightning song.

*Oh, oh, ill it does to me: This song could refer either to Earth Medicine Man, who according to legend sank straight through the earth to the underworld after a quarrel with I'itoi, or to I'itoi, who was killed, resurrected himself, then journeyed to the underworld by following the sun's path through the sky. The line on "do me ill" is generally attributed to I'itoi: he is said to have spoken this lamentation to Earth Medicine Man after rejoining him in the underworld. See Russell, *The Pima Indians,* 226, for a version of this meeting.

Emmett White believes that the reference is to neither god but to some or any present-day Pima dead person, whoever is poorly treated in life, dies, is buried, and remains in the burial place. It is a song from a contemporary grave.
†I remembered again: I became conscious again.

Silver lightning,
silver lightning
met me in a cloud;
four times killed me.
Four times I died;
then memory returned.
Now you call me Silver Meeting Lightning.

39

This is what I tell with them, * *which says, "What is the windiness that runs up there?" And he says, "It is the hard windiness. Along its path the land is swished wet"—wet to a certain amount of swishing—then it [the wind] stops, having wet enough.*

What windiness ran up here?
What windiness ran up here?
Must be the hard windiness
in whose path
land is swished wet.

40

Look, and after those follows this one, which are their songs, which you call whore woman.† "There is a whore woman, and she runs up first to their [birds'] songs." Then with someone's husband she runs singing eastward. He's not had.‡ "Ill he does to me [the wife says], and they [the good people] look askance in their midst."

Whore woman, whore woman,
first to run to the singing,
then runs to the dawn with my husband.
I don't have him; ill he does me,
here in people's glances.

41

Look, and this one then says, "Ill doing to me, are you making me a whore? Earth flower [you] wrap around my head"—threw earth flower on her

---

*with them: with the rest of them. This song was not one of Pablo's Oriole songs.
†whore women: Pima-Papago *ce:paowi* (the colon in this word signifies that the preceding vowel, *e*, is long). These are women who like to make love, especially at social dances. There are songs about them in many social-dancing sets.
‡He's not had: That is, he's not had by his wife.

head*—"*therefore my heart feels like a whore,*" *says this woman. These are women's songs that I pursue.*

Are you making me a whore?
Are you making me a whore
with earth flowers that you
wrap on my head?
Oh, oh, my heart
feels very whorish.

42

Now I've done the start.† Those two sound well together. Look, next he reaches one with a call to family: "My husband, my husband, I'm leaving you." She'll go alone in search of singing. "Here behind me people bother me; whore they call me. Oh, my husband, I'm leaving you."

Oh, oh, my husband,
oh, oh, my husband,
I left you and ran alone away to sing
where people call me whore and bother me.
Oh, oh, my husband,
I left you and ran alone away to sing.

43

This one next says, "Who is the woman? Who is the woman that clasps my hand?" They connected and ran to sing. "It's just the One-Flower-Having Woman who clasps my hand and runs off to sing," says this song.

Who is the woman?
Who is the woman
who clasps me
and runs far off to sing?
Must be One-Flower Woman
who clasps me
and runs far off to sing.

***earth flower:** a love potion said to grow in mountains. It is greatly discussed but is not shown to outsiders. When carried in a bag, its scent is said to make women crazy for love.
†**I've done the start:** I've begun the women's songs.

44

Look, and this one also sounds like crying,* but now it says, "Who is the woman? She acts slightly whorish, there circling behind us. With her hair she hides her face. She acts slightly whorish, circling there behind us."

Who is the woman
who acts so whorish,
circling there behind us,
hiding her face in her hair,
acting so whorish,
circling there behind us?

45

This now is the one with which he closes, which is an oriole bird. "It [the oriole] does me ill. With a jimsonweed flower at the end of his wing tip, he offers and makes me drink. And I drink it all and get dizzy"—that means "get drunk." "To standing sticks I cling."

White oriole truly mistreats me,
makes me drink jimsonweed liquor from his wing tip.
And I drink and get dizzy,
slantingly run,
on upright saplings clinging.

46

Look, and this says that they will stop singing. "And we stop singing. On top of our sitting place, our scrapers lie. With song marks marked on them they lie," says this one.

And now we stop singing and scatter.
Here on our seats our poor scraping sticks lie,
with song marks marked as they lie.

47

Well, and one comes on top that is the very end, which says, "And we stop singing, go in various directions. Here at our singing place a wind jumps out. It runs back and forth. People's traces—since they have stepped and it shows— people's traces it erases. They [the traces] won't remain after the wind has run," it says. Well, thus he ends.

*sounds like crying: The calling to the husband in song 42 is interpreted as crying (ṣuak in Pima-Papago).

And now we stop singing and scatter.
Wind springs from our singing place,
runs back and forth,
erasing the marks of people.
There's nothing left at the end.

ETHNOPOETIC RETRANSLATION
OF A ZUNI RITUAL
SONG SEQUENCE

▲

M. JANE YOUNG

INTRODUCTION

The following is my retranslation of a religious song set collected by
Ruth Bunzel in the 1930s from the Zuni Indians, a Pueblo group
located in western New Mexico.[1] I undertook the retranslation of
this text primarily to emphasize the ethnopoetic quality of the songs
but also to demonstrate that Zuni ritual poetry and sacred narratives
are generally organized into major divisions on the basis of temporal
components (such as the yearly and daily travels of the sun, the recurrent phases of the moon, the necessary number of days that have
passed on the ritual calendar, and so on). The reader will note, for
example, that the various sections of the song set (indicated primarily by the combinations of capital and lowercase roman numerals to
the right of the text) are determined by phrases that refer to temporal events or directional elements. It is significant that such temporal
and cosmological markers are also organizing principles of much of
Zuni visual art, operating in secular as well as sacred contexts.[2]

Since my retranslation is based on a text collected by Bunzel, I
cannot take into account important ethnopoetic elements that she
did not include, such as breath pauses, pitch, intonation, and vowel
lengthening; Bunzel did state that she arranged the text into lines
on the basis of "the important poetic stress . . . on the final syllable
of the line."[3] In most cases the lines of my retranslation parallel

Bunzel's; unlike Bunzel, however, I have spaced and indented these lines to reveal their structural parallelism. In addition to the repeated overall structure of certain lines, I have based my analysis on the use of identical or strikingly similar initial particles and, in some cases, on the occurrence of the same verb suffixes at the ends of lines. Since the Zuni text is not included here, I have tried to make this resonant poetic structure apparent both in the line indentations and spacing of my English translation and in the translation itself, following Zuni patterns of repetition where possible. The language in which Zuni sacred songs, poems, and narratives are rendered is quite different from the everyday language, which remains the language of social discourse today, although many tribal members are also fluent in English. Zuni sacred language, archaic Zuni, is an esoteric version of the language with its own special forms and meanings; this is evident linguistically and in the nearly codified metaphors and phrases that are repeated in these narrative forms.[4]

The songs that follow constitute the "Songs for Pouring in the Water" of the Great Fire Society, one of the Zuni medicine societies (societies of men and women whose main function is healing). Bunzel indicated that she was permitted to collect the text for only part of the song cycle; those most sacred songs that should not be shared with the non-Zuni were withheld from her.[5] Furthermore, she recorded only the words of the songs, not the accompanying music; to my knowledge, this music has never been recorded.

The various repetitions that conclude this sequence emphasize its songlike quality. It is especially significant that the three final songs, which I have set off from the rest of the text by single-spacing and asterisks, are the most songlike of the entire sequence and comprise six "stanzas" apiece. As is obvious in each song set (III, V, and VI), the number six is integral to the network of symbolic associations that the Zuni link with directionality. Each direction is related to a particular beast-god and color: this cosmological scheme also includes six rain priests of the six directions, six rain-bringing winds, six varieties of birds, six kinds of trees, and so on in an almost endless cycle of related elements. According to Zuni mythology, six Beast-Gods guard the world. They are the yellow mountain lion of the north, the blue bear of the west, the red badger of the south, the white wolf of the east, the speckled or all-colored eagle of the zenith, and the black mole of the nadir. Sometimes Knife Wing (the mythical being with wings and a tail of knives) rather than the eagle is associated with the zenith. These directional images are visually rendered on the walls of religious houses and meeting rooms, incorporated into the performance of most ritual actions (such as offering sacred cornmeal and smoke to the six directions), and repeated in the religious narratives that frequently describe, and are central to, these ceremonial activities. Zuni regard such repetition as essential to the efficacy of religious behavior and the fulfillment of the requests that conclude ritual prayers (for example, having long life, or "finishing" one's "road").

The song set is performed when the Great Fire Society convenes for the first time each year, in November at the full moon (the fifth through seventh lines of my translation: "there to the east now, / standing full above the horizon, / she makes her days into finished beings"; section II [i] indicates that this occurs before the winter solstice: "yet a little space remained," which is poetically referred to as being attained when the sun father reaches "his left-hand sacred dwelling place"). Before sunset on this day, the male members of this society assemble in their ceremonial house ("our healing water room"). Prior to this time they erected an altar against the west wall of the room, according to customary Zuni ritual practice. The female members of the society bring food to the ceremonial room as well as "perfect" corn ears, used as religious offerings, which will be placed on the altar. At sunset the society's choir begins to sing the songs that constitute "Songs for Pouring in the Water."

The initial part of the song sequence sets the temporal and ritual stage for the remaining lines. Essentially this part of the song describes the ritual actions (offering prayer sticks, sacred cornmeal, shells, seedlings) undertaken by the society members ("those who wish to grow old"). In the second sentence of section II [ii], the actions and pronouns change from third person plural to the first person singular as the medicine-society chief creates the cornmeal painting on the altar and on the floor between the altar and the door opposite ("having finished the cumulus cloud house" of his fathers and "having sent forth their life-giving sacred roads"). At this time he also sets up the corn ears brought by the women and adds other religious items to the altar, including seedlings that have been specially grown for this purpose. Then he positions the bowl for the medicine water (his "white-shell bowl"), mixes the medicine (invoking from the six directions the "healing waters" of the rainmaker priests, sections II[iii]–III[vi]). Integral to the act of mixing the medicine is that of pouring in water from four sacred gourds (four is a number that is related to directionality, as is the number six—both are central to Zuni ritual activity[6]). Next the medicine-society chief appeals to the beast-gods of the six directions (V[i]–VI[vi]), alluding to the fact that at the winter solstice the shamans of the medicine societies *become* these beast-gods ("we shall be one person") as the sick are cured. Finally the medicine-society chief adds sacred pebbles in the colors associated with the six directions to the medicine bowl (VI[i]–[vi]), stating that when society members ("our children") drink these "healing waters," they will have long life ("their roads will be finished"), and they will go to Dawn Lake upon their death.

As Bunzel noted, Zuni ritual poetry and narratives entail the creative and purposeful use of ambiguity, metaphor, and wordplay: "There are passages where subject and object are deliberately confounded, although there are excellent means for avoiding such ambiguity. These sentences are perfectly grammatical and can be correctly interpreted in two ways."[7] More recently, in her discussion of the Zuni system of aesthetics that encompasses both verbal and visual codes, Barbara Tedlock has suggested that the Zuni concept of beauty is predicated on a great love of variety in all things. She describes this aesthetic as dynamic, clear, exciting: multilayered, multilingual, multisensory, multitextured, and multicolored.[8] Although Tedlock does not precisely state this, I believe her discussion points to an aesthetic based on the kind of intentional ambiguity described by Bunzel—an elaborate redundancy of symbolism that gives rise to the operation of a multiplicity of meanings or interpretations in Zuni sacred and secular environments.

The Zuni creatively use multiple meanings or, as termed by Bunzel,[9] "double entendres" in daily conversation as well as in more formal genres of verbal art, such as folktales, myths, and ritual poetry. One might be surprised by the use of wordplay in ritual poems—that is, prayers that are integral to Zuni ceremonialism reveal a number of poetic features, and consist of highly stereotyped phrases and sequential arrangements that the Zuni consider efficacious only when rendered exactly as they were learned, with no change in wording or structure.[10] Yet Bunzel's analysis of Zuni ritual poetry yields a plethora of such examples, suggesting that humor and delight in the use of metaphor are as much a part of the verbal component of Zuni ritual as they are a part of the ceremonial enactments in which such speech occurs.

For instance, in the eighth line of the following text, the phrase "Our spring children" refers simultaneously to members of the Great Fire Society who have drunk from the sacred "spring," or bowl of medicine water on the altar, and to the bowl itself. Similarly, although the meaning is quite esoteric, "Those who at the First Beginning / were given the world, / the bushes, / the forest," in the fourteenth through seventeenth lines, alludes to the particular kind of wood that is used for prayer sticks (offerings made up of pieces of wood to which bird feathers, functioning to carry one's prayers to the gods, are tied). "First Beginning" refers to the myth time when the people traveled through four underworlds by means of four different trees (and with the aid of four different kinds of birds) to reach the surface of the earth; offering prayer sticks recalls that time. In the first line of the sentence that concludes section I[i], "our daylight fathers" indicates human beings—that is, "finished beings" who are "cooked" as opposed to the "divine ones" (also described as "those who are fortunate" in section I[i]), mentioned in section I[ii], who are "raw beings," a category that includes all the supernaturals and other sorts of nonhuman beings.[11]

Throughout the song set a person's "road" means that person's allotted life span, which may be cut short by various misfortunes; thus, one prays to "finish" one's "road." When the medicine-society members offer sacred cornmeal to the six directions (and the beast-gods who guard those directions), they are "making their sacred roads go forth" (that is, the sacred roads of the supernaturals); they also "bring their sacred roads in" when they invoke these beings to be present during the ritual that is taking place.

Due to the limitations of space, I cannot discuss all of the many ambiguous or highly metaphoric phrases employed in this poem-song; these examples should, however, give the reader some idea of the multivocality of Zuni sacred narrative. This ability to refer to or evoke a number of meanings at the same time contributes to an intensification of experience—a verbal interaction that frequently results in a "tremendous compression of both emotion and concepts" in the metaphoric utterance.[12] It is this compression of emotion and concept that accounts for the affect and, hence, the power of this verbal imagery.

NOTES

1. Ruth L. Bunzel, *Introduction to Zuñi Ceremonialism; Zuñi Origin Myths; Zuñi Ritual Poetry; Zuñi Katcinas: An Analytical Study*, in the Forty-seventh

Annual Report of the Bureau of American Ethnology for the Years 1929–1930 (Washington, D.C.: U.S. Government Printing Office, 1932), 782–91.

2. M. Jane Young, *Signs from the Ancestors: Zuni Cultural Symbolism and Perceptions of Rock Art* (Albuquerque: University of New Mexico Press, 1988), 95–119.

3. Bunzel, *Introduction to Zuñi Ceremonialism,* 620.

4. Stanley Newman, "Vocabulary Levels: Zuñi Sacred and Slang Usage," *Southwestern Journal of Anthropology* 11 (1955): 345–54.

5. Bunzel, *Introduction to Zuñi Ceremonialism,* 785.

6. See Young, *Signs from the Ancestors,* 98–107.

7. Bunzel, *Introduction to Zuñi Ceremonialism,* 619.

8. Barbara Tedlock, *The Beautiful and the Dangerous: Encounters with the Zuni Indians* (New York: Viking Press, 1992), 51, 191, 232, 269.

9. Bunzel, *Introduction to Zuñi Ceremonialism,* 619.

10. Ibid., 616, 618.

11. Young, *Signs from the Ancestors,* 56.

12. Robert J. Smith, *The Art of the Festival,* University of Kansas Publications in Anthropology no. 6 (Lawrence: University of Kansas Libraries, 1975), 99.

Now, enough days have passed   I[i]

    since the moon who is our mother,
      there to the west,
        still appeared to be small;
      there to the east now,
        standing full above the horizon,
          she makes her days into finished beings.
Our spring children,
    those who wish to grow old,
      carrying sacred cornmeal,
      carrying shells,
        there with prayer
          we make your sacred roads go forth.

    Those who at the First Beginning
      were given the world,
        the bushes,
        the forest,
          we meet them there.

    Those who are fortunate,
      at their feet
        sacred cornmeal,
        shell
          we offer
      from our fingertips
        as we look to the sacred directions.

    Those who are fortunate,
      pulling seedlings,
      drawing them toward them,
    those who stay there quietly,
      their finished roads holding,
      their old age holding,
          we bring their sacred roads in.

Our daylight fathers,
our mothers,
our children

to our healing water room
we make their sacred roads come in.

Enough days have passed   I[ii]

since the divine ones
with us, their children,
have lived their days on the earth.

Now this very day   I[iii]

for the beast-god priests—
for their ceremony—
we have prepared prayer sticks.

When the sun who is our father   II[i]
was about to go in to his sacred dwelling place
and sit down,
when yet a little space remained
before he could reach his left-hand sacred dwelling place,
to our fathers
we offered prayer sticks,
to our house,
bringing their sacred roads in.

There from all the directions   II[ii]

those who are our fathers,
the divine ones,
with none among them missing,
their sacred roads we will bring out.

My fathers,
having finished their cumulus-cloud house,
having spread out their mist blanket,
having sent forth their life-giving sacred roads,
having put down their rainbow-colored bow,
having put down their lightning arrow,
I shall sit down quietly.

I shall quietly set down my white-shell bowl.

▲

There from all the directions   II[iii]

you, our fathers, will come.

****

There from the north   III[i]
  rainmaker priests,
    carrying their healing water,
      will make their sacred roads come forth.

    Where my white-shell bowl lies,
      four times
        they will make their sacred roads come in.

There from the west   III[ii]
  rainmaker priests,
    carrying their healing water,
      will make their sacred roads come forth.

    Where my white-shell bowl lies,
      four times
        they will make their sacred roads come in.

There from the south   III[iii]
  rainmaker priests,
    carrying their healing water,
      will make their sacred roads come forth.

    Where my white-shell bowl lies,
      four times
        they will make their sacred roads come in.

There from the east   III[iv]
  rainmaker priests,
    carrying their healing water,
      will make their sacred roads come forth.

    Where my white-shell bowl lies,
      four times
        they will make their sacred roads come in.

▲

There from above   III[v]
  rainmaker priests,
    carrying their healing water,
      will make their sacred roads come forth.

    Where my white-shell bowl lies,
      four times
        they will make their sacred roads come in.

There from below   III[vi]
  rainmaker priests,
    carrying their healing water,
      will make their sacred roads come forth.

    Where my white-shell bowl lies,
      four times
        they will make their sacred roads come in.

****

When you have sat down quietly,   IV
  our children
    will drink
      your healing waters.

Then, their sacred roads reaching
  to Dawn Lake,
    their roads will be finished.

****

And furthermore,   V[i]
  there from the north
    you who are my father,
      mountain lion,
        the one who completes my road,
          you are my priest;
    carrying your medicine,
        you will make your sacred road come here.

    Where my white-shell bowl lies,
      four times

        you make your sacred road come in;
    watch over my spring.

    When you sit down quietly,
      we shall be one person.

And furthermore,   V[ii]
  there from the west
    you who are my father,
      bear,
        the one who completes my road,
          you are my priest;
    carrying your medicine,
        you will make your sacred road come here.

    Where my white-shell bowl lies,
      four times
        you make your sacred road come in;
    watch over my spring.

    When you sit down quietly,
      we shall be one person.

And furthermore,   V[iii]
  there from the south
    you who are my father,
      badger,
        the one who completes my road,
          you are my priest;
    carrying your medicine,
        you will make your sacred road come here.

    Where my white-shell bowl lies,
      four times
        you make your sacred road come in;
    watch over my spring.

    When you sit down quietly,
      we shall be one person.

* * * * * * * * *

And furthermore,   V[iv]
  there from the east

you who are my father,
  wolf,
    the one who completes my road,
      you are my priest;
carrying your medicine,
    you will make your sacred road come here.

Where my white-shell bowl lies,
  four times
    you make your sacred road come in;
watch over my spring.

When you sit down quietly,
  we shall be one person.

And furthermore,   V[v]
  there from above,
  you who are my father,
    knife wing,
      the one who completes my road,
        you are my priest;
carrying your medicine,
    you will make your sacred road come here.

Where my white-shell bowl lies,
  four times
    you make your sacred road come in;
watch over my spring.

When you sit down quietly,
  we shall be one person.

And furthermore,   V[vi]
  there from below,
  you who are my father,
    mole,
      the one who completes my road,
        you are my priest;
carrying your medicine,
    you will make your sacred road come here.

Where my white-shell bowl lies,
    four times
        you make your sacred road come in;
watch over my spring.

When you sit down quietly,
    we shall be one person.

****

And furthermore,   VI[i]
    there from the north
      the mossy mountains,
      the mountaintops,
      the middle slopes,
      the ravines opening out,
        you are the one who has the world in your keeping;
          ancient yellow stone,
            you will make your sacred road come here.

Where my white-shell bowl lies,
    four times
        you make your sacred road come in.

When you have sat down quietly,
    our children
      will drink
        your healing waters.

Then, their sacred roads reaching
    to Dawn Lake,
      their roads will be finished.

And furthermore,   VI[ii]
    there from the west
      the mossy mountains,
      the mountaintops,
      the middle slopes,
      the ravines opening out,
        you are the one who has the world in your keeping;
          ancient blue stone,
            you will make your sacred road come here.

Where my white-shell bowl lies,
    four times
        you make your sacred road come in.

When you have sat down quietly,
    our children
        will drink
            your healing waters.

Then, their sacred roads reaching
    to Dawn Lake,
        their roads will be finished.

And furthermore,   VI[iii]
  there from the south
    the mossy mountains,
    the mountaintops,
    the middle slopes,
    the ravines opening out,
        you are the one who has the world in your keeping;
            ancient red stone,
                you will make your sacred road come here.

Where my white-shell bowl lies,
    four times
        you make your sacred road come in.

When you have sat down quietly,
    our children
        will drink
            your healing waters.

Then, their sacred roads reaching
    to Dawn Lake,
        their roads will be finished.

And furthermore,   VI[iv]
  there from the east
    the mossy mountains,
    the mountaintops,
    the middle slopes,
    the ravines opening out,

you are the one who has the world in your keeping;
    ancient white stone,
        you will make your sacred road come here.

Where my white-shell bowl lies,
    four times
        you make your sacred road come in.

When you have sat down quietly,
    our children
        will drink
            your healing waters.

Then, their sacred roads reaching
    to Dawn Lake,
        their roads will be finished.

And furthermore,   VI[v]
    there from above,
        the mossy mountains,
        the mountaintops,
        the middle slopes,
        the ravines opening out,
            you are the one who has the world in your keeping;
                ancient many-colored stone,
                    you will make your sacred road come here.

Where my white-shell bowl lies,
    four times
        you make your sacred road come in.

When you have sat down quietly,
    our children
        will drink
            your healing waters.

Then, their sacred roads reaching
    to Dawn Lake,
        their roads will be finished.

And furthermore,   VI[vi]
    there from below,

the mossy mountains,
the mountaintops,
the middle slopes,
the ravines opening out,
   you are the one who has the world in your keeping;
     ancient black stone,
        you will make your sacred road come here.

Where my white-shell bowl lies,
   four times
      you make your sacred road come in.

When you have sat down quietly,
   our children
     will drink
       your healing waters.

Then, their sacred roads reaching
   to Dawn Lake,
     their roads will be finished.

BECAUSE HE MADE MARKS

ON PAPER,

THE SOLDIERS CAME

▴

DENNIS TEDLOCK

INTRODUCTION

Here is a Zuni story of two witches, a transvestite, and the U.S. Army, told by Andrew Peynetsa in 1965. In addition to the army, it is full of things that are missing from Zuni stories that took place "long ago" or "in ancient times," including a donkey, mules, writing, cannons, and a prison. Perhaps that is why it ended up as one of those numberless hidden stories that get left out of published collections, in this case my own *Finding the Center: Narrative Poetry of the Zuni Indians*.[1] If I had been working in the days of Franz Boas and his students, I certainly would have included it, since they were interested in stories that told not only of the mythical or distantly historical past but also of a world in which people from the other side of the Atlantic had already appeared.

It was in the late sixties that I began working on *Finding the Center*, a time when the recovery of lost worlds seemed one way in which to change the present one. Since then the story told here has come to look more and more like a missing chapter from that book. It would go at the end, not because it is the "final chapter" but because its events are recent. As it stands now, *Finding the Center* stays safely within ancient times, though in the story titled "The Boy and the Deer," three men ride horses, and in "The Shumeekuli" a man herds sheep. The book is not without politics: as Alasdair

MacIntyre pointed out, "The Sun Priest and the Witch-Woman" is about a person in high authority who undergoes a crisis of legitimacy.[2] But nowhere does politics break out of ancient times and jump into the lap of the polite non-Indian reader, as it does here. And when writing makes its appearance on the scene, it does so as an instrument of power.

Andrew Peynetsa told this story at To'ya, or Nutria, a farming hamlet northeast of Zuni, New Mexico, on the evening of March 26, 1965. We were in his farmhouse, with kerosene lamps lit and a fire in the corner fireplace. Also present were his wife, one of their sons, a couple of their grandchildren, and Walter Sanchez, a clan brother of Andrew's who was himself telling stories that evening. Andrew said the events took place around 1898. He seems to have combined incidents from two separate U.S. Army interventions in Zuni internal affairs, one taking place in 1891 and the other involving a six-month military occupation in 1897–98.[3]

Earlier in the same evening Andrew had told the first of three consecutive installments of his version of the Zuni origin story, "Chimiky'ana'kowa," literally, "When Newness Was Made"; he told the other two parts on March 29 and 31. I included the first two parts in *Finding the Center*[4]; the third part, which concerns the origin of the medicine society called Lheweekwe, or Stick People, has yet to be published. All three parts take place at a time when the earth was still soft, rather than hardened as it is now, and all three take place before the arrival of Europeans. Andrew considered a number of other stories, including the present one, to be further parts of "When Newness Was Made," though he did not attempt to construct narrative bridges that would connect them directly to the end of his long, three-part narrative. He remarked that in the present story, when the soldiers came along the edge of the valley that leads from Nutria down to the town of Zuni, their horses and wagons made deep tracks, meaning that the earth was still soft, as it was "when newness was made." On another occasion he commented, "There's a spot near Nutria where the soldiers camped; they fed hay to their horses, and there were tumbleweed seeds in it. Now only tumbleweeds grow on that spot, and they've spread all over."

The most important "newness" in this story is the abrogation of Zuni sovereignty by the U.S. Army. The Aapi'lha Aashiwani, or Bow Priests, a society of warriors that had long been the center of military and police power in the traditional Zuni government, suffered a blow from which it has never recovered. The most important result is that the Zuni were left defenseless against the internal enemies known as *aahalhikwi,* "witches"—or, as Andrew Peynetsa liked to put it, "the wicked people." The accused witch named Tumahka in his story, known in English as Nick, later became the head of the secular Zuni government (an institution set up during Spanish rule); he also served as a major informant for such ethnographers as Elsie Clews Parsons, Alfred Kroeber, Ruth Bunzel, and Ruth Benedict. The man named Weewa, a transvestite, served as an informant for Matilda Coxe Stevenson. The Society of Helical People, or Shumaakwe Tikyanne, is a medicine society that once included an order named Ts'u' Lhana, or Big Shell, devoted, as in the present story, to the subtler arts of warfare. Thunderers, or *towo"anaawe,* is the Zuni term for guns; "big" thunderers are cannons.

Bear Water, or Anshe Ky'an'a, is the Zuni name for Fort Wingate, which is located a short distance east of Gallup, New Mexico. "Midpoint," or *itiwan'a,* is the term for the solstice (in this case the winter solstice); it is also one of the names of the town of Zuni, which is located at the middle of the earth (as is explained in the second part of Andrew's version of "When Newness Was Made"). The place "where the Shalakos race" is an open area on the south bank of the Zuni River, opposite the central part of the town of Zuni, where the ten-foot kachinas called Shalakos race at the close of a ceremony that takes place shortly before the winter solstice. When Andrew says that "the soldiers passed through here," he is referring to Nutria, which lies on an old wagon road that connected Fort Wingate with Zuni. Luuna is the Zuni name for Los Lunas, south of Albuquerque, formerly the site of a prison.

Guide to Reading Aloud

Of all the features of oral storytelling, the suspenseful pauses, sudden shouts or prolonged whispers, and harsh or gentle tones are the easiest to translate from one language to another. Yet these are precisely the features most translators have left out until recently, even when they were working from sound recordings. In 1970, I began publishing narratives with a system of transcription designed to remedy this situation.[5] Since then others have used similar formats for oral performances in such Native American languages as Yupik, Koyukon, Tanacross, Chipewyan, Tlingit, Navajo, Hopi, Yaqui, Nahuatl, Yucatec Maya, Kuna, and Quechua. The conventions used in the present translation are given below; the duration of the original performance was eight minutes.

Pausing. A new line at the left-hand margin is preceded by a pause of at least half a second but no more than a full second; indented lines run on without a pause. Longer pauses are indicated by strophe breaks, with one dot (·) for each full second.

Amplitude. **Boldface type** indicates loud words or passages; soft-ness is indicated by small type.

Intonation. A lack of punctuation at the end of a line indicates a level tone; a dash indicates a rise; a comma, a slight fall; a semicolon, a more definite fall; and a period, the kind of fall that marks a complete sentence.

Comments. Most of Andrew Peynetsa's longer pauses serve as silent metaphors for the passage of time in his story, and the two that are doubly long, one of which is followed by a sigh, mark a mood of grave uncertainty. His voice turns gravelly when he speaks of what Bow Priests do to witches, what witches feel about their intended victims, and what an American prison did to the Bow Priests, forging a chain of force and the threat of force. When he tells of medicine-society members who were on a quiet religious retreat when the invasion came, he sounds as though he were in their house with them, speaking slowly and, again and again, in a soft voice that serves as a sonic metaphor for the passive acceptance of the possibility of violent death. It is in the very middle of this passage that he speaks in the voice of a child who prepares for death without knowing what it is.

After telling the story, Andrew said, "A long time ago they used to hang witches where the church is," referring to the ruins of a seventeenth-century Spanish mission abandoned in 1820. He explained that witches were not hanged by the neck but with their arms pulled back over a wooden rail and tied behind them, their legs dangling. As for the army occupation, he said he knew of a photograph in which "you can see the cannons all facing the village. Wicked people might be less so if they still had to go out to the old church in the daytime. They might be ashamed to go around doing things at night. Even if I catch a witch right now, I can't do anything." It should be noted that witches were strung up mainly in order to extract confessions; those who made convincing confessions were considered to have lost their power and were released.

Joseph Peynetsa, Andrew's nephew, who went over the tape of the story with me during the making of a transcription and a literal translation, offered further comments. When he heard how Suchiina had called a donkey to stand under her, he said, "Probably people said, 'She's a witch for sure.' " The way he had heard this story from his grandfather, "Suchiina confessed that she had made a powder from dead bodies and had sprinkled it down chimneys to cause the people to get sick." When we came to the part about what witches do "when you're living well," he cited a certain Zuni couple as an example of potential victims: "They have a nice car, sheep, money, clothes. They're respected, and the witches don't like people who have a lot of things." On hearing Tumahka mentioned, he said, "Another famous witch." At the point where the springs were poisoned and animals died, he said, "My grandfather said a lot of soldiers died, and horses and mules."

After we were finished with the tape, Joseph said, "Why *did* those soldiers come to Zuni? It was none of their business." He was reminded of a cartoon he'd seen recently: one Bureau of Indian Affairs official rushes into the office of another saying, "The Indians have got the bomb!"

NOTES

1. Dennis Tedlock, *Finding the Center: Narrative Poetry of the Zuni Indians* (New York: Dial Press, 1972; reprint, Lincoln: University of Nebraska Press, 1978).

2. Alasdair MacIntyre, review of *Finding the Center* by Tedlock, *New York Times Book Review*, December 24, 1972, 4.

3. See Watson Smith and John M. Roberts, *Zuni Law: A Field of Values*, Harvard University, Papers of the Peabody Museum no. 43 (Cambridge, Mass., 1954), 45–47, and C. Gregory Crampton, *The Zunis of Cibola* (Salt Lake City: University of Utah Press, 1977), 150–51.

4. Tedlock, *Finding the Center*, 223–98.

5. Tedlock, "Finding the Middle of the Earth," *Alcheringa* 1 (original series; 1970): 67–80; see also Tedlock, *The Spoken Word and the Work of Interpretation* (Philadelphia: University of Pennsylvania Press, 1983) and "From Voice and Ear to Hand and Eye," *Journal of American Folklore* 103 (1990): 133–56.

BECAUSE HE MADE MARKS ON PAPER,
THE SOLDIERS CAME

Well
it seems
some time ago, it was the usual thing,
with Zuni people,
that there were **witches** in their **town,**
and when one of them was **caught**
he was **strung up,** they **strung** him up themselves;
this, it seems, was the way they lived
and someone, it was Suchiina,
she was caught somewhere, it seems;
when she was **caught,** it seems, the **Bow Priests strung her up.**
They **strung her up**
that's how
Suchiina got strung up,
at that time donkeys wandered around town
she was calling the donkeys; when she called the donkeys
she went "chk-chk,"
the donkeys gathered around her,
[*tense voice*] she stood on one of them
on the back of a donkey, on its back,
resting her weight.
[*normal voice*] It seems that the **Bow Priests,** when this came to
  light

. .

they drove her donkey away;
[*gravelly*] and while she was up there she cried;
they beat her head with their clubs while she was up there—
[*normal*] this, it seems, is the way they were living
then
Tumahka,
it seems, was caught someplace in the same way.
When he was caught
he was **strung up.** Once he'd been strung up
that man stayed up
until he was **let down.**
Suchiina was let down first, then she was questioned;
[*evenly and close mouthed*] "When someone has handsome
  children,

this is something
[*gravelly*] that just shouldn't be," she said, probably
that's the way it probably **happened**
when she was **caught;**
she **told** about herself, when someone has handsome children
witches don't feel good about it.
That's why witches, if you're living well,
if you're just living well
witches will [*smooth, almost whispering*] test your strength.
[*gravelly again*] This is the way they were living

. .

[*normal*] when this **Tumahka** was caught,
strung up,
and let down, then it was his turn to talk about what he'd done,
he was strung up there,
then **released;**
because he knew the **ways** of the **Americans** quite well,
he made marks on paper
calling the soldiers to come from Bear Water;

. .

time went **on**
until it reached the **Midpoint;** when the medicine societies went
   into seclusion at the Midpoint
the **soldiers** came, they passed through here—
and it was down there
where the Shalakos race, that's where the soldiers camped.
At that time there were no houses, no stores in that place
and that's where the soldiers set up their tents.
Thunderers, **big** ones
were **set up** facing the **town.**

. .

The chief of the soldiers

. . . .

[*sighing*] now
went looking for
someone, the chief of the town.
Kwantooniyu, he's the one
who was singled out.
Someone, a
relative of his, it was **Weewa,**
a mere transvestite

but it seems he was **strong,**
had a fight
with the chief of the soldiers.
They fought **because of what this**
Tumahka had **done,** because he'd made **marks** on **paper** the
  soldiers had **come,**
but it **came** to be **known** just how **that man** had been living,
that it **wasn't just**
out of a **lack** of **goodness,**
or just because of **cruelty** that he came to be **strung up,** no such
  words
were behind all this.
The **truth** became **known,**
that he was **strung up** for being a **witch, that's** what
the chief of the soldiers **told** the other **soldiers**—
the matter of the Zuni people was settled.
And the **Society** of **Helical** People,
they had **fixed** the **springs.**
They notified the people;

         . .

when **everyone** had **hauled water, all** the **springs** were fixed.
  Once they were fixed,
when the **horses** drank, **mules** drank, they were **dying,**
there at **Zuni,**
by the time things were settled and the Zuni people were calm,
  the **soldiers** wanted to **break camp,**
a lot of the mules they had brought were just stretched out;
the **springs** had been fixed, **right** around here **all** the springs had
  been fixed,
as the **soldiers came by here their mules** drank, **dying** as they
  came,
and it seems they came through here again when they

         . .

went back to where they were stationed.
And the **Bow Priests** were captured. Having been captured, they
  were **taken** away to **Luuna.**
The Bow Priests were locked up at Luuna. Having been locked
  up, they lived on that way
[*gravelly*] they ended up stretched out.
[*normal*] Because of **Tumahka's** way of thinking.
Well, one **might** have **thought** he was just **living a peaceable** life,
  given the way the **Americans** got word of it—

living a peaceable life,
and **just** for **minding** his **own business** he got **strung up, he was**
   getting himself killed, strung up there,
so he got angry and sent paper with marks on it.
The **truth** was **brought** to **light,**
that it wasn't that way,
it was because he was not living a peaceable life that he was
   captured, then there was talk;
and that man
called the soldiers out of spite, in order to get the whole town
stretched out;
[*gravelly*] the Bow Priests were locked up;
[*normal*] they **strung that man** up, so they were **locked** up.
Ever since they were **locked up at Luuna,**
our Bow Priests have been in decline.

. .

And **this** was when the **Midpoint** had come. The **medicine**
   societies were in **seclusion.** Well, what happened wasn't happy.
A **life** was being threatened, and so

. . . .

the **soldiers** came.
The townspeople weren't happy, given that the whole town might
   end up stretched out. Since the medicine societies were in
   seclusion
food was brought to the **members,** but no one was thinking
"Yes, I'll eat," given that the whole town might end up stretched out.
They were not happy,
this is the way it **was**
when the medicine societies were in seclusion.
In the society we belong to now
our
late father
was a small boy then
and when **food** was brought **no one ate.**
[*in a child's voice*] "Let me eat now,
so I'll be good and full when I die."
[*normal*] That's what
our
late father said—
being a small boy, one doesn't know very much—
such were the words he **spoke**
while he sat there **eating;** the members of the society were not
   happy.

Because of **Tumahka's** way of **thinking**
the witches were saved.
The **way** things are going **now**
if a witch is caught, he doesn't get **strung up,**
because of the **American** way of thinking.
[*sharply*] **Things were going perfectly well** when **this** happened,
when he just had to expose his people. The **truth** of the **matter**
  came to **light.**
He wasn't strung up for no **reason.**
He got **strung up** because he was **caught** as a **witch**
and because the **true word** became **known,**
they were released, released—
the Zuni people were not mowed **down.**
That's all.

COYOTE, SKUNK,

AND THE PRAIRIE DOGS

BARRE TOELKEN

INTRODUCTION

This story, often referred to in print as "Coyote Makes Rain," was a favorite of Hugh Yellowman's and indeed is one of the most commonly told Coyote stories among the Navajo. Yellowman, a member of the Todich'ii'ni, or "Bitter Water" clan, was a gifted narrator who told Coyote stories to his family in the belief that their exposure to these dramatic enactments of moral issues would provide models for a sane and balanced life as well as clever and humorous entertainment in the richness of the Navajo language.

In Navajo tradition Coyote stories are actually told only during the winter, which for the Navajo starts with the first killing frost and ends at the first thunderstorm. Whatever the original reasons for this restriction may have been, the belief calls attention to the idea that spoken narratives are powerful, that they—like all other powerful dimensions of life—must operate in harmony with nature, and that the entertainment available in the content of the stories is overshadowed by larger, more important considerations of ritual propriety and proper use of the language. The Navajo assume that the reality we live in is created by speaking, by articulation; in their view language is affective more than it is descriptive. But Coyote stories can be mentioned, and scenes from them can be alluded to, during other parts of the year, especially when the reference clarifies or intensifies a healing ritual.

Typically stories are told by adults to one another and their children around the central fireplace of a one-room circular or octagonal hogan, the traditional Navajo form of housing. More recently, as more Navajo have moved to nearby off-reservation towns or into tribally built housing units in reservation communities, the stories are told around the kitchen table or in the living room, where the mother may be working nearby on an indoor loom. Someone in the family might request a favorite story, or the narrator might simply be reminded of one by some recent event or topic of conversation. Narration often lasts well into the night, with several stories being told, discussed, explained, and compared with others referred to only by theme or bare plot elements. The event thus can entail lengthy entertainment as well as a hearty discussion session about Navajo values, language, and cultural history.

The stories are narrated rather slowly, with care that key actions and words are stylistically foregrounded. The audience—and often the narrator—laugh when Ma'ii, Coyote, does or says something that runs counter to the behaviors that represent Navajo assumptions and values. (Anger, betrayal, selfishness, pushiness or intense competitiveness, immoderate or inconsiderate behavior, misuse of ritual, and mistreatment of the dead are common cultural discrepancies for the Navajo.) Since the Navajo often laugh in order to chastise their children for acting in ways considered dangerous to the culture or their health, the audience's laughter often marks those moments in which Coyote has done something that the listeners would avoid or find morally problematic. The stories dramatize values associated with proper behavior while embodying actions the Navajo believe have an effect on health.

The reader will notice that although the story line itself is quite understandable, the audience laughs in places where we non-Navajo probably would not. This is our indication that meanings and assumptions are "afloat" that are not stated directly in the text but are shared by members of the culture and can be touched off, or "excited," by an appropriate dramatic scene in the story. In the following story the audience laughs when Ma'ii causes it to rain because he hates the prairie dogs (*both* coyote and prairie dogs are associated with bringing rain; feelings of hatred and revenge are associated with mental imbalances); when Ma'ii gets swept away by his own flood (comeuppance for his arrogant behavior); when he asks the skunk to make him appear to be dead and decaying (the Navajo do not play around with death, for to do so would be to act like a "skin walker," a *yenaaldloshi*, the Navajo equivalent of a witch); when the skunk "urinates" (sprays) the small animals dancing around Ma'ii's presumed body (they are celebrating a death and mistreating what they think is a corpse; since they have blindly accepted the appearance of death, their blinding is ironically appropriate); when Ma'ii and Skunk club the small animals to death (comeuppance for their willful mistreatment of a "corpse"); when Ma'ii tries to get all or most of the meat and fails (selfishness is discouraged, as is betrayal or cheating of someone who has been helpful in getting food); when Ma'ii shows both exhaustion and triumph in "winning" the race with Skunk (serious personal striving and competition is a symptom of spiritual imbalance); when in digging out the four skinny prairie dogs, Ma'ii parallels the action and direction of a healing ritual— toward the east, then the south, then the west, then the north (throwing food away in the format of a ritual act is destructive and suggestive of witchery); and when Ma'ii is reduced to begging for only a few bones to gnaw on after assaying to obtain the whole meat supply (ironic deflation of ego).

Clearly without these responses of a Navajo audience to show us where the key moral dilemmas occur, we might easily misunderstand this story (and others like it) as merely another episode in the wily "Trickster cycle" so favored by Euro-American scholars and professional storytellers. While Ma'ii does occasionally trick someone, it is not the trick but the morally ironic juxtaposition of human emotions with human values that forms the dramatic core of the Navajo Ma'ii stories. And Ma'ii is not the humorously pitiful Wile E. Coyote from the Roadrunner cartoons; neither is he a canine caricature of Jerry Lewis; rather, Ma'ii is at once a sacred creator and a secular glutton with a dash of flash, bravado, klutz, and ego thrown in—a combination of Napoléon, Jesus, Peter Sellers's Inspector Clouseau, and Eddie Murphy.

In addition, the Navajo stories are full of actions that mirror the Navajo preoccupation with movement. Since there are 356,200 Navajo conjugations just for the verb *to go*, we are not surprised to find that the key scenes in Navajo stories focus on a series of active frames like the ones here: trotting, running, floating, planning, running, dancing, urinating, killing, digging, cooking, running, jumping, running, pacing, begging, and gnawing.

Phrases like "they say" or "it is said," which may seem redundant in English, are a way for the Navajo narrator to remind his audience constantly that the story and its details derive not from his own cleverness but from the Navajo culture, from the shared heritage of family, neighbors, and friends. Rather than giving the effect of a fresh entertainment by a gifted storyteller, this stylistic element functions as proverbs do for Euro-Americans, producing an aura of cultural authority: I'm not telling you this; the whole culture is telling you. Moreover, Yellowman reduces the potential egotism of his position by making it clear that there are details he does not himself understand, such as where the action took place (Where the Wood Floats Out) or what songs were being sung by the animals.

A few notes will help to make some of the terms and scenes in the story more understandable. Whenever Ma'ii wishes for something and articulates it, the language functions like the command "Let there be light" in the Hebrew Bible; the desired effect is achieved by speaking of it. The word Golizhii, "Skunk," literally means "the one who squirts [urinates] upward," an appropriate description, considering the action of the story. *Shiłna'ash*—literally, "one who walks along with me"—is used to designate a very close friend or buddy. Usually when Ma'ii refers to someone in this comradely fashion, he is trying to exploit the bonds and obligations of close friendship to their fullest. Toward the end of the story, when Ma'ii paces around and then tries to follow Golizhii's trail, it is clear that he has obliterated the very signs he is looking for. In this, as in many of his actions, his selfishness and impatience get in his way and thwart the achievement of his egotistical goals; this is an accurate dramatization of Navajo assumptions about the practical logic associated with moral weakness or misbehavior.

In the presentation of the text, indications of audience laughter are given in square brackets. Each line uttered by Yellowman is shown as starting at the left margin. Groups of lines are separated by a space representing a pause of one or more seconds in Yellowman's delivery. Indentation within an utterance signals a stylistic or grammatical shift for subordination or explanation.

Ma'ii was trotting along like he's always done.

At a place—I don't know where it is—called Where the Wood
    Floats Out,
  he was walking along, it is said.

Then, in an open area, it is said,
  he was walking along in the midst of many prairie dogs.

The prairie dogs were cursing him, it is said;
  they were all crowding together, yelling at him.

He went along farther into their midst, and
  then he walked along still farther.

He got angry, and soon he began to feel hostile.

After a while it was midday.

He wanted a cloud to appear
(his reason was that he was starting to hate those prairie dogs);
  so he thought about rain.
[*quiet laughter*]

Then a cloud appeared, it is said;
"If it would only rain on me," he said.
And that's what happened, it is said.

"If only there could be rain in my footprints."
And that's what happened, it is said.
"If only water would ooze up between my toes
  as I walk along," he said.

Then everything happened as he said, it is said.

"If only the water would come up to my knees," he said.
  And that's what happened.

"If only the water would be up to my back
  so that only my ears would be out of the water."

▲

"If I could only float," he said.
  Then, as he was starting to float:
"There where the prairie dogs are,
    if I could only land over there," he said.
  [*quiet laughter*]

He came to rest in the midst of the prairie dog town, it is said.

Someplace in the *diz*—
  [*quiet laughter*]
    (*diz* is the name of a plant that grows in clumps)—
    he landed, hung up in that clump, it is said.

And there he was lying after the rain.
And then Golizhii was running by to fetch water.
  (Ma'ii was pretending to be dead.)
Then Golizhii was running past him.

Ma'ii called out to him, it is said.
"Come here," he said, and Golizhii came over, it is said.

"Shiłna'ash," Ma'ii said.
  [*suppressed giggles*]
"Do something for me: tell those small animals,
  'The hated one has died and has washed up
    where the prairie dogs are';
    tell them that, shiłna'ash.

  'He's already got maggots,' you tell them," he said.

"Slendergrass it is called—shake that slendergrass
    so those crooked seeds fall off.
  In my crotch, in my nose, in the back part of my mouth,
    scatter some around; then put some inside my ears," he said.
" 'He's got maggots,' you tell them.
  'The hated one has been washed out.' "
  [*quiet laughter*]

"Make four clubs and put them under me,
    where I can get them.
  'We'll dance over him.
  We're all going to meet over there,' you tell them," he said.

▲

"This is how to do it," he said.
"Get them to make a circle,
    and when they're dancing around me, tell them,
'Hit Ma'ii in the ribs.'
But be careful not to hit me too hard!
'Slowly, gently, like this,' you tell them," he said.
[*laughter*]

This is what happened.
Golizhii ran home and gave out the word to the prairie dogs,
    it is said:
"The hated one is washed out."

There were rabbits and other animals
    and even ground squirrels.
Those animals that are food for Ma'ii were gathered together;
now they were dancing, it is said, at that meeting.

First Golizhii said, "It's true! It's true!
Let's have one of you fast runners run over there to find out."

Then Jackrabbit ran there and ran back saying,
"It's true!"
    it is said.
[*quiet giggling*]

Then Cottontail ran, and "It's true!" he said,
    running back, it is said.

Then Prairie Dog ran, and, they say, "It's true!" he said,
    running back, it is said.

At that time there was a big gathering.
They were dancing, it is said.
Whatever song they were singing, I don't know.
"The hated one is dead," they were saying;
    the club is beside him; they were hitting him in the ribs, it is
        said.

Then they continued with what they were doing,
    and more and more people came.
Then that evil Golizhii remembered Ma'ii's plan:

"When you are all dancing,
  while you are looking up, while you are saying, you say, 'Dance in
      that manner,' you tell them while you're in charge there,
      shiłna'ash," he had said.

Then they were dancing.
Then: "Waay, waay up there something is moving by overhead,"
  Golizhii said to them.

Then, when they were all looking up,
Golizhii urinated upward
  so that his urine fell in their eyes.
[*open laughter*]

The animals were rubbing his urine from their eyes.
"Oh, so 'the one who is hated is dead,' is he?" Ma'ii said,
  jumping up.
[*laughter*]

He grabbed the clubs from under him.
[*laughter*]

He used the clubs on them.
[*laughter*]
They were all clubbed to death.
[*laughter*]

Then: "Let us cook them by burying them in a fire pit,
  shiłna'ash," Ma'ii said.
"Dig right here," he said.
And he dug a trench, Golizhii did.

After he dug that ditch, he built a fire.
He put the food into the pit.
Then Ma'ii thought of something new.

"Let's have a footrace, shiłna'ash.
  Whoever comes back first,
      this will be his," he said.
  [*light laughter*]
"No," Golizhii said, but Ma'ii won the argument.
"I can't run fast," Golizhii said.

"I'll give you a head start;
  while I stay here, you start loping," Ma'ii said.

While Ma'ii pretended to be busy with something,
Golizhii started to run;
  then, just over the hill he ran and hid in an abandoned hole.

In a little while Ma'ii suddenly spurted away
    toward that mountain.

He had tied a torch to his tail,
    and the smoke was pouring out behind him as he ran.
[*laughter*]

While he was running over there,
Golizhii ran back, it is said,
    there where he had buried the food.
He dug them up and took them up into the rocks, it is said.
Four little prairie dogs he reburied;
    then he was sitting back up there, it is said.
Ma'ii ran back, it is said,
[*light laughter*]
    back to the place where the prairie dogs were buried.
He leaped over it.
[*laughter*]

"Whew!" he said.
[*extended loud laughter*]

"Shiłna'ash—I wonder how far back he's plodding along,
    Mr. His Urine," he said.
[*loud laughter*]

Sighing, he lay down,
    pretended to lie down, in the shade.
Then he jumped up and leaped over to the cooking pit.
[*laughter*]

He thrust a pointed object into the ground
    and grabbed the tail of the first prairie dog, it is said.
Only the tail came loose.
[*light laughter*]

"Oh no! the fire has gotten to the tail," he said.
  [*loud laughter*]

So he grabbed the stick and thrust it into the ground again;
    a little prairie dog he dug up, it is said.
"I'm not going to eat this," he said,
    and he flung it away toward the east.
  [*light laughter*]

He thrust it into the ground again;
    a little prairie dog he dug up.
"I'm not going to eat this," he said,
    and he flung it away toward the south.
  [*light laughter*]

He thrust it into the ground again;
    a little prairie dog he dug up.
"I'm not going to eat this," he said,
    and he flung it away toward the west.

He thrust it into the ground again;
    a little prairie dog he dug up.
"I'm not going to eat this," he said,
    and he flung it away toward the north.

He thrust repeatedly in many places, it is said,
    and couldn't find any more.
Nothing, it is said.
There weren't any, it is said.

He got frustrated; he walked around in circles.
So he went around, and he picked up those little prairie dogs
    he had thrown away.
Then he picked up every little bit and ate it all.
  [*soft laughter*]

Then he started to follow Golizhii's tracks, it is said,
    but he couldn't pick up the trail.
  [*quiet laughter*]
He kept following the tracks, back and forth,
    to where the rock meets the sand.
(He didn't bother to look up.)

▲

Golizhii dropped a bone, and Ma'ii looked up, it is said.
It dropped at his feet.
[*quiet laughter*]

"Shiłna'ash, share some meat with me again."
[*laughter*]

"Certainly not," Golizhii said to him, it is said.
Ma'ii was begging but to no avail, it is said.
Golizhii kept dropping bones down to him.
Ma'ii chewed the bones, it is said.
[*laughter*]

That's how it happened, it is said.

MẠ'II JOOLDLOSHÍ HANE':
STORIES ABOUT COYOTE,
THE ONE WHO TROTS

▲

TÓDÍCH'ÍÍ'NII BINALÍ BIYE'
(TIMOTHY BENALLY SR.)

In the beginning was the Black World, where the Holy People, First Man and First Woman, began. They came up through four worlds, and Coyote accompanied them from the first to the present, it is said.

INTRODUCTION

Navajo stories about Coyote are told to children in early evenings during the winter months, from about November through January. It is said that during these months the harmful creatures such as snakes, and lizards, and bears are hibernating. The lightning is recuperating for next summer's storms, it is said.

The term "it is said" (in Navajo, *jiní*) is used every now and then to indicate that the teller is retelling someone else's story. One of my maternal grandfather's older brothers, a singer of the Blessingway ceremony, used to say after telling a story, "I don't know; perhaps they told me a lie, and now I'm telling you a lie." Other times he would say, "I didn't actually witness these happenings. I just heard them being told while I was sitting by the entrance of the hogan." I think *jiní* is used in this manner, as a disclaimer.

Navajo elders, usually the grandparents, tell stories as a teaching tool. First children learn the skill of listening and develop their memory, and later they develop their own storytelling skills. Entertainment is the primary and obvious reason for the storytelling. Each storyteller may tell the story a little differently, but the main points each person emphasizes are the same.

Coyote is a mythological being in Navajo culture. He is considered semiholy and as such serves as a messenger between the Holy People (spiritual beings) and the Diné (Navajo people). The stories that a medicine man tells about Coyote usually relate to something Coyote did or said in the beginning of this world (the Fifth World) or in one of the previous four worlds.

Most of the stories refer to Coyote's setting the precedent for the kinds of behavior—good and bad—that humans practice in this world. It is said, for example, that when something harmful is about to occur, Coyote interferes with the daily harmony of life, perhaps by crossing the path of the intended victim, providing that individual with a warning so that he or she can do what is necessary to protect himself or herself. In this manner Coyote is considered good, and sacred crushed beads, called "hard rocks" (*ntł'iz*), are presented to him as his reward, usually by placing them in a spot where his tracks are found. In other ways Coyote sets a precedent for kinds of behavior that should not be followed. For example, Coyote kidnapped the Water Monster Being's baby because he was attracted by its smallness. Coyote was thus the first to kidnap another being. Coyote also had a daughter, and when she had grown into womanhood, he started scheming as to how he could marry her, thus committing the first act of incest, it is said.

The first story presented here, "Coyote's Sheep," was written as part of a small volume of Coyote stories that I gave to my two youngest children as a gift. My wife tape-recorded the stories as I told them. We then transcribed the tapes, trying to capture the flow of the story as it was told so that my son and daughter would be able to listen to the tape and read the words at the same time. The printed story therefore tries to capture the pauses and emphases contained in the oral version.

A middle-aged apprentice medicine man told this story to a group of us—stock owners and non–stock owners—who were working together to construct a well in our community. This was in the late 1950s or early 1960s. The apprentice medicine man did not own livestock. He seemed to be suggesting that modern-day stock owners had become lazy and that it was only because Coyote kept sheep in each herd that they would pay any attention to their animals. The story was not like other Coyote stories I had heard, in that it referred to modern-day issues.

The second story, "Coyote and Skunk," was told to me by my maternal grandfather when I was six or seven years old. I only remember him telling it to me once, and then I told it over and over again to my aunts. They were about my age, and we grew up together almost like brother and sisters. In the story my grandfather told me, the animals that Coyote was going to kill called Coyote *Doo Yildini* (literally, "the outcast" or "the one who is despised"). Coyote also referred to himself in that manner.

Coyote has a sheep or two
in every Navajo herd;
that is the reason,
now and then,
he doesn't hesitate
to steal one or two,
it is said.

In the beginning,
long, long ago,
the People were tired
of Coyote stealing sheep from their herds,
it is said.
So they told Coyote,
"Mą'ii,
separate your sheep from our herds,
and take care of them yourself.
That way
we will not hate you.
And just think,
then you could eat
anytime you want."

"No, no, my cousins!
What a horrible thought.
I couldn't do that.
I keep wandering around,
wandering around *all* the time;
therefore,
I could not tend to them.
Besides,
you would not tend to your herds
if I were not around to steal from you;
you would only become lazy.
Let my sheep stay
among your herds."

So,
to this day
Coyote keeps stealing sheep
and taking chances,
it is said.

There was a dark spot moving along the vast desert valley, the plains stretching in every direction. Over the dark spot two vultures were circling high up in the sky.

Coyote could not escape from the midmorning sun on this flat desert, and there was not a speck of cloud in the sky. He was sweating and getting thirstier as he plodded along. Even the reptiles were seeking shelter from the hot sun.

Coyote had traveled for days and nights in this condition, without water and food. He could see the buzzards circling high above him and thought, "This may be the end of me finally." His mouth would not stay open by itself; so he had to work it to keep from choking.

"You can wish, but I am not your meal yet," he yelled hoarsely at the buzzards, continuing to drag his feet one after another. His progress was slow, and his destination, the mountain, was barely visible in the distance. "It should be cool upon those mountains," he thought. "I'll make it. I have been in worse situations than this. I was even ground into pieces once, and look at me now."

Thinking about his past gave him an idea. "A cloud ought to appear above him," it is said he said, and a cloud formed directly above him. "His underfeet ought to be moist while he trots," he said again, and it began to sprinkle, and the soles of his feet were moist as he trotted.

After cooling off, Coyote regained some strength and became more lively. He said, "Rain water ought to gush out between his toes as he trots." It began to rain more heavily, and the water began to gush out between his toes. Then he said, "Water ought to reach his knees while he trots," and the rain became heavier, and the water rose till it reached his knees. Coyote trotted with the water splashing all around him, and he lapped and drank the rainwater as he went.

"Just his back ought to be above water as he trots," it is said he said again, and it started to rain much more heavily, until only his back was visible.

Again this he said, it is said: "One should float down the river, and one ought to wash ashore where prairie dogs, rabbits, squirrels, quails, and other edible beings are plentiful." And the water rose higher, till it began to carry him down the wash.

Coyote floated down the wash for quite some time. While he was floating, he was planning how he would lure the animals to him. He began to sing a song:

Prairie dogs, see me floating.
I am drowned, and soon I shall be washed ashore.
You will be so delighted by the reports of my
death,
that you will want to celebrate.
Gather around me
and sing songs of joy.

Coyote was washed ashore finally and played dead, just lying on the beach, barely breathing. He could hear the flies buzzing around him. After some while, he heard a rattle. The sound came closer and closer; then it stopped.

Coyote opened one eye and saw Skunk standing there looking at him, his mouth hanging open as if in surprise. Skunk had a jar in one hand, with a gourd dipper sticking out of it.

Coyote whispered to Skunk, "*Psst,* my cousin, my cousin. Come here. I need your help. Don't be afraid of me. I won't hurt you, I promise."

Skunk took several steps backward. Once he recovered from his initial surprise, he asked, "How can I help? You look like you are beyond help!"

"Come closer to me, my cousin," Coyote whispered. "I don't want anyone else to hear what I have to tell you."

"Well, all right," said Skunk as he reluctantly came closer to Coyote. "Now, what is it that's so important it has to be kept secret?"

"I just want to tell you how we can get plenty to eat later this evening. I'm so hungry! I haven't eaten for several days now. Getting us both fed will require your help," said Coyote.

Skunk was still recovering from the shock of seeing Coyote lying on the riverbank half-dead, and he just listened as Coyote continued.

"The first thing I want you to do is pick some grass seeds from the fields and put those seeds around my mouth, eyes, ears, anus and between my toes. Arrange them so that they look like the larvae of the blue flies," Coyote instructed. "I'll tell you the rest when you've done that."

Skunk said suspiciously, "I don't see how that is going to get us fed."

"Well, I am not through yet, my cousin," replied Coyote. "When you tell the people in your community that Doo Yildiní is dead, they will be curious and want to check your story. That is why I can't move from the spot where I am lying. I don't want to leave my tracks all over the place."

"So, when they check my story, you'll lie there as you are now, playing dead? When they come near, you'll grab them and then eat them? What a clever idea, my cousin. OK, I'll do it for you," said Skunk.

"No! No! Nothing like that. If the first one who comes does not return, they will know you are lying to them. But when they hear the same reports from different individuals, they will believe your story. They will want to celebrate my death. *That's* when we'll make our move."

"Oh! That's when we'll grab them and eat them, huh?" asked Skunk.

"You stupid skunk," Coyote thought disgustedly. "You still don't see the whole thing do you?" "Look," he said, "we can't catch but a few that way. So when they gather to celebrate my death, here is what I want you to do." He whispered again.

Skunk was delighted by Coyote's clever plan. He said, "OK, OK! I'll do just that," and left his cousin on the riverside.

After some time Skunk returned with the grass seeds and started placing them according to Coyote's instructions. When he had finished, he admired the fine work he had done. "It looks real enough even for me," he said aloud.

"One more thing," Coyote instructed; "before you go, make four wooden clubs, and bury two in front of me and the other two behind me so that at the proper moment we can grab and use them to kill our feast."

When everything was ready, Skunk filled his jar with water and headed home. When he got home, he said, "I saw Coyote washed ashore down by the river. The flash flood from this morning's heavy rainfall must have gotten him!"

Some of Skunk's neighbors gathered around and asked, "How could Coyote be dead? That's impossible!"

Skunk said, "I saw him with my own eyes as I was getting water just before noon. I checked *very* carefully. The flies had already laid their larvae around his mouth and eyes. We should celebrate his death. After all, it will mean we no longer have to hide in fear of him."

"It's a trick," said Prairie Dog, looking sideways at Skunk. "We should not trust Coyote to be dead. I don't even trust the one telling this story."

Cottontail Rabbit said, "Yes, Coyote is clever all right. Let's send someone else there to check him out. We shouldn't just come to a conclusion and start celebrating even though it is good news for many of us."

"Who wants to volunteer to check on Coyote's death?" asked Raccoon. No volunteer.

"I would volunteer, but my legs are too short. Coyote could easily overtake me," said Prairie Dog.

"That's it," said Raccoon. "We need someone who can easily outrun Coyote, and that is Jackrabbit, the rabbit that is big."

Jackrabbit stood up from behind the crowd and said, "I am getting old and can't run fast anymore. Get someone else." There was silence for a period of time.

"Come on, Jackrabbit. What do you mean you're old?" said Raccoon. "Why, you'd outrun Coyote so fast he wouldn't know what to do!"

A big cheer went up from the crowd. "Yea, yea, Jackrabbit! We know you are the fastest runner in the area."

"Well, OK, I'll go," said Jackrabbit.

Another big cheer!

As Jackrabbit disappeared over the hill, Skunk smiled to himself, thinking, "So they swallowed my story just like my cousin Coyote had predicted. I can taste my feast already!"

More animals had gathered around the two main speakers, Raccoon and Prairie Dog. Skunk thought, "The more the merrier!" One of the newcomers asked, "What's going on here? What's all the commotion about?"

Skunk replied, "Coyote is dead. He's washed ashore down by the river."

Prairie Dog interjected, "We just sent Jackrabbit to investigate the story. One just can't be too sure about these things, you know."

The newcomer, Quail, said, "It's a good idea to check it out to make sure. If it isn't true, lots of us would be at the mercy of Coyote."

Prairie Dog said, "True, true. We can't afford to take chances. Coyote is our worst enemy, and a very clever one too."

"What if Jackrabbit doesn't come back? Does that mean that Coyote still lives? What do we do then?" asked Ground Squirrel.

Skunk answered, "He'll come back! I was the one who reported Coyote was dead. I made sure he was *really* dead before I came back. I even kicked him in the stomach several times, and he didn't make a sound or make a move. I'm sure Jackrabbit will come back."

Prairie Dog thought Skunk seemed awfully sure of the answers he provided. He said, "If Jackrabbit does not get back, we will send someone else. And even if he comes back, we will check once more, just to be sure."

Skunk complained, "We should be celebrating the death of Coyote. What do we do instead? We check him out to see if he is really dead. I say let's celebrate and feast."

Just then Jackrabbit appeared in the distance. A loud cheer went up from the crowd, which had been growing in size since Skunk's return with the news. "It is true. Coyote is really dead, as Skunk reported," Jackrabbit shouted cheerfully. "He's dead! Coyote is dead! I jumped up and down on top of him, and he never moved at all. The larvae are all over his face now, as our friend Skunk had reported."

The crowd cheered louder at the news, and Prairie Dog had difficulties controlling them. He said, "I agree that is good news, but I am still not satisfied." The crowd was not listening to him.

Skunk took advantage of the situation. "Let's celebrate at the place where Coyote is lying dead," he said and started walking toward the river. Some started to follow him.

Prairie Dog shouted to the people, "Stop! Listen to me. We should send one more runner to check Coyote out. That way we will be certain that he is dead and that this is not a trick. Then you can celebrate if you like."

The followers stopped and returned to the main crowd.

Prairie Dog said, "Gopher, you go this time. Use your ability to dig fast in the ground for your getaway in case he is alive." Without any objections, Gopher took off toward the river and was gone.

"We could be celebrating right now," Skunk complained. "Instead, we have to listen to this worrier." He slunk off by himself and observed the discussions from a distance. He was forgotten.

Jackrabbit said, "When Gopher gets back, we ought to plan how to celebrate this special occasion, the death of Coyote."

The talk alerted Skunk once more, and he hurried back into the crowd and suggested, "Why wait till Gopher gets back? Let's start celebrating right now. I suggest that we go to the site and dance and feast for the rest of the day and all night!" A tremendous cheer went up again at the suggestion. "Bring your food, and we will share whatever we have," continued Skunk. "We no longer have to fear Coyote. He's dead! That calls for much celebration." More cheers!

Gopher in the meantime was approaching Coyote. He stopped at a distance, surveyed the situation carefully, and then decided to burrow his way. He didn't want to take the chance of being eaten. He burrowed right to the spot between the forelegs and the hind legs of Coyote and came up. He checked around and saw the larvae; then he bit into Coyote's ear. Nothing happened. He decided Coyote was dead just as had been reported by Skunk and Jackrabbit. Satisfied, he returned to the crowd and reported that Coyote was really dead.

"*Yaaah!*" the crowd yelled almost in unison as they started to move toward the river. Only Prairie Dog stayed behind. Once on the site, they formed four concentric circles around Coyote and began singing and dancing.

When they had really warmed up, Skunk moved a distance away from the crowd and pissed into the space above them. He yelled, "Look. Look. Look in the sky. There is something real pretty up there!" As they looked into the sky, Skunk's urine got into their eyes and momentarily obstructed their vision.

At that moment Skunk yelled to Coyote, "Now, my cousin, now!" Coyote sprang to his feet and grabbed the two clubs closest to him and started killing all the creatures who had been celebrating. Only a few got away after they recovered from the effects of Skunk's urine.

Over their horde of dead game, Coyote said to Skunk, "My cousin, gather some sticks so we can cook our meal and have a feast. We will make in-the-ground roast of them."

"You're going to do that here?" Skunk asked. "This is the killing ground. It is bad luck to cook and eat your kill right at the site. If you do, you may not have such luck again. Let's move the kill over by that cliff."

"All right! But let's hurry; I'm famished," replied Coyote.

The two moved their kill to the base of the cliff and built a fire. When the fire had burned to ashes, Coyote pushed the charcoal to one side and placed the game in the open pit. He covered the game with a light, dry dirt, then layered it evenly with hot ashes and charcoal all the way across. When he had finished, he said, "My cousin, what do you say we race around Crystal Mountain, to sort of work up our appetite?"

"No, no. I am short legged, my cousin. I can't win against your long legs. Besides, I am already hungry. My hunger doesn't need prompting," said Skunk.

"My cousin, be a good sport! Let's race. I'll even let you have a head start. I will not begin until you have passed the fourth hill from here. Crystal Mountain isn't all that far," urged Coyote.

Skunk knew that Coyote meant to cheat him out of his share of the meat and maybe even include him in as part of the meal. He also knew he wouldn't get out of the race by trying to reason or argue with Coyote. He thought, "Perhaps something will come up to my advantage along the way. The fourth hill is quite some distance.

That will give me time to think of a way to get back here first, I hope!" So he said to Coyote, "All right, we'll race. But whoever wins should get all the meat, every piece of it. How does that sound?"

Coyote laughed to himself. He thought, "What a silly wager for Skunk to propose. I am sure he can't win this race. He's right about his short legs being no competition against mine." He said aloud, "OK, my cousin. Whoever wins gets all the meat."

"So if I win, I get all the meat, right?" said Skunk. "And you won't come to me begging, even for a little piece!"

"Yes, yes, my cousin, and the same goes for you too!" replied Coyote. "Go now, my cousin. I won't start until you pass over the fourth hill."

Skunk wobbled from side to side as he slowly headed toward Crystal Mountain. While he waited for Skunk to get past the fourth hill, Coyote grabbed some strips of cedar bark and crushed them till they became soft. Then he tied the bunched cedar bark to the end of his tail with a thin yucca leaf and put a fire to it. Coyote was proud of his speed, and he wanted anyone who saw him to see how far in front of the smoke he could run. Then he started racing after his cousin Skunk.

In the meantime Skunk had come upon a raccoon hole in the ground. He took a tumbleweed and put it over the opening as he crawled in. He could see through the tumbleweed as he sat. Coyote passed in front of him after a while, with the blue smoke streaming behind him.

Skunk waited a few more moments before he left the hole and wobbled back to the cooking site. He pushed the ashes to the side and retrieved the roasted meat from the fire pit. He waited for the meat to cool and then carried it to the top of the cliff. Then he returned to the fire pit to make it look as if it had never been touched.

As he finished sticking the tails of the squirrels back in the ashes, Skunk saw smoke appearing just beyond his recent hiding place. He hurried up to the top of the cliff and waited.

Coyote returned to the cooking site. The torch on his tail had burned only about halfway through. He was sweating; the foam on his body was visible from where Skunk was sitting and observing. Coyote looked at the meat roasting in the fire pit, and he said, "Let the meat become even more tender."

While he let the meat cook awhile longer, Coyote rolled in the dirt and rubbed some sand on his belly. He laughed. "My poor cousin.

By the time he returns, I will have eaten every parcel and will be long gone."

After he had rested a bit, Coyote got up. He pulled the squirrels' tails out of the fire one at a time, commenting, "My, how tender the meat has become." As he threw the tails over his shoulder, he said, "These will only ruin my appetite for meat." Then he started to uncover the rest of the meat. Finding none, he became frantic. He scattered ashes all around, cussing, "You did this to me, Skunk! You did this to me, Skunk, Skunk, Skunk!"

Coyote found the tails he had thrown away and ate them. Then he started looking for Skunk's tracks. He found them and followed them to the base of the cliff, where they ended. Coyote returned to the fire, traced the tracks again, and still they ended at the base of the cliff. Four times he did this. Coyote could not figure out what had happened to Skunk and to the meat.

Finally, on his fourth trip to the cliff, Skunk called down, "My cousin, are you looking for me? I'm up here."

When Coyote looked up, Skunk threw him a small piece of bone, saying, "I shouldn't give you even a bone since we agreed that the winner takes all."

"Please give me some meat, my cousin," begged Coyote, as Skunk kept dropping him only bones.

"This is what you had planned to do to me, isn't it?" asked Skunk.

"No. No, my cousin. No. If I'd won, I would still have shared with you," Coyote replied.

"Then why did you say, 'my poor cousin, by the time he returns, I'll have eaten every parcel'? What were you referring to?" inquired Skunk.

"Oh, that. I was merely wishing, you know? People can say things they don't really mean. But I'm not really like that. I am a giving, sharing being. I would never have done that to you, so *please* give me some," pleaded Coyote.

"And I too am a giving, sharing being," replied Skunk as he threw Coyote a rat and more bones.

Coyote said, "The parcels you throw me are mere appetizers for my empty stomach. A fat rabbit or a fat prairie dog would do me fine."

Skunk ignored him and continued to eat until he was satisfied, throwing Coyote only small parcels and bones. When he was finally full, Skunk shoved off the cliff the things he didn't like himself and wobbled off toward the woods. Coyote ate only the scraps, it is said.

SINGING UP THE
MOUNTAIN

▲

PAUL G. ZOLBROD

INTRODUCTION

An early anecdote can help introduce this selection from the vast body of Navajo poetry either still unwritten or already translated. It comes from *To the Foot of the Rainbow*, Clyde Kluckhohn's account of a twenty-five-hundred-mile trip by horseback through the high desert country of Arizona and New Mexico in the 1920s. Somewhere near Gallup, New Mexico, at the end of that journey, Kluckhohn asked a medicine man named Hasteen Latsan Ih Begay for permission to attend a nine-day Nightway ceremony. Here is the answer he got:

> For many months you have lived among us, and now you are returning to your people. You are young; you will live many years; you will talk to many; you will tell them of us. Since ten generations has the white man talked to us of his religion. We know his beliefs; we do not want them. The white man knows not our religion, and yet he says that it is not good, that our ceremonies are unclean, that we must leave our gods and take his god. You white men do not pray, you grumble; but you shall see us here praying for nine days that our friend may regain health. I shall let you remain to see the most of what is to come, so that you will go back to your people to tell them that they must leave to us our gods.[1]

For its simple elegance alone this statement warrants pointed attention. But it also requires a broad awareness of what Hasteen Begay means when he links the ceremony with the Navajo gods and its characterization of Navajo expression.

Ceremonies like the one Hasteen Begay mentions here are dramatic reenactments of quests or exiles wherein a character nearly dies or is destroyed altogether. Sometimes the protagonist is male, sometimes female. In some cases two brothers or sisters may undergo the ordeal together. Or they may suffer two separate but parallel ordeals simultaneously. The hero brings misfortune on himself in some instances; in others he suffers innocently for an inadvertent wrongdoing.

In all cases, however, the protagonist is rescued by the very gods Hasteen Begay speaks of and is then cured by them. The deities administer medicine and restore strength with special food and by mending wounds and broken bones. They may even elect to reverse a death. But everything they do is accompanied by songs wherein the power to heal resides. Meanwhile the patient learns the songs along with the procedure so that once restored to full health, he or she can return home and teach them to fellow mortals.

The "friend"—the person whose healing ceremony Kluckhohn was permitted to watch—suffered from such a plight. Whatever the cause, he in effect became a prototypical hero whose illness the medicine man would cure, helped by trained assistants and chosen relatives. The same songs the gods had originally sung would be repeated in a reiterated tale. All supplementary treatment would get its power from the words themselves, which reverted to the story.

Every ceremony, then, is a dramatic reenactment of a narrative bearing underlying similarities to European epics, such as those of Homer and Virgil. A key difference, however, arises because the Navajo stories retain a power not associated with the narratives of Western classical traditions. Hasteen Begay's Nightway ceremony thus illustrates an important point. Aligned with a network of carefully recited songs and chants and climaxing with dancing and other kinds of ritualized, communal activities, Navajo storytelling has deep roots in a sacred mythical pàst. The story itself can be extracted from the ceremony and recited at gatherings large and small. When properly told, it retains ceremonial power because it preserves knowledge about the Haashch'ééh din'é, which is what the Navajo call their gods and in English translates as "Holy People."

It is important to understand that the Holy People demand balance in the world and throughout the cosmos. The Navajo word for that equilibrium is *hózhó,* which can also be represented by words like "beauty" and "harmony" but is best translated by combining those terms. Like the ceremonial patient, the protagonist in the stories suffers because *hózhó* has been lost. He or she has been chosen for the ordeal as a reminder that the restoration of balance requires the careful use of language—the source of all necessary power.

There are upward of two dozen such Chantway narratives—all ultimately part of a system of lore explaining how the Holy People fashioned this delicately balanced world that humans are to safeguard. Navajo tradition, therefore, is linked to the magic of creation and revival. It perpetuates the power of human speech to heal and restore through the careful assembly of story or song.

Sometimes the language is marked by a tight structure in which entire lines are repeated almost word for word. That happens most often in the songs the Holy People teach the ailing hero and the medicine man repeats during a healing ceremony. Or the language may be patterned more subtly, with lines whose wording and length may vary but match or complement each other in reiterated patterns of syntax. That can occur in public statements marking special occasions, such as Hasteen Begay's reply to Kluckhohn.

A careful look reveals that the passage begins with two compound sentences. The first contains two independent clauses parallel in structure. The second contains four, also parallel. The speaker closes with two compound-complex sentences, the first of which contains contrasting independent clauses alternately balancing and offsetting each other. It is worth noting too that his English exhibits the same kind of syntactic framing frequently found in formal Navajo discourse. The best Navajo singers and storytellers can adapt their speech to English in that way.

Between the two extremes of repetitive song and subtly balanced spoken discourse resides the language of spoken narrative, with its combination of repetition and reiterated phrasing that underscores how the entire cosmos exists in a harmonic array of dimension and color, darkness and light, and sunshine and rain—all carefully matched in strictly balanced counterpoise. In the exerpt below, from my translation of the Navajo creation story "Áłtsé Hastiin" ("First Man"),[2] the prototypical male literally sings his way to the summit of Ch'óol'í'í to reverse a loss of *hózhó* that now threatens a final band of survivors.

Such use of language is nothing short of poetic, even if it comes from a nonalphabetical people who preserved their poetry orally. Even the more loosely styled Coyote stories exhibit carefully crafted features. Although the language seems as unstructured as Coyote's disorderly behavior can be—he is, after all, the embodiment of the disorder so deeply feared in Navajo life and culture—it sustains subtle patterns of sound and syntax not recognizable at first.

For example, in the translation of "Coyote and Skunk" by Tódich'íi'nii Binalí Biye' that precedes this presentation, the cautious Prairie Dog speaks consistently in paired sentences that are sometimes parallel in structure. The scheming Coyote, meanwhile, and the equally devious Skunk vary their sentences in structure, length, and number as they contrive first against the other animals and then against each other. Coyote's language often replicates his actions in its unevenness just as episodes describing his exploits end in disarray. Thus, in Navajo storytelling poetic principles can sometimes convey an impression of their absence; and a good translator can adjust his or her language to match Navajo patterns of speech and word order.

For several reasons earlier translators often overlooked the poetry inherent in Navajo speech and storytelling and undervalued its presence in song. The Navajo language is as remote from the languages of Europe as the culture itself is, for one thing. For another, print-oriented Bible-bearing Europeans presumed that without written records and a scripted religion indigenous peoples like the Navajo could not possibly sustain poetry. Furthermore, the earliest translations of Navajo stories were recorded as prose; repetition was generally discarded as redundant, and the subtleties of Navajo syntax were ignored.

The result has been a serious oversight. To this day oral traditions abound in Navajo country, where stories are frequently repeated, and ceremonial life continues. To sing, narrate, or mark a special occasion with stylized speech is to invoke at once the Holy People and poetic art. The challenge now for the broader literary community is to accept into the full spectrum of American poetry the large, hitherto unrecognized corpus of sacred Navajo discourse, whether written, spoken or sung.

A Note on Pronunciation

For the newcomer wishing only to approximate Navajo sounds, consonants equate roughly with their counterparts, except for two that are rare or nonexistent in English—the voiceless *l* (ł), which sounds a little like *sh* in *push* or like the double *l* in Welsh place names, and the glottal stop ('), which resembles the medial clicklike sound in the English expression "oh oh."

There are only four basic vowels—*a* as in *art, e* as in *met, i* as in *sit,* and *o* as in *note.* However, vowels may be short or long, and length is designated by doubling a letter. A given vowel can take on a high tone, which is indicated by an overhead accent. Hence, the first part of the proper name Áłtsé Hastiin ("First Man") contains a voiceless *l* and ends in a high-tone vowel, while the second part includes a long *i.* Vowels may also be nasalized, but I have chosen not to designate those in the Navajo terms reproduced here.

NOTES

1. Clyde Kluckhohn, *To the Foot of the Rainbow: Twenty-five Hundred Miles on Horseback Through the Southwest* (New York: Century, 1927; reprint, Albuquerque: University of New Mexico Press, 1992), 261.

2. Paul G. Zolbrod, "Áłtsé Hastiin," in *Diné Bahane': The Navajo Creation Story* (Albuquerque: University of New Mexico Press, 1984).

Of a time long, long ago these things too are said.

It is said that the people had been continuing their flight from the monsters who pursued them.

By now they were calling themselves Ha'aznani dine'é. In the language of Bilagáana, the White Man, that name means "Emergence People." Those are the people destined to become known as the ancestors of the Navajo people who now live on the surface of this world.

In trying to escape the Binaayee', the Alien Giants, they went from place to place and from place to place, thinking themselves safe at each. They would settle and farm the land, planting corn and squash, beans and pumpkins in the spring. And they hoped that in the fall they could harvest what they had planted.

But then those dreaded creatures, the Binaayee', would locate them and again prey on them. They destroyed and devoured them unrelentingly as hungry wolves gobble sheep who stray.

Thus it was that the last survivors of that unending flight traveled to Tsé ligaii ii'ahi. In the language of Bilagáana, that name means "White Standing Rock."

By now there remained only Áltsé hastiin, the First Man, and Áltsé asdzáá, the First Woman, along with four other persons. Only an old man had also survived. And only his wife had survived with him. With them only two of their children had survived. One was a young man and the other was a young woman.

Those four were weary and meager. They were frightened and fully without hope. They now wondered what would be the good of clearing yet another patch of land. Surely Binaayee' would destroy them as they had destroyed everyone else.

• • • •

"They are sad," said Áltsé hastiin, the First Man, to Áltsé asdzáá, the First Woman.

"They have no heart for continuing such an existence."

That is what he said. And this is what she replied:

"Truly they are disheartened," she replied.

"And just as truly are they afraid. Indeed, I am afraid for them, just as I fear for myself and for you."

To which Áltsé hastiin, the First Man, then had this to say:

"In any case we must rest here," he said.

"We must try once more to settle. Perhaps the gods will help us somehow."

And Áłtsé asdzáá, the First Woman, had this to say in reply:

"Do not count on them," she replied.

"We do not yet altogether know what pleases them and what annoys them. We do not yet know when they will help us and when they will act against us."

. . . .

So they all settled themselves for the night, scarcely daring to try again to make a home for themselves and wondering how soon the final misfortune would befall all of them.

Indeed, these were not good times.

In the morning, however, Áłtsé hastiin, the First Man, observed that a dark cloud had covered the top of Ch'óol'í'í, the Giant Spruce Mountain, which stood yonder by some distance. Saying nothing to others about what he saw, however, he merely joined them in their work.

On the second morning he looked and noticed that the cloud had descended to the middle of Ch'óol'í'í and that it was raining on the upper half. But he said nothing to anyone else and joined those who were working.

When daylight brought the third morning, he looked and saw that the dark cloud had now settled farther down the sides of Ch'óol'í'í so that only the base of the mountain lay uncovered. But he still mentioned what he observed to no one, choosing instead to work along with the others.

On the fourth day, however, when he noticed that the dark cloud had now enveloped Ch'óol'í'í clear down to its base and that rain was falling on it in torrents, he spoke of what he saw to Áłtsé asdzáá, the First Woman, saying this to her:

"I wonder what is happening," he said to her.

"For four days Ch'óol'í'í has been covered with a dark cloud. Only the summit was covered at first. But each day the cloud has forced itself lower and lower, so that now even its flanks are entirely hidden.

"Perhaps I had better go there to investigate."

To which she had this reply to offer:

"It is better that you should stay here," she offered.

"There is great danger out there.

"Naayee', the Devouring Ones, will surely set upon you. Surely you will be devoured like so many others have been."

That is what she replied. And this is what he then had to say:

"Do not be afraid," said he.

"Nothing will go wrong. For I will surround myself with song.

"I will sing as I make my way to the mountain.

"I will sing while I am on the mountain.

"And I will sing as I return.

"I will surround myself with song.

"You may be sure that the words of my songs will protect me."

That is what Áłtsé hastiin, the First Man, said to his wife, Áłtsé asdzáá, the First Woman.

. . . .

So it was that Áłtsé hastiin, the First Man, set out for the cloud-covered mountain of giant spruces. On the very next morning he set out, singing as he went.

"I am Áłtsé hastiin, the First Man," he sang.

"Áłtsé hastiin, the First Man, am I, maker of much of the earth.

"Áłtsé hastiin, the First Man, am I, and I head for Ch'ool'í'í, the Giant Spruce Mountain, following the dark, rainy cloud.

"I follow the lightning and head for the place where it strikes.

"I follow the rainbow and head for the place where it touches the earth.

"I follow the cloud's trail and head for the place where it is thickest.

"I follow the scent of the falling rain and head for the place where the lines of rain are darkest."

For four days he traveled thus, singing as he went.

"I am Áłtsé hastiin," he sang, "and I head for Giant Spruce Mountain in pursuit of good fortune.

"In pursuit of good fortune, I follow the lightning and draw closer to the place where it strikes.

"In pursuit of good fortune, I follow the rainbow and draw closer to the place where it touches the earth.

"In pursuit of good fortune, I follow the trail of the cloud and draw closer to the place where it is thickest.

"In pursuit of good fortune, I follow the scent of the falling rain and draw closer to the place where the lines of rain are darkest."

On and on he traveled, continuing to sing as he made his way to Ch'ool'í'í, the Giant Spruce Mountain.

"I am First Man, and I head for Ch'ool'í'í in pursuit of old age and happiness," he sang.

"In pursuit of old age and happiness, I follow the lightning and approach the place where it strikes.

"In pursuit of old age and happiness, I follow the rainbow and approach the place where it touches the earth.

"In pursuit of old age and happiness, I follow the dark cloud's trail and approach the place where it is the thickest.

"In pursuit of old age and happiness, I follow the scent of the rainfall and approach the place where the lines of rain are darkest."

Thus it was that he continued traveling on and on until he reached the foot of the mountain. And thus it was that he continued on and on, making his way up toward the summit. As he made his way he continued singing boldly.

"Áltsé hastiin is who I am," sang he. "And here I am climbing Ch'óol'í'í in pursuit of long life and happiness for myself and my people.

"Here I am arriving at the place where the lightning strikes, in pursuit of long life and happiness for myself and my people.

"Here I am arriving at the place where the rainbow touches the earth, in pursuit of long life and happiness for myself and my people.

"Here I am where the trail of the dark cloud is thickest, in pursuit of long life and happiness for myself and my people.

"Here I am where the rich, warm rain drenches me, in pursuit of long life and happiness for myself and my people."

So it was that he made his way higher and higher on the mountain called Ch'óol'í'í because giant spruces grew thick and abundant upon it. And as he climbed, he continued to sing with confidence. Even when he reached the very summit he continued to sing.

"Long life and good fortune I attain for my people and for myself," he sang.

"There is long life and good fortune in front of me.

"There is long life and good fortune in back of me.

"There is long life and good fortune above me and below me.

"All around me there is long life and good fortune."

Thus singing as he reached the very point where the peak of Ch'óol'í'í meets the sky, he heard the cry of an infant.

And at precisely the moment when he first heard that cry, lightning was flashing everywhere; so brightly was it flashing that he could not see. Precisely when he first heard the cry, the tip of the rainbow showered the peak with intense colors; so intensely did those colors shower him that he could not see. Just when he first heard the infant crying, the dark cloud shut out the last bit of remaining daylight; so thick was the cloud's darkness that he could not see. Just at the moment when he heard the crying infant for the first time, the rain blinded him; so heavily did it fall that he could not see.

But although he could see nothing, he made his way to the spot where it seemed to him that the crying originated.

And as he reached that spot, the lightning ceased. The rainbow's intense shroud became a band of pastel softness. The dark cloud evaporated into a sky of blue. The rain stopped, and the rays of the morning sun shone upon him.

He looked down at his feet, where he had heard the baby crying. But he beheld only a turquoise figure. In it, however, he recognized the likeness of a female. It was no larger than a newborn child, but its body was fully proportioned like a woman's body. Not knowing what else to do, he picked it up and carried it back with him. Back he carried it to Áłtsé asdzáá, the First Woman, and the others.

"Take it," he bade them.

"Keep it and care for it as if it were real.

"Nurse it and nurture it as if it were our very own."

ENEMY SLAYER'S
HORSE SONG

▲

DAVID P. MCALLESTER

INTRODUCTION

In 1957, I was privileged to record the songs of the Blessingway
ceremony performed by Frank Mitchell at Chinle, Arizona. Among
the hundreds of Navajo songs I have studied in this and other ceremonies, I chose this text for inclusion here because of the extensive
flights of metaphor, unusual in Native American poetry.

The ceremony is used to ensure blessing, good luck, prosperity,
and the increase of livestock—horses are symbolic of all those desired ends. Blessingway may be used when someone is dedicating a
new house, going off on a journey, expecting a child, or in need of
psychic and spiritual renewal. It may be sung over a bundle of ceremonial paraphernalia that needs to have its power recharged. Horse
songs are not a part of every performance of Blessingway but are
likely to be included when the reason for the ceremony involves
travel, livestock, or the increase of wealth.

The first version of this particular song to be published was "The
War God's Horse Song," a much shorter text.[1] Several versions of
this translation and translations from other sources have been published since then; it is probably the most widely anthologized of
Navajo "poems."[2] This is the third of my own revisions, and I do
not expect it to be the last.

Of the poem's dozen or so appearances in print, only my *"War*

God's Horse Song" has been accompanied by the Navajo text,[3] but the Slim Curly version, as recorded in Navajo by Father Berard Haile, can be consulted in three repositories listed by Leland Wyman in *Blessingway*.[4] In this respect the "Horse Song" does better than most Native American texts in the anthologies, where no recourse to the original in the native language exists at all, and we are dependent on what was gleaned from an interpreter and then filtered through the poetic sensibilities of somebody who is usually quite outside the culture.

What follows thereafter, as subsequent editors "rework" the text from earlier translations, is increasing opacity regarding the original meaning of the song and the compounding of errors inevitable if there is no possibility of reference to an original Native text. In the case of the "Horse Song," there are at least the two texts mentioned above, and another translator can begin by comparing them. There are also several Navajo grammars and dictionaries available, college-level courses in the Navajo language, and sophisticated Navajo speakers who can be consulted. Some of these are ceremonial practitioners who know Blessingway and are fluent in English. An ideal would be to work from the Mitchell and Curly texts with the help of such a colleague, who would doubtless be much interested in the two other Native versions. Still in question would be the poetic gifts, in English, of the practitioner and the new translator. Such a collaborative effort might yield at least enough information to place subsequent translators on firmer ground than usual.

In what follows, the commentary is of particular importance in elucidating the meaning of the song. It was provided by Frank Mitchell in response to my questions. In addition, after Slim Curly's name I give Father Berard's translations of those phrases in Curly's version that come closest to matching parts of the song as Frank Mitchell performed it.[5] It is the same song but very different, raising considerable question concerning Washington Matthews's dictum that "if the slightest error is made, . . . the fruitless ceremony terminates abruptly."[6]

I include a short section of the song in musical notation to emphasize that this is a song, not a "poem" in the Western sense. I do not give the complete song because, to the Navajo, it is, as a song, a sacred entity with a life power of its own, susceptible to harm at the hands of casual strangers who are not trained in its use.

The syllables in italics are vocables, untranslatable text, like the English "hey nonny-no" or "fa-la-la." Many Native American song texts consist entirely or largely of vocables and so do not appear in our anthologies. Since Dell Hymes's seminal article, "Some North Pacific Coast Poems,"[7] reference to such vocables as "nonsense syllables" has been obsolete. Hymes showed how the vocables are an inseparable part of the structure and meaning of the text. Charlotte Frisbie has given the most thorough discussion of this aspect of Navajo texts.[8]

In the text given here, the ŋ as in the vocable ŋa is a soft *ng*, as in *doing*. The vowels in the vocables have the "continental values." Vowels marked with an acute accent are not stressed but pronounced with a high tone. Double vowels are long, and a hook under a vowel indicates nasality. An apostrophe indicates a glottal stop. Thus *dlǫ́ǫ́'* is pronounced with a high, long, nasal tone and concludes with a glottal stop. The lateral unvoiced *l* is written *ł*.

The word order in phrases like "Clouds, dark," are inversions of the usual English usage of adjective before noun. I keep the Navajo word order where possible in order to give the impact of ideas in their Navajo sequence. I cannot do this consistently, however, because in some cases it alters the sense. For example, if I rendered White Shell Woman in the Navajo order, Woman Shell White, it would imply a female white shell. It should be noted too that in the penultimate section the phrases "ever returning to long life" and "therefore blessed" are attempts to translate the two most potent phrases in Navajo ritual.[9]

One last explanation—about characters and story. White Shell Woman is one of the names of Changing Woman, the principal Navajo creator deity, and Enemy Slayer is one of her twin sons. In the songs about the origin of horses, he hears strange and beautiful voices calling, follows the sound up a rainbow into the sky, and finds that it comes from horses in the house of his father, the Sun. Enemy Slayer describes them and tells of his taking them into his possession, to bring them back to this world. This song, the fifth in a set of seventeen, tells of the journey to the sky and back again.

I am indebted to the Mitchell family of Chinle and Tsaile, Arizona, for many years of hospitality and teaching, and to the late Albert G. Sandoval and the late Albert G. Sandoval Jr. for painstaking interpreting. Curt Cacioppo and Brian Swann have contributed close reading and helpful suggestions to the present translation.

NOTES

1. Dane Coolidge and Mary Roberts Coolidge, *The Navajo Indians* (Boston and New York: Houghton Mifflin, 1930), 1.

2. For the publishing history and many interpretations of the song, see David P. McAllester, *"The War God's Horse Song": An Exegesis in Native American Humanities,* Selected Reports in Ethnomusicology no. 3 (Los Angeles: University of California, 1980), 1–21.

3. Ibid.

4. Leland C. Wyman, *Blessingway* (Tucson: University of Arizona Press, 1970).

5. The material from Slim Curly's version is in ibid., 260–62.

6. Washington Matthews, "Songs of the Navajos," *Land of Sunshine* 5 (1896): 197–201.

7. Dell Hymes, "Some North Pacific Coast Poems," *American Anthropologist* 67 (April 1965): 2.

8. Charlotte J. Frisbie, *Kinaaldá: A Study of the Navaho Girl's Puberty Ceremony* (Middletown, Conn.: Wesleyan University Press, 1967), 177–79, and "Vocables in Navajo Ceremonial Music," *Ethnomusicology* 24 (1980): 347–92.

9. Gary Witherspoon, *Language and Art in the Navajo Universe* (Ann Arbor: University of Michigan Press, 1977), 17–29.

FRANK MITCHELL'S HORSE SONG

One dot below note signifies staccato release; two dots indicate voice pulsation.

The E-flat as key signature indicates that the tone system used employs a minor third.

He-neye yaŋa,
 with their voices, for me they are calling,
 with their voices, for me they are calling,
 with their voices, for me they are calling,
 with their voices, for me they are calling,
 with their voices, for me they are calling,
 with their voices, for me they are calling, *ya'e, neye yaŋa.*

 With their voices, for me they are calling,
 with their voices, for me they are calling,
 with their voices, for me they are calling,
 with their voices, for me they are calling,
 with their voices, for me they are calling,
 with their voices, for me they are calling,
 with their voices, for me they are calling, *ya'e, neye yaŋa.*

[1] Now White Shell Woman, *ŋa,* her child, since that is who I am,
   na,
   with their voices, for me they are calling,
   with their voices, for me they are calling, *ya'e, neye yaŋa.*

[2] Now Day Disk Carrier, *ye,* his son, *'e,* since that is who I am, *na,*
   with their voices, for me they are calling,
   with their voices, for me they are calling, *ya'e, neye yaŋa.*

[3] Turquoise Boy, since that is who I am, *na,*
   with their voices, for me they are calling,
   with their voices, for me they are calling, *ya'e, neye yaŋa.*

[4] The rainbow, *iye,* where it is blue, *wo,* they are on it there, *iye,*
   now, where it arches over, now where it touches the earth,
   yiye,
   closer this way,
   with their voices, for me they are calling,
   with their voices, for me they are calling, *ya'e, neye yaŋa.*

*This means, "From where the rainbow arches over, edged with blue, a little
way from the end, they are calling me." His mother told him that sound was a
horse. He had asked, "What is that sound? Is that anything bad from battles I
have been through lately?" She said, "No, that is the sound of horses up where
your father lives." He was going to his father's house. The rainbow road went
clear up to the place where the Sun's house was. Before he reaches the end is
probably where he heard the horses.*

[5] Now Boy-Standing-Within-Day-Disk-Carrier, *ye,* his horses,
   i'e,
   with their voices, for me they are calling,
   with their voices, for me they are calling, *ya'e, neye yaŋa.*

*Sun-Standing-Within-Boy, his horses—it is speaking of the other brother, the
Sun's son who lived up there. Since horses came from up there, it is his horses
that Enemy Slayer hears. The Sun's boy's horses are calling me. The son of the
Sun, his horses are calling. "Standing Within" refers to his mother. Sun's boy,
descended from the Sun, his horses are calling me.*

[6] The turquoise horses, those are my horses, *i'e,*
   with their voices, for me they are calling,
   with their voices, for me they are calling, *ya'e, neye yaŋa.*

[7] Water jars, dark, *iye,* being their hooves,
    with their voices, for me they are calling,
    with their voices, for me they are calling, *ya'e, neye yaŋa.*

The little water jar is the horses' feet. It refers to their hooves.

[8] Arrowheads, *ye,* being the frogs of their underhooves,
    with their voices, for me they are calling,
    with their voices, for me they are calling, *ya'e, neye yaŋa.*

This refers to the arrowhead-shaped part of the hoof, underneath.

[9] Mirage stone, *ihiye,* being their striped hooves,
    with their voices, for me they are calling,
    with their voices, for me they are calling, *ya'e, neye yaŋa.*

CURLY: *Its hooves were striped mirage [verse 7].*

[10] Now wind, dark, *iye,* being their forelegs,
    with their voices, for me they are calling,
    with their voices, for me they are calling, *ya'e, neye yaŋa.*

[This] means in motion, running hard.
    CURLY: *Its legs were zigzag lightning [verse 8].*

[11] Cloud shadow, dark, *iye,* being their tails,
    with their voices, for me they are calling,
    with their voices, for me they are calling, *ya'e, neye yaŋa.*

This means the black shadows in the sky, coming down from the clouds.

[12] Fabrics of all kinds being their bodies,
    with their voices, for me they are calling,
    with their voices, for me they are calling, *ya'e, neye yaŋa.*

[13] Clouds, dark, *i,* with these being covered,
    with their voices, for me they are calling,
    with their voices, for me they are calling, *ya'e, neye yaŋa.*

This means their skin.

[14] Sun flare, red, *jiye,* being scattered over their bodies,
   with their voices, for me they are calling,
   with their voices, for me they are calling, *ya'e, neye yaŋa.*

"Sun flare, red"—this means little bits of rainbow. "Being scattered over their bodies"—the sparks that you can see at night in a horse's hair.

[15] Now Day Disk Carrier, *yeye, 'eye,* from before them is shining
     on them,
   with their voices, for me they are calling,
   with their voices, for me they are calling, *ya'e, neye yaŋa.*

The sun comes up in front of them, way over there, and shines on their hair.

[16] New moons, *iye,* being their cantles,
   with their voices, for me they are calling,
   with their voices, for me they are calling, *ya'e, neye yaŋa.*

"New moon" refers to his saddle.

[17] Sun rays, *iye,* being their crupper straps,
   with their voices, for me they are calling,
   with their voices, for me they are calling, *ya'e, neye yaŋa.*

"Crupper straps"—leather straps that go around behind, under the tail. You used to see them on saddles in the old days.

[18] Rainbow, *iye,* now being their girth straps,
   with their voices, for me they are calling,
   with their voices, for me they are calling, *ya'e, neye yaŋa.*

[19] Rainbow, *iye,* they are standing on it,
   with their voices, for me they are calling,
   with their voices, for me they are calling, *ya'e, neye yaŋa.*

"Standing on it" means the rainbow is its means of power, like electricity in a car. They can start up fast, as when you turn the key in a car.

[20] Rain horses, dark, *diye,* now with their manes streaming down,
   with their voices, for me they are calling,
   with their voices, for me they are calling, *ya'e, neye yaŋa.*

Dlǫ́ǫ́'—*anything that travels on four legs. It means "horse" here;* níłtsą́ dlǫ́ǫ́' *means "rain horses." And this refers to hair hanging down in a line along the neck, the mane.*

    CURLY: *Its neck fringed garment was hair [verse 10]; its tail was drooping rain [verse 17].*

[21] Sprouting plants, *iye*, being their ears,
    with their voices, for me they are calling,
    with their voices, for me they are calling, *ya'e, neye yaŋa.*

Nanise' *("it grows up") means his ears grow up like plants.*

    CURLY: *Its ears were reflected sunred [verse 11]; its face was vegetation [verse 16].*

[22] Now great stars, dark, *iye*, being their eyes,
    with their voices, for me they are calling,
    with their voices, for me they are calling, *ya'e, neye yaŋa.*

Since stars are always shining so bright at night, horses can see in the dark to where their home is.

    CURLY: *Its eyes were pointed big stars [verse 12].*

[23] Waters of all kinds, *iye*, being their faces,
    with their voices, for me they are calling,
    with their voices, for me they are calling, *ya'e, neye yaŋa.*

Water from springs and brooks, out of the ground. Some is sweet, some is salty; it is all colors too. Łanáschíin *means "all mixed together." Horses, anywhere, will drink any kind of water, and it won't hurt them unless it is poisoned. Any natural kind of water won't hurt them. Sometimes it gets a coating of dust, and horses blow it off. It's the same way they blow out to clean off the grass they are going to eat, so as not to swallow dirt or anything else that may be harmful. The marking on a horse's face, the whorl of hair, is a sign of that. It is the guiding point of a horse's whole being. The bridle is there. They can eat weeds with thorns, and it doesn't hurt them, or poisonous insects, and it doesn't hurt them.*

    CURLY: *It was eating pollen of beautiful flowers with collected waters [verse 21].*

[24] Great shell, *wheye*, being their lips,
    with their voices, for me they are calling,
    with their voices, for me they are calling, *ya'e, neye yaŋa.*

[This] refers to the big kind of seashell that has a lip and little points, like teeth.

[25] Shell, white, *ye*, being their teeth,
    with their voices, for me they are calling,
    with their voices, for me they are calling, *ya'e, neye yaŋa.*

CURLY: *Its teeth were white shell [verse 14].*

[26] Now flash lightning being their neighing,
    with their voices, for me they are calling,
    with their voices, for me they are calling, *ya'e, neye yaŋa.*

Lightning was put into their mouths to bite with. Horses' bite will hurt.
    CURLY: *Its speech was straight lightning [verse 15].*

[27] Music, dark, *iye*, sounding from their mouths,
    with their voices, for me they are calling,
    with their voices, for me they are calling, *ya'e, neye yaŋa.*

Dilí refers to any sound of a musical instrument. When you are going to make music, you put the instrument to your mouth. When horses were first made, dark sound makers were put in their mouths.

[28] Dawn, *iye*, filling it with their sounds,
    with their voices, for me they are calling,
    with their voices, for me they are calling, *ya'e, neye yaŋa.*

[29] Their voices, *he*, dark seeming, now reach me,
    with their voices, for me they are calling,
    with their voices, for me they are calling, *ya'e, neye yaŋa.*

[30] Dawn pollen, *iya*, lying within their mouths,
    with their voices, for me they are calling,
    with their voices, for me they are calling, *ya'e, neye yaŋa.*

In the early dawn everything new is coming up with it. The horse will receive new air into its mouth to breathe and sound forth, with dawn pollen. It is like when you learn something; then it is in your head, and then you are using it and teaching others with it. A horse does not know when it is tired or sleepy— they are not made like us. Whatever it was that was put in their mouth is what makes them not feel tired. It is put in its mouth and goes up in its mind so it cannot forget it.

[31]Flowers, blessed, *ye*, their pollen and dew lying within their
     mouths,
  with their voices, for me they are calling,
  with their voices, for me they are calling, *ya'e, neye yaŋa*.

*It is like a certain food we like: we all eat plenty of that. The horses will always
have flowers, pollen, dew, plenty of vegetation to eat. It means they will always
have plants and water, and so they will always be lively.*
  CURLY: *From it, it was eating pollen of beautiful flowers, with collected
waters [verse 21].*

[32]Sun rays, *iye*, now being their bridles,
  with their voices, for me they are calling,
  with their voices, for me they are calling, *ya'e, neye yaŋa*.

[33]To my right arm, *e*, beautifully to my hand they come,
  with their voices, for me they are calling,
  with their voices, for me they are calling, *ya'e, neye yaŋa*.

*This means the horses will not be harmed in the future in any way; they will
stay well.*

[34]On this day, *ye*, becoming my horses,
  with their voices, for me they are calling,
  with their voices, for me they are calling, *ya'e, neye yaŋa*.

It means the same for me.
  CURLY: *If on this day it makes me its partner, I should be winner [verse 27].*

[35]Increasing, now, not diminishing,
  with their voices, for me they are calling,
  with their voices, for me they are calling, *ya'e, neye yaŋa*.

CURLY: *Always increasing, never decreasing [verse 28].*

[36]Now ever returning to long life and therefore blessed, my
     horses,
  with their voices, for me they are calling,
  with their voices, for me they are calling, *ya'e, neye yaŋa*.

[37]Now, since I, myself, am the Boy of Ever Returning to Long
Life, and Therefore Blessed,

with their voices, for me they are calling,
with their voices, for me they are calling, *ya'e, neye yaŋa,*

with their voices, for me they are calling,
with their voices, for me they are calling,
with their voices, for me they are calling, *yehe,*
with their voices, for me they are calling,
with their voices, for me they are calling,
with their voices, for me they are calling, *ya'e, ne'eya!*

JOSEPH HOFFMAN'S
"THE BIRTH OF HE TRIUMPHS
OVER EVILS": A WESTERN
APACHE ORIGIN STORY

—

KEITH H. BASSO
AND
NASHLEY TESSAY SR.

INTRODUCTION

Shortly after dawn on July 21, 1933, two uncommon men sat down together in the dusty yard of a Lutheran mission overlooking the San Carlos Apache Indian Reservation in east-central Arizona. They stayed there throughout the day—an elderly Western Apache medicine man and a young linguist trained in anthropology—and by early evening had fashioned between them the most extensive text of the Western Apache origin story ever recorded. Skillfully narrated by Joseph Hoffman and meticulously transcribed in three small notebooks by Dr. Harry Hoijer, the story of "He Triumphs Over Evils" is a compelling piece of traditional American Indian literature. The opening portion of that work, which recounts the conception and birth of the man-god He Triumphs Over Evils to an extraordinary Apache woman, has never before been translated into English and is published here for the first time.

Over eighty-five years of age at the time he worked with Hoijer, Joseph Hoffman was recognized by his fellow Apache as an expert storyteller and a firsthand authority on a wide range of cultural topics.[1] Born to the north of San Carlos near the modern community of Cibecue, he was a young adult when his people were torn from their homes, herded onto reservations, and stripped of their freedom by the U.S. government. Prior to these calamitous events, the Western

Apache, whose name for themselves is Ndee (nDAY, "people"), ranged over an enormous territory that exceeded ninety thousand square miles. Living in highly mobile groups of between thirty and two hundred persons, they moved across the land to the complex rhythms of their own subsistence economy, a closely monitored mix of maize agriculture, wild-plant gathering, hunting, and mounted raids against other tribes. Hoffman himself was an experienced raider, having joined with other men from the Cibecue area in successful expeditions against the Navajo, Pima, and Yavapai.

But Hoffman was also a *diiyin* (deeYIN), a "person of power," and as part of his training for that esteemed position, he learned the ancient accounts of how the world and its inhabitants first came into being. He also learned to perform these accounts for Apache audiences, to dramatize their contents in rich and engrossing ways, to bring them to life with the artistry of his voice. Yet capturing Hoffman's narrative voice was not what Harry Hoijer set out to do when he took down the text of "He Triumphs Over Evils." A skilled phonologist and grammarian, Hoijer was engaged in a comparative study of Apachean verbs, and he was counting on Hoffman's narrative to supply him with a body of examples that could later be analyzed in detail. Such analysis required that close attention be given to the sounds of Hoffman's speech—to slight variations in the duration of vowels, subtle shifts in phonemic tones, intricate clusters of rapidly spoken consonants—and Hoijer's linguistic ear (he worked at San Carlos without the aid of a tape recorder) was superbly trained to hear them. So accurate was his transcription of Joseph Hoffman's words that today, some sixty years later, Western Apache people hearing them read aloud are astonished and amazed. They are pleased and grateful as well. A talented stranger searching for verbs preserved the heart of their storyteller's gift.

It is likely, however, that certain aspects of Hoffman's gift escaped the stranger's notice. Missing from Hoijer's record is any mention of several conventional techniques with which Western Apache storytellers enliven their performances and enhance their expressive effects. Nowhere, for example, did Hoijer note changes in the tempo of Hoffman's speech or alternations in the quality of his voice or strategic shifts in patterns of intonation. Nowhere did he comment on Hoffman's facial expressions or how he gestured with his hands or when—just at some crucial juncture—he might have paused to quicken a sense of suspense. Neither was Hoijer concerned with clarifying the organization of Hoffman's narrative to show textual units of varying size and complexity. Assuming that spoken sentences were the basic components of Apache narrative discourse, Hoijer failed to recognize that sentences are organized into successively larger groupings that together constitute a kind of hierarchy. Based on definite principles and reproduced again and again, these hierarchies impart structure to the narrative as a whole, investing it with added patterns and multiple levels of cohesion.

But whatever may be missing from Hoijer's record is more than offset by what the record contains. Using double exclamation marks, Hoijer registered heightened volume in Hoffman's speech, a prosodic feature that we have represented by means of small capital letters (for example, YOU'RE STEPPING ON ME!). He also identified with single exclamation marks a number of utterances delivered by Hoffman in a manner indicative of "urgency or anxiety." These statements, which charge the text with expectancy and pathos, have been rendered in italics (for example, *Can it really be that no one is alive!*).

With regard to textual units, our presentation reflects the following set of Western Apache conventions. The smallest elements of Hoffman's account take the form of narrative passages. Composed of one or more sentences, these units are bounded by a passage initial-temporal particle (*then* or *now*), a passage final-verb particle (*thus it was* or *they say*), or both. Narrative passages are grouped into narrative scenes (set apart below by four asterisks) on the recurrent theme of story characters leaving and returning home. Some scenes are partitioned into narrative episodes (set apart by two asterisks), which describe different activities or separate phases of the same activity that unfold at a single location. The most important of these activities is prayer (*'okąąhí*) (OKAwhee), a distinctive form of Apache speech that combines marked syntactic parallelism with pronounced lexical repetition. Because of these unusual linguistic features, and also to highlight their strong poetic qualities, passages of prayer have been arranged in lines and stanzas.

The opening segment of Joseph Hoffman's narrative centers on a heroic woman whose proper name is never mentioned. To the Apache, however, she is instantly recognizable as 'Isdzáń Naad-leeshé (isZAAN naaDLEHsheh), or "Changing Woman," the most deeply revered of female deities. As Hoffman's narrative begins, Changing Woman is sitting inside a hollow tree, riding the waters of a devastating flood that covers the earth and reaches to the sky. After the torrent subsides, she emerges from the tree and discovers to her horror that she alone survived the catastrophe. All other people, including her own, have been drowned and swept away. Changing Woman is the only human being in the world.

Against this gripping backdrop Changing Woman is drawn into a series of encounters with various beings—Yellow Snake, Growing Corn, and an enigmatic figure with yellow hair reaching to his waist—who challenge her character and test her will. Though alarmed and sometimes confused, she maintains her composure at every turn, demonstrating unshakable resolve, quick intelligence, and formidable presence of mind. But Changing Woman becomes increasingly unhappy. Desperate for human companionship, she yearns to become a mother and turns in prayer to In Charge of Life, the most sacred of all Apache deities, for help in conceiving a child. Soon her prayers are answered. At the conclusion of a four-day ceremony presided over by Growing Corn, she is made pregnant by rays from the Sun.

After returning to her home, Changing Woman learns that the baby she carries is male, a child named He Triumphs Over Evils (Naaye'nezghaané, pronounced naa YEHNEZGAANeh), whose manifold powers (acquired from the Sun and every bit as potent) will be used by him to rid the earth of everything wicked and bad. But Changing Woman is also warned that unless she complies with a demanding set of proscriptions, thereby ensuring her child's complete perfection, the birth will not occur. Closely supervised by Yellow Snake, she does exactly as she is told, and finally, after many months of anxious waiting, the crucial day arrives. Changing Woman leaves her home and walks slowly toward the east. Suddenly she cries out in pain—*"My belly hurts!"*—and at that precise moment In Charge of Life summons the most powerful forces of the universe to come to her aid. A short time later Changing Woman is enveloped in a cloud of misty rain, and He Triumphs Over Evils is born into the world. He is perfect in every way.

As with any piece of serious literature, Joseph Hoffman's version of the Western Apache origin story can be interpreted in different ways. From one perspective, and perhaps most affectingly, Hoffman's narrative is appreciated by Apache people as an epic of renewal and restoration, a moving depiction of how human life— Apache life—was rescued from extinction and set on a course that enabled it to flourish. But "He Triumphs Over Evils" is also understood as an account of the sacred origins of Apache social customs, a mythological treatise that offers inviolable explanations of how— and why—certain things are done as they are. Thus, owing to actions first taken by Changing Woman, Apache cornfields should be located at some distance from the permanent home of their owner; and permanent homes (where expectant mothers should always try to pass the night) should be located near the bottoms of foothills that descend to fertile valleys. Of the many cultural precedents described in Hoffman's narrative, none is more significant than the four-day ritual culminating in Changing Woman's impregnation by the Sun. Elaborate versions of this ritual, known to the Apache as *naa'ii'ees* (naaEEes, "she is prepared"), are regularly staged today to celebrate the onset of female puberty. Shortly after the puberty ceremony begins, Apache girls are symbolically transformed into living facsimiles of Changing Woman and later, having knelt before the sun, are invested with the same qualities of mind and body that enabled her to survive her ordeal and give birth to He Triumphs Over Evils. Enacted before hundreds of Apache spectators and accompanied by thunderous chants that allude repeatedly to Changing Woman's singular achievements, this episode of the Apache origin story comes stunningly alive.

Joseph Hoffman's achievements were of a different kind, of course, but these too remain suffused with life. Thanks to the work of Harry Hoijer, the world of Hoffman's narrative—dark and forbidding at first, later replete with triumph and joy—can be thoughtfully entered and imaginatively explored. For many readers this narrative world may seem strange and unattractive, a disquieting place where events are shaped by impersonal forces whose aims and purposes often appear obscure. But for Western Apache people, who know these forces only too well, Hoffman's story presents a riveting picture of how things were a long time ago—and how, despite the passage of time, they continue to be today. No mere relic of a lost or bygone age, "He Triumphs Over Evils" can thus be read as a statement of current Apache convictions about the nature of the universe and the perilous journey that mankind has taken within it. So prepare. Listen now for the roar of a murderous flood, and scan the horizon for a hollow tree tossing upon its waves. Changing Woman sits inside the tree. The Western Apache journey begins.

NOTE

1. Keith Basso, ed. *Western Apache Raiding and Warfare: From the Notes of Grenville Goodwin* (Tucson: University of Arizona Press, 1971), 73–92.

Then this woman lived where there were no people at all—thus it was.

She would become pregnant—thus it was.

* *

There being no place for people to live, she floated four times around the border of the sky inside a hollow tree—thus it was.

Then it came to rest on a small piece of land that pointed toward the east—thus it was.

Then she came out from inside the tree—thus it was.

Food-giving plants, which assuredly had been created for us, lay inside the tree. Two stones also lay inside there, a mano and a metate, with which she ground her food—thus it was.

These things had been placed with her inside the hollow tree—thus it was.

* * * *

Then she trailed a snake that had gone along near a gully—thus it was.

Its tracks were visible on the ground—thus it was.

"Somewhere I'll catch up with him," she was thinking—thus it was.

Then she looked up—they say.

"GAG! GAG!" A flock of crows was passing by ahead of her—they say.

Then she thought, *"If only there were some way I could question them!"*—they say.

▲

Then, after they had flown on beyond her, she continued trailing the snake—they say.

Then she scratched with her hands on the side of a rocky arroyo where he had gone inside—they say.

Then he came out to her—they say.

She questioned him when he appeared—they say.

"How can this be!" she said. *"You live in a place with no people!"*—they say.

"It's true," Yellow Snake told her. "They were swept away with everything they owned. No one was left alive. Now there is just myself. I am the sole survivor"—thus it was.

Then she said, "What are you going to do?"—they say.

"Since becoming a snake, I do nothing but crawl in the dirt," he told her—thus it was.

Then she said, "Why are flocks of crows headed in this direction?"—they say.

"They gather nearby where the bodies of people have washed up on land," he told her. "Those were the people with whom you used to live"—they say—thus it was.

Then she said, "Well, where is a good place for me to live?"—thus it was.

"Anyplace you wish," he told her. "Live wherever you choose"—thus it was.

Then she said, "Way over there, just below those foothills at the far end of the valley. That land will now belong to me"—thus it was.

Then he told her, "You have chosen to live exactly where the rays of the Sun touch the earth at dawn"—thus it was.

* * * *

Then she went to live there—they say.

Then she thought, *"What am I going to do?"*—they say.

Then those Food-Giving Plant People, those beings she already
knew, spoke to her by seeing her mind—thus it was.

"What shall I eat?" she said—thus it was.

Then they instructed her—thus it was.

"You are to plant this corn," they told her. "You are to plant it
over there, well away from your home"—thus it was.

Then they told her, "You are not to work it, but in just four days
you will see it appear. Meanwhile, you are to stay here. Don't go
over there and look at it"—thus it was.

Thus they spoke to her—thus it was.

Then she was thinking, "This is the day they told me about"—thus
it was.

Then she went there and looked—thus it was.

There was plenty of corn—thus it was.

There was corn in great abundance—thus it was.

They had spoken truly to her—thus it was.

"They spoke truly to me!" she thought—thus it was.

Then she felt happy and relieved—they say.

* * * *

Then, not far from where she was sitting, some birds were singing
in a bush covered with yellow blossoms—they say.

"Why is that?" she said. "I wonder why they are singing"—they
say.

Then she said, "I'd like to go over there and watch them"—they say.

Then she started off—they say.

Now she was looking about—they say.

High on the side of cliff, near the mouth of a circular cave where little streams of water were falling, there were many different birds—they say.

For a while, sitting there alone, she was content watching the birds—they say.

Then she thought at length about her own situation—they say.

She completely forgot that she was hungry—they say.

Then, shortly after noon, she remembered she needed to eat—they say.

Then she thought, *"Can it really be that no one is alive, here where people should be thriving?"*—they say.

Then she returned to her home—they say.

* * * *

She sat there preparing food for herself—they say.

Then she looked over at the stand of growing corn—they say.

Then, exactly in the middle of the corn, someone with long yellow hair reaching to his waist stood up before her again and again—they say.

Then she left immediately for where the water fell in little streams—they say.

Then she thought of the man she had seen in the corn—they say.

"I will find out later who and what he is," she said—they say.

Then she thought of nothing but returning to Water Streams Down—they say.

"There alone is it pleasant and safe!" she said—they say.

Then she arrived at Water Streams Down and looked again at all the different birds. There were speckled birds, red birds, white birds, black birds, yellow birds, birds with red on top of their heads—thus it was.

She began to feel better as she watched them—they say.

Then she thought at length about her own situation—they say.

"I wonder what will happen to me!" she thought—they say.

Then she thought, *"Is this really the way it will be? Am I to be the only person on this earth?"*—they say.

Then as she was sitting there, dusk came slowly upon her—they say.

Then she said, "I'd better go home"—they say.

She returned there in the evening—they say.

* * * *

She spent the night at her home—they say.

When dawn arrived, she was thinking again of her own situation—they say.

"This is what I will do," she thought. "I will return to Water Streams Down every day for the next four days"—they say.

Then she thought, "Something good might happen to me there"—they say.

Then she prepared food for herself—they say.

Then just as the Sun was rising above the horizon, the man she had seen before stood up again in the middle of the corn—they say.

▲

"Never mind," she thought. "Even though this has happened, I will go to Water Streams Down"—they say.

Then she left to go there—they say.

* *

Then she arrived at Water Streams Down—they say.

She had grown to like it there—they say.

"This is the only place I feel safe and secure!" she thought—they say.

Then her mind was torn between staying there and returning to where the man with yellow hair had stood up before her—they say.

"This is what I will do," she said. "I will stay here today. Then, if all goes well, I will go back there tomorrow evening"—they say.

Then she thought, "What kind of Water is this?"—they say.

"Perhaps this Water can inform me about the man I saw in the corn"—they say.

Then she thought, "I will spend the day right here. Perhaps this Water will do something good to me. *It may even give me a child!*"—they say.

"Would that I could be helped in this way!" she thought. *"Would that In Charge of Life, he who assuredly created mankind, would somehow give me a child!"*—they say.

"Let beauty and goodness return!" she thought. *"Would that he would give me a child so I can live among people!"*—they say.

Then she thought again of the man who had raised his head to her from inside the corn—they say.

"Perhaps he will speak to me," she thought—they say.

▲

Then she spent the night there—they say.

* *

Then when dawn arrived, her mind became confused—they say.

She was uncertain how to get back to the stand of growing corn—
they say.

Then she crossed some sticks and bound them together—they say.

She sighted between them to locate where she was going—they say.

Then, after standing the crossed sticks upright in the ground, she
left to go there—they say.

She went there in vain—they say.

No one was there—they say.

Then, she returned to the crossed sticks and sighted between them
again—they say.

"That is the place!" she said—they say.

Again she went there in vain—they say.

Again no one was there—they say.

She looked about in vain—they say.

"It was right here!" she said—they say.

The, she returned to the crossed sticks and sighted between them
again—they say.

"It was right there!" she said—they say.

Again she went there in vain—they say.

Again no one was there—they say.

▲

Then, having arrived a fourth time in vain, she said, *"It was right here he raised his head to me! Where has he gone!"*—they say.

* *

Then she was sitting there—they say.

She was looking about—they say.

Then she spoke again—they say.

"Where have you gone, you who kept raising your head to me? I have been searching for you. I want to see you! Today we were going to meet each other!"—they say.

"HERE!" he said. "YOU'RE STEPPING ON ME!"—they say.

"IT'S ME!" he said—they say.

Then he told her, "A long time has passed since I raised my head to you. You should have come to me right away"—they say.

Then he told her, "I was planning to enlighten you, but you didn't come to me quickly. You should have come immediately"—they say.

"Even so, I will enlighten you," he said—they say.

Then he said, "Who do you think I am?"

"I am the Growing Corn," he told her. "I have been helping you all this time"—they say.

* *

Then he told her, "Now I am going to instruct you. You must follow my instructions exactly"—they say.

Then he told her, "You will look squarely at the Sun as he pauses atop the horizon. Then his voice will shine upon you. You will kneel down before him. Raising your hands to the side of your face, you will beg the Sun in prayer. 'Give me something,' you will say to him"—thus it was.

▲

Then he told her, "You will kneel before him for four days"—thus it was.

Now she is begging the Sun in prayer—thus it was.

"Give me a baby!" she is saying—thus it was.

Two days passed with her that way—thus it was.

Four days passed with her that way—thus it was.

Then when she was nearly finished, she said, *"Black Sun, give me a child!"*—thus it was.

Then, after she had finished, her instructor told her, "Slap your body four times"—thus it was.

* *

Then he told her, "Now you must pray to In Charge of Life"—thus it was.

She did as she was told—thus it was.

Now she is begging in prayer to In Charge of Life—they say.

"Give me a baby!" she is saying—thus it was.

Then when she had finished, her instructor told her, "If a son should be given to you, he will rid the earth of everything evil and bad"—thus it was.

* *

Then he told her, "If clouds appear in four days, prepare for the one who will be given to you"—thus it was.

Then he told her, "If clouds appear in four days, you will say, 'Someone will be given to me' "—thus it was.

Then he told her, "If the clouds make four sounds, you will say with the fourth and final sound, 'Someone has been given to me' "—thus it was.

▲

Then he prayed for her—thus it was.

> "With the first sound,
>   if all is well,
> someone will be given to you.
>   There will be a sound.
>
> With the second sound,
>   if all is well,
> someone will be given to you soon.
>   There will be a sound.
>
> With the third sound,
>   if all is well,
> someone is being given to you.
>   There will be a sound.
>
> With the fourth sound,
>   if all is well,
> someone has been given to you.
>   There will be a sound.
>
> With the fourth sound,
>   you will truly be with child."

Then he told her, "White rays will slant toward you"—they say.

"You will give thanks to the Sun," he said—they say.

Then he told her, "As the white rays slant into you, you will beg him in prayer"—they say.

> "When my child is born,
>   all being well,
> take care of it for me.
>   Thus it shall be.
>
> When you give me this child,
>   all being well,
> look after it for me.
>   Thus it shall be.

▲

> This child of yours,
>   all being well,
> protect it for me.
>   Thus it shall be.
>
> This child of yours and
>   mine,
>   all being well,
> should live for us forever.
>   Thus it shall be."

Then she stood up—they say.

Then she said, *"Protect my child when you give it to me. I have begged you for this in prayer"*—they say.

Now the Sun was shining on her well—they say.

Then, right before her eyes, something beautiful and good was done to her—they say.

Then her instructor spoke to her again—they say.

"What has been done to you is perfect," he told her—they say.

"You will return to your home and stay there," he told her—they say.

Then he told her, "At sunrise you will kneel down and squarely face the Sun. You will kneel before him for four days. Then you will go to where the birds sing"—they say.

Then she returned to her home—thus it was.

* * * *

Then, having gone to where the birds sing, she followed his instructions not to make mistakes—they say.

"It is beautiful and good that you should be obedient," he had told her—they say.

▲

She was happy staying there—they say.

Then she was thinking, "Although I have had to beg for help, all is well. *A human being is going to live again!*"—they say.

"*Let it be a man!*" she said as she prayed—they say.

Then she became annoyed with the constant chattering of the birds—they say.

Then she thought about her own situation—they say.

"When will it happen?" she thought. "When will my child be born?"—they say.

Then she returned to her home—they say.

* * * *

Then as she was sitting there, a light started flashing at her—they say.

There was a flash from Yellow Snake, a constant flashing like that from a car as it moves along in the sunlight—they say.

After this happened four times, she became concerned, stopped what she was doing, and went to where the light was flashing—they say.

She came directly upon him there—they say.

"Why are you flashing light at me?" she said—they say.

Then he told her, "Someone has been given to you. He is already living inside you"—they say.

"Therefore you must be faithful and obedient," he told her. "Follow instructions exactly. Don't make any mistakes"—they say.

Then he told her, "Your child will be born at home"—they say.

▲

"Everything he will need for life on this earth is to be made for him at home," he told her—they say.

Then he told her, "Go to your home, and stay there. I will look after you from here. I will continue to instruct you as time goes on"—they say.

Then he told her, "I will see to it that all goes well. I will make sure that all goes well from now until the moment of birth . . . *but only if the baby is perfect!*"—thus it was.

"That is why you must follow my instructions exactly," he told her. "You must be faithful and obedient, for this man who will be born for In Charge of Life"—thus it was.

Thus he spoke to her—they say.

Then she returned to her home—thus it was.

* * * *

Then this woman began to dislike food—they say.

"You will be that way for a little while," he told her—thus it was.

"You will not want to eat until the baby inside you gets bigger," he told her. "Then your desire for food will return"—thus it was.

Then he told her, "I am helping you do what is beautiful and good. For that reason you must follow my instructions exactly"—they say.

Then the baby began to move inside her—thus it was.

Then her belly became heavy—thus it was.

Then she didn't go anywhere—thus it was.

"When the time comes, you will give birth inside a rain cloud," he told her—thus it was.

▲

Then he told her, "When He Triumphs Over Evils is born, all of his
father's powers, each and every one of them, will be passed on to
him"—thus it was.

* *

She knew already about the months of pregnancy—thus it was.

"Eleven or twelve months will pass this way with you," he told
her—thus it was.

Then eleven months passed with her there—they say.

Then she went toward the east—thus it was.

Then she said, *"My belly hurts!"*—thus it was.

Thus she spoke, though no one was there to hear her—thus it was.

Only In Charge of Life, he who sits up above, knew that she had
spoken—thus it was.

Then he made it happen—they say.

> Then he made Black Rain clouds
>   slant downward.
> Then he made Blue Rain clouds
>   slant downward.
> Then he made Yellow Rain clouds
>   slant downward.
> Then he made White Rain clouds
>   slant downward.

> Then Black Lightning
>   blessed her with his hand.

> Then Black Lightning
>   shook out her body with his voice.
> Then Blue Lightning

shook out her body with his voice.
Then Yellow Lightning
  shook out her body with his voice.
Then White Lightning
  shook out her body with his voice.

Then Black Whirlwind
  shook out her body with his voice.
Then Blue Whirlwind
  shook out her body with his voice.
Then Yellow Whirlwind
  shook out her body with his voice.
Then White Whirlwind
  shook out her body with his voice.

Then after all who came from the four directions had finished their work, she started to give birth—they say.

Then a fine, misty rain began to fall—they say.

It was raining lightly—they say.

Then her body made a sound, and the baby emerged—they say.

Then she said immediately, *"In Charge of Life, let him be perfect!"*— they say.

* * * *

There were no human beings to assist her at birth—they say.

Only Black Lightning and Black Whirlwind assisted her at birth— they say.

They were the only ones who helped her—they say.

Then, after she had given birth, she picked up her child and cradled it in her arms—they say.

Then, just at that moment, the sky above her began to clear—they say.

▲

Then, when the sky had cleared completely, she thought, "What shall I do with this baby?"—they say.

She put him down uncertainly—they say.

Then after carefully washing her son, she examined him closely and saw that his eyes were black—they say.

Then she said, *"For Black Sun, he before whom I knelt repeatedly, I have just given birth to a man like those who were formerly on earth!"*—they say.

THE BOY WHO WENT IN
SEARCH OF HIS FATHER

▲

EKKEHART MALOTKI

INTRODUCTION

Pressured by the material and social forces inherent in the dominant Euro-American society, the Hopi Indians of northeastern Arizona today are experiencing a steady, perhaps irreversible, erosion of their language and culture. Much of what is being lost can be linked directly to the rapid demise of their native tongue, as is evident in an informal survey of high school students conducted by the Hopi Health Department in 1986, in which 85 percent of the respondents claimed to be unable to speak or understand Hopi. With the fading of the linguistic substratum of Hopi culture, many Hopi concepts, beliefs, and religious ceremonies and much of the hitherto unrecorded oral literature also may slide into oblivion.

For all practical purposes Hopi storytelling, featuring a narrator and an audience in a face-to-face encounter, is already nonexistent. It has been replaced by the entertainment menu so readily available on television and at the local video-rental outlet. Ironically the cultural holocaust that is sweeping indigenous peoples on a global scale is largely voluntary. As Eugene Linden has pointed out, "Indigenous knowledge . . . also disappears because the young who are in contact with the outside world have embraced the view that traditional ways are illegitimate and irrelevant. . . . Entranced by images of the wealth and power of the First World, the young turn away from their elders, breaking an ancient but fragile chain of oral traditions."[1]

Alerted by the accelerating deterioration of the Hopi oral heritage, I began in the late seventies a massive effort to save as much of it as possible. This undertaking, in part supported by Organized Research Funds from Northern Arizona University, in Flagstaff, lasted through the mid-eighties. In the course of these years, I tape-recorded hundreds of Hopi stories, tales, legends, and myths in the vernacular. They were all collected from what I refer to as story rememberers. All of the individuals transmitted the narratives out of a sincere concern to see them preserved for posterity, and none of them had been established or recognized storytellers earlier in their lives. They had simply been exposed to a storehouse of narrative treasures in their adolescence and had retained them in their memory nearly verbatim. Most of the time when I recorded a tale, it was like pressing a button in the narrator's memory bank. A narrative spool would start to unwind and would not stop until the story was delivered in its entirety.

Such was the case with the man from the Second Mesa village of Shungopovi who remembered "Tiyo Nay Hepto" ("The Boy Who Went in Search of His Father").[2] The telling of the original Hopi version of this story, which I recorded in 1981, lasted nearly forty-five minutes. My awe of this mnemonic feat, and of that by other Hopi consultants of mine, has never diminished.

After recording these stories, I made initial transcriptions. Many of the stories, including the present one, were then edited by Michael Lomatuway'ma, my friend and research assistant from the Third Mesa community of Hotevilla. Michael worked with me from 1978 until his untimely death in 1987. Thoroughly versed in his native language and culture and familiar with a large corpus of Hopi narratives, he approached the material strictly from the Hopi point of view. Free, spontaneous storytelling always entails a certain number of unfinished sentences, rephrasings, repetitions, afterthoughts, instances of vagueness, syntactically awkward formulations, even grammatical mistakes. Michael addressed these "flaws" in order to render the text fit for printing. I then translated the text, again assisted by Michael whenever grammatical or semantic questions arose. Finally, the English translation was critiqued by my friend Ken Gary, whose writing skills and editing sense need be credited here as they have been in the acknowledgments of most of my publications.

▲

The present tale was selected from my corpus of Hopi oral literature for a number of reasons. To begin with, it is the length of a typical piece of verbal entertainment. Storytelling, in the days when it still exercised a functional role in Hopi society, was generally restricted to the moon period of *kyaamuya*, corresponding approximately to our December. During this winter month of imposed taboos, with many outdoor activities—especially those that would take place at night—discouraged or banned outright, long evenings were best passed in the comfort of a warm indoors and in the company of a *tuwutsmoki*. Literally meaning "story bag," the Hopi descriptive term for a storyteller implies that he is loaded with narratives. Many of the American Indian tales available in anthologies today, stripped of dialogue and other elements considered nonessential, are more like story abstracts than genuine narratives and would probably not have been much help to a listener eager to while away the long hours of a cold, dark winter night.

Another stock ingredient that distinguishes Hopi storytelling at its best—and is a frequently employed theme in Hopi narrative tradition—is the quest. This ingredient is central to "The Boy Who Went in Search of His Father," for its hero, having grown up without his father, is determined to learn his father's identity. To this intent, the boy embarks on a perilous journey to Taawa, "Sun," after his mother reveals to him that she was magically impregnated by the rays of the solar deity.

In the course of the journey, the protagonist encounters a series of tests, a plot device common to many Hopi tales. The boy overcomes all the tests with the advice and protective charms of Old Spider Woman, a beneficent earth goddess and *dea ex machina* par excellence as well as a favored Hopi story character.

The tests here not only serve to challenge the boy's courage but also prove him a worthy offspring of the powerful Sun: he is confronted with terrifying animals and snakes, among them the dreaded Paalölöqangw, "Water Serpent"; he has to traverse a hostile cactus-lined landscape; and he must pass between a pair of life-threatening cliffs that crash together at intervals, like the Symplegades of Greek mythology.

While the presence of Old Spider Woman lifts any tale above the level of the ordinary human experience, this narrative gains further significance in that its plot line is deeply enmeshed with the Hopi religious fabric as it pertains to the Sun.

Sun is a sky god who figures prominently in the Hopi belief system and mythology. While some origin myths have him exist a priori and portray him as participating in the creation of land and life, in emergence myths Sun is generally created by the people after their exit from the underworld. They are usually assisted in this endeavor either by Maasaw, owner of the upper world, or by Kookyangwso'-wuuti, "Old Spider Woman." In light of all the cultic and ritual attention directed toward Sun, the early-twentieth-century ethnologist Jesse W. Fewkes went so far as to label the Hopi "sun worshipers," a characterization that, in my view, does not do justice to Hopi religio-mythological reality.[3]

Although inferior in status to Maasaw, the supreme personage in the Hopi pantheon, the Sun is much more appealing to the Hopi, for the former is dreaded on account of his association with death. In the present story the Sun, perceived as a fecundator whose generative powers of warmth and light essentially sustain life, is also attributed sexual power through the motif of conception by sunlight. As the epitome of life force, Sun is therefore worshiped on a daily basis. For example, he is venerated during the early-morning rite of *kuyavato,* when a Hopi prays with a pinch of sacred cornmeal for good health and abundant crops. Also, every newborn child is presented to him at the conclusion of the twenty-day puerperal period, when paternal aunts, during the naming feast, bestow their names on the child.

Portrayed as a radiant youth whose face is adorned by a stylized sun disk, the anthropomorphized Taawakatsina, or "Sun kachina," is impersonated by a masked dancer during a *soyohim,* a mixed kachina dance.

Vestiges of a Hopi sun cult are further attested by the fact that the god is supplicated during *taawavaholalwa,* a brief summer-solstice ritual that consists primarily in the fashioning of prayer sticks for the god in the homes of the *taawangyam,* members of the Sun clan.

Soyalangw, a much more elaborate ceremony, on the other hand, once took place in December at the time of the winter solstice. Lasting as a rule for eight days, its major objective was to ensure, by means of sympathetic magic, the return of the Sun to a course that would guide him back again to his summer house.

The celestial body further played an important role in the realm of temporal orientation: the sun functioned as a chronometer not only during the span of the individual day but also throughout the entire year. The timing of both secular and ceremonial events was determined by the course of the sun along a monumental horizon calendar, where specific setting or rising points of the sun were observed by the *taawat wiiki'ymaqa,* or "sun watcher."[4]

NOTES

1. Eugene Linden, "Lost Tribes, Lost Knowledge," *Time* 138 (1991): 46–56.

2. Even now, several years after his death, I am obligated to honor his express wish to remain anonymous in conjunction with the oral traditions he shared with me.

3. Jesse Walter Fewkes, "The Tusayan Ritual: A Study of the Influence of Environment on Aboriginal Cults," *Smithsonian Institution, Annual Report* (Washington, D.C., 1896), 683–700.

4. For more specifics on horizon-based sun time, see Ekkehart Malotki, *Hopi Time: A Linguistic Analysis of the Temporal Concepts in the Hopi Language,* Trends in Linguistics, Studies and Monographs no. 20 (Berlin, New York, and Amsterdam: Mouton, 1983), 427–41.

*Aliksa'i.** People were living in many villages throughout the land. At the village of Walpi lived a young girl who had no desire at all for a lover. When young men came to call at night, she never invited them in. As a matter of fact, she became quite angry if they asked, and none of them, no matter how persistent, ever gained entrance to her house.

Despite this, she somehow became pregnant. As soon as she was sure, she told her mother and father, and they asked her, "Who have you been seeing that could be the father?"

"I don't know," said the girl. "I don't have a boyfriend; so I have no idea how I became pregnant. I've never been alone with a man, and you know that I have never allowed anyone inside the house, don't you?"

"Yes," said her parents, "but how can you be with child if you have never had a lover? Perhaps you did but just can't remember when it happened. Your child must have a father when it grows up; that's the main reason we're asking."

The girl thought hard, again and again. As the days stretched out, she kept searching her mind but couldn't think of anyone. She had never so much as spoken to a man; so how could she identify anyone as the father? Yet the fact remained—she was pregnant; there was no doubt about that.

One day she sat pondering the situation once again, and while deep in thought, her mind wandered back to one summer morning when she had awoken late, chiding herself because the sun was already well up. The night had been so hot that she had kicked off her light blanket during the night and awoke uncovered, with her legs spread apart. As she had become fully awake, she became aware that the Sun's rays had been coming through a vent hole in the wall and were shining directly between her legs. That's why her vagina had felt so strangely warm and glowing. As she sat thinking, all this came back to her.

The girl rushed to her parents and told them what she had remembered. Her father became very excited and said, "Perhaps it's the Sun who made you pregnant. He is a most powerful deity!"

Aliksa'i: the traditional story opener with which a storyteller of the Third Mesa dialect area signals to his audience that he is about to begin his narrative. Etymologically obscure, the formulaic locution may denote something like "hark" or "listen," but it is best left untranslated.

Her parents watched closely as the months passed and the girl's belly grew larger and larger until it was time for her to give birth. Before long she went into labor and delivered a beautiful, light-complexioned boy. When her father saw this, he was sure that his daughter had indeed borne a child of the Sun.

The girl's mother passed on the news of the birth to people of the Sun clan. Then, as is Hopi custom, she and the boy's paternal aunts and grandmothers got together to perform the proper rites for a newborn Hopi child, ceremonially washing the boy's hair and giving him a name. One of his aunts gave him the name Taawa, which means "sun," and said to him, "Bearing this name, strive toward old age." As such things sometimes happen, this name stuck and, as he grew, became the name by which he was known.

As he grew older, he learned to speak and to talk to his mother about things. In the course of playing with the other children, he began to observe that they all had fathers. Like all of them, he had a mother, grandparents, and aunts, but he became aware that he had no father. As he pondered this one day, he turned to his mother and said, "Mother, there's something I've been wondering about."

"What's that?" she asked.

"Well, all the other children here in Walpi seem to have fathers. The only ones who don't are those whose fathers have died, and me. Even those whose fathers have died must have known them before their death, but I don't remember ever having had a father. Whenever I think about it, it makes me very sad, and the other children tease me and call me names because of it. When they tease me, I feel ashamed because I have no father. So I want to know the truth: who is my father, and where is he?"

His mother then related the circumstances of her pregnancy and his birth and told him, "I've since come to realize that the Sun is indeed your father. You are the child of the very deity that travels the skies each day, and he is your true father."

"So that's why they call me Taawa, 'Sun'?"

"Yes," replied his mother. "You're named after your father. It was not long before you were born when it dawned on me that I must have been impregnated by his rays," and she related to him the details of his conception.

"And where does my father live?" the boy asked.

"Well, no one really knows. He rises in the east, and people say that he sets beyond the horizon, somewhere in the middle of the ocean. Perhaps he lives in both places, for he rises in the east and sets in the west," his mother explained.

Taawa thought about this for a moment and then said firmly, "I'd like to go and find my father."

His mother was surprised and exclaimed, "Goodness, no! You can't go looking for him. You're just a young child and will give up after only a short distance. Besides, you have never gone anyplace by yourself, and there are always enemies around. Put this idea out of your mind. When you are older and stronger, then you can think about it again."

The son obeyed, but as he grew older, he constantly thought about going to find his father. The years passed, and when he was about fifteen years old, he once again came to his mother to talk about the trip. He was now quite strong and able-bodied, capable of contributing to the family welfare and accompanying his grandfather or maternal uncles to distant places.

When the time was right, he said to his mother, "Mother, I'm now almost fifteen years old, and still I don't know my father. I know you said that he is the Sun, but other than that, I know nothing about him. I don't know what he looks like or anything about his personality. Is he kind, benevolent? I would also very much like to find out if he knows I am his son. These questions are constantly on my mind, and I must get the answers. The only way I can do that is to seek him out. So please, get a few things ready for me," he instructed his mother. "Prepare what food I'll need for the trip. I'll also ask my grandfather to make some new moccasins for me. My present pair is about to fall apart at the seams." With these plans Taawa eagerly made preparations to leave.

Later that same day the youth approached his grandfather and told him of his plans. "Are you serious?" his grandfather exclaimed. "Is that your intention? Well, I guess it was inevitable that when you grew older, you'd want to go looking for your father.

"However, since he's not in the habit of mingling with humans, he may not be aware that you are his son; so don't be disappointed if you find him and he doesn't recognize you. I understand, though, that you want to know the truth about this, whatever it turns out to be.

"As to the matter of where he lives—who can say? We all can see that he rises every morning in the east and sets every evening in the west, but I have no idea in which direction you should seek him."

The youth listened to his grandfather carefully and when he had finished said, "I think I will head east. Surely that is where he lives. I know it is a long way, and I may not make it, but at least I can give it a try."

"There is no telling what you may have to face as you search for him," said his grandfather, "but if you are truly determined, you will find him. Think it over carefully, for I repeat, who knows what hardships await you if you go?"

That night as he lay on his bed of sheepskins, Taawa thought long and hard about his desire to go in search of his father. He wrestled with it in his heart, turning it over and over, looking at it from every angle. Finally he decided that he must find his father no matter what might happen. Relieved by his decision, he fell quickly to sleep.

The next day Taawa revealed his decision to his mother and grandparents, who all gave their consent, and he informed them that he would be departing in four days.

Right away his grandfather set to work making a bow and some arrows, a quiver and shield, and a hunting knife. When he had finished these, he also made a new pair of moccasins and presented all these things to Taawa, saying, "I made these things for you. It's the least I can do to help you on what is sure to be a long and difficult journey."

In addition, Taawa's mother and grandmother carefully prepared some journey food, which they presented to him early on the morning of the fourth day after he had announced his plans. As the sun rose, Taawa and his grandfather descended from the village of Walpi to the plain below, stopping on a small rise. There his grandfather encouraged him with these words: "All right, proceed onward with a happy heart, and seek your father." As he said these words, he laid out a path of white cornmeal to the east for Taawa to follow. Pausing slightly, Taawa turned and set a course toward the rising sun.

As the day bore on, the heat became nearly unbearable, and he began to look for shade. Before too long he reached a large stand of junipers and settled down in the shade of one of the trees to rest. He opened his canteen, poured some water into the gourd bowl his mother had given him, and mixed some sweet cornmeal into it. Eagerly he dipped some piki bread into it and ate it all.

His hunger satisfied, and resting easily, he felt like taking a nap. Just at that moment, however, he had a strong urge to defecate and went looking for a suitable spot. When he had found it and was making ready, he heard an urgent voice instructing him, "Phew! Move somewhere else, and do it there! When you are finished, return here and come into my place."

Somewhat bewildered, Taawa did as he was told. Looking around for the source of the voice, he moved off to another spot and, when he was done, returned to the original place. He scanned the area, but there was no one in sight. Getting down on his hands and knees, he examined the immediate patch of ground where he stood. Finally he found a small hole and shouted into it, "Hey, did someone speak to me from down there?"

"Yes, I did," came a voice from below the surface of the ground. "Come on in."

Taawa stood there peering at the hole, not sure whether to believe what he was hearing. "But I can't get in. Your entrance is much too small," he protested.

"That's all right," said the voice, which by now Taawa was sure came from the hole; "just rotate your heel into the hole before you, and it will get bigger."

The youth did as suggested and much to his surprise instantly found himself in a room, with the voice saying, "Have a seat. I felt sorry for you, and that's why I've been waiting here for you to arrive." Recovering his composure and looking up to see where the voice was coming from, he recognized Old Spider Woman.

"I felt sorry for you because I know why you are here and what hardships lie ahead. You are headed in the right direction, but your destination is a long, long way off, and there are many pitfalls still in store for you along the way.

"Your father is not an ordinary being, and if you are to find him, you must undergo many tests of your courage. If you are truly the offspring of the Sun, you will pass these tests without harm and find your father. Nevertheless, you will not be able to make it completely on your own; so I have some things for you."

Saying this, she presented him with a piece of medicinal root about the length of his longest finger. "Always chew this root when you encounter danger," she instructed him. "I've also packed for you some of my cobweb, a club, and these high-topped moccasins. I'm sure you'll make good use of all these things somewhere along the way."

As she handed him all these gifts, she encouraged him: "Don't worry, I won't forsake you. When you arrive at your destination, I'll be there waiting for you. So go forward now with a happy heart."

Taawa thanked Old Spider Woman and continued on. Some time later he was plodding along with his mind on other things when he suddenly heard a loud, hissing noise. He looked up, startled. Blocking the trail not far away lay a huge striped black snake! It was coiled as if ready to strike and had a mean look in its eyes.

Taawa froze in his tracks, petrified at the sight of the monstrous reptile, which just lay there swaying back and forth, flicking its forked tongue in and out. He expected it to strike any moment, but it did not. The snake made a move toward Taawa as if to test him, and when Taawa stepped back, the snake stopped.

Growing extremely anxious, Taawa frantically calculated how he could get by the horrible creature. He bolted to one side of the trail, but fast as lightning, the snake blocked his path. Stunned, Taawa paused, then dashed to the other side of the trail, hoping to get past. Once more the snake shot in front of him and this time quickly wrapped himself around Taawa's body and began squeezing.

Taawa tried mightily to resist, but the snake just squeezed tighter until the youth was on the point of suffocation. Just then he coughed and spattered the snake with his saliva, which had become mixed with the herbal medicine he had been chewing.

The medicine had a powerful effect on the reptile, for it released Taawa, uncoiled, and slithered away. His heart still pounding, but greatly relieved, he said to himself, "Well, I guess that's why Old Spider Woman gave me that medicine. She must have known that I'd run into this snake." When he had calmed down, he resumed his journey.

Traveling on, after many days he came to a place so thickly forested with pine trees that he could not see very far ahead. He was picking his way through the forest when he heard an angry snarl. Blocking his path just a short distance ahead was a vicious wolf! Taawa pulled up abruptly when he saw the ravenous animal pacing nervously back and forth, growling all the while. The wolf turned to face Taawa and without warning suddenly charged straight toward him!

Standing there, his mind racing with fear, Taawa knew it would do no good to run, and besides, his legs would not move. The wolf leaped at him and made a move to sink its fangs into his neck, but regaining a little of his composure, Taawa grabbed hold of the creature's ears and wrapped his legs around its body. Over and over they rolled, the wolf snapping at Taawa's throat. Finally Taawa was able to hold off the attack just long enough to whip out the cobweb that Old Spider Woman had given him and quickly bind the wolf's muzzle. Try as it might, the wolf could not break the strands of the cobweb. Finally it gave up the struggle and bounded away, leaving Taawa alone. "So that's why Old Spider Woman gave me the cobweb!" he thought. "It appears that the medicine she gave me worked only on the snake I encountered."

When he had recovered from the wolf's attack, he continued on through the forest until he arrived deep in its midst. So thick were the trees there that few rays of the sun penetrated the gloomy darkness.

As he pressed on, he became aware of a black mound in his way, but he was too far away to recognize what it was. As he got closer, he was still not able to see clearly what it was, although it seemed vaguely familiar. There was so little light that he almost stumbled over it when he got near.

He was peering through the dim light to examine it more closely when the thing reared up on its hind legs, growling furiously, and began moving toward him! Taawa, to his horror, could now see all too clearly that it was a huge bear!

Towering over him, it moved forward, its red tongue hanging out and saliva dripping from its mouth. Long, curved claws grew from its outstretched paws, claws that Taawa knew could rip his chest wide open. He stumbled backward a few steps before he became paralyzed with fear, staring into the bear's gleaming eyes. How terrifying it was!

As Taawa just stood there in terror, the gigantic beast reached out and threw its massive arms around him in a tight embrace, seemingly impossible to break. Taawa struggled with all his strength to free himself but was soon completely exhausted. Just as he thought in despair, "This is the end of me for sure!" the bear spoke to him. Taawa was amazed!

"I'm not going to hurt you, Taawa," said the bear. "I only wanted to test your courage—that's why I frightened you this way. At first you were scared indeed, but despite your fear, you struggled with all your might. I can see now that you have courage, and because I am your uncle, I don't really intend to do you any harm.

"The snake, the wolf, and I—we all tried to scare you, but it was just a test. There seems to be no doubt; you are the courageous child of the Sun, or you would never have gotten this far.

"Be patient, however, for you have a long way yet to go. The fearlessness that brought you this far will no doubt carry you all the way to your destination. Your father may already be waiting there for your arrival; so go forward with a glad heart." With these words of encouragement, the bear vanished into the mysterious darkness of the pine forest.

Taawa once again struck out toward the east, finally coming out of the forest onto a well-established trail. Some time later, however, the trail disappeared into an enormous thicket of thorns and burrs, which stretched as far as he could see and grew almost waist-high.

He just stood there, dumbfounded. How would he ever get

through such an impenetrable and sharp mass? But then as he stood there pondering his dilemma, he remembered the pair of high-topped moccasins that Old Spider Woman had given him. "This must be why she gave me these," he thought as he pulled them on. They were so high that they came all the way to his crotch. Taking the club that she had also given him, he waded into the mass of thorns and burrs, whacking them this way and that! By great effort he was able to clear a narrow path, which closed almost immediately behind him. From every side the thorns menaced him but failed to penetrate the moccasins. How dense the thicket was! He hacked away for so long that he almost lost track of time, but just as he was almost exhausted, he crashed through the mass and collapsed to the ground.

He was so tired that he simply had to rest. After a while he was rested enough to eat again and did so eagerly. After he had finished eating, he again felt a strong urge to defecate. Apparently the old woman had been expecting him, for as soon as he found a spot, he heard her say, "All right my grandchild, you are coming to the ocean. From now on you'll have to travel on the water, and on the way you'll have to pass between two stone cliffs. These cliffs move back and forth, smashing into each other with great force. If you time it right, you'll make it through without getting crushed." After that warning Old Spider Woman told the youth how to pass successfully between the menacing cliffs.

She instructed him further: "If you manage to pass these cliffs, you will travel on until you arrive at the very middle of the ocean, where you will see a ladder jutting into the air. That is your destination. The minute you arrive, the waters will part to reveal a small patch of land where you can leave your boat. There will be a kiva nearby.

"By the kiva will be one more creature lying in wait to test you. For this one chew on your medicine root and spray it with your saliva. It should then allow you to go near the kiva."

The old woman went on: "The beast is bound to ask you, 'All right, why are you here; what is your purpose for coming?' It will also want to know who you are. Say this to the beast: 'My name is Taawa, and I am named after my father. I have come in search of him, and I have been told that he lives here. Is that true?' " This is the way she advised him.

He agreed, and together they walked toward the shore of the ocean. When they arrived there, Old Spider Woman said, "This is the place," and pulled something from the edge of the water. It was a small boat, cleverly fashioned from willow saplings and animal skins, made in much the same way as a war shield except that it was much larger and shaped like a bowl. Apparently it had also been coated with pitch, probably from the piñon pine, to prevent water from soaking through its walls.

The old woman also gave him a broad piece of dry corn husk and instructed him: "Here, paddle the boat with this." Taawa climbed into the boat, which was just large enough for him and his baggage. "Well then," she said in farewell, "carry on with a happy heart!"

Taawa made his way out onto the open water, paddling with the corn husk. It felt as if he were pushing the water backward, and although his paddle was merely this piece of dried husk, it had plenty of strength and did not get soaked. As near as he could tell, he was moving along quite swiftly.

Before long he began to get dizzy from the rocking of the boat over the waves, but after a while he got used to the rocking and continued at a brisk pace. Eventually he saw the two cliffs that Old Spider Woman had warned him about, and as he got closer, he could see them moving back and forth.

They would move ponderously away from each other, pause slightly, and then quickly crash into each other with such force that the resulting boom sounded like a clap of thunder. Each time they crashed, a loud echo resonated through the air, causing huge waves, which threatened to swamp the small boat.

He was terrified of going between them but paddled doggedly on. Following Old Spider Woman's advice, he waited until the two cliffs crashed together and then, as they began to separate, speeded up his paddling. Watching them carefully, he entered the space between them as they opened. He had barely passed the midpoint when the two massive cliffs began moving toward each other again. Paddling still faster, he reached the other side just before they smashed together, missing him by inches. The shock of the waves almost capsized his little willow-and-skin boat once again.

He was so frightened that he was sweating heavily. He just drifted in his boat for a while until he caught his breath and was able to go on.

"I was told to row straight ahead," he said to himself as he pressed on. Finally he came to the middle of the ocean, and sure enough there was a ladder jutting out of the water, with a kiva nearby. "This must be the place," he thought. "Old Spider Woman's directions have brought me right to it." Just as she had said, the waters parted as he got near, and a mound appeared, where he left his boat.

As he approached the kiva, he saw a creature on its roof, rearing up and making a terrible hissing noise like the rapids of a large river. It was a *ka'to'ya,* a gigantic snake, angrily moving about. Though frightened, Taawa slowly crept toward it, watching its every movement. As soon as he was close enough, he sprayed the magic medicine over it.

Immediately the huge snake settled down and said to Taawa, "I am surprised to see you, for no one has ever made it here before. You must be someone special to have arrived here without harm, and no doubt you have a good reason for coming."

"Yes," Taawa replied, "I came to find my father. I was told by Old Spider Woman that this is where he lives."

"Is that so?" hissed the snake. "What is your name, then?"

"Well," he said, "since I am the child of the Sun, I was named after him; my name is Taawa, 'Sun.' Since I bear his name, I started out on a quest for him. Isn't this his home?"

"Indeed it is," admitted the snake. "I believe you really are his son, for who else could have made it all the way here despite all those obstacles and dangers? Why don't you just go on in?"

Taawa climbed into the kiva. As he entered, he stopped on the east side of the ladder. Across the room was a man, who looked up as he entered and invited him to take a seat.

Taawa sat down and watched the man, who was very handsome. He had light skin, and his long hair was hanging freely. He wore an ornate costume, just like that of a kachina, with an embroidered kilt around his loins and a wide brocaded sash and narrow belt around his waist. Hanging down from the back of his waist was a gray fox pelt, and over his right shoulder hung a bandolier of red cloth. His feet were bare, but he wore colorful anklets.

The man's body was painted all over in splendid color. The area from his right shoulder to a point just beneath his breast and in the back just down to his shoulder blade was painted turquoise blue. His right leg from the knee down and his left arm from the elbow to the wrist were painted the same color blue. A wash of yellow pigment had been used on the corresponding areas of the opposite side of his body. All the areas not covered with blue or yellow were tinted a light red. Along with this ornate costume and brilliant paint, he wore a pure-white eagle breast plume tied to the hair on top of his head.

The man sat down by the kiva fire pit and lit his pipe. When he had finished smoking, he refilled the pipe and motioned the boy to join him. Taawa stepped up to him and sat down at his side.

Near the fire pit were two fox pelts, gray and yellow. Between the pelts was a large war shield whose rim was fringed with flowing red horsehair. Taawa did not know what to make of these objects and did not ask about them.

The man lit his pipe, took several puffs, and addressed Taawa. "My son," he said. In utter disbelief, Taawa at first failed to make the proper response. Only after the man repeated, "My son," did he acknowledge by saying, "My father." Taawa now knew without a doubt that this man was his father, the Sun.

His father took four more puffs before he handed the pipe to Taawa, who smoked and said once again, "My father." His father replied again, "My son."

After the smoking ritual was over, a few moments passed. Then the Sun asked his child, "Did you know before you arrived here that you are my son?"

"Yes," Taawa replied. "My mother told me that she bore me for you. Also, the women who claim you as their clan totem attended me at the time of my birth and bestowed your name on me. Bearing this name, I traveled all the way here in search of you, my father."

"Thanks," acknowledged his father. "Indeed I am aware that you are my son, and this gives me additional strength to carry out my daily rounds."

Taawa now told his father all about his childhood—how he had endured the other children's taunts for being without a father and how he had then become determined to set out in search of him. Taawa was so moved by the memory of these things that he got a lump in his throat and nearly cried as he told his father about them.

When the Sun heard these things, he felt pity for his son and said to him, "Yes, I found out soon after you were born that I had a son of my own. I learned of this on the twentieth day after your birth, following the hair-washing and naming rite, when your grandmother, one of my clan relatives, took you out to pray to me.

"I was overjoyed to have you as a son, but it was impossible for me to raise you myself, and it was not possible for me to live there on earth with you. That is not my purpose for existing, to look after you alone. My task is to tend to the needs of all people.

"But you are constantly on my mind. When I learned of your coming, I looked forward to your arrival with great anticipation. I'm glad that you had the willpower and courage to journey here and that you are now at my side." With these words the Sun embraced him, and as he took Taawa in his arms, intense heat radiated from his body but did not burn the boy.

"I have someplace to go," said the Sun. "I'll take you along with me and show you how I care for the people. I will also reveal to you the wishes they convey to me in their prayers. We'll take the route that I travel daily, but before we set out, I must do something else."

The Sun then stood up, picked up the gray fox skin, and left the kiva. As Taawa watched him, wondering what he would do with the skin, the Sun hung the pelt from the end of a stick standing at the south end of the kiva's entrance. To Taawa's amazement, at that very moment gray dawn appeared along the horizon. This done, the Sun reentered the kiva.

He sat down alone by the fire pit and smoked over the yellow fox pelt, just sitting there for a while after finishing. At the proper time he gathered up the yellow pelt, went outside, and replaced the gray pelt with the yellow one. This time the yellow dawn appeared and brought light to the world.

Returning inside the kiva, he put the gray pelt back in its place and said to Taawa, "All right, it's almost time for us to go. But first let me bring in the other skin." When he had put the yellow pelt back in its place, he took down his shield and said to Taawa, "Now we're ready to go."

When they had climbed out, the Sun placed the shield flat on the roof of the kiva and instructed the boy: "Climb on this shield right behind me. It's time for us to leave."

As soon as they boarded the shield, the sun rose full up in the east, and bright sunlight flooded the world. "We'll be heading west," said the Sun as they began moving across the sky at a steady rate.

As they began, people on the earth were going out to say their early-morning prayers to the Sun, carrying with them their pahos—prayer sticks, or prayer feathers. Placing these on the ground in various spots, they prayed for the things they had in mind when they made them. Some wished for good, some for ill; some pleaded for a good life for all people, some lusted after women, and some asked for things meant to hurt others.

"That's the way people go about doing things," the Sun explained to Taawa. "When they go out for their morning prayers, these are the kinds of things they ask for. Then, whether their wishes are good or evil, I pick them up and carry them forward with me."

Thus the two moved along. Traversing the sky, they gathered up everyone's petitions, and it was the same everywhere. Finally they arrived in the middle of the ocean to the west, where there was another kiva just like the one in the east. When they had landed on the roof, the Sun explained, "All right, this is the place where I go in every day after traveling the route we just traveled, caring for the people of the earth. Now let us enter my other home."

Inside, the Sun bade Taawa have a seat. Here not only did the Sun have a second home, but relatives lived there who fed Taawa and made him comfortable. He feasted on such fine things as watermelon and muskmelon, and when he was finished, the Sun said, "Now I will show you what I do with these things," whereupon he sat down next to the prayer feathers and prayer sticks he had collected as they traveled.

He picked them up one by one and inspected each one carefully. As he went about this task, he separated them into two piles. Those made with evil intentions he tossed to a place between the kiva ladder poles. The others, fashioned with good thoughts, he laid gently to the side. This task took a long time, but finally he was finished.

"Now follow me," he said to his son as he took all the good pahos and carried them into an inner room of the kiva. This room was filled with so many pahos that their number was beyond counting. "Take a good look around," said the Sun. "Here is where I keep all the good prayers. Most of them have been here for a long time. They were deposited by the old people, people with good hearts, who are no longer alive. I will also put these most recent pahos, from our trip today, in here."

In great awe Taawa marveled at everything in his father's second home and began to think what he would relate when he returned to Hopi. His father, however, warned him: "When you arrive back home, I don't want you to reveal to anyone what you have seen here, not even your grandfather, in spite of the fact that he is the village chief. What you have learned here is for your use only. He will want to know why you will not tell him; so just say, 'My father forbade me to give these secrets away. I'm to be the only one with this knowledge.'" This is how the Sun instructed him.

"But for now you will spend the night here. Tomorrow morning you can begin your return trip home from where we started this morning.

"The trip back will be the same as when you first came. When you reach the cliffs, however, this time there will be yet another test in store for you. A horrible creature will guard the approach to the cliffs. This creature, the Water Serpent, will test your courage. When it threatens to attack you, show it this paho, and it will disappear back into its underwater home.

"When you reach the cliffs, do as you did before, and you will pass safely. On the other side, your grandmother, Old Spider Woman, will have some instructions for you. If you follow them, you're bound to arrive home safely."

By this time it was dark, and they both retired for the night.

Taawa was still in a deep sleep when his father shook him and said, "Taawa, it's time to get up."

When he was fully awake, he discovered that he was no longer at the kiva in the west but had awakened back at the kiva from where he had first set out with his father. Apparently while he was still asleep, his father had taken him underneath the earth, and he had not noticed a thing.

"All right," said his father. "This is how it will be. I've instructed you in everything that I do from day to day. Do not reveal these things to anyone when you arrive back home. Tell those who ask only this: When you make pahos, do not make them with evil intent. Exclude all bad thoughts as you pray to me, the Sun, as I don't care to take all those negative thoughts along with me. That's all you may tell your grandfather as well," he admonished Taawa. "Tell him only that when he makes prayer feathers for me in the future, to do so only with good thoughts in mind."

"Very well," his son obediently replied. "So be on your way," his father urged him. "The time has come for you to go. I too have to set out on my daily rounds." With that his father went out of the kiva first. Taawa followed and indeed the sun had risen and was casting its bright rays over all the land.

He jumped into his boat and set out upon the ocean. After some time the waters began to churn and swirl, spinning him so rapidly that he thought he might be thrown out. It was all he could do just to hold on. As he spun, he caught sight of a large, dark shape emerging from the sea. As it rose from the water, it grew taller and taller. It was simply incredible!

Bigger around and taller than the biggest pine tree, it stood there, swaying back and forth. It resembled a rattlesnake but was immensely larger. As his father had warned him, looming before him was Paalölöqangw, the "Water Serpent"!*

He could hardly stand to look at it as it looked down on him and his fragile, swaying boat. Its belly showed a tint of green, its entire back was black, and on its neck were two sets of parallel lines representing the tracks of the Pöqangw brothers.†

Its head was massive and round and held a mouth filled with many

*Paalölöqangw, the "Water Serpent": the controller of all bodies of water, such as springs, pools, lakes, and oceans. As a powerful god, he is both feared and revered by the Hopi.
†the Pöqangw brothers: the grandchildren of Kookyangwso'wuuti, "Old Spider Woman." Endowed with greater than human powers, their names are Pöqangwhoya and Palöngawhoya.

teeth, which it constantly ground. Its eyes were so huge and round that they bulged out. On top of its head were feathers much like those worn by the snake dancers. The loose plumes were tied in a huge bunch and smeared with red ocher. To each feather tip was attached a pair of bluebird-wing feathers.

At the back of the serpent's head was a fan of eagle-tail feathers, which swung back and forth as the serpent swayed, and about its neck it wore strands of seashells and turquoise beads. It was simply monstrous in appearance!

Taawa feared for his life, but coming back to his senses, he remembered the paho his father had given him. Groping about the bottom of his boat, he found it and held it out to the serpent, who promptly calmed down and sank below the surface of the ocean.

Breathing a sigh of relief, he pressed on toward the cliffs. When he arrived there, he carefully calculated their opening and closing as he had done before and paddled rapidly through without harm.

After a while he arrived back at the shore from which he had first embarked. Beaching the boat and placing the corn-husk paddle inside, he set out on foot across the land. Soon he felt the need to defecate again. "Perhaps it's because my grandmother, Old Spider Woman, is waiting here for me," he thought. "Why else would I have the urge to relieve myself when I haven't had much food lately?"

Sure enough, when he had gone off a little ways, he heard her say, "Shame on you, young man! Move a little farther away, and do it there! Then after you've finished your business, come in and see me."

When Taawa was done, he came back to the original spot and entered her home again, turning his heel into her hole as before. "Thank goodness," she said. "You found your father without suffering any harm. Now that you've come to know him, I hope that the matter will no longer trouble you."

"Yes, that is right, thank you," the boy replied.

"Well, then," she continued, "I'm sure your father gave you some instructions. Follow them and return to your home. You will, of course, be put to the test by the same creatures that menaced you when you came this way before. Use the medicine I gave you, and you will be all right." She added, "And by the way, you still have a long way to go. I suggest you put on the moccasins I gave you."

Taawa obeyed and put on his high-topped moccasins. Not too much later, he came to the thorny thicket and once again with great effort made it through with the aid of these moccasins and his club.

As he continued on his way back home, he encountered once again the gargantuan bear and the angry, growling wolf. He was ready for both of them and sprayed them with the root medicine, whereupon they slunk away, defeated.

He emerged from the pine forest and after some time reached the place where the huge snake blocked the trail, but it also let him pass when he used the magic root medicine.

In his desire to reach home, he picked up his pace but was once again struck with the urge to relieve himself. He went off the path and once again found himself in Old Spider Woman's home, where she said to him, "All right, you're now getting close to home. From now on you'll have to travel alone, without my help. But I warn you, as you set out from here, don't look back, not even once. If you do, you'll never get home." With this caution to him, she laid out a trail of cornmeal for him to journey on.

From there on Taawa traveled alone. As he approached the land of the Hopi from the east, he could see smoke rising in the distance and knew that he was getting close to home.

It was about sunset when he reached the foot of the mesa on which Walpi sits. Climbing the trail to the mesa top and arriving at his home, he climbed up to the second story. His mother, who had seen him coming, rushed up to him and embraced him, followed closely by his grandmother and grandfather. How happy they were to see him! How good it felt to be back home after all he had been through!

After they had all had supper and Taawa had rested for a while, his grandfather asked whether he had found his father.

"Yes," the boy replied. "I did find him. But I experienced many hard times getting there and back. And before you ask, he also told me not to reveal to anyone, not even you, Grandfather, what I observed.

"However, he did say that there is one thing I should relate to those who make pahos. They should offer them to him."

"Yes," his grandfather acknowledged, "we do that, for he tends constantly to our wants. The Sun is everyone's father. We pray to him for the food we grow, for rain, and for long life. We implore him for these things when we make pahos."

"Yes, that is true," asserted Taawa, "but there is one thing he asked me to mention specifically. Do not have bad thoughts while making pahos, and do not ask him to perform evil deeds. This is what he specifically ordered me to tell you.

"As for me, I bring good news. I know now for certain that I am the son of this deity, the Sun. He's a most handsome man to look at, and I saw for myself how he tends to our needs every single day of our lives. Therefore, we must live out our lives in a good manner, and he will never forsake us. My mind is at rest now, and I can live knowing for sure who my father is."

This is how Taawa was born, grew, traveled, and came to discover who his father really is. And here the story ends.

TWO HOPI
SONGPOEMS

▲

DAVID LEEDOM SHAUL

INTRODUCTION

Many Hopi songpoems deal with summer. Life at this time of year is at its fullest, and the imagery of summer and life pervades the lyrics: light, sunlight, sunflowers, butterflies, water in many forms, rainbows, frogs, corn plants, bean plants, and the blossoms of other kinds of flowers. These symbols of happiness, fulfillment, and long life are the basic texture of each piece.

Some of the summer songpoems are for masked kachina dances, whereas others are intended for the Butterfly Dance, in which both men and women participate. The object of both the kachina and the butterfly forms is to realize what the summer songs talk about. To do this, the songpoems are performed in the context of public ritual. Nevertheless, both kachina and butterfly songpoems are often sung to oneself or others outside the context of public ritual.

Some comment about the kachina figures for which these songs were intended is of interest, although not of real relevance to the issue of translation. The Angaktsina ("Long-Hair") Kachina has long hair, long bangs, long side bangs, and a long beard below the nose; the hair and beard represent the shoals of "walking rain" typical of the monsoon season in the American Southwest. The chest of this kachina bears a yellow depiction of lightning against a black background. The Korowista Kachina is said to have come to the

Hopi from the Keres pueblos of New Mexico. Dressed in a green and white manta, it carries a stick and seeds, which the audience may receive. Although both figures relate to different aspects of agriculture, the lyrics of both songpoems are remarkably similar in style and comment.

Hopi stylistics includes some repetition, which, along with parallelism, varies slightly for the sake of imagery (for example, references to the colors that represent the cardinal directions). It has been suggested that repetition and parallelism in Native American poetic texts have a supernatural value. I only wish to note in the texts translated here that these two common devices may be used in a sophisticated way as well.

There are two sections of music that make up the songpoems. The first one, labeled *a,* is lower in pitch than the second one, labeled *b*. Both sections are repeated twice, with a final repetition of *a,* creating a five-part structure *(aabba).* The rhythms and melodies of the *b* sections are usually more complex than those of the *a* sections. The *b* section of a songpoem is also the semantic core, and the *b* sections of kachina songpoems are made up entirely of vocables (song words having only emotional value; a commonplace English example is *tra-la-la*). In the lyrics of songpoems, each line of poetry consists of half lines, which are words or wording of about the same length and meaning. In translation it is possible to echo sections, lines, and half lines; it is harder to find English interjections or vocables to approximate the Hopi vocables.[1]

The Korowista kachina songpoem, composed by one Koyanimptiwa, was recorded and published early in this century by Natalie Curtis.[2] It is a series of four metaphors. The maidens (referred to specifically in my translation) are symbolic of flowering plants in the fields, their facial powdering (typical of female participants in a Butterfly Dance) symbolic of pollination. Perhaps *chasing* (also in my translation) is reminiscent of the physical motion of the Butterfly Dance, with the buzzing of bees equivalent to the singing of the male dance partners.

In the Angaktsina lyric, composed by one Làahu (bark) and also collected by Curtis,[3] the theme of dancing corn maidens is also used, but the subimage of the maidens' taking part in a Butterfly Dance seems absent. The maidens in this lyric enjoy themselves, refreshed and delighted by the rain. The *b* section is a set of vocables that make up the song the corn maidens are singing. This song within a song serves to make the imagery immediate.

There are previously published translations of these songpoems: the ones "elicited" by Curtis and those by Emory Sekaquaptewa.[4]

The translations by Curtis appear below for reference to my own translations; those by Sekaquaptewa are fairly literal and are thus not requoted. Curtis does not indicate how she worked toward translation. Although she must have employed an interpreter in the field (she spent limited amounts of time with a score of different Native American groups), we do not know who this person was. She states that her contemporary, the Mennonite missionary H. R. Voth, reviewed her translations.[5] Yet she did not always take his advice, and translated the lyrics into the "rhymed" mode of her day.[6]

My own translations differ in that I make use of English interjections to approximate the vocables, echo the half lines of the Hopi lyric (especially in the Korowista kachina songpoem), let the melodic envelope shape the overall translation, and indicate the vivid sense of motion of the Hopi text. The imagery of the Hopi lyrics is dynamic, serving to point up the green, growing plants swaying in the cool breeze after a shower, drops of water glistening on their leaves and pollen blown onto their "faces," just like maidens dancing in a Butterfly Dance.

In my translation of the Korowista songpoem, *magnificently* echoes the glistening, prismatic brilliance of the Hopi word; initially I chose *resplendent* and rejected *colorfully. Corn maidens* (and *bean maidens*) is the usual translation in English spoken by the Hopi and is common in the published literature. Moreover, both expressions approximate the length and rhythm of the Hopi words.

Similar problems in usage occur in the Angaktsina songpoem, which presents structural complications for translation as well. The *a* and *a'* sections have a very short lyric that frames a scene after a rain: the plant maidens, delighted with the fresh coolness, sway in the breeze, entertaining one another in song. The word *nascent* suggests pubescent girls, the core image of the Hopi text; "nascent maidens" are on the verge of motherhood: as potential new mothers, they embody a newness and a potential for newness. Vocables of delight, along with the mention of the singing, constitute the *b* and *b'* sections. The return *a* section repeats, as a quotation, the maidens' song.

In both songpoems the audience is addressed. In the Korowista songpoem the bees assure the people that abundant rain will come to their maturing plants, which will sway resplendently in the breeze. In the Angaktsina songpoem the song of the swaying, dancing plant maidens is quoted (as the entire last section); it consists of vocables, thus mimicking the structure of most kachina songpoems, whose *b* section is usually made up of vocables.

Appreciation of these Hopi texts depends on a word-by-word

gloss; this is given in Curtis for both songpoems presented here, along with a transcription of the music.[7] The relation of the lyric to the melodic envelope can be ascertained from these, as well as the relation of the translations here to the Hopi texts.

NOTES

1. For a bibliography and more information on Hopi songpoem poetics, see David L. Shaul, "A Hopi Song-Poem in 'Context,' " in *On the Translation of Native American Literatures,* ed. Brian Swann (Washington, D.C.: Smithsonian Institution Press, 1992).

2. Natalie Curtis, *The Indians' Book: An Offering by the American Indians of Indian Lore, Musical and Narrative, to Form a Record of Songs and Legends of Their Race* (New York: Harper and Brothers, 1907), 483–89, 508–16, 559.

3. Ibid., 483, 505–7, 559.

4. Emory Sekaquaptewa's translations appear in Mary E. Black, "Maidens and Mothers: An Analysis of Hopi Corn Metaphors," *Ethnology* 23 (1984).

5. Curtis, *The Indians' Book,* 478.

6. That Curtis did not always follow Voth's advice can be seen in the manuscript notes for *The Indians' Book* (Denver Art Museum, Denver, Colo.).

7. Curtis, *The Indians' Book,* 559.

[*a*] Sikyavolimu humisimantu
talasiyamuy pitsangwatimakyangw
tuvenngöyimani.

[*a'*] Sakwavolimu morisimanatu
talasiyamuy pitsangwatimakyangw
tuvenngöyimani.

[*b*] [vocables]

[*b'*] [vocables]

[*a*] Humisimantuy amunawita
taatangayatu töökiyuyuwintani:
umu'uuyiy amunawita
yoy'umumutimani, taawanawita.

[*a'*] Morisimanatuy amunawita
taatangayatu töökiyuyuwintani:
umu'uuyiy amunawita
yoy'hoyoyotimani, taawanawita.

Yellow butterflies,
Over the blossoming virgin corn,
  with pollen-painted faces
Chase one another in brilliant throng.

  Blue butterflies,
Over the blossoming virgin beans,
  With pollen-painted faces
Chase one another in brilliant streams.

  Over the blossoming corn,
  Over the virgin corn
Wild bees hum:

  Over the blossoming beans,
  Over the virgin beans,
Wild bees hum.

Over your field of growing corn
  All day long hang the thunder-clouds;
Over your field of growing corn
  All day shall come the rushing rain.

Yellow butterfly   corn maidens
  skim along,   their pollen on their faces,
    chasing along magnificently.

Blue butterfly   bean maidens,
  going along, pollen   powdering their faces,
    chasing splendidly.

Hmmmmmmmmmm.

Hmmmmmmmmmm.

Among the corn girls,
bees, dancing along,   call out:
  "Amid your plants,
  rain will go along, thundering all day long."

Among the bean girls,
the bees dance along,   calling out:
  "Amid your plants,
  rain will be moving along all day long."

[*a and a'*] Uyisonaqa yooki,
tuvelvolimanatu
nangu'ymani.
Yooyangw yaalaqw, puma'a

[*b and b'*] *La' i' i' i, ihihi' i.*

Ta'a'a'a hin pa natayawinma,
yang uyisonaqa

Ahaha' a, ha' aha' ay, owa' elo.
Ahaha' a, ha' aha' ay, owa' elo.

Yan'i puma tuwat tatawyuyuywina,
Yang'a'a'ay.

Rain all over the corn fields,
Pretty butterfly-maidens
Chasing one another when the rain is done,
   Hither, thither, so.
How they frolic 'mid the corn,
   Laughing, laughing, thus:
      A-ha, ha-ha
      O-ah, e-lo.
How they frolic 'mid the corn,
   Singing, singing thus:
      A-ha, ha-ha
      O-ah, e-lo.

Rain on the plants,
the nascent maidens
will grasp each other.
Rain abates, and they

    Aaaaaaaah!   Mmmmmmmmm!

[Okay!] They go along delighting each other*
  this way among the plants:

    Aaaah . . .   mmmmm . . .   delightful!

They go along this way, teasing with a song,
    and this is how it goes:

    Aaaah . . .   mmmmm . . .   delightful!

*[Okay!]: The interjection is an intrusion into the songpoem of an outside voice, an indefinite identity.

THE FAREWELL
SONG

^

LEANNE HINTON

INTRODUCTION

The Havasupais are a small tribe in Arizona who speak a language that belongs to the Yuman family. They live in a tributary of the Grand Canyon, a lush oasis of spectacular color and beauty. Also under their stewardship is a large area above the canyon, on the Coconino Plateau, a sweeping landscape of great vistas. Their love of the land is illustrated in "The Farewell Song."

This was one of the first songs I heard in Supai (as they call their home) when I began my work there in 1964. It was performed for me by Dan Hanna, a great singing poet. "The Farewell Song" was first sung, he said, by an ancestor of his, named Horned Heart. It was passed down the generations, finally reaching Dan. This kind of Havasupai song, sometimes called the "old men's songs" and "old women's songs," used to be composed by Havasupais very frequently. The songs are partially improvised, the way stories are. That is, the basic content and many of the more often repeated lines will be the same each time, but in any given rendition one can expect more or fewer verses and some different subsections, with lines coming in different orders and a number of them being unique to that performance.

The old men's and old women's songs are composed to express a deeply felt emotion. They are love songs, songs of anger, and songs of pride in a family member, and they are almost always directed to a certain person; and some, like this one, are addressed directly to the land.

Traditionally the Havasupais did not talk about their emotions but sang them instead. In what to me has always seemed one of the most beautiful illustrations of how the pieces of a well-integrated culture fit together, this practice of the Havasupai is practiced as well by the mythical characters of Havasupai stories. Traditional Havasupai tales are told objectively, always in the third person, and the emotions of the characters are not described. Nonetheless, the stories contain songs that are like the old men's and old women's songs: they are in the first person and always express some emotion felt by one character toward another. Like the old men's and old women's songs, the songs in the traditional tales express anger, love, derision, sadness at leaving a place, fear of impending weakness and death, or some other strong emotion.

The translation of a song creates special challenges. The song has a melody, a meter, and dynamics that are lost in a written translation, and the text has various instances of alliteration and consonance that cannot be approximated in English. On the other hand, features of the melodic structure of the song are retained in the organization of this translation. Each line of melody, separable for musical reasons (melodic repetition, meter, and so on), coincides with a line of text, and these lines have been arranged in verses, like an English song. In "The Farewell Song" each line has a falling melodic contour (see the musical transcription). The first line, which for this discussion I will label *a*, begins at a high melodic level; the second line, *b*, begins at a lower melodic level, and the third line, *c*, begins at the lowest level. The verse may consist of as few as five lines and as many as fifteen and will always have the melodic form of *abc(bc)*, where *(bc)* may be repeated more than once.

Line *c* always ends in the vocable syllables *haŋa* or some variant of that sequence. In the translation I have replaced this refrain with an Anglicized version, *ha na*. Dan Hanna explained to me that although these are indeed vocables, they are not meaningless: they bear the connotation of mourning, something like the English *alas*. (In the same manner, the vocables *tra-la-la* in English bear a connotation of happiness.) In Havasupai as in English, when melody and rhythm are removed from a song, leaving the bare text, a feature such as the frequent repetition of a refrain seems overly repetitive and intrusive. Although my goal is always to remain as true to the original rendition as possible, so many friends and colleagues reading drafts of "The Farewell Song" complained about the tiresomeness of the refrain that I reduced its frequency, including it only once per verse. One important function of the refrain is to mark the song's structure. To retain this structure in the translation, I have indented each line that bears the refrain in the sung version.

A fascinating aspect of Havasupai songs that I had to give up in translation is the practice of changing words so that their sound when sung is quite different from their sound spoken. As I have written elsewhere,[1] the Havasupai singer inserts many vowels and syllables not found in speech and substitutes many sounds. Here are two lines for illustration:

spoken: yač məʔevək
sung: gayaǰ moʔevoga
English: "listen to me"

spoken: ičʔaləmo
sung: yaʔajeyʔalamo
English: "to the very top"

The first five lines of the song are displayed here so that the final translation may be compared with the literal, word-for-word translation (in the left-hand column).

Baqey dispayva,
Water-spring dripping,   Spring water dripping,

mate ʔeyamo,
land I-wander-[nominalizer],   land that I wandered,

nyevo geyowe, heŋe.
[demonstrative] that-place [vocables].   that place.

Gayaǰ mu ʔevaga:
This you-listen-to-me: Listen to me,

wameǰemavəga, haŋm
bear-up-under-adversity [vocables]   forget about me, ha na.

The demonstrative *nyevo* in the line above that translates as "that place" is for a referent designating one that used to be in sight but is now gone. In normal speech it may be used for someone who was here but left, someone who has passed away, or someone the speaker once knew or lived with but now does not.

The vocables *heŋe* and *haŋm* are variants of the vocable syllables written earlier as *haŋa*. The vowel in the vocable always rhymes with the last vowel of the line it follows. I tried in earlier drafts to use this same rhyming device in the translation, but somehow "Forget about me, heenee" doesn't maintain the beauty of the original.

I have tried to remain as true as possible to the semantic intent of each line, and I have retained the order of lines within the song. Although I have attempted to be consistent in giving the same translation for each instance of the same line in Havasupai, in some cases I have found it necessary to change the translation when the line occurs in different contexts. For example, because the Havasupai verbs are tenseless in this song, an option that for the most part is not available in English, I have sometimes translated a line in the past tense and have sometimes translated the same line in the present tense, depending on the context.

I have also very often used Dan Hanna's own translation of a given line even when it is not as literal as other alternatives, for he was the best judge of the underlying sense. As an example, the line in the first verse that translates as "forget about me" is far from literal. Havasupai speakers have interpreted the verb as "to bear pain" or "to tolerate a bad situation." But Dan Hanna himself said the line in the song means "Don't mourn for me," "Forget about me," or "Learn to live without me." I thus felt free to choose from these alternatives.

"The Farewell Song" expresses the understanding that youth believes itself immortal, and displays the deep disappointment of old age's realization that this youthful belief is false. And even more strikingly, the song communicates poignantly the expression of the Havasupai belief that the land is a living being and has a close and loving relationship with humans. As I learned from other Havasupais, the land is always treated as sentient. A person traveling to a land he has not been to before talks to it about who he is, why he is there, and where he is going. The widespread practice of planting prayer sticks at springs is based on this same belief in the land's awareness. As a Havasupai woman once said to me, "We believe that the land knows you're there, and it misses you when you're gone." The lesson of her words and of the song went straight to my heart during the intense learning experience of my early fieldwork. It is a fine thought with which to travel through life.

Guide to Special Symbols

č is ch, as in *church*.

ə is a nondescript vowel sound, like the *a* in *sofa* or *calamity*.

ǰ is the *j* sound in Jesse.

ŋ is an *n*-like sound pronounced with the back of the tongue touching the roof of the mouth. In English this sound occurs before *g* or *k* and is written as *n*, as in *sing*.

q is a sound that does not occur in English and is something like a *k* but is uttered farther back in the throat.

ʔ is a brief stoppage of sound, such as between the two syllables of the informal English word for "no," *uh-uh*.

NOTE

1. Leanne Hinton, "Vocables in Havasupai Songs," in *Southwestern Ritual Drama*, ed. Charlotte J. Frisbie (Albuquerque: University of New Mexico Press, 1980) and "Havasupai Songs: A Linguistic Perspective," *Ars Linguistica* 6 (Tubingen, Germany; 1984).

Spring Water Dripping,
land that I wandered,
  that place.
Listen to me:
  forget about me,
                ha na.

I thought I'd live forever,
thought I'd travel forever;
  that's how I was.
I thought I'd always be that way,
  but now my strength is gone,
                ha na.

I thought I'd always be that way.
That's how I was,
  but now my strength is gone.
Land that I wandered,
  that place.
Listen to me:
  forget about me,
                ha na.

Horned animals,
I used to hunt them;

I thought I'd always be that way,
I'd be that way forever.
  But now my strength is gone,
          ha na.

That's how I was,
I was,
  I was.
Thicket of bushes,
  that place,
          ha na.

I ran and ran
all around them;
  listen to me.
Forget about me;
  forget about me,
          ha na.

Fallen logs
that I'd jump over,
  that place.
Listen to me:
  forget about me,
          ha na.

Sitting boulders
that I stumbled over,
  that place.
Listen to me;
  forget about me,
          ha na.

Trail lying there
that I once followed,
  once followed.
That place.
  Listen to me.
Forget about me;
  forget about me,
          ha na.

▲

Arroyo,
arroyo,
   that I used to dash across.
That place.
   Listen to me.
Listen to me:
   forget about me,
               ha na.

Pointed Hill,
Pointed Hill,
   that place,
that I used to run up,
   that place.
Listen to me:
   forget about me.
To the very top
   I would come.
I'd stand there;
   I'd look into the distance.
That place.
   Listen to me.
Forget about me;
   forget about me,
               ha na.

Faraway jackrabbit,
a young one,
   a brown one.
He leaped out of hiding,
   leaped out of hiding.
I went after him,
   went after him,
               ha na.

I caught right up;
I came up beside him;
   that's what I did.
The hunting cane
   that belonged to me:
I hooked him,
   caught him,
               ha na.

I roasted him,
roasted him
  and ate him.
I thought I'd live forever,
  thought I'd travel forever.
That's how it seemed to me,
  but now my strength is gone,
          ha na.

Faraway antelope
Faraway antelope
  a young one.
He leaped out of hiding;
  he came out suddenly.
He started off,
  and I went after him,
          ha na.

I caught right up,
I came up beside him;
  that's what I did.
The hunting cane
  that belonged to me:
I hooked him,
  caught him.
Roasted him,
  ate him,
          ha na.

I thought I'd live forever,
thought I'd travel forever,
  thought I'd always be that way;
that's how it seemed to me.
  But now my strength is gone.
Land that I wandered,
  that place.
Listen to me:
  forget about me.
That's what I say;
  that's what I say,
          ha na.

Land that I wandered,
that place,
  listen to me.
I thought I'd always be that way;
  that's how I was.
But it wasn't true.
  I thought I'd be that way forever,
but it wasn't true.
  I thought I'd be that way forever,
but now my strength is gone.
  I thought I'd be that way forever,
           ha na.

Deer hides
that belonged to me,
  I hung them on a juniper.
I filled a tree with them;
  I looked at them there.
I felt
  so proud,
           ha na.

Deer hides
that belonged to me,
  I hung them on junipers.
I filled two trees;
  I filled three trees.
I looked at them there.
  I felt
so proud.
  I thought I'd be that way forever,
           ha na.

I thought I'd always be that way,
but now my strength is gone.
  I thought I'd always be that way.
That's how I was,
  how I was,
           ha na.

I thought I'd live forever,
thought I'd travel forever;

that's how I was.
I'd be with the land,
   it seemed.
That's how I was,
   it seemed,
That's how I'd always be.
   But now my strength is gone,
          ha na.

The sky
spreading over me,
   it seemed
I'd be with it forever,
   it seemed.
I thought I'd always be that way,
   but now my strength is gone,
          ha na.

Listen to me:
forget about me,
   Forget about me.
Now my strength is gone.
   I thought I'd always be that way.
That's how I was,
   how I was,
          ha na.

Standing water,
I came there;
   I knelt down.
The drinking place
   where I always drank,
that place,
   listen to me.
Forget about me;
   forget about me,
          ha na.

Painted water hole
in the rock,
   I came there;

I knelt down.
  That place:
forget about me;
  forget about me,
        ha na.

The sun
over the hill,
  I saw it go down.
I started out running,
  started out running.
That's how I was;
  I didn't go slow,
        ha na.

That's not what I did;
I wasn't that way,
  that way.
I ran fast,
  ran fast.
I got home quickly,
  got home quickly,
        ha na.

I outran the sun;
I outran the sun.
  That's what I used to do.
That's how I was,
  how I was,
        ha na.

I didn't sleep late,
didn't wait for the sun;
  that's not what I did.
I wasn't that way,
  that way,
        ha na.

The dawn,
when it came,
  I saw it.

I got up,
  I got up.
The dawn,
  I ran toward it,
          ha na.

I thought I'd always be that way;
that's how I used to travel;
  I thought I'd be that way forever,
but now my strength is gone.
  I thought I'd be that way forever;
that's how I was.
  Listen to me,
          ha na.

Land that I wandered,
that place,
  listen to me:
forget about me,
  forget about me.
That's what I want,
  what I want,
          ha na.

My strength is gone.
I thought I'd always be that way,
  that's how I was.
I thought I'd live forever,
  I thought I'd live forever.
I'd always be with the land,
  it seemed,
          ha na.

I'd always be with the mountains,
it seemed;
  that's how I was,
that's what I believed.
  I felt
so proud.
  I thought I'd be that way forever.

But now my strength is gone.
   I thought I'd be that way forever.
That's how I was,
   how I was,
                     ha na.

TWO KOASATI
TRADITIONAL NARRATIVES

▲

GEOFFREY KIMBALL

INTRODUCTION

The Koasati language, a member of the Muskogean family that includes Creek, Choctaw, and Mikasuki, is presently spoken by about
five hundred to one thousand people in two communities, one in
southwestern Louisiana and the other in eastern Texas. The speech
of the Texas community has been greatly influenced by the Alabama
language also spoken there; the Louisiana community is considered
to speak the "best" form of the language.

Koasati traditional narratives have been gathered primarily by two
persons, John R. Swanton, who collected them from speakers in
Texas and Louisiana in 1910,[1] and me; I have been collecting them
in Louisiana since 1977. In former times Koasati traditional narratives were told by older men and women of a household as entertainment for household members at night, during bad weather, or
whenever stories were requested of them. At the present time traditional narratives are most likely to be told to interested non-Koasati
visitors, as most younger people have little interest in them. Few
people younger than forty know even one story well enough to retell
it; it seems likely that the corpus of traditional narratives will disappear long before the Koasati language does.

The genre of traditional tales is called *cokfa:łihilká,* "rabbit
story," in Koasati, since the trickster-hero Rabbit is the protagonist

of many of the notable ones. Rabbit is known primarily as Cokfi, although when talking about him outside of story he is often called Cokfi Holá:si, "Rabbit the Trickster" (the word *holá:si* also means "liar"). An old name for Rabbit, Hapá:sa, of no other meaning, occurs in "Rabbit and the Turkeys," the first tale presented here. Rabbit stories are considered quite funny by the Koasati. Laughter is elicited by Rabbit's droll comments or by the outrageous tricks he plays. The behavior of the Koasati audience in listening to an amusing story is rather different from that of a non-Koasati audience; the latter will burst out laughing as soon as an event strikes them funny, often drowning out the narrator; the former wait until the narrator has finished the verse before beginning to laugh.

The Native concept of narrative gives free range to the creativity of the narrator by requiring only the skeleton of a story to remain the same from narration to narration. For any particular tale all that is required is that certain events be related in a certain order. The narrator can at will expand or contract the narrative or embroider elements she or he finds interesting or attractive. Given the lack of an obligatory structure aside from the basic plot, it is the responsibility of the narrator to give the tale a form and shape.

Narratives also vary according to their audience. Most notably, they are censored by speakers when told to non-Indians: scenes pertaining to sex or excretion are deleted, or whole stories may not be told at all. These acts of self-censorship clearly seem to have resulted from the negative reaction of non-Indians to such stories. Note that Swanton, in his translations of oral narratives from the Southeast, either tacitly omitted material he considered salacious or translated it into turgid Latin.

A Koasati narrative is composed of lines, which are generally equivalent to a sentence and are determined by linguistic and semantic criteria. The appearance of a conjunction at the beginning of a sentence indicates the beginning of a line, and quoted speech frequently begins a new line. Lines can also consist of two or more verses, which are phrases that combine to form a line. They have the stylistic function of highlighting important sections of a narrative. The narrator marks important sections by combining four or five verses and uses combinations of six to eight verses to indicate the climactic action of a narrative.

Lines can be arranged into larger groups, called scenes. A scene consists of a number of lines that are semantically bound together. The number of scenes in a narrative appears not to be fixed, although narratives consisting of four, eight, or twelve scenes seem to be very common. That these numbers are multiples of four, the Koasati ritual number, may not be due to chance. Narratives with more than eight scenes seem to have larger-scale structures. Such narratives often can be divided into halves, the first half initiating the action of the story and the second completing the action. Furthermore, it is possible to associate the scenes in pairs.

Selin Williams, the narrator of these two tales, is almost completely forgotten by the present-day Indians, so only a bare biographical sketch of her can be made. She was born in 1841, and the names of her father and mother are unknown. In the 1860s she married a Koasati Indian named Joe Henderson, who adopted the surname Langley from an Acadian in Louisiana. Her brother-in-law was the chief John Abbey, and she herself may have been of a chiefly lineage, since her son, Jackson Langley, became chief on the death of John Abbey, in 1910. Traditional ritual specialists were also found in her family; her brother was the last known traditional weather worker.

John R. Swanton came and worked with her son in 1910, and she also provided him a large number of traditional narratives. At the time she had five living children and seventeen grandchildren, making up the large family prized by the Indians. Only one photograph of her survives; it shows a slender, old-looking woman.[2]

The only clue to her personality can be found in the stories she related to Swanton. That she was not reticent about sexual matters can be inferred from several stories, in one of which, "The Origin of Crow," two boys create Crow by rubbing a bowstring across the anus of their dead father, who had tried to kill them; and in another, "The Deer Women," a man has sexual intercourse with a doe. She seemed to be fascinated by Rabbit as the trickster; her best tales, like the two translated here, are the ones concerned with Rabbit playing tricks on various animals and humans. She also seemed to like the idea of the trickster tricked and told Swanton two different tales on that theme. She was apparently very traditional, which is not unexpected in a person raised without contact with non-Indians in the nineteenth century. Such is the outline of the personality of the woman who helped preserve some of the oldest traditional narratives of the Koasati.

"Rabbit and the Turkeys" was dictated to, and recorded by, John R. Swanton in Koasati in 1910.[3] An edited version based on his interlinear glosses was published in his *Myths and Tales of the Southeastern Indians*.[4] I retranslated this narrative from Swanton's original Koasati version. Great assistance was given by Martha John, a contemporary Koasati storyteller, who helped me understand the narrative and pointed out the humor in it.

The second narrative presented here, "Rabbit Tricks Great One Who Eats Human Beings," was taken by dictation in Koasati by John R. Swanton in 1910.[5] In 1929, Swanton published a translation based on the interlinear glosses in the 1910 manuscript.[6] It is notable that he censored in his publication the lines in scene 3 in which Rabbit tells that his testicles will pop. Such censoring and the translation into Latin of salacious matters in other narratives seem to be concessions on his part to standards of "decency" expected of scientific publications of the period.

In the translation of this narrative, I was aided by the late Bel Abbey (1916–92), another Koasati storyteller.

Guide to Pronunciation

Koasati words are written with a phonemic orthography. Different from standard English pronunciation are *c*, pronounced *ch*, and ł, which is a sound that does not occur in English but is like *sh* and *l* pronounced together. In addition, vowels have the continental values, and accented vowels do not receive more stress but, rather, are higher in pitch than unaccented vowels. A colon (:) written after a vowel indicates that the vowel is long.

NOTES

1. John Reed Swanton, "Koasati Texts," 2d series, 1910, manuscript 1818, National Anthropological Archives of the Natural History Museum, Smithsonian Institution, Washington, D.C.

2. John Reed Swanton, *The Indians of the Southeastern United States,* Smithsonian Institution, Bureau of American Ethnology Bulletin no. 137 (Washington, D.C.: 1946), plate 27.

3. Swanton, "Koasati Texts," 2d series, 19.

4. John Reed Swanton, *Myths and Tales of the Southeastern Indians,* Smithsonian Institution, Bureau of American Ethnology Bulletin no. 88 (Washington, D.C., 1929), 210.

5. Swanton, "Koasati Texts," 2d series, 17.

6. Swanton, *Myths and Tales of the Southeastern Indians,* 207–8.

RABBIT AND THE TURKEYS

RABBIT PLAYS ROLLING-DOWN-A-HILL   *[SCENE 1]*

Rabbit climbed up and stood on a hill,
   then got in a sack,
      rolled down in it,
         and was laughing and laughing.
There were some turkeys eating acorns at a distance,
   and they watched him from there, so it is said.
And as they watched,
   they became interested,
      and then
         they came up close, so it is said.

RABBIT CONVINCES THE TURKEYS THAT IT IS FUN   *[SCENE 2]*

And then Rabbit spoke to them.
   "Here, by doing it this way,
      I am really having a great time," he said, so they say.
On hearing him,
   "You are lying!" they said.
"Well then,
   one of you get in,
      and let me roll it for you!" he said.
And then one got in,
   and he began rolling it,
      and having rolled to the bottom, the Turkey laughed;
         "Indeed, it is good!
            Indeed, it pleased me!" he said.

RABBIT TRICKS THE TURKEYS   *[SCENE 3]*

At that they all got in,
   and he rolled it;
      it went down with them inside,
         and he grabbed the bag with them,
            threw it over his arm,
               and carried them off, so it is said.
He took them
   and brought them to where his grandmother lived.

He closed them up in a corncrib that stood there.
"Do not open the corncrib now or later!" he said to his
    grandmother, so people say.
Then he went off.

RABBIT'S GRANDMOTHER ALLOWS THE TURKEYS TO ESCAPE   [SCENE 4]

And then she was staying there with nothing to do,
    and when she opened the corncrib,
        "Flippity-flap!" was the noise they made as they came out,
            and grabbing for them,
                she caught both feet of only one turkey, so they say.
Then she called out,
    "Hapá:sa! I have got a turkey by the feet!" she said, so they say.
When Rabbit arrived,
    "I told you, 'Do not do this now or later!' " he said, so people
        say.
Having killed that one mere turkey,
    "Cook it then! I am planning for a *lot* of people to come to
            dinner," he said.
    "As you cook it, I will go away and tell people," he said,
        and having gone away,
            just anywhere he was wandering.
He merely wandered about,
    and coming back,
        "Many people are about to arrive," he said, so they say.

RABBIT PRETENDS TO BE A CROWD   [SCENE 5]

At that,
    "The people are arriving," he said,
        and he himself talked a lot;
            he kept on pretending to be a lot of people,
                and he conversed with himself, so it is said.
Then he spoke to his grandmother,
    "Ladle out the food!" he said,
        and she ladled it up,
            and there on a cane platform that he had made,
              having fully laid out the meal,
                "Now! Let us eat!" he said, so people say.
Again he pretended to be a lot of people;

he made all kinds of noises;
    in one place he hopped up and ate,
        in another place he climbed and ate;
           he kept on going around and around to every place and
             eating, so it is said.
He pretended to be a lot of people,
    and so it is said that he ate up all the turkey.

RABBIT TRICKS HIS GRANDMOTHER   [SCENE 6]

After that he mashed up rotten linden wood
    and put it in the soup
        and set it out for his grandmother;
           "This is all that is left. Eat!" he said.
She ate it;
    "It is like rotten wood," she said.
        "I guess that's how turkey is at this time of year," he said, so
           they say.
Then they say he said,
    "The people have all left."
At which they ate the soup, so it is said.

RABBIT TRICKS GREAT ONE WHO EATS HUMAN BEINGS

*RABBIT ENCOUNTERS GREAT ONE WHO EATS
HUMAN BEINGS* [SCENE 1]

Great One Who Eats Human Beings was working off in his field
when Rabbit came over to where he was working.
They say that Rabbit said,
"What are you working at?"
Then Great One Who Eats Human Beings said,
"I am going to plant string beans."

*RABBIT TRICKS THE WIFE OF GREAT ONE WHO EATS
HUMAN BEINGS* [SCENE 2]

Then Rabbit went off;
when he arrived at the house of the wife of Great One Who
Eats Human Beings, he spoke.
"Your husband said that you should boil up some string beans
for me," he said.
The wife of Great One Who Eats Human Beings replied,
"But we're planning to plant these string beans."
"You can boil them up for me," he said,
and they say that the woman did not believe him.
Then Rabbit spoke.
"Well, I shall call out to him and ask him for you," he said,
and she replied;
"All right," she said,
and Rabbit went outside and called out to him,
"Did you talk to me about it?"
and Great One Who Eats Human Beings spoke.
"Indeed, I did," he called back, so they say.

*RABBIT PRETENDS TO PERMIT GREAT ONE WHO EATS
HUMAN BEINGS TO KILL HIM* [SCENE 3]

Afterward Great One Who Eats Human Beings arrived and spoke to
him.
"You have devoured my beans!" he said,
and Rabbit spoke.
"Are you really angry with me?" he replied, people say.
"I shall lie down on a large box,

and you can chop me up and cut me in two!" he then said, they
say.
Then Rabbit lay down,
   and when Great One Who Eats Human Beings chopped at him,
   he jumped away,
      and the Great One Who Eats Human Beings chopped the
         box,
      and destroyed it, so it is said.
Thereupon Rabbit spoke again.
   "Well, I shall lie over on a large stone,
      over where it sits,
      and you chop me up and cut me in two!" he said.
Thereupon Rabbit went over to a large stone and lay on it,
   and when Great One Who Eats Human Beings chopped at him,
   he jumped away,
      and the Great One Who Eats Human Beings chopped against
         the stone;
      he destroyed the ax on it, so it is said.
"No one can kill me," Rabbit said,
   "unless, closing me up in the house,
      and burning it down,
      I shall die in the fire," he told him, they say.
"It will make a noise as I die;
   something also will make a popping sound;
      they will make a noise as I die;
      my balls will pop," he said.
Then in the house
   he dug underneath the bed;
      he crawled through the tunnel and got out far away
      and stayed there, so it is said.
Great One Who Eats Human Beings went on doing it;
   having shut up the house,
   it is said they set it on fire.
Right then Rabbit came running back from far away
   and came out
   and, arriving there,
      "Ho!" he said, so they say.
      "Nothing can kill me.
      Let us become friends with each other!" he said,
      and it is said that Great One Who Eats Human Beings
         became friends with him.

RABBIT AND GREAT ONE WHO EATS HUMAN BEINGS
GO WANDERING   [SCENE 4]

Then the two of them were going about, so it is said.
> Then as the two of them were going about, Rabbit said,
> "There is a tree split by lightning.
> We will sleep there."
Then when they arrived there, he spoke again.
> "When we've found a lot of wood,
>> we will sleep," he said.
Soon he stood shaking an almost-fallen dead tree.
> He thought that the two of them would lie down near to that,
> having kindled a fire.
> And he kindled a fire.
Then while Great One Who Eats Human Beings slept,
> he decided to pick up some hot coals,
> and pouring them out on him,
>> he himself poured out for himself a little bit on some cold
>> food.
>> Great One Who Eats Human Beings, having been suddenly
>> awakened,
>> it is said that he stayed awake the rest of the night.
Then again the next day the two of them went on.
"There is a river for jumping back and forth across there," Rabbit
said.
"Soon we will arrive there," he said,
> and when they arrived there,
> there was a narrow little creek.
As soon as they arrived there,
> Rabbit went and jumped across the creek.
> "You too!" he said,
>> and Great One Who Eats Human Beings came jumping
>> across and stood there with him.
> When Rabbit came jumping back,
>> the river was cut down the middle and widened.
>> Great One Who Eats Human Beings stood alone on the
>> other side,
>> and it floated off with him and disappeared with him,
>> and afterward took him to the other side of the ocean.

CALIFORNIA

TWO STORIES FROM
THE YANA

▲

HERBERT W. LUTHIN

INTRODUCTION

The Yana were a mountain people of northern California. Their homelands were the rugged slopes, steep valleys, and upland plateaus that rise northeastward from the banks of the Sacramento River to the volcanic peaks and ridges of the southern Cascades. Mount Lassen is the tallest peak in their old stretch of range, which ran from Pit River south almost to the Feather River. Modern-day Redding lies just west of their old territory.

Yana belongs to the ancient, deep-rooted Hokan family of languages. It was spoken in four closely related dialects: Northern, Central, Southern, and Yahi. (Yahi was the language spoken by Ishi, the famed and so-called "last wild Indian in North America."[1]) The stories I have translated here come from the Northern and Central dialects and were collected early in this century by the great linguist Edward Sapir.

The Yana suffered early and hard at the hands of the white settlers and miners. Perhaps three thousand strong before contact, they were all but wiped out in 1864 in one of the most brutal and comprehensive massacres in California history. Jeremiah Curtin, visiting in 1884, put the number of speakers at a mere thirty-five.[2] By 1934, only the smallest handful of knowledgeable persons remained. Today there will still be people—not many, though—who can claim

Yana heritage, whose families endured only because the survivors of those times were sheltered and absorbed by neighboring tribes. Although the truth is hard to face, the Yana no longer exist as a people, and the language itself is extinct.

Sapir did his fieldwork among the Yana in 1907, while there were still a few men and women who could recall the traditional culture and speak the language with authority. His *Yana Texts* was published in 1910,[3] to be followed by some dozen other publications involving the language. Sapir's work stands today as the richest and most reliable repository of knowledge on Yana language and culture.

Unfortunately, we know more about the language and the culture than we do about the individuals who told these stories. Sapir's first consultant was Betty Brown (whose Yana name was C'iidaymiya), a Northern Yana speaker. At the time Sapir knew her, she did washing for white families in the Montgomery Creek area three days a week. That left only four days a week for Sapir, who worked with her, at the then-standard rate of $1.50 a day, through the summer and fall of 1907. Betty Brown died not long after Sapir completed his work with her. In the time they spent together, she gave him—in addition to the fundamental elements of Yana grammar—three myth texts and a series of charms, reminiscences, and ethnographic vignettes. Her stories are sometimes halting and often confused (Sapir rated her a poor storyteller overall), but her reminiscences are invaluable, emotionally charged recreations of Yana life and customs. Without them we would know far less than we do about her people.

In December of 1907, Sapir moved down to Redding to begin work with Sam Batwi (Yana name, Bat^hwii), a Central Yana speaker. Unlike Betty Brown, Sam was already an experienced linguistic consultant, having worked as a translator for Jeremiah Curtin in 1884 and then as a narrator for Roland Dixon in 1900.[4] After his work with Sapir, Sam was brought down to Berkeley by Alfred Kroeber to help interpret for Ishi. By most accounts, Sam Batwi was a lively but crotchety old man. He was also a natural-born storyteller, and the texts he gave Sapir in 1907 are full of detail, humor, suspense, and wisdom—stories that convey both the essential rhythms of Yana life and the fullest, freest swing of Yanan verbal art.

Sam Batwi's "Story of Wildcat, Rolling Skull," the second story presented here, is a widespread and favorite Native American horror story. In the Yana version of the tale, an unfortunate Wildcat is so disturbed by a bad dream that he acts out the dream in real life, dismembering himself limb by limb until he's nothing but a skull.

(How he is able to do this, and how a legless skull can bound around the countryside so fearsomely, are matters for the imagination. Sam Batwi told Sapir that "when the older Indians first saw the trolley cars of the whites, they compared them with the wildly rushing *P͟ʻu'tǃukǃuyā'* or Human Skull."[5]) As Person's Skull he devours his newborn son and then sets off on a terrible superhuman rampage, frightening or killing everybody for miles around. Then he meets Coyote. Coyote disguises himself as an old woman and somehow tricks the Skull into letting himself be roasted alive in a pit. The story ends with the world restored to order—one of Coyote's more serious functions, after all—with the people coming out of hiding and Coyote bragging up a storm.

"A Story of Wildcat, Rolling Skull" was the ninth and final text that Sam Batwi dictated, and it would seem he was on a roll by the time he told it. There is even some linguistic evidence to back up this impression. Prosodically the performance is very smooth, with no chafing or champing, as if Sapir and Batwi had finally settled into a working rhythm that transcended the halting, artificial constraints of the dictation.

By contrast, Betty Brown's traditional stories, even the one included here, are distinctly jagged and hard to follow, as if she had been rusty or perhaps intimidated by the strangeness of the dictation process. In her traditional stories it is not uncommon for characters to appear without introduction, for scenes to change without warning, for stories to end without closure and new ones to begin without transition. For example, Betty Brown never actually identifies *any* of the characters in the story presented here. We only know who is speaking and what their names are because Sapir worked it out afterward—and even then we cannot always be sure. Still, it would be a mistake not to look beneath the sometimes rumpled surface of her words. By looking deep, we may recognize one of her texts for what it is: a rare gem of a story.

That gem, "Dragonfly Woman: The Drowning of Young Buzzard's Wife," is a strange, disquieting tale, one that has the feel of a tragedy that may really have happened, but so long ago that it has entered the domain of legend. In the story Young Buzzard is chief of his people. It is the time of year to move camp and search for winter food, so he calls everyone together to announce his plans. Young Buzzard's wife is Dragonfly Woman. She is headstrong, and it seems that something has antagonized her, because she will not take anyone's counsel: if there's a dare, she'll dare it; if it's forbidden, she'll do it; if it's denied her, she'll have it.

Dragonfly sets out with a group that will climb for pine nuts.

They come to a river, and she decides to try to swim it. Her companions try to talk her out of it, but she insists, and she drowns. Her body is not recovered. When Buzzard arrives on the scene, he doesn't know what to do. In his speeches we can hear shock and denial, anger and grief, confusion and despair, all in rapid succession. Finally he gathers his wits and tries to rescue her. He details a group of people to divert the flow of the river, though he knows it's hopeless. Disconsolate, the people return home and begin their mourning. Now Young Buzzard must confront the girl's parents. Her mother accuses him of carelessness; Buzzard despairs. It is clear that he just can't understand why Dragonfly behaved as she did. The story ends with a long, difficult scene in which the mother tells about an alarming conversation she had with her daughter months before—how Dragonfly had had a dream of death and how she had then made her farewells to her parents, cautioning them to fast in mourning and not to weep too much.

Is Dragonfly, like Wildcat in "Rolling Skull," driven to her strange, suicidal behavior by her premonition of death? The very last line of the story is critical to understanding the mysterious dynamics at work here: the mother quotes Dragonfly as having said, "I never thought I should have taken a husband." Was this an arranged marriage, then, decided against her will? Was Young Buzzard, a chief, perhaps too old for her? Too autocratic, too conservative, too responsible? Or is this her mother once again fixing the blame on Young Buzzard for not controlling his wife? At this remove from the original culture, I'm not sure we ever *can* know the answer, and in the end Dragonfly's motivations remain a mystery. But that's why the story is so haunting.

In working with these stories, I wanted to do more than just modernize Sapir's translations and bring a contemporary slant to the English. Though still with his glosses as my inevitable partner, I have gone all the way back to the original Yana and sought to restore the sound of Betty Brown's and Sam Batwi's voices just as they told these stories to Sapir. I have done my best to read the clues preserved in the amber of Sapir's phonetic transcriptions and found where the storytellers must have paused for thought or breath or dramatic effect—or just to wait for Sapir's pen to catch up. In Betty Brown's story the short lines reflect the frequent breaks that are phonetically evident in her delivery. And in Sam Batwi's story the passages delineated by bullets (·) represent the rests—something like oral paragraphs—in his delivery, which Sapir marked with a period. The arrangement of lines on the page is meant to slow the eye as it follows down the page, to guide the flow of the voice in reading aloud. Punctuation is made to serve a similar function, with commas representing less of a pause or finality than a period or semicolon.

I have kept my editorial amendments to a minimum, and I have chosen not to vary or eliminate repeated words or phrases. Sometimes, though, I felt I had to insert the name of a speaker in dialogue or specify the subject or object of an action. Indeed, in Betty Brown's story almost all the "he said's" and "she said's" (but none of the "they say's") are added, as are *all* of the names and dialogue attributions; seven lines, each noted in the text with an asterisk, have been inserted in their entirety. The alternative was to present the story as a play, something it was not intended to be.

I was unable to translate some of the place-names mentioned in these stories (and have guessed at others, like "Cross-Meadow Creek" and "South-Flowing Salt"). The Yana words and names you do encounter here may be pronounced more-or-less as follows: Bathwii (BAH-twee), C'iidaymiya (ch-EE-die-me-yah), K'aasip'u (k-AH-sheep-oo), Unchunaha (OON-choo-nah-ha), Wamaarawi (wa-MAH-ra-wee). The word for "Human Skull," P'u't!uk!uyā' (PUT-ook-oo-YAH), is cited in Sapir's now archaic phonetic orthography.

NOTES

1. Theodora Kroeber, *Ishi in Two Worlds: A Biography of the Last Wild Indian in North America* (Berkeley: University of California Press, 1963).

2. Jeremiah Curtin, *Creation Myths of Primitive America, in Relation to the Religious History and Mental Development of Mankind* (Boston: Little, Brown, 1898; reprint, New York: Benjamin Blom, 1969).

3. Edward Sapir, *Yana Texts (together with Yana Myths, collected by Roland B. Dixon)*, University of California Publications in American Archaeology and Ethnography, vol. 9, no. 1 (Berkeley: University of California Press, 1910).

4. Roland B. Dixon, "Yana Field Notes," 1900, Valory Collection, manuscript 70, Bancroft Library, University of California, Berkeley.

5. Sam Batwi quoted in Sapir, *Yana Texts,* 125.

DRAGONFLY WOMAN:
THE DROWNING OF YOUNG
BUZZARD'S WIFE

1

Young Buzzard spoke as a chief does:*

> "Now then,
> you will all dig for roots—
> they are already getting ripe.
> Let us climb sugar pines!
> We shall move out at dawn.
> You will all set up camp.
>
> Now then,
> I shall go climbing for pine nuts—
> they are already getting ripe.
> All the people will move out there.
> We shall all set up camp there.
> There is a good spring.
> Perhaps others will be arriving too.
> We shall wait for them, what do you say?"

There were lots of people gathered, they say.
Then Young Buzzard spoke again as chief:*

> "Now then,
> let us climb for them.
> Bring food along!
>
> Now then,
> some of you will dig for tiger lilies.
>
> Now then,
> gather food for winter!
> You women will probably want to dig instead of climb.
> If we should succeed in this—
> well then, we will all get winter food."

*Lines marked with an asterisk have been added to the original.

2

"I could wade out into that water there,"
    said Dragonfly Woman, Young Buzzard's wife.*
"Let's see!" she said; "let's go for a drink!"

"Do not go for a drink!" said the people.

"Why should I be afraid?" she said;
"I'm going for a drink."

She saw these logs, they say,
bobbing up and down in the water.

"Let's see!" she said.
"I could swim across there to the west."

They lost sight of her, they say.
They looked around, they say.

"Look out, I'm going to try it," she said.
"I could swim through that water."

"You could *not* swim through that water!" the people said.

She took off her skirt, they say.

"I'm going to swim out into that water," she said.
"Just keep watching me."

She swam to the west, they say.
There were lots of people there, they say.
Everybody saw her, they say.

Now then,
    there in the middle,
        she sank down, they say.

Now then,
"We warned you beforehand!" the people said.

They just lay there on the bank, they say:
her buckskin shirt,
her pine-nut-beaded tassels.

3

Now then,
everybody cried, they say.

"What are you crying for?" asked Young Buzzard.

"She has sunk down!" the people said.

" 'Don't take her near the water!' " cried Young Buzzard,
"I *told* you that!
  This is all your fault!
  It would have been better
  if I had been there instead!
  Could it be for this
  that I have come to this place?
  I'm going to give it up. . .

  No, let's search for her!
  Please do it—
  see if we can find her.
  Let's try!
  She was a good person.
  Run back to get the rest of the people—
  they should all come here."

Someone ran back to get them, they say.
"All right!" the people said.

"Let's see, just go ahead!" Young Buzzard said.
"I'm going to try something."
  They channeled off the water, they say.

"Channeling off the water probably won't work.
  You won't be able to channel off the water," said Young Buzzard.

"Please, what should we do?" the people asked.

"Channel it off!" Young Buzzard said.
"But I doubt we'll ever find her.
  We'll never find her.
  She must have sunk straight down,

maybe right between two logs.
That place is bad."

4

They broke camp for going back, they say.
They all went home together, they say.

Young Buzzard lamented:*
"No more shall I gather winter food.
Now I have done with all of that.
Alas! that I was happy once.
Is there more that I can do?
Then I shall do no more."

"Why did you let her wander off?" her mother asked.
"You should have packed some water for the trail.
You were foolish."

"I don't know," said Buzzard.
"I should have packed some water.
But she just runs off by herself.
'Let's go for a drink!' she says.
I should have been told about that.
She was made angry.
I am no good.
My heart feels grieved."

They all came home, they say.
They lay down in the ashes of the fire pit, they say.
The men too, they say.

Her people,
    they wept, so they say—
        all those who had been climbing.

They dumped all their pine nuts in the fire, they say.

5

Now her mother told a story:*
"A long time ago my daughter told me,

▲

'Perhaps I shall never enter this house again:
I dreamed about my own death.
So please, burn up all my things.'

'I am afraid of the way you're talking,' I told her.

'We'll probably be gone camping for two moons
while we're climbing,' she told me.
'Maybe I'm going to die.
I will never come back into my house.'

'I'm going to cry,' I said,
'from the way you are talking.'

'Really,' she said,
'in the end you will find out it's true.' "

Now her mother wept, they say.

"She is dead," she cried.
"Now her hair comes flying back home,
comes drifting back home."

Then she went on with her story:*
"Long ago my daughter told me,*

'I will surely have died
if my hair ever drifts back home.'

'Take along your western mountain skirt,
your fringed white-grass apron,' I told her;
'swing your pine nut beads around your neck!'

'All right,' she said.
'Now then,' she said.

'Mother!
Farewell!
You will not see me again.'

'I am afraid,' I told her.
'Stay at home!
I am afraid for you!'

▲

'Daddy!' she cried,
'Please don't feel bad;
please just cry a little.

Father!
You have grown old.

Mother!
Please don't cry,
much.

If you see feasting,
you must not go over to the next house.
If you see food over there,
please look away.

You were happy once,
raising me.

I never thought I should have taken a husband.' "

1

.

Lots of people were there, they say, dwelling at Unc^hunaha.
Little Wildcat had his wife pregnant for him.

.

She bore him a child. The woman gave birth, so Wildcat's
not going deer hunting—she's bearing him a child.

.

Said Wildcat, "Let's go get pine nuts; there's nothing else
I can do but go pine-nutting.

.

And make your child look pretty."
And then they went east with their child.

«««   »»»»

.

There were lots of them there, they say—pine nuts, that is.
The branches were loaded down toward the ground, they
say.

"I'm going to climb up after them here. Let's get some
pine nuts."

"Yes," said the woman.

.

Already Little Wildcat has climbed up the tree.

.

And then he showered down pine nuts—pinecones—then
he knocked more pinecones down to the ground. The
woman laid her baby down flat on the ground. She
pounded out the nuts down below, while Little Wildcat
knocked the pinecones down from up above.

.

He shouted back down to his wife from above, "Are they
big nuts?"

Said the woman, "Yes! Knock them all down!"
Said the woman, "They are big nuts."

▲

He threw down pinecones. "There!"
He threw them down again. "There!"

"Yes!" the woman said.
•

In his heart, they say, Little Wildcat spoke to her, calling
down to her from up above: "Hey-héy!
•

What could be happening to me that my sleep is so bad?"

But the woman's not answering.

"There!"

He knocked one loose down to the south,
   he knocked one loose down to the north,
      he knocked one loose down to the east,
         he knocked one loose down to the west.

"I dreamed during the night while I was sleeping:
I dreamed about tearing myself down in pieces.

I threw down my shoulder,
   I threw down my other shoulder;
      I threw down my thigh,
         I threw down my other thigh."
•

The woman's not looking up from her nut-pounding.
•

The baby's lying flat in its cradle.
•

"I dreamed about throwing down my backbone.
•

I dreamed that I ran all over as nothing but my skull. I
dreamed about it."

The woman looked east toward the pitch-pine place, they
say.
•

Blood was dripping down from the pitch-pine tree. The
woman put her hand over her mouth, staring at the blood.
•

The woman was afraid. The woman ran away home.

Wildcat hopped around all by himself up above, nothing but a skull.

The woman ran off without her child. The woman forgot about her child, ran all the way back to her house.

《《《《   》》》》

"What could he be going to do? He throws his own limbs down, hops around up above as nothing but his skull. Blood drips down from the pitch-pine tree. I am afraid," the woman said.

"No wonder!" the people said. "Let's run away; he might kill us all!"

The people did: they have already run away, it is said, running away to the south then. They went all the way down into Wamaarawi. They blocked off the smoke hole with a sandstone rock. The people were all crowded in—children, women, men.

《《《《   》》》》

Said Little Wildcat, "Huuh!" But the woman's not there to answer. Little Wildcat's skull bounded down from above.

He bounded down to earth, lay there resting quietly, not seeing his wife anywhere. Then he started bounding around, nothing but a skull.

He saw his child, gobbled his child right up.

"Ahmm!" Little Wildcat said to his missing wife. He bounded back west, came bounding back home to his house. There were no people. He bounded around to every house. There were no people.

"Ahmm! What has been going on, that they have run away? I shall find you." Then he started tracking them all around, bounding from place to place. He found their footprints, all heading south.

"Ahmm! I shall find you."

Bounding southward now, he mowed down trees, bottom oaks. He mowed down bushes. He bounded onto rocks, smashed the rocks to splinters. He bounded south to Red Clay Village, a skull person rushing along. He came on like a strong wind, they say.

.

He came along like that, they say.

.

He bounded south uphill to Bear Creek Village, tracking the people's footprints. Then he came bounding into Wamaarawi. People's voices could be heard inside the lodge.

.

"Let me come in! I'm going to come inside," said the Person's Skull.

.

"Keep quiet! Absolutely don't let him come in!" said the people.

.

He was not allowed to get in.

"Let me come in!"

"Absolutely don't let him come in! Everybody just sit still!"

"Há-ha-háah!" he said then in his heart, outside. "You people are not . . . not letting me come in."

He bounded off a long ways to the north. And then Person's Skull came rushing back south across the earth.

.

Powerful.

.

He mowed down all the bushes one after another.

.

He mowed down all the trees one after another. He nearly broke through into the lodge. . .

.

But they made it too strong.

.

He bounded to the east, he bounded back from the east; he nearly broke through westward into the lodge. The lodge shook, but it was too strong for him to break down.

He bounded south, he came bounding back from the south; he nearly burst in from the south . . . but they made it too strong.

People could be heard talking inside the lodge.

He bounded to the west, he came bounding back from the west. But it was just like that flint, they say: holding strong. They just made it too strong for him.

He lay still to rest; he lay there. "Hey-héy!" Person's Skull said.

.

"You have been clever, people!" He bounded up into the air.

.

He was about to burst down into the lodge from above the smoke-hole door. He hurtled back down from above, but they made it too strong for him, up on top. He bounced back up again.

"Look out, I'm going to try it again; maybe I can burst down into the lodge."

He did: he bounded up into the air, he bounded back down from above—but that skull person just bounced back up again. He nearly burst down into the lodge. The sandstone door was already wearing thin, they say. Those inside were afraid.

"Hey! It looks like we're all going to die. It seems he's about to burst down into the lodge," the people said.

.

Little Wildcat bounded back north, downhill across the earth. And then he just lay there like a stone.

"What do I keep trying to burst in for? The house has been made too strong for me."

《《《   》》》

He bounded back north, rushed back as far as East River Side, came rushing back there to his old house. "Oh, where am I going to?"

He bounded north, overtook some people, killed those people. Then he rushed on to the north, rushed north, downhill toward South-Flowing Salt.

He killed ten people. He rushed uphill to the north. It was heard by all the people, they say, his rushing forth.

It was making a *wind,* his rushing forth.

He rushed as far as K'aasip'u there.

2

Coyote came along from the north past Bone Place.

Coyote had on an elk-skin belt, they say. He carried an otter-skin quiver.

Coyote stood still, listened. "That must be the Person's Skull," Coyote said. He was coming along from the north. "I'm going to be crossing his path," said the Coyote in his heart.

"But maybe I won't be killed. I have heard about him killing people."

Then Person's Skull came rushing down from the south. Likewise from the north came Coyote. There Coyote stood his ground, at Cross-Meadow Creek.

"Hey! What am I doing?"

He unloosened his belt, hid away his otter-skin quiver in the brush, hid away his net cap in the brush.

•

Person's Skull rushed from the south, they say, getting closer and closer.

•

Said Coyote:
  "Let there be an old pack basket!
  Let there be an old fringed maple-bark apron!
  Let there be a woman's skirt for me!
  This could get bad!"

It happened:
  a shredded-bark apron came to him,
  an old pack basket,
  a woman's skirt.

"Let there be some pitch, some white clay!"

He smeared his own head with pitch, smeared it onto his face. He could just barely see out his eyes through the pitch.

•

And then Person's Skull came bounding out of the south.

•

"I should probably be weeping," Coyote said. And then he hiked the old pack basket up on his back.

Coyote did: he came from the north.
Person's Skull: getting closer from the south.

"Héy-héy-héy-héy-héy-héy!" Coyote sobbed.

Coyote poked along leaning on his stick. Person's Skull, he lay there resting quietly, listening to the weeper.

Coyote, as a woman, walked right up to Person's Skull.

•

Coyote looked at Person's Skull.

•

Cried Coyote, "I have heard about your badness in the south. Why do they say you are behaving like that?"

Person's Skull, he spoke.

•

"I was dreaming," he said to Coyote, "about having had a

child born for me. I dreamed about throwing my own
limbs down. I dreamed I was bounding about as nothing
but my skull."

Then Coyote started talking to Person's Skull, just whining
away.
•
"Hey-héy! Wouldn't I like to roast you down inside a pit!
Because you are going to die from acting that way,
bounding about as nothing but your skull.
•
I once saw a person act that way, acting just like you
because of a dream, and I helped him to be a person
again," he was saying to Person's Skull.
•
He's just lying there, big-eyed, Person's Skull.
•
He just sat there as nothing but his eyes.
•
"I fetched rocks in a basket, I dug a round hole, I gathered
some wood."

Wildcat listened to him, to what he was saying, to Coyote.
•
"Next, I made a fire down in the fire pit. I put lots of
wood on the fire, till it was burning along. Next, I put
rocks into the fire, big rocks. And then the rocks were
glowing hot. Next I . . . I looked around for some
pitch—soft, honey-colored pitch. I mixed it in with some
old red pitch.

Huuh! I smeared pitch around here on your skull. I
smeared the pitch smoothly all over it.

Huuh! Next, I put you down in the fire pit."

That's what he said to Wildcat.
•
"*Sssss!* went the pitch, spluttering as it blazed."

"Let's see you do it to me!" Person's Skull said.
•
"Then I placed glowing-hot rocks down on top, big rocks.

Huuh! And then, *Sssss!* the pitch was saying. It stretched
out, turning into a person again.

And then, huuh! He rose up again out of the fire, having
turned into a person again."
•

It shuddered all over. After that Wildcat didn't move
around at all anymore, being dead already, just as he was
about to burst up out of the pit.
•

"Ahá, hey-héy!" Coyote said, speaking as a man again.
"You did not beat *me!* I have never been beaten *any*
place."

He reached back there for his quiver and bow,
 threw away his one-time pack basket,
  threw away his shredded-bark apron,
   cast them all away.
He put on his belt, tying his hair up into a topknot.

"Never will I be the one who is beaten!"
    ««« »»»
•

Coyote then went south.
He went up-mountain to the south,
 he went up over the crest,
  he went south,
   he went down as far as South-Flowing Salt.
•

Then, going south, he got down all the way to
Wamaarawi. There were lots of people in the lodge.

"Everybody come back out again!" Coyote said, shouting
to those inside. "I have killed the Person's Skull; I have
killed him there at Cross-Meadow Creek."

The people did: already they were coming back out again,
moving back east,
 moving back south,
  moving back west,
   moving back north.
•

They have now all moved back on home again, it is said.

SILVER-GRAY FOX CREATES
ANOTHER WORLD

▲

DARRYL BABE WILSON

INTRODUCTION

Susan Brandenstein Park (as Susan Brandenstein) graduated from
the University of California, Berkeley, in 1930 with a degree in anthropology. Her major professor was Alfred L. Kroeber, and her
chief adviser was Robert Lowie. She dreamed of going to Fiji to
study the customs and songs of the Fijians, but Dr. Kroeber sent her
instead to the extreme northeastern corner of California, to the land
of my father's people, the Atsugewi.

In 1931 and again in 1933, Susan was among my people, recording our stories and songs and making her own census of the Hat
Creek and Dixie Valley Natives. Soon thereafter she was married to
Mr. Park and was off to Ethiopia, but she still cherished her experiences among my people.

With sad tenderness Susan recalled her first "informant," Mr. Lee
Bone: "I had no idea how to start [interviewing]. So I wandered
around and found a great many Indians sitting in front of the post
office—just sitting, not talking. Just sitting.

"I approached Lee Bone because he had such a pleasant face. He
was a roly-poly, sweet-looking man, and I asked him if he would like
to talk to me about his people and about his history. He said he
would like to, very much.

"So we got in my car, and we drove to his house, and we sat down on the porch—a very dilapidated old porch—and talked and talked."[1]

So Susan listened to my people and diligently wrote in her note-books. She traveled around the country—over some very rutted roads, along the whispering creeks and crashing rivers, and into the silent, vast valleys—seeking people who were willing to talk with her. She recorded verbatim in order to preserve the voice, the flavor, and the intent of the narration. Thus, I present here her original field notes for "Silver-Gray Fox Creates Another World," an Atsugewi story told by Lee Bone. To make some of the "rough" spots flow, I have added, in brackets and in footnotes, explanations of the original text.

To me, my children, and my people, it was a precious labor that Susan Park performed. It takes an immense amount of inner strength to accomplish what Susan has accomplished and to collect all that she was given by my people.

Iss is our identity. Iss means "we, this people dwelling here." Ajumawi and Atsugewi are identities academicians have issued us so various disciplines can have an identifiable focus of study—a study that qualifies them for funding or research. In some instances the study has been for the purpose of publication. Approaching the lives of my people in this manner is not an isolated incident. Historically academicians have altered the identity of many Native nations in order to suit their own purposes.

The ancestral homeland of Iss is east of the Wintun-Yana home-land, south of the Klamath-Modoc homeland, west of the Paiute homeland, and north of the Maidu homeland. The Pit River is the major river, with Fall River and Hat Creek the major tributaries; there are in addition numerous creeks joining the Pit as it meanders and crashes through the high mountain terrain.

Originally there were eleven large communities comprising thou-sands of Iss. Today there are only remnants of some of the communities, and there are fewer than five hundred people. Of that five hundred, fewer than a quarter are full-blooded. Yet the old stories are still told. There are still giggles about Old Coyote, and there are still worries that the language and the songs will melt, like spring snow, but not return with the following winter.

My intention in reviving these lesson-legends is to furnish my people with a new vigor by revealing our recent history of the land, of the time when it was open and free of barbed wire and NO TRES-PASSING signs, when it was so good to sing to the rising sun and when it was a "way" to behave toward one another—to be concerned with the entire well-being of our little nation from season to season.

It is said that Silver-Gray Fox possesses the awesome power to create and that Coyote has the power only to change. That, the old ones say, is why Coyote, in a fit of jealousy, always changes things. Coyote cannot leave anything unchanged. Coyote was born smart but not wise, conniving but not thinking, quick to suspect but unable to solve a situation that requires fidelity—and always and forever he wants to be "chief." Coyote is constantly getting killed by Fox, but Coyote returns somehow—not any wiser, but he returns, nevertheless.

The old people still say, "Early in the morning Fox was listening. To the east he listened; then to the south he listened; then to the west he listened. He heard nothing. Then he listened north. Yes! There it was. Coyote calling from far north. And Fox knew Coyote was returning."

Coyote's greed is never satisfied, even when he possesses more than enough. His ability to shrug off danger and proceed through life is always honed to precision. His irresponsibility seems to fortify his ability to defy death. Death just misses him by a hair of his tail, and he nonchalantly dogtrots crookedly away. The human disposition to do that which is usually silly and often damaging is displayed in the errors of Coyote.

Silver-Gray Fox is a creator who makes things that are good. He is a teacher who forgives the errors of Coyote and continues creating, knowing all the while that Coyote is coming behind him, changing the creation (and changing it for the worse). Again and again Fox gives lessons to Coyote, and again and again Coyote does not learn. In this story Fox tires of "killing" Coyote; so he devises a plan to make another world—a world without Coyote. But a little basket in the above world tells Coyote that Fox has gone down through the hole under the center post of the sweat house. Finding only water, Fox begins singing and sings until there is some earth. When there is enough earth, Fox sings a sweat house into being. He has made another world—a world without Coyote. And so the human desire to do what is proper is displayed in the spirit of Fox. Susan Park captured this message in her field notes long ago.

Soon after entering the University of California at Davis in the fall of 1987, I began writing articles for *News from Native California,* a publication from Berkeley. I usually sign my tribal identity as A-juma-wi/Atsuge-wi, being Ajumawi (the people who live beside the Pit River) on my mother's side and Atsugewi (the people who live beside the Hat Creek and in unison with the Oporegee of Dixie Valley) on my father's side.

In 1990, while reading *News from Native California*, Susan Park was startled to find the name Atsuge-wi, the people Dr. Kroeber had instructed her to study sixty years ago.

She soon wrote to me, introducing herself and wondering whether I was related to any of the people she listed (I am related to almost all of them). We exchanged a few letters, and I visited her home in Carson City, Nevada. We looked over the materials, and I was startled! There, in old field notes written with a number-two lead pencil, were the shadows and the spirits of my people. They "talked" to me, and the more I studied her notes, the more the people took on form, and presence, and voice. Sampson Grant was peering across Goose Valley, dreaming. Lee Bone was telling his rendition of "The Creation." Bob Rivers was telling of a time when "doctors" had a war in which they threw their poisons into enemy camps like artillery shells. Ida Piconom was doctoring, interpreting, singing, doctoring again. I cried. I saw them as if they were deer grazing in the open fields, jumping, darting—dancing to the music of the universe and peering into the future. Ever alert, beautiful, real.

With a mini-grant from the Women's Research and Resource Center at UC Davis, my twin boys, Hoss and Theo, then ten years old, and I were able to travel to Susan's home and get her notes, photocopy them, and return the originals to her at Carson City. The fragile pages tore with every quick movement. The binding, brittled by age, cracked if we opened the pages too quickly. The cautious labor accomplished, we were happy.

Elated that her field notes were of some "use," Susan gathered other materials, such as genealogies, profiles, and photographs for me when I would next visit. But before I returned, a fire in her home office destroyed this material. A precious part of our history had vanished. Susan was devastated, and I was crushed. Nevertheless, we gathered ourselves together and continued getting the stories out of the original field notes. The result is the completion of a first volume, which will display the legends and lessons that have been returned to us as a gift, a gift from our old ones who had talked with Susan long ago in an era when our ancestral homeland was a more magical place in which to dwell. Perhaps in this manner the Iss will recall a time, only moments ago, when the songs of our doctors were more powerful than the bullets of the American military and the laughter of our children was more beautiful than the "music" of the Euro-Americans.

NOTE

1. Susan Brandenstein Park, interview with author, Carson City, Nev., July 14, 1992.

There was nothing here, and there was above in the other side of the sky lots of people.*

Coyote was too rough up there, and Fox doesn't know how to get rid of him, and he, Fox, had a big sweat house, and that sweat had a big center post.†

And Fox lifted up the center post.‡ And Fox, he came down through the hole and put the post down so Coyote couldn't see.§ He had a cane—which he brought with him.

And he put it down upright on the water,‖ and he sat on the top and was singing.

And with his singing he made a little ground around. And when it big enough, he sang a sweat house.

Coyote tried to find out where Fox was. And no one would tell him. And one little basket told him; he said, "Fox is down there," to that post.# And that's why Coyote went down.

He went same way Fox did, and he could do same things that Fox did.

So he went down and pulled up the sweat-house post in the same way.

He went down with another cane just like Fox's,** and he came down on Fox's *chemaha*,†† and he see Fox in sweat house.

Fox saw Coyote when he came to his house, and so he live with him, and so he make big singing all the time and make a big world— just as it now.

Fox went out to get *dalsi* away out on a hill,‡‡ and he call it§§: "Bring down acorn bread." And he sat down and crossed his arms and covered his eyes, and bread came down, and he come down on

*and there was . . . : that is, but there was . . .
†center post: the post in the center of the sweat house, or round house, that holds up the roof.
‡lifted up: that is, pulled up.
§put the post down: that is, put the post back in the hole.
‖it: the cane.
#he said . . . to that post: he said . . . as he was pointing to the center post.
**He went down: He went through the hole.
††*chemaha:* a sweat house. It is sometimes used only for ceremonies; at other times it is used as a dwelling place for the community and may also be referred to as the winter house.
‡‡*dalsi:* bread made from the acorns of a variety of oak trees. The acorns are dried, ground into meal, and then cooked.
§§he call it: he called to the creation power.

his back. And when everything done the way he wanted it, he woke up.

Acorn bread came. Fox made that. He don't eat till he go back to his home and he find Old Coyote. He see the bread, and he glad to see the acorn bread.

And it give half to Old Coyote.*

"Where you get this?"

"I went up in the hill and right on the hill and I sat with my head in my arms and I told him to come down, and then he come down on my back. When we done, I wake up and I see the bread around my back"; that's what he told Old Coyote.

Old Coyote think, "That's a good way to get grub. I can take lots of 'em after a while. I better eat first."

Coyote, he ate up all that bread.

So he go another place.

So he sat there same way on a hillside,† and he told them to come down, and they come down, and He look down,‡ and he come down with a big rock.

And Old Coyote thought a big bread come down on his back, and he said, "Gimme some more." And more rocks came till he was all crippled up.

And he go back without grub because it was all rock.

And he go back crying and said, "I don't see how you eat that way. And you might to have to pound up [acorns] and then make bread. That's the way they used to do."

And Fox never said a word.

And Fox went out in the morning. He called grouse. Went on a big tree [limb] that had pitch in. He sat again with his head in his arms, and he built a fire on one thick limb of tree and sit down, and the grouse came down, and he picked it up.

He looked around and saw lots of grouse on the ground, and he picked them up, and he went back, and when he got back to the chemaha, Old Coyote is there, and he give him half. He like 'em pretty good.

And he ask Fox, "How you done this?"

And Fox told him, "I put a little fire on top,§ and I sit my head in my arms, and I don't see."

---

*it: that is, Fox.
†he sat there same way: he sat as Fox had sat.
‡He: the Great Power.
§on top: that is, on top of a limb in the tree.

Coyote went out and he got a big tree with lots of pitch on it,* and he put a fire on a limb, and he put his head in his arms and didn't look and: "Bring down lots of grouse!"

And it did come down, lots of grouse, on his back. And he got up. He see lots of grouse. Old Coyote, he glad to see lots of grouse.

"Well," he said, "I can get lots next time. I can build fire again."

And he eat 'em up right there. Then when he eat 'em up, he go to another place, and he do same. He build fire on limb, sit down same way again, and He bring down lots of pitch.

And Old Coyote think, "Oh! It comes! Lots of grouse."

And pitch came all over head and back, and he shook off so more could come. He didn't want to get up, and he jump up,† and he didn't get anything but pitch on his back.

And he go back, and Fox, he said nothing. He knows what going to happen. So Old Coyote was lying, and he told him what happened.

"You have to shoot [grouse] with a bow and arrow; that how you can get it."

And that's how it happened that we do it that way now. If he'd call behind Fox,‡ we could have lots good to eat.

And Fox went out again trying to get something to eat, and he wanted roots—*jatu*.§ And he went to a cedar where limbs break easy.

He sat down, and all limbs came down on his back, and when he got up, there was lots of jatu.

And he picked 'em up and put 'em in his basket, and he take 'em home.

He don't eat outside. He waits till it gets back.|| That's why Coyote is punished when he eats way out.#

And he finds old Coyote, who say, "Where you get this? It's fine!"

And Fox told him he pulled limbs down with stick.

---

*he got . . . : that is, he found . . .

†He didn't want . . . and he jump up. . . . : He could barely get up, and finally he jumped up. . . .

‡If he'd call behind Fox . . . : If he'd asked for enough and not been greedy . . .

§*jatu:* "roots"; also called *epos* or *apas*. The top of this plant resembles that of a carrot. The roots grow in bunches of three to six, with each root about the size of a person's little finger. The roots are sweet and are often eaten immediately. They are also dried for making bread and soup during the winter.

||it: Coyote.

#Coyote is punished when he eats way out: The punishment is that Coyote usually eats carrion. By "way out" the narrator meant "alone."

Old Coyote thought, "I can do that." All right, and they have lots to eat. So in morning he went out, and he went to a nice cedar tree, and he sat down just as he always did, and he come down, lots of them.*

And Old Coyote thought, "I can make lots that way. I'm glad." And he laughed. And he eat 'em up because—"I'll have plenty, after a while, when I get home." And he thought, "When I go to another place, I get a little more." And he ate them all up. He didn't have any at all.

And he go to another tree, bigger tree, and he sat down, same way, again and said, "Bring down lots of them." And, [Great Power] bring down big limb right straight over his back, nearly killed him. He jumped out and go away, and he went home.

He didn't get anything. Fox said nothing. He knows what's going to happen every time when he does that.† And he told the Fox, "It's no use to have it that way. Let woman get jatu."

So he said nothing and went out again in the morning, Fox, and he went to a yellow jacket nest. And Fox put a little fire to smoke out the yellow jackets. So it did this,‡ and [Fox] got a bunch of yellow jacket eggs, and he take them back and built a fire and roast them, and he give half to Coyote.

And he asked him how he did it, and Coyote said, "I guess I can do that."

And Coyote went out in the morning. He did the same as Fox did, killing the yellow jackets with fire. So he took them out, and he found lots of them there.§

And so Old Coyote, when he wake up,‖ he eats it right then, and he said, "I can get lots. I'll eat them up." So he did. And—"I can get another place. And I can get more!"

And he went same way again, and when he sat down with his head in his arms, the yellow jackets got him all over his ear, and he swell up.

And he said, "That's not right!"

All his face all swell up, and he went back, and Fox never said a word when Coyote got back, and Coyote told Fox what he did, and he said,# "You didn't tell me what to do!"

---

*he: that is, the *jatu*.
†when he does that: when Coyote does that.
‡it: the smoke.
§lots of them: a lot of the yellow jacket eggs.
‖when he wake up: Coyote had closed his eyes and sung in accordance with Fox's explanation of what he had done.
#he said: Coyote said.

And Coyote got mad because his face was all swell up. Coyote put his thing in the yellow jacket nest just as Fox had done,* and he couldn't pee, and he got mad at Fox.

Fox said, "We'll get a rabbit." And he said, "[Over there] I find lots of rabbit." And he said, "I'm going to get this string."

And all day he made that string. He put sugar pine nuts inside [on] the *rassouou,*† and he eats 'em that way.

So Old Coyote couldn't see what he was doing, and he sleep all the time. Old Coyote, he hasn't much grub. So Old Coyote woke up, and he thought in his head, "I know that's pine nuts." And Coyote said to Fox, "You better give me one. I want to see what you got!"

And Fox gave it to him, and the pine nuts were all [strung] out on the thread. Fox wanted to make a trap. That's why he made the thread. Fox wouldn't let Coyote see him. And when they had made string,‡ Fox made it all right.

He wanted to make a net quick. And Old Coyote sleep sound. And he measured Coyote with the nose.§

And Coyote jumped up and said, "You measure me, huh?"

And Fox said. "No. You got lots of dirt on you; I brush off." So Coyote sleep again, and Fox make net all night, and he fixed net, and he said, "We'll get lots of rabbit."

He told Coyote to come around the other side and send the rabbit into the net, and he said, *"Keep your eyes closed so rabbit can come in net."*

And Old Coyote thought, "All right. I'll go there."

Fox set nets across so rabbit will get in.

And after a while Coyote thought, "Lots of rabbit." And he kept his eyes shut so when he opened them there would be lots of rabbit, and Fox gave Coyote half the rabbit, and Coyote thought, "That's pretty good. We're going to have lots to eat."

And the [next] day they went together to get rabbit, and he told him to go round and bring lots of rabbit, and Fox put net across, way back so Coyote wouldn't see. And, when he run behind, he went into the net, and Old Fox got a big club.

---

*his thing:** his penis.
†*rassouou:* string made from milkweed. The stem of the milkweed is made of very tough fibers that may be carefully pulled apart in long strands, dried, and twisted together into twine. The *rassouou* is difficult to break, and it does not deteriorate quickly under any condition—except fire.
‡**they:** that is, he, Fox.
§**And he measured Coyote with the nose:** Fox measured Coyote's nose to make certain the net fit exactly.

As soon as Coyote was in net, Fox knocked him in head, and Coyote said, "Don't do that to me!"

And Fox beat him dead, right there.

And he kill Coyote. He knows that Coyote is pretty tough to kill.* He said, "He'll come back all right, but I'll try to get rid of him."

He went through all the world—that Old Coyote traveled. And [Fox] covered up all Coyote's dirt, all his tracks.† He went back and forth, two days.

He doesn't make noise.‡ He listened.§ Two times [he] went out [and listened].

[Coyote called] early in the morning—and he thought he'd killed him good.

One place he had missed. And early daylight Coyote made a noise, and Fox got scared out, and he nearly cried.

Coyote was over in the middle of Tule Lake, on the little island.||

Coyote made a bridge of ground, and he came right out. "I'll fix you all right after what you did to me!" That's what Coyote think, and he come back.

Coyote made fire, and fire came behind him.

Old Fox saw him and saw the big fire coming, and he thought, "What am I going to do? I'm gonna get sick."#

So he made crickets and plums, and he made chokecherries, and he made manzanita berries—so Coyote would eat this.

Coyote see the crickets, and he eat one, and he eat all this food, and fire comes behind.

When he's pretty close, he eats and eats, and he gets over his desire to kill the fellow, as long as he makes all that grub.

He told fire to go back, and he went to the chemaha with his belly full, and he goes in and sees the Fox lying down and so sick he could hardly talk.

So Old Coyote liked when he saw how sick Fox was. And Coyote said, "What's the matter?" And Fox said, "I'm pretty sick." And Coyote: "Why?"

And so he couldn't kill the fellow, and they come together again.

***Coyote is pretty tough to kill:** It is difficult to keep Coyote dead.

†**all his tracks:** all the places where Coyote had urinated.

‡**He:** Coyote.

§**He:** Fox.

||**the little island:** where Coyote had urinated and Fox had missed in cleaning up after him.

#**I'm gonna get sick:** Fox knows Coyote wants to kill him with fire, and he gets sick so that Coyote will feel sorry for him.

And we still have the same burns*; they never much change.

Coyote told Fox, "I'm the one you hit, me!"

Coyote told Fox this. He said, "I'm the one,† but you hit me anyway!"

And Fox said he was pretty deaf and he didn't hear.‡

---

*And we still have the same burns: Earth still, many layers down, shows where Coyote long ago brought fire for revenge, and Silver Fox still has the singed ends on his silver-gray coat. Lee Bone, in this lesson-legend, is attempting to validate the length of time it has been since Coyote came with fire to burn the *chemaha* of Silver Fox. "Long ago there was fire. You can see under coals when you dig way down and find a burned rock. You know that you're digging under the trail where Coyote brought fire"—meaning that it was a very long time ago, and by digging down into the earth, it is possible to find burned rocks almost everywhere.

†I'm the one: that is, I am your friend and companion.

‡Fox said . . . he didn't hear: Fox said that he couldn't hear Coyote; so Coyote ceased pursuing the argument.

TWO MAIDU MYTHS

▲

WILLIAM SHIPLEY

INTRODUCTION

The two Maidu tales that follow are from a large collection of stories written down in the original language by Roland Dixon of Harvard University. In 1902–3, Dixon went to California as a member of the Huntington Expedition, a group of scholars whom the American Museum of Natural History sent to California to study, among other things, the cultures and languages of Native California. Dixon made a study of the Maidu language. He said of these stories, "All of the texts were secured at Genesee, Plumas County, from Tom Young, a half Maidu, half Atsugewi man, who, although only about thirty years of age, possessed an extensive knowledge of the myths of the Maidu of this region." Dixon published the stories (with English translations) in 1912.[1]

I did fieldwork on Maidu during several summers in the 1950s. I soon found out from my Maidu teacher that Tom Young, whose real name was Hánc'ibyjim, was considered by the Indians to be the last great Maidu storyteller. I also quickly came to know that Dixon's transcriptions were full of mistakes and misrecordings. My teacher and I were fascinated by the wonderful stories; we worked together to reconstitute a small part of the corpus, but time and circumstance intervened—most of the material remained in its original form when my teacher died.

Many years later I took Dixon's book off the shelf and set out to reconstitute the beginning of the Creation Myth. To my considerable surprise, I was able to infer what Hánc'ibyjim had really said with an amazing amount of confidence. I took up the task of restoring the material to its proper phonological form. Next it was necessary to break down the reconstituted text and establish its literal meaning. Only when the original Maidu was clear to me did I attempt to come up with an artful English version—one that would be as close as possible to the meaning of the Maidu but at the same time would satisfy and delight an English ear.[2]

In preconquest times the Maidu lived at the northern end of the Sierra Nevada, in a series of beautiful and well-watered high mountain meadows. Politically they were not a tribe in the formal sense; they were organized in clusters of villages, typically around the margins of one of the meadows. Winter houses were large, communal, semisubterranean structures, sod covered, snug and cozy, with open-hearth fires and smoke holes in the roofs. It was in these lodges that myths and stories were told—some of them only in winter and only at night.

The first story here, "Coyote the Spoiler," is the fourth and last part of an unusually long and complex creation myth. In the beginning the Creator (whose name means, literally, "earth maker") and Coyote are floating on an endless sea, searching for a bit of land from which to make the world. They find the nest of Meadowlark, which, at Earth Maker's behest, Coyote stretches out by lying on his belly and pushing with all four feet, thus bringing the world into being. Earth Maker creates all different sorts of creatures, assigning to each a name and a place to live. In an uncannily intuitive account, the storyteller represents these various protocreatures as plantlike entities that become their animal selves only after a sort of prenatal period of growing and sprouting in the ground.

In the second part of the creation myth, Earth Maker and Coyote have a falling-out over whether there will be death in the world—Coyote is for it; Earth Maker is against it. They angrily part company. Coyote becomes a solitary fugitive while Earth Maker, abetted by the people he has created, sets out to track Coyote down and kill him. Three attempts are made—an unusual number in North American Indian mythology—and all three fail. The last try is of particular interest: Earth Maker has his people build a boat; then he floods the world in order to drown Coyote. But Coyote, disguised, joins the people in the boat and thereby saves himself. Earth Maker, defeated, abandons his plan to kill his adversary.

In the third part Earth Maker and Coyote continue their controversy about death and also argue about procreation. As before, Earth Maker advocates a deathless world and a world where children are brought into being overnight by the simple act of laying a stick in the bed between the parents; in the morning the stick will have turned into a baby. But Coyote again argues for death as well as for his greatest invention, sexual love. Earth Maker admits defeat on both counts and, as he wanders away, contrives the death of Coyote's only son, leaving Coyote with a bitter victory.

The fourth part of the myth, "Coyote the Spoiler," concludes the story with Coyote triumphant. So in the end the land itself was made from Meadowlark's nest, the creatures that inhabit it were made by Earth Maker, and the human condition—the circumstances of love and death—were the work of Coyote.

The other story here is "The Sisters Who Married the Stars." This tale is unusual in that it has no animal characters. In fact, there is only one other story in the collection that is similar to it: "The Great Serpent." In both stories young girls have secret lovers who are mythical beings—in one case a Great Serpent and in the other two Star Men. And in both stories the girls come to accept their parents' advice, reject their lovers, and return home. In "The Sisters Who Married the Stars," there is an overt reference to the girls' puberty ceremony, which was a very important event in Maidu life. Undoubtedly these two stories were meaningful in ways we will never know.

NOTES

1. Roland B. Dixon, *Maidu Texts,* Publications of the American Ethnological Society, vol. 4, ed. Franz Boas (Leiden, Holland: E. J. Brill, 1912).

2. William Shipley, *The Maidu Indian Myths and Stories of Hánc'ibyjim* (Berkeley, Calif.: Heyday Books, 1991).

Now Earth Maker came along this way,
and after he had walked for a while,
he crossed over a river and arrived there at the Pissing Place.
He went along the side of the hill beyond.

There was a sweat house across the river—
the house of the Pissing Women,
who rushed forth from time to time
and massacred the people round about.
Whenever someone came along,
they swooped down on him from their sweat house
and killed him!

They looked out and saw Earth Maker,
and they shot streams of piss at him across the river.
But he managed to get safely over the ridge
by sticking his flint flaker into the ground.
That way he kept going along until he was out of danger.

He went along
until he came to where the Mink brothers were living,
and there he camped for the night.

In the morning those two youngsters spoke.

"Why don't you help us set our trap?" they asked.
"Whenever we set it, the creatures always escape from it.
Why don't you set it for us?"

So Earth Maker went down and set the trap,
and when he had done so, he said,
"Don't say anything, you two, about what you've seen.
Keep your mouths shut, and take off after those Pissing Women.
Grab up some of that grease there, and take it with you.
When you get to the Pissing Women's sweat house
and they have crawled in to sweat,
then throw it down through the smoke hole,
and run away as fast as you can!
And when they breathe in the smell of that grease,
they will suffocate."

"All right," said the Mink brothers.
And Earth Maker went away.

Now the two Mink boys kept watch,
and in the morning, just as the sun was rising,
a condor was circling overhead.

Then the younger brother said,
"There's a condor circling around—
something must be caught in our trap!"

Then they jumped up,
and hurrying along, they ran down to it.
As the condor,
who was going to carry the trapped thing up into the sky,
was just halfway to it, the brothers ran up.
And after they had sprung up to where it was,
they cut it in two.
They saved back only the part toward the tail
and threw the rest of it up into the air.
Milk, dripping down, dripped on those two as they looked up.
Drops of milk fell on their mouths.
Drops of white milk fell on their chins.
Drops of milk were on their breasts.

And then, as it got along toward evening,
the Mink brothers took the grease
and carried it along to the Pissing Women's house.

Just at dark those women were sweating
and dancing the bear dance.
They were terrible to see!

The boys flung the grease in through the smoke hole
and then ran away.
And then that sweat house caught fire
and burned to the ground.

Those two Mink brothers didn't stop running
until they got back to their home.
They stayed there.

All this time Earth Maker was traveling along.
He arrived in Nearby Valley, where the Crow brothers lived.
He made camp there.
Then those two brothers said to him,
"Elder brother, you'd better sharpen our knives for us.
Having them dull doesn't seem to do us any good."

So he sharpened the beaks on those two Crow brothers,
and after he had camped out there for a while,
he walked away.

As he came walking along,
the pet porcupine of the Two-Boys-Who-Stab-People-in-Boats
was lying on top of a rock.
He was a pet who always saw everything, they say,
but he didn't see Earth Maker!
Earth Maker dodged down out of sight
and got himself under the rock,
and having reached up,
and having grabbed the porcupine,
and having killed it,
and having tucked it into his belt,
he took himself silently away.

Meanwhile the two boys just kept on talking with each other.
And then they took a look at the knife they used
to cut people's heads off with.
They said as they were talking together,
"This is the kind of a thing we two always use
when we go around cutting off people's heads!"

The Great Being stepped down to where they were,
and when he had gotten there, he stood on the bank of the river,
and they saw him.
Those two started to hide, but they couldn't.
Earth Maker saw them.
"Hey, you two, get me a boat!" he said.
The two boys pushed the boat out of the water,
but when they got it partway onto the bank,
they couldn't push it any farther.
"Jump on from where you are," one of them said.
He climbed down
and started to jump into the boat from the bank of the river.

But just as he was about to jump,
the boys moved the boat a little
so that he might slip and fall
and the boys could attack with their knives
and cut his head off.
So they crouched to spring on him,
but as he jumped aside, he said,
"Now then! Let me have a look at your knives!
Which of your knives is better?"

Then the boys stood up,
took out their knives, and gave them to him.
Earth Maker took them and said,
"Well! You certainly seem to have very fine knives!
I'm going now.
I suppose you two know your way around in this country.
You must feel at home in all these mountains around here.
On this mountain here, in olden times,
the people came out of a boat and left it there.
They abandoned the boat.
Before then deep waters covered all this land,
all these mountains round about."
Then as he spoke,
Earth Maker took one of the knives and pointed all around.
He pointed toward each and every part of the countryside.
Then he stuck one of the knives in their throats
and cut their heads off. He killed them both.
And after that he put them on his back
and lifted them up out of the boat.

Now there was an earth oven there, nearby,
with a fire burning round it.
He laid the two boys down there
and pulled off their pissers.
He put the two bodies in the oven,
and when they were covered up,
he laid a trap by bending their pissers over,
and he went away.
After he had done things with those two bodies—
when he had covered them up—
he went away.

▲

Then he came to where the grandmother of the two boys lived.
He took the porcupine that was tucked under his belt
and flung it across at her.
"Take that porcupine, bake it in the ashes, and eat it!"
he said to her as he threw it across.
But she threw it back at him and said as she threw it,
"Take that porcupine, bake it in the ashes, and eat it!"
Earth Maker picked it up and threw it back again.
"Take that porcupine, bake it in the ashes, and eat it!" he said.
But she flung it back again and said, "Bake it and eat it!"

So then he spread the embers apart
and laid the porcupine down into them.
He covered it over,
stretched himself out with his back to the fire,
and went to sleep. He usually slept with his back to the fire.
In truth, only a shadow of his real self was there—
a log—a rotten log.
That old woman reached across and picked up her stone pestle,
and when she had taken careful aim, she bashed the log with it.
She made the log burst and fly all to pieces.
"Well, well!" she said,
"I didn't think that was really you there.
I really did believe that was some old thing!"
The rotten log did look like him,
but Earth Maker, who had been lying with his back to the fire,
had already gone away to some other place.
Only his shadow remained there.
Though he seemed to be lying with his back to the fire,
it was really only his shadow.

Later on the old woman jumped up and ran away.
"I suppose he must have eaten my two grandsons long since!"
she said. Talking to herself like that,
she ran to the trap and stooped down,
and at that very moment she was caught in the trap.
Thus, Earth Maker killed off all three of them.
But he paid no mind to that and went on his way.

After he had traveled for a long time,
he came to where Grouse Old Woman lived.
He made camp there and then went on again in the morning.

He set out and went along
until he came to Grizzly Old Woman's house.
When he got there, he had her two cubs tucked under his belt.
"Singe the hair off these squirrels, and let's eat them," he said.
Then while she gave him a bewildered look,
he lay down with his back to the fire.
But in fact he had already gone away,
and it was only a shadow that seemed to be sleeping there.
She grabbed up her digging stick
and brought it around to hit him,
but what she hit was a log.
"I guessed that it wasn't you but something else," she said.
"Well, well! I'm sure you'll outlive us all!"
And she set out to find him,
whirling her skirt so that it fluttered about.
Then the countryside caught fire.
It seemed as if the fire swept over the land everywhere.
Everywhere, it seemed.

And then Earth Maker asked of Water, "How is it with you?"
And Water answered, "I'm boiling and bubbling. I'm very hot!"
And he asked Rock, "How is it with you?"
And Rock answered, "I'm hot, and from time to time I burst!"
And he asked Tree, "How is it with you?"
And Tree answered, "I'm burning mightily, and I'll stay very
    hot!"
And he asked Milkweed, "And how is it with you?"
And Milkweed answered, "When the fire has come and gone,
I'm left standing behind!"
And Milkweed crawled out into the midst of the fire
and stayed there.

The country kept burning until it was all burned up.
And when it had cooled,
Grizzly Old Woman kept following Earth Maker's tracks.
She kept tracking him all around, going all around.
But she gave up and went home.

Earth Maker traveled along, coming this way.
He climbed up to the top of a ridge.
"Well," he said, "it seems to me that this sugar pine
is something for human beings to eat.

So people will have to climb up,
throw the cones down, and gather them."
He said to the sugar pine,
"You're going to be short and low limbed."
He left and came farther this way.

But Coyote, angry, came along after him.
When he got to where the sugar pine tree was, he said,
"I wonder how in the world this tree got to be so short!"
And he pissed on it.
"Now most of the pinecones are high in the top of the tree
so that when people see them,
they won't be able to climb up to them," he said.
And he went on his way.

Now when Earth Maker had come along this way for a while,
he sat down and took a look around.
"Here is where people will fish for salmon with nets," he said.
"They will stretch the nets wide and throw them in,
time after time. And on the other side of the river,
they will do the same thing."

He set out again and traveled and traveled,
coming always this way, they say.
And there, at the Place-of-the-Little-White-Root,
he sat down and ate little white roots for lunch.
And when he had eaten, he got to his feet.
He stood awhile and gazed all around him.
He started off downhill and kept going and going
until he came to Hanýlekim Valley.
"Well, I still have this beautiful country left," he said.
"While Coyote is spoiling the world,
here I'll make a place where old people may reawake!
A place where human beings—old human beings—
may bathe and become young again!"
And he made a little hill.
He kept climbing up it as fast as he could until he got to the top.
"Here," he said, "old people who are about to die
will climb and climb until they get to the very top,
and then when they have bathed in this pool,
they will be young again!" And then he went away.

He set out from there
and crossed over to where the sun comes up.

But Coyote was going around here and there.
He saw the hill and said,
"I wonder why this hill is the way it is."
He looked it all over. He stared at it for a while.
"I think I'll just piss on it!" he said.
He took another quick look at the hill,
there in the middle of the valley.

Then that hill toppled over,
and when it had fallen, it broke open,
and the water spilled out into the house of the Great Serpent,
and the water flooded everything
until it had filled up the whole valley.
And the valley is filled with water to this very day!

"People will say of me, talking and laughing,
'Long ago Coyote pissed on Oskypem Mountain
and made it tumble down! In olden times
Coyote was very powerful.
He got the best of Earth Maker and made him angry!'
That's what they'll say when they talk to each other,
and they'll laugh. I will be Coyote forever!"
That's what Coyote said.

Then he went along by where Oskypem Mountain had been.
And when he had howled, *"Wowowowowowowo!"*
he ran away. He said, "People will talk about me!"
And as he went away from there,
he was not thinking about anything at all
because all his work was done.

That's all, they say.

Two women, who were just old enough to dance, were dancing,
and when they had stopped dancing, at daybreak,
they both went to sleep.
They slept until sometime along toward the next morning;
then they woke up and went to dig for tiger lily bulbs.
And when the women got back at dark,
everyone was dancing around again.
After they had danced round and round,
they danced stepping forward and back.
Then, just as the daylight came down over the rim of the hills,
when everyone had chased the singers away,
the two women went to sleep again.

Then in a little while one of them dreamed.
Their mother said, "If you dream something bad,
then when you have pierced your earlobes,
you must dive into the water. Afterward
you must blow all the bad things away from yourselves.
Then sleep will heal you, and you will wake up feeling well."

Now when those two women dreamed,
they dreamed of Star Beings,
and they did not blow the dream away!
They did not pierce their ears!
They did not bathe in the stream!
And when the dance was done,
they went with their mother to the spring,
planning to stay there and dig for tiger lily bulbs.
And when they got there, they made camp.
They lay down there to go to sleep,
and as they lay on their backs and stared up into the sky,
they talked with each other.
One of them asked the other,
"Would you like to go up there?
If I could just get up there,
I would like to have a look at that very red, bright star!"
"I feel the same way," said the other;
"I would like to get up to that star that looks bluish!
I wonder what he looks like!"

Then those two went to sleep,
and when they woke up in the morning,
they found themselves with the Star Beings in the sky.

That old woman, their mother,
who was left behind down here,
went searching for them.
She sought to find out where they might have gone.
She tried to find their footprints
but could not see them anywhere.
Since she could find no footprints to follow,
she trudged along back home, weeping.
When she got back, the people came home from hunting.
They kept coming, and when they arrived,
they too searched for the daughters.
They looked and looked for tracks,
but when they could not find any, they came back home.
And when they got back, they all stayed there.

Meanwhile the two women were in the Meadows Above.
They married the Star Men and stayed there.
Then the younger one said to the other,
"Our mother, our father, our kinsmen must all feel bad
since they can't find any trace of us.
It was you, of course, who wanted so much to come here.
When you said so, I believed you,
and I have come with you so far as this.
We have made my father unhappy.
We have made my mother unhappy.
We have made my kinsmen unhappy.
It was all your idea!
Our mother gave us very good advice,
but you didn't believe her!
When you had a bad dream,
then you didn't pierce your ears.
That's what you did, and now here we are!
But I'm going back. If you want to stay here, stay here!
It makes me feel miserable to think of my parents.
I'm sorry to say these things, but I have said them.
When I think about it, I feel terrible."
It was the younger sister who was talking.

Then her elder sister spoke:
"So then, let's both go back, some way or another.
But in the meantime let's go gather some kind of food.
Perhaps in time we can find a way to get back home."

So they stayed there, and each one of them had a child.
They went a little way off together, and there they built a house.
And when they had built it, they lived there.
And after some time had passed, they said,
"These children of ours want some sinew."
So their two husbands gave them sinew.
And then again, later, the women said, "They want sinew."
The husbands gave it.

The women rolled the sinew on their thighs.
Every day they said, "The children want sinew."
And their husbands gave it to them.
And those two women kept rolling it on their thighs,
and when it was dark, they made a rope, those two.
And, letting it down toward the earth,
they took its measure.
"It might be hanging down just far enough!" they said.
But it didn't hang very far down;
so still the women said to their husbands,
"The children want sinew!
These children eat a lot, and nothing but sinew!"
And their husbands believed them.

The two women kept making rope until they had enough.
It reached all the way down,
all the way down to the ground below.
And then those two, leaving their children behind,
tied the rope and came down,
and when they were halfway down,
the children began to cry. They cried and cried.
Then one of the Star Men said,
"What's the matter with those children?
Perhaps you'd better go see."

So the other one went to the women's house,
but when he got there, no one was there
except the children, crying.

He looked all around,
and there was the rope, hanging straight down.
Then he cut it,
and the two women, who had almost reached the ground,
fell and died.

One of their brothers who was still hunting for them saw them.
The rope was also there.
He took it back home and told the others,
"Those sisters of ours, those two women, are dead!"
Then the kinsmen went,
and when they got to where the women lay,
they lifted them up and carried them home.
And when they had carried them there,
they laid them down in the water.
Then in the morning the two women awoke,
and they came up out of the water and went home.

After a while the younger sister said,
"My sister spoke to me first,
and then we talked together
about how we looked with great wonder at those Star Men.
I went along with her.
During the dancing time we dreamed of those Star Men,
but there seemed to be no way for us to get to them.
We talked so much, talking of everything with delight!
That's what we did, talking together.
And then our Star Men brought us to themselves
and made love to us, and we all played together.
But when we set out to return home, they found out about it
and cut the ropes as we were climbing down, and so we died."
That's what the younger sister said.
The two sisters told their mother all about it.
The younger sister said, "One of the Star Men looked very red,
and he ate only hearts! Another looked bluish,
and *he* ate only fat! There seem to be a lot of Star Beings,
each one eating just one kind of thing or another.
Some eat just liver. Some eat just flesh.
That's the way the Star Beings are!"
The elder sister said nothing,
and then long ago they all stayed there together.
That's all of it, they say.

MYTH, MUSIC, AND MAGIC:
NETTIE REUBEN'S KARUK LOVE
MEDICINE

▲

WILLIAM BRIGHT

INTRODUCTION

The Karuk tribe (also called Karok) lives on the upper Klamath
River, in northwestern California; the distinctive culture of the area
is shared by the neighboring Yurok and Hupa, although the tribes
concerned speak totally unrelated languages. The traditional oral
literature of the region consists in large part of myths set in an ancient time before human beings existed. The characters in the myths
are spirit people (in Karuk, *ikxaréeyav*), many of whom have names
like Coyote, Bear, and Deer. Typically myths end with a statement
by a spirit person that the life of human beings, who are about to
come into existence, will be as the spirit person ordains: thus, at the
end of one narrative, Coyote provides salmon and acorns and says
that humans will live on them. At the end of the story, many spirit
people are transformed into the prototypes of the animal species
that we know today, whereas others remain in the world in intangible form.[1]

All the spirit people may be addressed by humans who seek their
favor; thus, a hunter, before he goes out to the mountains, will
"make medicine," asking Deer for permission to kill him. Typically
he uses a "formula" (to use the word that has been applied by anthropologists) involving memorized prayer and/or song. These formulas are often learned from an elder member of one's family; they

are valuable property and may be kept secret from outsiders.[2] The sung material, like other types of song in the region, is typically brief. Sometimes it consists entirely of "song words"—meaningless vocables comparable to the English *tra-la-la*. Others consist of a few short phrases, repeated several times; for example, a song to keep a boat from sinking in rough water consists simply of the words "Let's not capsize! Let's not capsize!"

The type of song called *chiihvíichva* in Karuk—"love song" in English—is in fact a form of "love medicine"—not simply an expression of amorous feelings but, specifically, a type of magic to attract a lover. Thus, on a recent visit to Karuk friends, I heard that a tradition-oriented man had been asked to sing a "love song" at the wedding of a young, nontraditional couple: "Hell, no," he said, "I've got enough women pestering me already." Some typical songs of this type are the following. First is a song sung by a woman to bring back a departed lover:

> Oh, I'm lonely! Oh, I'm lonely!
> He went off toward the ocean,
> He went off far away.

These lines are repeated numerous times. The second example is sung by a woman who wishes to become attractive to men. It is addressed to the spirit person Chishihtunvêenach, "Bitch-in-Heat," and invokes her powers of attracting males:

> This is the way she did,
> Bitch-in-Heat, Bitch-in-Heat.
> They smell her from over the river.
> Come on, honey, swim across!

Many myths and songs were taught to me in 1949–50 by Nettie Reuben, a Karuk woman of Orleans, California, who was about seventy years old at the time. Nettie was a famous basket maker and traditionalist who spoke little English. At first she didn't want to talk to me; after she agreed to talk to me, she didn't want to speak into a microphone for recording; and after she agreed to do that, she didn't want to sing her love medicine. But finally she decided that since she had no daughter to whom she could teach her songs, she would give them to me: *"Pananipákuri pa'apxantiich tanivíriv-shav,"* she said; "I've willed my songs to the white man."

The most elaborate formula that I learned from Nettie, her "Evening Star" love magic, illustrates the interaction of speech and song. The main framework is that of a myth: a prose narrative about a pair of lovers among the spirit people. The boy is Evening Star; the girl is not named, except as Evening Star's Lover. They quarrel, and Evening Star goes off to the upriver end of the world—a place far in the north, variously identified as Klamath Lakes (in Oregon) or the North Pole. The girl is lonely and decides to make medicine to bring the boy back. She does this by composing a magical song. In the song she expresses her loneliness; then she says that the boy will feel likewise and will return to her; and finally she predicts that when human beings come to exist, they will use this story and song to the same effect. After the embedded song the narrative relates how the medicine works, how the lovers are reunited, and how the girl once more predicts that the same medicine will also work for humans.

In this translation the myth is presented in terms of the ethnopoetic realization that many traditional narratives of the American Indian are structured not as prose but as a type of "measured verse," in which lines are definable in terms of their grammatical and semantic structures.[3] But in embedded songs the lines are definable in terms of the melodic structure to which they are sung. In the present case the song of Evening Star's Lover consists of ten stanzas of five lines each plus a final one of three lines.

The musical notation is given along with the words for the first stanza of the song. The first three lines are meaningless vocables, or song words; the last two lines are *"Ii, tanéepshaamkir"* ("Oh, he left me"); *"Ii, nanikeech'ikyav"* ("Oh, my lover"). An acute accent in a Karuk word indicates high level pitch; a circumflex accent indicates falling pitch.

Like other Karuk love medicine, this song is characterized by repeated self-reflexiveness. A woman, abandoned by her lover, decides to use this magic: she tells the story of a spirit girl who had a similar experience and whose tradition the human woman has inherited. In the story the spirit girl decides to make magic by singing a song. The song repeats how the lovers were separated and predicts that they will be united. After she sings the song, her prediction comes true. Then she makes a further prediction, that human women will use this same magic—and this, of course, comes true by the very fact that a human woman is reciting and singing it. The performance *of* the myth reflects the action *in* the myth; the magic of the song is activated in the story, and the magic of the story is activated by the fact of its recitation.

I am indebted to Violet Super, P. J. Atkinson, and Elizabeth Snapp for helping me understand the Karuk text of this song. I'm grateful to the ethnomusicologist Richard Keeling for the musical notation provided here—and for pointing out that this song is highly unusual among Native California songs in the length and complexity of its musical and linguistic structure.

NOTES

1. I have published a collection of these myths in bilingual format; see William Bright, *The Karok Language,* University of California Publications in Linguistics no. 13 (Berkeley, 1957).

2. For a detailed description, see Richard Keeling, *Cry for Luck: Sacred Song and Speech Among the Yurok, Hupa, and Karok Indians of Northwestern California* (Berkeley: University of California Press, 1992).

3. The bases for this kind of interpretation are given in Dell Hymes, *"In Vain I Tried to Tell You": Essays in Native American Ethnopoetics* (Philadelphia: University of Pennsylvania Press, 1981); I have applied them to Karuk myths in *American Indian Linguistics and Literature* (Berlin: Mouton, 1984).

Small notes are something like "grace notes."

Slowly (♩. = ca. 60)

Ii— ii ii ii ya,

aa ii ii— ii ya,

aa ii ii— ii ya,

Ii, ta - néep - shaam - kir/,

Eleven times

Ii, na - ni - keech' - ik - yav.

Scale

Evening Star lived there,
    along with his lover.
And for a long time they lived beautifully.
But one day they had a quarrel,
    oh, they got cranky,
    they had a quarrel.
And he went home,
    Evening Star did.
And finally he went all the way around,
    around the whole world,
  he went off far away.

And the woman thought,
 "Oh, my lover!
 How will I ever see him again,
  my sweetheart?"

Oh, she was lonely,
 she sat back down on the doorstep.
"Oh, how lonely I am!
 Oh, how he left me!"
 she thought.
So once more the next day,
 at evening she sat back down there.
"Whatever shall I do?"
And she thought,
 "Perhaps I'll make a song,
 that way I'll get to see him again,
  my lover."

And again the next day,
 she sat back down on the doorstep.
And she sang a song,
 she thought,
"That way I'll get to see him again."

  Ii ii ii iiya
  aa ii ii iiya
  aa ii ii iiya
  oh, he left me
  oh, my lover

  Oh, I'm lonely
  oh, we had a quarrel
  oh, my lover
  oh, Evening Star
  oh, *ina ina*

  oh, he left me
  oh, we had a quarrel
  oh, my lover
  oh, my lover
  oh, my lover

even though you think *ina*
"to the upriver end of the earth
I'll go far away upriver,"
then you think *inaa*
oh, my lover

"Oh, let's be together again
oh, let's be together again
oh, my lover
oh, I'm lonely
oh, my lover"

then you think *ina*
"oh, my lover
oh, we had a quarrel"
you've gone there
to the upriver end of the earth

you just have no home
then you must roll around
here to the middle of the earth
at that place, when you arrive
here we'll roll together again

then just on your breast
there we'll roll together again
"oh, my lover
oh, Evening Star
oh, Evening Star

then you think *inaa*
"when Humans come to exist
then they will do that too"
even though you may quarrel
you and your lover

So you'll be together again
so you'll be together again
when Humans come to exist there
when they find my song
when they know it *ina*

so we live together
you have learned it from me *ina*
oh, my lover

When she finished it,
    singing the love song,
then Evening Star thought,
    "Oh, I'm lonely,
    I'm thinking of my lover,
    let me go see her again!"
In fact his heart was lost,
    but he would find his heart again.
In fact, here at the center of the earth,
    the two would see each other again,
    and so he would find his heart again
        when Evening Star and his lover embraced each other.

And she said this,
    the woman did,
    "When Humans come into existence,
    even though a woman is abandoned,
    she will find him again,
        by means of my song.
    He will come back from there,
        even though he's gone off to the end of the earth."

And Evening Star was transformed,
    into a big star in the sky.

SUGGESTED READING

Works cited in the Notes should also be considered suggested reading.

TOM LOWENSTEIN

Asatchaq, Tukummuq, and Tom Lowenstein. *The Things That Were Said of Them: Shaman Stories and Oral Histories of the Tikiġaq People.* Berkeley: University of California Press, 1992.

Burch Jr., Ernest S. *The Traditional Eskimo Hunters of Point Hope, Alaska: 1800–1875.* Barrow, Alaska: North Slope Borough, 1981.

Lowenstein, Tom. *Ancient Land: Sacred Whale. The Inuit Hunt and Its Rituals.* London: Bloomsbury, 1993; New York: Farrar, Strauss and Giroux, 1994.

Rainey, Froelich. *The Whale Hunters of Tigara.* American Museum of Natural History Anthropological Paper no. 41, pt. 2. New York, 1947.

Vanstone, James. *Point Hope: An Eskimo Village in Transition.* Seattle: University of Washington Press, 1962.

ANTHONY C. WOODBURY AND PHYLLIS MORROW

Burch, Ernest, ed. *The Central Yupik Eskimos.* Études/Inuit/Studies. Supplementary ed. Québec: Laval University, 1984.

Dauenhauer, Nora, Richard Dauenhauer, and Gary Holthaus. "Alaska Native Writers, Storytellers, and Orators." *Alaska Quarterly Review* 4 (1986).

Fitzhugh, William, and Aron Crowell. *Crossroads of Continents: Cultures of Siberia and Alaska.* Washington, D.C.: Smithsonian Institution Press, 1988.

Fitzhugh, William, and Susan Kaplan. *Inua: Spirit World of the Bering Sea Eskimo.* Washington, D.C.: Smithsonian Institution Press, 1982.

Holtved, Erik. *The Polar Eskimos: Language and Folklore.* 2 vols. Medelelser om Grønland, no. 152. Copenhagen: Kommissionen for videnskabelige undersøgelser i Grønland, 1951.

Kaplan, Lawrence D., ed. *Ugiuvangmiut Quliapyuit: King Island Tales*. Fairbanks: Alaska Native Language Center and the University of Alaska Press, 1988.

Nelson, Edward William. *The Eskimo About Bering Strait*. In The Eighteenth Annual Report of the Bureau of American Ethnology for the Years 1896–97. Washington, D.C.: General Printing Office, 1899. Reprint. Washington, D.C.: Smithsonian Institution Press, 1983.

Sherzer, Joel, and Anthony C. Woodbury, eds. *Native American Discourse: Poetics and Rhetoric*. Cambridge, England: Cambridge University Press, 1987.

Tennant, Edward A. and Joseph N. Bitar, eds. *Yuut Qanemciit: Yupiit Cayaraita Qanrutkumallrit/Yupik Lore: Oral Traditions of an Eskimo People*. Bethel, Alaska: Lower Kuskokwim School District, 1981.

Woodbury, Anthony C., ed. *Cev'armiut Qanemciit Qulirait-llu/Eskimo Narratives and Tales from Chevak, Alaska*. Fairbanks: Alaska Native Language Center and University of Alaska Press, 1984.

ANN FIENUP-RIORDAN AND MARIE MEADE

Fienup-Riordan, Ann. *The Nelson Island Eskimo*. Anchorage: Alaska Pacific University Press, 1983.

———. *Eskimo Essays: Yup'ik Lives and How We See Them*. New Brunswick, N.J.: Rutgers University Press, 1990.

Lantis, Margaret. "The Social Culture of the Nunivak Eskimo." *Transactions of the American Philosophical Society* 35 (1946).

Tennant, Edward A. and Joseph N. Bitar, eds. *Yuut Qanemciit: Yupiit Cayaraita Qanrutkumallrit/Yupik Lore: Oral Traditions of an Eskimo People*. Bethel, Alaska: Lower Kuskokwim School District, 1981.

ELIZA JONES AND CATHERINE ATTLA

Chapman, John, and James Kari. *Athabaskan Stories from Anvik*. Fairbanks: Alaska Native Language Center, 1981.

Kari, James, and James A. Fall, eds. *Shem Pete's Alaska*. Fairbanks: Alaska Native Language Center, 1987.

Nelson, Richard K. *Make Prayers to the Raven: A Koyukon View of the Northern Forest*. Chicago: University of Chicago Press, 1983.

Tenenbaum, Joan. *Dena'ina Sukdu'a: Traditional Stories of the Tanaina Athabaskans,* translated and edited by Joan M. Tenenbaum and Mary Jane McGary. Fairbanks: Alaska Native Language Center, 1984.

JANE MCGARY

Kari, James, Priscilla Russell Kari, and Jane McGary. *Dena'ina Elnena: Tanaina Country*. Fairbanks: Alaska Native Language Center, 1983.

Osgood, Cornelius. *Contributions to the Ethnography of the Tanaina*. Yale University Publications in Anthropology, vol. 16. 1937. Reprint. New Haven, Conn.: Yale University Press, 1976.

Townsend, Joan B. "Tanaina." In *Subarctic*. Vol. 6 of *Handbook of North American Indians,* edited by June Helm. Washington, D.C.: Smithsonian Institution Press, 1981.

JAMES KARI

Kalifornsky, Peter. *Kahtnuht'ana Qenaga: The Kenai People's Language.* Fairbanks: Alaska Native Language Center, 1977.

———. *K'tl'egh'i Sukdu/The Remaining Stories.* Fairbanks: Alaska Native Language Center, 1984.

Kari, James, and James A. Fall, eds. *Shem Pete's Alaska.* Fairbanks: Alaska Native Language Center, 1987.

Osgood, Cornelius. *Contributions to the Ethnography of the Tanaina.* Yale University Publications in Anthropology, vol. 16. 1937. Reprint. New Haven, Conn.: Yale University Press, 1976.

CATHARINE MCCLELLAN

Cruikshank, Julie. *The Stolen Women: Female Journeys in Tagish and Tutchone Narrative.* National Museum of Man Mercury Series, Canadian Ethnology Service Paper no. 87. Ottawa: National Museums of Canada, 1983.

Hallowell, A. Irving. "Bear Ceremonialism in the Northern Hemisphere." *American Anthropologist* 28 (1926): 1–175.

McClellan, Catharine. *My Old People Say: An Ethnographic Survey of Southern Yukon Territory.* 2 pts. National Museum of Man Publications in Ethnology no. 6. Ottawa: National Museum of Canada, 1975.

McClellan, Catharine, et al. *Part of the Land, Part of the Water: A History of Yukon Indians.* Vancouver and Toronto: Douglas and McIntyre, 1987.

Rockwell, David. *Giving Voice to Bear: North American Indian Myths, Rituals and Images of the Bear.* Niwot, Colo.: Roberts Rinehart, 1991.

JULIE CRUIKSHANK

Chowning, Ann. "Raven Myths in Northwestern North America and Northeastern Asia." *Arctic Anthropology* 1 (1962).

Cruikshank, Julie. *Reading Voices/Dän Dhá Ts'edenintth'é: Oral and Written Interpretations of the Yukon's Past.* Vancouver: Douglas and McIntyre, 1991.

Cruikshank, Julie, with Angela Sidney, Kitty Smith, and Annie Ned. *Life Lived Like a Story: Life Stories of Three Athapaskan Elders.* Lincoln: University of Nebraska Press, and Vancouver: University of British Columbia Press, 1990.

Radin, Paul. *The Trickster.* New York: Philosophical Library, 1956.

Sidney, Angela. *Place Names of the Tagish Region, Southern Yukon.* Whitehorse, Yukon: Yukon Native Languages Project, Council for Yukon Indians, 1980.

———. *Tagish Tlaagú/Tagish Stories,* recorded by Julie Cruikshank. Whitehorse, Yukon: Yukon Native Languages Project, Council for Yukon Indians, 1982.

———. *Haa Shagóon/Our Family History.* Whitehorse, Yukon: Yukon Native Languages Project, Council for Yukon Indians, 1983.

Sidney, Angela, Kitty Smith, and Rachel Dawson. *My Stories Are My Wealth,* recorded by Julie Cruikshank. Whitehorse, Yukon: Yukon Native Languages Project, Council for Yukon Indians, 1977.

ROBIN RIDINGTON

Brody, Hugh. *Maps and Dreams.* Vancouver: Douglas and McIntyre, 1981.

Ridington, Robin. *Swan People: A Study of the Dunne-za Prophet Dance.* National Museum of Man Mercury Series, Canadian Ethnology Service Paper no. 38. Ottawa: National Museums of Canada, 1978.

———. *Trail to Heaven: Knowledge and Narrative in a Northern Native Community.* Iowa City: University of Iowa Press, 1988.

———. *Little Bit Know Something: Stories in a Language of Anthropology.* Iowa City: University of Iowa Press, 1991.

ROBERT BRIGHTMAN

Ahenakew, Edward. "Cree Trickster Tales." *Journal of American Folklore* 42 (1929).

Beardy, Lazarus. *Pisiskiwak Ka-Pisiskwecik: Talking Animals.* In Algonquian and Iroquoian Linguistics Memoir no. 5, edited and translated by H. C. Wolfart. Winnipeg: University of Manitoba, 1988.

Bloomfield, Leonard. *Sacred Stories of the Sweet Grass Cree.* National Museums of Canada Anthropological Series no. 11, Bulletin no. 60. Ottawa, 1930.

———. *Plains Cree Texts.* Publications of the American Ethnological Society no. 16. New York: G. E. Stechert, 1934.

Vandall, Peter, and Joe Douquette. *Waskahikaniwiyiniw-Ācimōwina: Stories of the House People,* edited and translated by F. Ahenakew. Winnipeg: University of Manitoba Press, 1987.

LAWRENCE MILLMAN

Cabot, W. B. *Labrador.* Boston: Small, Maynard, 1920.

Speck, Frank. *Naskapi.* Norman: University of Oklahoma Press, 1935.

Turner, Lucien. *Ethnology of the Ungava District.* Washington, D.C.: Smithsonian Institution, 1889–90.

ROBERT BRINGHURST

Bringhurst, Robert. "That Also Is You: Some Classics of Native American Literature." In *Native Writers and Canadian Writing,* edited by W. H. New. Vancouver: University of British Columbia Press, 1990.

———. "A Story as Sharp as a Knife, Part 3: The Polyhistorical Mind." *Journal of Canadian Studies* 29:2 (1994).

Drucker, Philip. *Indians of the Northwest Coast.* New York: McGraw-Hill, 1955.

Lévi-Strauss, Claude. *The Way of the Masks.* Seattle: University of Washington Press, 1982.

MacDonald, George F. *Haida Monumental Art.* Vancouver: University of British Columbia Press, 1983.

JUDITH BERMAN

Berman, Judith. "George Hunt and the Kwakw'ala Texts." *Anthropological Linguistics* 36 (1994).

Boas, Franz. *Kwakiutl Tales.* Columbia University Contributions to Anthropology, vol. 2. New York: Columbia University Press, 1910.

———. *Ethnology of the Kwakiutl.* The Thirty-first Annual Report of the Bureau of American Ethnology. Washington, D.C.: U.S. Government Printing Office, 1921.

————. *Religion of the Kwakiutl*. Columbia University Contributions to Anthropology, vol. 10. Pt. 1, "Texts," and pt. 2, "Translations." New York: Columbia University Press, 1930.

————. *Kwakiutl Tales, New Series*. Columbia University Contributions to Anthropology, vol. 26. Pt. 1, "Texts," and Pt. 2, "Translations." New York: Columbia University Press, 1935 and 1943.

————. *Kwakiutl Ethnography*, edited by Helene Codere. Chicago: University of Chicago Press, 1966.

Boas, Franz, and George Hunt. *Kwakiutl Texts*. Memoir of the American Museum of Natural History, Jesup North Pacific Expedition, no. 3. New York: G. E. Stechert, 1905.

————. *Kwakiutl Texts, Second Series*. Memoir of the American Museum of Natural History, Jesup North Pacific Expedition, no. 10. New York: G. E. Stechert, 1906.

Maud, Ralph. *A Guide to B.C. Indian Myth and Legend: A Short History of Myth-Collecting and a Survey of Published Texts*. Vancouver: Talonbooks, 1982.

ANTHONY MATTINA

Cline, Walter, Rachel S. Commons, May Mandelbaum, Richard H. Post, and L.V.W. Walters, *The Sinkaietk or Southern Okanagon of Washington*. Contributions from the Laboratory of Anthropology, General Series in Anthropology no. 6. Menasha, Wis.: George Banta, 1938.

Hill-Tout, Charles. *The Thompson and the Okanagan*. Vol. 1 of *The Salish People: The Local Contributions of Charles Hill-Tout*, edited by Ralph Maud. 1899. Reprint. Vancouver: Talonbooks, 1978.

Mattina, Anthony. "North American Indian Mythography: Editing Texts for the Printed Page." In *Recovering the Word: Essays on Native American Literature*, edited by Brian Swann and Arnold Krupat. Berkeley: University of California Press, 1987, 129–48.

Mattina, Anthony, ed. *The Golden Woman: The Colville Narrative of Peter J. Seymour*. Tucson: University of Arizona Press, 1985.

Ray, Verne F. *The Sanpoil and Nespelem: Salishan Peoples of Northeastern Washington*. University of Washington Publications in Anthropology no. 5. Seattle: University of Washington Press, 1932.

————. "The Bluejay Character in the Plateau Spirit Dance." *American Anthropologist* 39 (1937): 593–601.

Spier, Leslie, ed. *The Sinkaietk or Southern Okanagon of Washington*. By Walter Cline, Rachel S. Commons, May Mandelbaum, Richard H. Post, and L. V. W. Walters. General Series in Anthropology, no. 6, Contributions from the Laboratory of Anthropology, Menasha, Wisconsin: George Banta Publishing Company, 1938.

Teit, James A. "Okanagon Tales." In *Folktales of Salishan and Sahaptin Tribes*, edited by Franz Boas. Memoirs of the American Folklore Society, vol. 11. Boston: Houghton Mifflin, 1917, 65–97.

————. "The Okanagon." In *The Salishan Tribes of the Western Plateau*, edited by Franz Boas. The Forty-fifth Annual Report of the Bureau of American Ethnology for the Years 1927–28 (Washington, D.C.: U.S. Government Printing Office, 1930, 198–294.

Turney-High, Harry. "The Bluejay Dance." *American Anthropologist 35* (1933): 103–7.

JAROLD RAMSEY

Aoki, Haruo, and Deward E. Walker. *Nez Perce Oral Narratives.* University of California Publications in Linguistics no. 104. Berkeley, 1989.

McWhorter, L. V. *Hear Me My Chiefs: Nez Perce History and Legend.* Caldwell, Idaho: Caxton Press, 1952.

Phinney, Archie. *Nez Perce Texts.* Columbia University Contributions to Anthropology, vol. 25. New York: Columbia University Press, 1934.

Slickpoo Sr., Allen. *Noon Nee-me-poo: Culture and History of the Nez Perce.* Lapwai, Idaho: Nez Perce Tribe, 1973.

Stern, T., M. Schmitt, and A. Halfmoon. "A Cayuse–Nez Perce Sketchbook." *Oregon Historical Quarterly* 81 (1980).

JUDITH VANDER

Herzog, George. "Plains Ghost Dance and Great Basin Music." *American Anthropologist* 37, no. 3 (1935).

Hittman, Michael. *Wovoka and the Ghost Dance.* Carson City, Nev.: Grace Dangberg Foundation, 1990.

Mooney, James. *The Ghost-Dance Religion and Sioux Outbreak of 1890.* The Fourteenth Annual Report of the Bureau of American Ethnology for the Years 1892–93. Pt. 2. 1896. Reprint with an introduction by Raymond J. DeMallie. Lincoln: University of Nebraska Press, 1991.

DOUGLAS PARKS

Densmore, Frances. *Pawnee Music.* Smithsonian Institution, Bureau of American Ethnology Bulletin no. 93 (Washington, D.C., 1929).

Grinnell, George Bird. "Pawnee Mythology." *Journal of American Folklore* 6 (1893): 113–20.

———. "A Pawnee Star Myth." *Journal of American Folklore* 7 (1894): 197–200.

———. "The Girl Who Was the Ring Hoop," *Harper's Monthly Magazine* 102 (1901): 425–30.

Parks, Douglas R. "An Historical Character Mythologized: The Scalped Man in Arikara and Pawnee Folklore." In *Plains Indian Studies: A Collection of Essays in Honor of John C. Ewers and Waldo R. Wedel.* Smithsonian Contributions to Anthropology no. 30, edited by Douglas H. Ubelaker and Herman J. Viola. (Washington, D.C., 1982), 47–58.

JULIAN RICE

Picotte, Agnes. *An Introduction to Basic Dakota, Lakota, and Nakota.* Chamberlain, S.D.: Dakota Indian Foundation, 1987.

Rice, Julian. *Black Elk's Story: Distinguishing Its Lakota Purpose.* Albuquerque: University of New Mexico Press, 1991.

———. *Deer Women and Elk Men: The Lakota Narratives of Ella Deloria.* Albuquerque: University of New Mexico Press, 1992.

————. *Ella Deloria's Iron Hawk*. Albuquerque: University of New Mexico Press, 1993.

————. *Ella Deloria's The Buffalo People*. Albuquerque: University of New Mexico Press, 1994.

Taylor, Allan R. and David S. Rood. *Beginning Lakhota*. 2 vols. Boulder: University of Colorado Lakhota Project, 1976.

Vestal, Stanley. *Sitting Bull: Champion of the Sioux*. Norman: University of Oklahoma Press, 1980.

ELAINE A. JAHNER

Deloria, Ella C. *Dakota Texts*. Publications of the American Ethnological Society no 14. New York: G. E. Stechert, 1932. Reprint. New York: AMS Press, 1974.

————. *Speaking of Indians*. New York: Friendship Books, 1944.

Jahner, Elaine A. "Finding the Way Home: The Interpretation of American Indian Folklore." In *Handbook of American Indian Folklore*, edited by Richard M. Dorson. Bloomington: Indiana University Press, 1986.

Walker, James R. *Lakota Belief and Ritual*. Edited by Raymond J. DeMallie and Elaine A. Jahner. Lincoln and London: University of Nebraska Press, 1980.

————. *Lakota Myth*. Edited by Elaine A. Jahner. Lincoln: University of Nebraska Press, 1984.

CALVIN W. FAST WOLF

Bad Heart Bull, Amos. *A Pictographic History of the Oglala Sioux*. Lincoln: University of Nebraska Press, 1967.

Buechel, S. J., Eugene. *A Lakota-English Dictionary*, edited by Paul Manhart, S.J. Pine Ridge, S.D.: Red Cloud Lakota Language and Cultural Center, 1970.

Buechel, S.J., Eugene, et al. *Lakota Tales and Texts*, edited by Paul Manhart, S.J. Pine Ridge, S.D.: Red Cloud Lakota Language and Cultural Center, 1978.

Feraca, Stephen E. *Wakinyan: Contemporary Teton Dakota Religion*. Museum of the Plains Indian, Studies in Plains Anthropology and History no. 2. Browning, Mont., 1963.

Lewis, Thomas H. *The Medicine Man: Oglala Sioux Ceremony and Healing*. Lincoln: University of Nebraska Press, 1990.

Powers, William K. *Oglala Religion*. Lincoln: University of Nebraska Press, 1977.

RIDIE WILSON GHEZZI

Barnouw, Victor. *Wisconsin Chippewa Myths and Their Relation to Chippewa Life*. Madison: University of Wisconsin Press, 1977.

Hallowell, A. Irving. "Ojibwa Ontology, Behavior and World View." In *Culture in History*, edited by Stanley Diamond. New York: Columbia University Press, 1960.

Johnston, Basil. *Ojibway Heritage*. New York: Columbia University Press, 1976.

Landes, Ruth. *Ojibwa Religion and the Midewiwin*. Madison: University of Wisconsin Press, 1968.

Overholt, Thomas W., and J. Baird Callicott. *Clothed-in-Fur and Other Tales: An Introduction to an Ojibwa World View.* Washington, D.C.: University Press of America, 1982.

Vizenor, Gerald. *The Everlasting Sky: New Voices from the People Named the Chippewa.* New York: Crowell-Collier Press, 1972.

Warren, William W. *History of the Ojibways, Based upon Traditions and Oral Statements.* 1885. Reprint. Minneapolis, Minn.: Ross and Haines, 1957.

BLAIR A. RUDES

Johnson, Elias. *Legends, Traditions and Laws of the Iroquois, or Six Nations, and History of the Tuscarora Indians.* Lockport, N.Y.: Union Printing and Publishing, 1881.

Johnson, F. Roy. *Mythology, Medicine, Culture.* Vol. 1 of *The Tuscaroras.* Murfreesboro, N.C.: Johnson Publishing, 1967.

Smith, Erminne A. *Myths of the Iroquois.* The Second Annual Report of the Bureau of American Ethnology. Washington, D.C.: Smithsonian Institution, 1883.

JOHN BIERHORST

Bierhorst, John. *Mythology of the Lenape: Guide and Texts.* Tucson, Az.: University of Arizona Press, 1995.

———. *The White Deer and Other Stories Told by the Lenape.* New York: William Morrow, 1995.

Goddard, Ives. "Delaware." In *Handbook of North American Indians,* edited by William C. Sturtevant. Washington: Smithsonian Institution, 1978, 15: 213–39.

Heckewelder, John G. E. *An Account of the History, Manners, and Customs of the Indian Nations.* 1819. Reprinted as *History, Manners, and Customs of the Indian Nations Who Once Inhabited Pennsylvania and the Neighboring States.* Philadelphia: Historical Society of Pennsylvania, 1876, and New York: Arno Press, 1971.

Kraft, Herbert C. *The Lenape: Archaeology, History, and Ethnography.* Newark: New Jersey Historical Society, 1986.

Weslager, C. A. *The Delaware Indians: A History.* New Brunswick, N.J.: Rutgers University Press, 1972.

Zeisberger, David. "History of the Northern American Indians," edited by Archer B. Hulbert and William N. Schwarze. *Ohio State Archaeological and Historical Quarterly* 19 (1910): 1–189.

DAVID A. FRANCIS AND ROBERT M. LEAVITT

Leavitt, Robert M., and David A. Francis, eds. *Wapapi Akonutomakonol/The Wampum Records: Wabanaki Traditional Laws.* Fredericton: Micmac-Maliseet Institute, University of New Brunswick, 1990.

Mechling, W. H. *Malecite Tales.* Geological Survey of Canada Memoir no. 49. Ottawa: Government Printing Bureau, 1914.

Nowlan, Alden. *Nine Micmac Legends.* Hantsport, Nova Scotia: Lancelot Press, 1983.

Parkhill, Thomas. " 'Of Glooscap's Birth, and of His Brother Malsum, the Wolf': The Story of Charles Godfrey Leland's 'Purely American Creation.' " *American Indian Culture and Research Journal* 16, no. 1 (1992).

Rand, Silas T. *Legends of the Micmacs.* 1894. Reprint. New York and London: Johnson Reprint, 1971.

Simmons, William S. *Spirit of the New England Tribes: Indian History and Folklore, 1620–1984.* Hanover, N.H.: University Press of New England, 1986.

Whitehead, Ruth Holmes. *Stories from the Six Worlds: Micmac Legends.* Halifax, Nova Scotia: Nimbus, 1988.

LARRY EVERS AND FELIPE S. MOLINA

Spicer, Edward H. *The Yaquis: A Cultural History.* Tucson: University of Arizona Press, 1980.

M. JANE YOUNG

Hymes, Dell. *"In Vain I Tried to Tell You": Essays in Native American Ethnopoetics.* Philadelphia: University of Pennsylvania Press, 1981.

Tedlock, Dennis. *Finding the Center: Narrative Poetry of the Zuni Indians.* 1972. Reprint. Lincoln: University of Nebraska Press, 1978.

———. *The Spoken Word and the Work of Interpretation.* Philadelphia: University of Pennsylvania Press, 1983.

DENNIS TEDLOCK

Burns, Allan F. *An Epoch of Miracles: Oral Literature of the Yucatec Maya.* Austin: University of Texas Press, 1983.

Dauenhauer, Nora Marks, and Richard Dauenhauer. *Haa Shuká/Our Ancestors: Tlingit Oral Narratives.* Seattle: University of Washington Press, 1987.

Howard-Malverde, Rosaleen. "Storytelling Strategies in Quechua Narrative Performance." *Journal of Latin American Lore* 15 (1989).

Knab, Tim. "Three Tales from the Sierra de Puebla." *Alcheringa* 4 (new series, 1980).

Scollon, Ron, and Suzanne B. K. Scollon. *Linguistic Convergence: An Ethnography of Speaking at Fort Chipewyan, Alberta.* New York: Academic Press, 1979.

Sherzer, Joel. "Poetic Structuring of Kuna Discourse: The Line." In *Native American Discourse: Poetics and Rhetoric,* edited by Joel Sherzer and Anthony C. Woodbury. Cambridge, England: Cambridge University Press, 1987.

Toelken, Barre, and Tacheeni Scott. "Poetic Retranslation and the 'Pretty Languages' of Yellowman." In *Traditional Literatures of the American Indian: Texts and Interpretations,* edited by Karl Kroeber. Lincoln: University of Nebraska Press, 1981.

Wiget, Andrew. "Telling the Tale: A Performance Analysis of a Hopi Coyote Story." In *Recovering the Word: Essays on Native American Literature,* edited by Brian Swann and Arnold Krupat. Berkeley: University of California Press, 1987.

BARRE TOELKEN

Brady, Margaret K. *"Some Kind of Power": Navajo Children's Skinwalker Narratives.* Salt Lake City: University of Utah Press, 1984.

Kluckhohn, Clyde. *Navaho Witchcraft.* 1944. Reprint. Boston: Beacon Press, 1967.

Reichard, Gladys A. *Navaho Religion: A Study of Symbolism.* Bollinger Foundation Series no. 10. Princeton, N.J.: Princeton University Press, 1950. Reprint. 1963, 1974.

Toelken, Barre. "Life and Death in the Navajo Coyote Tales." In *Recovering the Word: Essays on Native American Literature,* edited by Brian Swann and Arnold Krupat. Berkeley: University of California Press, 1987.

———. "Ma'ii Jołdlooshi lá Eeyá: The Several Lives of a Navajo Coyote." *The World and I,* April 1990.

Zolbrod, Paul G. "Navajo Poetry in Print and in the Field: An Exercise in Text Retrieval." In *On the Translation of Native American Literatures,* edited by Brian Swann. Washington, D.C.: Smithsonian Institution Press, 1992.

Witherspoon, Gary. *Language and Art in the Navajo Universe.* Ann Arbor: University of Michigan Press, 1977.

TÓDÍCH'ÍI'NII BINALÍ BIYE' (TIMOTHY BENALLY SR.)

Gilpin, Laura. *The Enduring Navajo.* Austin: University of Texas Press, 1968.

PAUL G. ZOLBROD

Matthews, Washington. "Songs of Sequence of the Navajos." *Journal of American Folklore* 7 (1894).

———. *Navajo Legends.* Boston: American Folklore Society, 1897.

———. *Navajo Texts,* edited by Pliny Earl Goddard. New York: American Museum of Natural History, 1933.

———. *Navajo Myths, Prayers and Songs.* Berkeley: University of California Press, 1907.

DAVID P. MCALLESTER

Matthews, Washington. *The Navajo Mountain Chant.* In The Fifth Annual Report of the Bureau of American Ethnology for the Years 1883–84. Washington, D.C.: Smithsonian Institution. Reprinted as *The Mountain Chant: A Navajo Ceremony.* 1887.

———. *The Night Chant: A Navajo Ceremony.* American Museum of Natural History Memoirs, Anthropology Series no. 5, New York, 1902.

Mitchell, Frank. *Navajo Blessingway Singer: The Autobiography of Frank Mitchell, 1881–1967,* edited by Charlotte J. Frisbie and David P. McAllester. Tucson: University of Arizona Press, 1978.

Wyman, Leland C. *Beautyway: A Navajo Ceremonial.* Bolinger Series no. 53. New York: Pantheon Books, 1957.

Young, Robert W., and William Morgan. *The Navajo Language: A Grammar and Colloquial Dictionary.* Albuquerque: University of New Mexico Press, 1980.

KEITH H. BASSO AND NASHLEY TESSAY SR.

Basso, Keith. *The Cibecue Apache.* New York: Holt, Rinehart and Winston, 1970.

———. *Western Apache Language and Culture: Essays in Linguistic Anthropology.* Tucson: University of Arizona Press, 1990.

Goddard, P. E. *San Carlos Apache Texts.* American Museum of Natural History Anthropological Paper no. 24. Pt. 3. New York, 1919.

Goodwin, Grenville. *Myths and Tales of the White Mountain Apache.* Memoirs of the American Folklore Society vol. 33. New York: J. J. Augustin, 1939.

————. *The Social Organization of the Western Apache*. Chicago: University of Chicago Press, 1942.

EKKEHART MALOTKI

Curtis, Edward S. *The Hopi*. Vol. 12 of *The North American Indian*. Reprint. New York and London: Johnson Reprint, 1970.

Malotki, Ekkehart. *Hopitutuwutsi/Hopi Tales: A Bilingual Collection of Hopi Indian Stories*. Flagstaff: Museum of Northern Arizona Press, 1978.

Malotki, Ekkehart and Michael Lomatuway'ma. *Stories of Maasaw, a Hopi God*. Vol. 10 of *American Tribal Religions*, edited by Karl Luckert. Lincoln: University of Nebraska Press, 1987.

Voth, Henry R. *The Traditions of the Hopi*. Field Columbian Museum Publication no. 96, Anthropological Series vol. 8. Chicago, 1905.

DAVID LEEDOM SHAUL

Rhodes, Robert W. *Hopi Music and Dance*. Tsaile, Ariz.: Navajo Community College Press, 1978.

Shaul, David L. "A Hopi Song-Poem in 'Context.'" In *On the Translation of Native American Literatures*, ed. Brian Swann. Washington, D.C.: Smithsonian Institution Press, 1992.

LEANNE HINTON

Hinton, Leanne. "Song: Overcoming the Language Barrier." *News from Native California* 5 (1988).

————. "Songs Without Words." *News from Native California* 6 (1992).

HERBERT W. LUTHIN

Luthin, Herbert W. *Restoring the Voice in Yanan Traditional Narrative*. Ph.D. diss., University of California, Berkeley. Ann Arbor: University Microfilms International, 1991.

Sapir, Edward, and Leslie Sapir. *Notes on the Culture of the Yana*. Anthropological Records, vol. 3, no. 3. Berkeley: University of California Press, 1943.

DARRYL BABE WILSON

Angulo, Jaime de. *Indians in Overalls*. San Francisco: Turtle Island Foundation, 1950.

————. *How the World Was Made*. San Francisco: Turtle Island Foundation, 1976.

Dixon, Roland B. "Achomawi and Atsugewi Tales." *Journal of American Folklore* 21 (1908).

Garth, Thomas R. *Atsugewi Ethnography*. University of California Anthropological Records no. 14. Berkeley, 1953.

Gifford, Edward W., and Gwendoline Harris. *California Indian Nights*. Lincoln: University of Nebraska Press, 1990.

Merriam, C. Hart, and Istet Woiche. *Annikadel: The History of the Universe As Told by the Achumawi Indians of California*. Tucson: University of Arizona Press, 1990.

WILLIAM SHIPLEY

Shipley, William. *Maidu Texts and Dictionary*. University of California Publications in Linguistics no. 33. Berkeley, 1963.

CONTRIBUTORS

CATHERINE ATTLA was born in 1927 in the old village of Cutoff on the Koyukuk River. She learned her storytelling skills from her grandmother and is now one of Alaska's leading storytellers, active in presenting and promoting Koyukon traditions.

DORA AUSTIN lives in Carcross, Yukon. Like her recently deceased sister, Angela Sidney, she continues to transmit the oral traditions of her gifted mother, Maria Johns, and often participates in public storytelling events.

DONALD BAHR is Professor of Anthropology at Arizona State University, Tempe. A long-time student of Pima-Papago culture, he has published on this people's theory of sickness and curing and on the varieties and structures of their oral literature.

KEITH H. BASSO is Professor of Anthropology at the University of New Mexico. He has conducted linguistic and ethnographic research among the Western Apache since 1959.

KNUT BERGSLAND was, before his retirement in 1981, Professor of Finno-Ugric languages at the University of Oslo. Among his publications are *Aleut Dialects of Atka and Attu* (1959), *Atkan Aleut–English Dictionary* (1984), *Aleut Dictionary* (1994), and with Moses L. Dirks, *Atkan Aleut School Grammar* (1981).

JUDITH BERMAN is a Guest Curator at the University of Pennsylvania Museum of Archaeology and Anthropology. Her current research traces the last two hundred years of a family of prominent Indian storytellers, oral historians, and scholarly collaborators from the north Pacific coast.

JOHN BIERHORST is the author-editor-translator of more than twenty-five books on Native American literature, including *Four Masterworks of American Indian Literature* (1974), *Cantares Mexicanos: Songs of the Aztecs* (1985), and *The Way of the Earth: Native America and the Environment* (1994).

TÓDÍCH'II'NII BINALÍ BIYE' (Timothy Benally Sr.) is Director of the Office of Navajo Uranium Workers. He is of the Táchii'nii ("Red-Streak-Running-into-Water") clan; his paternal clan is 'Áshįįhi ("Salt"). Chairman of the Navajo Tribal Council's Education Committee at the time the Navajo Community College was established, in 1968, he later served as an administrator of that college.

WILLIAM BRIGHT taught linguistics and anthropology at the University of California, Los Angeles, from 1959 to 1988. He is now Professor Adjoint in Linguistics at the University of Colorado. He was editor of the *International Encyclopedia of Linguistics* (1992) and wrote *A Coyote Reader* (1993).

ROBERT BRIGHTMAN is Associate Professor of Anthropology and Linguistics at Reed College. His research focuses on Native Americans, hunter-gatherer societies, social theory, and sociolinguistics. He is the author of two books and is currently completing a third, on the interpretation of dreams in Cree society.

ROBERT BRINGHURST is the author of a dozen volumes of poetry and several books on Native American, European, and American colonial cultural history. His recent works include *The Black Canoe* (1991), a study of Haida myth and culture as portrayed in the work of Haida sculptor Bill Reid, *The Elements of Typographic Style* (1992), and *The Calling: Selected Poems 1970–1995* (1995).

JULIE CRUIKSHANK has spent more than a decade working in the Yukon. Much of her research is summed up in her recent books, *Life Lived Like a Story: Life Stories of Three Athapaskan Elders,* written with Angela Sidney, Kitty Smith, and Annie Ned (1990), and *Reading Voices/Dän Dhá Ts'edenintth'é: Oral and Written Interpretations of the Yukon's Past* (1991). She is Associate Professor of Anthropology at the University of British Columbia.

NORA MARKS DAUENHAUER was born in Juneau, Alaska. Her first language is Tlingit, and she has worked extensively—doing fieldwork, transcription, translation, and explication—with Tlingit oral literature. Her own poetry, prose, and drama have been widely published. She is Principal Researcher in Language and Cultural Studies at Sealaska Heritage Foundation, Juneau.

RICHARD DAUENHAUER has lived in Alaska since 1969. He has published three volumes of poetry and is Director of Language and Cultural Studies at Sealaska Heritage Foundation, Juneau. He is former poet laureate of Alaska.

STEVEN M. EGESDAL has written *Stylized Characters' Speech in Thompson Salish Narrative* (1992) as well as several articles on Salish narratives. Since 1992, he has been a bilingual-education instructor at the Salish Kootenai College on the Flathead Indian Reservation in Pablo, Montana. He is developing teaching materials in the Flathead Salish and Kutenai languages for use in local schools.

LARRY EVERS is Professor in the Department of English and in the American Indian Studies Program at the University of Arizona. With Felipe S. Molina he has written *Yaqui Deer Songs/Maso Bwikam* (1987), *Woi Bwikam/Coyote Bwikam* (1990), and *Hiakim: The Yaqui Homeland* (1992).

CALVIN W. FAST WOLF was born on the Pine Ridge Indian Reservation in South Dakota. His first and primary language is Lakota, which he has been translating and teaching for the past twenty years. In 1992, he began teaching Lakota in the Department of Linguistics at Stanford University.

ANN FIENUP-RIORDAN is an independent scholar who has lived in Alaska since 1973. Her books include *The Nelson Island Eskimo* (1983), *The Yup'ik Eskimos* (1988), *Eskimo Essays* (1990), *The Real People and the Children of Thunder* (1991), and *Boundaries and Passages* (1994).

MICHAEL K. FOSTER was Curator of Iroquoian Ethnology at the Canadian Museum of Civilization in Ottawa from 1970 to 1989 and is now retired. He has published a monograph on Cayuga ceremonialism and is currently translating a body of traditional Iroquois political speeches and preparing a Cayuga grammar and dictionary.

DAVID A. FRANCIS, a Passamaquoddy elder and teacher, is Language Coordinator at the Wabanaki Resource Center, Pleasant Point, near Eastport, Maine. He has co-authored several books and articles with Robert M. Leavitt.

RIDIE WILSON GHEZZI received her doctorate from the Department of Folklore and Folklife at the University of Pennsylvania in 1990. She received her master of science degree in Information Studies in 1993 and is currently a librarian at the University of Pennsylvania.

LEANNE HINTON is Associate Professor of Linguistics at the University of California, Berkeley. She is author of numerous publications on Havasupai language, story, and song. She also co-edited *Spirit Mountain* (1984), a book of tales from the Yuman languages, and authored a children's book, *Ishi's Tale of Lizard* (1992). Her most recent book is *Flutes of Fire: Essays on California Indian Languages* (1994).

DELL HYMES was Dean of the Graduate School of Education at the University of Pennsylvania and is now Commonwealth Professor of Anthropology and English at the University of Virginia. He began the study of the languages and narratives of the Oregon country in 1951. He is the author of many books.

ELAINE A. JAHNER is Professor of English at Dartmouth College. She has edited, translated, and commented on Lakota texts. She has written on cross-cultural issues as they affect literary criticism.

MARIA JOHNS, born in the late nineteenth century, spent most of her life in Yukon, but she also had Alaskan coastal connections. She was both a song composer and a splendid raconteur.

ELIZA JONES grew up in the Huslia area in Alaska. She has taught her native Koyukon Athabaskan language at the Alaska Native Language Center, at the University of Alaska, Fairbanks, and around the state. She has published books in her language.

VINCENT JOSEPH was a Pima singer from Casa Blanca, a village of the Gila River Indian community in Arizona. Besides Oriole songs, he was versed in Blackbird and Swallow songs, all of which are used for social dancing.

PETER KALIFORNSKY, a Dena'ina Athabaskan from Cook Inlet, Alaska, was born in 1911 and died in 1993. His writings have been collected in *A Dena'ina Legacy* (1991).

JAMES KARI is Professor of Linguistics at the Alaska Native Language Center, Fairbanks. He has worked with many of the outstanding Alaskan Athabaskan storytellers, recording, transcribing, and editing Native-language texts, and he has published widely.

GEOFFREY KIMBALL is a Postdoctoral Fellow in the Department of Anthropology at Tulane University. He is the author of two books on the Koasati language, *Koasati Grammar* (1991) and *Koasati Dictionary* (1994). He has written numerous articles on the linguistics of southeastern and other American Indian languages.

ROBERT M. LEAVITT is Professor on the Faculty of Education of the University of New Brunswick, where he is also Director of the Micmac-Maliseet Institute. He has co-authored several books and articles with David A. Francis.

HENRY LINKLATER, a Cree Indian, was born around 1910 and lived in and around Brochet, Manitoba. His occupations included trapping, caribou hunting, and employment with the Hudson's Bay Company. He died in the mid-1980s.

TOM LOWENSTEIN teaches at Chelsea School of Art and Design in London. His first two books in a three-volume series on Tikiġaq narrative and ritual were published in 1992–93, and his most recent book of poetry is *Filibustering in Samsāra* (1987).

HERBERT W. LUTHIN teaches at Clarion University of Pennsylvania. He has worked on Yana since 1986, producing a dissertation on Yana ethnopoetics, "Restoring the Voice in Yanan Traditional Narrative. He is currently editing *A California Indian Reader* for the Smithsonian Institution Press.

DAVID P. MCALLESTER is Professor Emeritus of Anthropology and Music at Wesleyan University. Among his books and articles are *Peyote Music* (1949) and *Enemy Way Music* (1954). He edited *The Myth and Prayers of the Great Star Chant and the Myth of the Coyote Chant* (1956) and with Susan W. McAllester wrote *Hogans, Navajo Houses and House Songs* (1980).

Contributors

CATHARINE MCCLELLAN is Professor Emerita at the University of Wisconsin, Madison. She has done fieldwork in Alaska, Yukon, and British Columbia and has served as president of the American Ethnological Society and as editor of *Arctic Anthropology*. She contributed to *Subarctic*, volume 6 of the *Handbook of North American Indians*, edited by June Helm (1981).

JANE MCGARY was editor at the Alaska Native Language Center, Fairbanks, from 1975 through 1984, concentrating on Athabaskan languages and culture. She now works as a freelance editor and writer in Oregon.

EKKEHART MALOTKI is Professor of Languages at Northern Arizona University. In addition to bilingual works on Hopi semantics and oral literature, he has published a children's book, *Mouse Couple* (1988), and has contributed the Hopi titles to Godfrey Reggio's movies *Koyaanisqatsi* and *Powaqqatsi*. Since 1986 he has been part of the Hopi Dictionary Project.

ELSIE MATHER was born in the Yupik village of Kwigillingok and has lived in Bethel, Alaska, since 1959. She is the author of *Cauyarnariuq* (1985), a description of pre-Christian Yupik ceremonialism, and co-author, with Osahito Miyaoka, of the standard college text on Yupik orthography.

ANTHONY MATTINA has edited *The Golden Woman: The Colville Narrative of Peter J. Seymour* (1985) and has taught linguistics at the University of Montana since 1971. He is currently on assignment at the En'owkin Centre, Penticton, British Columbia, where he continues to study the language and literature of the Colville-Okanagon.

MARIE MEADE is a Yupik Eskimo who has worked as a translator and Yupik-language instructor since 1970. With Osahito Miyaoka she has written *Survey of Yup'ik Grammar* (1991), and she has worked on the Central Yup'ik Oral History Project.

LAWRENCE MILLMAN has written works of poetry and fiction as well as books on ethnology, folklore, and travel, including a travel narrative about the North, *Last Places* (1990). His most recent work is a collection of Innu stories and myths, *Wolverine Creates the World* (1993).

FELIPE S. MOLINA works as a language specialist for the Yaqui-English Bilingual Program in the Tucson Unified School District and lives in the Yoem Pueblo, a Yaqui community near Tucson. With Larry Evers he has written *Yaqui Deer Songs/Maso Bwikam* (1987), *Woi Bwikam/Coyote Bwikam* (1990), and *Hiakim: The Yaqui Homeland* (1992).

PHYLLIS MORROW is Associate Professor of Anthropology at the University of Alaska, Fairbanks. From 1979 through 1981, she directed the Yupik Eskimo Language Center of Kuskokwim College and developed bilingual-bicultural curricula for the Lower Kuskokwim School District until 1987. She has published widely on Yupik culture.

LEO MOSES was born in the Yupik village of Kashunuk, where he was trained in traditional subsistence skills and heard the words of his elders in the *qasgiq*. He now lives in Chevak, Alaska, where he has served as mayor and in other civic capacities. He is widely recognized for his oratory in both Yupik and English and is frequently called to serve as an interpreter.

DOUGLAS PARKS teaches anthropological linguistics and is Associate Director of the American Indian Studies Research Institute at Indiana University. He is the author of *A Grammar of Pawnee* (1976), editor of *Ceremonies of the Pawnee* by James R. Murie (1981), and collector, editor, and translator of *Traditional Narratives of the Arikara Indians* (1991).

JAROLD RAMSEY is a poet, essayist, and playwright. His books on Native American literature include *Reading the Fire* (1983) and *Coyote Was Going There* (1977), the latter an anthology of traditional Indian verbal art from the Oregon country. He teaches English at the University of Rochester.

JULIAN RICE is Professor of English at Florida Atlantic University. He is the author of five books on the Lakota oral tradition: *Lakota Storytelling* (1989), *Black Elk's Story* (1991), *Deer Women and Elk Men* (1992), *Ella Deloria's Iron Hawk* (1993), and *Ella Deloria's The Buffalo People* (1994).

ROBIN RIDINGTON has done fieldwork with the Dunne-za since 1964. His publications on the Dunne-za include *Trail to Heaven: Knowledge and Narrative in a Northern Native Community* (1988) and *Little Bit Know Something: Stories in a Language of Anthropology* (1991). He is Professor of Anthropology at the University of British Columbia.

BLAIR A. RUDES is President of First Americans Research, an Indian-owned company in Washington, D.C. Since 1974, he has worked with the few living speakers of Tuscarora and is currently preparing a Tuscarora-English dictionary.

DAVID LEEDOM SHAUL is Research Linguist at the Bureau of Applied Research in Anthropology at the University of Arizona. He is the author of the forthcoming *Hopi Ethnoliterature: An Overview; Language, Music and Dance in the Pimería Alta; Language and Culture* (with Louanna Furbee).

WILLIAM SHIPLEY is Emeritus Professor of Linguistics at the University of California, Santa Cruz. He has worked with Maidu phonology, grammar, and lexicon and has maintained a strong interest in the mythologies of, and the historical relationships among, the languages of California.

ANGELA SIDNEY's collaboration with anthropologists and linguists during her lifetime (1902–91), documenting Tagish and Tlingit oral traditions from southern Yukon, earned her the Order of Canada in 1984. Her publications include *My Stories Are My Wealth* (1983), *Haa Shagoon/Our Family History* (1983), and *Tagish Tlaaguu* (1982), all published by the Yukon Native Language Center. She is also a co-author of *Life Lived Like a Story* (1990).

DENNIS TEDLOCK is James H. McNulty Professor of English at the State University of New York, Buffalo. His books are *Finding the Center: Narrative Poetry of the Zuni Indians* (1972), *Teachings from the American Earth: Indian Religion and Philosophy,* edited with Barbara Tedlock (1975), *The Spoken Word and the Work of Interpretation* (1983), *Popol Vuh: The Mayan Book of the Dawn of Life* (1985), *Days from a Dream Almanac* (1990), and *Breath on the Mirror: Mythic Voices and Visions of the Living Maya* (1994).

NASHLEY TESSAY SR. lives in Cibecue, Arizona. A ceremonial specialist, he is a member of the White Mountain Apache Tribe and of the White Mountain Apache Tribal Council.

M. TERRY THOMPSON has published numerous articles and books on the Salish languages. She is currently completing dictionaries of three of these languages.

BARRE TOELKEN has been, since 1985, Professor of English and History at Utah State University, where he directs the Folklore Program and the American Studies Graduate Program. He was editor of the *Journal of American Folklore* and is an associate editor of *Oral Tradition.*

TUKUMMIQ is a bilingual Iñupiaq woman living in Tikiġaq.

JUDITH VANDER has worked with the Wind River Shoshone in Wyoming since 1977. She has published *Ghost Dance Songs and Religion of a Wind River Shoshone Woman* (1986) and *Songprints: The Musical Experience of Five Shoshone Women* (1988). She is currently writing a book on the Shoshone Ghost Dance religion, presenting the music and texts of 130 songs and placing them within their Great Basin cultural context.

DARRYL BABE WILSON was born at the confluence of the Fall and Pit rivers. A graduate of the University of California, Davis, he has recently completed a master's degree in American Indian studies at the University of Arizona and is entering the doctoral program in Comparative Cultural and Literary Studies.

ANTHONY C. WOODBURY is Associate Professor of Linguistics at the University of Texas, Austin. He has worked in Yupik country since 1978. With Joel Sherzer he has edited *Native American Discourse: Poetics and Rhetoric* (1987); he has also published a number of articles on Yupik and on linguistic theory.

M. JANE YOUNG is Associate Professor of American Studies at the University of New Mexico. She has published *Signs from the Ancestors: Zuni Cultural Symbolism and Perceptions of Rock Art* (1988) and has co-edited a collection of articles, *Feminist Theory and the Study of Folklore* (1993).

PAUL G. ZOLBROD is Professor of English at Allegheny College and Senior Curator, Laboratory of Anthropology, at the Museum of Indian Arts and Culture in Santa Fe. He has written extensively about Native American oral poetry and is the author of *Diné Bahane': The Navajo Creation Story* (1984) and *Reading the Voice* (1995).

INDEX

•

ABOUT THE EDITOR

BRIAN SWANN is professor of English at the Cooper Union in New York City. He is the author of a number of books of poetry and fiction as well as the translator of collections of poetry. He has written *Song of the Sky: Versions of Native American Song-Poems* (1994) and *Wearing the Morning Star: Native American Song-Poems* (1996). He has edited *Smoothing the Ground: Essays on Native American Oral Literature* (1983) and *On the Translation of Native American Literatures* (1992). With Arnold Krupat he has edited *Recovering the Word: Essays on Native American Literature* (1987), *I Tell You Now: Autobiographical Essays by Native American Writers* (1987), and *Everything Matters: Autobiographical Essays by Native American Writers* (1996).